Write nothing
in this margin
but the number
of your answer.

j

[A]. O sauron túle nukumna ...lantaner
and   came   humble(d)   they fell

turkildi nuhuinenna ... tarkalion
        under-shadow

ohta káre valannar ... númeheruvi
war made   on-Powers   Lords-of-West

arda sakkante lenéme ilúvatáren ...
Earth   rent   with-leave

ëari ullier ikilyanna ... númenóre
seas should pour into-chasm   Numenor

ataltane .
fell down

Kadō zigūrun zabathān unakkha ...
and so   humbled   he-came

ēruhīnim dubdam ugru-dalad ...ar-
          fell   ?shadow beneath

pharazōnun azaggara avalōiyada ...
              was warring   against Powers

bārim an-adūn yurahtam dāura sāu-
Lords . of West   they rent   Earth   with

bēth-mā ēruvō ... azriya duphursā
assent   from Eru   that seas should gush

akhāsada ... anadūnē zīrān hikalba ...
into Chasm   Anadune the beloved she fell

[A].

O sauron túle nukumna ...lantaner
  and   came   humble(d)   they fell

turkildi nuhuinenna ... tarkalion
            under-shadow

ohta káre valannar ... númeheruvi
 war made   on-Powers   Lords-of-West

arda sakkante lenéme ilúvatáren ...
 Earth   rent   with-leave

ëari ullier ikilyanna ... númenóre
 seas should pour into-chasm   Numenor

ataltane .
    fell down

Kadō zigūrun zabathān unakkha ...
 and so   humbled   he-came

ēruhīnim dubdam ugru-dalad ... ar-
       fell   ?shadow beneath

pharazōnun azaggara avalōiyada ...
      was warring   against Powers

bārim an-adūn yurahtam dāura sāi-
 Lords . of West They rent   Earth   with

bēth-mā ēruvō ... azriya duphursā
 assent   from Eru that seas should gush

akhāsada ... anadūnē ziran hikalba ...
 into Chasm   Anadune the beloved she fell

bawība dulgū ... balik hazad annimru-
winds (were)   black   ships   seven   of   ?

zīr azūlada ...
   eastwards

ii

[B] Agannālō burōda nēnud ... zāira
death-shadow   very heavy   on us   longing

nēnud ... adūn izindi batān tāidō
on us   west   straight (right?) road then (once?)

ayadda: īdō katha batīna lōkhī.
it went   now   all   ways (are) bent

[A] Vahaiya sín andóre.
   far away   now (is) Andóre (Land of Gift)

[B] Ephalak īdō Yōzāyan.
   far away   now   Gift-land.

[B] Ephal-ephalak īdō hi Akallabēth.
   for far away   now   She that hath fallen

[A] Haiya vahaiya sín atalante.
   far for away   now (is) the Down-fallen.

SAURON DEFEATED

THE HISTORY OF MIDDLE-EARTH

I
THE BOOK OF LOST TALES, PART ONE

II
THE BOOK OF LOST TALES, PART TWO

III
THE LAYS OF BELERIAND

IV
THE SHAPING OF MIDDLE-EARTH

V
THE LOST ROAD

VI
THE RETURN OF THE SHADOW

VII
THE TREASON OF ISENGARD

VIII
THE WAR OF THE RING

IX
SAURON DEFEATED

J. R. R. TOLKIEN

SAURON DEFEATED

THE END OF THE THIRD AGE
(The History of The Lord of the Rings Part Four)

THE NOTION CLUB PAPERS
and
THE DROWNING OF ANADÛNÊ

Edited by Christopher Tolkien

Boston   New York   London
HOUGHTON MIFFLIN COMPANY
1992

For information about permission to reproduce selections from
this book, write to Permisssions, Houghton Mifflin Company,
215 Park Avenue South, New York, New York 10003.

Library of Congress Cataloging-in-Publication Data
Tolkien, J. R. R. (John Ronald Reuel), 1892–1973.
Sauron defeated : the history of the Lord of the rings, part four.
The Notion Club papers, and, The drowning of Anadûnê / J.R.R.
Tolkien ; edited by Christopher Tolkien.
p.   cm. — (The History of Middle-earth ; 9)
ISBN 0-395-60649-7
1. Tolkien, J. R. R. (John Ronald Reuel), 1892–1973.   Lord of the
rings—Criticism, Textual.   2. Fantastic fiction, English—
Criticism, Textual.   3. Middle Earth (Imaginary place).
I. Tolkien, Christopher.   II. Tolkien, J. R. R. (John Ronald Reuel),
1892–1973.   Notion Club papers.   1992.   III. Tolkien, J. R. R. (John
Ronald Reuel), 1892–1973.   Drowning of Anadûnê.   1992.   IV. Title.
V. Series: Tolkien, J. R. R. (John Ronald Reuel), 1892–1973.
History of Middle-earth ; 9.
PR6039.O32L63743   1992
823'.912 — dc20   92-14587
CIP

Printed in the United States of America
HAD   10   9   8   7   6   5   4   3   2   1

CONTENTS

PART THREE: THE DROWNING OF ANADÛNÊ

ILLUSTRATIONS

To
TAUM SANTOSKI

FOREWORD

With this book my account of the writing of *The Lord of the Rings* is completed. I regret that I did not manage to keep it even within the compass of three fat volumes; but the circumstances were such that it was always difficult to project its structure and foresee its extent, and became more so, since when working on *The Return of the King* I was largely ignorant of what was to come. I shall not attempt a study of the history of the *Appendices* at this time. That work will certainly prove both far-ranging and intricate; and since my father soon turned again, when *The Lord of the Rings* was finished, to the myths and legends of the Elder Days, I hope after this to publish his major writings and rewritings deriving from that period, some of which are wholly unknown.

When *The Lord of the Rings* had still a long way to go – during the halt that lasted through 1945 and extended into 1946, *The Return of the King* being then scarcely begun – my father had embarked on a work of a very different nature: *The Notion Club Papers*; and from this had emerged a new language, Adunaic, and a new and remarkable version of the Númenórean legend, *The Drowning of Anadûnê*, the development of which was closely entwined with that of *The Notion Club Papers*. To retain the chronological order of writing which it has been my aim to follow (so far as I could discover it) in *The History of Middle-earth* I thought at one time to include in Volume VIII, first, the history of the writing of *The Two Towers* (from the point reached in *The Treason of Isengard*) and then this new work of 1945–6, reserving the history of *The Return of the King* to Volume IX. I was persuaded against this, I am sure rightly; and thus it is in the present book that the great disparity of subject-matter appears – and the great difficulty of finding a title for it. My father's suggested title for Book VI of *The Lord of the Rings* was *The End of the Third Age*; but it seemed very unsatisfactory to name this volume *The End of the Third Age and Other Writings*, when the 'other writings', constituting two thirds of the book, were concerned with matters pertaining to the Second Age (and to whatever Age we find ourselves in now).

Sauron Defeated is my best attempt to find some sort of link between the disparate parts and so to name to the whole.

At a cursory glance my edition of *The Notion Club Papers* and *The Drowning of Anadûnê* may appear excessively complicated; but I have in fact so ordered them that the works themselves are presented in the clearest possible form. Thus the final texts of the two parts of the *Papers* are each given complete and without any editorial interruption, as also are two versions of *The Drowning of Anadûnê*. All account and discussion of the evolution of the works is reserved to commentaries and appendages which are easily identified.

In view of the great disparity between Part One and Parts Two and Three I have thought that it would be helpful to divide the Index into two, since there is scarcely any overlap of names.

I acknowledge with many thanks the help of Dr Judith Priestman of the Bodleian Library, and of Mr Charles B. Elston of Marquette Unversity, in making available photographs for use in this book (from the Bodleian those on pages 42 and 138–41, from Marquette those on pages 19 and 130). Mr John D. Rateliff and Mr F. R. Williamson have very kindly assisted me on particular points in connection with *The Notion Club Papers*; and Mr Charles Noad has again generously given his time to an independent reading of the proofs and checking of citations.

This book is dedicated to Taum Santoski, in gratitude for his support and encouragement throughout my work on *The Lord of the Rings* and in recognition of his long labour in the ordering and preparation for copying of the manuscripts at Marquette, a labour which despite grave and worsening illness he drove himself to complete.

Since this book was set in type Mr Rateliff has pointed out to be the source of Arundel Lowdham's allusion to 'the Pig on the Ruined Pump' (p. 179), which escaped me, although my father knew the work from which it comes well, and its verses formed part of his large repertoire of occasional recitation. It derives from Lewis Carroll, *Sylvie and Bruno*, chapter X – where however the Pig sat beside, not on, the Pump:

> *There was a Pig, that sat alone,*
> *Beside a ruined Pump.*
> *By day and night he made his moan:*

It would have stirred a heart of stone
To see him wring his hoofs and groan,
Because he could not jump.

In *Sylvie and Bruno Concluded*, chapter XXIII, this becomes the first verse of a poem called *The Pig-Tale*, at the end of which the Pig, encouraged by a passing Frog, tries but signally fails to jump to the top of the Pump:

Uprose that Pig, and rushed, full whack,
Against the ruined Pump:
Rolled over like an empty sack,
And settled down upon his back,
While all his bones at once went 'Crack!'
It was a fatal jump.

On a very different subject, Mr Noad has observed and communicated to me the curious fact that in the Plan of Shelob's Lair reproduced in *The War of the Ring*, p. 201, my father's compass-points 'N' and 'S' are reversed. Frodo and Sam were of course moving eastward in the tunnel, and the South was on their right. In my description (p. 200, lines 16 and 20) I evidently followed the compass-points without thinking, and so carelessly wrote of the 'southward' instead of the 'northward' tunnels that left the main tunnel near its eastern end.

PART ONE

THE END OF THE
THIRD AGE

I

THE STORY OF FRODO AND SAM
IN MORDOR

Long foreseen, the story of the destruction of the Ring in the fires of Mount Doom was slow to reach its final form. I shall look back first over the earlier conceptions that have appeared in *The Return of the Shadow* and *The Treason of Isengard*, and then give some further outlines of the story.

The conception of the Fiery Mountain, in which alone the Ring could be destroyed, and to which the Quest will ultimately lead, goes back to the earliest stages in the writing of *The Lord of the Rings*. It first emerged in Gandalf's conversation with Bingo Bolger-Baggins, predecessor of Frodo, at Bag End (VI.82): 'I fancy you would have to find one of the Cracks of Earth in the depths of the Fiery Mountain, and drop it down into the Secret Fire, if you really wanted to destroy it.' Already in an outline that almost certainly dates from 1939 (VI.380) the scene on the Mountain appears:

> At end
> When Bingo [> Frodo] at last reaches Crack and Fiery Mountain *he cannot make himself throw the Ring away*. ? He hears Necromancer's voice offering him great reward – to share power with him, if he will keep it.
> At that moment Gollum – who had seemed to reform and had guided them by secret ways through Mordor – comes up and treacherously tries to take Ring. They wrestle and Gollum *takes Ring* and falls into the Crack.
> The mountain begins to rumble.

Two years later, in a substantial sketch of the story to come ('The Story Foreseen from Moria') it was still far from clear to my father just what happened on the Mountain (VII.209):

> Orodruin [*written above:* Mount Doom] has three great fissures North, West, South [> West, South, East] in its sides. They are very deep and at an unguessable depth a glow of fire is seen. Every now and again fire rolls out of mountain's heart down the terrific channels. The mountain towers above Frodo. He comes to a flat place on the mountain-side where the fissure is full of fire – Sauron's well of fire. The Vultures are coming. He *cannot* throw Ring in. The Vultures are coming. All goes dark in his eyes and he falls to his

knees. At that moment Gollum comes up and wrestles with him, and takes Ring. Frodo falls flat.

Here perhaps Sam comes up, beats off a vulture and hurls himself and Gollum into the gulf?

Subsequently in this same outline is found:

They escape [from Minas Morgol] but *Gollum follows.*
It is *Sam* that wrestles with Gollum and [?throws] him finally in the gulf.

Not long after this, in the outline 'The Story Foreseen from Lórien' (VII.344), my father noted that 'Sam must fall out somehow' (presumably at the beginning of the ascent of Mount Doom) and that Frodo went up the mountain alone:

Sam must fall out somehow. Stumble and break leg: thinks it is a crack in ground – really Gollum. [?Makes ?Make] Frodo go on alone.

Frodo toils up Mount Doom. Earth quakes, the ground is hot. There is a narrow path winding up. Three fissures. Near summit there is Sauron's Fire-well. An opening in side of mountain leads into a chamber the floor of which is split asunder by a cleft.

Frodo turns and looks North-west, sees the dust of battle. Faint sound of horn. This is Windbeam the Horn of Elendil blown only in extremity.

Birds circle over. Feet behind.

Since the publication of *The Treason of Isengard* there has come to light an outline that is obviously closely related to this passage from 'The Story Foreseen from Lórien' (which does not necessarily mean that it belongs to the same time) but is very much fuller. This I will refer to as I. The opening sentences were added at the head of the page but belong with the writing of the text.

(I)   Sam falls and hurts leg (really tripped by Gollum). Frodo has to go alone. (Gollum leaps on Sam as soon as Frodo is away.)

Frodo toils on alone up slope of Mt.Doom. Earth quakes; the ground becomes hot. There is a narrow path winding up. It crosses one great fissure by a dreadful bridge. (There are three fissures (W. S. E.).) Near the summit is 'Sauron's Fire-well'. The path enters an opening in the side of the Mt. and leads into a low chamber, the floor of which is split by a profound fissure. Frodo turns back. He looks NW and sees dust and smoke of battle? (Sound of horn – the Horn of Elendil?) Suddenly he sees birds circling above: they come down and he realizes that they are Nazgûl! He crouches in the chamber-opening but still dare not enter. He hears feet coming up the path.

At same moment Frodo suddenly feels, many times multiplied, the impact of the (unseen) *searching eye*; and of the enchantment of the Ring. He does not wish to enter chamber or to throw away the Ring. He hears or feels a deep, slow, but urgently persuasive voice speaking: offering him life, peace, honour: rich reward: lordship: power: finally a share in the Great Power – *if* he will stay and go back with a Ring Wraith to Baraddur. This actually terrifies him. He remains immovably balanced between resistance and yielding, tormented, it seems to him a timeless, countless, age. Then suddenly a new thought arose – not from outside – a thought born inside *himself*: he would keep the Ring himself, and be master of all. Frodo King of Kings. Hobbits should rule (of course he would not let down his friends) and Frodo rule hobbits. He would make great poems and sing great songs, and all the earth should blossom, and all should be bidden to his feasts. *He puts on the Ring!* A great cry rings out. Nazgûl come swooping down from the North. The *Eye* becomes suddenly like a beam of fire stabbing sheer and sharp out of the northern smoke. He struggles now to take off the Ring – and fails.

The Nazgûl come circling down – ever nearer. With no clear purpose Frodo withdraws into the chamber. Fire boils in the Crack of Doom. All goes dark and Frodo falls to his knees.

At that moment Gollum arrives, panting, and grabs Frodo and the Ring. They fight fiercely on the very brink of the chasm. Gollum breaks Frodo's finger and gets Ring. Frodo falls in a swoon. Sam crawls in while Gollum is dancing in glee and suddenly pushes Gollum into the crack.

Fall of Mordor.

Perhaps better would be to make Gollum repent in a way. He is utterly wretched, and commits suicide. Gollum has it, he cried. No one else shall have it. I will destroy you all. He leaps into crack. Fire goes mad. Frodo is like to be destroyed.

Nazgûl shape at the door. Frodo is caught in the fire-chamber and cannot get out!

Here we all end together, said the Ring Wraith.

Frodo is too weary and lifeless to say nay.

You first, said a voice, and Sam (with Sting?) stabs the Black Rider from behind.

Frodo and Sam escape and flee down mountain-side. But they could not escape the running molten lava. They see Eagles driving the Nazgûl. Eagles rescue them.

Make issue of fire *below* them so that bridge is cut off and *a sea of fire bars their retreat* while mountain quivers and crumbles. Gandalf on *white* eagle rescues them.

Against the sentence 'He is utterly wretched, and commits suicide' my father subsequently wrote *No*.

Another outline, which I will call II, is closely related to outline I just given. It is written in ink over a briefer pencilled text, very little of which can be read – partly because of the overwriting, partly because of the script itself (my father could not read the conclusion of the first sentence and marked it with dots and a query).[1]

(II)   Frodo now feels full force of the Eye . . . . ? He does not want to enter Chamber of Fire or throw away the Ring. He seems to hear a deep slow persuasive voice speaking: offering life and peace – then rich reward, great wealth – then lordship and power – and finally a share of the Great Power: if he will take Ring intact to the Dark Tower. He rejects this, but stands still – while thought grows (absurd though it may seem): he will keep it, wield it, and himself have Power alone; be Master of All. After all he is a great hero. Hobbits should become lords of men, and he their Lord, King Frodo, Emperor Frodo. He thought of the great poems that would be made, and mighty songs, and saw (as if far away) a great Feast, and himself enthroned and all the kings of the world sitting at his feet, while all the earth blossomed.

(Probably now Sauron is aware of the Ring and its peril, and this is his last desperate throw to halt Frodo, until his messenger can reach Orodruin.)

Frodo puts on Ring! A great cry rings out. A great shadow swoops down from Baraddur, like a bird. The Wizard King is coming. Frodo feels him – the one who stabbed him under Weathertop. He is wearing Ring and has been seen. He struggles to take off Ring and cannot. The Nazgûl draws near as swift as storm. Frodo's one idea is to escape it, and without thinking of his errand he now flies into the Chamber of Fire. A great fissure goes across it from left to right. Fire boils in it. All goes dark to Frodo and he falls on his knees. At that moment *Gollum* arrives panting and grabs at the Ring. That rouses Frodo, and they fight on the brink of the chasm. Gollum breaks Frodo's finger and gets Ring. Frodo falls in swoon. But Sam who has now arrived rushes in suddenly and pushes Gollum over the brink. Gollum and Ring go into the Fire together. The Mountain boils and erupts. Barad-dur falls. A great dust and *a dark shadow* floats away NE on the rising SW wind. Frodo suddenly thinks he can hear and smell Sea. A dreadful shuddering cry is borne away and until it dies far off all men and things stand still.

Frodo turns and sees door blocked by the Wizard King. The mountain begins to erupt and crumble. Here we will perish together, said the Wizard King. But Frodo draws Sting. He no longer has any fear whatsoever. He is master of the Black Riders. He

commands the Black Rider to follow the Ring his master and drives
it into the Fire.

Then Frodo and Sam fly from the chamber. Fire is pouring out of
the mountain-side by three great channels W, SE, S, and makes a
burning moat all round. They are cut off.

Gandalf, of course, now knows that Frodo has succeeded and the
Ring has perished. He sends Gwaihir the Eagle to see what is
happening. Some of the eagles fall withered by flame?[2] But Gwaihir
sweeps down and carries off Sam and Frodo back to Gandalf,
Aragorn, etc. Joy at the reunion – especially of Merry and Pippin?

There seems to be no certain way in which to date this text, but the
reference to the coming of the Wizard King from Barad-dûr shows at
any rate that his fate on the Pelennor Fields had not yet arisen. I incline
to think that it is relatively late, and would associate it tentatively with
the end of the outline 'The Story Foreseen from Forannest' (VIII.362):

> Gandalf knows that Ring must have reached fire. Suddenly
> Sauron is aware of the Ring and its peril. He sees Frodo afar off. In a
> last desperate attempt he turns his thought from the Battle (so that
> his men waver again and are pressed back) and tries to stop Frodo.
> At same time he sends the Wizard King as Nazgûl to the Mountain.
> The whole plot is clear to him. ...
> Gandalf bids Gwaihir fly swiftly to Orodruin.

With this cf. the words of outline II just given: 'Probably now *Sauron
is aware of the Ring and its peril*, and this is his *last desperate throw to
halt Frodo*'; and 'Gandalf, of course, now knows that Frodo has
succeeded and the Ring has perished. He sends Gwaihir the Eagle to
see what is happening.'

I turn now to other outlines that preceded any actual narrative
writing of Book VI. The first of these, Outline III, also only came to
light recently; it is a somewhat disjointed page, with deletions and
additions, but all belonging to the same time. I believe that time to be
the brief period of work (October 1944) when my father began
writing 'Minas Tirith' and 'The Muster of Rohan', and wrote also
many outlines for Book V; with the opening of the present text cf.
VIII.260: '[12] Gandalf and Aragorn and Éomer and Faramir defeat
Mordor. Cross into Ithilien. Ents arrive and Elves out of North.
Faramir invests Morghul and main force comes to Morannon. Parley.'
It will be seen that the story of the fighting and slaughter in the Tower
of Kirith Ungol had not yet arisen.

(III) They pass into Ithilien [12 >] 11[3] [and turn >] Éomer and
Faramir invest Minas Morghul. The rest turn / north to Moran-
non. Joined by Ents and Elves out of Emyn Muil. Camp on [*added:*
S. edge (of)] Battle Plain [14 >] evening of 12. Parley. Messengers

[*sic*] of Sauron. Gandalf refuses. [*Added:* begins assault on Morannon.]
    Sam rescues Frodo night of 11/12. They descend into Mordor. [Gollum comes after them. They see a vast host gathering in Kirith Gorgor, and have to lie hid (12). 12/13 They go on and are tracked by Gollum. *This was struck out and replaced by the following:*] Frodo from the high tower holds up phial and as if with Elvish sight[4] sees the white army in Ithilien. On the other side he sees the vast secret host of Mordor (not yet revealed) gathered on the dead fields of Gorgor. ? Sauron delays to take Frodo because of the defeat at Gondor.
    Mt.Doom (Orodruin) stands in plain at inner throat of Kirith Gorgor, but a complete darkness comes over land, and all they can see is Mt.Doom's fire and far away the Eye of Baraddur. They cannot find a path? It is not until night of 12 that they reach rocky slopes above the levels of Kirith Gorgor. There they see an immense host camped: it is impossible to go further. They remain in hiding during 13 – and are tracked down by Gollum. Suddenly the whole host strikes camp and pours away leaving Mordor empty. Sauron himself has gone out to war.[5] They cross plain and climb Mt.Doom. Frodo looks back and sees the white army driven back.

    Frodo captured on night 10/11. But Shagrat persuades Gorbag not to send message at once,[6] until he's had a look for the *real* warrior still loose. Orcs scatter and hunt in Kirith Ungol (11). Sam at last finds way in – he has to go back and down pass[7] – then he finds quite a small fort[8] of many houses and a gate and a path leading up to the cliff. It is not until [evening >] night of 11 that he manages to get in.
    Rescue of Frodo early on 12. Shagrat sends message to Lugburz. [*Added:* How do messages work. Signal from Tower to Eye. News.] Nazgûl arrives at Tower and takes coat of mail and [clothes etc. >] a sword to Baraddur (12).
    Frodo and Sam hide in rocks. The Gorgor plain is covered with armies. They are in despair, for crossing is impossible. Slowly they work their way north to where the defile narrows, to a point nearer Mt.Doom [> Dûm].[9]

Another outline (**IV**) describes the capture of Frodo and his rescue by Sam from the Tower of Kirith Ungol; and this is yet another text of which I was not aware until recently. Like outline II it is written in ink over an underlying, and much briefer, pencilled text. It was written, very obviously at the same time, on the reverse of a page that carries a rejected preliminary version (also in ink over pencil) of the outline 'The march of Aragorn and defeat of the Haradrim' given in VIII.397–9, which preceded the writing of 'The Battle of the Pelennor Fields' and very probably accompanied the outline 'The Story Foreseen from

Forannest' (see VIII.397). This preliminary version of 'The march of Aragorn and defeat of the Haradrim', which contains remarkable features, is given at the end of this chapter (p. 14).

In this outline IV Gorbag is expressly the 'Master of the Tower', whereas in the fair copy manuscript of 'The Choices of Master Samwise' he is the Orc from Minas Morghul, as in RK. It is notable however that at his first appearance in this text he is the Orc from Minas Morghul, changed immediately to Shagrat – which is however marked with a query. This query suggests to me that after so much changing back and forth of the names of these beauties (see VIII.225, note 46) my father could not remember what decision he had come to, and did not at this time check it with the manuscript of the end of Book IV (cf. the case of 'Thror' and 'Thrain', VII.159–60). The same uncertainty is seen in outline III above (see note 6).

(IV) Frodo is captured night of 10–11. Mar.12 Frodo in prison. (Sauron is distracted by news of the Ents and defeat of his forces in Eastemnet by Ents and Elves of Lórien.)

No message is sent for some time to Dark Tower – partly because of general . . . .[10] Frodo is stripped, and the *Mithril* coat is found.

[Gorbag >] Shagrat (?) covets this, and tries to stop Gorbag sending message: at first pleading need of searching for confederate. But quarrel breaks out, and Shagrat and Gorbag fight and their men take sides. Sam at last finds way in – by a front gate overlooking Mordor – and a steep descent down into a long narrow dale or trough beyond which is a lower ridge.[11] In end Gorbag (Master of the Tower) wins, because he has more men, and Shagrat and all his folk are slain. Gorbag then sends tidings to Baraddur together with the Mithril coat – but overlooks Lórien cloak.[12] Gorbag has only very few men left, and has to send two (since one won't go alone for fear of the missing spy) to Baraddur. Sam slips in and slays one of Gorbag's remaining two at the gate, another on stair, and so wins his way in to the Upper Chamber. There he finds Gorbag. Sam takes off his Ring and fights him and slays him. He then enters Frodo's chamber. Frodo lying bound and naked; he has recovered his wits owing to a draught given him by orcs to counter poison – but he has talked in his delirium and revealed his name and his country, though not his errand.[13] Frodo is filled with fear, for at first he thinks it is an orc that enters. Then hatred for the bearer of the Ring seizes him like a madness, and he reproaches Sam for a traitor and thief. Sam in grief; but he speaks kindly, and the fit passes and Frodo weeps. This is night of 13th. Sam and Frodo escape from Tower on 14th.

It might be a good thing to increase the reckoning of time that Frodo, Sam and Gollum took to climb Kirith Ungol by a day, so that Frodo is not taken until night of 11–12. Quarrel between Orcs on 12th and sending of message that night or morning of 13th when

Gorbag is victorious. Sam gets in on 13th. Otherwise Sam will have to spend all 11, 12 and part of 13 trying to get into Tower. Make Sam get in before fight and get mixed up with it. And so let Sam hear message sent to Baraddur?

The last outline (V), while written independently of IV, evidently belongs closely with it, and has the same story of the Tower of Kirith Ungol – Gorbag is the captain of the garrison, and Sam slays him. This text, giving the first detailed account of the journey of Frodo and Sam to Mount Doom, is identical in appearance to 'The Story Foreseen from Forannest' and was clearly a companion to it.

At the head of the page are written these notes on distances, which were struck through:

Minas Tirith to Osgiliath (W. end) 24–5 miles. Width of city [*written above:* ruin] 4 miles. East end of Osgiliath to Minas Morghul about 60 miles (52 to Cross Roads?). Minas Morghul to top of Kirith Ungol (and pass below Tower) 15 miles on flat. Kirith Ungol to crest of next (lower) ridge beyond Trough is about 15 miles.

The opening paragraph of the main text is enclosed in square brackets in the original. All the changes shown were made subsequently in pencil, including the reduction of most of the dates by a day.

(V)   [Gorbag sends swift runner to Baraddur on morn(ing) of 13th. He does not reach plain and make contact with any horseman until end [> morn(ing)] of 14th? A rider reaches Baraddur on 15th [> night of 14], and at same time by Nazgûl news of the defeat before Gondor and the coming of Aragorn is brought to him [Sauron].[14] He sends the Nazgûl to Kirith Ungol to learn more. The Nazgûl discovers Tower full of dead and the prisoner flown.]

Sam rescues Frodo and slays Gorbag on 14th [> 13]. Frodo and Sam escape: when clear of the Tower, they disguise themselves in orc-guise. In this way they reach the bottom of the Trough at night on 14th [> 13]. They are surprised that there seems no guard and no one about; but they avoid the road. (A steep stair-path leads down from Tower to join the main road from Minas Morghul over Kirith Ungol pass to the Plain of Mordor and so to Baraddur.) The darkness is that of night.[15]

On 15th [> 14] March they climb the inner ridge – about 1000 feet at most, sheer on W. side, falling in jumbled slopes on E. side. They look out on the Plain of Mordor, but can see little owing to dark [*added:* but the clouds are blown away]. Though by the wizardry of Sauron the air is clear of smokes (so that his troops can move) it hangs like a great pall in the upper air. It seems largely to issue from Orodruin – or so they guess, where far away (50 miles) under the pall there is a great glow, and a gush of flame. Baraddur (further and S. of the Mountain) is mantled in impenetrable shadow. Still, Frodo and Sam can see that all plain is full of troops. Hosts of fires dot the land as far as they can see. They cannot hope to cross. Frodo decides to try and find a point where the open land is narrower, in or nearer to Kirith Gorgor. They descend into Trough again and work north. They begin to count their food anxiously. They are very short of water. Frodo weak after poison – though the orcs gave him something to cure it, and *lembas* seems specially good as antidote; he cannot go fast.[16] They manage 10 miles along Trough.

On 16th [> 15] they continue to crawl along Trough, until they are some 25–30 miles north of Kirith Ungol.

On 17th [> 16] they climb ridge again, and lie hid. They hardly dare move again even in the gloom, since they can see below them great hosts of warriors marching into the defile out of Mordor. Frodo guesses they are going to war and wonders what is happening to Gandalf etc. [*Added:* No, most of troops are now *coming back in.*]

On 19th [> 18] being desperate they go down and hide in the rocks at the edge of the defile. At last Sauron's troop-movements cease. There is an ominous silence. Sauron is waiting for Gandalf to come into trap. Night of 19–20 [> 18–19] Frodo and Sam try to cross the defile into Ered-Lithui. (About this time let Sam have suspicion that Gollum is still about, but say nothing to Frodo?)

After various adventures they get to Eredlithui at a point about 55 miles NW of Orodruin. 20 (part), 21, 22, 23 they are working along slopes of Eredlithui.[17]

On 24th their food and water is all spent – and Frodo has little strength left. Sam feels a blindness coming on and wonders if it is due to water of Mordor.

24th. Frodo with a last effort – too desperate for fear – reaches foot of Orodruin and on 25 begins the ascent. There is a constant rumble underground like a war of thunder. It is night. Frodo looks round fearing the ascent – a great compulsion of reluctance is on him. He feels the weight of the Eye. And behold the mantle of shadow over Baraddur is drawn aside: and like a window looking into an inner fire he sees the Eye. He falls in a faint – but the regard of the Eye is really towards Kirith Gorgor and the coming battle, and it sweeps past Orodruin.

Frodo recovers and begins ascent of Mt.Doom. He finds a winding path that leads up to some unknown destination; but it is cut across by wide fissures. The whole mountain is shaking. Sam half-blind is lagging behind. He trips and falls – but calls to Frodo to go on: and then suddenly Gollum has him from behind and chokes his cries. Frodo goes on alone not knowing that Sam is not behind, and is in danger. Gollum would have killed Sam but is suddenly filled with fear lest Frodo destroy Ring. Sam is half throttled, but he struggles on as soon as Gollum releases him.

Here the text ends, and at the end my father wrote in pencil: 'Carry on now with old sketch.' Possibly he was referring to outline II (p. 6), although there seems reason to think (p. 7) that that outline belongs to much the same time as the present text.

★

The chronology of writing

I take it as certain that my father took up *The Lord of the Rings* again, after the long halt at the end of 1944, in the latter part of 1946: this was when he returned to the abandoned openings of the chapters 'Minas Tirith' and 'The Muster of Rohan'. For the subsequent chronology of writing there is little evidence beyond the rather obscure statements in his letters. On 30 September 1946 (*Letters* no.106, to Stanley Unwin) he said that he 'picked it up again last week' and wrote a further chapter, but there is really no knowing what this was; and on 7 December 1946 (*Letters* no.107, to Stanley Unwin) he wrote: 'I still hope shortly to finish my "magnum opus": the Lord of the Rings: and let you see it, before long, or before January. I am on the last chapters.'

In an unpublished letter to Stanley Unwin of 5 May 1947 he wrote: 'It [Farmer Giles] is hardly a worthy successor to "The Hobbit", but on the real sequel life hardly allows me any time to work'; and in another of 28 May 'I have not had a chance to do any writing.' On 31 July 1947 (*Letters* no.109) he was saying: 'The thing is to finish the thing as devised and then let it be judged'; and a further eight months on (7 April 1948, *Letters* no.114, to Hugh Brogan) he wrote: 'Only the difficulty of writing the last chapters, and the shortage of paper have so far prevented its printing. I hope at least to finish it this year ...' Then, on 31 October 1948 (*Letters* no.117, again to Hugh Brogan), he said, 'I managed to go into "retreat" in the summer, and am happy to announce that I succeeded at last in bringing the "Lord of the Rings" to a successful conclusion.'

The only other evidence that I know of is found in two pages on which my father made a list of candidates for an academic post with notes on their previous experience. Against several of the names he noted both date of birth and present age, from which it is clear that the year was 1948. On the reverse of one of these pages is drafting for the passage in 'The Land of Shadow' in which Frodo and Sam see the darkness of Mordor being driven back (RK p. 196); the second part is overwritten with drafting for the discussion of food and water in 'The Tower of Kirith Ungol' (RK p. 190), while the reverse of it carries very rough sketching of the discovery of Frodo by Sam in the Tower.

Thus in December 1946 he was 'on the last chapters' of *The Lord of the Rings*, and hoped to finish it 'before January'; but in 1948 he was drafting the opening chapters of Book VI. The explanation must be, I think, that by the end of 1946 he had completed or largely completed Book V, and so (in relation to the whole work) he could feel that he was now 'on the last chapters'; and greatly underestimating (as he had so often done before) how much needed to be told before he reached the end, he thought that he could finish it within the month. But 1947 was largely unproductive, as the letters imply; and Book VI was not written until 1948.

NOTES

1   The few words and sentences that I can make out are sufficient to show that the story in the underlying text was substantially the same. The ink overwriting ends before the pencilled text does, and the last sentence of the latter can be read: 'Thorndor sweeps down and carries off Sam and Frodo. They rejoin the host on Battle Plain.' The naming of the rescuing eagle *Thorndor* (earlier form of *Thorondor*) is very surprising, but is perhaps to be explained as an unconscious reminiscence (when writing at great speed) of the rescue of Beren and Lúthien in *The Silmarillion*.

2   Cf. the fate of the Nazgûl in RK (p. 224): 'And into the heart of the storm ... the Nazgûl came, shooting like flaming bolts, as caught in the fiery ruin of hill and sky they crackled, withered, and went out.'

3   The dates are still in February. For the change in the month see VIII.324–5; and with the chronology of this text cf. that given in VIII.226.

4   Cf. the outline 'The Story Foreseen from Fangorn' (VII.438): 'Then return to Frodo. Make him look out onto impenetrable night. Then use phial which has escaped ... By its light he sees the forces of deliverance approach and the dark host go out to meet them.' On this I remarked (VII.440, note 15): 'The light of the Phial of Galadriel must be conceived here to be of huge power, a veritable star in the darkness.'

5   *Sauron himself has gone out to war*: despite the apparent plain significance of the words, it is impossible that my father should have meant that Sauron was no longer present in the Dark Tower.

6   *Gorbag* replaced *Yagûl* as the name of the Orc from Minas Morghul in the fair copy manuscript of 'The Choices of Master Samwise' (see VIII.225, note 46). Here 'Shagrat persuades Gorbag not to send message at once' suggests that Gorbag is the Orc from the Tower, whereas a few lines later 'Shagrat sends message to Lugbûrz'; see further outline IV, p. 9.

7 *he has to go back and down pass:* i.e., Sam had to go back out of the tunnels and up to the pass, then down the other side of it (cf. RK pp. 173–5).

8 *quite a small fort:* I think that this means, not 'only a *small* fort', but 'an actual fort, if not very large, not simply a tower'.

9 For the spelling *Mount Dûm* see VII.373, VIII.118.

10 My father could not read the pencilled words here and wrote queries against them.

11 This is the first description of the Morgai (which is marked and named on the Second Map, VIII.435, 438).

12 The outline 'The march of Aragorn and defeat of the Haradrim', closely associated with the present text, has a brief passage about the rescue of Frodo concerned with the cloak of Lórien (VIII.398):

> Rescue of Frodo. Frodo is lying naked in the Tower; but Sam finds by some chance that the elven-cloak of Lórien is lying in a corner. When they disguise themselves they put on the grey cloaks over all and become practically invisible – in Mordor the cloaks of the Elves become like a dark mantle of shadow.

13 Cf. 'The Story Foreseen from Forannest' (VIII.361):

> He [the ambassador of Sauron to the Parley] bears the Mithril coat and says that Sauron has already captured the messenger – a *hobbit*. How does Sauron know? He would of course guess from Gollum's previous visits that a small messenger might be a *hobbit*. But it is probable that either Frodo *talked in his drugged sleep* – not of the Ring, but of his name and country; and that Gorbag had sent tidings.

14 A pencilled X is written against this sentence. Cf. 'The Story Foreseen from Forannest' (VIII.360): 'Sauron ... first hears of Frodo on 15 of March, and at the same time, by Nazgûl, of the defeat in Pelennor and the coming of Aragorn. ... He sends the Nazgûl to Kirith Ungol to get Frodo ...'

15 Against this paragraph is written in the margin: 'Frodo's horror when Sam comes in and looks like a goblin. Hate for the Ringbearer seizes him and bitter words of reproach for treachery spring to his lips.'

16 In the margin is written here: 'Ring a great burden, worse since he had been for a while free of it.'

17 Beside these dates is written '10 miles, 15, 15, 15'.

★

The rejected preliminary version of 'The March of Aragorn and defeat of the Haradrim'

I have mentioned (pp. 8–9) that on the reverse of the page bearing outline IV (describing the capture and rescue of Frodo) is the original form of the outline given in VIII.397–9, entitled 'The march of Aragorn and defeat of the Haradrim'. This is a very puzzling text, and I give it in full. It was in fact written in three forms. The first is a pencilled text (a) as follows:

Aragorn takes Paths of the Dead early on March 8th. Comes out of the tunnel (a grievous road) and reaches head of the Vale of Morthond at dusk. He blows horns [*struck out*: and unfurls standard] to amazement of the people; who acclaim [him] as a king risen from the Dead. He rests three hours and bidding all to follow and send out the war-arrows he rides for the Stone of Erech. This is a stone set up between the mouths of Lamedui and the Ethir Anduin delta to commemorate the landing of Isildur and Anárion. It is about 275 miles by road from the issuing of the Paths of the Dead. Aragorn rides 100 miles and reaches the Ringlo Vale (where men are assembling) on March 9. There he gathers news and men. He rides after short rest into Lamedon (10) and then goes to

Here this version was abandoned and a new start made, also in pencil, at 'Aragorn takes Paths of the Dead'; but this text (b) was overwritten in ink and can only be read here and there. The overwritten form (c) reads thus:

Aragorn takes Paths of the Dead morn(ing) 8 March, passes tunnels of the mountains and comes out into the head of Morthond Vale at dusk. Men of the Dale are filled with fear for it seems to them that behind the dark shapes of the living riders a great host of shadowy men come nearly as swift as riders. Aragorn goes on through night and reaches Stone of Erech at morn(ing) on March 9. Stone of Erech was black stone fabled to have been brought from Númenor, and set to mark the landing of Isildur and Anárion and their reception as kings by the dark men of the land. It stood on the shores of Cobas, near the outflow of Morthond, and about it was a ruined wall within which was also a ruined tower. In the vault under the tower forgotten was one of the Palantir[i]. From Erech a road ran by [the] sea, skirting in a loop the hills of Tarnost, and so to Ethir Anduin and the Lebennin.

At Stone of Erech Aragorn unfurls his standard (Isildur's) with white crown and star and Tree and blows horns. Men come to him. (The Shadow-men cannot be seen by day.) Aragorn learns that what he saw in Palantir was true indeed: Men of Harad have landed on the coasts near the Ethir, and their ships have sailed up the estuary as far as Pelargir. There the men of Lebennin have made a block – on the basis of an ancient defence. The Haradwaith are ravaging the land. It is nearly 350 miles by coast road from Erech to Pelargir. Aragorn sends out swift riders north into the Dales, summoning what men remain to march on Pelargir. He does not himself take coast-road, since it is infested, but after a rest he sets out at dusk of March 9 – and goes like wind by rough paths over Linhir and so to Fords of Lameduin (about 150 miles away). The Shadow Host is seen to follow. He crosses Morthond at Linhir, passes into Ringlo Vale, and sets all land aflame for war. He reaches Lameduin evening of March 10. Men are assembled there, and are resisting an attempt of the Haradwaith to cross Lebennin > NW. Aragorn and the Shadow Host come out of the dark with the white star shining on the banner and the Haradwaith are terrified. Many drowned in the river Lameduin. Aragorn camps and crosses Lameduin into Lebennin and marches on Pelargir morn(ing) of 11 March. The terror of 'the Black King' precedes him, and the Haradwaith try to fly: some ships escape down Anduin, but Aragorn comes up driving Haradwaith before him. The Shadow Host camps on shores of Anduin before Pelargir on evening of March 11th. By night they set fire in guarded ships, destroy the Haradwaith and capture 2 vessels. On morn(ing) of 12th they set out up Anduin, with Haradwaith captains rowing.

The extraordinary thing about this, of course, is the site of Erech. It seems plain beyond any question from all the evidence presented in *The War of the Ring* (see especially the chapter 'Many Roads Lead Eastward (1)') that from its first emergence Erech was in the southern foothills of Ered Nimrais, near the source of Morthond: Erech stands self-evidently in close relationship with the Paths of the Dead. Why then did my father now move it, first (in **a**) to the coast between the mouths of Lameduin and Ethir Anduin, and then (in **b** and **c**) to Cobas Haven (north of Dol Amroth: see the Second Map, VIII.434)? I am unable to propose any explanation.

The geography of the **c**-version is at first sight hard to follow. In **a** Aragorn's route can be understood: all that is said here is that he rode from the head of Morthond Vale 'for the Stone of Erech'; he reaches the Ringlo Vale, and then continues into Lamedon (which at this stage lay east of the river Lameduin: see VIII.437). The distance of 275 miles from the issuing of the Paths of the Dead to Erech 'between the mouths of Lamedui and the Ethir Anduin delta' is however much too great, and was perhaps an error for 175. (On the form *Lamedui* see VIII.436.) In version **c**, however, Aragorn leaves Erech 'on the shores of Cobas, near the outflow of Morthond', and 'goes like wind by rough paths *over Linhir and so to Fords of Lameduin* (about 150 miles away). ... *He crosses Morthond at Linhir, passes into Ringlo Vale ... He reaches Lameduin.*' As it stands this makes no sense; but the explanation is that his journey is described twice in the same passage. The first statement is comprised in the words 'He goes like wind by rough paths over Linhir, and so to Fords of Lameduin (about 150 miles away).' The second statement is 'He crosses Morthond at

Linhir, passes into Ringlo Vale ... He reaches Lameduin.' This must mean that Linhir is here in the earlier position, above Cobas Haven (see VIII.437).

It is said in c that the coast road from Erech skirted in a loop 'the Hills of Tarnost'. This name is written in pencil against a dot on the square Q 12 of the Second Map, at the northern extremity of the hills between the rivers Lameduin and Ringlo (see VIII.434, 437, where I said that so far as I then knew the name *Tarnost* does not occur elsewhere).

Lastly, in the concluding lines of b, which were not overwritten, the name *Haradrians* is given to the Haradwaith.

II

THE TOWER OF KIRITH UNGOL

It seems that my father returned to the story of Frodo and Sam more than three years after he had 'got the hero into such a fix' (as he said in a letter of November 1944, VIII.218) 'that not even an author will be able to extricate him without labour and difficulty.' As one of the outlines given in the preceding chapter shows, however, he had continued to give thought to the question, and while Book V was still in progress he had discovered the essential element in Sam's rescue of Frodo: the quarrel of Shagrat and Gorbag in the Tower of Kirith Ungol, leading to the mutual slaughter of almost all the orcs both of the Tower and of Minas Morgul before Sam arrived (p. 9).

His first draft ('A') of the new chapter extended as far as the point where Sam, descending the path from the Cleft, sees the two orcs shot down as they ran from the gateway of the Tower, and looking up at the masonry of the walls on his left realises that to enter in 'the gate was the only way' (RK p. 178). In this draft the text of RK was largely achieved, but not in all respects. In the first place, the chapter begins thus: 'For a while Sam stood stunned before the closed door. Far within he heard the sounds of orc-voices clamouring . . .' It is clear that he was not physically stunned, as he was in the final story. On this see pp. 21–2.[1]

Secondly, when Sam, groping his way back from the under-gate in the tunnel, wondered about his friends (RK p. 173), 'Out in the world it was the dark before dawn on the twelfth of March in Shire-reckoning, the third day since he and Frodo came to the Cross Roads, and Aragorn was drawing near to Anduin and the fleet of Umbar, and Merry was beginning the third day of his ride from Dunharrow, and the forest of Druadan lay before him; but in Minas Tirith Pippin stood sleepless on the walls [?waiting] for [the] Causeway Forts had fallen and the enemy was coming.'

Thirdly, the fortress of Kirith Ungol was at first conceived as rising 'in four great tiers', not three as in RK (p. 176), and its strange structure, as it were flowing down the mountain-side, is sketched on the page of the draft (reproduced on p. 19) beside the description in the text; this description, originally in pencil but overwritten in ink, runs as follows:

And in that dreadful light Sam stood aghast; for now he could see the Tower of Kirith Ungol in all its strength. The horn that

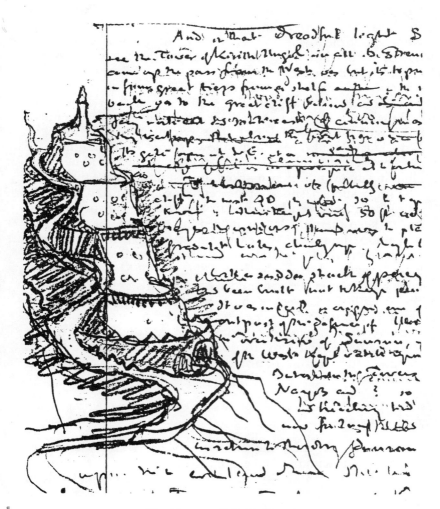

The Tower of Kirith Ungol

those could see who came up the pass from the West was but its topmost turret. Its eastern face stood up in four great tiers from a shelf in the mountain wall some 500 feet below. Its back was to the great cliff behind, and it was built in four pointed bastions of cunning masonry, with sides facing north-east and south-east, one above the other, diminishing* as they went up, while about the lowest tier was a battlemented wall enclosing a narrow courtyard. Its gate open[ed] on the SE into a broad road. The wall at the [?outward] .... was upon the brink of a precipice.

　*[The bottom one was probably projected some 50 yards from the cliff, the next 40, the next 30, the top 20 – and on the top [*or* tip] of it was the turret-tower. Their heights were 50 ft., 40 ft., 30 ft., 20 ?]

With black blank eyes the windows stared over the plains of Gorgoroth and Lithlad; some [?form(ed)] a line of red-lit holes, climbing up. Maybe they marked some stair up to the turret.

　With a sudden shock of perception Sam realized that this stronghold had been built not to keep people out of Mordor, but to keep them in! It was indeed in origin one of the works of Gondor long ago: the easternmost outpost of the defence of Ithilien and Minas Ithil, made when after the overthrow of Sauron, in the days of the Last Alliance, the Men of the West kept watch upon the evil land where still his creatures lurked. But as with the Towers of the Teeth that watch[ed] over Kirith Gorgor, Nargos and ? [*sic*][2], so here too the watch and ward had failed and treachery had yielded up the Tower to the Ringwraiths. [?And] now for long it had been occupied by evil things. And since his return to Mordor Sauron had found it useful.

　The pencilled passage that follows the end of the overwriting in ink reads as follows:

... keep watch upon the evil land where still his creatures lurked. But as with the Towers of the Teeth upon Kirith Gorgor, so here the watch and ward had failed and treachery had yielded up the Tower. But Sauron too had found it useful. For he had few servants and many slaves. Still its purpose was as of old to keep people in.

　Sam looked and he saw how the tower commanded the main road from the pass behind; the road he was on was only a narrow way that went corkscrewing down into the darkness and seemed to join a broad way from the gate to the road.

This page was removed from the original draft text A on account of the illustration (the only one that my father ever made of the Tower of Kirith Ungol), which was squared off with rough lines, and placed with the second fair copy manuscript (E), although by then the fortress was built in three tiers not four.

This original draft continues on to its end thus, and in this appears the most important difference from the story of RK (pp. 176–8):

There was no doubt of the path he must take, but the longer he looked the less he liked it. He put on the Ring again and began to go down. Now he could hear the cries and sounds of fighting again. He was about halfway down when out of the dark gate into the red glow came two orcs running. They did not turn his way but were making for the main road, when they fell and lay still. Apparently they had been shot down by others from the wall of the lower course or from the shadow of the gate.[3] After that no more came out. Sam went on. He came now [to] the point where [the] descending path hugged the lower wall of the tower as it stood out from the rock behind. There was a narrow angle there. He stopped again, glad of the excuse; but he soon saw that there was no way in. There was no purchase in the smooth rock or [?jointed] masonry and 100 feet above the wall hung beetling out. The gate was the only way.

Here the first draft stops. Thus the entire passage in RK (p. 177) in which Sam is tempted to put on the Ring and claim it for his own, his mind filling with grandiose fantasies (deriving from those of Frodo on Mount Doom in outlines I and II, pp. 5–6), is lacking; but at the point where the draft ends my father wrote (clearly at the same time): *Sam must not wear Ring*. No doubt it was this perception that caused him to abandon this text.

He began at once on a second draft, '**B**', for most of its length written legibly in ink, with the number 'LII'[4] and the title 'The Tower of Kirith Ungol'. This opened in the same way as did A (p. 18): 'For a while Sam stood stunned before the closed door. Far within he heard the sounds of orc-voices clamouring ...' In the fair copy manuscript of 'The Choices of Master Samwise' it had been said (following the original draft) that 'Sam hurled himself against it, and fell', changed in pencil to 'Sam hurled himself against the bolted plates, and fell to the ground.' This was repeated in the first typescript of that chapter; only in the second typescript was the word 'senseless' introduced. The explanation of this is that while writing the present draft B of 'The Tower of Kirith Ungol' my father was struck by a thought which he noted in the margin of the page, telling himself that he 'must leave time for Frodo to recover and to fight'[5] and that in order to achieve this

'Sam must *swoon* outside the undergate.' It was no doubt at this time that he changed the opening of B:

For a while Sam stood dumb before the closed door. Then desperate and mad he charged at the brazen door, and fell back stunned; down into darkness he sank. How long it lasted he could not tell; but when he came to himself still all was dark.

Against the passage in the draft A referring to other events in the world at that hour (p. 18) my father noted: 'Make Frodo and Sam one day more in Epheldúath. So Frodo is captured night of 12, when Merry was in Druadan Forest and Faramir lay in fever and Pippin was with the Lord, but Aragorn was manning his fleet.' In B the passage now becomes:

Out westward in the world it was deep night upon the twelfth of March by Shire-reckoning, three days since he and Frodo had passed the peril of Minas Morgul; and now Aragorn was manning the black fleet on Anduin, and Merry in the Forest of Druadan was listening to the Wild Man, while in Minas Tirith the flames were roaring and [the great assault upon the Gates had begun >] the Lord sat beside the bed of Faramir in the White Tower.

Against 'March' in this passage my father scribbled in the margin: 'Make Hobbit names of months.'

At the point where Sam at the crest of the pass looked out over Mordor to Orodruin ('the light of it ... now glared against the stark rock faces, so that they seemed to be drenched with blood', RK p. 176) my father halted briefly and wrote the following note across the page:

Change in the Ring as it comes in sight of the furnace where it was made. Sam feels *large* – and naked. He knows that he must *not* use the Ring or challenge the Eye; and he knows he is not big enough for that. The Ring is to be a desperate burden and no help from now onwards.

The Tower of Kirith Ungol is still built in four tiers, not three, and the note concerning the dimensions of the bastions was retained (see p. 20), though the dimensions were changed:

[The bottom tier projected some 40 yards from the nearly perpendicular cliff, the second 30, the third 20, the topmost 10; and their height diminished similarly, 80 ft., 70 ft., 60 ft., 40 ft., and the topmost turret some 50 ft. above the top of .... mountain wall.]

The road from Minas Morgul over the Pass of Morgul is said here to pass 'through a jagged cleft in the inner ridge out into the valley of Gorgor on its way to the Dark Tower'; the name *Morgai* had not yet been devised (cf. RK p. 176). *Gorgor* was changed, probably immediately, to *Gorgoroth* (cf. VIII.256). The Towers of the Teeth were at first not named in this text, but *Narchost and Carchost* was added in subsequently.

Following the note on the subject of the Ring just given, this draft now effectively reaches the text of RK in the account of Sam's temptation and his refusal of it, as far as the point where A ended ('The gate was the only way', RK p. 178). From this point B becomes rough and is partly in outline form.

Sam wonders how many orcs lived in the Tower with Shagrat and how many men Gorbag had [*marginal note:* Make Gorbag's men more numerous in last chapter of Book IV][6] and what all the fighting was about. 'Now for it!' he cried. He drew Sting and ran towards the open gate – only to feel a shock, as if he had run into some web like Shelob's but *invisible*. He could see no obstacle, but something too strong for his will to overcome barred the way. Then just inside the gate he saw the Two Watchers. They were as far as he could see in the gloom like great figures sitting on chairs, each had three bodies, and three heads, and their legs facing inward and outward and across the gateway. Their heads were like vulture-faces, and on their knees were laid clawlike hands.[7] They were carved of black stone, it seemed, moveless, and yet they were aware; some dreadful spirit of evil vigilance dwelt in them. They knew an enemy, and forbade his entry (or escape). Greatly daring, because there was now nothing else to do, Sam drew out the phial of Galadriel. He seemed to see a glitter in the jet-wrought eyes of the Watchers, but slowly he felt their opposition melt into fear. He sprang through, but even as he did so, as if it was some signal given by the Watchers, far up in the Tower he heard a shrill cry.

In RK (p. 179), even as Sam sprang through the gateway, 'he was aware, as plainly as if a bar of steel had snapped to behind him, that their vigilance was renewed. And from those evil heads there came a high shrill cry that echoed in the towering walls before him. Far up above, like an answering signal, a harsh bell clanged a single stroke.' In the margin of the present text, against the foregoing passage, is a note: 'Or make Watchers close with a snap. Sam is in a trap once more.'

The courtyard was full of slain orcs. Some lay here and there, hewn down or shot, but many lay still grappling one another, as they throttled or stabbed their opponents. Two archers right in the gateway – probably those who shot down the escaping orcs – lay pierced from behind with spears. [Sting, Sam noticed, was only shining faintly.]

Sam rushed across the court, and to his relief found the door at the base of the Tower ajar. He met no one. Torches are flaring in brackets. A stair, opening on right, goes up. He runs up it, and so out into the narrow yard before the second door. 'Well!' he said to himself, his spirits rising a little, 'Well! It looks as if Shagrat or Gorbag was on my side and has done my job for me. There's nobody left alive!' And with that he halted, suddenly realizing the full meaning of what he had said: nobody was left alive. 'Frodo! Frodo!' he called, forgetful of all else, and ran to the second door. An orc leaps out at him [*in margin:* Two orcs].

Sam kills the [> one] orc and the other runs off yelling for Shagrat. Sam climbs warily. The stair now rises at the back of the entrance passage, and climbs right up to the Turret (the Brazen Gate enters about on a level with the courtyard?). Sam hears voices, and stalks them. The orc is pattering away up the stairs. 'Shagrat!' he calls. 'Here he is, the other spy.' Sam follows. He overhears the orc reporting to Shagrat. Shagrat is lying wounded by dead body of Gorbag. All Gorbag's men have been killed, but they have killed all Shagrat's but these two.

An isolated slip of paper seems very likely to be the continuation of this outline, and the first sketching of the new story of the escape from the Tower. The writing declines towards the end into such a scrawl that many words and phrases are impossible to make out.

Shagrat has in vain tried to get messages away to Baraddûr. The Quarrel arose about the treasures. Gorbag coveted the mithril coat, but pretended that they must search for the missing spy first. He sent his men to capture wall and gate, and demanded mithril coat. But Shagrat won't agree. Frodo was thrust in chamber of turret and stripped. Shagrat gives him some medicine and begins to question him. Shagrat puts things together to send to Baraddur (Lugburz). Gorbag tries to fight way in and slay Frodo.

Gorbag and Shagrat fight.

When Shagrat hears news (although orc says the other spy is not a large warrior) he is frightened, as he is wounded. He makes the treasures into a bundle and tries to creep off. He must get to Lugburz. So when Sam leaps out with phial and shining sword he flees. Sam pursues; but gives up for he [?hears] Frodo

[?crying]. He sees Shagrat far below rushing out of gate – and does not at first realize the misfortune of news getting to Lugburz. The orc left behind is tormenting Frodo. Sam rushes in and slays him.

Scene of yielding up Ring. Frodo has lost his cloak and ....[8] He has to dress in the orc's clothes [or in orcs' clothes]. Sam does likewise but keeps cloak and Sting. Frodo has to have orc-weapons. The sword is gone.[9] He tells Sam about the fight. They make their plans.

The opposition of the Watchers. The Tower seems full of evil. Cry goes up as they escape. And as if in answer a Nazgûl comes dropping down out of the black sky, [?shining .... ?with] a fell red, and perches on the wall. Meanwhile they dash down the road, and as soon as they can leave it and climb into the shelter of the rocks near bottom of trough. They wonder what to do.

Food.[10] Drink. They had found Frodo's sack and ..... [?in corner] rummaged – but orcs would not touch *lembas*. They gathered up what was left of it, in broken fragments. Orcs must drink. [?They see] [a] well in the courtyard. Sam tastes it – says Frodo not to risk it. It seems all right. They fill their water bottles. It is now 13th of March, make it 14th? They reckoned they have [?enough] for about a week with care or at a desperate pinch ten days. How far is it.

They climb to lower ridge and find they dare not go across the plain at that point – where it is broad and full of enemies.

The Nazgûl [?explores] Tower and sees there is [??trouble] and flies off. Frodo thinks it best to go north to where the plain narrows – he had seen sketch of Mordor in Elrond's house – and away from Kirith Ungol to which [??attention is now directed]. He bemoans fact that Shagrat had got away with *tokens*.

Chapter ends with the Nazgûl shining red circling over Tower [??and he cries as] ..... of orcs begin to search the [?pass] and the road and lands about.

I believe that at this stage my father began the chapter again, and this was the first completed manuscript ('D'). It was numbered 'LII' but given a new title 'The Orc-tower'; the number was later changed to 'L' (which I cannot explain) and the title 'The Tower of Kirith Ungol' (which it had borne in the draft B) restored.

New initial drafting begins at the point where Sam enters the gate of the Tower, but up to this point the final text was now written out on the basis of the drafts A and B described above, in a form only differing in a few minor points from that in RK. The chapter now opens exactly as it does in the published work (see p. 22), and Sam now has to climb back over the stone door leading into the passage to the under-gate, since he still cannot find the catch (note 1). The events 'out westward in the world' are described in the same words as in RK (with the addition, after 'Pippin watched the madness growing in the eyes of Denethor', of 'and Gandalf laboured in the last defence'); but the date ('noon upon the fourteenth day of March' in RK) is now 'morning upon the thirteenth day of March'. The name *Morgai* appears as an early addition to the text (p. 22). The Tower now has three tiers, and the note about the dimensions of the bastions, still present (see pp. 20, 22), was accommodated to this: the tiers now projected 40, 30 and 20 yards from the cliff, and their heights were 80, 70, and 60 feet, changed at the time of writing to 100, 75, and 50 feet. 'The top was 25 feet above Sam, and above it was the horn-turret, another 50 feet.'[11]

From ' "That's done it!" said Sam. "Now I've rung the front-door bell!" ' a draft text ('C') takes up. This is written in a script so difficult that a good deal of it would be barely comprehensible had it not been closely followed in the fair copy D.[12] The final story was now reached, and there is little to record of these texts. At the point in the narrative where Sam climbed up to the roof of the third (topmost) tier of the Tower there is a little diagram in D showing the form of the open space (not clearly seen in the drawing reproduced on p. 19): rectangular at the base but with the sides drawing together to a point (cf. the 'pointed bastions' referred to in the description of the Tower), roughly in the shape of a haystack. To the statement that the stairhead was 'covered by a small domed chamber in the midst of the roof, with low doors facing east and west' D adds 'Both were open': this was omitted in the second manuscript ('E'), perhaps inadvertently. The name of the sole surviving orc beside Shagrat is *Radbug* in both C and D (*Snaga* in RK; see LR Appendix F, p. 409), *Radbug* being retained in the final story as the name of an orc whose eyes Shagrat says that he had squeezed out (RK p. 182); in C the orcs whom Sam saw running from the gate and shot down as they fled are *Lughorn* and *Ghash* > *Muzgash* (*Lagduf* and *Muzgash* in D, as in RK). Where in RK Snaga declares that 'the great fighter' (Sam) is 'one of those bloody-handed Elves, or one of the filthy *tarks*', and that his getting past the Watchers is '*tark's* work',[13] C has 'that's Elvish work'; D has 'one of these filthy wizards maybe' and 'that's wizard's work' ('wizard' being changed in pencil to '*tark*', which appears in the second manuscript E as written).

Only in one point does the story as told in the draft C differ from that in D. When Gorbag rouses himself from among the corpses on the roof Sam sees in the latter, as in RK (p. 183), that he has in his hand 'a broad-headed spear with a short broken haft'; in C on the other hand he has 'a red [?and shining] sword. It was his own sword, the one he left by Frodo.' With this cf. text B (p. 25 and note 9): 'Frodo has to have orc-weapons. The sword is gone.'

Sam's song as he sat on the stair in the horn-turret was much worked on.[14] I give it here in the form that it has in D, which was preceded by rougher but closely similar versions.

> *I sit upon the stones alone;*
> *the fire is burning red,*
> *the tower is tall, the mountains dark;*
> *all living things are dead.*
> *In western lands the sun may shine,*
> *there flower and tree in spring*
> *is opening, is blossoming:*
> *and there the finches sing.*
>
> *But here I sit alone and think*
> *of days when grass was green,*
> *and earth was brown, and I was young:*
> *they might have never been.*
> *For they are past, for ever lost,*
> *and here the shadows lie*
> *deep upon my heavy heart,*
> *and hope and daylight die.*
>
> *But still I sit and think of you;*
> *I see you far away*
> *Walking down the homely roads*
> *on a bright and windy day.*
> *It was merry then when I could run*
> *to answer to your call,*
> *could hear your voice or take your hand;*
> *but now the night must fall.*
> *And now beyond the world I sit,*
> *and know not where you lie!*
> *O master dear, will you not hear*
> *my voice before we die?*

The second verse was altered on the manuscript:

> *For they are gone, for ever lost,*
> *and buried here I lie*
> *and deep beneath the shadows sink*
> *where hope and daylight die.*

At the same time the last two lines of the song became:

> *O Master, will you hear my voice*
> *and answer ere we die?*

In this form the song appears in the second manuscript E. At a later stage it was rewritten on this manuscript to become virtually a different song, but still retaining almost unchanged the second half of the original first verse, which now became the opening lines:

> In western lands the Sun may shine;
> there flower and tree in Spring
> are opening, are blossoming,
> and there the finches sing.

Further correction of these lines on the manuscript produced the final form (RK p. 185).

A last point concerns the ladder: 'Suddenly the answer dawned on Sam: the topmost chamber was reached by a trap-door in the roof of the passage', RK p. 185. In my account of the fair copy manuscript of 'The Choices of Master Samwise' I did not describe a development in the last words of Shagrat and Gorbag that Sam overheard before they passed through the under-gate of the Tower (TT p. 351). In the draft text, only Shagrat speaks:

> 'Yes, up to the top chamber,' Shagrat was saying, 'right at the top. No way down but by the narrow stair from the Look-out Room below. He'll be safe there.'

In the fair copy this was retained, but Shagrat begins 'Yes, that'll do' (as if the suggestion had come from Gorbag), and 'the ladder' was substituted for 'the narrow stair'. It is thus seen that this element in the story was already present when Book IV was completed. The further development in the conversation of the orcs, in which Gorbag argues against Shagrat's proposal, and Shagrat declares that he does not trust all of his own 'lads', nor any of Gorbag's, nor Gorbag himself (and does not mention that the topmost chamber was reached by ladder), was added to the first typescript of 'The Choices of Master Samwise' at this time, as is seen from the fact that rough drafting for it is found on a page carrying drafts for passages for 'The Land of Shadow'. Curiously, my father wrote at the head of this: 'No way up but by a ladder', as if this idea had only now emerged.[15]

NOTES

1 When Sam came back to the stone door of the orc-passage 'on the inner side he found the catch' (whereas in RK he could not find it and had to climb over). This was retained in the second draft B.

2 For earlier names of the Towers of the Teeth see the Index to *The War of the Ring*, entries *Naglath Morn, Nelig Myrn*. The name *Nargos* here is a reversion to one of the original names (*Gorgos* and *Nargos*) of the towers guarding Kirith Ungol, when that was

still the name of the chief pass into Mordor: see VII.344 and note 41.

3 These two orcs, who survived into the final text (RK p. 178), originally appeared in outline IV (p. 9) as messengers sent to Barad-dûr. At that time there was no suggestion that they did not make good their errand.

4 At this stage, presumably, 'The Pyre of Denethor' and 'The Houses of Healing' constituted the two parts of Chapter XLIX (VIII.386), while the remainder of Book V was divided between L and LI (the fair copy manuscript of 'The Black Gate Opens' is numbered LI).

5 In the event, of course, Frodo did not fight, and no draft of this period suggests that he did. Possibly at this stage, before he had come to write the new story of the rescue of Frodo, my father was still thinking in terms of the original plot in 'The Story Foreseen from Lórien', when Frodo was more active (VII.335 ff.).

6 In the fair copy manuscript of 'The Choices of Master Samwise' Sam asked himself: 'How many are there? Thirty, forty, or more?' The change to 'Thirty of forty from the tower at least, and a lot more than that from down below, I guess' (TT p. 344) was made on the first typescript of the chapter. – In outline IV (p. 9) the orcs of the Tower are the more numerous.

7 Cf. the original conception of the Sentinels guarding the entrance to Minas Morgul in 'The Story Foreseen from Lórien' written years before (VII.340–1): 'It was as if some will denying the passage was drawn like invisible ropes across his path. He felt the pressure of unseen eyes. ... The Sentinels sat there: dark and still. They did not move their clawlike hands laid on their knees, they did not move their shrouded heads in which no faces could be seen ...' See also the diagrammatic sketch of the Sentinels in VII.348.

8 The illegible word might possibly be *jewel* (i.e. the brooch of his elven-cloak).

9 *The sword is gone:* this is Sam's sword from the Barrow-downs; cf. 'The Choices of Master Samwise' (TT p. 340): ' "If I'm to go on," he said, "then I must take your sword, by your leave, Mr. Frodo, but I'll put this one to lie by you, as it lay by the old king in the barrow ..." ' See pp. 26–7.

10 This passage concerning their provision of food and water is marked to stand earlier – no doubt after the words 'They make their plans'. The illegible words in the sentence following 'Food. Drink.' could conceivably be read as *stick thrust,* i.e. 'They had found Frodo's sack and stick thrust in corner, rummaged.'

11 A few other differences of detail are worth recording. Where in RK (p. 176) the text reads: 'not even the black shadows, lying deep where the red glow could not reach, would shield him long

from the night-eyed orcs' D continues: 'that were moving to and fro.' This was taken up from the draft B, and remained into the second manuscript of the chapter (E), where it was removed. – Sam's rejection of the temptation to claim the Ring as his own was expressed thus: 'The one small garden of a free gardener was all his need and due, not a garden swollen to a realm; his own hands to command, not the hands of others. Service given with love was his nature, not to command service, whether by fear or in proud benevolence.' – After the words 'He was not really in any doubt' (RK p. 177) there follows in D: 'but he was lonely and he was not used to it, or to acting on his own.' To this my father subsequently added, before striking it all out, 'Since no one else was there he had to talk to himself.'

12 Some passages are absent from the draft C, but not I think because pages are lost: rather D becomes here the initial narrative composition. Thus the passage in RK p. 181 from 'Up, up he went' to ' "Curse you, Snaga, you little maggot" ' is missing; and here the D text becomes notably rougher and full of corrections in the act of writing. The very rough draft C stops near the beginning of Sam's conversation with Frodo in the topmost chamber (RK p. 187), and from that point there are only isolated passages of drafting extant; but the latter part of D was much corrected in the act of writing, and was probably now to a large extent the primary composition.

13 Cf. LR Appendix F (RK p. 409): in Orkish Westron '*tark*, "man of Gondor", was a debased form of *tarkil*, a Quenya word used in Westron for one of Númenorean descent'.

14 For my father's original ideas for the song that Sam sang in this predicament see VII.333.

15 When Frodo and Sam passed out through the gate of the Tower Frodo cried: *Alla elenion ancalima! Alla* was not changed to *Aiya* until the book was in type (cf. VIII.223, note 29).

III

THE LAND OF SHADOW

It seems plain that 'The Land of Shadow' was achieved swiftly and in a single burst of writing; the draft material (here compendiously called 'A') consists largely of very roughly written passages immediately transferred to and developed in the first continuous manuscript ('B'), which was given the number 'LIII' (see p. 25) and the title 'Mount Doom', subsequently changed to 'The Land of Shadow'. Only in a few passages did my father go momentarily down an unsuccessful turn in the story.

The first of these concerns the overhearing by Sam and Frodo of the conversation of orcs in the valley beneath the Morgai, which was at first conceived very differently from the story in RK (pp. 202–3). The draft text A is here, as throughout, exceedingly difficult to read.

Presently [three >] two orcs came into view. They were in black without tokens and were armed with bows, a small breed, black-skinned with wide snuffling nostrils, evidently trackers of some kind. .... they were talking in some hideous unintelligible speech; but as they passed snuffling among the stones scarcely 20 yards from where the hobbits lurked Frodo saw that one was carrying on his arm a black mail-shirt very like the one that he had abandoned. He sniffed it as [he] went as if to recall its scent. All at once lifting his head he let out a cry. It was answered, and from the other direction (from Kirith Ungol now some miles behind) ... large fighting orcs came up with shields .... [?painted] with the Eye.

A [?babble] of talk in the common tongue now broke out. 'Nar,' said the tracker, 'not a trace further along. Nor o' this smell, but we're not [?easy]. Somebody that has no business here has been about. Different smell, but a bad smell: we've lost that too, it went up into the mountains.'

'A lot of use you little snufflers are,' grunted a bigger orc. 'I reckon eyes are better than your snotty noses. Have you seen anything?'

'What's to look for?' grunted the tracker.

Amid much further orcish dissension in confused drafting the final story emerges, with two orcs only, a soldier and a small tracker: my father had some trouble in deciding which offensive remark belonged to which speaker.

Drafting for the passage in which Sam described to Frodo all that had happened (RK p. 204) runs thus:

When he had finished Frodo said nothing for some time, but took Sam's hand and pressed it. At length he stirred. 'So this is what comes of eavesdropping, Sam,' he said. 'But I wonder if you'll ever get back. Perhaps it would have been safer to have been turned into a toad as Gandalf threatened. Do you remember that day, Sam,' he said, 'and clipping the edges under the window?'

'I do, Mr. Frodo. And I bet things are in [a] nasty mess there now with [?that] Lobelia and her Cosimo,[1] begging your pardon. There'll be trouble if ever we get back.'

'I shouldn't worry about that if I were you,' said Frodo. 'We've got to go on again now. East, East, Sam, not West. I wonder how long it will be before we are caught and all this slinking and toiling will be over?'

It is curious that Sam, speaking darkly of the state of affairs in the Shire, should ascribe it to Lobelia and Cosimo Sackville-Baggins. In the original sketch of the Mirror of Lothlórien, when it was King Galdaran's Mirror, and when it was Frodo who saw the visions of the Shire, he was to see 'Cosimo Sackville-Baggins very rich, buying up land'; but there is no mention of Cosimo in the first narrative of the scene (VII.249, 253).

Frodo's entrusting of Sting and the Phial of Galadriel to Sam entered in the first manuscript (B) in this form:

'You must keep the Lady's gift for me, Sam,' he said, 'I've nowhere to store it now, except in my hand, and I need both in the dark. And you must keep Sting too, since I have lost your sword. I have got an orc-blade, but I do not think it is my part to strike any blows again.'

It was at this time, as it appears, that my father came to a new perception of the lands in the north-western extremity of Mordor, and saw that the vale behind the Morannon was closed also at the southward end by great spurs that thrust out from Ephel Dúath and Ered Lithui. As first written in B, Frodo told Sam this concerning his knowledge of Mordor (cf. RK p. 204):

'No very clear notion, Sam,' said Frodo. 'In Rivendell before I set out I saw old maps made before the Dark Lord came back here, and I remember them vaguely. I had a little secret plan with names and distances: it was given to me by Elrond, but that has gone with all my other things. I think it was ten leagues or even a dozen from the Bridge to the Narrows, a point where the western and northern ranges send out spurs and make a sort of gate to the deep valley that lies behind the Morannon. The Mountain stands out alone on the plain, but nearer the northern range. Nearly fifty miles I think from the Narrows, more, of course, if we have to keep to the edge of the hills on the other side.'

In a revised version of this Frodo says: 'I guess, not counting our wasted climb, we've done say [twenty miles >] six or seven leagues north from the Bridge since we started.' The final version in this manuscript gives seven leagues as the distance they have traversed, 'ten leagues or so' from the Bridge to the meeting of the mountain-spurs, and still fifty miles from there to Mount Doom. In RK these distances are twelve leagues, not seven; twenty leagues, not ten; and sixty miles, not fifty: see further the Note on Geography at the end of this chapter.

When Frodo and Sam at last set eyes on the north-western confines of Mordor as seen from the south (RK p. 205) the names *Durthang* and *Carach Angren 'the Iron Jaws'* appear in the original draft, but the valley behind Carach Angren is named *the Narch*.[2] The draft text is here partly illegible, but enough can be read to show that the landscape was perfectly clear to my father's eyes as soon as he reached this point in the narrative. In the B text the name *Isenmouthe* appears, though the valley behind is still called 'the deep dark valley of Narch.'[3]

A notable feature in the original draft of the story is that there is no mention of Gollum (see RK p. 206). While Frodo slept Sam went off by himself and found water, as in RK, but then 'the rest of that grey day passed without incident. Frodo slept for [?hours]. Sam did not wake him, but trusting once more to "luck" slept for a long while beside him.' Gollum enters in the B text in these words:

At that moment he thought he caught a glimpse of a black form or shadow flitting among the stones above, near to Frodo's hiding. He was almost back to his master before he was sure. There was Gollum indeed! If his will could have given him strength for a great bound Sam would have sprung straight on his enemy's back; but at that moment Gollum became aware of him and looked back. Sam had a quick glimpse of two pale eyes now filled with a mad malevolent light, and then Gollum, jumping from rock to rock with great agility, fled away onto the ridge and vanished over its crest.

The end of the chapter, the story of Frodo and Sam being forced to join the orc-band coming down from Durthang and their escape from it in the confusion at the road-meeting near the Isenmouthe, was achieved in all but minor details unhesitatingly.[4]

NOTES

1 For Cosimo Sackville-Baggins, later Lotho, see VI.283, VII.32.

2 It was while working on the latter part of 'The Land of Shadow' that my father first mapped this new conception of the north-western extremity of Mordor, on a slip of paper that bears on the reverse drafting for the story of the forced march of Frodo and Sam in the troop of orcs moving from Durthang to the Isen-mouthe. On this little sketch-map the closed vale between the Morannon and the Isenmouthe is named *The Narch*, subsequently overwritten *Udûn*. In my description of the Second Map in VIII.438 I noted that the vale was first marked *Gorgoroth*, but that this was struck out, 'and in its place was pencilled here the name *Narch Udûn*.' It is in fact clear that *Narch* alone was first written, and that *Udûn* was intended as a replacement.

3 This was changed later to 'the deep dale of Kirith Gorgor', and then to 'the deep dale of Udûn' (see note 2).

4 A few such details from the earliest form of the conclusion of the chapter may be mentioned. The orc 'slave-drivers' are called 'two of the large fierce *uruks*, the fighting-orcs', and this seems to be the first time that the word was used (though the name *Uruk-hai* had appeared long since, VII.409, VIII.22, see also p. 436); and it is said that 'one of the slave-drivers *with night-sighted eyes* spied the two figures by the roadside.' Where in RK this orc says 'All your folk should have been inside Udûn before yesterday evening' he says here 'inside the Narch-line'; and following his words 'Don't you know we're at war?' he adds: 'If the elvish folk get the best of it, they won't treat you so kindly.'

Note on the Geography

In the first draft of the chapter, when Frodo and Sam climbed to the crest of the Morgai and looking out eastwards saw Mount Doom, it was 'still 30 miles away, perhaps, due East from where the hobbits stood.' In the B text, in the following manuscript, and in the final typescript for the printer, the distance became 'seven leagues or more', and was only altered to 'forty miles at least' (RK p. 200) at a late stage. It is impossible to relate '30 miles', still less 'seven leagues', to any of the maps. On the Second Map the distance due East from the Morgai to Mount Doom (in its second, more westerly, position, see VIII.438) is just under 50 miles, while on the Third Map (the last general small-scale map that my father made) it became 80 miles. On the large-scale map of Rohan, Gondor and Mordor the distance is somewhat under 60 miles, as Mount Doom was first placed; but when it was moved further to the west it became about 43 miles (under 40 in my redrawing of the map published in *The Return of the King*), with which the text of RK agrees.

The distance from the Morgai bridge below Kirith Ungol to the Isenmouthe was roughly estimated from memory by Frodo (p. 33) as 'ten leagues or even a dozen' (30–36 miles); and 'ten leagues at least' remained into the final typescript before being changed to the figure in RK (p. 204), 'twenty leagues at least'. The Second Map does not allow of precise measurement of the distance from the Morgai bridge to the Isenmouthe, since the conception of the closing of the vale behind the Morannon by spurs of Ephel Dúath and Ered Lithui had not arisen when it was made, but it could be minimally calculated as between 30 and 40 miles; on the large-scale map it becomes 56 miles or just under 19 leagues, agreeing with the twenty leagues of RK.

Frodo's estimation of the distance from the Isenmouthe to Mount Doom as about fifty miles likewise remained through all the texts until replaced at the very end by sixty. This distance is roughly 50 miles on the Second Map, about 80 on the Third Map, and 62 on the large-scale map as Mount Doom was first placed; when it was moved further west the distance from the Isenmouthe became 50 miles. The change of 50 to 60 at the end of the textual history of RK is thus, strangely, the reverse of the development of the map.

In the original draft Sam and Frodo joined the road to the Isenmouthe 'after it had already run down some 4 miles from the orc-hold of Durthang and turned away somewhat northward so that the long descent behind was hidden from them [?hurrying] on the stony road. They had been going an hour and had covered perhaps some 3 miles without meeting any enemy when they heard what they had all along dreaded ...' In B 'they came at last to the road where, after descending swiftly from Durthang, it became more level and ran under the ridge towards the Isenmouthe, a distance of perhaps ten miles.' As in A, they had only been on the road for an hour when they were overtaken by the orcs, and it is added in B at this point 'it was maybe six miles yet before the road would leave its high shelf and go down into the plain.' In the following manuscript and in the final typescript for the printer the hobbits still reached the road 'at the point where it swung east towards the Isenmouthe ten miles away', and it was still after only an hour on the road that they halted, and were shortly afterwards overtaken. On the typescript my father emended 'ten miles' to 'twenty miles', and 'an hour' to 'three hours', but the final reading of RK was 'after doing some twelve miles, they halted.' On the large-scale map the track of Frodo and Sam up the valley below the Morgai is marked, and the point where their track joined the road from Durthang is 20 miles from the Isenmouthe; the change in the text was thus very probably made to accommodate it to the map. The change whereby the hobbits had gone for three hours or twelve miles along the road before being overtaken clearly followed from the increased distance to the Isenmouthe, in order to reduce the time that Frodo and Sam had to submit to the punishing pace set by the orcs before they escaped.

Note on the Chronology

Dates are written in the margins of the original texts of this chapter. At this stage the chronology of the journey from Kirith Ungol can be set out thus:

March 14 Dawn: Frodo and Sam climb down into the valley below the Morgai. Wind changes and the darkness begins to be driven back.

Night of March 14–15: They sleep below the crest of the Morgai; Sam sees a star.

March 15 They reach the top of the Morgai and see Mount Doom; descend and continue up the valley; overhear the two orcs quarrelling.

Night of March 15–16: They continue up the valley northward.

March 16 They spend the day in hiding in the valley.

Night of March 16–17: They continue up the valley.

March 17 In hiding. They see Durthang and the road descending from it. Gollum reappears.

Night of March 17–18: They take the road from Durthang and are forced to join the orc-company.

This chronology accords with the date March 14 of the Battle of the Pelennor Fields (see VIII.428–9); in both the drafting A and the first manuscript B of the chapter 'It was the morning of the fourteenth of March ... Théoden lay dying on the Pelennor Fields.' Here in RK (p. 196) it was the morning of March 15; and all the dates as given above are in the final story one day later.

IV
MOUNT DOOM

The original draft of the chapter 'Mount Doom' was written continuously with the first completed manuscript B of 'The Land of
Shadow', which at this stage was called 'Mount Doom' (see p. 31); but
the division into two chapters was soon made.

The latter part of the original single chapter (which I will continue
to call 'B') is remarkable in that the primary drafting constitutes a
completed text, with scarcely anything in the way of preparatory
sketching of individual passages, and while the text is rough and full
of corrections made at the time of composition it is legible almost
throughout; moreover many passages underwent only the most minor
changes later. It is possible that some more primitive material has
disappeared, but it seems to me far more probable that the long
thought which my father had given to the ascent of Mount Doom and
the destruction of the Ring enabled him, when at last he came to write
it, to achieve it more quickly and surely than almost any earlier
chapter in *The Lord of the Rings*. He had known from far back (see
p. 3) that when Frodo (still called 'Bingo') came to the Crack of Doom
he would be unable to cast away the Ring, and that Gollum would
take it and fall into the chasm. But how did he fall? In subsequent
outlines Sam's part was pondered. My father knew that Sam was
attacked by Gollum on the way up the Mountain and delayed, so that
Frodo made the final ascent alone; and he knew that Gollum got hold
of the Ring by taking Frodo's finger with it. But for a long time he
thought that it was Sam who, finally making his way to the Chamber
of Fire, pushed Gollum with the Ring into the abyss. In none of the
later outlines given in Chapter I did he achieve the final articulation of
the story; but there seems good reason to think that these belong to the
period of the writing of Book V, and if my chronological deductions
are correct (see pp. 12–13), he had had plenty of time to 'find out what
really happened' before he came actually to describe the final moments
of the Quest.

As I have said, the final form of 'Mount Doom' was quite largely
achieved in the first draft (B), and I give the following brief passage
(interesting also for another reason) as exemplification (cf. RK
p. 223):

'Master!' he cried. Then Frodo stirred, and spoke with a clear
voice, indeed a voice clearer and more powerful than Sam had

ever heard him use, and it rose above the throb and turmoils of the chasm of Mount Doom, echoing in the roof and walls.

'I have come,' he said. 'But I cannot do what I have come to do. I will not do it. The Ring is mine.' And suddenly he vanished from Sam's sight. Sam gasped, but at that moment many things happened. Something struck Sam violently in the back, his legs were knocked from under him and he was flung aside striking his head against the stony floor. He lay still.

And far away as Frodo put on the Ring the Power in Baraddur was shaken and the Tower trembled from its foundations to its proud and bitter crown. The Dark Lord was suddenly aware of him, the Eye piercing all shadows looked across the plain to the door in Orodruin, and all the plot [> devices] was laid bare to it. Its wrath blazed like a sudden flame and its fear was like a great black smoke, for it knew its deadly peril, the thread upon which hung its doom. From all its policies and webs its mind shook free, and through all its realm a tremor ran, its slaves quailed, and its armies halted and its captains suddenly steerless bereft of will wavered and despaired. But its thought was now bent with all its overwhelming force upon the Mountain; and at its summons wheeling with a ...ing cry in a last desperate race there flew, faster than the wind, the Nazgûl, the Ringwraiths, with a storm of wings they hurtled towards Mount Doom.

Frodo's words 'But *I cannot do* what I have come to do' were changed subsequently on the B-text to 'But *I do not choose now to do* what I have come to do.' I do not think that the difference is very significant, since it was already a central element in the outlines that Frodo would *choose* to keep the Ring himself; the change in his words does no more than emphasize that he fully willed his act. (In the second text of the chapter, the fair copy manuscript 'C',[1] Sam cried out just before this not merely 'Master!' as in the first text and in RK but 'Master! Do it quick!' – these words being bracketed probably at the time of setting them down.)

This passage is notable in showing the degree to which my father had come to identify the Eye of Barad-dûr with the mind and will of Sauron, so that he could speak of 'its wrath, its fear, its thought'. In the second text C he shifted from 'its' to 'his' as he wrote out this passage anew.

Some other differences in the original text are worth recording. On the morning after they escaped from the orc-band marching to the Isenmouthe, following Frodo's words 'I can manage it. I must' (RK p. 211) text B at first continued:

In the end they decided to crawl in such cover as they could towards the north-range [and then turn south >] until they were further from the vigilance on the ramparts, and then turn south.

As they went from hollow to hollow or along cracks in the stony ground, keeping always if they could some screen between them and the north, they saw that the most easterly of the three roads went also in the same direction. It was in fact the road to the Dark Tower, as Frodo guessed.

He looked at it. 'I shall wear myself out in a day of this crawling and stooping,' he said. 'If we are to go on we must risk it. We must take the road.'

Here my father stopped, struck this out, and replaced it by a passage very close to that in RK, where it is Sam who sees that they can go no further in this fashion and must risk taking the road to the Dark Tower.

Another slight difference in the original text follows Frodo's words to Sam on the morning on which they left the road and turned south towards Mount Doom: 'I can't manage it, Sam. It is such a weight to carry, such a weight' (RK p. 214).

Sam knew what he meant, but seeking for some encouragement amid despair he answered: 'Well, Mr Frodo, why not lighten the load a bit. We're going that way as straight as we can make.' He pointed to the Mountain. 'No good taking anything we're not sure to need.'

Like a child, distracted from its trouble by some game of make-believe, Frodo considered his words seriously for a moment. Then 'Of course,' he said. 'Leave everything behind we don't want. Travel light, that's the thing, Sam!' He picked up his orc-shield and flung it away, and threw his helmet after it; and undoing his heavy belt cast it and the sword and sheath with it clattering on the ground. Even his grey cloak he threw away.

Sam looked at him with pity.

This was struck out immediately and replaced by the text of RK, in which Sam suggests that he should bear the Ring for a while. But neither in the text B nor in the fair copy C is there mention of the phial of Galadriel or of the little box that she gave to Sam.[2]

The height of Mount Doom was at first differently conceived: 'It was indeed some 3000 feet or so from foot to the .... broken crater at its crown. A third of that height now lay below him ...' Text C still differs from RK (p. 218): 'The confused and tumbled shoulders of its great sprawling base rose for maybe three[3] thousand feet above the

plain, and above them was reared, *almost as high again*, its tall central
cone, like a vast oast or chimney capped by a jagged crater. But
already Sam stood *half way up* the base ...' (where RK has 'half as
high again' and 'more than half way up'). My father's drawing,
reproduced in *Pictures by J. R. R. Tolkien* no. 30, and in this book on
p. 42, from a small page that carries also a scrap of drafting for this
part of the chapter, seems to show the final conception, with the cone
'half as high again' in relation to the 'base'; but in this drawing the
door of the Sammath Naur is at the foot of the cone, whereas in all
versions of the text the climbing road came 'high in the upper cone,
but still far from the reeking summit, to a dark entrance'.[4]

When Gollum fell upon Sam as he carried Frodo up the road, both
in the original text and in the fair copy C Sam not only tore the backs
of his hands as he crashed forward (RK p. 220) but also cut his
forehead on the ground. In B, against the words 'But Sam gave him no
more heed. He suddenly remembered his master. He looked up the
path and could not see him' (RK p. 222) my father wrote in the
margin: 'his head was bleeding?' This was not taken up in C, but a
little earlier, after the words 'Sam's hand wavered. His mind was hot
with wrath and the memory of evil' (RK p. 221) C has: 'Blood trickled
down his forehead.' Both these references to Sam's bleeding forehead
were later struck from C. It is not clear to me what my father had in
mind here. At first sight there might seem to be a connection with
Sam's blindness in outline V (p. 11): 'Sam feels a blindness coming on
and wonders if it is due to water of Mordor ... Sam half-blind is
lagging behind', but that seems to have been introduced to explain
how it was that when Gollum attacked Frodo went on unaware of
what had happened; whereas here the blood in Sam's eyes was the
result of Gollum's attack, and he himself urged Frodo to go on.
Possibly the cutting of his forehead was intended to explain why Sam
could not see Frodo when he looked up the path, and was removed
when my father came to the point when Sam was again felled by
Gollum in the Sammath Naur: 'He was dazed, and blood streaming
from his head dripped in his eyes' (RK p. 223).

When Sam urged Frodo to go on up alone while he dealt with
Gollum Frodo replied, both in B and C: 'The Quest shall now be all
fulfilled', where in RK he said: 'This is the end at last.'

At the end of the chapter, after the words 'Down like lashing whips
fell a torrent of black rain' (RK p. 224), the first text moves at once to
' "Well, this is the end, Sam," said a voice by his side.' Here my father
wrote in the margin soon after: 'Put in here (or in next chapter?) vision
of the cloudwrack out of Baraddur [?growing] to shape of a vast black
[?man] that stretches out a menacing unavailing arm and is blown
away.' The word 'man' is very unclear but I cannot see how else it
could be read. Later at this point in the manuscript he wrote 'Fall of
Ringwraiths' with a mark of insertion, and the passage 'And into the

heart of the storm, with a cry that pierced all other sounds ...' appears in C.

Lastly, Sam's feelings were thus described in B: 'If he felt anything in all that ruin of the world, it was perhaps most of all a great joy, to be servant once again, and know his master [*added:* and surrender to him the leadership].' This was repeated in C, but rejected and replaced by the reading of RK. In Frodo's final words he did not, in the original text, speak of forgiving Gollum.[5]

NOTES

1   The fair copy manuscript C is entitled 'Mount Doom' and numbered 'LIV' (see pp. 31, 37), the number changed subsequently to 'LII' (see p. 25).

2   Sam's vain use of the Phial when he entered the Sammath Naur (RK p. 222) appears in B. The addition concerning the Phial and the box was made later to text C.

   The passage in which Sam remembered paddling in the Pool at Bywater with the children of Farmer Cotton (RK p. 216) is also absent from B. This is one of the few passages in this chapter for which a separate draft is found (before its introduction into text C), and here the names of the Cotton children are seen emerging.

3   *three* was changed in pencil to *two* on the manuscript (C), but *three* survived.

4   In both B and C, despite the earlier statement (as in RK p. 219) that the road came 'high in the upper cone ... to a dark entrance', it is said in the passage corresponding to that in RK p. 222 that the road 'with a last course passed *across the base of the cone* and came to the dark door', where in RK 'with a last eastward course [it] passed *in a cutting along the face of the cone* and came to the dark door'.

   In B there is a little sketch of Mount Doom which my father struck through, and here the entrance to the Sammath Naur is placed about a third of the way up the cone (which is here shorter in relation to the base than in the drawing reproduced on p. 42). The road here disappears round the eastern side of the cone, below the door, and seems (the drawing is hard to make out) to reappear further up, coming from the left (east) and ending at the door.

5   A couple of points concerning names in this chapter may be mentioned. In the opening paragraph both B and C have 'He heard the scuffling and cries die down as the troops passed on into the Narch', where RK has 'passed on through the Isenmouthe'; see p. 33. The name *Sammath Naur* does not appear in B, but enters in C without any initial hesitation as to its form.

Mount Doom

Note on the Chronology

The chronology was still a day behind that of RK (see p. 36). At nightfall of the day on which they escaped from the orc-band at the Isenmouthe my father wrote in the margin of text B '18 ends'; this was March 19 in RK (in *The Tale of Years* 'Frodo and Samwise escape and begin their journey along the road to the Barad-dûr'). The reference to the passing of the Cross Roads by the Captains of the West and the burning of the fields of Imlad Morghul (so spelt) is however present in B at the same point as in RK (p. 212): see VIII.432.

In B, against the words 'There came at last a dreadful evening; and even as the Captains of the West drew near the end of the living lands, the two wanderers came to an hour of blank despair' (cf. RK p. 212), my father wrote 'end of 22'. This was the same date as in RK, and thus there follows in the original text 'Five days had passed since they escaped the orcs' (i.e. March 18–22), where RK has 'Four'.

V

THE FIELD OF KORMALLEN

In the first draft of this chapter my father again achieved for most of its
length an extraordinarily close approach to the final form, and this is
the more remarkable when one considers that he had no plan or
outline before him. There had been many mentions of a great feast to
follow the final victory (VII.212, 345, 448; VIII.275, 397), but
nothing had ever been said of it beyond the fact that it was to take
place in Minas Tirith.[1] That this text ('A') was indeed the first setting
down on paper of the story and that nothing preceded it seems
obvious from the nature of the manuscript itself, which has all the
marks of primary composition.[2] It was followed by a fair copy
manuscript ('B'), bearing the number and title 'LV   The Field of
Kormallen', which was also pencilled in later on A.

Not until the end of the minstrel's song of Frodo of the Nine Fingers
and the Ring of Doom did the first text A diverge in any narrative
point, and little even in expression, from the form in RK. There are
however several interesting details.

One of these concerns the Eagles. As the passage (RK p. 226)
describing their coming above the Morannon was first written it read:

There came Gwaihir, the Wind-lord, and Lhandroval his
brother, greatest of all the eagles of the north, mightiest of the
descendants of [added: Great > old] Thorondor who built his
eyries in the immeasurable peaks of Thangorodrim [changed
immediately to the Encircling Mountains] when Middle-earth
was young.

In the *Quenta* §15 (IV.137) it is told that after the Battle of
Unnumbered Tears 'Thorndor King of Eagles removed his eyries from
Thangorodrim to the northward heights of the Encircling Mountains
[*about the plain of Gondolin*], and there he kept watch, sitting upon
the cairn of King Fingolfin.' In the *Quenta Silmarillion* of 1937 there is
no mention of the Eagles dwelling on Thangorodrim, and at the time
of the fall of Fingolfin in his duel with Morgoth, before the Battle of
Unnumbered Tears, Thorondor came for the rescue of the king's body
'from his eyrie among the peaks of Gochressiel' (i.e. the Encircling
Mountains; V.285, §147). On the other hand, in the abandoned story
'Of Tuor and the Fall of Gondolin' given in *Unfinished Tales*, a story
that I believe to have been written in 1951, Voronwë speaks to Tuor of

'the folk of Thorondor, who dwelt once even on Thangorodrim ere Morgoth grew so mighty, and dwell now in the Mountains of Turgon since the fall of Fingolfin' (p. 43).

Gwaihir the Windlord had of course appeared often before this in *The Lord of the Rings* (for long *Gwaewar*, but becoming *Gwaihir* in the course of the writing of 'The White Rider', VII.430). In the *Quenta Silmarillion* (see V.301) Gwaewar had been one of the three eagles that came to Angband for the rescue of Beren and Lúthien; the earliest form of that passage reads:

Thorondor led them, and the others were Lhandroval (Wide-wing) and Gwaewar his vassal.

The following text (also belonging to 1937) has:

Thorondor was their leader; and with him were his mightiest vassals, wide-winged Lhandroval, and Gwaewar lord of the wind.

In a revision of the passage which can be dated to 1951 *Gwaewar* was changed to *Gwaihir*. As I have noticed in V.301, the names of the vassals of Thorondor were suppressed in the published *Silmarillion* (p. 182) on account of the present passage in RK, but this was certainly mistaken: it is clear that my father deliberately repeated the names. As in so many other cases in *The Lord of the Rings*, he took the name *Gwaewar* for the great eagle, friend of Gandalf, from *The Silmarillion*, and when *Gwaihir* replaced *Gwaewar* in *The Lord of the Rings* he made the same change to the eagle's name in *The Silmarillion*. Now he took also *Lhandroval*[3] to be the name of Gwaihir's brother; and added a new name, *Meneldor* (RK p. 228).

At the fall of the Black Gate Gandalf said only: 'The Realm of Sauron is ended'; but to this my father added, probably immediately: 'So passes the Third Age of the World.' This was placed within brackets, and 'The Ringbearer has fulfilled his Quest' written in the margin.

To Gwaihir Gandalf said: 'You will not find me a burden any greater than when you bore me from Zirakinbar where my old life burned away.' *Zirakinbar* remained through all the texts of the chapter and was only changed to *Zirakzigil* on the galley proof. On these names see VII.174 and 431 with note 6.

Another difference in A which survived long (into the final typescript of the chapter) was the absence of Sam's expression of astonishment at seeing Gandalf at his bedside ('Gandalf! I thought you were dead! But then I thought I was dead myself. ...', RK p. 230).

The date of the Field of Kormallen (as the name was spelt until the final typescript) was expressed by Gandalf thus in A:

'Noon?' said Sam, puzzling his brains. 'Noon of what day?'
'The third day of the New Year,' said Gandalf, 'or if you like

the twenty-eighth day of March in the Shire-reckoning. But in Gondor the New Year will always begin upon the 25th of March when Sauron fell, and when you were brought out of the fire to the King. ...'[4]

If March 25th was New Year's Day, the 28th was the fourth day of the New Year in Gondor, and my father wrote 'fourth' above 'third', without however striking out 'third'. In pencil he wrote 'seventh' against this, and 'the last day' above 'the twenty-eighth day', although this would give 31 days to the month. His reason for this is obscurely indicated by a note in the margin: 'More time required for [?gathering] of goods, say' (i.e., 'say the seventh').[5]

In the fair copy B as written Gandalf said 'The Seventh of the New Year; or if you like, the last day of March in the Shire-reckoning'; this was changed later to 'The Fourteenth of the New Year' and 'the sixth day of April in the Shire-reckoning'. Even allowing 31 days to the month, the sixth of April would be the thirteenth day of the New Year, and 'sixth' was afterwards changed to 'seventh', and finally to 'eighth', as in RK. I do not know precisely what considerations impelled my father so greatly to prolong the time during which Sam and Frodo lay asleep.

Their first conversation with Gandalf ends thus in A:

'What shall we wear?' said Sam, for all he could see were the old and tattered clothes that they had journeyed in, lying folded on the ground beside their beds.

'The clothes that you were found in,' said Gandalf. 'No silks and linen, nor any armour or heraldry, could be more honourable. But afterwards we shall see.'

This survived through all the texts to the galley, where 'The clothes that you were found in' was changed to 'The clothes that you journeyed in'. It was not until the Second Edition of 1966 that the passage was altered and extended, by changing Gandalf's words to 'The clothes that you wore on your way to Mordor.[6] Even the orc-rags that you bore in the black land, Frodo, shall be preserved', and by his return of the Phial of Galadriel and the box that she gave to Sam (RK pp. 230–1; cf. p. 39 and note 2).

The crying of praise as Frodo and Sam came to the Field of Kormallen underwent many changes. In all the texts of the chapter Old English phrases cried by the Riders of Rohan were mingled. The form of the 'Praise' in A runs thus (with some punctuation added from the B-text, which is closely similar):

Long live the halflings! Praise them with great praise! Cuio i Pheriannath anann, aglar anann! Praise them with great praise!

Hale, hale cumath, wesath hale awa to aldre. Fróda and Samwís! Praise them! Kuivië, kuivië! laurea'esselínen![7] Praise them!

In the fair copy B the Old English words were changed to *Wilcuman, wilcuman, Fróda and Samwís!* and the Quenya words became *Laitalle, laitalle, andave laita!* In the first typescript the Old English *Uton herian holbytlan!* was added before *Laitalle, laitalle*; and in the second (final) typescript the Quenya words became *A laituvar, laituvar, andave laita!* This was then changed on the typescript to *A laita te, laita te! Andave laituvalme!* Thus the form as it appears on the galley proof is:

Long live the Halflings! Praise them with great praise! Cuio i Pheriannath anann! Aglar anann! Praise them with great praise! Wilcuman, wilcuman, Fróda and Samwís! Praise them! Uton herian holbytlan! A laita te, laita te! Andave laituvalmet! Praise them! The Ringbearers, praise them with great praise!

The final text of the 'Praise', as it appears in RK, was typed onto the galley proof.

From the end of the minstrel's song (RK p. 232) the original text A runs thus:

And then Aragorn stood up and all the host rose, and they passed to a pavilion made ready, there to eat and drink and make merry.

But as Sam and Frodo stepped down with Aragorn from the throne Sam caught sight of a small man-at-arms as it seemed in the silver and sable of the guards of the king: but he was small and he wondered what such a boy was doing in such an army. Then suddenly he exclaimed: 'Why, look Mr Frodo. Look here. Bless me if it's not Pippin, Mr Peregrin Took I should say. Bless me but I can see there's more tales than ours to hear. It'll take weeks before we get it all right.'

'Yes,' said Frodo. 'I can see myself locked up in a room somewhere making notes for days or Bilbo will be bitterly disappointed.'

And so they passed to the feast and at a sign from Aragorn Pippin went with them.[8]

The page carrying this text was rejected; on the back of it is an outline of the story to come (see p. 51, 'The Story Foreseen from Kormallen'). A replacement page was substituted, but again the development turned out to be unsatisfactory:

But first Frodo and Sam were led apart and taken to a tent, and there their old raiment was taken off, but folded and set aside with honour; and clean linen was brought to them. But Gandalf came and with him went an esquire, no more than a small lad he seemed, though clad in the silver and sable of the king's guard, and to the wonder of Frodo and Sam they bore the sword and the elven-cloak and the mithril-coat that had been taken from them; and for Sam they brought a coat of gilded mail, and on Frodo's right hand upon the middle[9] and little fingers they set small rings of mithril set each with a gem like a star. But the wonder of all these things was as little to the wonder on Sam's face as he looked on the face of the esquire and knew him.

And he cried out: 'Why look, Mr. Frodo. Look here! Save me, if it isn't Pippin, Mr. Peregrin Took, I should say. Why bless us all, but I can see there's more tales to tell than ours. It will take weeks of talk before we get it all sized up.'

'It will indeed,' said Pippin. 'But at present it is time for a feast, and you must not keep it waiting. Later on, Frodo must be locked up in a tower in Minas Tirith till he's made notes of all our doings, or Bilbo will be dreadfully disappointed.'

This passage was at once reconstructed to remove Pippin from the scene, and Gandalf comes to the tent alone, as in RK (p. 233). When he has set the rings of mithril on Frodo's fingers the feast follows at once:

... and on Frodo's right hand, upon the middle and little fingers, he set fine rings of mithril, slender as threads of silk but bearing each a small gem shining like a star.[10] And when they were made ready, and circlets of silver were set upon their heads, they went to the feast, and sat with Gandalf, and there was Aragorn and King Éomer of Rohan and all the Captains of the West, and there too were Legolas and Gimli.

[Struck out at once: 'That's six of the Company,' said Sam to Frodo. 'Where are the o(thers)] But when wine was brought there came in an esquire to serve the Kings of Gondor and Rohan, or so he seemed, and he was clad in the silver and sable of the guards of the King; but he was small, and Sam wondered what such a boy was doing in an army of mighty men. [Then follows Sam's recognition of Pippin, as above.]

'It will indeed,' said Pippin, 'and we'll begin as soon as this feast is ended. In the meantime you can try Gandalf. He's not as close as he used to be, though he laughs now more than he talks.'

And so at last the glad day ended; and when the sun was gone and the crescent moon[11] rode slowly above the mist of Anduin and flickered through the fluttering leaves, Frodo and Sam sat amid the night-fragrance of fair Ithilien, and talked deep into the night with Pippin and Gandalf and Legolas and Gimli.

At last Gandalf rose. 'The hands of the King are hands of healing, dear friends,' he said. 'But you went near to the very brink of death, and though you have slept long and blessedly, still it is now time to rest again. Not you only, Frodo and Sam, but you Peregrin also. For when they lifted you from under the slain it is said that even Aragorn despaired of you.'

Probably at once, this was emended throughout to make Merry also present (see note 8), and the last part of it (Gandalf's parting words) was in turn rejected. In very rough further drafting the final text was approached, though not achieved, in the manuscript A. Gimli's speech (RK p. 234) at this time ended thus:

'... And when I heaved that great carcase off you, then I made sure you were dead. I could have torn out my beard. And that was but a week ago. To bed now you go. And so shall I.'

From this it is seen that it was 'the seventh day of the New Year': see p. 46.[12] The draft continues to its end thus:

'And I,' said Legolas, 'shall walk in the woods of this fair land, which is rest enough. And in days to come, if my Elven lord will allow it, some of our folk shall remove hither, for it is more lovely than any lands they have yet dwelt in;[13] and then it will be blessed for a while. But Anduin is near and Anduin leads down to the sea. To the sea, to the sea, and the white gulls crying, to the sea and the sea and the white foam flying,' and so singing he went away down the hill.

And then the others departed and Frodo and Sam went to their beds and slept; and in the morning the host prepared to return to Minas Tirith. The ships had come and they were lying under Cair Andros, and soon all would be set across the Great River, and so in peace and ease fare over the green swards of Anórien and to the Pelennor and the towers under tall Mindolluin, the city of the men of Gondor, last memory of Westernesse.

Thus the name *Kormallen* did not enter in the original text of the chapter, and it is not said that the Field was near to Henneth Annûn; but scribbled drafting put in later on the last page of the manuscript shows the final text emerging:

And in the morning they rose again and spent many days in Ithilien, for the Field of Kormallen where the host was encamped was near to Henneth Annûn, and they wandered here and there visiting the scenes of their adventures, but Sam lingered ever in some shadow of the woods to find maybe some sight of the Oliphaunt. And when he heard that in the seige of Gondor there had been fifty of them at the least, but all were dead, he thought it a great loss. And in the meanwhile the host rested, for they had laboured much and had fought long and hard against the remnant of the Easterlings and Southrons; and they waited also for those that were to return.

In the fair copy B the final text of the First Edition was present in all but a few points, most of which have been mentioned in the foregoing account and in the notes;[14] but an important change in the description of the dressing of Frodo and Sam before the feast (RK p. 233) was made in the Second Edition. As the text stood in the First Edition (going back unchanged to the fair copy manuscript B) it ran:

... For Sam he brought a coat of gilded mail, and his elven-cloak all healed of the soils and hurts that it had suffered; and when the Hobbits were made ready, and circlets of silver were set upon their heads, they went to the King's feast, and they sat at his table with Gandalf ...

In the Second Edition the passage was added in which Gandalf brought Sting and Sam's sword, and Frodo had to be persuaded to wear a sword and to accept back Sting. At this time also the reference was added to 'the Standing Silence' before the feast began.

NOTES

1 There had been a suggestion (VIII.397) that the tale of the passage of the Paths of the Dead should be told at the 'feast of victory in Minas Tirith', but that idea had of course been overtaken.

2 It may be that the first draft of 'The Field of Kormallen' was written before the fair copy manuscript of 'Mount Doom'. A pointer to this is the fact that where in RK (p. 228) 'a great smoke and steam belched from the Sammath Naur' A has 'a great fire belched from the cave': see p. 41 note 5.

3 The first draft A has the spelling *Lhandroval* at all occurrences, but the fair copy B has *Landroval*, as in RK.

4 Both in A and B it is Frodo who asks 'What king, and who is he?' On the first typescript Sam's question 'What shall we wear?' was transferred to Frodo, but in the final typescript given back to Sam.

5 Perhaps to be compared is the sentence in 'The Steward and the King', RK pp. 241–2: 'Merry was summoned [*from Minas Tirith*] and rode away with the wains that took store of goods to Osgiliath and thence by ship to Cair Andros.'

6 Frodo was naked when Sam found him in the Tower of Kirith Ungol; he had to dress in 'long hairy breeches of some unclean beast-fell, and a tunic of dirty leather' (RK p. 189).

7 *laurea'esselínen* was changed at the time of writing to *an-kalim'esselínen*.

8 At this stage, when only a little time had passed since the fall of Sauron, Merry would still have been in Minas Tirith; cf. note 5.

9 My father named the penultimate finger (the 'fourth finger' or 'ring-finger') the 'third finger'; so Frodo's 'third finger was missing' (RK p. 229).

10 The rings of mithril set on Frodo's fingers were retained in the fair copy B, where the passage was struck out.

11 The 'crescent moon' remained in B and in the first typescript, where it was changed to 'the round moon'.

12 It is strange that in B Gimli said here, not as in RK 'And it is only a day yet since you were first up and abroad again', but 'a few days' (this being corrected on the manuscript).

13 This sentence was retained in B and the first typescript, where it was struck out.

14 To these may be added the retention of the name *Narch* in 'And they passed over the Narch and Gorgoroth' (RK p. 228), subsequently emended to *Udûn*. At the end of the chapter it was said at first in B that 'when the month of May was passed seven days the Captains of the West set out again', but this was changed to 'when the month of May was drawing near', and at the same time the last sentence of the chapter was changed from 'for the King would enter his gates with the rising of the Sun' by the addition of the words 'it was the Eve of May, and (the King would enter ...)'.

THE STORY FORESEEN FROM KORMALLEN

This page (see p. 47) was scribbled down in pencil in my father's most impossible handwriting. I have not marked with queries a number of words that I think are probable but not altogether certain, and I have expanded several names given only as initials. The first sentence was written separately from the rest of the outline, whether before or after.

Gimli explains how Pippin was saved.

Next scene – The Host sets out from Cair Andros and [*read* in] the ships and passes into Gondor.
Scene shifts to Merry and to Faramir and Éowyn.
Return of King Elessar. His crowning. His judgements . . . . . of Berithil.
The hobbits wait. For there is to be a wedding. Elrond and Galadriel and Celeborn come and bring Finduilas.
The wedding of Aragorn and Finduilas.
Also Faramir and Éowyn.
The end of the Third Age is presaged. What the Rings had done. Their power waned. Galadriel and Elrond prepare to depart.
The hobbits return with Éomer to the funeral of Théoden and then on through the Gap of Rohan [?with . . . . . and the Dúnedain].
They come on Saruman and he is [?pardoned].
They come to Rivendell and see Bilbo. Bilbo gives him Sting and the coat. But he is getting old.
They come back to the Shire [*added in margin:* via Bree, pick up pony] and drive out Cosimo Sackville-Baggins. Lobelia is dead – she had a fit in [?quarrel]. Sam replants the trees. Frodo goes back to Bag End. All is quiet for a year or two. And then one day Frodo takes Sam for a walking [?tour] to the Woody End. And [?behold there go many] Elves. Frodo rides to the Havens and says farewell to Bilbo. End of the Third Age.
Sam's Book.

It is plain that my father wrote this outline while he was working on 'The Field of Kormallen', and indeed the precise stage in that work can probably be deduced: for Gimli's words at the end of the evening, in which he spoke of finding Pippin under the heap of slain, had not entered ('Gimli explains how Pippin was saved'). The precise placing of these notes in the history of the composition of Book VI gives them a particular interest. Several features of the end of the story now appear for the first time: as the marriage of Faramir and Éowyn; Bilbo's giving of the mithril-coat and Sting to Frodo ('forgetting that he had already done so', RK p. 265); the time of peace and quiet after the return of the hobbits to the Shire (but that 'Sam's casket restores Trees' had been known for a long time, VII.286); and Frodo's walk with Sam to the Woody End. But the death, before the return of the hobbits, of Lobelia Sackville-Baggins in a fit (of fury? – the word I have given as *quarrel* is scarcely more than a guess) was not permanent: she would be resurrected, survive her imprisonment during the troubles of the Shire, and end her days in a much more enlightened fashion.

This outline is as elliptical as were so many of my father's sketches of the further course of the story, concentrating on particular elements and ignoring or only hinting at others; and it is hard to know what narrative idea underlay the words 'Frodo rides to the Havens and says farewell to Bilbo'. Many years before (VI.380) he had written that when 'Bingo' returned to the Shire he would make peace, and would then 'settle down in a little hut on the high green ridge – until one day he goes with the Elves west beyond the towers' (cf. also another note of that time, VI.379: 'Island in sea. Take Frodo there in end'). In the outline 'The Story Foreseen from Moria' (VII.212) he had concluded his synopsis thus:

XXVIII What happens to Shire?

Last scene. Sailing away of Elves [*added:* Bilbo with them] . . .

XXIX Sam and Frodo go into a green land by the Sea?

In another note of that period (VII.287) he said: 'When old, Sam and Frodo set sail to island of West . . . Bilbo finishes the story.' Probably about the time of the writing of 'The King of the Golden Hall' he had written (VII.451) that in old age Frodo with Sam had seen Galadriel and Bilbo. On the other hand, in his letter to me of 29 November 1944 (see VIII.219) he was entirely clear – and accurate – in his prevision:

> But the final scene will be the passage of Bilbo and Elrond and Galadriel through the woods of the Shire on their way to the Grey Havens. Frodo will join them and pass over the Sea (linking with the vision he had of a far green country in the house of Tom Bombadil).

Since this is of course the story in the last chapter of *The Lord of the Rings* it is strange indeed to find in the present text that he had departed from it – for 'Frodo rides to the Havens and says farewell to Bilbo' can obviously be interpreted in no other way. I suspect therefore that there is in fact no mystery: that in notes written at great speed my father merely miswrote 'Bilbo' for 'Sam'.

Remarkable also is the reference to the encounter with Saruman – the word *pardoned* here is not certain, but can hardly be read otherwise. That they would meet Saruman again on the homeward journey was an old idea (see 'The Story Foreseen from Moria', VII.212), but then it had taken place at Isengard, and the matter of that scene had of course been removed to a much earlier place in the narrative (VII.436). A later note (VII.287) says that 'Saruman becomes a wandering conjuror and trickster', but nothing further has been told of him since he was left a prisoner in Orthanc guarded by the Ents until now.

VI

THE STEWARD AND THE KING

My remarks about 'The Field of Kormallen' (p. 44) can be repeated of 'The Steward and the King': the preliminary draft ('**A**') of this chapter, though written roughly and rapidly, was changed very little afterwards. There are nonetheless a number of differences in detail.[1]

A had no title, but 'Faramir and Éowyn' was pencilled in subsequently. A fair copy manuscript '**B**' followed, with the chapter-number 'LVI' but no title; to this text the title 'The Watchers on the Walls' was added in pencil, and this was changed to 'The Steward and the King'. In B the page-numbers run only as far as 'And she abode there until King Éomer came' (RK p. 243); at 'All things were now made ready in the City', at the top of a new page, a new numbering from '1' begins.

Of this chapter my father made a third, very fine manuscript '**C**', numbering it 'LIV'. Beneath the title 'The Steward and the King' he pencilled '(i) The Steward'; but although there is a large space in the text after 'And she remained there until King Éomer came', where the new page-numbering begins in B, there is no second sub-title.

At the beginning of the chapter in A the Warden of the Houses of Healing, after the words 'He sighed and shook his head' (RK p. 237), continues:

'It may come thus to us all yet,' he said, 'choosing or not choosing. But in the meantime we must endure with patience the hours of waiting. It is not always the easier part. But for you, Lady, you will be the better prepared to face evil that may come in your own manner, if you do as the healers bid, while there is still time.'

This was rejected before the chapter had proceeded much further, for similar words were given to Faramir subsequently in the initial text (RK p. 238). And when the Warden looked out from his window and saw Faramir and Éowyn, finding in the sight a lightening of his care, it is said: 'For it had been reported to him that the Lord Aragorn had said "If she wakes to despair then she will die, unless other healing comes which I cannot give."'

The blue mantle set with stars which Faramir gave to Éowyn when the weather turned cold is in A said to have been made for his mother 'Emmeril', changed in the act of writing to 'Rothinel of Amroth, who died untimely'. This name survived into the following manuscript B, where it was changed to Finduilas (see pp. 58–9).

The words of the Eagle that bore tidings to Minas Tirith of the fall of the Dark Tower were first reported thus:

The realm of Sauron hath ended and the Ring of Doom is no more and the King is victorious, he has passed through the Black Gate in triumph and all his enemies are fled.

The name *Kormallen* entered in this text. My father left a blank for the name as he wrote: 'And Éowyn did not go, though her brother sent word begging her to come to the field of ___ [between Henneth Annûn and Cair Andros]' (cf. RK p. 242 and p. 50 above), but he evidently wrote the name in the margin at once, since it appears in the text as written a few lines later.

In the conversation between Éowyn and Faramir that follows she said, in A, 'I love or have loved another.' This survived in B, where her words were changed to 'I hoped to be loved by another', and then at once to 'I wished'.

Somewhat later in the chapter (RK p. 244) Ioreth (now so spelt; hitherto Yoreth) names the hobbits *Periannath* (cf. *Ernil i Pheriannath* in the chapter 'Minas Tirith', RK p. 41, *Ernil a Pheriannath* VIII.287), and this survived into the First Edition of LR, changed to *Periain* in the Second.

There were substantial differences in the original account of Aragorn's coming to Minas Tirith and his coronation before the walls from the story in RK (pp. 244–6). The entry of Aragorn, Gandalf, Éomer, Imrahil and the four hobbits into the cleared space before the Gateway was very briefly described in A: there was no mention of the Dúnedain nor of Aragorn's apparel. The casket in which the White Crown was laid was not described ('of black *lebethron* bound with silver' B, as in RK; cf. VIII.180). When Faramir, surrendering his office as 'the Last Steward of Gondor', gave Aragorn the white rod Aragorn did not return it to him; he said nothing to Faramir at this point, and Faramir at once proclaimed: 'Men of Gondor, you have no longer a Steward, for behold one has returned to claim the kingship at last. Here is Aragorn son of Arathorn ...' Among Aragorn's titles Faramir names him 'chieftain of the Dúnedain of the North' and does not name him 'bearer of the Star of the North'. After the description of the crown there follows:

And Aragorn knelt, and Faramir upon the one hand and upon the other the Prince Imrahil set the crown upon his head, and then Gandalf laid his hand on Aragorn's shoulder and bade him arise. And when he arose all that beheld him gazed in silence ...

and a light was about him. And then Faramir said 'Behold the King!' and he broke his white rod.

Lastly, when Aragorn came to the Citadel a marginal addition to A says that 'the banner of Tree Crown and Stars was raised above it' ('the banner of the Tree and the Stars' B, as in RK); see VIII.279, 389, 399.

The reference to the Dúnedain 'in silver and grey' and the description of Aragorn's black mail and white mantle clasped with a great green stone was added to B, but the 'star upon his forehead bound by a slender fillet of silver' did not enter until the Second Edition; similarly Faramir still proclaimed him 'chieftain of the Dúnedain of the North' ('of Arnor', Second Edition) and did not name him 'bearer of the Star of the North' in the First Edition (see VIII.299, 309; 389 and note 10).

Rough marginal additions to A make Aragorn return the white rod to Faramir with the words 'That office is not yet wholly at an end' (cf. RK p. 245: 'That office is not ended, and it shall be thine and thy heirs' as long as my line shall last'), and give a first draft of his wish that he should be crowned by those 'by whose labours and valour I have come to my inheritance'. Here the ceremony takes this form: 'Gandalf took the crown and bade Frodo and Sam lay their hands also upon it, and they set the White Crown of Gondor upon the head of Aragorn'; whereas in RK, at Aragorn's request, Frodo brought the crown to Gandalf, who then performed the crowning alone. In B the text of RK was reached at all points in this scene apart from the words of Elendil repeated by Aragorn when he held up the crown,[2] which take the form: *Et Ëarello Endorenna lendien. Símane maruvan, ar hildinyar, kenn' Iluve-metta!* A translation pencilled in later is virtually the same as that in RK (p. 246): 'Out of the Great Sea to Middle-earth have I come. Here will I abide, and my heirs, unto the ending of the world.' In the third manuscript C the words remained the same as in B, apart from *tenn'* (as in RK) for *kenn'*, but were subsequently changed to *Et Ëarello Endorenna nilendie. Sinome nimaruva yo hildinyar tenn' Ambar-metta!*

A notable visitor to Minas Tirith among the many embassies that came to the King is found in A:

... and the slaves of Mordor he set free and gave them all the lands about Lake Núrnen for their own. And last of all there came to him Ghân-buri-Ghân of the Wild Woods and two of the headmen, and they were clad in garments of green leaves to do honour to the king, and they laid their foreheads on his feet; but he bade them rise up and blessed them and gave them the Forest of Druadan for their own, so that no man should ever enter it without their leave.

This was not rejected on the manuscript, but it is not present in B. For the further history of the last encounter with the Wild Men of the Woods see pp. 61–2, 67–8.

Éowyn's words to Faramir (RK p. 248), saying that she must now return to Rohan with Éomer, but that after the funeral of Théoden she will return, are absent from A (but were added to B). The statements in RK that the Riders of Rohan left Minas Tirith on the eighth of May and that the sons of Elrond went with them are not found in any of the texts, and they remain absent in the First Edition; on the other hand the return of Elladan and Elrohir to Minas Tirith with the company from Rivendell and Lothlórien (RK p. 250) is already found in A. It is told in A that 'the Companions of the Ring lived with Gandalf in a house in the Citadel, and went to and fro as they wished; but Legolas sat most[ly] on the walls and looked south towards the sea.' That the house was in the Citadel was not repeated in B, which retained however the words concerning Legolas; these were lost, possibly unintentionally, in C.

In the story of the ascent of Mindolluin by Gandalf and Aragorn (RK pp. 248–50) there are some differences from the final form to mention. In the original text it is not said that they went up by night and surveyed the lands in the early morning, nor is there mention of the ancient path to the hallow 'where only the kings had been wont to go'; and Gandalf in his words to Aragorn does not speak of the Three Rings, but says:

'... For though much has been saved, much is passing away. And all these lands that you see, and those that lie about, shall be dwellings and realms of Men, whom you must guide. For this is the beginning of the Dominion of Men, and other kindreds will depart, dwindle, and fade.'

B has the final text in all this. In A Aragorn says 'I have still twice the span of other men'; this was retained through the following texts and not changed until the galley proof to the reading of RK (where there is a difference between the First and Second Editions: in the First he says 'I may have life far longer than other men', but in the Second 'I shall').

When Aragorn saw the sapling at the edge of the snow he cried, in A, *En túvien!*, which in B becomes *En a túvien!* This was retained in C but corrected to *En [?in]túviet*; on the final (typescript) text of the chapter this was retained, but then erased and *Yé! utúvienyes* written in its place. The passage continues in A, in extremely difficult handwriting:

'... I have found it, for here is a scion of Nimloth eldest of trees. And how comes it here, for it is not yet itself seven years old?'

And Gandalf said: 'Verily here is a sapling of the line of Telperion Ninquelóte that the Elves of Middle-earth name Nimloth. Nimloth the fair of many names, Silivros and Celeborn³ and Galathilion of old. But who shall say how it comes here in the hour that is appointed? But the birds of the air are many, and maybe down the ages as lord followed lord . . . . . in the City and the tree withered, here where none looked for it the [?race] of Nimloth has [?flowered already] hidden on the mountain, even as Elendil's race lay hid in the wastes of the North. Yet the line of Nimloth is older far than your line, lord Elessar.'

With the names that appear in this passage cf. the *Quenta Silmaril-lion* in V.209, §16:
Silpion the one was called in Valinor, and Telperion and Ninquelótë and many names in song beside; but the Gnomes name him Galathilion.
A footnote to the text (V.210) adds:
Other names of Silpion among the Gnomes are Silivros glimmering rain (which in Elvish form is Silmerossë), Nimloth pale blossom, Celeborn tree of silver . . .
B has here the text of RK, in which Aragorn does not name 'the Eldest of Trees', and Gandalf says: 'Verily this is a sapling of the line of Nimloth the fair; and that was a seedling of Galathilion, and that a fruit of Telperion of many names, Eldest of Trees.' In *The Silmarillion* chapter 5 (p. 59) it is told that Yavanna made for the Elves of Tirion
. . . a tree like to a lesser image of Telperion, save that it did not give light of its own being; Galathilion it was named in the Sindarin tongue. This tree was planted in the courts beneath the Mindon and there flourished, and its seedlings were many in Eldamar. Of these one was afterwards planted in Tol Eressëa, and it prospered there, and was named Celeborn; thence came in the fullness of time, as is elsewhere told, Nimloth, the White Tree of Númenor.⁴
In A the sapling did not 'hold only lightly to the earth', but 'Aragorn and Gandalf dug deep.'

In the account of the riding from Rivendell and Lórien at the end of the chapter it is not said in any of the texts that Elrond brought the sceptre of Annúminas and surrendered it to Aragorn; this was only inserted on the final proof. Elrond's daughter is named Finduilas (VIII.370, 386, 425; at this stage Faramir's mother was named Rothinel, p. 54); and in A my father added, after 'Finduilas his daughter', '[and daughter of Celebrian child of Galadriel].' This is the first mention of Celebrian, by this or any name. In the last sentence of the chapter in A Aragorn 'wedded Finduilas Halfelven'; this name survived into B, where Faramir's mother Rothinel was changed to

Finduilas, and Elrond's daughter Finduilas was changed to Arwen, called Undómiel.[5]

NOTES

1   All names in RK not mentioned in my account can be presumed to be present already in A, with the exception of *Beregond*, which was only changed from *Berithil* on manuscript C. Thus Elfhelm is called 'Elfhelm the Marshal' (RK p. 244; cf. VIII.352); and the last king of the line of Anárion is Eärnur, here first named (RK p. 245; cf. VIII.153). The rather puzzling reference to Min-Rimmon (RK p. 245: 'tidings had gone out into all parts of Gondor, from Min-Rimmon even to Pinnath Gelin and the far coasts of the sea') goes back to A.

2   The words of Elendil do not appear in A.

3   In A the name *Celeborn* is spelt with *C*; so also *Celebrian*. In this chapter and in the next the *C* spelling reverted to *K* in the finely-written third manuscripts, but on both it was then corrected back to *C*.

4   Cf. also the *Akallabêth* in *The Silmarillion*, p. 263, and *Of the Rings of Power and the Third Age*, ibid. p. 291.

5   Arwen first emerged in the fair copy of the following chapter, 'Many Partings': see p. 66.

Note on the Chronology

A curious point of chronology that arises in this chapter concerns the lapse of time between the departure of the host from Minas Tirith and the destruction of the Ring.

At the beginning of the chapter, against the words 'When the Captains were but two days gone', the figure '19' is written in the margin of A, i.e. March 19. This is the chronology described in VIII.432, according to which the march from Minas Tirith began on the 17th (the 18th in RK).

When in RK (p. 239) it is said that 'the fifth day came since the Lady Éowyn went first to Faramir', and that was the day of the destruction of the Ring and the fall of the Dark Tower, the same is said in A (and subsequent texts); and at the head of that page my father noted: 'F. sees E. on 19. 20, 21, 22, 23, 24, 25.' This day was therefore the 24th of March. But this is strange, since already in the first draft of 'The Field of Kormallen' Gandalf had declared that 'in Gondor the New Year will always begin on the 25th of March when Sauron fell ...' (p. 46). In A, Éowyn says that this day was 'seven days since [Aragorn] rode away' (RK p. 240), which agrees with the date of March 24 for the destruction of the Ring. But my father changed 'seven', as he wrote, to 'nine', which would presumably give March 26 as the day of deliverance. He then changed 'nine' to 'eight', giving the

25th as the day, and 'eight' is the reading in B and C, changed in C to 'seven' as in RK: this presumably implies that the date of the departure from Minas Tirith had been changed to the 18th. – On the significance of the date 25 March see T. A. Shippey, *The Road to Middle-Earth* (1982) pp. 151–2.

VII
MANY PARTINGS

The original draft of this chapter ('**A**') was paginated continuously with that of 'The Steward and the King' and bore no title. In comparison with its subsequent form my father's initial account of the 'many partings' was remarkably brief and spare; and though his handwriting is very difficult and here and there altogether illegible I shall give a substantial part of it in full, for it differs in very many points from the story in RK.

The opening, however, remained almost unchanged from first draft to final text (apart from *Queen Finduilas* for *Queen Arwen*), as far as '"Then I beg leave to depart soon," said Frodo.' Then follows (with no mention of the Queen's gift):

'In three days we will go,' said Aragorn. 'For we shall ride with you great part of the way. We too have errands to do.'

And so it was that the King of Gondor and his Queen set out once more upon the North Roads, and many knights rode with them; and the Princes of Dol Amroth and of Ithilien; and King Éomer and his householdmen were also in that riding, for he had come to the wedding of his lord and brother. And with slow songs of the Mark they brought from the Halls [*probably for Hallows*] and his resting in Rath Dínen King Théoden upon a golden bier; and as one that still slept deeply they laid him upon a great wain with Riders of Rohan all about it, and his banner borne before. And Merry being his esquire, and a Knight of the Riddermark, rode upon the wain and kept the arms of the dead king. But for the other companions steeds were furnished according to their stature, and Frodo and Sam rode at the king's side with Gandalf upon Shadowfax; and with them also went Legolas and Gimli upon Hasufel[1] who had borne them so far.[2]

And slowly and at peace they passed into Anórien. And .... the Greywood[3] under Amon Dîn.

Here my father stopped and asked whether the homage of the Wild Men should be put here – referring, presumably, to the story in the original text of 'The Steward and the King', where Ghân-buri-Ghân and two of his headmen actually came to Minas Tirith (p. 56). He then wrote: 'and there stood Ghân-buri-Ghân by the eaves of the trees, and did them homage as they passed' (see p. 67). The text continues:

And so at last after many days (15?) they brought King Théoden back to his own land, and they came to Edoras, and there they stayed and rested; and never so fair and full of light was the Golden Hall, for no king of the City of the South had ever come thither before. And there they held the funeral of Théoden, and he was laid in a house of stone with many fair things, and over him was raised a great mound, the eighth of those upon the east side of the Barrowfields, and it was covered with green turves of grass [and] of fair Evermind. And then the Riders of the King's House rode about it, and one among them sang a song of Théoden Thengel's son that brought light to the eyes of the folk of the Mark and stirred the hearts of all, even those that knew not [that] speech. And Merry who stood at the foot of the mound wept.[4]

And when the burial was over and the last song was ended there was a great feast in the hall, and when they came to the time when all should drink to the memories of mighty men forth came Éowyn Lady of Rohan, golden as the sun and white as snow, and she brought forth the cup to Éomer King of the Mark, and he drank to the memory of Théoden. And then a minstrel sang naming all the kings of the [?Mark] in their order, and last King Éomer; and Aragorn arose and [?wished him] hail [and] drank to him. And then Gandalf arose and bid all men rise, and they rose, and he said: 'Here is a last hail[5] ere the feast endeth. Last but not least. For I name now [one >] those who shall not be forgotten and without whose valour nought else that was done would have availed; and I name before you all Frodo of the Shire and Samwise his servant. And the bards and the minstrels should give them new names: *Bronwe athan Harthad* and *Harthad Uluithiad*, Endurance beyond Hope and Hope unquenchable.'[6]

And to those names men drank in honour; but Sam went very red, and murmured to Frodo: 'I don't know what my Dad would think of the change: he was always against outlandish names. "The gentry can do as they please," he said, "with their Roriuses and Ronshuses, but for plain folk something shorter wears better." But even if I could say the name, I think it don't suit. My hope ... . low, Mr. Frodo, ...'[7]

The announcement by Éomer of the betrothal of Faramir and

Éowyn and the words of Éowyn with Aragorn are particularly hard to read, but the passage does not differ significantly from that in RK (pp. 255–6). The text then continues:

And after the feast those that were to go took leave of King Éomer, and Faramir abode with him, for he would not be far from Éowyn any longer. And Finduilas also remained and took leave of her father and brethren. But Aragorn rode on with the companions, and they passed on to Helm's Deep and there rested. And then Legolas repaid his vow to Gimli and went into the Glittering Caves; and when he returned he was silent, for he said that only Gimli could find fit words. 'And now,' said he, 'we will go to Fangorn', at which Gimli looked little pleased.

And so they passed . . . . to Isengard and saw how the Ents had busied themselves, for all the stone circle was removed and was planted with trees, but in the midst of the orchards Orthanc rose up still, tall and [? unapproachable]. And there was Treebeard and other Ents to welcome them, and he praised all their deeds, of which it seemed he had full tidings. 'But Ents played their part,' said he. 'And there would have been no Golden Hall to return to but for Treebeard and his folk. For we caught a great army of those – *burarum* – those orcs that were coming down through the Wold and we drove them away. Or otherwise the king of the grassland would [?have never] ridden far.'

And Gandalf praised his work, and at last he said farewell with many long words, saying that he had added some new lines. And when Merry and Pippin at last said farewell he . . . . them and said 'Well, my merry folk! Take a draught before you go!' And they said 'Yes, indeed!' And he looked at them over the bowl, and he said 'Take care! For you have already grown since I saw you!' And they laughed, and then he [?went] sad, and he said 'And don't forget that if you ever hear news of the Entwives you must send word to us.' And Aragorn said 'The East lands now lie open.' But Treebeard shook his head and said that it was far away.

But Legolas and Gimli here said goodbye, and went into Fangorn, and from there they purposed [? to journey] together to their own countries. 'Alas, that our lands lie so far apart! But we will send word to Rivendell.' And Elrond looked at them and said: 'Send rather to the Shire.'

Then they rode to the Gap of Rohan, and Aragorn took leave of them in that very place where Pippin had looked in the Palantír. And Pippin said 'I wish we could have one to see all our friends.' 'But one only now remains,' said Aragorn . . . . ., 'and the king must keep that. But forget not that my realm lies now also in the North; and later on I may come again.'

And so slowly they passed in[to] the waste lands west of the mountains and fared north, and summer wore away; and Galadriel and Celeborn and their folk passed over the Dimrill Stair and went back to Lórien. But Elrond and Gandalf and the hobbits came back at last to Rivendell.

The chapter ends in this earliest form with very rough sketching of the time that the hobbits spent with Bilbo, but most of the essentials of the final form are present. The chief difference lies in Bilbo's gifts: 'Then Bilbo gave Frodo his coat and sword, and he gave Sam a lot of books of lore, and he gave Merry and Pippin a lot of good advice.' Bilbo's verse (*The Road goes ever on and on*) is lacking, but that there should be a verse at this point is indicated on the manuscript. Gandalf's intimation that he would go with the hobbits 'at least as far as Bree' is lacking; and at the departure from Rivendell Elrond's words of farewell to Frodo, though the same as in RK (suggesting that 'about this time of the year' he should 'look for Bilbo in the woods of the Shire'), were heard also by the others: 'And they did not fully understand what he meant, and Gandalf of course would not explain.' The text then runs straight on into what would become the opening of the next chapter, 'Homeward Bound'.

This first manuscript was greatly enlarged by the insertion of new material. The story of the visit to Isengard was elaborated, and Treebeard's account of the release of Saruman from Orthanc now enters – the necessary prelude, of course, to the encounter with Saruman and Wormtongue on the northward journey of the remaining company. There are a number of differences from the text of RK, but they are minor.[8] The farewell speeches of Treebeard with Celeborn and Galadriel now appear, differing from the final form only in the Quenya phrase: *O vanimar vanimalion ontari* (see note 16).

A long rider takes up at the words 'Then they rode towards the Gap of Rohan' (cf. RK p. 260), and the departure of Aragorn is told in almost the same words as in RK; but Galadriel said to him: 'Elfstone, through darkness you have come to your desire. Use well the days of light', and Celeborn said: 'Kinsman, farewell, but your doom is like to mine; for our treasure shall outlast us both' (see pp. 124–5 and note 16).

The story of the meeting with Saruman, which had been very obliquely referred to in 'The Story Foreseen from Kormallen' ('They come on Saruman and he is [?pardoned]', p. 52), was now fully told, but with a number of differences, one very notable. No indication is given of where or when the encounter took place: after the company had crossed the Isen they 'passed into the waste land west of the mountains, and they turned north, and summer wore away. And many days afterward they overtook an old man leaning on a staff ...' See further p. 69.

To Saruman's remark 'I am seeking a way out of his realm' Gandalf at first replies:

'Then you are going the wrong way [*bracketed*: as seems to be your doom], unless you wish to pass into the utter North and there freeze to death. For from the Sea in the West to Anduin and thence many days' march east is the realm of the King, and east ere long it will spread beyond the water of Rúnaeluin.'[9]

Without striking this out my father replaced it by:

'Then you have far to go,' said Gandalf, 'and should be going eastward. Yet even so you would have to travel far, and find the border of his realm ever marching up behind you.'

This was struck through, and the final text here is: ' "Then you have far to go," said Gandalf, "and I see no hope in your journey...." ' Wormtongue still names himself *Frána*, not *Gríma* (cf. VII.445, VIII.55). Most curious is my father's remarkably different initial conception of Saruman's response to Merry's generosity (the sentence that I have bracketed was presumably rejected):

'Mine, mine, yes, and dearly paid for,' said Saruman, clutching at the pouch. And then suddenly he seemed touched. 'Well, I thank you,' he said. '[You do not crow, and your kind looks maybe are not feigned.] You seem an honest fellow, and maybe you did not come to crow over me. I'll tell you something. When you come to the Shire beware of Cosimo, and make haste, or you may go short of leaf.'

'Thankyou,' said Merry, 'and if you get tired of wandering in the wild come to the Shire.'

My father knew that Saruman acquired his supply of pipe-weed from the Shire (see VIII.59, note 8). There is no certain indication that he had at this stage begun to conceive of any more far-reaching relations between Saruman and Cosimo Sackville-Baggins, but in the original draft of 'The Scouring of the Shire' this idea was very fully present (see p. 84). On the other hand, it is a very notable feature of that draft that Saruman was *not* present in person in the Shire and did not preside over the last stages of its spoliation.

Since as will be seen subsequently the whole of the conclusion of *The Lord of the Rings* from 'Many Partings' to the 'Epilogue' was written in one continuous draft, it seems perfectly possible that all this new material was introduced into the original draft of 'Many Partings' *after* the first draft of 'The Scouring of the Shire' had been written. If this is so, it was very probably when writing and developing the present passage that my father first conceived of Saruman's visit to the Shire (as in the story itself the decision to do so also arose in Saruman's mind at this juncture, RK p. 298); possibly it was in fact Merry's extraordinarily artless invitation (though immediately abandoned, as will be seen in a moment) that was the germ of the story.

Precisely what my father had in mind when he wrote Saruman's words here, 'When you come to the Shire beware of Cosimo, and make haste, or you may go short of leaf', I do not know. It certainly shows that Saruman knew what was going on there, but equally certainly it was intended to be taken as good advice on Saruman's part to repay Merry for his gift. But my father marked Merry's reply with a large query, and at once, on the same page, recognising that the pride, bitterness and malevolence of Saruman could never be pierced by such a gesture on the part of Merry Brandybuck, he wrote the passage that stands in RK (p. 262): 'This is but a repayment in token. You took more, I'll be bound . . .'

The first draft A was followed by a much-needed fair copy 'B', and that (as in 'The Steward and the King') by a third text 'C' in my father's most handsome script. B was subsequently given the number and title 'LVII Many Partings'.[10] While the final form of the chapter was very largely achieved in B, there remain a number of minor differences from the text of RK; I mention here some of the more noteworthy, and collect a few further details in note 16.

It was in B that the name *Arwen* at last emerged. In the opening paragraph of the chapter in this text the Queen was named *Ellonel*, but this was at once changed back to *Finduilas*, and she is *Finduilas* at the two following occurrences (and *Evenstar* in 'But wear this now in memory of Elfstone and Evenstar with whom your life has been woven,' RK p. 253). It must have been at this point that my father determined that her name was not *Finduilas*, and that he must find out what it was; for on a page of rough drafting for sentences in the opening of the chapter he is seen experimenting with other names, as *Amareth, Emrahil*. He wrote *Elrond Elladan Elrohir Emrahil, Finduilas > Emrahil*, and beside this (evidently to avoid the clash with *Imrahil*) *Imrahil > Ildramir*; but then, clearly and firmly, *Arwen Undómiel*. Immediately after this in text B as written Éomer says to Gimli 'But now I will put Queen Arwen Evenstar first' (RK p. 253).

In a first form of Arwen's words to Frodo she says: 'Mine is the choice of Lúthien, and I have chosen as she at last', the words 'at last' being omitted in a second version of the passage; and of her gift to him she says in B:

'. . . But in my stead you shall go, Ringbearer, when the time comes, and if you then desire it: for your wounds have been grievous and your burden heavy. But you shall pass into the West until all your wounds and weariness are healed. [*Struck out at once:* Take this token and Elrond will not refuse you.' And she took from her hair a white gem like a star] Take with you the Phial of Galadriel and Círdan will not refuse you. But wear this now in memory of Elfstone and Evenstar with whom your life has been woven!' And she took a white gem . . .

In the third manuscript C the text of RK was reached.

Merethrond, the Great Hall of Feasts in Minas Tirith (RK p. 253) is said in B to be 'in the Citadel' (a statement omitted in C). On a page of rough drafting for this passage my father dashed off a little plan of the Citadel. This is shown as a circle with seven small circles (towers) at equal distances within the circumference, one of these standing beside the entrance. Beyond the Court of the Fountain is marked, at the centre, the White Tower and Hall of the Kings, and beyond that again, on the west side of the Citadel, the King's House. To the right (north) of the White Tower is the Hall of Feasts. The outlines of other buildings are roughed in between the towers.

When Aragorn and Éomer came to the Hallows 'they came to the tomb that had been built in Rath Dínen' (where C has the reading of RK, 'the tombs in Rath Dínen'); and returning with the bier they 'passed through the City, where all the people stood in silence; but the knights of Rohan that followed the bier sang in their own tongue a lament for the fallen' (so in A, p. 61, 'with slow songs of the Mark'). This was changed to 'the knights of Rohan . . . walked also in silence, for the time for song was not yet come' (cf. RK p. 253).

The encounter with Ghân-buri-Ghân (see pp. 61–2) was further developed, re-using the original passage in the previous chapter (p. 56) where Ghân-buri-Ghân came to Minas Tirith:

. . . and they came to the Grey Wood under Amon Dín. And there beside the road in the shadow of the trees stood Ghân of the Wild Woods and two of his headmen beside him, and they were clad all in garments of green leaves to do honour to the king. For Ghân-buri-Ghân said: 'He was great king; he drove away dark with bright iron. And now men of Stonehouses have king, he will not let dark come back.' And he and his headmen laid their foreheads upon Aragorn's feet; and he bade them rise up, and he blessed them, and gave them the Forest of Druadan to be their own, so that no man should ever enter it without their leave. Then they bowed and vanished into the trees.

This was struck through, and a version replacing it is found written on the last page of text B of 'The Steward and the King', almost as in

RK (p. 254), in which the Wild Men remain invisible and only their drums are heard. In this version the heralds added: 'and whoso slays one of his people slays the king's friends.'

All the names of the Kings of the Mark, recited by the minstrel in the Golden Hall, are now given, but my father missed out *Folcwine*, great-grandfather of Théoden: this was a mere slip, since Folcwine appears in the earliest list of the kings (VIII.408), and without him there are only seven mounds on the east side of the Barrowfield. But the omission escaped notice, and Folcwine was not inserted until the Second Edition. The eleventh king (*Háma* in the original list) now becomes *Léof* (changed to *Léofa* in the Second Edition).[11]

In the parting of Merry from Éomer and Éowyn (RK p. 256) they address him as 'Meriadoc of the Shire and of the Mark' – the name *Holdwine* ('of the Mark') was only introduced on the galley proof; and Éomer says this of the gift of the horn, which he does not attribute to Éowyn:

'... but you will take naught but the arms that were given to you. This I suffer, because though we are of other lands and kind, still you are to me a dear kinsman whose love can only be requited with love. But this one gift I beg you now to take ...'

The horn is described in the same words as in RK; but then follows:

'This is an heirloom of our house,' said Éowyn, 'and in the deeps of time it was made for our forefathers by the dwarves [*struck out:* of Dale], and Eorl the Young brought it from the North.'

The statement that the horn 'came from the hoard of Scatha the Worm' entered on the galley proof.

The meeting with Treebeard reaches in this text B the form in RK at almost all points. Treebeard's denunciation of the Orcs runs here: *henulka-morimaite-quingatelko-tingahondo-rakkalepta-sauri-kumba*.[12] A curious point is that Gandalf says here 'The Third Age begins', which was repeated in C but there emended to 'The New Age begins' as in RK. With this may be compared my father's letter of November 1944 (*Letters* no. 91, also VIII.219): 'So ends the Middle Age and the Dominion of Men begins', and, further back, Saruman's speech to Gandalf in Isengard (VII.150): 'The Elder Days are gone. The Middle Days are passing. The Younger Days are beginning'; but in 'The Story Foreseen from Kormallen' (p. 52) is found 'The end of the Third Age is presaged' and 'End of the Third Age'.

Gandalf's response to Treebeard's report that he had allowed Saruman to go free remains as it was in A (see note 8): Treebeard now says 'A snake without fangs may crawl where he will', but this does not yet prompt Gandalf to the observation that Saruman 'had still one tooth left ... the poison of his voice', which entered in C. Gimli, in his farewell, still concludes as in A (p. 63): 'Alas! that our lands lie so far apart. But we will send word to Rivendell when we may'; to which Elrond now replies: 'Send rather to Gondor, or else to the Shire!'

Again as in A (note 8), Treebeard does not say when the release of Saruman had taken place, and this remained into the First Edition; in the Second Edition 'Yes, he is gone' was changed to 'Yes, he is gone seven days.'[13]

The actual encounter with Saruman now differed virtually not at all from RK, but the placing of it was somewhat different in the First Edition from the revised version in the Second. The text of the First Edition ran thus (RK pp. 260–1):

Soon the dwindling company came to the Isen, and crossed over it, and came into the waste lands beyond, and then they turned northwards, and passed by the borders of Dunland. And the Dunlendings fled and hid themselves, for they were afraid of Elvish folk, though few indeed ever came to their country. But the travellers did not heed them, for they were still a great company and were well provided with all that they needed; and they went on their way at their leisure, setting up tents when they would; and as they went the summer wore away.

After they had passed by Dunland and were come to places where few folk dwelt, and even birds and beasts were seldom to be seen, they journeyed through a wood climbing down from the hills at the feet of the Misty Mountains that now marched on their right hand. As they came out again into open country they overtook an old man leaning on a staff ...

As noted above, in the Second Edition Treebeard told Gandalf that Saruman had been gone seven days; and in the revision of the passage just cited the First Edition text 'After they had passed by Dunland and were come to places where few folk dwelt, and even birds and beasts were seldom to be seen, they journeyed through a wood ...' was altered to 'On the sixth day since their parting from the King they journeyed through a wood ...' By this change the company was still in Dunland when they came upon Saruman, and a little later in the narrative, after 'I fancy he could do some mischief still in a small mean way' (RK p. 263), my father added in the Second Edition: 'Next day they went on into northern Dunland, where no men now dwelt, though it was a green and pleasant country' (northern Dunland, rather than the country north of Dunland, now becoming the uninhabited region).

From this point, the end of the Saruman episode, the text B continues:

September came in with a golden morning shimmering above

silver mists; and looking out they saw away to the east the sun catching three peaks that thrust up through floating cloud into the sky: Caradhras, Celebras, and Fanuiras.[14] They were near once more to the Gates of Moria. And now came another parting . . .

This must mean that it was on the first of September that they saw the Mountains of Moria. This was developed by a late emendation to C to the reading of the First Edition:

September came in with golden days and silver nights. At last a fair morning dawned, shimmering above gleaming mists; and looking from their camp on a low hill the travellers saw away in the east the Sun catching three peaks that thrust up into the sky through floating clouds: Caradhras, Celebdil, and Fanuidhol. They were near to the Gates of Moria.

Here now for seven days they tarried, for the time was at hand for another parting . . .

In the Second Edition this passage (from 'September came in . . .') was extended by references to the Swanfleet river, the falls, and the ford by which the company crossed.[15]

In various small points B received further alteration in the story of the sojourn of the hobbits in Rivendell, but effectively the final form was now reached.[16]

NOTES

1　*Hasufel* was presumably no more than a slip of memory, though it survived until emended on the third manuscript. Hasufel was Aragorn's horse of Rohan, and the horse that carried Legolas and Gimli was Arod.

2　Pippin is not mentioned, but in a rejected form of the passage it is said that he 'rode with the Prince of Ithilien, for he was the esquire of the Steward.'

3　*the Greywood*: previously named ('Grey Woods') only on a small map in a draft text of 'The Ride of the Rohirrim', VIII.353.

4　Here there is a mark of insertion, probably referring to verses that would be given at this point (although there are no verses here in the second and third manuscripts: see note 16).

5　In *wished him hail* (if correctly read) in the preceding sentence *hail* means 'health, happiness, welfare'; in Gandalf's *Here is a last hail* the word seems to be used elliptically, as if 'Here is a last drinking (of) hail'.

6　The word that I give as *athan* is very unclear and uncertain.

7　Gandalf's praise of Frodo and Sam, and this engaging glimpse of the Gaffer amid the ceremoniousness of Edoras, had disappeared in the second text. *Ronshus* is evidently his clipped form of *Gerontius*, the name of the Old Took; and I suppose that he attached the 'learned' or high-falutin ending *-us* to Rory (Brandybuck). But the Gaffer's views were not entirely lost. When discussing with Frodo the name of his eldest child ('The Grey Havens', RK p. 306) Sam said: 'I've heard some beautiful names on my travels, but I suppose they're a bit too grand for daily wear and tear, as you might say. The Gaffer, he says: "Make it short, and then you won't have to cut it short before you can use it."' – Sam's final remark is unfortunately altogether illegible; the word preceding *low* might possibly be *getting*, or *pretty*, but the word preceding that is certainly not *was*.

8   The two sentinel trees that grew now where the gates of Isengard had stood do not appear. The words of Aragorn and Gandalf with Treebeard after his mention of the destruction of the Orcs (whom he apostrophises only in English adjectives) in the Wold were different from those in RK (p. 258), though a part of this dialogue was used a little later in the final text:

> 'We know it,' said Aragorn, 'and never shall it be forgotten, nor your storming of Isengard, and it is our hope that your forest may grow again in peace. There is room and to spare west of the mountains.'
>
> 'Forest may grow,' said Treebeard sadly; 'woods may spread, but not Ents; there are no Entings now.'
>
> 'Never at least while the Mark and Gondor remain,' said Gandalf; 'and that will have to be very long indeed to seem long to Ents. But what of your most important task, Fangorn? ...'

Treebeard does not say how long it was since Saruman had gone (see p. 69); and Gandalf does not tell him that Saruman had found his soft spot and persuaded him by 'the poison of his voice', but says merely 'Well, he's gone then, and that is all there is to be said' (reminiscent of his resigned 'Well, well, he is gone' when he heard from Legolas at the Council of Elrond of Gollum's escape, FR p. 269). Quickbeam does not appear in the handing over of the keys to Orthanc: ' "It is locked," said Treebeard, "locked by Saruman, and here are the keys," and he gave three black keys to Aragorn.'

9   *Rúnaeluin*: the last four letters are not perfectly clear, but this seems much the most probable interpretation. Can *Rúnaeluin* be the Sea of Rhûn?

10   The third manuscript C was given the chapter-number 'LV'. This reduction of the numbers by two begins with 'The Tower of Kirith Ungol' (p. 25).

11   In the First Edition, while the eleventh king is named *Léof* by the minstrel in Edoras in 'Many Partings', in the list of the Kings of the Mark in Appendix A (II) the eleventh king is *Brytta*, with no explanation given. In the Second Edition the explanation was added: 'He was called by his people *Léofa*, for he was loved by all; he was openhanded and a help to all the needy.'

12   The English adjectives in B are the same as those in RK: 'evileyed, blackhanded, bowlegged, flinthearted, clawfingered, foulbellied, bloodthirsty'. In C the words *quingatelko* and *rakkalepta* were omitted, and then *henulka* and *saurikumba* were struck out and *tingahondo* changed to *sincahondo*. Finally *sincahondo* was changed on the printer's typescript to *sincahonda* as in RK.

13   On a copy of the First Edition that my father used to make alterations for incorporation in the Second Edition he added to the section 'The Chief Days from the Fall of the Barad-dûr to the End of the Third Age' in Appendix B the entry *'August 15   Treebeard releases Saruman'*, but this was not for some reason included in the Second Edition. See the Note on Chronology below.

14   On the names *Celebras* and *Fanuiras* see VII.174, 306.

15   The course of this river was marked already on the First Map (VII.305), flowing down from the Misty Mountains to join the Greyflood above Tharbad. It was not referred to in the text of the First Edition, but was named the *Glanduin* in Appendix A (I, iii, first paragraph). The accidents or misunderstandings that be-devilled its representation on the map accompanying *The Lord of the Rings* are detailed in *Unfinished Tales* pp. 263–5.

16   It is not said in B that the only part of the hobbits' story that really interested Bilbo was the account of the crowning and marriage of Aragorn; nor that he had forgotten that he had already given Sting and the mithril-coat to Frodo; nor that his books of lore had red backs. All these changes entered in the third manuscript C. The books were labelled *Translations from the Elvish, by B. B. Esquire*; *Esquire* was removed on the galley proof.

   I record here various other details, mostly concerning names, in which B differed from RK.

   The reference to Merry as 'a Knight of the Riddermark' was retained from A (p. 61) and then struck out. On *Hasufel* for *Arod* see note 1.

   The alliterative verses of the song of the Riders of Rohan as they rode round Théoden's barrow were only introduced on a rider to the fourth text, the typescript for the printer, together with the passage preceding them in which the song of the Riders brought to mind 'the voice of Eorl crying above the battle upon the Field of Celebrant', and 'the horn of Helm was loud in the mountains'. The king's minstrel, who made the song, was

Gleowin in B, *Gléowine* in C; and *the Barrowfields* of A become *the Barrowfield* in B.

In Éomer's farewell words to Merry (RK p. 256) he speaks of his deeds 'upon the fields of Mundberg', emended on C to *Mundburg* (see VIII.355–6).

Treebeard's name of Lórien was spelt *Laurelindórinan*, and this survived into the First Edition, becoming *Laurelindórenan* in the Second. He still says to Galadriel and Celeborn *O vanimar vanimalion ontari* (p. 64), *O* being changed to *A* on text B and *ontari* to *nostari* on C. The comma after *vanimar* was added in the Second Edition. In VIII.20 I mentioned late notes of my father's on the fragments of other languages found in *The Lord of the Rings*, which for the greater part of the book are so hastily written as to be mostly unusable. His translation of *O vanimar, vanimálion nostari* can however be made out (in the light of the Quenya words themselves): 'fair ones begetters of fair ones', and with this is a note '*nosta* beget'; cf. the *Etymologies* in Vol.V, stems BAN, NŌ, ONO.

Wormtongue's name remained *Frána* (p. 65) in B and C, but was changed to *Gríma* on the final typescript; and Gandalf still calls Butterbur *Barnabas* (RK p. 265).

Note on the Chronology

In the original draft A of this chapter there were scarcely any indications of chronology: Aragorn tells Frodo (p. 61) that they will depart from Minas Tirith in three days' time, but this only relates to the end of 'the days of rejoicing', of indeterminate length; and it was fifteen days' journey from Minas Tirith to Rohan.

In B Aragorn tells Frodo that they will leave in seven days, and that 'in three days now Éomer will return hither to bear Théoden back to rest in the Mark', as he duly did; and all this is retained in *The Lord of the Rings*, together with the fifteen days of the journey to Rohan. But neither B nor C give much more indication than did the original draft of the time taken over the stages of the journey from Edoras to Rivendell, and it may be that my father did not attend to the matter closely until the final preparation of the book. It is a curious fact that the chronology of 'The Chief Days from the Fall of the Barad-dûr to the End of the Third Age' in Appendix B (and which is the same in this respect in both editions) does not agree with the text of 'Many Partings' in respect either of Éomer's return in relation to the setting out for Edoras or of the time taken on that journey. In the chronology of 'The Chief Days' Éomer returned to Minas Tirith on July 18, and the riding from the City with King Théoden's wain took place on the following day, July 19, not four days later as in 'Many Partings'; while the arrival at Edoras is dated August 7, eighteen days later, not fifteen as in the text.

As I have noted already, no indication of date was given for the meeting of Saruman with the travellers as they rode north even in the First Edition; in the Second Edition the passage was altered to say that the meeting took place on the sixth day since they parted from the King, and they were still in Dunland (see p. 69). But in fact this dating was already present in the First Edition, in the chronology of 'The Chief Days' in *The Tale of Years:*

August 22   They come to Isengard; they take leave of the King of the West at sunset.

August 28   They overtake Saruman; Saruman turns towards the Shire.

As the third text C was written it was still on September 1 that the travellers saw the Mountains of Moria, but late emendation (see p. 70) produced, or satisfied, the chronology of 'The Chief Days':

September 6   They halt in sight of the Mountains of Moria.

September 13   Celeborn and Galadriel depart, the others set out for Rivendell.

On September 21, the day before Bilbo's birthday, Gandalf and the hobbits returned to Rivendell, having taken (being mounted) a much shorter time than they took to reach Moria on their outward journey, nine months before.

VIII
HOMEWARD BOUND

The original draft A of 'Many Partings' continued on into the opening
of 'Homeward Bound' (see p. 64), but my father drew a line of
separation, and began a new pagination, probably at an early stage. At
the same time he scribbled in a title for the new chapter: 'Homecoming'. This text runs on with continuous pagination right through to the
end of *The Lord of the Rings*, and included the Epilogue.

This last of the first drafts ends the work in style: if not the most
difficult of all the manuscripts of *The Lord of the Rings* it certainly has
few rivals. As far as the Battle of Bywater (see p. 93) it gives the
impression of having been written in one long burst, and with
increasing rapidity. Ideas that appear in earlier reaches of the text are
contradicted later without correction of the former passages. In the
part of it that corresponds to 'Homeward Bound' and the beginning of
'The Scouring of the Shire', however, the text does not present
excessive difficulty, chiefly because the final form of the story was not
very substantially changed from that in the original draft, but also
because my father's handwriting, while very rough throughout,
declined only gradually as the text proceeded.

I break the text here into three chapters as in RK. Throughout, the
original draft is of course called 'A'. Of the tale of the visit to *The
Prancing Pony* there is not a great deal to record. It opens thus (RK
p. 268):

So now they turned their faces for home; and though they
rode now they rode but slowly. But they were at peace and in no
haste, and if they missed their companions of their adventures,
still they had Gandalf, and the journey went well enough when
once they passed beyond Weathertop. For at the Fords of
Bruinen Frodo halted and was loth to ride through, and from
here on to Weathertop he was silent and ill at ease; but Gandalf
said nothing.

And when they came to the hill he said 'Let us hasten', and
would not look towards it. 'My wound aches,' he said, 'and the
memory of darkness is heavy on me. Are there not things,
Gandalf, that cannot ever be wholly healed?'

'Alas, it is so,' said Gandalf.

'It is so I guess with my wounds,' said Frodo. ...

This page of A (carrying the end of the later 'Many Partings' and the beginning of 'Homeward Bound') was replaced, in all probability very soon, by a new page with a chapter number, 'LVIII', and in this the opening passage draws nearer to that in RK: the date of the crossing of the Fords of Bruinen is given (the sixth of October, as in RK), and Frodo speaks of his pain there, not below Weathertop; but he says: 'It's my shoulder, my wound aches. And my finger too, the one that is gone, but I feel pain in it, and the memory of darkness is heavy on me.'[1]

When Butterbur came to the door of *The Prancing Pony* he did not, as in RK, misunderstand Nob's cry 'They've come back' and come rushing out armed with a club:

And out came Barnabas wiping his hand on his apron and looking as bustled as ever, though there seemed few folk about, and not much talk in the Common Room; indeed he looked in the dim lamplight rather more wrinkled and careworn.

'Well, well,' he said, 'I never expected to see any of you folk again and that's a fact: going off into the wild with that Trotter ...'

Whatever response Butterbur made to Gandalf's request 'And if you have any tobacco we'll bless you. Ours has long since been finished' is not reported. When Butterbur objects (RK p. 272) that he doesn't want 'a whole crowd of strangers settling here and camping there and tearing up the wild country' Gandalf tells him:

'... There's room enough for realms between Isen and Greyflood, and along the shores between Greyflood and Brandy-wine. And many folk used to dwell north away, a hundred miles and more from you, on the North Down[s] and by Nenuial or Evendimmer, if you have heard of it. I should not wonder if the Deadmen's Dike is filled with living men again. Kings' Norbury is its right name in your tongue. One day the King may come again.'[2]

Apart from these passages the text of 'Homeward Bound' in RK was virtually present in the draft text,[3] though naturally with many small changes in the dialogue still to come, until the end of the chapter: here there is a notable difference in the story. The conversation of the hobbits as they left Bree is much as in RK, but without Merry's reference to pipe-weed and without Gandalf's reference to Saruman and his interest in the Shire:

'I wonder what he [Butterbur] means,' said Frodo.

'I can guess some of it at any rate,' said Sam gloomily. 'What I saw in the Mirror. Trees cut down and all, and the old gaffer turned out. I ought to have turned back sooner.'

'Whatever it is it'll be that Cosimo at the bottom of it,' said Pippin.

'Deep but not at the bottom,' said Gandalf.

This stands near but not at the foot of a page. Across the empty space my father wrote this note:

Gandalf should stay at Bree. He should say: 'You may find trouble, but I want you to settle it yourselves. Wizards should not interfere in such things. Don't crack nuts with a sledge-hammer, or you'll crack the kernels. And many times over anyway. I'll be along some time.'

The empty space had perhaps been intended to mark a pause; at any rate this note was written in later (though not much later), since the text continues on the following page and Gandalf has not left the hobbits: he is present at and plays a part in the encounter with the gate-guards on the Brandywine Bridge (at the beginning of the next chapter in RK, 'The Scouring of the Shire': pp. 79–80).

They passed the point on the East Road where they had taken leave of Bombadil, and half they expected to see him standing there to greet them as they went by. But there was no sign of him, and there was a grey mist over the Barrow-down[s] southward and a deep veil hid the Old Forest far away.

Frodo halted and looked wistfully south. 'I should like to see the old fellow again. I wonder how he's getting on.'

'As well as ever, you may be sure,' said Gandalf. 'Quite untroubled, and if I may say so not at all interested in anything that has happened to us. There will be time later to visit him. If I were you I should press on for home now, or we'll not come to Brandywine Bridge till the gates are locked.'

'But there aren't any gates,' said Merry, 'at least not on the Road. There's the Buckland Gate of course.'

'There weren't any gates, you mean,' said Gandalf. 'I think you'll find some now.'

They did. It was long after dark when tired and wet they came to the Brandywine and found the way barred at both ends of the Bridge ...

The first draft was followed by a fair copy ('B') of 'Homeward Bound' with that title, and then by a fine and elegant manuscript ('C').

Already in B the final form of the chapter was achieved at almost every point.[4]

NOTES

1 The reason for the change was that the recurrence of the pain of Frodo's wound should depend on the date, not on the place. See further p. 112, notes 3 and 4.

2 The name *Nenuial* first occurs here. The curious (but certain) form *Evendimmer* I cannot explain; *Evendim* (and *Fornost Erain*) appear in the second text of the chapter.

3 The return of Bill the Pony is recorded by Butterbur in almost the same words as in RK (cf. VII.448, VIII.219). – Two other minor points may be mentioned here. Gandalf's sword (RK p. 272) is called *Orcrist* (the name of the sword of Thorin Oakenshield): this was a mere slip, which however survived into the third manuscript of the chapter, where it was changed to *Glamdring*. The entrance into Bree by the road from Weathertop was called 'the East-gate', and only changed to 'the South-gate' on the typescript for the printer; cf. the plan of Bree, VI.335.

4 In his parting words to the hobbits Gandalf says in B: 'I am not coming to the Shire. You must settle its affairs yourselves. To bring me in would be using a sledgehammer to crack nuts.' With the last sentence cf. the note, written on text A, given on p. 77. – *Trotter* and *Cosimo* survived into the third manuscript C and were only then changed to *Strider* and *Lotho*; *Barnabas* survived into the final typescript and was corrected on that to *Barliman*.

IX

THE SCOURING OF THE SHIRE

As has been seen in the last chapter, the long draft text A moves on into what became 'The Scouring of the Shire' without break; Gandalf's departure to seek out Tom Bombadil, where the chapter break would come, was not yet present. When the travellers came to the Brandywine Bridge their reception was just as in RK, but Sam's shouted 'I'll tear your notice down when I find it' is followed by:

'Come along now!' said the wizard. 'My name is Gandalf. And here is a Brandybuck, a Took, a Baggins, and a Gamgee, so if you don't open up quick there will be more trouble than you bargain for, and long before sunrise.'

At that a window slammed, and a crowd of hobbits poured out of the house with lanterns, and they opened the far gate, and some came over the Bridge. When they looked at the travellers they seemed more frightened than ever.

'Come, come,' said Merry, recognizing one of the hobbits. 'If you don't know me, Hob Hayward, you ought to. ...'

Before the narrative had proceeded much further the text was corrected and Gandalf's words were given to Frodo: ' "Come along now!" said Frodo. "My name is Frodo Baggins. And here is a Brandybuck, a Took, and a Gamgee..." '

The questioning of Hob Hayward (RK p. 277) is a tangle of names and titles. So far as I can see, it ran thus as first written, with some changes made immediately:

'I'm sorry, Mr. Merry, but we have orders.'
'Whose orders?'
'The Mayor's, Mr. Merry, and the Chief Shirriff's.'
'Who's the Mayor?' said Frodo.
'Mr. [Cosimo >] Sackville of Bag-End.'
'Oh is he, indeed,' said Frodo. 'And who's the Chief Shirriff?'
'Mr. [Baggins >] Sackville of Bag-End.'
'Oh, indeed. Well, I'm glad he's dropped the Baggins at least. And he'll leave Bag-End too if I hear any more nonsense.'

A hush fell on the hobbits beyond the gate. 'It won't do no good to talk that way,' said Hob. 'He'll get to hear of it. And if you make so much noise you'll wake up the Big Man.'

'I'll wake him up in a way that'll surprise him,' said Gandalf. 'If you mean that your precious Mayor is employing ruffians out of the wild, then we've not come back too soon.' He leaped from his horse and put his hand to the gate and tore the notice from it, and threw it on the path in the faces of the hobbits.[1]

This was the last appearance of Gandalf before the final leave-taking at the Grey Havens.[2] 'Gandalf' was changed here to 'Frodo', and 'horse' to 'pony', and it was presumably at this point that the note given on p. 77 ('Gandalf should stay at Bree ...') was written on the manuscript. It will be seen in what follows that in this original version of the story Frodo played a far more aggressive and masterful part in the events than he does in RK, even to the slaying of more than one of the ruffians at Bywater and their leader at Bag End, despite his words to Sam already present in the first manuscript of 'The Land of Shadow' (p. 32; RK p. 204): 'I do not think it is my part to strike any blows again' (see the added sentence given in note 23).

The account of the hobbits' lodging that night in the guard-house by the Brandywine Bridge is much as in the final form, but lacks a few details (as Hob Hayward's remark that stocks of pipe-weed had been 'going away quietly' even before Frodo and his companions left the Shire, and the remonstrance of other hobbits against Hob's indiscretion, RK p. 279). It is Frodo, not Merry, who threatens Bill Ferny and gets rid of him. In the story of their 'arrest' at Frogmorton[3] 'one of the Shirriffs' told them that on the orders of the Chief Shirriff (see note 1) they were to be taken to the *Lock-holes* in Michel Delving (cf. RK p. 280), which is where the term first appears (see pp. 98–9). It turns out that, unlike the later story, Robin Smallburrow was actually the leader of the band of Shirriffs (see p. 95):

To the discomfiture of the Shirriffs Frodo and his companions all roared with laughter. 'Go on,' said Frodo. 'Robin Smallburrow, you're Hobbiton-bred. Don't be silly. But if you're going our way we'll go with you as quiet as you could wish.'

'Which way be you going, Mister Baggins?' said Shirriff Smallburrows,[4] a grin appearing on his face which he quickly smoothed away.

'Hobbiton, of course,' said Frodo. 'Bag End. But you needn't come any further than you wish.'

'Very well, Mr. Baggins,' said the Shirriff, 'but don't forget we've arrested you.'

Sam's conversation with Robin Smallburrows was concluded more abruptly in A (cf. RK pp. 281–2):

'... You know how I went for a Shirriff seven years ago, before all this. Gave you a chance of walking round the Shire and seeing folk and hearing the news, and keeping an eye on the inns. But we all has to swear to do as the Mayor bids. That was all right in the days of old Flourdumpling. Do you remember him? – old Will Whitfoot of Michel Delving. But it's different now. Yet we still has to swear.'

'You shouldn't,' said Sam, 'you should cut out the Shir-riffing.'

'Not allowed to,' said Robin.

'If I hear "not allowed" much oftener,' said Sam, 'I'm going to get angry.'

'Can't say I'd be sorry to see it,' said Robin, and he dropped his voice. 'Tell you the truth, your coming back and Mr. Frodo and all is the best that's happened in a year. The Mayor's in a fine taking.'

'He'll be in a fine getting before many days are over,' said Sam.

The Shire-house[5] at Frogmorton was as bad as the gate-houses. ...

It was Frodo, not Merry, who made the Shirriffs march in front on the journey from Frogmorton, and there is no mention of his looking 'rather sad and thoughtful' as his companions laughed and sang. The incident of the old 'gaffer' by the wayside who laughed at the absurd scene, and Merry's refusal to allow the Shirriffs to molest him, is absent;[6] but when the Shirriffs gave up their forced march at the Three-Farthing Stone while Frodo and his friends rode on to Bywater, the leader saying that they were breaking arrest and he could not be answerable, it was again Frodo, not Pippin, who said 'We'll break a good many things yet, and not ask you to answer.'

The horror especially of Frodo and Sam when they came to Bywater and saw what had been done there is told in A very much as in the final form; but from Sam's words 'I want to find the Gaffer' (RK p. 283) I give the text in full, for differences now begin to multiply, and before long the story evolves in a way totally unlike that of the final form of the chapter. By this point my father's handwriting is of extraordinary difficulty, and gets worse; it has been a struggle to elucidate it even to the extent that it is printed here. I have supplied much of the punctuation, and I have silently entered omitted words where these are obvious, corrected words given wrong endings, and so forth.

'It'll be dark, Sam, before we can get there,' said Frodo. 'We'll get there in the morning. One night now won't make any difference.'

'I wish we'd turned down into Buckland first,' said Merry. 'I feel trouble's ahead. We'd have heard all the news there and got some help. Whatever Cosimo's been up to it can't have gone far in Buckland. Bucklanders wouldn't stand any dictating from him!'

All the houses were shut and no one greeted them. And they wondered why, till coming to the Green Dragon, almost the last house on the Hobbiton side, they were astonished and disturbed to see four ill-favoured men lounging at the street-end. Squint-eyed fellows like the one they saw at Bree. 'And at Isengard too,' muttered Merry. They had clubs in their hands and horns in their belts. When they saw the travellers they left the wall they had been leaning on and walked into the road, blocking the way.

'Where do you think you're going?' said one. 'This ain't the road to Michel Delving. And where's the perishing Shirriffs?'

'Coming along nicely,' said Frodo. 'A bit footsore maybe. We'll wait for them.'

'Garn, I told the Boss [> Big Sharkey] it was no good sending the little fools. We ought to have a'gone, but the Boss [> Sharkey] says no, and .... [> the Boss let him have his way.][7]

'And if you had gone, what difference would that have made, pray?' said Frodo quietly. 'We are not used to footpads in this country, but we know how to deal with them.'

'Footpads, eh,' said the man, 'so that's your tone, is it? I'll learn you manners if you ain't careful. Don't you trust too much to the Boss's kind heart. [*Added in margin:* He's all right if you treat him right, but he won't stand talk of that sort.] He's soft enough. But he's only a hobbit. And this country needs something a bit bigger to keep it in order. It'll get it, too, and before the year's out, or my name's not Sharkey. Then you'll learn a thing or two, you little rat-folk.'

'Well,' said Frodo, 'I find that very interesting. I was thinking of waiting here and calling in the morning, but now I think I had better call on the Boss at once, if you mean my cousin Mr. Cosimo. He'd like to know what's afoot in good time.'

The squinting man laughed. 'Oh, he knows alright though he pretends not to. When we've finished with bosses we get rid of them. And of anyone who gets in our way, see?' [*Added in margin, as a replacement or variant:* 'O, Cosimo,' he said, and he laughed again and looked sidelong at his mates. 'Ah, Boss

Cosimo! [*Struck out:* He knows all right, or he did.] Don't you worry about him. He sleeps sound, and I shouldn't try and wake him now. But we're not going to let you pass. We get enough of .... in our way.']

'Yes, I see,' said Frodo. 'I'm beginning to see a great deal. But I fear you're behind the times and the news here, Ruffian Sharkey. Your day's over. You come from Isengard, I think. Well, I have myself come from the South, and this news may concern you. The Dark Tower has fallen, there is a King in Gondor, Isengard is no more, and Saruman is a beggar in the wilderness. You are the fingers of a hand that has been cut off, and arm and body too are dead. The King's messengers will be coming soon up the Greenway, not bullies of Isengard.'

The man stared at him, taken aback for a moment. Then he sneered. 'Swagger it, swagger it, little cock-a-whoop on your pony,' he said. 'Big words and fat lies won't scare us. King's messengers?' he said. 'When I see them I'll take notice maybe.'

This was too much for Pippin. As he thought of the minstrel upon Kormallen and the praise of all the fair host, and here this squint-eyed rascal calling the Ringbearer little cock-a-whoop. [*sic*]

He flashed out his sword and rode forward, casting aside his cloak so that the silver and sable of Gondor which he still wore could be seen. 'We are the King's messengers,' he said. '[And I'm the squire of Frodo of the Nine Fingers, Knight of Gondor, and down you go in the road on your knees or we'll deal with you. >] And I am the esquire of the Lord of Minas Tirith, and here is Frodo of the Nine Fingers renowned among all peoples of the West. You're a fool. Down on your knees in the road, or I'll set this troll's bane in you.' His sword glinted red in the last rays of the sun. Merry and Sam drew and rode up beside him; but Frodo made no move.

The man and his fellows taken aback by the weapons and the sudden fierce speech gave way and ran off up the road to Hobbiton, but they blew their horns as they ran.

'Well, we've come back none too soon,' said Merry.

'Not a day too soon,' said Frodo. 'Poor Cosimo. I hope we haven't sealed his doom.'

'What do you mean, Frodo?' said Pippin. 'Poor Cosimo? ... I'd seal his doom if I could get at him.'

'I don't think you understand it all quite,' said Frodo. 'Though you should. You've been in Isengard. But I've had

Gandalf to talk to, and we've talked much on the long miles.
Poor Cosimo! Well, yes. He's both wicked and silly. But he's
caught in his own net. Can't you see? He started trading with
Saruman and got rich secretly and bought up this and that on
the quiet, and then he's [?hired] these ruffians. Saruman sent
them to "help" him, and show him how to build and [??repair]
... all ...   And now of course they're running things in his
name – and not in his name for long. He's a prisoner [?really] in
Bag End, I expect.'

'Well, I am staggered,' said Pippin. 'Of all the ends to our
journey this is the last I expected: to fight half-orcs in the Shire
itself to rescue Cosimo the Pimple of all people!'[8]

'Fight?' said Merry. 'Well, it looks like it. But we're after all
only 4 hobbits even if we're armed. We don't know how many
ruffians there are about. I think we may really need the
sledgehammer for this nut after all.'[9]

'Well, we can't help Cousin Pimple tonight,' said Frodo. 'We
must find cover for the night.'

'I've an idea, Mr. Frodo,' said Sam. 'Let's go to old Jeremy
Cotton's.[10] He used to be a stout fellow, and he has a lot of lads,
all friends of mine.'

'What, Farmer Cotton down South Lane?' said Frodo. 'We'll
try it!' They turned and a few yards back rode into the lane, and
in a quarter of a mile came to the gates. Though it was early all
the farmhouse was dark, and not a dog barked. ' "Not
allowed", I suppose,' grunted Sam. They knocked on the door,
twice. Then slowly a window was opened just above and a head
peered out.

'Nay, it's none o' them ruffians,' whispered a voice. 'It's only
hobbits.'

'Don't you pay no heed anyway, Jeremy,' said a voice (the
farmer's wife by the sound of it). 'It'll only bring trouble, and
we've had enough.'

'Go away, there's good fellows,' said the farmer hoarsely.
'Not the front door anyway. If there's anything you want badly
come round to the back first thing in the morning before they're
about. There's a lot in the street now.'

'We know that,' said Frodo. 'But we've sent them off. It's Mr.
Frodo Baggins and friends here. We've come back. But we want
shelter for a night. The barn will do.'

'Mr. Frodo Baggins?' gasped the farmer. 'Aye, and Sam with
him,' added Sam.

'All right! But don't shout,' said the farmer. 'I'm coming down.'

The bolts were drawn back stealthily and it crossed Sam's mind that he had never known that door to be locked let alone bolted before. Farmer Cotton put a head round and looked at them in the gloaming. His eyes grew round as he looked at them and then grave. 'Well,' he said, 'voices sound all right, but I wouldn't a' knowed you. Come in.' There was dim light in the passage, and he scanned their faces closely. 'Right enough,' he said, and laughed with relief. 'Mr. Baggins and Sam and Mr. Merry and Mr. Pippin. Well, you're welcome, more than welcome. But it's a sorry homecoming. You've been away too long.'

'What's come of my gaffer?' said Sam anxiously.

'Not too well, but not too bad,' said Farmer Cotton. 'He's in one of [?they new] Shire-houses, but he comes to my backdoor and I sees he's better fed than some of the poor things. He's not too bad.'

Sam drew a breath of relief. 'Shire-houses,' he said. 'I'll burn the lot down yet.'

They went into the kitchen and sat down by the fire, which the farmer blew up to a blaze. 'We go to bed early these days,' he said. 'Lights o'night bring unwelcome questions. And these ruffians, they lurk about at night and lie abed late. Early morning's our best time.'

They talked for a while and learned that Frodo's guesses had been near the mark. There were some twenty ruffians quartered in Hobbiton, and Cosimo was up at Bag End; but was never seen outside of it. 'His ma, they took her and put her in the Lockholes at Michel Delving three [?months] ago,' said the farmer. 'I'm less sorry for her than I am for some as they've took. But she did stand up to them proper, there's no denying. Ordered them out of the house, and so they took her.'

'Hm,' said Frodo. 'Then I am afraid we've brought you trouble. For we've threatened four of them and sent them off. The chief of them is one Sharkey by his own naming. I feared there were more. They blew horns and went off.'

'Ah, I heard 'em,' said the farmer. 'That's why we shut down. They'll be after you soon enough, unless you've scared 'em more than I guess. Not but what I think they'd run quick enough from anything of their own size. We'd clear 'em out of the country if only we'd get together.'

'Have they got any weapons?'

'They don't show 'em, no more than whips, clubs, and knives, enough for their dirty work,' said the farmer. 'But maybe they have. Some have got bows and arrows, anyhow, and shoot [?pretty quick] and straight. They've shot three in this district to my knowledge.' Sam ground his teeth.

There came a great bang at the front door. The farmer went quietly down the passage putting out the light and the others followed him. There was a second louder bang. 'Open up you old rat, or we'll burn you out,' shouted a hoarse voice outside.

'I am coming,' said the farmer, all of a [?quake.] 'Slip up and see how many there is,' said Sam. And he [?rattled the chains] and . . . . ed the bolts as the farmer ran up the stairs and back.

'I should say a dozen at the least, but all the lot, I guess,' he said.

'All the better,' said Frodo. 'Now for it.'

The four hobbits stood back to the wall towards which the door swung. The farmer [?unbolted] the bolts, turned the key, and then [?slipped back] up the stairs. The door swung open and in [?peered] the head and shoulders of Sharkey. They let him come in; and then quickly Frodo drove the point of his sword into his neck. He fell, and there was a howl of rage outside. 'Burn them, burn them,' voices cried, 'go and get fuel.' 'Nar, dig them out,' said two, and thrust into the passage. They had swords in their hands, but Frodo now behind the door swung it suddenly in the face of the rear one, while . . . Sam ran Sting through the other.[11] Then the hobbits leaped out. The ruffian who had been down on his face was [?leaning against the doorpost]. He fled, blood pouring from his nose. The farmer . . . took the sword from the fallen ruffian and stood guard at the door. The hobbits ranged about the yards stealthily. They came on two ruffians bringing wood from the woodpile and . . . . ed and killed them before they knew they were attacked. 'It is like a rat hunt,' said Sam. 'But that's only four and one with a broken nose.'

At that moment they heard Merry shouting, 'Gondor to the Mark', and they ran and found him in a corner of the stack yard with four ruffians [?pressing] on him, but held at bay by his sword. They had only knives and clubs. Frodo and Sam came running from one side and Pippin from another. The ruffians fled blowing horns, but one more fell to Frodo's sword before he could escape.

They heard the farmer calling. They ran back. 'One less,' said Farmer Cotton. 'I got him as he ran. The rest have run off down the lane blowing like a hunt.'

'That's six altogether,' said Frodo. 'But no doubt the horns will bring more. How many are there in the neighbourhood?'

'Not many,' said the farmer. 'They mostly bide here or at Michel Delving, and go anywhere's there's any dirty work. No more of [?them's] come in since last spring. I ... say there's not much [more than] a hundred in the whole Shire. If we could only join together.'

'Then let's start tonight,' said Frodo. 'Rouse up the folk. Put lights in the houses. Get out all the lads and grown hobbits. Block the road south and send out scouts round the place.'

It was not long before all Bywater was alive and awake again. Lights shining in windows and people at their doors. And there were even cheers for Mr. Frodo. Some lit a bonfire at the Road Bend[12] and danced round it. It was after all not more than [the] six[th of] October[13] on a fair evening of late autumn. Others went off to spy the land round about.

Those that went up Hobbiton way said that there was quite a hubbub there. News of Mr. Frodo's return had come in and folk were coming out. The ruffians seemed to have left the place clear. 'Bolted towards Michel Delving where they've made the Lockholes into a fortress, that's what they've a' done, I guess,' said Farmer Cotton. 'But they'll come back. There's no way from the West.[14] They don't go down the Tuckborough way. They've never given in there. And they've [?beaten] up more than one ruffian in the Took-house.[15] There is a kind o' siege going on.'

'We'll send word to them. Who'll go?' No answer.

'I'll go of course,' said Pippin. 'It's my own country. I'm proud of it. It's not more than 14 miles, as the crow flies or as Took goes who knows all the ways, from here where I stand to the Long Smial of [?Tuckborough] where I was born.[16] Anyone come with me? Well, never mind. I'll be bringing some [?stout] Tooklanders this way in the morning.'

Frodo sent out other messengers to all hamlets and farms near enough for folk to be willing to run to them.

Nothing more that night.

In the morning from Hobbiton and Bywater and round about there were about 100 fullgrown hobbits gathered together with sticks, staves, knives, pitchforks and mattocks and axes and scythes. Messages came in to say that a dozen or more ruffians had been seen going west to Michel Delving the evening before. Then a hobbit ran in to say that about fifty Tooklanders had come in on ponies to the East Road junction and a couple of hundred were marching up behind. 'Whole country's up, like a fire,' he said. 'It's grand! Right glad we are you came back, Mr. Frodo. That's what we needed.'

Frodo now had forces enough. He had [?the] block .. ... the East .....[17] and put a lot of them behind the hedge on each side of the way. They were under Pippin's command. 'I don't know what you think,' he said to Merry and Sam. 'But it seems to me that either the ruffians are all going to gather in Michel Delving and fight it out there: in that case we'll have to raise the Shire and go and dig them out; or more likely they'll come back in full force this way to their precious Boss. It's forty miles if it's a foot to Michel Delving. Unless they get ponies (which wouldn't help much) or have got horses they can't come back for a day or two.'

'They'll send a messenger,' said Sam, 'and wait somewhere till their friends arrive; that'll speed things up a bit. Even so I don't see how they can do it till the day after tomorrow at quickest.'

'Well then,' said Frodo, 'we'd best spend the time by going to Hobbiton and have a word with Cousin Cosimo.'

'Right you are, Mr. Frodo,' said Sam, 'and I'll look up the gaffer.'

So leaving Pippin in charge on the Road and Farmer Cotton in Bywater, Frodo, Sam and Merry rode on to Hobbiton. It was one of the saddest days of their lives. The great chimney rose up before them, and as they came in sight of the village they saw that the old mill was gone and a great red brick building straddled the stream. All along the Bywater road every tree was felled, and little ugly houses with no gardens in [?desert] ..... of ash or gravel. As they looked up the hill they gasped. The old farm on the right had been turned into a [?long ?big] workshop or [?building] with many new windows. The chestnuts were gone. Bagshot Row was a yawning sand-pit, and Bag End up beyond could not be seen for a row of sheds and ugly huts.[18]

[*The following was struck out and replaced immediately:* A [?surly dirty] ill-favoured hobbit was lounging at the new mill-door. He was [?smut]-faced and [?chewing]. 'As good a small model of Bill Ferny as I've seen,' said Sam.

Ted Sandyman did not seem to recognize them but stared at them with a leer until they had nearly passed.

'Going to see the Boss?' he said. 'It's a bit early. But you'll see the notice on the gate. Are you the folks that have been making all the row down at Bywater? If you are, I shouldn't [?try] the Boss. He's angry. Take my advice and sheer off. You're not wanted. We've got work to do in the Shire now and we don't want noisy riffraff.'

'You don't always get what you want, Ted Sandyman,' said Sam. 'And I can tell you what's coming to you, whether you like it or no: a bath.' He jumped from his pony and before the astonished Ted knew what was coming Sam hit him square on the nose, and lifting him with an effort threw him over the bridge with a splash.]

A dirty surly-looking hobbit was lounging on the bridge by the mill. He was grimy-faced and grimy-handed, and was chewing. 'As good a small copy of Bill Ferny as you could ask for!' said Sam. 'So that's what Ted Sandyman admires, is it. I'm not surprised.'

Ted looked at him and spat. 'Going to see the Boss?' he said. 'If you are you're too early. He don't see no visitors till eleven, not even them as thinks themselves high and mighty. And he won't see you anyway. You're for the Lockholes, where you belong. Take my advice and sheer off before they come for you. We don't want you. We've work to do in the Shire now.'

'So I see,' said Sam. 'No time for a bath, but time for wall-propping. Well, never you mind, Ted, we'll find you something to do before this year's much older. And in the meantime keep your mouth shut. I've a score to pay in this village, and don't you make it any longer with your sneers, or you'll foot a bill too big for you to pay.'

Ted laughed. 'You're out o' date, Mr. Samwise, with your elves and your dragons. If I were you I'd go and catch one of them ships that [are] [?always] sailing, according to your tale. Go back to Babyland and rock your cradle, and don't bother us. We're going to make a big town here with twenty mills. A hundred new houses next year. Big stuff coming up from the South. Chaps who can work metals, and make big holes in the ground. There'll be forges a-humming and [?steamwhistles] and wheels going round. Elves can't do things like that.'

Sam looked at him, and his retorts died on his lips. He shook his head.

'Don't worry, Sam,' said Frodo. 'He's day-dreaming, poor wretch. And he's right behind the times. Let him be. But what we shall do with [him] is a bit of a worry. I hope there's not many caught the disease.'

'If I had known all the mischief Saruman had been up to,' said Merry, 'I'd have stuffed my pouch down his throat.'

They went sadly up the winding road to Bag End. The Field of the Party was all hillocks, as if moles had gone mad in it, but by some miracle the tree was still standing, now forlorn and nearly leafless.[19] They came at last to the door. The bell-chain dangled loose. No bell could be rung, no knocking was answered. At last they pushed and the door opened. They went in. The place stank, it was full of filth and disorder, but it did not appear to have been lived in for some time. 'Where is that miserable Cosimo hiding?' they said. There was nothing living to be found in any room save mice and rats.

'This is worse than Mordor,' said Frodo. 'Much worse in some ways.' 'Ah,' said Sam, 'it goes home as they say, because this is home, and it's all so, so mean, dirty [and] shabby. I'm very sorry, Mr. Frodo. But I'm glad I didn't know before. All the time in the bad places we've been in I've had the Shire in mind, and that's what I've rested on, if you take my meaning. I'd not have had a hope if I'd known all this.'

'I understand,' said Frodo. 'I said much the same to Gandalf long ago.[20] Never mind, Sam. It's our task to put it all right again. Hard work, but we'll not mind. Your box will come in useful.'

'My box?' said Sam. 'Glory and sunshine, Mr. Frodo, but of course. She knew, of course she knew. Showed me a bit in the Mirror. Bless her. I'd well-nigh forgotten it. But let's find that Boss first.'

'Hi you, what're you doing? Come out of it!' A loud voice rang out. They ran to the door and saw a large man, bowlegged, squinteyed, [?painfully ??bent] coming up the field from one of the sheds. 'What in Mordor do you mean by it?' he shouted. 'Come out of it. Come here, you Shire-rats. I [?saw] you.'

They came out and went to meet him. When they drew near enough for him to see them he stopped and looked at them, and to Frodo it seemed that he was .... [?and] a little afraid. 'We're looking for the Boss,' he said, 'or so I think you call him. Mr. Cosimo of Bag End. I'm his cousin. I used to live here.'

'Hi lads, hi, [?come here],' shouted the man. 'Here they are. We've got 'em.'

But there was no answer.

Frodo smiled. 'I think, Ruffian Sharkey, [?we] should cry "We've got him"? If you're calling for your other ruffians I'm afraid they've made off. To Michel Delving, I'm told. I am told you sleep sound.²¹ Well, what about it now.' The hobbits drew their swords and pressed near him; but he backed away. Very orc-like all his movements were, and he stooped now with his hands nearly touching the ground. 'Blast and grind the fools,' he said. 'Why didn't they warn me?'

'They thought of themselves first, I expect,' said Frodo, 'and anyway you've given strict orders that your sleep is not to be disturbed. It's on every notice. Come. I want to see the Boss. Where is he?'

The man looked puzzled. Then he laughed. 'You're looking at him,' he said. 'I'm the Boss. I'm Sharkey all right.'

'Then where is Mr. Cosimo of Bag End?'

'Don't ask me,' said the man. 'He saw what was coming, and he legged it one night. Poor booby. But it saved us the trouble of wringing his neck. We'd had enough of him. And we've got on better without him. He hadn't the guts of his ma.'

'I see,' said Frodo. 'So you ruffians from Isengard have been bullying this country for a year, and [??pretending] to be Mayor and Shirriff and what not, and eating most of the food and ...ing folk and setting up your filthy hutches. What for?'

'Who are you,' said the man, 'to "what for" me? I'm the Boss. And I do what I like. These little swine have got to learn how to work and I'm here to learn 'em. Saruman wants goods and he wants provisions, and he wants a lot of things lying idle here. And he'll get them, or we'll screw the necks of all you little rats and take the land for ourselves.'

'Isengard is a ruin and Saruman walks as a beggar,' said Frodo. 'You've outlived your time, Ruffian Sharkey. The Dark Tower has fallen and there is a King in Gondor, and there is a King also in the North. We come from the King. I give you three days. After that you are outlaw, and if you're found in this Shire you shall be killed, as you killed the [?wretch] Cosimo. I see in your eye that you lie, and in your hands that you strangled him. Your way leads downhill and [to] the East. Quick now!'

The orc-man looked at them with such a leer of hatred as they had not seen even in all their adventures. '... you're liars like all

your kind. Elf-friends and . . . . And four to one, which makes
you so bold.'

'Very well,' said Frodo, 'one to one.' He took off his cloak.
Suddenly he shone, a small gallant figure clad in mithril like an
elf-prince. Sting was in his hand;[22] but he was not much more
than half Sharkey's stature. Sharkey had a sword, and he drew
it, and in a [?fury] hewed double-handed at Frodo. But Frodo
using the advantage of his size and [?courage] ran in close
holding his cloak as a shield and slashed his leg above the knee.
And then as with a groan and a curse the orc-man [?toppled]
over him he stabbed upwards, and Sting passed clean through
his body.

So died Sharkey the Boss [?on the] . . . . where Bilbo's garden
had been. Frodo [??crawling] from under him looked at him as
he wiped Sting on the grass. 'Well,' he said, 'if ever Bilbo hears
of this he'll believe the world has really changed! When Gandalf
and I sat here long ago, I think that at least one thing I could
never have guessed would be that the last stroke of the battle
would be at this door.'[23]

'Why not?' said Sam. 'Very right and proper. And I'm glad
that it was yours, Mr. Frodo. But if I may say so, though it was a
grand day at Kormallen, and the happiest I have known, I never
have felt that you got as much praise as you deserve.'

'Of course not, Sam,' said Frodo. 'I'm a hobbit. But why
grumble? You've been far more neglected yourself. There's
never only one hero in any true tale, Sam, and all the good folk
are in others' debt. But if one had to choose one and one only,
I'd choose Samwise.'

'Then you'd be wrong, Mr. Frodo,' said Sam. 'For without
you I'm nothing. But you and me together, Mr. Frodo: well,
that's more than either alone.'

'It's more than anything I've heard of,' said Merry. 'But as for
the last stroke of battle, I'm not so sure. You've finished the
beastly Boss, while I only looked on. I've a [?feeling] from the
horns in the distance you'll find that Pippin and the Tooks have
had the last word. Thank heaven my . . . . . is Took Brandybuck.'

It was as he said. While they had dealt with the Boss things
had flared up in Bywater. The ruffians were no fools. They had
sent a man on a horse to [?within] horn cry of Michel Delving
(for they had many horn-signals). By midnight they had all
assembled at Waymoot,[24] 18 miles west of the Bywater Road
[?crossing]. They had [?horses of their own] on the White

Downs and rode like the fire. They charged the road-barrier at 10 a.m. but fifty were slain. The others had scattered and escaped. Pippin had killed [?five] and was wounded himself.

So ended the [??fierce] battle of Bywater, the only battle ever fought in the Shire. And it has at least a chapter all to itself in all standard histories.

It was some time before the last ruffians were hunted out. And oddly enough, little though the hobbits were inclined to believe it, quite a number turned out to be far from incurable.

This ends a page, and with it the now fearsomely difficult writing comes to an end: for the next page is perfectly legible, and this better script continues to the end of the draft, which is also the end of *The Lord of the Rings*. The pagination is continuous, however, and the likeliest explanation seems to be that there was simply a break in composition at this point.

The division between 'The Scouring of the Shire' and 'The Grey Havens' occurs at a point in RK that has nothing corresponding in the original draft, but it is convenient to make a break here, after one further paragraph concerning the fate of the 'ruffians', and to give the further continuation of the draft in the following chapters.

If they gave themselves up they were kindly treated, and fed (for they were usually half-starved after hiding in the woods), and then shown to the borders. This sort were Dunlanders, not orc-men/halfbreeds, who had originally come because their own land was wretched, and Saruman had told them there was a good country with plenty to eat away North. It is said that they found their own country very much better in the days of the King and were glad to return; but certainly the reports that they spread (enlarged for the covering of their own shame) of the numerous and warlike, not to say ferocious, hobbits of the Shire did something to preserve the hobbits from further trouble.

It is very striking that here, virtually at the end of *The Lord of the Rings* and in an element in the whole that my father had long meditated, the story when he first wrote it down should have been so different from its final form (or that he so signally failed to see 'what really happened'!). And this is not only because the original story took a wrong direction, as it turned out, when all four of the 'travellers' went to Farmer Cotton's house, nor because he did not perceive that it was Saruman who was the real 'Boss', Sharkey, at Bag End, but most of all because Frodo is portrayed here at every stage as an energetic and commanding intelligence, warlike and resolute in action; and the final text of the chapter had been very largely achieved when the changed conception of Frodo's part in the Scouring of the Shire entered.

It is perhaps a minor question, to try to resolve how my father was developing the idea of 'Sharkey' as he wrote this text, but it is certainly not easy to do so. The statements made are as follows:

– The chief of the orcish men at Bywater said (p. 82) that he had told the Boss that it was no good sending hobbits, and that the men ought to have gone, but the Boss had said no. This was changed to make the man say that he had given this advice to 'Big Sharkey', but Sharkey had said no, and 'the Boss let him have his way'.

– Later in the same conversation, this man says: 'It'll get it too, and before the year's out, or my name's not Sharkey.' Then Frodo calls him (p. 83) 'Ruffian Sharkey'.

– When the ruffians came to Farmer Cotton's house it was 'Sharkey' who peered in at the door; and Frodo slew him with his sword.

– The man who accosted the hobbits at Bag End (whose orc-like character is much emphasised) is called by Frodo 'Ruffian Sharkey' (p. 91).

– Frodo tells this man that he wants to see the Boss; to which he replies: 'I'm the Boss. I'm Sharkey all right.'

– Subsequently Frodo again calls him 'Ruffian Sharkey'; and he slays him with Sting in single combat.

As the text stands there can be no solution to this unless it is supposed that my father changed his conception as he wrote without altering the earlier passages. This would probably mean that the name 'Sharkey', whatever its basis as a name, was transferred from the squint-eyed rascal at Bywater when my father saw that 'the Boss' (Cosimo Sackville-Baggins) was being used now purely nominally by some more ruthless and sinister presence at Bag End: this was 'Sharkey'.[25] Then, suddenly, after the present draft was completed, my father saw who it really was that had supplanted Cosimo, and Saruman took over the name 'Sharkey'.[26]

At any rate, it is altogether certain that Saruman only entered the Shire in person in the course of the development of the present chapter. On the other hand, his previous baleful association with Cosimo Sackville-Baggins was present in the original draft, as is seen from Frodo's remarks at Bywater (p. 84) and Merry's at Bag End (p. 90: 'If I had known all the mischief Saruman had been up to, I'd have stuffed my pouch down his throat').

It required much further work to attain the story as it stands in *The Return of the King*, and the vehicle of this development was the complicated second manuscript 'B', which was numbered 'LIX' and at first given the title 'The Mending of the Shire'. It seems very probable that Saruman's presence at Bag End had already arisen when my

father began writing this text, and the references to 'Sharkey' are as in
RK; but while in detail and in wording it advances far towards the
final form he was still following A in certain features, and the major
shift in the plot (whereby the fight at Farmer Cotton's house was
removed) took place in the course of the writing of the manuscript.

Before that point in the story is reached the most notable feature is
that Frodo retains his dominance and his resolute captaincy. The
incident of the old 'gaffer' who jeered at the band of Shirriffs on their
forced march from Frogmorton entered in B, but it was Frodo, not
Merry, who sharply ordered their leader to leave him alone. The
leader was still, and explicitly, Robin Smallburrow (' "Smallburrow!"
said Frodo. "Order your fellows back to their places at once" '); but
his displacement by the officious and anonymous leader took place in
the course of the writing of this manuscript.[27]

There was a notable development in B of Frodo's exposition to
Pippin concerning Cosimo and Saruman and the pass to which the
Shire has been brought (see pp. 83–4). This was removed (cf. RK
p. 285) when, on a rider inserted into B, it became Farmer Cotton who
recounted from personal knowledge the recent history; but Cotton, of
course, did not know who Sharkey was, and presumably would not
have been much enlightened to learn that he was Saruman.

'I don't think you understand it quite,' said Frodo. 'Though
you were at Isengard, and have heard all that I have since. Yes,
Poor Cosimo! He has been a wicked fool. But he's caught in his
own net now. Don't you see? Saruman became interested in us
and in the Shire a good while ago, and began spying. [Added: So
Gandalf said.] A good many of the strange folk that had been
prowling about for a long while before we started must have
been sent by him. I suppose he got into touch with Cosimo that
way. Cosimo was rich enough, but he always did want more. I
expect he started trading with Saruman, and getting richer
secretly, and buying up this and that on the quiet. [Added:
Saruman needed supplies for his war.]'

'Ah!' said Sam, 'tobacco, a weakness of Saruman's. [> 'Yes!'
said Pippin. 'And tobacco for himself and his favourites!] I
suppose that Cosimo must have got his hands on most of it. And
on the South-farthing fields, too, I shouldn't wonder.'

'I expect so,' said Frodo. 'But he soon got bigger ideas than
that. He began hiring [> He seems to have hired] ruffians; or
Saruman sent them to him, to "help him". Chimneys, tree-
hacking, all those shoddy little houses. They look like imitations
of Saruman's notions of "improvement". But now, of course,
the ruffians are on top . . .'

The text then becomes that of RK; but after Frodo's admonition on the subject of killing (RK p. 285) it continues thus, following and expanding A (p. 84):

'It depends on how many of these ruffians there are,' said Merry. 'If there are a lot, then it will certainly mean fighting, Frodo. And it isn't going to be as easy after this. It may prove a nut tough enough for Gandalf's sledgehammer. After all we're only four hobbits, even if we're armed.'

'Well, we can't help Cousin Pimple tonight,' said Pippin; 'we need to find more out. You heard that horn-blowing? There's evidently more ruffians near at hand. We ought to get under cover soon. Tonight will be dangerous.'

'I've an idea,' said Sam. 'Let's go to old Cotton's. He always was a stout fellow, and he's a lot of lads that were all friends of mine.'

'D'you mean Farmer Cotton down South Lane?' said Frodo. 'We'll try him!'

They turned, and a few yards back came on South Lane leading out of the main road; in about a quarter of a mile it brought them to the farmer's gates.

In the story of their arrival at the farm, their welcome there and conversation with Farmer Cotton, my father followed A (pp. 84–6) closely, with some minor expansion but no movement away from the draft narrative (except that the imprisonment of Lobelia Sackville-Baggins is made longer: ' "They took his ma six months ago," said Cotton, "end o' last April" '). But from the bang on the front door the story changes:

There came at that moment a loud bang on the door. Farmer Cotton went softly down the passage, putting out the light. The others followed. There was a second louder bang.

'Open up, you old rat, or we'll burn you out!' shouted a hoarse voice outside. Mrs. Cotton in a nearby room stifled a scream. Down the stairs that led into the kitchen five young hobbits came clattering from the two upper rooms where they slept. They had thick sticks, but nothing more.

'I'm coming,' shouted the farmer, rattling the chains and making a to-do with the bolts. 'How many is there?' he whispered to his sons. 'A dozen at least,' said Young Tom, the eldest, 'maybe all the lot.'

'All the better,' said Frodo. 'Now for it! Open up and then get back. Don't join in, unless we need help badly.'

The four hobbits with swords drawn stood back to the wall against which the door swung. There came a great blow on the lock, but at that moment the farmer drew the last bolt, and slipped back with his sons some paces down the passage [*added: and round the corner out of sight*]. The door opened slowly and in peered the head of the ruffian they had already met. He stepped forward, stooping, holding a sword in his hand. As soon as he was well inside, the hobbits, who were now behind the opened door, flung it back with a crash. While Frodo slipped a bolt back, the three others leaped on the ruffian from behind, threw him down on his face and sat on him. He felt a cold blade of steel at his neck.

'Keep still and quiet!' said Sam. 'Cotton!' called Merry. 'Rope! We've got one. Tie him up!'

But the ruffians outside began attacking the door again, while some were smashing the windows with stones. 'Prisoner!' said Frodo. 'You seem a leader. Stop your men, or you will pay for the damage!'

They dragged him close to the door. 'Go home, you fools!' he shouted. 'They've got me, and they'll do for me, if you go on. Clear out! Tell Sharkey!'

'What for?' a voice answered from outside. 'We know what Sharkey wants. Come on, lads! Burn the whole lot inside! Sharkey won't miss that boob; he's no use for them as makes mistakes. Burn the lot! Look alive and get the fuel!'

'Try again!' said Sam grimly.

The prisoner now desperately frightened screamed out: 'Hi, lads! No burnings! No more burnings, Sharkey said. Send a messenger. You might find it was you as had made a mistake. Hi! D'you hear?'

'All right, lads!' said the other voice. 'Two of you ride back quick. Two go for fuel. The rest make a ring round the place!'

'Well, what's the next move?' said Farmer Cotton. 'At least they won't start burning until they've ridden to Bag-end and back: say half an hour, allowing for some talk. The murdering villains! Never thought they'd start burning. They burned a lot of folk out earlier, but they've not done [any] for a long while. We understood the Boss had stopped it. But see here! I've got the wife and my daughter Rosie to think of.'

'There's only two things to be done,' said Frodo. 'One of us has got to slip out and get help: rouse the folk. There must be

200 grown hobbits not far away. Or else we've got to burst out
in a pack with your wife and daughter in a huddle, and do it
quick, while two are away and before more come.'

'Too much risk for the one [that] slips out,' said Cotton.
'Burst out together, that's the ticket, and make a dash up the
lane.'

The concluding passage, from 'There's only two things to be done,'
was written in a rapidly degenerating scribble, and the text ends here,
not at the foot of a page. The story of the attack on the farmhouse had
already shifted strongly away from that in the original draft (in which
Frodo and Sam slew two of the marauders at the front door and four
others were killed in the yard before the remainder fled); and at this
point my father decided that he had taken a wrong turning. Perhaps he
could not see any credible way in which they could burst out of the
house (with the young Cottons and their mother in the midst) and
through the ring of men unscathed. At any rate, the whole of this part
of the B text, from ' "D'you mean Farmer Cotton down South Lane?"
said Frodo' (p. 96), was removed from the manuscript and replaced by
a new start, with Frodo's saying in response to Sam's suggestion that
they all go to Farmer Cotton's: 'No! It's no good getting "under
cover" ', as in RK (p. 286), where however it is Merry who says this. It
is Frodo also, not Merry, who answers Pippin's question 'Do what?'
with 'Raise the Shire! Now! Wake all our people!', and tells Sam that
he can make a dash for Cotton's farm if he wants to; he ends 'Now,
Merry, you have a horn of the Mark. Let us hear it!'

The story of the return of the four hobbits to the middle of Bywater,
Merry's horn-call, Sam's meeting with Farmer Cotton and his sons, his
visit to Mrs. Cotton and Rose, and the fire made by the villagers, is
told in virtually the same words as in RK (pp. 286–8), the only
difference being that it was on the orders of Frodo, not of Merry, that
barriers were set up across the road at each end of Bywater. When
Farmer Cotton tells that the Boss (as he is still named throughout B,
though emended later to 'the Chief') has not been seen for a week or
two B diverges a little from RK, for Tom Cotton the younger
interrupts his father at this point:

'They took his ma, that Lobelia,' put in Young Tom. 'That'd
be six months back, when they started putting up sheds at Bag
End without her leave. She ordered 'em off. So they took her.
Put her in the Lock-holes. They've took others that we miss
more; but there's no denying she stood up to 'em bolder than
most.'

'That's where most of them are,' said the farmer, 'over at
Michel Delving. They've made the old Lock-holes into a regular

fort, we hear, and they go from there roaming round, "gathering". Still I guess that there's no more than a couple of hundred in the Shire all told. We can master 'em, if we stick together.'

'Have they got any weapons?' asked Merry.

This perhaps implies that the *Lock-holes* were a prison in the days before any 'ruffian' came to the Shire. Subsequently Young Tom's story of Lobelia was removed from this part of the narrative, and replaced by Pippin's question 'Hobbiton's not their only place, is it?', which leads into Farmer Cotton's account of where else the 'ruffians' hung out beside Hobbiton, as in RK (p. 288), and a different idea of the origin of the Lock-holes: 'some old tunnels at Michel Delving'.

Merry's question 'Have they got any weapons?' leads, as in RK, to Farmer Cotton's account of the resistance of the Tooks, but without his reference to Pippin's father (Paladin Took), the Thain, and his refusal to have anything to do with the pretensions of Lotho (Cosimo):

'There you are, Frodo!' said Merry. 'I knew we'd have to fight. Well, they started it.'

'Not exactly,' said Farmer Cotton, 'leastways not the shooting. Tooks started that. You see, the Tooks have got those deep holes in the Green Hills, the Smiles[28] as they call 'em, and the ruffians can't come at 'em ...'

With Frodo still firmly in the saddle at Bywater, Merry rode off with Pippin to Tuckborough (as he does not in RK). After they had gone, Frodo reiterated his injunction against any killing that could be avoided (as in RK, p. 289), but then continued: 'We shall be having a visit from the Hobbiton gang very soon. It's over an hour since we sent the four ruffians off from here. Do nothing, until I give the word. Let them come on!' In RK it is Merry who gives the warning that the men from Hobbiton will soon be coming to Bywater, and he concludes 'Now I've got a plan'; to which Frodo merely replies 'Very good. You make the arrangements.' The arrival of the men, and the trapping of them beside the fire where Farmer Cotton was standing apparently all alone, follows exactly as in the final story, except that it is of course Frodo, not Merry, who accosts the leader; and when this encounter is over, and the men bundled off into one of their own huts, Farmer Cotton says 'You came back in the nick, Mr. Frodo.'

Then follows Cotton's account to Sam of the condition of the Gaffer ('he's in one of them new Shire-houses, Boss-houses I call 'em'), and Sam's departure to fetch him, virtually as in RK (p. 291). Once again, it is Frodo not Merry who posts look-outs and guards, and he goes off alone with Farmer Cotton to his house: 'He sat with the family in the kitchen, and they asked a few polite questions, but were far more concerned with events in the Shire. In the middle of the talk in burst

Sam, with the Gaffer.' The farmer's account of the 'troubles', ending with Young Tom's story of the carting off of Lobelia to the Lock-holes (RK p. 291–3), was inserted into B on a long rider; and at this time Frodo's earlier suppositions about how it all began (p. 95) and Young Tom's earlier remarks about Lobelia (p. 98) were removed.[29]

The incursion of the Gaffer into the Cottons' kitchen is told as in RK (pp. 293–4); but then follows in B:

In the morning early they heard the ringing call of Merry's horn, and in marched nearly a hundred of Tooks and other hobbits from Tuckborough and the Green Hills. The Shire was all alight, they said, and the ruffians that prowled round Tookland had fled; east to the Brandywine mostly, pursued by other Tooks.

There were now enough forces for a strong guard on the East Road from Michel Delving to Brandywine, and for another guard in Bywater. When all that had been settled and put in the charge of Pippin, Frodo and Sam and Merry with Farmer Cotton and an escort of fifty set out for Hobbiton.

The text then continues with the story of their coming to Hobbiton and meeting with Ted Sandyman, and their entry into Bag End, told almost word for word as in RK (pp. 296–7);[30] and ends with the advent of Saruman and his murder by Wormtongue (on which see pp. 102–3). The text B ends just as does the chapter in RK, with Merry's saying 'And the very last end of the War, I hope', Frodo's calling it 'the very last stroke', and Sam's saying 'I shan't call it the end, till we've cleared up the mess.' But there is thus no Battle of Bywater!

The Battle is found on inserted pages that are numbered as additional ('19a, 19b') to the consecutive pagination of the text just described. If this pagination means that these pages were written and inserted subsequently, and it is hard to see what else it could mean, it might seem that my father (still following the story in A, in which the visit to Hobbiton preceded the battle, p. 92) had driven on to the end of the Bag End episode without realising that the story of the Battle of Bywater had yet to be told. But this seems incredible. Far more likely he saw, as he wrote the story of the visit to Hobbiton, that the order of the narration in A must be reversed, so that the chapter would end with the last stroke of the War 'at the very door of Bag End'; but he postponed the battle, and inserted it subsequently into the text already continuously paginated.

Whenever this was done, the existing text (in which the dispositions for defence next morning were followed at once by the visit to Hobbiton) was altered to that of RK (p. 294), and the approach of the men along the road from Waymoot and their ambush on the high-banked road to Bywater was told almost as in the final story: the few differences in this passage are chiefly caused by Merry's having gone to Tuckborough with Pippin. The messenger from the Tookland does not refer to the Thain (see p. 99), and tells that 'Mr. Peregrin and Mr. Merry are coming on with all the folk we can spare'; it was Nick Cotton, not Merry, who had been out all night and reported the approach of the men, whom he estimated to number 'fifty or more' ('close on a hundred', RK); and when the Tooks came in 'the ringing call of Merry's horn was heard.' But from the point where the way back out of the ambush was blocked against the ruffian men, when the hobbits pushed out more carts onto the road, the B text diverges remarkably from the story told in RK:

A voice spoke to them from above. 'Well,' said Frodo, 'you have walked into a trap. Your fellows from Hobbiton did the same, and are all prisoners now. Lay down your weapons! Then go back twenty paces and sit down. Any who try to break out will be shot.'

Many of the men, in spite of the curses of their more villainous mates, at once obeyed. But more than a score turned about and charged back down the lane. Hobbit archers at gaps in the hedges shot down six before they reached the waggons. Some of them gave up, but ten or more burst through and dashed off, and scattered across country making for the Woody End it seemed.

Merry blew a loud horn-call. There were answering calls from a distance. 'They won't get far!' he said. 'All that country is now alive with hunters.'

The dead ruffians were laden on waggons and taken off and buried in an old gravel-pit nearby, the Battle Pits as they were called ever afterwards. The others were marched off to the village to join their fellows.

So ended the Battle of Bywater, 1419, the [only >] last battle fought in the Shire, and the only battle since the Greenfields, 1137,[31] away up in the North Farthing. In consequence, although it only cost six ruffian lives and no hobbits it has a chapter to itself in all the standard histories, and the names of all those who took part were made into a Roll and learned by heart. The very considerable rise in the fame and fortunes of the Cottons dates from this time.

The connection with the visit to Hobbiton was made in these words:

When all was settled, and a late midday meal had been eaten, Merry said: 'Well now, Frodo, it's time to deal with the Chief.'

Farmer Cotton collected an escort of some fifty sturdy hobbits, and then they set out on foot for Bag End: Frodo, Sam, Merry and Pippin led the way.

The words 'When all was settled' are used now to refer to the ending of the battle and the disposal of the dead and captured ruffians; previously (p. 100) they had referred to the arrangements made to meet the approaching enemy.

The story of the meeting with Saruman at Bag End was written out twice in B, the first form soon declining into a scribble when my father thought better of the opening of the episode. The first opening I give here:

'No doubt, no doubt. But you did not, and so I am able to welcome you home!' There standing at the door was Saruman, looking well-fed and a great deal less wretched than before; his eyes gleamed with malice and amusement.

A sudden light broke on Frodo. 'Sharkey!' he said. Saruman laughed. 'So you've heard that, have you? I believe all my men used to call me that in the better times. They were so devoted. And so it has followed me up here, has it? Really I find that quite cheering.'

'I cannot imagine why,' said Frodo. 'And what are you doing here anyway? Just a little shabby mischief? Gandalf said he thought you were still capable of that.'

[*Struck out:* 'Need you ask?' said Saruman.] 'You make me laugh, you hobbit lordlings,' said Saruman. 'Riding along with all these great people so secure and so pleased with yourselves; thinking you have done great things and can now just come back and laze in the country. Saruman's home can be ruined, and he can be turned out. But not Mr. Baggins. Oh, no! He's really important.

'But Mr. Baggins is a fool all the same. And can't even mind his own affairs, always minding other people's. To be expected of a pupil of Gandalf. He must dawdle on the way, and ride twice as far as he need. The Shire would be all right. Well, after our little meeting I thought I might get ahead of you and learn you a lesson. It would have been a sharper lesson if only you had dawdled longer. Still I have done a little that you'll find it hard to mend in your time. It'll be a warning to you to leave other folk alone, and not to be so cocksure. And it will give me something quite pleasant to think about, to set against my own injuries.'

The second version of the episode in B is virtually as in RK, except that it entirely lacks any reference to the dreadful corpse of Saruman and the mist that rose above it and loomed 'as a pale shrouded figure' over the Hill of Hobbiton; and this passage did not enter until my father wrote it in on the page proofs of *The Return of the King*.

A note that he pencilled against the episode in a copy of the First Edition is interesting:

Saruman turned back into Dunland[32] on Aug. 28. He then made for the old South Road and then went north over the Greyflood at Tharbad, and thence NW. to Sarn Ford, and so into the Shire and to Hobbiton on Sept. 22: a journey of about 460 [miles] in 25 days. He thus averaged about 18 miles a day – evidently hastening as well as he could. He had thus only 38 days in which to work his mischief in the Shire; but much of it had already been done by the ruffians according to his orders – already planned and issued before the sack of Isengard.

September 22 is the date given in *The Tale of Years* for Saruman's coming to the Shire, and October 30 for the coming of the 'travellers' to the Brandywine Bridge.

At a late stage of work on the B text (but before the insertion of the long rider in which Farmer Cotton recounts the history of the Shire since Frodo and his companions left, see p. 100 and note 29) my father perceived that Frodo's experience had so changed him, so withdrawn him, as to render him incapable of any such rôle in the Scouring of the Shire as had been portrayed. The text as it stood required no large recasting; the entirely different picture of Frodo's part in the events was brought about by many small alterations (often by doing no more than changing 'Frodo' to 'Merry') and a few brief additions. Virtually all of these have been noticed in the foregoing account.

A third, very fine manuscript ('C') followed B, and here the text of RK was reached in all but a few passages, most of these being very minor matters. It was on this manuscript that Cosimo Sackville-Baggins became Lotho, and the references to the Thain were introduced (see pp. 99, 101). The number of men at the Battle of Bywater had been enlarged to 'more than seventy', and the battle had become much fiercer, with the trapped men climbing the banks above the road and attacking the hobbits, already as C was first written; by later emendation the numbers of the men and of the slain on both sides were further increased. The original reading of C 'Merry himself slew the largest of the ruffians' was altered to '... the leader, a great squint-eyed brute like a huge orc'; with this cf. the description of the orc-man 'Sharkey' at Bag End in the A version, pp. 90–1. Lastly, an important addition was made to C concerning Frodo: 'Frodo had been in the battle, but he had not drawn sword, and his chief part had been to prevent the hobbits in their wrath at their losses from slaying those of their enemies who threw down their weapons' (RK pp. 295–6).

There lacked now only the passage describing the departure of the spirit of Saruman, and his corpse.

NOTES

1   Subsequently the passage was corrected in pencil. The question 'Who's the Mayor?' was given to Merry, and the answer became 'The Boss at Bag End'; Frodo's 'And who's the Chief Shirriff?' received the same answer. Then follows: 'Boss? Boss? You mean Mr. Cosimo, I suppose.' 'I suppose so, Mr. Baggins, but we have to say just The Boss nowadays.'

   Further on, where in RK (p. 279) it is said that 'The new "Chief" evidently had means of getting news', A has 'the New Mayor [?or] Chief Shirriff'; but this was changed to 'the Boss or Chief Shirriff'. When 'arrested' at Frogmorton Frodo and his companions are told that 'It's [Mayor's >] the Chief Shirriff's orders', where RK (p. 280) has 'It's the Chief's orders'.

2   But see p. 111.

3   The village was named *Frogbarn*, with *Frogmorton* written above as an alternative (and *Frogmorton* occurs in the text subsequently); and the date of their ride from the Brandywine Bridge was 'the fifth of November in the Shire-reckoning', with '1st' (the date in RK) written above. The village was 'about 25 miles from the Bridge' ('about twenty-two miles' in RK).

4   The name *Smallburrow* was written so, as in RK, at the first occurrence, but thereafter *Smallburrows*.

5   'Shire-house' is used in A for 'Shirriff-house' in RK. Sam asks what the term means, and Robin Smallburrows replies: 'Well, you ought to know, Sam. You were in one last night, and didn't find it to your liking, we hear.'

6   See p. 95.

7   The text here is very difficult. Above '(I told) the Boss' my father first wrote 'Long Tom' before changing this to 'Big Sharkey'. The end of the ruffian's remarks as first written cannot be read: 'but the Boss says no, and [?Long Tom] ..... way' (just possibly 'goes his way').

8   There is a note on the manuscript here which is partly illegible: '....... only Cosimo .... What happened to Otho?' In 'Three is Company' (*The Fellowship of the Ring* p. 75) it is said that Otho Sackville-Baggins 'had died some years before, at the ripe but disappointed age of 102', and this goes back to an early stage.

9   See the note given on p. 77 ('Gandalf should stay at Bree ...').

10 In RK Farmer Cotton is named Tom.
11 Sting had been given to Sam by Frodo in 'The Land of Shadow' (p. 32; RK p. 204); but Frodo wields Sting in his combat at Bag End with the chief of the orc-men (p. 92). In a passage that was introduced in the Second Edition Frodo was induced to receive it back at the Field of Cormallen (see p. 50).
12 *the Road Bend:* the westward turn in the road to Hobbiton at Bywater Pool. On the large-scale map of the Shire that I made in 1943 (VI.107) the bend is more marked and more nearly a right angle than it is on the small map in *The Fellowship of the Ring.*
13 *October* is a slip for *November:* see note 3.
14 By 'There's no way from the West' Farmer Cotton meant, I suppose, that there was no other way back from Michel Delving but by taking the East Road, since the ruffians could not or would not pass through the Tookland.
15 There are a couple of pages of roughly pencilled text which repeat, with minor alterations and extensions, this section of the chapter in A, made perhaps because my father recognised the near-illegibility of the original, and these pages have provided help in elucidating it here and there (characteristically, the words or phrases that defy elucidation in the original text are expressed differently in the second). At this point the pencilled text has: 'They've caught a ruffian or two and thrashed 'em in the Tookus' (*Tookus* < *Took-house,* as *workhouse* became *workus*).
16 I do not know whether *the Long Smial* is to be equated with *the Took-house.* – This is the first appearance of the word *smial,* which seems clearly to be written thus, although in the second text of 'The Scouring of the Shire' it is written *Smiles* (see p. 99 and note 28). Since Pippin was born in the Long Smial, it must be the forerunner of the Great Smials. These were at Tuckborough (Pippin speaks in Fangorn Forest of 'the Great Place of the Tooks away back in the Smials at Tuckborough', TT p. 64), but the name as written here is not in fact *Tuckborough:* it looks more like *Tuckbery* (not *Tuckbury*). However, there are many words wrongly written in this manuscript (in the next line of the text, for instance, the word I have given as '[?stout]' can really only be interpreted as 'stood').
17 The text could conceivably be interpreted as 'he had the block on the East [Road] strengthened', although no road-block on the East Road has been mentioned. The second, pencilled text of this part of the chapter (see note 15) has here: 'He had a block made on the Road at the waymeet.' This text gives out a few lines beyond this point.
18 It is interesting to look back at early references to the destruction in the Shire. In a note probably belonging to the time of the outline 'The Story Foreseen from Moria' (VII.216) my father

wrote: 'Cosimo has industrialised it. Factories and smoke. The Sandymans have a biscuit factory. Iron is found'; and in the earliest reference to the Mirror in Lothlórien Frodo was to see 'Trees being felled and a tall building being made where the old mill was. Gaffer Gamgee turned out. Open trouble, almost war, between Marish and Buckland on one hand – and the West. Cosimo Sackville-Baggins very rich, buying up land' (VII.249; cf. also VII.253, where there is a reference to the tall chimney being built on the site of the old mill).

In 'The old farm on the right' one should possibly read 'left' for 'right'; cf. my father's painting of Hobbiton, and the words of the final text of 'The Scouring of the Shire' (RK p. 296): 'The Old Grange on the west side had been knocked down, and its place taken by rows of tarred sheds.'

19 Later in this manuscript (p. 108) the Tree in the Party Field had been cut down and burned.

20 The reference is to 'The Shadow of the Past' (FR p. 71): 'I feel that as long as the Shire lies behind, safe and comfortable, I shall find wandering more bearable: I shall know that somewhere there is a firm foothold, even if my feet cannot stand there again.'

21 *I am told you sleep sound*: cf. the words of the orc-man at Bywater, speaking of Cosimo (an addition to the text, p. 83): 'He sleeps sound, and I shouldn't try and wake him now.'

22 Earlier in this narrative Sam wielded Sting: p. 86 and note 11.

23 At the top of the page on which Frodo's words appear my father wrote: 'Ah, and you said in Mordor you'd never strike another blow,' said Sam. 'Just shows you never know.' See p. 80.

24 *Waymoot*: *Waymeet* in RK. My original large-scale map of the Shire made in 1943 (VI.107) has *Waymoot*, as also that published in *The Fellowship of the Ring*; but the second manuscript of 'The Scouring of the Shire' has *Waymeet*. Presumably my father changed his mind about the form but neglected the map.

25 It is not explained how Frodo knew that this person, when he met him at Bag End, was called 'Sharkey'.

26 Cf. Saruman's words at the end of the chapter (p. 102): 'I believe all my men used to call me that in the better times. They were so devoted' (RK: 'All my people used to call me that in Isengard, I believe. A sign of affection, possibly'). The footnote to the text in RK p. 298 'It was probably Orkish in origin: *Sharkū* [Second Edition *Sharkû*], "old man"' was not added until the book was in page proof.

27 A rewritten account of the arrest at Frogmorton and Sam's conversation with Robin Smallburrow was inserted into manuscript B. This is almost as in RK, but as first written Robin's reply to Sam's question 'So that's how the news of us reached you, was it?' was different:

'Not directly. A message came down from the Chief at Bag End, about two hours ago, that you were to be arrested. I reckon someone must have slipped down from the Bridge to Stock, where there's a small gang of his Men. Someone went through Frogmorton on a big horse last night.'

This was changed at once to the text of RK (p. 282), but with 'One [runner] came in from Bamfurlong last night'. *Bamfurlong* was the reading of the First Edition here. In the Second Edition it was changed to *Whitfurrows* (which though shown on the map of the Shire was never mentioned in the text of the First Edition), and the name *Bamfurlong* was given to Maggot's farm in 'A Short Cut to Mushrooms' (FR p. 100): 'We are on old Farmer Maggot's land' of the First Edition became 'This is Bamfurlong; old Farmer Maggot's land.'

28 Cf. *the Long Smial* in A (note 16). A draft for the present passage has: 'those deep places the Old Smiles in the Green Hills'. I would guess that my father introduced *Smiles* as being the most natural spelling if the old word had survived into Modern English, but then abandoned it (it was changed to *Smials* on the B text) as being capable of an absurd interpretation. Cf. Appendix F (II, 'On Translation'): '*smial* (or *smile*) "burrow" is a likely form for a descendant of *smygel*'.

29 This rider was inserted at a late stage, for as in RK Merry interrupts Farmer Cotton with a question ('Who is this Shar-key?'); thus he was no longer away in Tuckborough with Pippin, but had assumed his rôle as commander of the operations at Bywater.

30 The only differences worth noting are that the trees had been felled along the Bywater Road 'for fuel for the engine'; and that a few men were still present in the huts at Hobbiton, who 'when they saw the force that approached fled away over the fields.'

31 It is said in the Prologue to *The Lord of the Rings* that 'before this story opens' 'the only [battle] that had ever been fought within the borders of the Shire was beyond living memory: the Battle of Greenfields, S.R.1147, in which Bandobras Took routed an invasion of Orcs.' The date 1137 was corrected to 1147 on the text C. – See p. 119.

32 In the First Edition the meeting with Saruman took place after the company had left Dunland: see p. 69.

X

THE GREY HAVENS

The original writing down of the last chapter of *The Lord of the Rings* was the continuation of the long uninterrupted draft text ('A') that extends back through 'The Scouring of the Shire' and 'Homeward Bound' (see pp. 75, 79), and which I left at the end of the Battle of Bywater on p. 93. That text continues:

And so the year drew to its end. Even Sam could find no fault with Frodo's fame and honour in his own country. The Tooks were too secure in their traditional position – and after all their folkland was the only one that had never given in to the ruffians – and also too generous to be really jealous; yet it was plain that the name of Baggins would become the most famous in Hobbit-history.

From this point the text of A, rough but now fully legible, differs chiefly from the final form of the chapter not in what is actually told nor in how it is told but in the absence of several significant features and a good deal of detail that were added in later. For example, while the rescue of Lobelia Sackville-Baggins from the Lockholes in Michel Delving and the disposition of her property is told much as in RK, there is no mention of Fredegar Bolger; and nothing is said of the hunting out of the gangs of men in the south of the Shire by Merry and Pippin. Frodo became the Mayor, not the Deputy Mayor, although the difference was only one of title, since he made it a condition of his acceptance that Will Whitfoot should become Mayor again 'as soon as the mess is cleared up'; and his inactivity in the office is not mentioned. As my father first set it down the account in RK (pp. 302–4) of the work of restoration and repair, of Sam's planting of young trees, of the fruitfulness of the year 1420,[1] and of Sam's marriage to Rose Cotton was very largely reached. In this text there is no reference to 'Sharkey's Men', and the jocular name given in Bywater to the restored Bagshot Row was 'Ruffians' End'. The seed in Galadriel's box is described as 'like a nut or a dried berry', its colour golden-yellow; Sam planted it in the Party Field 'where the tree had been burned' (see p. 90).

There is in A no reference to Frodo's first illness in March of 1420, when in Sam's absence Farmer Cotton found him on his bed 'clutching a white gem that hung on a chain about his neck' (the gift of Arwen recorded in 'Many Partings'). The passage in RK (p. 305) describing the finery and magnificence of Merry and Pippin, in contrast to the 'ordinary attire' of Frodo and Sam, is lacking, and so the further reference to the white jewel that Frodo always wore is also absent. Since my father had written a couple of pages earlier that 'Even Sam could find no fault with Frodo's fame and honour in his own country', the sharply contrasting picture in RK is of course lacking: 'Frodo dropped quietly out of all the doings of the Shire, and Sam was pained to notice how little honour he had in his own country. Few people knew or wanted to know about his deeds and adventures . . .'

Frodo's illness on the sixth of October 1420, the date of the attack of the Ringwraiths at Weathertop two years before, is recorded, but not that in March 1421. The naming of Sam's eldest daughter *Elanor* ('born on 25 March as Sam duly noted') on Frodo's suggestion is told, and the big book with red leather covers is described, without however any mention of the title page and the sequence of Bilbo's rejected titles; the writing in the book ended at Chapter 77 (the number being marked with a query).[2]

The last part of the chapter was set down with great sureness, though not all elements in the final story were immediately present. At the meeting of Frodo and Sam with the Elves in the Woody End there is no mention of the Great Rings of Elrond and Galadriel;[3] at Mithlond Círdan the Shipwright does not appear (but enters in a later marginal addition), nor is Gandalf said to bear the Third Ring; and Frodo's sight of the 'far green country under a swift sunrise' is absent (though this also is roughed in marginally; the linking of Frodo's passage over the Sea 'with the vision he had of a far green country in the house of Tom Bombadil' had been referred to in my father's letter of November 1944, see p. 53). I give here the text of A from the coming of the company to Mithlond:

And when they had passed the Shire by the south skirts of the White Downs they came to the Far Downs and the Towers and looked on the Sea; and rode down at last to Mithlond the Grey Havens in the long firth of Lūne. And there was a ship lying at the haven, and upon the quays stood one robed also in white. It was Gandalf, and he welcomed them; and they were glad for then they knew that he also would take ship with them.

But Sam was now sad at heart, and it seemed to him that if the parting would be bitter, even worse would be the lonely ride home. But even as they stood there and were ready to go aboard, up rode Merry and Pippin in great haste. And amid his tears Pippin laughed. 'You tried to give us the slip once before and failed, Frodo, and this time you have nearly done it, but you've failed again.' 'It was not Sam this time who gave you away,' said Merry, 'but Gandalf himself.'

'Yes,' said Gandalf. 'It will be better to ride back three together than one alone. Well, here at last, dear friends, on the shores of the Sea comes an end of our fellowship in Middle-earth. Go in peace; and I will not say, do not weep, for not all tears are an evil.'

Then Frodo kissed Merry and Pippin and last of all Sam, and went aboard, and the sails were drawn up, and the wind blew, and slowly the ship sailed away down the [?pale] Gulf of Lune. And it was night again; and Sam looked on the grey sea and saw a shadow on the waters that was lost in the West. And he stood a while hearing the sigh and murmur of the waves on the shores of Middle-earth, and the sound of it remained in his heart for ever, though he never spoke of it. And Merry and Pippin stood silent beside him.

The long ride back to the Shire is told in almost the same words as in *The Return of the King*. And thus the Third Age was brought to its final end, in this most memorable of partings, without hesitation and with assured simplicity; the unmistakeable voices of Merry and Pippin, the still more unmistakeable voice of Gandalf in his last words on Middle-earth, and the beginning of the voyage that was bearing away into the True West the hobbits, Bilbo and Frodo, leaving Sam behind.

A manuscript of the chapter as a separate entity ('B') followed, subsequently numbered 'LX' and entitled 'The Grey Havens'. It was written before the changed view of Frodo's reputation in the Shire had entered, but with emendations and additions it reached the final form in almost all the features in which A differed from it. My father did not yet realise, however, that Fredegar Bolger languished in the Lockholes along with Will Whitfoot and Lobelia Sackville-Baggins; and of Lobelia it was said in a first draft of the passage concerning her that 'She never got over the news of poor Cosimo's murder, and she said that it was not his fault; he was led astray by that wicked Sharkey and never meant any harm.'

Frodo's first illness was still absent as B was originally written, and when it was introduced it was in these words:

Sam was away on his forestry work in March, and Frodo was glad, for he had been feeling ill, and it would have been difficult to conceal from Sam. On the twelfth of March[4] he was in pain and weighed down with a great sense of darkness, and could do little more than walk about clasping the jewel of Queen Arwen. But after a while the fit passed.

An idea that was never carried further appears in a hastily scribbled passage on this manuscript, apparently intended for inclusion before 'Little Elanor was nearly six months old, and 1421 had passed to its autumn' (RK p. 306):

At midsummer Gandalf appeared suddenly, and his visit was long remembered for the astonishing things that happened to all the bonfires (which hobbit [?children] light on midsummer's eve). The whole Shire was lit with lights of many colours until the dawn came, and it seemed that the fire [??ran wild for him] over all the land so that the grass was kindled with glittering jewels, and the trees were hung with red and gold blossom all through the night, and the Shire was full of light and song until the dawn came.

No other trace of this idea is found. Perhaps my father felt that when Gandalf declared that his time was over he meant no less.[5]

The title page of the Red Book of Westmarch first appears in B, with Bilbo's titles written one above the other and all struck through (which was the meaning of the word 'so' in 'crossed out one after another, so:', RK p. 307):

Memoirs of An Amateur Burglar
My Unexpected Journey
There and Back Again   and What Happened After
Adventures of Five Hobbits
The Case of the Great Ring (compiled from the records
    and notes of B. Baggins and others)
What the Bagginses Did in the War of the Ring
(here Bilbo's hand ended and Frodo had written:)
The
Downfall
of
The Lord of the Rings
and
The Return of the King
(as seen by B. and F. Baggins, S. Gamgee, M. Brandybuck, P. Took,
    supplemented by information provided by the Wise)

In the typescript that followed B the following was added:

Together with certain excerpts from Books of Lore
translated by B. Baggins in Rivendell[6]

In B appeared the Three Rings of the Elves on the fingers of their bearers, but they were not yet named. It was not until the book was in galley proof that 'Vilya, mightiest of the Three' was added to the description of Elrond's Ring, Gandalf's Ring was named 'Narya the

Great', and that of Galadriel became 'Nenya, the ring wrought of *mithril*'.

Lastly, both in A and in B my father set within square brackets, his usual sign of doubt, certain of Frodo's words to Sam in the Woody End, thus: 'No, Sam. Not yet anyway, not further than the Havens. [Though you too were a Ringbearer, if only for a little while: your time may come.]'

NOTES

1 Absent from the account of the year 1420 is the sentence in RK, p. 303: 'All the children born or begotten in that year, and there were many, were fair to see and strong, and most of them had a rich golden hair that had before been rare among hobbits.' This entered in the first typescript text. See p. 134, note 12.

2 In the following text the last, unfinished chapter in the Red Book was numbered '72', and on the first typescript this was changed to '80', as in RK.

3 The chant to Elbereth began thus:
> O Elbereth Gilthoniel
> Silivren pennar oriel!
> Gilthoniel O Elbereth . . .

Cf. VI.394. This was repeated in the second text of the chapter, but *oriel* was emended to *íriel*. This in turn was repeated on the first typescript, and then the opening was changed to its form in RK:
> A! Elbereth Gilthoniel
> silivren penna míriel
> o menel aglar elenath . . .

To Bilbo's question (RK p. 309) 'Are you coming?' Frodo replies here: 'Yes, I am coming, *before the wound returns*. And the Ringbearers should go together.' Frodo was speaking of the sickness that had come on him on October the sixth, the date of his wounding at Weathertop, in each of the following years. It was now 22 September (Bilbo's birthday); on the twenty-ninth of the month the ship sailed from the Grey Havens. On the third anniversary of the attack at Weathertop *The Lord of the Rings* ends, for it was on that day, according to *The Tale of Years*, that Sam returned to Bag End.

4 The date was corrected to the thirteenth of March on the following typescript text. This in the final chronology was the anniversary of the poisoning of Frodo by Shelob, as noted in *The Tale of Years*. Frodo's third illness, in the following year, also fell on March 13, according to *The Tale of Years*.

5 But he had perhaps intended that a final visit by Gandalf to the Shire should be recorded; as Gandalf said when he parted from the

hobbits in the note on the draft manuscript of 'Homeward Bound' (p. 77): 'I'll be along some time.'

6 In the two typescript texts of the chapter the crossings-out were omitted, and Bilbo's first title 'Memoirs of an Amateur Burglar' was replaced by 'My Diary'. 'What Happened After' was still shown as an addition, and the words 'and friends' were added after 'Bagginses' in Bilbo's final title; in the margins of both typescripts my father noted that the corrections were to be printed as such, representing the original title-page. The final form of the page was introduced on the galley proof.

XI

THE EPILOGUE

The words that end *The Lord of the Rings*, ' "Well, I'm back," he said', were not intended to do so when my father wrote them in the long draft manuscript A which has been followed in the previous chapters. It is obvious from the manuscript that the text continued on without break;[1] and there is in fact no indication that my father thought of what he was writing as markedly separate from what preceded. I give now this last part of A: very rough, but legible throughout. The ages of Sam's children were added, almost certainly at the time of writing: Elanor 15, Frodo 13, Rose 11, Merry 9, Pippin 7.

And one evening in March [*added:* 1436][2] Master Samwise Gamgee was taking his ease by a fire in his study, and the children were all gathered about him, as was not at all unusual, though it was always supposed to be a special treat.

He had been reading aloud (as was usual) from a big Red Book on a stand, and on a stool beside him sat Elanor, and she was a beautiful child more fair-skinned than most hobbit-maids and more slender, and she was now running up into her 'teens; and there was Frodo-lad on the heathrug, in spite of his name as good a copy of Sam as you could wish, and Rose, Merry, and Pippin were sitting in chairs much too big for them. Goldilocks had gone to bed, for in this Frodo's foretelling had made a slight error and she came after Pippin, and was still only five and the Red Book rather too much for her yet. But she was not the last of the line, for Sam and Rose seemed likely to rival old Gerontius Took in the number of their children as successfully as Bilbo had passed his age. There was little Ham, and there was Daisie in her cradle.

'Well dear,' said Sam, 'it grew there once, because I saw it with my own eyes.'

'Does it grow there still, daddy?'

'I don't see why it shouldn't, Ellie. I've never been on my travels again, as you know, having all you young folk to mind –

regular ragtag and bobtail old Saruman would have called it. But Mr. Merry and Mr. Pippin, they've been south more than once, for they sort of belong there too now.'

'And haven't they grown big?' said Merry. 'I wish I could grow big like Mr. Meriadoc of Buckland. He's the biggest hobbit that ever was: bigger than Bandobras.'

'Not bigger than Mr. Peregrin of Tuckborough,' said Pippin, 'and he's got hair that's almost golden. Is he Prince Peregrin away down in the Stone City, dad?'

'Well, he's never said so,' said Sam, 'but he's highly thought of, that I know. But now where were [we] getting to?'

'Nowhere,' said Frodo-lad. 'I want to hear about the Spider again. I like the parts best where you come in, dad.'

'But dad, you were talking about Lórien,' said Elanor, 'and whether my flower still grows there.'

'I expect it does, Ellie dear. For as I was saying, Mr. Merry, he says that though the Lady has gone the Elves still live there.'

'When can I go and see? I want to see Elves, dad, and I want to see my own flower.'

'If you look in a glass you'll see one that is sweeter,' said Sam, 'though I should not be telling you, for you'll find it out soon enough for yourself.'

'But that isn't the same. I want to see the green hill and the white flowers and the golden and hear the Elves sing.'

'Then maybe you will one day,' said Sam. 'I said the same when I was your age, and long after, and there didn't seem no hope, and yet it came true.'

'But the Elves are sailing away still, aren't they, and soon there'll be none, will there, dad?' said Rose; 'and then all will be just places, and very nice, but, but ...'

'But what, Rosie-lass?'

'But not like in stories.'

'Well, it would be so if they all was to sail,' said Sam. 'But I am told they aren't sailing any more. The Ring has left the Havens, and those that made up their mind to stay when Master Elrond left are staying. And so there'll be Elves still for many and many a day.'

'Still I think it was very sad when Master Elrond left Rivendell and the Lady left Lórien,' said Elanor. 'What happened to Celeborn? Is he very sad?'

'I expect so, dear. Elves are sad; and that's what makes them so beautiful, and why we can't see much of them. He lives in his own land as he always has done,' said Sam. 'Lórien is his land, and he loves trees.'

'No one else in the world hasn't got a Mallorn like we have, have they?' said Merry. 'Only us and Lord Keleborn.'[3]

'So I believe,' said Sam. Secretly it was one of the greatest prides of his life. 'Well, Keleborn lives among the Trees, and he is happy in his Elvish way, I don't doubt. They can afford to wait, Elves can. His time is not come yet. The Lady came to his land and now she is gone;[4] and he has the land still. When he tires of it he can leave it. So with Legolas, he came with his people and they live in the land across the River, Ithilien, if you can say that, and they've made it very lovely, according to Mr. Pippin. But he'll go to Sea one day, I don't doubt. But not while Gimli's still alive.'

'What's happened to Gimli?' said Frodo-lad. 'I liked him. Please can I have an axe soon, dad? Are there any orcs left?'

'I daresay there are if you know where to look,' said Sam. 'But not in the Shire, and you won't have an axe for chopping off heads, Frodo-lad. We don't make them. But Gimli, he came down to work for the King in the City, and he and his folk worked so long they got used to it and proud of their work, and in the end they settled up in the mountains up away west behind the City, and there they are still. And Gimli goes once every other year to see the Glittering Caves.'

'And does Legolas go to see Treebeard?' asked Elanor.

'I can't say, dear,' said Sam. 'I've never heard of anyone as has ever seen an Ent since those days. If Mr. Merry or Mr. Pippin have they keep it secret. Very close are Ents.'

'And have they never found the Entwives?'

'Well, we've seen none here, have we?' said Sam.

'No,' said Rosie-lass; 'but I look for them when I go in a wood. I would like the Entwives to be found.'

'So would I,' said Sam, 'but I'm afraid that is an old trouble, too old and too deep for folks like us to mend, my dear. But now no more questions tonight, at least not till after supper.'

'But that won't be fair,' said both Merry and Pippin, who were not in their teens. 'We shall have to go directly to bed.'

'Don't talk like that to me,' said Sam sternly. 'If it ain't fair for Ellie and Fro to sit up after supper it ain't fair for them to be born sooner, and it ain't fair that I'm your dad and you're not mine. So no more of that, take your turn and what's due in your time, or I'll tell the King.'

They had heard this threat before, but something in Sam's voice made it sound more serious on this occasion. 'When will you see the King?' said Frodo-lad.

'Sooner than you think,' said Sam. 'Well now, let's be fair. I'll tell you all, stay-uppers and go-to-bedders, a big secret. But don't you go whispering and waking up the youngsters. Keep it till tomorrow.'

A dead hush of expectancy fell on all the children: they watched him as hobbit-children of other times had watched the wizard Gandalf.

'The King's coming here,' said Sam solemnly.

'Coming to Bag End!' cried the children.

'No,' said Sam. 'But he's coming north. He won't come into the Shire because he has given orders that no Big Folk are to enter this land again after those Ruffians; and he will not come himself just to show he means it. But he will come to the Bridge. And —— ' Sam paused. 'He has issued a very special invitation to every one of you. Yes, by name!'

Sam went to a drawer and took out a large scroll. It was black and written in letters of silver.

'When did that come, dad?' said Merry.

'It came with the Southfarthing post three days ago [*written above:* on Wednesday],' said Elanor. 'I saw it. It was wrapped in silk and sealed with big seals.'

'Quite right, my bright eyes,' said Sam. 'Now look.' He unrolled it. 'It is written in Elvish and in Plain Language,' said Sam. 'And it says: *Elessar Aragorn Arathornsson the Elfstone King of Gondor and Lord of the Westlands will approach the Bridge of Baranduin on the first day of Spring, or in the Shire-reckoning the twenty-fifth day of March next, and desires there to greet all his friends. In especial he desires to see Master Samwise Mayor of the Shire, and Rose his wife, and Elanor, Rose, Goldilocks and Daisie his daughters, and Frodo, Merry, and Pippin and Hamfast his sons.* There you are, there are all your names.'

'But they aren't the same in both lists,' said Elanor, who could read.

'Ah,' said Sam, 'that's because the first list is Elvish. You're the same, Ellie, in both, because your name is Elvish; but Frodo is *Iorhail*, and Rose is *Beril*, and Merry is *Riben* [> *R..el* > *Gelir*], and Pippin is *Cordof*, and Goldilocks is *Glorfinniel*, and Hamfast is *Marthanc*, and Daisy [*so spelt*] is *Arien*. So now you know.'

'Well that's splendid,' said Frodo, 'now we all have Elvish names, but what is yours, dad?'

'Well, that's rather peculiar,' said Sam, 'for in the Elvish part, if you must know, what the King says is *Master Perhail who should rather be called Lanhail*, and that means, I believe, "Samwise or Halfwise who should rather be called Plain-wise". So now you know what the King thinks of your dad you'll maybe give more heed to what he says.'

'And ask him lots more questions,' said Frodo.

'When is March the 25th?' said Pippin, to whom days were still the longest measures of time that could really be grasped. 'Is it soon?'

'It's a week today,' said Elanor. 'When shall we start?'

'And what shall we wear?' said Rose.

'Ah,' said Sam. 'Mistress Rose will have a say in that. But you'll be surprised, my dears. We have had warning of this a long time and we've prepared for the day. You're going in the most lovely clothes you've ever seen, and we're riding in a coach. And if you're all very good and look as lovely as you do now I shouldn't be at all surprised if the King does not ask us to go with him to his house up by the Lake. And the Queen will be there.'

'And shall we stay up to supper?' said Rose, to whom the nearness of promotion made this an ever-present concern.

'We shall stay for weeks, until the hay-harvest at least,' said Sam. 'And we shall do what the King says. But as for staying up to supper, no doubt the Queen will have a word. And now if you haven't enough to whisper about for hours, and to dream about till the sun rises, then I don't know what more I can tell you.'

The stars were shining in a clear sky: it was the first day of the clear bright spell that came every year to the Shire at the end of March, and was every year welcomed and praised as something surprising for the time of the year.

All the children were in bed. Lights were glimmering still in Hobbiton and in many houses dotted about the darkening countryside. Sam stood at the door and looked away eastward. He drew Mistress Rose to him and held her close to his side. 'March 18th [> 25th]',[5] he said. 'This time seventeen years ago, Rose wife, I did not think I should ever see thee again. But I kept on hoping.'

THE EPILOGUE

['And I never hoped at all, Sam,' she said, 'until that very day; and then suddenly I did. In the middle of the morning I began singing, and father said "Quiet lass, or the Ruffians will come," and I said "Let them come. Their time will soon be over. My Sam's coming back." And he came.']⁶

'And you came back,' said Rose.

'I did,' said Sam; 'to the most belovedest place in all the world. I was torn in two then, lass, but now I am all whole. And all that I have, and all that I have had I still have.'

Here the text as it was written ends, but subsequently my father added to it the following:

They went in and shut the door. But even as he did so Sam heard suddenly the sigh and murmur of the sea on the shores of Middle-earth.

It cannot be doubted that this was how he intended at that time that *The Lord of the Rings* should end.

A fair copy ('**B**') followed, and this was headed 'Epilogue', without chapter-number; subsequently 'Epilogue' was altered to 'The End of the Book', again without number. The changes made to the original draft were remarkably few: very minor adjustments and improvements in the flow of the conversation between Sam and his children, and the alteration or enlargement of certain details.

Merry Gamgee now knows that Bandobras Took 'killed the goblin-king': the reference is to 'An Unexpected Party' in *The Hobbit*, where it is told that the Bullroarer 'charged the ranks of the goblins of Mount Gram in the Battle of the Green Fields, and knocked their king Golfimbul's head clean off with a wooden club.' Of the sailing of the Elves Sam now says, not that 'they aren't sailing any more', but that 'they are not sailing often now', and he continues: 'Those that stayed behind when Elrond left are mostly going to stay for good, or for a very long time. But they are more and more difficult to find or to talk to.' Of Ents he observes that they are 'very close, very secret-like, and they don't like people very much'; and of the Dwarves who came from Erebor to Minas Tirith with Gimli he says 'I hear they've settled up in the White Mountains not very far from the City', while 'Gimli goes once a year to see the Glittering Caves' (in Appendix A III, at end, it is said that Gimli 'became Lord of the Glittering Caves').

The King's letter now begins *Aragorn Arathornsson Elessar the Elfstone*; and the date of his coming to the Brandywine Bridge was now 'the eighth day of Spring, or in the Shire-reckoning the second of April', since my father had decided, already while writing A (see note 5), that the 25th of March was not the day on which the King would come to the Bridge, but the day on which *The Lord of the Rings* came to an end.[7]

Daisie Gamgee's name is now *Erien* (*Arien* in A); and in the King's letter he calls Sam *Master Perhail who should rather be called Panthail*, which Sam interprets as 'Master Samwise who ought to be called Fullwise'.

Other changes were made to B later, and these were taken up into the third and final text 'C' of this version of the 'Epilogue', a typescript. To this my father gave the revised title of B, 'The End of the Book', with a chapter-number 'LVIII',[8] but he then struck out both title and number and reverted to 'Epilogue.' The text now opens thus:

One evening in the March of 1436 Master Samwise Gamgee was taking his ease by the fire in his study, and his children were gathered round him, as was not at all unusual. Though it was always supposed to be a special occasion, a Royal Command, it was one more often commanded by the subjects than by the King.

This day, however, really was a special occasion. For one thing it was Elanor's birthday;[9] for another, Sam had been reading aloud from a big Red Book, and he had just come to the very end, after a slow progress through its many chapters that had taken many months. On a stool beside him sat Elanor ...

Sam now says of the Entwives: 'I think maybe the Entwives don't want to be found'; and after his words 'But now no more questions tonight' the following passage was introduced:

'Just one more, please!' begged Merry. 'I've wanted to ask before, but Ellie and Fro get in so many questions there's never any room for mine.'

'Well then, just one more,' said Sam.

'About horses,' said Merry. 'How many horses did the Riders lose in the battle, and have they grown lots more? And what happened to Legolas's horse? And what did Gandalf do with Shadowfax? And can I have a pony soon?' he ended breathlessly.

'That's a lot more than one question: you're worse than Gollum,' said Sam. 'You're going to have a pony next birthday, as I've told you before. Legolas let his horse run back free to Rohan from Isengard; and the Riders have more horses than ever, because nobody steals them any longer; and Shadowfax went in the White Ship with Gandalf: of course Gandalf couldn't have a' left him behind. Now that'll have to do. No more questions. At least not till after supper.'

The letter of the King now begins *Aragorn Tarantar* (at which Sam explains 'that's Trotter') *Aranthornsson* &c. *Tarantar* was altered on the typescript to *Telcontar* ('that's Strider'): see VIII.390 and note 14. Rose's name in Elvish becomes *Meril* (for *Beril*), and Hamfast's *Baravorn* (for *Marthanc*); the Elvish name of Daisy (so spelt in C) reverts to *Arien* (for *Erien*), the form in A.

Though never published, of course, this version of the Epilogue is, I believe, quite well known, from copies made from the text at Marquette University. My father would never in fact have published it, even had he decided in the end to conclude *The Lord of the Rings* with an epilogue, for it was superseded by a second version, in which while much of Sam's news from beyond the Shire was retained its framework and presentation were radically changed.[10] Of this there are two texts. The first is a good clear manuscript with few corrections; it has neither title nor chapter-number. The second is a typescript, which though made by my father followed the manuscript very closely indeed; this is entitled 'Epilogue', with the chapter-number 'X' (i.e. of Book Six). I give here the text of the typescript in full.

The second version of the Epilogue

EPILOGUE

One evening in the March of 1436 Master Samwise Gamgee was in his study at Bag End. He was sitting at the old well-worn desk, and with many pauses for thought he was writing in his slow round hand on sheets of loose paper. Propped up on a stand at his side was a large red book in manuscript.

Not long before he had been reading aloud from it to his family. For the day was a special one: the birthday of his daughter Elanor. That evening before supper he had come at last to the very end of the Book. The long progress through its many chapters, even with omissions that he had thought advisable, had taken some months, for he only read aloud on great days. At the birthday reading, besides Elanor, Frodo-lad had been present, and Rosie-lass, and young Merry and Pippin; but the other children had not been there. The Red Book was not for them yet, and they were safely in bed. Goldilocks was only five years old, for in this Frodo's foretelling had made a slight error, and she came after Pippin. But she was not the last of the line, for Samwise and Rose seemed likely to rival old Gerontius Took as successfully in the number of their children as Bilbo had in the number of his years. There was little Ham, [and there was Daisy still in her cradle >] and Daisy, and there was Primrose still in her cradle.[11]

Now Sam was 'having a bit of quiet'. Supper was over. Only Elanor was with him, still up because it was her birthday. She sat without a sound, staring at the fire, and now and again glancing at her father. She was a beautiful girl, more fair of skin than most hobbit-maidens, and more slender, and the firelight glinted in her red-gold hair. To her, by gift if not by inheritance, a memory of elven-grace had descended.[12]

'What are you doing, Sam-dad[13] dear?' she said at last. 'You said you were going to rest, and I hoped you would talk to me.'

'Just a moment, Elanorellë,' said Sam,[14] as she came and set her arms about him and peered over his shoulder.

'It looks like Questions and Answers,' she said.

'And so it is,' said Sam. 'Mr. Frodo, he left the last pages of the Book to me, but I have never yet durst to put hand to them. I am still making notes, as old Mr. Bilbo would have said. Here's all the many questions Mother Rose and you and the children have asked, and I am writing out the answers, when I know them. Most of the questions are yours, because only you has heard all the Book more than once.'

'Three times,' said Elanor, looking at the carefully written page that lay under Sam's hand.

Q. *Dwarves, &c.* Frodo-lad says he likes them best. What happened to Gimli? Have the Mines of Moria been opened again? Are there any Orcs left?

A. *Gimli:* he came back to work for the King, as he said, and he brought many of his folk from the North, and they worked in Gondor so long that they got used to it, and they settled there, up in the White Mountains not far from the City. Gimli goes once a year to the Glittering Caves. How do I know? Information from Mr. Peregrin, who often goes back to Minas Tirith, where he is very highly thought of.

Moria: I have heard no news. Maybe the foretelling about Durin is not for our time.[15] Dark places still need a lot of cleaning up. I guess it will take a lot of trouble and daring deeds yet to root out the evil creatures from the halls of Moria. For there are certainly plenty of Orcs left in such places. It is not likely that we shall ever get quite rid of them.

Q. *Legolas.* Did he go back to the King? Will he stay there?

A. Yes, he did. He came south with Gimli, and he brought many of his people from Greenwood the Great (so they call it now). They say it was a wonderful sight to see companies of Dwarves and Elves journeying together. The Elves have made the City, and the land where Prince Faramir lives, more beautiful than ever. Yes, Legolas will stay there, at any rate as long as Gimli does; but I think he will go to the Sea one day. Mr. Meriadoc told me all this, for he has visited the Lady Éowyn in her white house.

Q. *Horses.* Merry is interested in these; very anxious for a pony of his own. How many horses did the Riders lose in the battles, and have they got some more now? What happened to Legolas's horse? What did Gandalf do with Shadowfax?

A. *Shadowfax* went in the White Ship with Gandalf, of course. I saw that myself. I also saw Legolas let his horse run free back to Rohan from Isengard. Mr. Meriadoc says he does not know how many horses were lost; but there are more than ever in Rohan now, because no one steals them any longer. The Riders also have many ponies, especially in Harrowdale: white, brown, and grey. Next year when he comes back from a visit to King Éomer he means to bring one for his namesake.

Q. *Ents.* Elanor would like to hear more about them. What did Legolas see in Fangorn; and does he ever see Treebeard now? Rosie-lass very anxious about Entwives. She looks for them whenever she goes in a wood. Will they ever be found? She would like them to be.

A. Legolas and Gimli have not told what they saw, so far as I have heard. I have not heard of any one that has seen an Ent since those days. Ents are very secret, and they do not like people much, big or little. I should like the Entwives to be found, too; but I am afraid that trouble is too old and deep for Shire-folk to mend. I think, maybe, Entwives do not want to be found; and maybe Ents are now tired of looking.

'Well dear,' said Sam, 'this top page, this is only today's batch.' He sighed. 'It isn't fit to go in the Book like that. It isn't a bit like the story as Mr. Frodo wrote it. But I shall have to make a chapter or two in proper style, somehow. Mr. Meriadoc might help me. He's clever at writing, and he's making a splendid book all about plants.'

'Don't write any more tonight. Talk to me, Sam-dad!' said Elanor, and drew him to a seat by the fire.

'Tell me,' she said, as they sat close together with the soft golden light on their faces, 'tell me about Lórien. Does *my* flower grow there still, Sam-dad?'

'Well dear, Celeborn still lives there among his trees and his Elves, and there I don't doubt your flower grows still. Though now I have got you to look at, I don't hanker after it so much.'

'But I don't want to look at myself, Sam-dad. I want to look at other things. I want to see the hill of Amroth where the King met Arwen, and the silver trees, and the little white niphredil, and the golden elanor in the grass that is always green. And I want to hear Elves singing.'

'Then, maybe, you will one day, Elanor. I said the same when I was your age, and long after it, and there didn't seem to be no hope. And yet I saw them, and I heard them.'

'I was afraid they were all sailing away, Sam-dad. Then soon there would be none here; and then everywhere would be just places, and'

'And what, Elanorellë?'

'And the light would have faded.'

'I know,' said Sam. 'The light is fading, Elanorellë. But it won't go out yet. It won't ever go quite out, I think now, since I have had you to talk to. For it seems to me now that people can remember it who have never seen it. And yet,' he sighed, 'even that is not the same as really seeing it, like I did.'

'Like really being in a story?' said Elanor. 'A story is quite different, even when it is about what happened. I wish I could go back to old days!'

'Folk of our sort often wish that,' said Sam. 'You came at the end of a great Age, Elanorellë; but though it's over, as we say, things don't really end sharp like that. It's more like a winter sunset. The High Elves have nearly all gone now with Elrond. But not quite all; and those that didn't go will wait now for a while. And the others, the ones that belong here, will last even longer. There are still things for you to see, and maybe you'll see them sooner than you hope.'

Elanor was silent for some time before she spoke again. 'I did not understand at first what Celeborn meant when he said goodbye to the King,' she said. 'But I think I do now. He knew that Lady Arwen would stay, but that Galadriel would leave him.[16] I think it was very sad for him. And for you, dear Sam-dad.' Her hand felt for his, and his brown hand clasped her slender fingers. 'For your treasure went too. I am glad Frodo of the Ring saw me, but I wish I could remember seeing him.'

'It was sad, Elanorellë,' said Sam, kissing her hair. 'It was, but [it] isn't now. For why? Well, for one thing, Mr. Frodo has gone where the elven-light isn't fading; and he deserved his reward. But I have had mine, too. I have had lots of treasures. I am a very rich hobbit. And there is one other reason, which I shall whisper to you, a secret I have never told before to no one, nor put in the Book yet. Before he went Mr. Frodo said that my time maybe would come. I can wait. I think maybe we haven't said farewell for good. But I can wait. I have learned that much from the Elves at any rate. They are not so troubled about time. And so I think Celeborn is still happy among his trees, in an Elvish way. His time hasn't come, and he isn't tired of his land yet. When he is tired he can go.'

'And when you're tired, you will go, Sam-dad. You will go to the Havens with the Elves. Then I shall go with you. I shall not part with you, like Arwen did with Elrond.'

'Maybe, maybe,' said Sam kissing her gently. 'And maybe not. The choice of Lúthien and Arwen comes to many, Elanorellë, or something like it; and it isn't wise to choose before the time.

'And now, my dearest, I think that it's time even a lass of fifteen spring-times should go to her bed. And I have words to say to Mother Rose.'

Elanor stood up, and passed her hand lightly through Sam's curling brown hair, already flecked with grey. 'Good night, Sam-dad. But'

'I don't want *good night but*,' said Sam.

'But won't you show it me first? I was going to say.'

'Show you what, dear?'

'The King's letter, of course. You have had it now more than a week.'

Sam sat up. 'Good gracious!' he said. 'How stories do repeat themselves! And you get paid back in your own coin and all. How we spied on poor Mr. Frodo! And now our own spy on us, meaning no more harm than we did, I hope. But how do you know about it?'

'There was no need for spying,' said Elanor. 'If you wanted it kept secret, you were not nearly careful enough. It came by the Southfarthing post early on Wednesday last week. I saw you take it in. All wrapped in white silk and sealed with great black seals: any one who had heard the Book would have guessed at once that it came from the King. Is it good news? Won't you show it me, Sam-dad?'

'Well, as you're so deep in, you'd better be right in,' said Sam. 'But no conspiracies now. If I show you, you join the grown-ups' side and must play fair. I'll tell the others in my own time. The King is coming.'

'He's coming here?' Elanor cried. 'To Bag End?'

'No, dear,' said Sam. 'But he's coming north again, as he hasn't done since you was a mite.[17] But now his house is ready. He won't come into the Shire, because he's given orders that no Big Folk are to enter the land again after those Ruffians, and he won't break his own rules. But he will ride to the Bridge. And he's sent a very special invitation to every one of us, every one by name.'

Sam went to a drawer, unlocked it, and took out a scroll, and slipped off its case. It was written in two columns with fair silver letters upon black. He unrolled it, and set a candle beside it on the desk, so that Elanor could see it.

'How splendid!' she cried. 'I can read the Plain Language, but what does the other side say? I think it is Elvish, but you've taught me so few Elvish words yet.'

'Yes, it's written in a kind of Elvish that the great folk of Gondor use,' said Sam. 'I have made it out, enough at least to be sure that it says much the same, only it turns all our names into Elvish. Yours is the same on both sides, Elanor, because your name *is* Elvish. But Frodo is *Iorhael*, and Rose is *Meril*, and Merry is *Gelir*, and Pippin is *Cordof*, and Goldilocks is *Glorfinniel*, and Hamfast is *Baravorn*, and Daisy is *Eirien*. So now you know.'

'How wonderful!' she said. 'Now we have all got Elvish names. What a splendid end to my birthday! But what is your name, Sam-dad? You didn't mention it.'

'Well, it's rather peculiar,' said Sam. 'For in the Elvish part, if you must know, the King says: "Master *Perhael* who should be called *Panthael*". And that means: Samwise who ought to be called Fullwise. So now you know what the King thinks of your old father.'

'Not a bit more than I do, Sam-dad, *Perhael-adar*[18] dearest,' said Elanor. 'But it says the second of April, only a week today![19] When shall we start? We ought to be getting ready. What shall we wear?'

'You must ask Mother Rose about all that,' said Sam. 'But we *have* been getting ready. We had a warning of this a long time ago; and we've said naught about it, only because we didn't want you all to lose your sleep of nights, not just yet. You have all got to look your best and beautifullest. You will all have beautiful clothes, and we shall drive in a coach.'

'Shall I make three curtsies, or only one?' said Elanor.

'One will do, one each for the King and the Queen,' said Sam. 'For though it doesn't say so in the letter, Elanorellë, I think the Queen will be there. And when you've seen her, my dear, you'll know what a lady of the Elves looks like, save that none are so beautiful. And there's more to it even than that. For I shall be surprised if the King doesn't bid us to his great house by Lake Evendim. And there will be Elladan and Elrohir, who still live in Rivendell – and with them will be Elves, Elanorellë, and they will sing by the water in the twilight. That is why I said you might see them sooner than you guessed.'

Elanor said nothing, but stood looking at the fire, and her eyes shone like stars. At last she sighed and stirred. 'How long shall we stay?' she asked. 'I suppose we shall have to come back?'

'Yes, and we shall want to, in a way,' said Sam. 'But we might stay until hay-harvest, when I must be back here. Good night, Elanorellë. Sleep now till the sun rises. You'll have no need of dreams.'

'Good night, Sam-dad. And don't work any more. For I know what your chapter should be. Write down our talk together – but not to-night.' She kissed him, and passed out of the room; and it seemed to Sam that the fire burned low at her going.

The stars were shining in a clear dark sky. It was the second day of the bright and cloudless spell that came every year to the Shire towards the end of March, and was every year welcomed and praised as something surprising for the season. All the children were now in bed. It was late, but here and there lights were still glimmering in Hobbiton, and in houses dotted about the night-folded countryside.

Master Samwise stood at the door and looked away eastward. He drew Mistress Rose to him, and set his arm about her.

'March the twenty-fifth!' he said. 'This day seventeen years ago, Rose wife, I didn't think I should ever see thee again. But I kept on hoping.'

'I never hoped at all, Sam,' she said, 'not until that very day; and then suddenly I did. About noon it was, and I felt so glad that I began singing. And mother said: "Quiet, lass! There's ruffians about." And I said: "Let them come! Their time will soon be over. Sam's coming back." And you came.'

'I did,' said Sam. 'To the most belovedest place in all the world. To my Rose and my garden.'

They went in, and Sam shut the door. But even as he did so, he heard suddenly, deep and unstilled, the sigh and murmur of the Sea upon the shores of Middle-earth.

★

In this second Epilogue Sam does not read out the King's letter (since Elanor could read), but associated with it (as is seen from the name-forms *Eirien, Perhael, Panthael*) are three 'facsimiles' of the letter, written in *tengwar* in two columns.

The first of these ('I') is reproduced on p. 130. It is accompanied by a transliteration into 'plain letters' of both the English and the Sindarin. The transliteration of the English does not precisely correspond to the *tengwar* text, for the former omits *Arathornsson*, and adds *day* where the *tengwar* text has 'the thirty-first of the Stirring'. The words *and Arnor, ar Arnor* were added in to both the *tengwar* texts and are lacking in the transliterations. As my father wrote them they read as follows:

Aragorn Strider The Elfstone, King of Gondor and Lord of the Westlands, will approach the Bridge of Baranduin on the eighth day of Spring, or in the Shire-reckoning the second day of April. And he desires to greet there all his friends.
In especial he desires to see Master *Samwise*, Mayor of the Shire, and *Rose* his wife; and *Elanor, Rose, Goldilocks*, and *Daisy* his daughters; and *Frodo, Merry, Pippin* and *Hamfast* his sons.

To Samwise and Rose the King's greeting from Minas Tirith, the thirty-first day of the Stirring, being the twenty-third of February in their reckoning.
A · E ·

Elessar Telcontar: Aragorn Arathornion Edhelharn, aran

Gondor ar Hîr i Mbair Annui, anglennatha i Varanduiniant
erin dolothen Ethuil, egor ben genediad Drannail erin
Gwirith edwen. Ar e aníra ennas suilannad mhellyn în
phain: *edregol* e aníra tírad i Cherdir *Perhael* (i sennui
Panthael estathar aen) Condir i Drann, ar *Meril* bess dîn,
ar *Elanor, Meril, Glorfinniel,* ar *Eirien* sellath dîn; ar
Iorhael, Gelir, Cordof, ar *Baravorn,* ionnath dîn.
   A *Pherhael* ar am *Meril* suilad uin aran o Minas
Tirith nelchaenen uin Echuir.
                            A · E ·

The change of pen after *ar Elanor* was no doubt made in order to fit
the Sindarin text onto the page.
   The second 'facsimile' ('II'), not accompanied by a transliteration
and not reproduced here, is very similar to I, but *and Arnor, ar Arnor*
is part of the texts as written, there is no variation in the boldness of
the lettering, and the texts end at the words *his sons, ionnath dîn,*
followed by the initials A · E ·, so that there is here no mention of the
date and place of the letter.
   The third of these pages ('III'), preserved with the typescript text of
the second Epilogue and accompanied by a transliteration, is reproduced on p. 131. In this case the use of vowel-*tehtar* above consonants in the Sindarin text greatly reduced its length. The English text is
the same as in I, but the note of the date is different: 'From Minas
Tirith, the twenty-third of February 6341' [= 1436]. The Sindarin text
differs from that of I and II in the word order:
   Aragorn Arathornion Edhelharn anglennatha iVaranduiniant
   erin dolothen Ethuil (egor ben genediad Drannail erin Gwirith
   edwen) ar ennas aníra i aran Gondor ar Arnor ar Hîr iMbair
   Annui [*written* Anui][20] suilannad mhellyn in phain . . .
The note of date at the end of the Sindarin text reads:
   a Pherhael ar am Meril suilad uin aran o Minas Tirith
   nelchaenen ned Echuir: 61.[21]

It emerges from the account of his works that my father wrote for
Milton Waldman in 1951 that the second version of the Epilogue was
written at a very late stage. In this account he included what he called
'a long and yet bald résumé' of the story of *The Lord of the Rings*; this
was omitted in *Letters* (no. 131), and I give here its closing passages.

The 'Scouring of the Shire' ending in the last battle ever fought there
occupies a chapter. It is followed by a second spring, a marvellous
restoration and enhancement of beauty, chiefly wrought by Sam
(with the help of gifts given him in Lórien). But Frodo cannot be
healed. For the preservation of the Shire he has sacrificed himself,
even in health, and has no heart to enjoy it. Sam has to choose

First copy of the King's letter

Third copy of the King's letter

between love of master and of wife. In the end he goes with Frodo on a last journey. At night in the woods, where Sam first met Elves on the outward journey, they meet the twilit cavalcade from Rivendell. The Elves and the Three Rings, and Gandalf (Guardian of the Third Age) are going to the Grey Havens, to set sail for the West, never to return. Bilbo is with them. To Bilbo and Frodo the special grace is granted to go with the Elves they loved – an Arthurian ending, in which it is, of course, not made explicit whether this is an 'allegory' of death, or a mode of healing and restoration leading to a return. They ride to the Grey Havens, and take ship: Gandalf with the Red Ring, Elrond (with the Blue) and the greater part of his household, and Galadriel of Lórien with the White Ring, and with them depart Bilbo and Frodo. It is hinted that they come to Eressëa. But Sam standing stricken on the stone quay sees only the white ship slip down the grey estuary and fade into the darkling West. He stays long unmoving listening to the sound of the Sea on the shores of the world.

Then he rides home; his wife welcomes him to the firelight and his first child, and he says simply 'Well, I've come back.'[22] There is a brief epilogue in which we see Sam among his children, a glance at his love for Elanor (the Elvish name of a flower in Lórien) his eldest, who by a strange gift has the looks and beauty of an elven-maid; in her all his love and longing for Elves is resolved and satisfied. He is busy, contented, many times mayor of the Shire, and struggling to finish off the Red Book, begun by Bilbo and nearly completed by Frodo, in which all the events (told in The Hobbit and The Lord [of the Rings]) are recorded. The whole ends with Sam and his wife standing outside Bag-end, as the children are asleep, looking at the stars in the cool spring sky. Sam tells his wife of his bliss and content, and goes in, but as he closes the door he hears the sighing of the Sea on the shores of the world.

It is clear from the words 'we see Sam among his children' that my father was referring to the first version of the Epilogue.

He was persuaded by others to omit the Epilogue from The Lord of the Rings. In a letter to Naomi Mitchison of 25 April 1954 (Letters no. 144) he wrote:

Hobbit-children were delightful, but I am afraid that the only glimpses of them in this book are found at the beginning of vol. I. An epilogue giving a further glimpse (though of a rather exceptional family) has been so universally condemned that I shall not insert it. One must stop somewhere.

He seems both to have accepted and to have regretted that decision. On 24 October 1955, a few days after the publication of The Return of the King, he wrote to Katherine Farrer (Letters no. 173):

I still feel the picture incomplete without something on Samwise and Elanor, but I could not devise anything that would not have destroyed the ending, more than the hints (possibly sufficient) in the appendices.

NOTES

1 The 'Epilogue' text begins at the head of a page, but this is merely because the words ' "Well, I'm back," he said' stand at the foot of the preceding one.

2 '1436' was pencilled in subsequently. Apparently my father first wrote 'And one evening Master Samwise . . .', but changed this at once to 'And one evening in March Master Samwise . . .' This does not suggest the passage of many years since the sailing of the ship from Mithlond, but that such was the case is immediately plain in the same opening sentence ('and the children were all gathered about him'); the absence of a date in the text as first written must therefore be casual and without significance.

3 *Keleborn:* immediately above the name was spelt *Celeborn*; here, the *K* was changed from *C* in the act of writing the letter.

4 On the development of the legends of Galadriel and Celeborn see *The History of Galadriel and Celeborn* in *Unfinished Tales*, Part Two §IV.

5 *March 18th [> 25th]:* the King had declared in his letter that he would be coming to the Brandywine Bridge on March 25; Elanor had said that that was 'a week today'; and as my father wrote this concluding passage Sam said to Rose at the door of Bag End 'March 18th'. On the change to the 25th, apparently made immediately, see note 7.

6 The brackets are in the original.

7 The change in the King's letter from March 25 to April 2 was in fact, and at first sight very oddly, an emendation made on the B text. This question of the dates is minor, complicated, and explicable. When my father wrote the text A the great day of the King's coming north to the Brandywine Bridge was to be the 25th of March, the date of the destruction of the Ring and the downfall of Sauron (see pp. 59–60); and Elanor said (p. 118) that that was 'a week today', so that the occasion of Sam's conversation with his children recorded in the Epilogue was March 18. When Sam and Rose stood outside Bag End that night Sam said: 'March 18th. Seventeen years ago . . .' (p. 118). My father changed '18' to '25' on the manuscript A (and probably at the same time added in the words '*This time* (seventeen years ago)') because he decided, just at that point, that the end of *The Lord of the Rings* (in its Epilogue) should fall on that date (possibly also because he recalled that it was Elanor's birthday, which had of

course been chosen for the same reason); but he failed to postpone the date in the King's letter earlier in A (p. 117).

Writing out the fair copy B, in which he followed A very closely, he momentarily forgot this decision, and repeated the date in A of the King's coming to the Bridge, March 25. Subsequently, while writing B, he realised that this was now erroneous, and changed it to April 2; so at the end of B Sam says (as he had in A): 'March the twenty-fifth! This time seventeen years ago ...'

Elanor's answer to Pippin's question 'When is the second of April?' was changed subsequently on B from 'a week today' to 'a week tomorrow', which is the reading in the typescript C. This, however, was erroneous, since it gives March thirty-one days; 'a week today' was restored in the second version of the Epilogue, p. 127.

8 Chapter-number 'LVIII': the basis of the revised numbering of the chapters of Book Six is not clear to me. The sequence ran from LII 'The Tower of Kirith Ungol' (p. 25) to LX 'The Grey Havens' (p. 110), but on some of the chapters these numbers were reduced by two; here the reduction is by three.

9 Elanor's birth on 25 March (1421) was mentioned in the original draft of 'The Grey Havens', p. 109.

10 In this second version Sam is making notes, which are cited and which are an essential part of the Epilogue, for the filling of the empty pages at the end of the Red Book; and it seems odd that the title 'The End of the Book', so suitable to the second version, should have been used, and rejected, on texts B and C of the first (pp. 119–20).

11 This emendation was made on the typescript only. In 'The Longfather-tree of Master Samwise' in Appendix C Daisy Gamgee was born in 1433 and Primrose in 1435; Bilbo Gamgee was born in the year of the Epilogue, 1436, and was followed by three further children, making thirteen in all.

12 A footnote to the record of the birth of Elanor in *The Tale of Years* states: 'She became known as "the Fair" because of her beauty; many said that she looked more like an elf-maid than a hobbit. She had golden hair, which had been very rare in the Shire; but two others of Samwise's daughters were also golden-haired, and so were many of the children born at this time.' Cf. the reference in 'The Grey Havens' to the golden-haired children born in the Shire in the year 1420 (RK p. 303; see p. 112, note 1).

13 *Sam-dad:* this address to Sam by his children entered in text B of the first version.

14 In the manuscript 'said Sam' is followed by 'sucking his pen-holder'; this was probably omitted inadvertently, as were other phrases afterwards picked up and reinserted in the typescript.

15   Sam was no doubt thinking of the end of Gimli's song in Moria, by which he was greatly struck (FR p. 330):
    There lies his crown in water deep,
    Till Durin wakes again from sleep.
Or else of Gimli's words when Frodo and Sam looked with him into Mirrormere: 'O Kheled-zâram fair and wonderful! There lies the crown of Durin till he wakes.' '"What did you see?" said Pippin to Sam, but Sam was too deep in thought to answer' (FR p. 348).

16   Elanor's words refer to RK p. 260 ('Many Partings'): 'But Celeborn said: "Kinsman, farewell! May your doom be other than mine, and your treasure remain with you to the end!"' For the original form of Celeborn's farewell to Aragorn see p. 64.

17   I do not know of any other reference to this northern journey of Aragorn in the early years of his reign.

18   In the manuscript (which had *ai* forms, later emended, in the names *Iorhail, Perhail, Panthail*) Elanor calls her father *Panthail-adar*.

19   *only a week today:* see note 7, at end.

20   My father's transliteration has *ar ennas i aran Gondor ar Arnor ar Hîr iMbair Annui aníra* ...

21   61 = 16, i.e. year 16 of the Fourth Age, which means that the Fourth Age began in 1421 (see Appendix D to *The Lord of the Rings*, at end).

22   In all the texts of 'The Grey Havens' from the earliest draft Sam said to Rose when he returned to Bag End 'Well, I'm back.' 'Well, I've come back' does not mean the same thing.

APPENDIX

Drawings of Orthanc and Dunharrow

When I wrote Volume VIII, *The War of the Ring*, it entirely and most regrettably escaped my memory that there are several unpublished drawings of Orthanc and Dunharrow in the Bodleian Library. As these are of much interest I reproduce them belatedly here, as a final appendix to the history of *The Lord of the Rings*.

The upper drawing on the page called here 'Orthanc I' shows a conception essentially similar to that of the little sketch 'Orthanc 3' reproduced in VIII.33 and described in the first manuscript of the chapter 'The Voice of Saruman', VIII.61. In this, the tower was founded on a huge arch spanning the great cleft in the rock; flights of stairs led up on two sides to a narrow platform beneath the arch, whence further stairs ran up 'to dark doors on either side, opening in the shadow of the arch's feet'. But in the present drawing the rock of Orthanc is enormously much greater in relation to the tower than in 'Orthanc 3'; the tower has only three tiers (seven in 'Orthanc 3' and in the description associated with it, VIII.32–3); and the horns at the summit are very much smaller.

In the lower drawing on this page, showing the Circle of Isengard in Nan Gurunír between the mountains' arms, is seen the feature described in the original drafting of the chapter 'The Road to Isengard' but rejected from the first completed manuscript (VIII.43, note 23): the western side of the Circle was formed by the mountain-wall itself. The dark letter C was a change made later to the faintly pencilled name of the Wizard's Vale, *Nan Gurunír* becoming *Nan Curunír*.

The page 'Orthanc II' carries two designs for 'Orthanc's roof'; and on 'Orthanc III' the final conception is seen emerging, in which the 'rock' of Orthanc becomes itself the 'tower'. The drawing on the right has in fact been previously published: it was used in *The Lord of the Rings Calendar 1977*, and so appears in *Pictures by J. R. R. Tolkien*, no. 27 (see VIII.44, note 26).

The two pages of drawings of Dunharrow are not easy to interpret, more especially 'Dunharrow I' (for the early conceptions of Dunharrow and the first sketches see VIII.235 ff.). Of 'Dunharrow I' it can at least be said that this idea of the approach to the Hold was never described in words. Apparently, the path winding up from the valley passed near the top of the cliff through the great door in the foreground and entered a steeply ascending tunnel, climbing up by stairs inside the cliff, the head of which can be seen emerging from a large opening or hole in the flat land above. The single menhir, first mentioned in the text F of the original work on the chapter 'The Muster of Rohan' (VIII.246) as standing in the rock-ringed floor of the Hold, is seen; but since there is no sign of the lines of standing stones across the upland (nor of the Púkel-men at the turns in the climbing path) I would be inclined to place this drawing after the earliest drafts of the chapter and the little sketches reproduced in VIII.239 but before the writing of the text F.

A very puzzling feature of this drawing is the wavy line at bottom left, hiding one of the bends in the climbing path.

The upper drawing on the page 'Dunharrow II' has a general likeness in the lie of the mountain side to the coloured drawing reproduced as the first frontispiece (but which should have been the second) to *The War of the Ring*, but there the resemblance ceases. In that other picture a double line of huge standing stones crosses the upland from the brink of the cliff to a dark cleft in the mountain, where the road so marked out disappears; and I suggested (VIII.250) that the dark cleft is ' "the gate of the Hold", the "Hold" itself, the "recess" or "amphitheatre" with doors and windows in the cliff at the rear, being in this picture invisible.' In the present drawing the Púkel-men are seen at the turns of the path coming up from the valley; at the top of the cliff the road continues to wind, but the turns are now marked by pointed stones. There is then a straight stretch across the upland field, unmarked by stones; and the road passing (apparently) between two stones or pillars leads into the Hold, in which the door into the cliff behind can be seen. In the left-hand lower drawing the Púkel-men reappear, and in the right-hand drawing a double line of cone-shaped stones leads across the upland and into the Hold, with a single stone standing in the middle of the 'amphitheatre'.

My guess is that the upper drawing on this page shows a stage in the development of the conception of Dunharrow when the Púkel-men had emerged, but not the double line of stones: these are seen at the moment of their emergence in one of the lower sketches. In relation to the manuscript evidence, 'Dunharrow I' would then belong with, but actually precede, the text F of 'The Muster of Rohan', in which both the Púkel-men (then called the Hoker-men) and the lines of stones are present.

Orthanc I

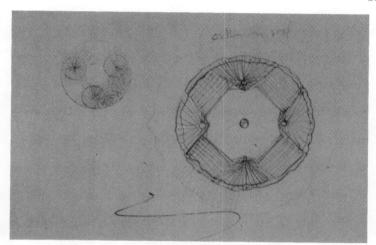

Orthanc II

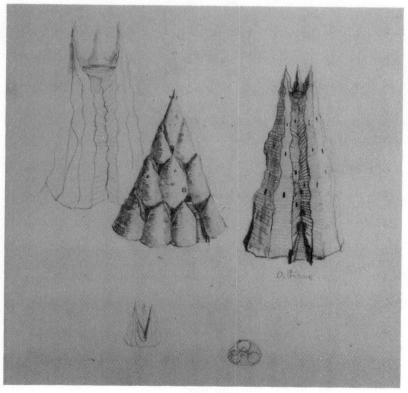

Orthanc III

Dunharrow I

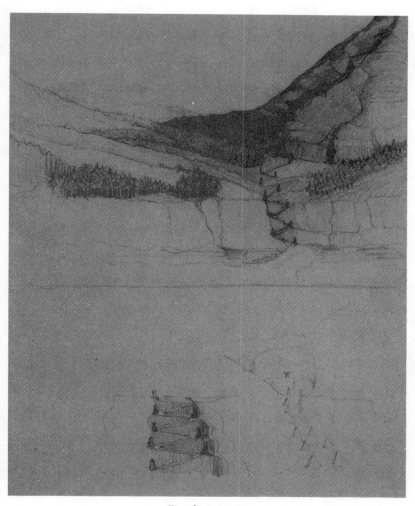

Dunharrow II

PART TWO

THE NOTION CLUB
PAPERS

THE NOTION CLUB PAPERS

Introduction

On 18 December 1944, when *The Lord of the Rings* had reached the end of what would become *The Two Towers* (and a few pages had been written of 'Minas Tirith' and 'The Muster of Rohan' at the beginning of Book V), my father wrote to me (*Letters* no. 92) that he had seen C. S. Lewis that day: 'His fourth (or fifth?) novel is brewing, and seems likely to clash with mine (my dimly projected third). I have been getting a lot of new ideas about Prehistory lately (via Beowulf and other sources of which I may have written) and want to work them into the long shelved time-travel story I began. C. S. L. is planning a story about the descendants of Seth and Cain.' His words are tantalizingly difficult to interpret; but by 'clash with mine' he surely meant that the themes of their books ran rather close.[1]

Whatever lies behind this, it is seen that he was at this time turning his thoughts to a renewed attempt on the 'time-travel story', which would issue a year later in *The Notion Club Papers*. In his letter to Stanley Unwin of 21 July 1946 (*Letters* no. 105) he said that he hoped very shortly 'actually to – write', to turn again to *The Lord of the Rings* where he had left it, more than a year and a half before: 'I shall now have to study my own work in order to get back to it,' he wrote. But later in that same letter he said:

> I have in a fortnight of comparative leisure round about last Christmas written three parts of another book, taking up in an entirely different frame and setting what little had any value in the inchoate *Lost Road* (which I had once the impudence to show you: I hope it is forgotten), and other things beside. I hoped to finish this in a rush, but my health gave way after Christmas. Rather silly to mention it, till it is finished. But I am putting *The Lord of the Rings*, the *Hobbit* sequel, before all else, save duties that I cannot wriggle out of.

So far as I have been able to discover there is no other reference to *The Notion Club Papers* anywhere in my father's writings.

But the quantity of writing constituting *The Notion Club Papers*, and the quantity of writing associated with them, cannot by any manner of means have been the work of a fortnight. To substantiate this, and since this is a convenient place to give this very necessary information, I set out here the essential facts of the textual relations of all this material, together with some brief indication of their content.

As the development of *The Notion Club Papers* progressed my father divided it into two parts, the second of which was never completed, and although he ultimately rejected this division[2] I have found it in every way desirable to preserve it in this book. Part One was 'The Ramblings of Michael Ramer: *Out of the Talkative Planet*', and this consists of a report in direct speech of the discussions at two successive meetings[3] of 'the Notion Club' at Oxford far in the future at the time of writing. On the first of these occasions the conversation turned on the problem of the vehicle, the machine or device, by which 'space-travellers' are transported to their destination, especially in respect of its literary credibility in itself and its effect on the story contained within the journeys; on the second, of which the report is much longer, one of the members, Michael Ramer, expounded his ideas concerning 'true dreams' and his experiences of 'space-travel' in dream.

The earliest manuscript, here called '**A**', is a complete text of Part One. It is roughly written and hastily expressed, there is no title or explanatory 'scene-setting', and there are no dates; but while the text would undergo much expansion and improvement, the essential structure and movement of the dialogue was already largely present.

The second manuscript, '**B**', is also a complete text of Part One, but is much fuller than A, and (with many changes and additions) advances far towards the final form. Here also the two meetings, as the text was first written, have no dates, and the numbers given to the meetings imply a much longer history of the Club than is suggested for it subsequently. For the elaborate title or prolegomenon to this version see pp. 148–9.

The third manuscript, '**C**', is written in a fine script, but is not quite complete: it extends to Ramer's words 'So there does appear to be at least one other star with attendant planets' (p. 207), and it is clear that no more was written of this text (which, incidentally, it would have taken days to write).

A typescript '**D**', made by my father, is the final form of Part One. In one section of the text, however, D seems to have preceded C, since it has some B readings which were then changed to those of C; but the final form of the text is scarcely ever in doubt, and even where it is the differences are entirely trivial. Where C ends, the typescript follows B, the place of transition being marked on the B manuscript. (A second typescript – not, I think, made by my father – was begun, but abandoned after only a few pages; this has no independent value.)

Part Two, 'The Strange Case of Arundel Lowdham', records a number of further meetings of the Notion Club, continuous with those of Part One. This second Part is largely devoted to the intrusion of the Matter of Númenor into the discussions of the Notion Club, but of this there are only two texts, a manuscript ('**E**') and a typescript ('**F**').

Both end at the same point, with the next meeting of the Club arranged and dated, but never written.

The typescript F is a complex document, in that my father rejected a substantial section of it ('F 1') as soon as he had typed it, replaced it ('F 2'), and then continued on to the end, the structure of the text being thus F 1, F 1 > F 2, F 2 (see p. 237 and note 37).

For both Parts, but especially for Part Two, there is a quantity of rough, discontinuous drafting, often scarcely legible.

While Part Two was being further developed (that is, after the completion of the manuscript E so far as it went) the Adunaic* language emerged (as it appears), with an abandoned but elaborate account of the phonology, and *pari passu* with *The Notion Club Papers* my father not only wrote a first draft of an entirely new version of the story of Númenor but developed it through further texts: this is *The Drowning of Anadûnê*, in which all the names are in Adunaic.

How is all this to be equated with his statement in the letter to Stanley Unwin in July 1946 that 'three parts' of the work were written in a fortnight at the end of 1945? Obviously it cannot be, not even on the supposition that when he said 'a fortnight' he greatly underestimated the time. Though not demonstrable, an extremely probable explanation, as it seems to me, is that at the end of that fortnight he stopped work in the middle of writing the manuscript E, at the point where *The Notion Club Papers* end, and at which time Adunaic had not yet arisen. Very probably Part One was at the stage of the manuscript B.[4] On this view, the further development of what had then been achieved of Part One, and more especially of Part Two (closely associated with that of the Adunaic language and the writing of *The Drowning of Anadûnê*), belongs to the following year, the earlier part of 1946. Against this, of course, is the fact that the letter to Stanley Unwin in which my father referred to the *Papers* was written in July 1946, but that letter gives no impression of further work after 'my health gave way after Christmas'. But it is to be remembered that *The Lord of the Rings* had been at a halt for more than a year and a half, and it may well be that he was deeply torn between the burgeoning of Adunaic and Anadûnê and the oppression of the abandoned *Lord of the Rings*. He did not need to spell out to Stanley Unwin what he had in fact been doing! But he said that he was 'putting *The Lord of the Rings* before all else', which no doubt meant 'I am *now going to put it* before all else', and that included Adunaic. To the interrupted *Notion Club Papers* he never returned.

The diverse and shifting elements in all this work, not least the complex but essential linguistic material, have made the construction

---

*Adunaic is always so spelt at this time (not *Adûnaic*), and I write it so throughout.

of a readily comprehensible edition extremely difficult, requiring much experimentation among possible forms of presentation. Since *The Notion Club Papers* are now published for the first time, the final typescripts D of Part One and F of Part Two must obviously be the text printed, and this makes for difficulties of presentation (it is of course very much easier to begin with an original draft and to relate it by consecutive steps to a final form that is already known). The two Parts are separated, with notes following each Part. Following the text of the *Papers* I give important sections that were rejected from or significantly changed in the final text, earlier forms of the 'Númenórean' fragments that 'came through' to Arundel Lowdham and of the Old English text written by his father, and reproductions of the 'facsimiles' of that text with analysis of the *tengwar*.

Although the final text of Part Two of the *Papers* and *The Drowning of Anadûnê* were intimately connected,[5] especially in respect of Adunaic, any attempt to combine them in a single presentation makes for inextricable confusion; the latter is therefore treated entirely separately in the third part of this book, and in my commentary on Part Two of the *Papers* I have not thought it useful to make continual reference forward to *The Drowning of Anadûnê*: the interrelations between the two works emerge more clearly when the latter is reached.

There are some aspects of the framework of the *Papers*, provided by the Foreword of the Editor, Mr. Howard Green, and the list of members of the Notion Club, which are better discussed here than in the commentary.

The Foreword

The original manuscript A of Part One, as already noticed, has no title or introductory statement of any kind, but begins with the words 'When Ramer had finished reading his latest story . . .' The first page of B begins thus:

Beyond Lewis
or
Out of the Talkative Planet

Being a fragment of an apocryphal Inklings' Saga, made by some imitator at some time in the 1980s.

Preface to the Inklings

While listening to this fantasia (if you do), I beg of the present company not to look for their own faces in this mirror. For the mirror is cracked, and at the best you will only see your countenances distorted, and adorned maybe with noses (and other features) that are not your

own, but belong to other members of the company –
if to anybody.

Night 251

When Michael Ramer had finished reading his latest story . . .

This was heavily emended and then struck through, and was replaced
by a new, separate title-page (made when B had been completed):

Beyond Probability[6]
or
Out of the Talkative Planet

———

The Ramblings of Ramer
being Nights 251 and 252 of *The Notion Club Papers*

[Little is known about this rare book, except that
it appears to have been written after 1989, as an
apocryphal imitation of the *Inklings' Saga Book*. The
author identifies himself with the character called in the
narrative Nicholas Guildford; but Titmouse has shown
that this is a pseudonym, and is taken from a mediaeval
dialogue, at one time read in the Schools of Oxford. His
real identity remains unknown.]

An aside to the audience. While listening to this hotch-
potch (if you do), I beg of the present company not to
look for their own faces in my mirror. For the mirror is
cracked . . .

This is followed by a list of the persons who appear (see p. 151). It
seems clear that at the stage when the text B was written my father's
idea was far less elaborate than it became; intending perhaps, so far
as the form was concerned, no more than a *jeu d'esprit* for the
entertainment of the Inklings – while the titles seem to emphasise that
it was to be, in part, the vehicle of criticism and discussion of aspects
of Lewis's 'planetary' novels. Perhaps he called to mind the witty and
ingenious method that Lewis had devised for his criticism of *The Lay
of Leithian* in 1930 (see *The Lays of Beleriand*, p. 151). – So far as I
can see, there is no indication that at this stage he envisaged the form
that Part Two of the *Papers* would take, and definite evidence to the
contrary (see pp. 281–2).

There are several drafts for a more circumstantial account of the
Papers and of how they came to light, preceding the elaborate form in
the final text that follows. They were found at the University Press
waiting to be pulped, but no one knew how they had got there; or they
were found 'at Messrs. Whitburn and Thoms' publishing house'.[7]

The mediaeval dialogue from which the name Nicholas Guildford is derived is *The Owl and the Nightingale*, a debate in verse written between 1189 and 1216. To the Owl's question, who shall decide between them, the Nightingale replies that *Maister Nichole of Guldeforde* is the obvious choice, since he is prudent, virtuous, and wise, and an excellent judge of song.

The List of Members

At the top of a page that preceded the manuscript A and is almost certainly the first setting down of the opening passage of Night 60 of the *Papers* (see p. 211, note 7) my father wrote these names:

> *Ramer   Latimer   Franks   Loudham   Dolbear*

Beneath *Ramer* he wrote 'Self', but struck it out, then 'CSL' and 'To', these also being struck out. Beneath *Latimer* he wrote 'T', beneath *Franks* 'CSL', beneath *Loudham* 'HVD' (Hugo Dyson), and beneath *Dolbear* 'Havard'.

This is the only actual identification of members of the Notion Club with members of the Inklings that is found. The name *Latimer* (for *Guildford*) remained that of the Club's 'reporter' in manuscript A; it is derived from Old French *latinier* ('Latiner', speaker of Latin), meaning an interpreter. *Loudham* (so spelt in A and B, and initially in the manuscript E of Part Two) would obviously be Dyson even without 'HVD' written beneath (see Humphrey Carpenter, *The Inklings*, pp. 212–13); and since *Franks* (only becoming *Frankley* in the third text C) is here Lewis, I suppose that my father felt that the name was appropriate to his character. The other two names were presumably 'significant', but I do not know what the significance was. *Dolbear* is an uncommon surname, but there was a chemist's shop in Oxford called Dolbear & Goodall, and I recollect that my father found this particularly engaging; it may be that he simply found in Dolbear the chemist a comic appropriateness to Havard, or to Havard as he was going to present him. *Ramer* is very puzzling; and here there is no certain identification with one of the Inklings in the list. The various dictionaries of English surnames that I have consulted do not give the name. The only suggestion that I can make is that my father derived it from the dialectal verb *rame*, with these meanings given in the *Oxford English Dictionary*: 'to shout, cry aloud, scream; keep up the same cry, continue repeating the same thing; obtain by persistent asking; repeat, run over'; cf. also the *English Dialect Dictionary*, ed. Joseph Wright (with which he was very familiar: he called it 'indispensable', *Letters* no. 6), *ream* verb 3, also *raim*, *rame*, etc., which gives similar meanings, and also 'to talk nonsense, rave'. But this seems far-fetched.

At any rate, this list is interesting as suggesting that my father started out with the idea of a series of definite 'equivalences', distorted no doubt but recognisable. But I think that this plan very quickly dissolved, because he found that it would not suit his purpose; and not even in the earliest text does there seem to be any clearer association with individual Inklings than there is in the final form of the *Papers*, with the possible exception of Lowdham. In A his interventions are limited to jocular facetiousness, and the interest that in the later form of Part One (pp. 199–201) he shows in 'Old Solar' and in Ramer's names of other worlds is in A given to Dolbear (and then in B to Guildford).

It would not suit my father's purpose, because in 'The Ramblings of Ramer' he wished to allow his own ideas the scope, in the form of a discussion and argument, that they would never have had in fact, in an actual meeting of the Inklings. The professional knowledge and intellectual interests of the members of the Notion Club are such as to make this symposium possible. On p. 149 I have given the second version of a title-page, in which after the author's 'aside to the audience', warning them 'not to look for their own faces in my mirror', there follows a list of the members of the Club. At this stage only six members were listed (plus Cameron); and of these six, Ramer is Professor of Finno-Ugric, Guildford is a Comparative Philologist, and Loudham has 'special interests in Icelandic and Anglo-Saxon', while the chemist Dolbear 'concerns himself with psychoanalysis and related aspects of language'. At this stage Frankley is a lecturer in French, changed to the Clarendon Reader in English Literature, 'with a taste for the Romance literatures and a distaste for things Germanic', while the statement of Jeremy's position and interests is much as in the final list. Ramer, Jeremy, Guildford and Frankley all have 'a taste for romances of travel in Space and Time.'

The enlarged list of members in the final form (pp. 159–60), most of whom do not have even walk-on parts, served the purpose, I suppose, of creating an impression of a more amorphous group surrounding the principals. The polymathy of the monk Dom Jonathan Markison extends to some very recondite knowledge of Germanic origins, while Ranulph Stainer appears in Part Two as a sceptical and rather superior onlooker at the strange proceedings. The surname of the apparently speechless undergraduate John Jethro Rashbold is a translation of *Tolkien* (*Toll-kühn*: see *Letters* no. 165 and note 1). In Part Two appears 'old Professor Rashbold at Pembroke', the Anglo-Saxon scholar described by Lowdham as 'a grumpy old bear' (p. 256 and note 72). There are no doubt other hidden puns and jokes in the list of members.

In my view it would be useless to seek even any 'intellectual equivalence' with historical persons, let alone portraiture (for a list of those who came often – but not all at the same period – to the Inklings, with brief biographies, see Humphrey Carpenter, *The Inklings*, Appendix A). The fact that Lowdham is 'loud' and makes jokes often at inappropriate moments derives from Dyson (but he was wittier than Lowdham), yet Lowdham is the very antithesis of Dyson in his learning and interests; no doubt Frankley's *horror borealis* is a reminiscence of

Dyson also, though it is profoundly un-Dysonian to have read mediaeval works on Saint Brendan (p. 265). In earlier drafts of the list of members Dolbear has no position in the University, and with his red hair and beard and his nickname in the Club (see *Letters* no. 56) he can be seen as a sort of parody of Havard. But these things are marginal to the ideas expounded and debated in the *Papers*; essentially, the members of the Notion Club are fictions, and become more obviously so in Part Two.

Scarcely a sentence remained entirely unchanged between text A and text D of Part One, but in my notes all this development is largely ignored when (as for the most part it is) it is a matter of improvement in the expression or of amplification of the argument. Similarly, the ascription of speeches to speakers underwent many changes in the earlier texts, but in general I do not record them.

I do not enter in this book into any critical discussion of the topics and issues raised in 'The Ramblings of Michael Ramer'. This is partly because I am not well qualified to discuss them, but also because they fall somewhat outside the scope and aim of *The History of Middle-earth*, which is above all to present accurate texts accurately ordered (so far as I am able) and to elucidate them comparatively, within the context of 'Middle-earth' and the lands of the West. With very limited time at my disposal for this book I have thought that I could better devote it in any case to clarification of the complexities of the 'Númenórean' material. The notes are therefore very restricted in scope and are often trivial in relation to the content of the discussion, being mostly concerned with the elucidation of references that may be obscure and not easily tracked down, with comparison of earlier forms of certain passages, and with citation of other writings of my father's. I do not suppose that many readers of this book will be unacquainted with the novels of C. S. Lewis, *Out of the Silent Planet* (1938), *Perelandra* (1943), and *That Hideous Strength* (1945), but I have provided a few explanations and references.

Why my father abandoned *The Notion Club Papers* I do not know. It may be that he felt that the work had lost all unity, that 'Atlantis' had broken apart the frame in which it had been set (see pp. 281–2). But I think also that having forced himself to return to *The Lord of the Rings*, and having brought it to its end, he was then deflected into the very elaborate further work on the legends of the Elder Days that preceded the actual publication of *The Lord of the Rings*. However it was, the Notion Club was abandoned, and with it his final attempt to embody the riddle of Ælfwine and Eadwine in a 'tale of time'. But from its forgotten *Papers* and the strange figure of Arundel Lowdham there emerged a new conception of the Downfall of Númenor, embodied in a different tradition, which would come to constitute a major element in the *Akallabêth* many years later.

NOTES

1   In a note to this passage in my father's letter Humphrey Carpenter remarks: 'Lewis's next published novel after *That Hideous Strength* and *The Great Divorce* was *The Lion, the Witch and the Wardrobe.* Tolkien is, however, almost certainly referring to some other book of Lewis's that was never completed.' *The Great Divorce* was published in 1946; Lewis was reading it aloud in April and May 1944 (*Letters* no. 60, 69, 72).

    It may be mentioned here that my father had evidently discussed with Lewis the matter of 'true dreams': an important element in the plot of *That Hideous Strength* is Jane Studdock's 'tendency to dream real things', in the words of Miss Ironwood (Chapter 3, §iii), and this can hardly be a mere coincidence. It is presumably not coincidental either that there should be so many references to 'Numinor' in *That Hideous Strength* (published in 1945); see p. 303 and note 15.

2   On the final text D of Part One the heading of the first page (after 'Leaves from the Notion Club Papers'):'Part I / The Ramblings of Michael Ramer / *Out of the Talkative Planet*' was struck out. The final text F of Part Two has no heading at the beginning. A pencilled title page apparently accompanying the manuscript E has 'Leaves from the Notion Club Papers / II / The Strange Case of Arundel Lowdham'.

3   A very brief report of an earlier meeting was added at the beginning of the text in the course of the development of Part One.

4   A pointer to this is the fact that in B the name is spelt *Loudham* throughout; in E it begins as *Loudham* but becomes *Lowdham* in the course of the writing of the manuscript; in C it is *Lowdham* from the first. See further p. 282.

5   Cf. the close relation of the manuscript of *The Lost Road* and the original text of *The Fall of Númenor*, V.9.

6   *Beyond Probability* is a pun on the title of Lewis's book *Beyond Personality*, which had been published in 1944.

7   That *Whitburn* (*and Thoms*) is a play on the name *Blackwell*, the Oxford bookseller and publisher, is seen from the fact that the firm was originally *Basil Blackwell and Mott*.

Leaves

from   the

ᕬOᏟIOᕬ
ᏟᏞᏌᏴ
ᑭᎪᏢᎬᏒᏚ

edited by
Howard Green

Second edition

MMXIV

Leaves from

THE NOTION CLUB PAPERS

FOREWORD

These Papers have a rather puzzling history. They were found
after the Summer Examinations of 2012 on the top of one of
a number of sacks of waste paper in the basement of the
Examination Schools at Oxford by the present editor, Mr.
Howard Green, the Clerk of the Schools. They were in a
disordered bundle, loosely tied with red string. The outer sheet,
inscribed in large Lombardic capitals:

ꝶOᴄIOꝶ   CLᴜꝶ   ꝮAꝮEꝰꙅ,

attracted the notice of Mr. Green, who removed them and
scrutinized them. Discovering them to contain much that was to
him curious and interesting, he made all possible enquiries,
without result.

The Papers, from internal evidence, clearly had no connexion
with any examinations held or lectures given in the Schools
during Mr. Green's many years of office. Neither did they
belong to any of the libraries housed in the building. Advertise-
ment has failed to find any claimant to ownership. It remains
unknown how the Papers reached the waste-paper sack. It
seems probable that they had at some time been prepared for
publication, since they are in many places provided with notes;
yet in form they are nothing more than an elaborate minute-
book of a club, devoted to conversation, debate, and the
discussion of 'papers', in verse or prose, written and read by its
members, and many of the entries have no particular interest for
non-members.

The minutes, or reports, covered probably about 100 meetings or 'nights' during the years of last century, approximately
1980 to 1990. It is, however, not the least curious fact about
these Papers that no such club appears ever to have existed.
Though certain resemblances are inevitable between a group of
imaginary academic persons and their real contemporaries, no
such persons as those here depicted, either with such names, or

such offices, or such tastes and habits, can be traced in the Oxford of the last generation, or of the present time.

The author appears in one or two passages, and in the occasional notes, to identify himself with the character called in the dialogues Nicholas Guildford. But Mr. J. R. Titmass, the well-known historian of twentieth-century Oxford, who has given all possible assistance to the present editor, has shown that this is certainly a fictitious name and derived from a mediaeval dialogue at one time read in the Schools of Oxford.

On examination the bundle was found to contain 205 foolscap pages, all written by one hand, in a careful and usually legible script. The leaves were disarranged but mostly numbered. The bundle contains the entries for Nights 51 to 75, but they are defective and several leaves appear to have been lost; some of the longer entries are incomplete. It is probable that three other bundles, containing Nights 1–25, 26–50, 76–100, once existed. Of the missing sections, however, only a few scattered sheets were found in the sack, and these, so far as can be discerned, belonged originally to the entries 1–25. Among them was a crumpled and much corrected sheet, of a different paper, containing a list of members.

The total on this scale would have made a volume of considerable bulk, but its size will be overestimated, if calculation is based on the length of the extracts here printed. Many Nights are represented only by a few lines, or by short entries, of which Nights 54 and 64 have been included as specimens. As a rule these short items have been omitted, unless they bear closely on the longer reports here selected and presented to those interested in literary curiosities.

Note to the Second Edition

Mr. W. W. Wormald of the School of Bibliopoly, and Mr. D. N. Borrow of the Institute of Occidental Languages, found their curiosity aroused by the published extracts, and asked Mr. Green for permission to examine the manuscript of the Papers. They have now sent in a joint report, which raises some interesting points.

'Paper of this kind,' they write, 'is, of course, very difficult to trace or to date. The sheets submitted to us are of a poor quality much inferior to the paper now in general use for such purposes. Without venturing on a definite opinion, we record our suspicion that these sheets are much older than the dates of the supposed meetings of the Club, perhaps 40 to 50 years older, belonging, that is, to the period during or just after the Six Years' War. This suspicion is supported by various items of internal evidence, notably the idiom of the dialogues, which is old-fashioned and does not represent with any fidelity the colloquial language either of the nineteen-eighties or of the present time. We conclude, then, that *The Notion Club Papers* were written sixty years ago, or more.

'It remains, nonetheless, on this hypothesis a puzzling fact that the Great Explosion of 1975 is referred to, and even more precisely, the Great Storm, which actually occurred on the night of Thursday, June 12th, 1987;[1] though certain inaccuracies appear in the account given of the progress and effects of the latter event. Mr. Green has proposed to us a curious explanation of this difficulty, evidently suggested to him by the contents of the Papers: the future events were, he thinks, "foreseen". In our opinion a less romantic but more probable solution is this: the paper is part of a stock purchased by a man resident in Oxford about 1940. He used the paper for his minutes (whether fictitious or founded on fact), but he did not use all his stock. Much later (after 1987) he copied out his matter again, using up the old paper; and though he did not make any general revision, he moved the dates forward and inserted the genuine references to the Explosion and the Storm.'

Mr. Green rejoins: 'This is one of the most fantastic "probable solutions" I have yet met, quite apart from the unlikelihood of an inferior paper being stored for about fifty years and then used for the same purpose again. The writer was not, I think, a very young man; but the handwriting is certainly not that of an old man. Yet if the writer was not young in 1940, he must have been old, very old, in 2000. For it is to that date, not to 1987, that we must look. There is a point that has escaped the notice of Messrs. Wormald and Borrow: the old house, no. 100 Banbury Road, the last private dwelling house in that block, was in fact the scene of "hauntings",* a remarkable display of poltergeist activity, between the years 2000 and 2003, which only ended when the house was demolished and a new building, attached to the Institute of National Nutrition, erected on the site. In the year 2003 a person possessed of the paper, the

* See Night 61, p. 179.

pen-habits,* and the idiom of the period of the Six Years' War would have been an oddity that no pseudonym could conceal from us.

'In any case, the Storm is integral to all the entries from Night 63 to Night , [sic] and is not just "inserted". Messrs. Wormald and Borrow must either neglect their own evidence and place the whole composition after 1987, or else stick to their own well-founded suspicions of the paper, the hand,* and the idiom, and admit that some person or persons in the nineteen-forties possessed a power of "prevision".

'Mr. Titmass informs me that he cannot find any record in the nineteen-forties of the names given in the list. If therefore, any such club existed at that earlier period, the names remain pseudonyms. The forward dating might have been adopted as an additional screen. But I am now convinced that the Papers are a work of fiction; and it may well be that the predictions (notably of the Storm), though genuine and not coincidences, were unconscious: giving one more glimpse of the strange processes of so-called literary "invention", with which the Papers are largely concerned.'

MEMBERS OF THE NOTION CLUB

The Notion Club, as depicted, was informal and vague in outline. A number of characters appear in the dialogues, some rarely or fitfully. For the convenience of readers the List of Members found among the Papers is here printed, though several of the persons named do not appear in this selection. The order is not alphabetical and seems intended to represent some kind of seniority: the first six names were written earlier and larger; the rest were added at various times and in different inks, but in the same hand. There are also later entries inserted after some of the names, recording details of their tastes or history. A few further details, gleaned from the Papers themselves, have been added in brackets.

---

*Mr. Wormald himself, something of an expert in such matters, before he proposed his 'probable solution', ventured the opinion that the handwriting of the Papers in general character went with the old-fashioned idiom and belonged to the same period. The use of a pen rather than a typewriter would indeed, in itself, already have been most unusual for a man of 1990, whatever his age.

MICHAEL GEORGE RAMER. Jesus College. Born 1929 (in Hungary). Professor of Finno-Ugric Philology; but better known as a writer of romances. His parents returned to England when he was four; but he spent a good deal of time in Finland and Hungary between 1956 and 68. [Among his interests are Celtic languages and antiquities.]

RUPERT DOLBEAR. Wadham. Born 1929. Research Chemist. Has many other interests, notably philosophy, psychoanalysis, and gardening. [A close friend of Ramer. He is redhaired and redbearded, and known to the Club as Ruthless Rufus.]

NICHOLAS GUILDFORD. Lincoln. Born 1937. Archaeologist. The Club reporter; because he likes it and knows shorthand. [He is seldom recorded as reading anything to the Club, and it is then not reported; but he appears to have written several novels.]

ALWIN ARUNDEL LOWDHAM. B.N.C. Born 1938. Lecturer in English Language. Chiefly interested in Anglo-Saxon, Icelandic, and Comparative Philology. Occasionally writes comic or satirical verse. [Known as Arry.]

PHILIP FRANKLEY. Queen's. Born 1932. A poet, once well-known as a leader of the Queer Metre movement; but now just a poet, still publishing volumes of collected verse; suffers from *horror borealis* (as he calls it) and is intolerant of all things Northern or Germanic. [He is, all the same, a close friend of Lowdham.]

WILFRID TREWIN JEREMY. Corpus Christi. Born 1942. University Lecturer in English Literature. He specializes in Escapism, and has written books on the history and criticism of *Ghost-stories*, *Time-travel*, and *Imaginary Lands*.

James Jones. Born 1927. Has been a schoolmaster, journalist, and playwright. Is now retired, living in Oxford, and divides his time between producing plays and his hobby of private printing. A very silent man, but assists the Reporter with his retentive memory.

Dr. Abel Pitt. Trinity. Born 1928. Formerly Chaplain of Trinity College; now Bishop of Buckingham. Scholar, occasional poet.

Colombo Arditi. St. John's. Born 1940. Tempestosa Professor of Italian. Is fond of (and not unskilled in) singing (basso), swimming, and the game of bowls. Collects books and cats.

Dom Jonathan Markison, O.S.B.[2] New College, Master of St. Cuthbert's Hall. [Polymath.]

Sir Gerard Manface. All Souls. Lawyer. Mountaineer; much travelled. Has many children, for whom he wrote many (unpublished) books and tales. [Seldom appears. A special friend of Frankley, but not resident in Oxford.]

Ranulph Stainer. University College. Born 1936. Professionally an expert in banking and economics; privately devoted to the history and practice of music, and has composed several works, major and minor, including one (moderately successful) opera: *Midas*.

Alexander Cameron. Exeter. Born 1935. Modern historian, specially interested in Spanish and South American history. Collects coins and stamps. Plays a pianola. [No one remembers his being invited to join the Club, or knows why he comes; but he appears from time to time.]

John Jethro Rashbold. Magdalen. Born 1965. Undergraduate. Classical scholar; apprentice poet. [Introduced by Frankley, to whom he is much attached.]

Note. It is represented as the habit of the Club for all members to initial the record of any meeting at which they were present, whether they are reported as speaking or not. Presumably the initialling, which in the extant Papers is in the same hand as the text, took place after N.G.'s report has been seen and passed, and before the fair copy was made. Mr. Cameron's initials never appear.

Leaves from
The
NOTION CLUB PAPERS

[PART ONE]³

Night 54.   Thursday, November 16th, 1986.⁴

A wet night. Only Frankley and Dolbear arrived (Dolbear's
house). Dolbear reports that Philip never said a word worth
recording, but read him an unintelligible poem about a Mechanical Nightingale (or he thought that was the subject). Frankley
reports that Rufus was drowsy and kept on chuckling to
himself. The only clearly audible remark that he made was
going off the deep end, I think. This was in reply to an enquiry
about Michael Ramer, and whether D. had seen him lately.
After F. had read a poem (later read again) called *The Canticle
of Artegall* they parted. R.D. P.F.⁵

[One or two minor entries, defectively preserved, are here
omitted.]

Night 60.   Thursday, February 20th, 1987.⁶ [Defective at the
beginning. Ramer's story is lost.]

[When Michael Ramer had finished] reading his story, we sat
in silence for a while. He had not read us anything for a long
time; in fact he had seldom appeared at meetings for a year or
more. His excuses for absence, when he gave any, had been
vague and evasive. On this occasion the Club was better
attended than usual, and no more easy to please. That hardly
accounted for Ramer's nervousness. He is one of our oldest
members, and was at one time one of our most frequent
performers; but to-night he read hastily, boggling and stumbling. So much so that Frankley made him read several sentences
over again, though these interruptions, which only made matters worse, are omitted above. Now he was fidgetting.

'Well?' he said at last. 'What do you think of it? Will it do?'

A few of us stirred, but nobody spoke.

'Oh, come on! I may as well get the worst over first. What
have *you* got to say?' he urged, turning to Guildford in the next
chair.

'I don't know,' Guildford answered reluctantly. 'You know
how I dislike criticizing ...'

'I've never noticed it before,' said Frankley.

'Go on, Nicholas!' laughed Lowdham. 'You dislike it about as much as Philip dislikes interrupting.'

'At any rate I don't criticize unfinished sentences,' said Guildford. 'If I'd not been interrupted, I was going to say *I dislike criticizing off-hand, and still in the heat of listening.*'

'In the chill's your more usual temperature,' said Lowdham.[7]

'Most unfair! I'm a voracious reader, and I like stories.'

A chorus of incredulous shouts followed, but Guildford could just be heard amending his words, first to *I read a good many tales and like most of them*, and finally to *I do like some stories, including one or two of Ramer's.* 'But it's much more difficult,' he went on at last, 'to say anything about the *liking*, especially so soon. Liking is often much more complex than dislike. And it's less necessary to say anything about it in a hurry. The feeling of liking has a very lasting flavour; it can wait, it's often better for being stored for a bit. But defects stick out all hard and painful, while one's still close at hand.'

'For those who have the knack of seeing them in *every* literary landscape,' Ramer interposed.

'There are minor ones,' Guildford went on unperturbed, 'that may, of course, get forgotten, or be overlooked by familiarity; but they are better removed while fresh.'

'The sort that Philip corrects at once while you are reading?' said Ramer.

'Yes,' said Guildford. 'But there are more serious faults than his anacolutha and split infinitives that may also get passed, if the thing's allowed to harden. It may be painful for the author to have the blindness of paternal love removed, but it seems the most useful thing to do on the spot. What's the good of sitting here, hearing things before they're in print, if all we're to do is to pat the father's back and murmur: *Any child of yours is welcome, Mr. Ramer. Your fiftieth, is it? Well, well! How they do all take after their dear father, don't they?*'

Lowdham laughed. 'And what you're longing to say, I suppose, is: *Why don't you wipe the brat's nose, and get its hair cut?*'

'*Or strangle it!*' said Ramer impatiently.

'No, seriously,' Guildford protested, 'I only objected to parts, not to the whole of your latest infant, Michael. Only to the first chapter and the end of the last one, really. But there! I suppose no one has ever solved the difficulty of arriving, of getting to another planet, no more in literature than in life. Because the difficulty is in fact insoluble, I think. The barrier cannot and will not ever be passed in mortal flesh. Anyway, the opening chapters, the journey, of space-travel tales seem to me always the weakest. Scientifiction, as a rule: and that is a base alloy. Yes it is, Master Frankley, so don't interrupt! Just as much as the word is an ill-made portmanteau: rotten for travelling with. And that goes for your machine, too, Ramer. Though it's one of the better failures, perhaps.'

'Thankyou for that!' Ramer growled. 'But it's just like you, Nicholas, to pick on the frame, which is an awkward necessity of pictures, and easy to change anyway, and say nothing about what's inside it. I suppose you must have seen something to praise inside: we know how painful you find praising anything. Isn't that the real reason why you postpone it?'

'Nonsense!' said Guildford. 'I thought what was inside was very good, if you must have it. Though I felt there was something very odd about it.'

'I'm sure you did!'

'I mean *odd* coming from you. And in its setting. For you won't get away with that framed excuse. A picture-frame is not a parallel. An author's way of getting to Mars (say) is part of *his* story of *his* Mars; and of *his* universe, as far as that particular tale goes. It's part of the picture, even if it's only in a marginal position; and it may seriously affect all that's inside.'

'Why should it?' said Frankley.

'Well, if there are space-ships at all in your imagined universe, you'll fail to sell it to me, for one thing,' said Guildford.

'That's carrying your anti-machine mania too far,' said Lowdham. 'Surely poor writers can include things *you* don't like in their stories?'

'I'm not talking about dislike at the moment,' Guildford returned. 'I'm talking about *credibility*. I don't like heroic warriors, but I can bear stories about them. I believe they exist, or could. I don't think space-ships do, or could. And anyway, if you pretend that they do, and use them for space-journeys in the flesh, they'll land you in space-ship sort of adventures. If you're spaceship-minded and scientifictitious, or even if you let your characters be so, it's likely enough that you'll find things of that order in your new world, or only see sights that interest such folk.'

'But that isn't true,' Frankley objected. 'It's not true of this story of Ramer's.'

'It's generally true, all too ghastly true,' said Guildford. 'But of course there is a way of escape: into inconsistency, discord. Ramer takes that way, like Lindsay,[8] or Lewis, and the better post-Lewis writers of this sort of thing. You *can* land on another world in a space-ship and then drop that nonsense, if you've got something better to do there than most of the earlier writers had. But personally I dislike that acutely. It makes the scientifictitious bunkum all the worse by contrast. Crystal torpedoes, and "back-rays", and levers for full speed-ahead (faster than light, mark you), are bad enough inside one of those hideous magazines – Dead Sea fruit with gaudy rinds; but in, say, *A Voyage to Arcturus** they are simply shocking. All the more so for being unnecessary. David Lindsay had at least two other better methods up his sleeve: the séance connexion; or the suggestion of the dark tower at the end. Thank goodness, there was at any rate no return by crystal torpedo in that tale!'[9]

'But the trick in *Out of the Silent Planet*, getting the hero kidnapped by space-ship villains, so as to explain how an interesting man ever got inside one, was not bad,' said Frankley. 'And the stupid villainy of the space-ship folk was essential. They behaved as such people would, and the plot depends on that.'

'Not bad, I agree,' said Guildford. 'Still it was, as you say, a trick. And not first rate, not if you want sheer literary credibility, the pure thing, rather than an alloy with allegory and satire. Ramer is not after any such Lewisite alloy; and I think his device of letting an intelligent artist get into a contraption by accident, not knowing what it is, is a mere trick. But what I really object to, in any such tale, however tinged, is the pretence that these contraptions could exist or function at all. They're indefinitely less probable – as the carriers of living, undamaged, human bodies and minds – than the wilder things in fairy-stories; but they pretend to be probable on a more material mechanical level. It's like having to take Heath-Robinsons seriously.'

'But you've got to have some kind of removal van,' said Frankley, 'or else do without this kind of story. They may not be

---

* This book had recently been rescued from oblivion by Jeremy's book on *Imaginary Lands*. See the account of his reading parts of this to the Club, above, Nights 30, 33, 40 [not preserved]. Most of the members are fairly well-read in twentieth-century books of travel in Space and Time. N.G.

your sweetmeat, Nicholas, but I've got a tooth for them; and I'm not going to be done out of them by you.'

'You can wallow in Scientifiction mags, for all I care,' said Guildford; 'but I've got to have literary belief in my removal van, or I won't put my furniture into it. I have never met one of these vehicles yet that suspended my disbelief an inch off the floor.'

'Well, your disbelief evidently needs a power-crane,' said Frankley. 'You should look at some of the forgotten Old Masters, like Wells, if you've ever heard of him. I admit that what his first men found in the Moon was a bathos after the journey. But the machine and the journey were splendid. I don't of course, believe in a gravitation-insulator outside the story, but inside the story it worked, and Wells made damned good use of it. And voyages can end in grubby, vulgar, little harbours and yet be very much worth while.'

'It wouldn't be easy to miss the name of Wells with Jeremy always about,' said Guildford. 'And I *have* read *The First Men in the Moon*, and *The Time Machine*. I confess that in *The Time Machine* the landfall was so marvellous that I could have forgiven an even more ridiculous transport – though it would be difficult to think of one! All the same, the machine was a blemish; and I'm quite unconvinced that it was a necessary one. And if it had been removed – the effect on the whole thing! Enormous enhancement even of that remarkable tale.

'No doubt authors are in as great a hurry to get there as we are; but eagerness doesn't excuse carelessness. And anyway, we're older. We may allow the primitives their ingenuousness: we can't imitate it. Isn't it always so? What might do once won't do any longer. I used to read with gusto romances in which the hero just pushed off into the Blue, over mountains and deserts, without water supplies. But now I feel that procedure is slipshoddy.'

'There's no such word,' said Frankley.

'Shut up!' said Lowdham.

'I want my man to have his adventures in the Blue, as much as ever, but I want to be made to feel that the author has faced the difficulties and not ignored them, or fudged them. It's usually all the better for the tale in the long run.

'Certainly I'll admit that if I allow Wells his "cavorite",[10] then he makes good use of it. If I'd been a boy when the tale was new, I should have allowed it and enjoyed it. But I can't allow it now. I'm post-Wells. And we're not criticizing him but Ramer, for using at this much later date a rather similar device. Any one who touches space-travel now has got to be much more convincing: if indeed a convincing machine is at present possible. Command of power has prodigiously increased, but the problems have become more complex, and not simpler. Scientists can't destroy simple faith and hope still to keep it for themselves. A gravitation-insulator won't do. Gravity can't be treated like that. It's fundamental. It's a statement by the Universe of where you are in the Universe, and the Universe can't be tricked by a surname with *ite* stuck on the end, nor by any such abracadabra.

'And what of the effect on a man of being hurled out of one gravitational field through zero into another? Even on so elementary a journey as one to the Moon?'

'Oh! difficulties of that sort will be got over all right,' said Frankley. 'At least that is what most of the scientists say who are concerned with space-projects.'

'Scientists are as prone to wishful thinking (and talking) as other men, especially when they are thinking about their own romantic hopes and not yours,' said Guildford. 'And they like opening vague, vast, vistas before gapers, when they are performing as public soothsayers.'

'I'm not talking about that kind,' said Frankley. 'There are quiet unpublicized people, quite scientific medicos, for instance, who'll tell you that your heart and digestive arrangements, and all that, would function all right, even at, say, zero gravity.'

'I dare say they will,' said Guildford. 'Though I still find it difficult to believe that a machine like our body, made to function under definite earth-conditions, would in fact run on merrily when those were greatly changed – and for a long time, or permanently. Look how quickly we wilt, even on this globe, if we're transferred to unusual heights or temperatures. And the effect on you of greatly *increased* gravity is rather hushed up, isn't it?* Yet after all that is what you'd be most likely to get at the other end of your journey.'

'That's so,' said Lowdham. 'But people of this blessed century think primarily of travelling and speed, not of destination, or

---

* Not, of course, in Scientifiction. There it is usually exorcized by mere abracadabra in bogus 'scientific' form.   N.G.

settling. It's better to travel "scientifically", in fact, than to get anywhere; or the vehicle justifies the journey.'

'Yes, and it is *speed* that really bothers me,' said Guildford, 'more than these other difficulties. I don't doubt the *possibility* of sending a rocket to the Moon. The preparations were knocked back by the Great Explosion,[11] but they say they're under way again. I'll even admit the eventual possibility of landing undamaged human goods on the lunar landscape – though what they'll do there is dubious. But the Moon is very parochial. Rockets are so slow. Can you hope to go as fast as light, anything like as fast?'

'I don't know,' said Frankley. 'It doesn't seem likely at present, but I don't think that all the scientists or mathematicians would answer that question with a definite *no*.'

'No, they're very romantic on this topic,' said Guildford. 'But even the speed of light will only be moderately useful. Unless you adopt a Shavian attitude and regard all these light-years and light-centuries as lies, the magnitude of which is inartistic. If not, you'll have to plan for a speed greater than light; much greater, if you're to have a practical range outside the Solar System. Otherwise you will have very few destinations. Who's going to book a passage for a distant place, if he's sure to die of old age on the way?'

'They still take tickets on the State Railways,' said Lowdham.

'But there's still at least a chance of arriving before death by coach or train,' said Guildford. 'I don't ask for any greater degree of probability from my author: just a possibility not wholly at variance with what we know.'

'Or think we know,' Frankley murmured.

'Quite so,' Guildford agreed. 'And the speed of light, or certainly anything exceeding it, is on that basis incredible: if you're going to be "scientific", or more properly speaking "mechanical". At any rate for anyone writing now. I admit the criteria of credibility may change; though as far as I can see, genuine Science, as distinct from mechanical romance, narrows the possibilities rather than expands them. But I still stick to my original point: the "machine" used sets the tone. I found space-ships sufficiently credible for a raw taste, until I grew up and wanted to find something more useful on Mars than ray-guns and faster vehicles. Space-ships will take you to that kind of country, no doubt. But I don't want to go there. There's no need now to travel to find it.'

'No, but there is an attraction in its being *far away*, even if it's nasty and stupid,' said Frankley. 'Even if it's the same! You could make a good story – inevitably satirical in effect, perhaps, but not really primarily so – out of a journey to find a replica of Earth and its denizens.'

'I daresay! But aren't we getting a bit mixed?' said Lowdham. 'Nick's real point, which he seems to have forgotten as well as the rest of us, was incoherence – discord. That was really quite distinct from his dislike, or his disbelief in mechanical vehicles; though actually he dislikes them, credible or not. But then he began confusing *scientific probability* with *literary credibility*.'

'No, I didn't and I don't,' said Guildford. 'Scientific probability *need* not be concerned at all. But it *has* to be, if you make your vehicle mechanical. You cannot make a piece of mechanism even sufficiently credible in a tale, if it seems outrageously incredible *as a machine* to your contemporaries – those whose critical faculties are not stunned by the mere mention of a machine.'

'All right, all right,' said Lowdham. 'But let's get back to the incoherence. It's the discord between the objects and the findings of the better tales and their machines that upsets you. And I think you have something there. Lewis, for instance, used a space-ship, but he kept it for his villains, and packed his hero the second time in a crystal coffin without machinery.'

'Half-hearted,' said Guildford. 'Personally, I found the compromise very unconvincing. It was wilfully inefficient, too: poor Ransom[12] got half toasted, for no sound reason that I could see. The power that could hurl the coffin to Venus could (one would have thought) have devised a material that let in light without excessive heat. I found the coffin much less credible than the Eldils,[13] and granted the Eldils, unnecessary. There was a page or two of smoke-screen about the outward journey to Perelandra, but it was not thick enough to hide the fact that this semi-transparent coffin was after all only a material packing-case, a special one-man space-ship of unknown motive power. It was necessary to the tale, of course, to have safe delivery of Ransom's living terrestrial body in Venus: but this impossible sort of parcel-post did not appeal to me as a solution of the problem. As I say, I doubt if there is a solution. But I should prefer an old-fashioned wave of a wizard's wand. Or a word of power in Old Solar[14] from an Eldil. Nothing less would suffice: a miracle.'

'Why have anything at all?' little Jeremy asked suddenly. So far he had sat curled up on the floor, as near to the fire as he could get, and he had said nothing, though his black birdlike eyes had hopped to and fro from speaker to speaker. 'The best stories I know about imaginary times and lands are just stories about them. Why a wizard? At least, why a wizard, outside the real story, just to waft you into it? Why not apply the *Once-upon-a-time* method to Space? Do you need more than author's magic? Even old Nick won't deny authors the power of seeing more than their eyes can. In his novels he lets himself look into other people's heads. Why not into distant parts of Space? It's what the author has really got to do, so why conceal it?'

'No, of course I don't deny authors their right of invention, *seeing*, if you like to call it that,' said Guildford.

At that point Dolbear stirred and seemed about to wake up; but he only settled more comfortably into his chair, and his loud breathing went on, as it had since the early part of Ramer's story.

'But that's a different kind of story, Jeremy,' objected Frankley. 'Quite good in its way. But I want to travel in Space and Time myself; and so, failing that, I want people in stories to do it. I want contact of worlds, confrontation of the alien. You say, Nick, that people cannot leave this world and live, at least not beyond the orbit of the Moon?'

'Yes, I believe they could not, cannot, and never will.'

'Very well then, all the more reason for having stories about *they could* or *they will*. Anybody would think you'd gone back to all that old-fashioned stuff about escapism. Do you object to fairy-tales?'

'No, I don't. But they make their own worlds, with their own laws.'

'Then why can't I make mine, and let its laws allow space-ships?'

'Because it won't then be your private world, of course,' said Guildford. 'Surely that is the main point of that kind of story, at an intelligent level? The Mars in such a story *is* Mars: the Mars that is. And the story is (as you've just admitted) a substitute for satisfaction of our insatiable curiosity about the Universe as it is. So a space-travel story ought to be made to fit, as far as we can see, the Universe as it is. If it doesn't or doesn't try to, then it does become a fairy-story – of a debased kind. But there is no need to travel by rocket to find Faërie. It can be anywhere, or nowhere.'

'But supposing you did travel, and did find Fairyland?' asked Ramer, suddenly. For some time now he had been staring at the fire, and had seemed to take very little interest in the battle that had been going on about him. Jeremy gaped at him, and jumped to his feet.

'But not by space-ship surely!' he cried. 'That would be as depressingly vulgar as the other way about: like an awful story I came across once, about some men who used a magic carpet for cheap power to drive a bus.'

'I'm glad to get *you* as an ally!' laughed Guildford. 'For you're a hardened sinner: you read that bastard stuff, scientific-tion, not as a casual vice, but actually as a professional interest.'

'The stuff is extremely interesting,' said Jeremy. 'Seldom as art. Its art level is as a rule very low. But literature may have a pathological side – still you've heard me on all that often enough. On this point I'm with you. Real fairy-stories don't pretend to produce impossible mechanical effects by bogus machines.'

'No. And if Frankley wants fairy-tales with mechanized dragons, and quack formulas for producing power-swords, or anti-dragon gas, or scientifictitious explanations of invisibility, well, he can have 'em and keep 'em. No! For landing on a new planet, you've got your choice: miracle; magic; or sticking to normal probability, the only known or likely way in which any one has ever landed on a world.'

'Oh! So you've got a private recipe all the time, have you?' said Ramer sharply.

'No, it's not private, though I've used it once.'

'Well? Come on! What is it?'

'Incarnation. By being born,' said Guildford.[15]

At that point Dolbear woke up. He yawned loudly, lifted his heavy lids, and his blue-bright eyes opened wide under his red brows. He had been audibly sleeping for a long while,* but we

---

* He often slept loudly, during a long reading or discussion. But he would rouse up in the middle of a debate, and show that he had the odd faculty of both sleeping and listening. He said that it was a time-saving habit that long membership of the Club had forced him to acquire. N.G.

were used to the noise, and it disturbed us no more than the sound of a kettle simmering on the fire.

'What have you got to say to that, Ramer?' he asked. He shot a sharp glance at him, but Ramer made no reply. Dolbear yawned again. 'I'm rather on Nick's side,' he said. 'Certainly about the first chapter in this case.'

'Well, that was read at the beginning, before you settled down for your nap,' said Lowdham.

Dolbear grinned. 'But it was not that chapter in itself that interested me,' he said. 'I think most of the discussion has been off the point, off the immediately interesting point. The hottest trail that Nicholas got on to was the *discord*, as you said yourself, Arry.[16] That's what you should follow up now. I should feel it strongly, even if space-ships were as regrettably possible as the Transatlantic Bus-service. Michael! Your real story is *wholly* out of keeping with what you called the frame. And that's odd in you. I've never felt such a jar before, not in any of your work. I find it hard to believe that the machine and the tale were made by the same man. Indeed, I don't think they were. You wrote the first chapter, the space-voyage, and also the homecoming (rather slipshod that, and my attention wandered): you *made it up*, as they say. And as you've not tried your hand at that sort of thing before, it was not much above the average. But I don't think you wrote the story inside. I wonder what you've been up to?'

'What are you driving at?' said Jeremy. 'It was typical Ramer all through, nearly every sentence was hall-marked. And even if he wanted to put us off with borrowed goods, where could he get them from?'

'You know his itch to re-write other people's bungled tales,' said Lowdham. 'Though certainly he's never tried one on us before, without telling us.'

'I know all that,' said Jeremy, hopping about angrily. 'I mean: where could he get this tale from? If he has found any printed space-travel story that I don't know, then he's been doing some pretty hot research. I've never met anything like it at all.'

'You're missing my point,' said Dolbear. 'I shouldn't have said *wrote*. I should have said *made up*, *invented*. I say again: I wonder what you've been up to, Ramer?'

'Telling a story,' answered Ramer glumly, staring at the fire.

'Yes,' said Dolbear. 'But don't try to do that in the nursery sense, or we'll have to roast you.' He got up and looked round at us all. His eyes looked very bright under bristling brows. He turned them sharply on Ramer. 'Come!' he said. 'Come clean! Where's this place? And how did you get there?'

'I don't know where it is,' said Ramer quietly, still staring at the fire. 'But you're quite right. I went there. At least ... well, I don't think our language fits the case. But there is such a world, and I saw it – once.' He sighed.

We looked at him for a long while. All of us – except Dolbear, I think – felt some alarm, and pity. And on the surface of our minds blank incredulity, of course. Yet it was not quite that: we did not feel the underlying emotion of incredulity. For apparently all of us, in some degree, had sensed something odd about that story, and now recognized that it differed from the norm like seeing does from imagining. I felt that it was like the difference between a bright glimpse of a distant landscape: threadlike waters really falling; wind ruffling the small green leaves and blowing up the feathers of birds on the branches, as that can be seen through a telescope: limited but clear and coloured; flattened and remote, but moving and real – between that and any picture. Not, it seemed to me, an effect to be explained simply by art. And yet – the explanation offered was nonsense outside the pages of a romance; or so I found that most of us felt at that moment.

We tried a few more questions, but Ramer would not say any more that night. He seemed disgruntled, or tired; though we had not scoffed. To relieve the tension, Frankley read us a short poem he had recently written. It was generous of him, for it was a good piece; but inevitably it fell rather flat. It is, however, pretty well-known now, as it appeared as the opening poem of his 1989 volume: *Experiments in Pterodactylics*.

We broke up soon after he had read it.

'Ramer,' I said at the door, 'we *must* hear some more about this, if you can bear it. Can't you come next week?'

'Well, I don't know,' he began.

'O don't go off to New Erewhon again just yet!' cried Lowdham, a bit too jocularly. [I don't think so. A.A.L.] 'We want more News from Nowhere.'[17]

'I did not say it was Nowhere,' said Ramer gravely. 'Only that it was Somewhere. Well, yes, I'll come.'

I walked part of the way home with him. We did not talk. It was a starry night. He stopped several times and looked up at the sky. His face, pale in the night, had a curious expression, I thought: like a man in a strange country trying to get the points of the compass, and wondering which way his home lies.

In the Turl[18] we parted. 'I think what the Club really needs is not more stories – yet,' I said. 'They need, I specially want, some description of the method, if you could manage it.' Ramer said nothing. 'Well, good night!' I said. 'This has been one of the great Club evenings, indeed! Who'd have thought that in starting up that literary hare about the most credible way of opening a space-tale I'd blunder on the lair of a real winged dragon, a veritable way of travelling!'

'Then you do believe me?' said Ramer. 'I thought that all of you but Dolbear thought I was spoofing, or else going batty. You in particular, Nick.'

'Certainly not spoof, Michael. As for battiness: well, in a sense, your claim is a batty one, even if genuine, isn't it? At least, it is, if I've any inkling of it. Though I've nothing to go on but impressions, and such hints as I've managed to get out of Rufus about your recent doings. He's the only one of us that has seen much of you for quite a time; but I rather fancy that even he does not know a great deal?'

Ramer laughed quietly. 'You're a hound, I mean a sleuth-hound, by nature, Nicholas. But I am not going to lay down any more trail tonight. Wait till next week! You can then have a look at my belfry and count all the bats. I'm tired.'

'Sleep well!' I said.

'I do,' said Ramer. 'Very well indeed. Good night!'

MGR. NG. AAL. PF. WTJ. RD. JJ.

Night 61.   Thursday, February 27th, 1987.[19]

A week later we were all together again, in Frankley's rooms this time; and even Cameron had come. As will be seen, he actually made a remark on this occasion, more than his stock 'Thanks for a very enterrtaining evening.' It was generally understood that Ramer was going to read a paper on *Real Space-travel.*

He was the last to arrive, and we were pleasantly surprised to see that he looked quite well, quite normal, and had not even the rather haggard look he used to have after writing a paper. He spends a frightful lot of late hours on such things, and burns more paper than he keeps.

Arry Lowdham[20] tapped him all over and pretended to be disappointed by the result. 'No models!' he cried. 'No plans of cylinders, spheres, or anything! Not even a Skidbladnir for a pocket-handkerchief!'[21]

'Now, none of that Nordic stuff, please!' groaned Frankley, who regards knowledge of his own language at any period before the Battle of Bosworth as a misdemeanour, and Norse as a felony.[22]

'No, not even a paper,' said Ramer.

'Why not?' we all cried.

'Because I haven't written one.'

'Oh I say!' we protested. 'Then you were spoofing all the time?' said Lowdham.

'No,' said Ramer. 'But I'm not going to read a paper. I didn't write one, because it would have been a great sweat; and I wasn't sure that you'ld really want to hear any more about it all. But if you do, I'm ready to talk.'

'Come on!' we said. Frankley shoved him down into a chair, and gave him a tankard of beer, and a box of matches – for him to strike, hold over a dead pipe, and throw away, as usual.

'Well,' he said after a short silence. 'It begins some way back. And the threads may seem a bit disconnected at first. The origins were literary, of course, like the discussion last week. I've always wanted to try a space-travel story, and have never dared. It was one of my earliest ambitions, ever since *Out of the Silent Planet* appeared, when I was a small boy. That puts it back a bit.'

'Yes, 1938,' said Cameron,[23] whose memory is like that. I doubt if he has ever read the book. The memoirs of minor modern diplomats are more in his line. The remark was his sole contribution.

'I never did write one,' said Ramer, 'because I was always bothered by the machinery, in a literary sense: the way of getting there. I didn't necessarily object to machines; but I never met and couldn't think of any credible vehicle for the purpose. I really agree very much with Nicholas on that point.'

'Well, you tried a pretty ordinary machine on us in that tale,' said Frankley.

'And seemed pretty disgruntled with me for objecting to it,' said Guildford.

'I was not really disgruntled,' said Ramer. 'A bit put out,

perhaps, as one is when one's disguise is pierced too quickly. Actually I was interested in the way you all felt the discord: no more than I did myself. But I felt that I had to tell that story to somebody, to communicate it. I wanted to get it out. And yet, and yet now I'm rather sorry. Anyway, I put it in that quickly-made cheap frame, because I didn't want to discuss the way I came by it – at least not yet. But Ruthless Rufus with his "third degree" has landed me here.'

'Yes, he has!' said Dolbear. 'So get on with your confession!'

Ramer paused and considered. 'Well, thinking about methods of getting across Space, I was later rather attracted by what you may call the telepathic notion – merely as a literary device, to begin with. I expect I got the idea from that old book you lent me, Jeremy: *Last Men in London*, or some name like that.[24] I thought it worked pretty well, though it was too vague about the *how*. If I remember rightly, the Neptunians could lie in a trance and let their minds travel. Very good, but *how* does the mind travel through Space or Time, while the body is static? And there was another weakness, as far as I was concerned: the method seemed to need rational creatures with minds at the other end. But I did not myself particularly want to see – or I should say at that stage, perhaps, write about – what Lewis called *hnau*.[25] I wanted to see things and places on a grand scale. That was one thread.

'Another thread was dreams. And that had a literary origin, too, partly. Because Rufus and I have long been interested in dreams, especially in their story-and-scene-making, and in their relation to waking fiction. But as far as I could judge such things, it did seem to me that a pretty good case had been made out for the view that in dream a mind can, and sometimes does, move in Time: I mean, can observe a time other than that occupied by the sleeping body during the dream.'

'But of course it can, and without sleeping,' said Frankley. 'If we were confined to the present, we couldn't think at all, even if we could perceive or feel.'

'But I mean *moving* not by memory, or by calculation, or by invention, as the waking mind can be said to *move*; but as a perceiver of the external, of something new that is not yet in the mind. For if you can see, in other times than the time of dreaming, what you never saw in waking life, so that it is not in your memory – seeing the future, for instance, would be a clear

case, and it cannot reasonably be doubted that that occurs –
then obviously there is a possibility of real first-hand seeing of
what is "not there", not where your body is.'

'Not even your eyes?' said Frankley.

'Ah,' said Ramer, 'that is of course a point. I shall come to
that later. It is probably a case of "translation"; but leave it for
a bit. I was thinking of dreaming chiefly, though I don't suppose
the possibility is really limited to that state. Only, if you live in a
never-ending racket of sense-impressions, other more distant
noises have to be very loud to be heard. And this *movement,* or
transference of observation: it is clearly not limited to Other
Time; it can occur in Other Space, or in both. A dreamer is not
confined to the events of Other Time occurring in his bedroom.'

'But wouldn't you expect to be limited to the places where
you yourself *have been,* or *will be,* in Other Time?' asked
Guildford.

'That's not the general human tradition about visions,' said
Ramer. 'Nor is it borne out by authenticated modern instances.
And it is not my experience, as you will see. But naturally I
thought about that point. I think, actually, that it is clear that
the mind can be in two places at one time: two or more; once
you have made it more than one, the figure is, perhaps, not very
important. For I suppose, as far as the mind goes, you can't get
nearer to saying where it is than to say where its attention is.
And that, of course, may be decided by various causes, internal
and external.

'You can get a sort of literary parallel. I think it is a pertinent
one, actually; for I don't think literary invention, or fancy, is
mixed up in all this by accident. When you are writing a story,
for instance, you can (if you're a vivid visualizer, as I am, and
are clearly visualizing a scene) *see* two places at once. You can
see (say) a field with a tree and sheep sheltering from the sun
under it, and be looking round your room. You are really seeing
both scenes, because you can recollect details later. Details of
the waking scene not attended to, because you were *abstracted*:
there's no doubt of that. I should as certainly add: details of the
inner scene, blurred because you were to some extent *distracted.*

'As far as my own visualizing goes, I've always been impres-
sed by how often it seems independent of my will or planning
mind (at the moment). Often there is no trace of composing a
scene or building it up. It comes before the mind's eye, as we
say, in a way that is very similar to opening closed eyes on a

complete waking view.*[26] I find it difficult, usually quite impossible, to alter these pictures to suit myself, that is my waking purpose. As a rule I find it better, and in the end more right, to alter the story I'm trying to tell to suit the pictures. If the two really belong together – they don't always, of course. But in any case, on such occasions you are really seeing double, or simultaneously. You tend to associate the two views, inner and outer, though the juxtaposition of them may be, usually is, their only connexion. I still associate a view of a study I no longer possess and a pile of blue-and-yellow-covered exam-scripts (long burnt, I hope) with the opening scene of a book I wrote years ago: a great morain high up in the barren mountains.'

'I know', said Jeremy, 'the foot of the Glacier in *The Stone-eaters*.'[27]

'I think a connexion could be made out between those two scenes,' said Frankley.

'It's very difficult to find any two things that the story-making faculty cannot connect,' said Ramer. 'But in this case the story-scene came into my head, as it is called, long before the examination reality. The two are connected only because I was re-visualizing, revisiting, the Glacier-foot very strongly that day.'

'That doesn't quite get rid of some connexion other than coinciding in time,' said Frankley.

'Well, never mind. They did coincide,' said Ramer. 'And that is my point at the moment. The mind can be in more than one place at a given time; but it is more properly said to be where its attention is. And that, I suppose, is in one place only: for most human minds, or at any rate for my mind.

'But I'm afraid this is a digression. To go back to dreams. Of course, the memory of such true dreams, or free dreams, is notoriously rarish and chancy, and also scrappy as a rule. But it is not legitimate, it is pretty plainly wrong, to assume that what is ordinarily remembered by ordinary people of their dreaming is either most of the total, or the most important part of it. And the will to remember can be strengthened, and the memory can

* Ramer said later: 'It is still more like re-viewing in memory a place that one has really been to; it is like *memory* in its quality as compared with *sightseeing*, but on the first occasion of its arising in the mind it does not seem to be "remembering".' N.G.

be enlarged. Rufus has had a good deal of experience in that direction, and he has helped me from time to time.'

Dolbear stirred and opened his eyes. 'So his suspicion was not due to pure literary criticism of discords?' said Frankley.

'Well, I haven't the faintest idea of what Michael is driving at, yet – if that's what you mean,' said Dolbear. 'Or rather, I understand what he's saying and more or less agree with it, but what it has to do with that vision of, of what was it?'

'Emberü,' said Ramer. 'I don't yet see,' Dolbear ended.[28]

'Well, here is a third thread,' Ramer went on. 'I had the notion, as others probably have too, that for movement or travelling the mind (when abstracted from the flood of sense) might use the memory of the past and the foreshadowing of the future that reside in all things, including what we call "inanimate matter". Those are not the right words, but they'll have to do: I mean, perhaps, the causal descent from the past, and the casual probability in the present, that are implicit in everything. At any rate, I thought that might be one of the mind's vehicles.[29] But an incarnate mind seemed rather a problem to me.'

'Not a very new one!' said Guildford.

Ramer laughed. 'Don't be too hard on me,' he said. 'I'm not at all original. And anyway my problem was practical rather than philosophical. I was puzzled about *jumping*. I didn't see how it could be done. I'm not a philosopher, but an experimenter, a man driven by desires – if not very fleshly ones, still very incarnate ones. Being an *incarnate* mind, I am conditioned by Time and Space, even in my curiosities; though being a *mind*, I want to get beyond the range of my own body's senses and history.

'Of course, you might imagine the mind, by some special effort of its own, doing something analogous to the body's leaping from place to place, especially in a less trammelled state like sleep, or trance. But I thought the analogy probably false – for a living man, anchored even in trance to the body, however long and thin the rope. The mind may be neither in Time nor Space, except in so far as it is specially associated with a body; but while you're alive the bond holds, I thought. Mind-body: they jump together, or neither jumps at all.

'I hardly need to say again that by *jump* I do not mean the movement of thought to objects already in its grasp, or memory: shifting instantaneously from, say, considering the peculiar configuration of Rufus's face to thinking of Table Mountain (which I once saw). I wanted to observe new things far off in Time and Space beyond the compass of a terrestrial animal.'

'And so,' said Lowdham, 'like the Pig on the Ruined Pump, day and night you made your moan, because you could not jump?'[30]

'Exactly,' said Ramer; 'for of course by this time I was really thinking more about travelling myself than writing a travel-story. But I didn't want to die. And I thought that all I could do was to refine my observation of other things that have moved and will move: to inspect the history of things whose paths have, at some point of time and space, crossed the path of my body.

'The mind uses the memory of its body. Could it use other memories, or rather, records? What kind of record of past events and forms could there be? In the time-sequence the disintegration of a form destroys the memory – or the special record – of the history of that form, unless it has got into a mind first. The fragments, right down to the smallest units, no doubt preserve the record of their own particular history, and that may include some of the history of the combinations that they've entered into. But take a haunted house, for instance.'

'Take a house!' interrupted Jeremy. 'All houses are haunted.'

'I agree,' said Ramer. 'But I'm using the words, as they're commonly used, to mean a house where some particular detail of the haunting has become specially perceptible; how or why that occurs is another question.'

'But *haunting*, and *atmosphere* (which I suppose is what Jeremy means), are something added by accident of history,' objected Frankley. 'They're not part of the house itself, *qua* house.'

'I'm not sure I understand you,' said Ramer. 'But I'm quite sure that I personally am not interested in 'housiness' in itself, but in this or that thing which you may class as a house, part of which (the most interesting part to me) is its history. If I say No. 100 Banbury Road,[31] I mean the shape which you call house *and* all that you call the accidents of its history: what it is at present. So do you. And if you destroy an actual house *qua* house, you also destroy, or dissipate, the special haunting. If a haunted house were pulled to pieces, it would stop being haunted, even if it were built up as accurately as possible again. Or so I think, and so-called 'psychical' research seems to bear me out. In a way analogous to life in a body. If all the king's horses and all his men had put Humpty Dumpty together again, they'ld have got, well, an egg-shell.'

'But you can go a long way, short of destruction, without wholly banishing atmosphere or quite laying ghosts,' said Jeremy. 'Bricking up windows, changing staircases, and things like that.'

'Quite right,' said Lowdham. 'There was one poor ghost I heard of, and when they raised the floor of his favourite corridor, he went on walking on the old level. So people in the passage below could see the old fellow's feet trudging along under the ceiling. That's how they discovered he had holes in his soles. Don't laugh!' he said indignantly. 'It's a most melancholy case, and well authenticated.'

'I dare say!' said Ramer. 'But quite apart from such forlorn ghosts, and Arry's authorities (whoever they may be), I expect there are in fact lots of neglected chances of historical research, with proper training; especially among old houses and things more or less shaped by man. But that was not my chief interest. I wanted to travel a long way.

'So I tried various experiments, on myself; various forms of training. It's difficult to concentrate, chiefly because it's difficult to get quiet enough. The body makes such a noise itself, quite apart from the din of sensations coming from outside. I wanted to discover if my mind had any power, any trainable latent power, to *inspect* and *become aware* of the memory or record in other things, that would be in them anyway, even if not inspectable by me. For, I suppose, what we call memory, human memory, is both the power to inspect and be aware of the record within us, *and* the record that would be there anyway. The power of inspection and awareness is always there; and so is the material and record, I suppose, unless it is smashed up. Though the inspector cannot always get at the records. We aren't in full control of ourselves, even, so obviously it wouldn't be easy to deal with other things.'

'But the mind seems also to have its own storehouses, as well as keys of inspection, doesn't it?' said Guildford. 'I mean, it can remember past inspections, and retains what it has noted.'

'Yes, I think so,' said Ramer; 'but it is difficult, of course, when you're dealing with a mind-body, an association in which neither can do anything without having some effect on the other. I don't think an incarnate mind ever gets really free of its body, wherever it strays, until a man dies, if then. However, I went on trying to train myself for this kind of, well, historical inspection and awareness. I don't think I have any special talent for it. I don't *know*, for so few people seem to have tried it. But I fancy that Jeremy, for instance, has more of a bent in this direction than I have.

'It is difficult, and it's also frightfully slow. Less slow, of course, with things that have organic life, or any kind of human associations: but they don't carry you very far. It's slow, and it's *faint*. In inorganic things too faint to surmount the blare of waking sense, even with eyes shut and ears stopped.

'But here the threads begin to join. Remember, I was also training my memory on dreams at the same time. And that is how I discovered that the other experiments affected them. Though they were blurred, blurred by the waking senses beyond recognition, I found that these other perceptions were not wholly unnoted; they were like things that are passed over when one is abstracted or distracted, but that are really "taken in". And, asleep, the mind, rootling about, as it does, in the day's leavings (or the week's), would inspect them again with far less distraction, and all the force of its original desire. I dare say it enjoyed it.

'But it couldn't make much of it. By which I suppose I mean that I couldn't remember much about such inspections, although I was now becoming pretty good at remembering large passages of more vivid and pictorial dreams. And that means I suppose also, that my mind was not able (at least not without more practice) to translate the notes into the terms of the senses which I can handle when awake. All the same, I used to get at that time very extraordinary geometric patterns presented to me, shifting kaleidoscopically but not blurred; and queer webs and tissues, too. And other non-visual impressions also, very difficult to describe; some like rhythms, almost like music; and throbs and stresses.

'But all the time, of course, I wanted to get off the Earth. That's how I got the notion of studying a meteorite, instead of mooning about with houses, ruins, trees, boulders, and all sorts of other things. There is a very large meteorite in a park, Gunthorpe Park in Matfield,[32] where I lived as a boy, after we came back from abroad; even then it had a strange fascination for me. I wondered if it could have come from Malacandra. I took to hobnobbing with it again, in the vacs. Indeed, I made

myself ridiculous and an object of suspicion. I wanted to visit
the stone alone at night – to lessen the distractions; but I was
not allowed to: closing hours were closing hours. So I gave that
up. It seemed to be quite without results.'

'So the poor old stone was left all alone?' said Lowdham.

'Yes,' said Ramer. 'It was. It is a very long way indeed from
home, and it *is* very lonely. That is, there is a great loneliness in
it, for a perceiver to perceive. And I got a very heavy dose of it.
In fact I can't bear to look at such things now. For I found,
about the end of the long vac. two years ago, after my final visit,
that there *had* been results. It had evidently taken some time to
digest them, and even partially translate them. But that is how I
first got away, out beyond the sphere of the Moon, and very
much further.'

'Travelling on a dream-meteor!' said Frankley. 'Hm! So that's
your method, is it?'

'No,' said Ramer. 'Not if you mean how I got the news of
Emberü that I put into my tale.[33] But I did work back into the
meteorite's history, I think; though that sort of vehicle does not
readily give any place or time references that can be related to
our waking point. I did get, all the rest of that term, and I still do
get occasionally, some very odd dreams or sleep-experiences:
painful often, and alarming. Some were quite unpictorial, and
those were the worst. Weight, for instance. Just Weight with
a capital W: very horrible. But it was not a weight that was
pressing on *me*, you understand; it was a perception of, or
sympathy in, an experience of almost illimitable weight.[34] And
Speed too. Heavens! waking up from that one was like hitting a
wall, though only a wall of light and air in my bedroom, at a
hundred miles a second – or rather, like knowing about it.

'And Fire! I can't describe that. Elemental Fire: fire that is,
and does not consume, but is a mode or condition of physical
being. But I caught sight of blazing fire, too: some real pictures.
One, I think, must have been a glimpse of the meteorite hitting
our air. A mountain corroded into a boulder in a few seconds of
agonizing flame. But above, or between, or perhaps through all
the rest, I knew endlessness. That's perhaps emotional and
inaccurate. I mean Length with a capital L, applied to Time;
unendurable length to mortal flesh. In that kind of dream you
can know about the feeling of aeons of constricted waiting.

'Being part of the foundations of a continent, and upholding
immeasurable tons of rock for countless ages, waiting for an

explosion or a world-shattering shock, is quite a common situation in parts of this universe. In many regions there is little or no "free will" as we conceive it. Also, though they are large and terrific, events may be relatively simple in plan, so that catastrophes (as we might call them), sudden changes as the end of long repeated series of small motions, are "inevitable": the present holds the future more completely. A perceiving but passive mind could see a collapse coming from an immense distance of time.

'I found it all very disturbing. Not what I wanted, or at least not what I had hoped for. I saw, anyway, that it would take far too much of a mortal human life to get so accustomed to this kind of vehicle that one could use it properly, or selectively, at will. I gave it up. No doubt, when any degree of control was achieved, my mind would no longer have been limited to that particular vehicle or chunk of matter. The waking mind is not confined to the memories, heredity, or senses, of its own normal vehicle, its body: it can use that as a platform to survey the surroundings from. So, probably, it could, if it ever mastered another vehicle: it could survey, in some fashion, other things where the meteorite (say) came from, or things it had passed in its historical journey. But that second transference of observation would certainly be much more difficult than the first, and much more uncertain and inefficient.

'So I turned more than ever to dream-inspection, trying to get "deeper down". I attended to dreams in general, but more and more to those least connected with the immediate irritations of the body's senses. Of course, I had at times experienced, as most people have, parts of more or less rationally connected dreams, and even one or two serial or repeating dreams. And I have had also the not uncommon experience of remembering fragments of dreams that seemed to possess a "significance" or emotion that the waking mind could not discern in the remembered scene.[35] I was not at all convinced that this "significance" was due to obscured symbols, or mythical values, in the dream-scenes; or at least I didn't and don't think that that is true of most of such dream-passages. Many of these "significant patches" seemed to me much more like random pages torn out of a book.'

'But you didn't wriggle out of Rufus's clutches that way, did you?' said Guildford. 'He'll analyse a whole book as cheerfully as a page.'

'It depends on the contents,' said Ramer. 'But I'll come back to that. For at about that time something decisive happened. It seemed to sweep away all other trials and experiments; but I don't think they were really wasted. I think they had a good deal to do with precipitating the, well, catastrophe.'

'Come on, come on! What was it?' said Dolbear. He stopped snoring and sat up.

'It was most like a violent awakening,' said Ramer. He was silent for almost a minute, staring at the ceiling as he lay back in his chair.

At last he went on. 'Imagine an enormously long, vivid, and absorbing dream being shattered – say, simultaneously by an explosion in the house, a blow on your body, and the sudden flinging back of dark curtains, letting in a dazzling light: with the result that you come back with a rush to your waking life, and have to recapture it and its connexions, feeling for some time a shock and the colour of dream-emotions: like falling out of one world into another where you had once been but had forgotten it. Well, that was what it was like *in reverse*; only recapturing the connexions was slower.

'I was awake in bed, and I *fell wide asleep*: as suddenly and violently as the waker in my illustration. I dived slap through several levels and a whirl of shapes and scenes into a connected and remembered sequence. I could remember all the dreams I had ever had, of that sequence. At least, I remember that I could remember them while I was still "there", better than I can "here" remember a long sequence of events in waking life. And the memory did not vanish when I woke up, and it hasn't vanished. It has dimmed down to normal, to about the same degree as memory of waking life: it's edited: blanks indicating lack of interest, some transitions cut, and so on. But my dream-memories are no longer fragments, no longer like pictures, about the size of my circle of vision with fixed eyes, surrounded with dark, as they used to be, nearly always. They are wide and long and deep. I have visited many other sequences since then, and I can now remember a very great number of serious, free, dreams, my deep dreams, since I first had any.'

'What a lumber-room!' said Lowdham.

'I said *my serious dreams*,' said Ramer. 'Of course, I can't, don't want to, and haven't tried to remember all the jumble of marginal stuff – the rubbish the analysts mostly muck about with, because it's practically all they've got – no more than you try to recollect all the scribbling on blotting-paper, the small talk, or the idle fancies of your days.'

'How far have you gone back?' Lowdham asked.

'To the beginning,' Ramer answered.

'When was that?'

'Ah! That depends on what you mean by *when*,' said Ramer. 'There are seldom any data for cross-timing as between waking and dreaming. Many dreams are in, or are concerned with, times remote from the standpoint of the body. One of those dreams might be said to occur before it started; or after. I've no idea how far I've gone *back* in that sense, backward in the history of the universe, you might say. But sticking to the waking time, then I suppose I cannot have begun dreaming until I had begun to be: that is, until the creation of my mind, or soul. But I doubt if any ordinary time-reference has any real meaning with regard to that event considered in itself; and the word *dreaming* ought to be limited to the ... er ... spare-time, off-duty, activities of an incarnate mind. So I should say my dreaming began with the entry of my mind into body and time: somewhere in the year 1929. But that fifty-odd years of our time *could* contain various indefinite lengths of experience, or operation, or journeying. My earlier experiments were not necessary, except perhaps to help in the precipitation of memory, as I said. My mind "asleep" had long done that sort of thing very much better.'

He paused, and we looked at him, some of us a bit queerly. He laughed. 'Don't imagine me walking about "in a dream", as people say. The two modes are no more confused than before. If you had two homes in quite different places, say in Africa and Norway, you'ld not usually be in doubt which one you were staying in at any given time, even if you could not remember the transition. No, at the worst my situation is only like that of a man who has been reading a deeply interesting book, and has it "on his mind", as he goes about his affairs. But the impression can pass off, or be put aside, as in the case of a book. I need not think about my dreams, if I don't wish to, no more than I need think about any book or re-read it.'

'You say *re-read*. Can you will, now when awake, to go back to any particular dream, to repeat it or go on with it?' asked Frankley. 'And can you remember your waking life while in a dream?'

'As to the last question,' Ramer replied, 'the answer is: in a sense *yes*. As clearly as you can remember it while writing a story, or deeply engrossed in a book. Only you can't give direct attention to it. If you do, you wake up, of course.

'The other question's more difficult. Dreams are no more all of one sort than the experiences of waking life; less so in fact. They contain sensations as different as tasting butter and understanding a logical argument; stories as different in length and quality as one of Arry's lower anecdotes and the Iliad; and pictures as unlike as a study of a flower-petal and those photographs of the explosion in the Atomic Reservation in the seventies,[36] which blew the Black Hole in the States. Dreams happen, or are made, in all sorts of ways. Those that people mostly remember, and remember most of, are marginal ones, of course, or on the upper levels . . .'

'Margins? Upper levels? What d'you mean?' snapped Jones,[37] breaking in, to our surprise. 'Just now you spoke of diving. When do we get to the bottom?'

'Never,' Ramer laughed. 'Don't take my words too literally, at any rate no more literally than I suppose you take the *sub* in *subconscious*. I'm afraid I haven't thought out my terminology very carefully, James; but then I didn't mean to talk about these things to you, not yet. I've been put on the mat. I think I meant *deep* as in *deeply interested*; and down, lower, upper, and all the rest have crept in afterwards, and are misleading. Of course there isn't any *distance* between dreams and waking, or one kind of dream and another; only an increase or decrease of abstraction and concentration. In some dreams there's no distraction at all, some are confused by distractions, some just *are* distractions. You can lie "deep" and sodden in body-made dreams, and receive clear visions in "light" sleep (which might seem on the very margin of waking). But if I use "deep" again you'll know that I mean dreams as remote as may be from disturbance, dreams in which the mind is seriously engaged.

'By the marginal ones I meant those that are produced when the mind is playing, idling, or fooling, as it often is, mooning aimlessly about among the memories of the senses – because it's tired, or bored, or out of mental sorts, or worried by sense-messages when its desires or attention are elsewhere; the devil's tattoo of dreaming as compared with the piano-playing. Some minds, perhaps, are hardly capable of anything else, sleeping or waking.

'And the machinery may go on ticking over, even when the mind is not attending. You know how you've only got to do something steadily for hours – like picking blackberries, say – and even before you're asleep the manufacture of intricate trellises of briars and berries goes on in the dark, even if you're thinking of something else. When you begin to dream you may start by using some of those patterns. I should call that "marginal". And anything else that is largely due to what is actually going on, in and around the body: distraction complexes in which such things as "noises off", indigestion, or a leaking hot-water-bottle play a part.

'Asking if you can re-visit that stuff is like asking me if I can will to *see* (not make) rain tomorrow, or will to be waked up *again* by two black cats fighting on the lawn. But if you're talking about serious dreams, or visions, then it's like asking if I shall walk back up the road again last Tuesday. The dreams are for your mind events. You can, or might – waking desire has some effect, but not much – go back to the same "places" and "times", as a spectator; but the spectator will be the you of now, a later you, still anchored as you are, however remotely, to your body time-clock here. But there are various complications: you can re-inspect your memories of previous inspections, for one thing; and that is as near to dreaming the same dream over again as you can get (the closest parallel is reading a book for a second time). For another thing, thought and "invention" goes on in dreams, a lot of it; and of course you can go back to your own work and take it up again – go on with the story-making, if that is what you were doing.'

'What a busy time we all seem to have been having without knowing it,' said Lowdham. 'Even old Rufus may not be quite such a sloth as he looks. Anyway you've given him a jolly good excuse to fall back on. "Goodbye all! I'm off to my dream-lab to see if the retorts are bubbling," says he, and he's snoring in two ticks.'

'I leave the bubbling retorts to you,' said Dolbear, opening his eyes. 'I am afraid I've not yet got down to such high levels as Michael, and I muck about still with the marginal stuff, as he calls it. Tonight at any rate I've been having a bit of a dream: in the rootling stage, I suppose, owing to the distraction of this discussion going on round my body. I got a picture of Ramer, equipped with Frankley's long nose, trying to extract whiskey out of a bottle; he couldn't pour it out, as he had no arms, only a pair of black wings, like a devil in a stuffed M.A. gown.'

'The whiskey-bottle was not derived from the sense-data in this room,' said Lowdham.

'Now I can sympathize with the psychoanalysts,' said Frankley, rising and getting a bottle out of the cupboard. 'The difficulty they must have in sorting out dreams from the malicious inventions of the patient's waking mind!'

'No difficulty with Rufus,' said Lowdham. 'The drink-urge explains most of him. And I don't think he's got a Censor, sleeping or waking.'

'Hm! I'm glad I'm so transparent,' said Dolbear. 'Not everyone is so simple, Arry. You walk in disguises, even when awake. But they'll slip, my lad, one day. I shouldn't wonder if it was fairly soon.'[38]

'Lor!' said Lowdham. 'Have I come out in a false beard and forgotten it, or something?' But at that moment he caught a glint in Dolbear's eye, and stopped suddenly.

'Go on, Michael, and don't take any notice of them!' said Jeremy.

'Shall I?' he asked, absentmindedly drinking the whiskey that Frankley had put at Dolbear's elbow.

'Of course!' we said. 'We are fortified now.'

'Well, seriously,' he went on, 'I don't think the marginal stuff is very interesting in normal people: it's so ravelled, and more bother to unravel than it's worth. It's very much like the idleness and foolery of the waking mind. The chief distinction is, I think, that when a man's awake he's attending more to the foolery; and when he's asleep his attention is probably already far away: so the foolery is less good of its kind. But as for his mind being *busy*, Arry: I only said, if you remember, that your life *could* contain a lot of dream-work or events. I don't think it usually does. Minds can be lazy on their own account. Even for the energetic ones sleep is largely a rest. But of course, for a mind rest is not oblivion, which is impossible for it. The nearest it can get to that is passivity: the mind can be very nearly passive, contemplating something worthy of it, or what seems worthy. Or it can take the kind of holiday we call "a change", doing something different to the work imposed on it by needs or duties when it is awake. If it has by nature, or has acquired, some dominant interest – like history, or languages, or mathematics – it may at times work away at such things, while the old body is recuperating. It can then construct dreams, by no means always pictorial. It can plan and calculate.

'My mind, like many others, I imagine, makes up stories, composes verse, or designs pictures out of what it has got already, when for some reason it hasn't at the moment a thirst to acquire more. I fancy that all waking art draws a good deal on this sort of activity.[39] Those scenes that come up complete and fixed that I spoke of before, for instance; though some of them, I believe, are visions of real places.

'And that strong feeling of hidden significance in remembered fragments: my experience now, though it is still very imperfect, certainly bears out my guess, as far as my own dreams go. *My significant fragments were actually often pages out of stories, made up in quieter dream-levels, and by some chance remembered. Occasionally they were bits of long visions of things not invented.*

'If long ago you'd either read or written a story and forgotten it, and then in an old drawer you came on a few torn pages of it, containing a passage that had some special function in the whole, even if it had no obvious point in isolation, I think you'ld get very similar feelings: of hidden significance, of lost connexions eluding you, and often of regret.'

'Could you give us any examples?' asked Jeremy.

Ramer thought for a moment. 'Well,' he said, 'I could have done so. I've placed several of my fragments in their proper setting now. But the difficulty is that when once you've got the whole story, you tend very soon to forget which part of it was the bit you used to remember torn out. But there are a couple that I still remember, for I only placed them recently; and I still remember my disappointment. The whole stories are often not particularly good or interesting, you know; and the charm of the fragments is often largely in being unfinished, as sometimes happens in waking art. The sleeping mind is no cleverer than itself; only it can be less distracted and more collected, more set on using what it has.

'Here's one case: it's only interesting as an illustration.

A row of dark houses on the right, going up a slight slope. Their backs had little gardens or yards fenced with hedges, and a narrow path behind them. It was miserably dark and gloomy. Not a light in the houses, not a star, no moon. He was going up the path for no particular reason, in a heavy aimless mood. Near the top of the slope he heard a noise: a

*door had opened at the back of one of the houses, or it had
closed. He was startled and apprehensive. He stood still. End
of fragment.*
What would you expect the emotion to be that this aroused?'

'Like going round to the back-door after closing-time and
hearing that just being shut as well?' suggested Lowdham.

'It sounds reasonable enough,' agreed Ramer with a laugh.
'Actually it was a happiness that brings tears, like the thrill of
the sudden turn for good in a dangerous tale; and a kind of dew
of happiness was distilled that spilled over into waking, lasted
for hours, and for years was renewed (though diminishingly) on
recollection.

'All my waking mind could make of it was that the picture
was sombre. It did rather remind me of – or rather, I identified
it, in spite of some misfit, with a row of cottages near where I
lived as a small boy. But that did not explain the joy. And, by
the way, if it had really been a picture of that row, there should
have been a pump just at the top of the slope. I put it in. I see it
now in dark silhouette. But it was not there in my earliest
recollection, not in the original version. Also, I was only the *he*
of the scene in the way one does (or I do) identify oneself
variably with this or that character in a tale, especially with
regard to the point of vision. The scene was observed more or
less from *his* point of view, though I (the producer) was just
behind (and a little above) *him* – until he stopped. At the
emotion-point I took his place.

'The story that scene came out of is known to me now; and
it's not very interesting. Apparently it's one I made up years
ago,[40] somewhere in the fifties, at a time when, while awake, I
wrote lots of things of the sort. I won't bother you with it all: it
had a long and complicated plot,[41] mainly dealing with the Six
Years' War; but it wasn't very original, nor very good of its
kind. All that matters at the moment is that this scene came just
before a lovers' reunion, beyond the hope of either the man or
the woman. On hearing the noise he halted, with a premonition
that something was going to happen. The woman came out of
the door, but he did not recognize her till she spoke to him at the
gate. If he hadn't halted, they would have missed one another,
probably for ever. The plot, of course, explained how they both
came to be there, where neither of them had been before; but
that doesn't matter now. The interesting thing is that the
remembered fragment, for some reason, ended with the sound

of the door and the halting; but the *emotion* left over was due to part of the story immediately following, which was not remembered pictorially at all. But there was no trace of the emotions of still later parts of the story, which did not finally have a happy ending.

'Well, there it is. Not very exciting, but suggestive, perhaps. Do you want the other case?'

Dolbear gave a loud snore. 'Hark at him!' said Lowdham. 'I expect he's analysed you enough already, and doesn't want any more of your juvenilia to interrupt his slumber.'

'Oh go on, Ramer!' said Jeremy. 'Let's have it!'

'It's your evening, and we asked for it,' said Guildford. 'Carry on!'

'Well, here's another picture,' said Ramer.

A pleasant small room: a fire, a lot of books, a large desk; a golden light from a lamp. He is sitting at the desk. The dreamer's attention, from slightly above his head, is concentrated on the circle of light, but is vaguely aware of dim figures away in front, moving about, taking books from shelves, reading in corners. He is looking at an open book at his left hand, and making notes on a paper. General air of cheerfulness and quiet. He pauses and looks up as if thinking, knocking his pipe-stem between his teeth. He turns a leaf of the book – and sees a new light, makes a discovery; but the fragment ends.

What do you make of that?'

'He'd solved the acrostic with the aid of a dictionary?' said Frankley.

'Emotion: Jack-Hornerism, quiet bibliophilous gloating?' said Lowdham.

'No!' said Ramer. 'Though you're getting warm, Arry. But the emotion associated was *worry*, with a heavy hang-over into waking hours of a dull sense of loss, as heavy as anything you felt in childhood when something precious was broken or lost.'

'Well, New Readers now go back to Chapter One,' said Lowdham. 'What is it?'

'Rather more unusual than the first case, so I'll tell it more fully,' said Ramer. 'He was the librarian in a small university. The room was his office-study: quite comfortable, but it had a glass wall on one side, through which he could overlook the main hall of the library. He was feeling cheerful, for a few years back a local magnate had left the university a splendid book-collection, and most of his money for the enlargement and upkeep of the library. The library had become important; so had he, and his salary as curator of the endowed collection was generous. And after a lot of delay a new wing had been built, and the books transferred. For some time he'd been carefully re-examining the more interesting items. The book to his left was a volume made up of various manuscript-fragments bound together, probably in the sixteenth century, by some collector or pilferer.

'In the remembered bit of the dream I knew I had been able to read the page before he turned over, and that it was not English; but I could remember no more than that – except that I was delighted, or he was. Actually it was a leaf, a unique fragment of a MS. in very early Welsh, before Geoffrey,[42] about the death of Arthur.

'He turned to look at the back of the leaf – and he found, stuck between it and the next, a document. It turned out to be a will made by the Donor. This book of fragments was one of the last things the magnate had acquired, just before his death. The will was later than the proved and executed will by nearly two years. It was in form, and witnessed, and it did not mention the university, but directed that the books should be dispersed and sold, and the proceeds should go to found a Chair of Basic English in London; while the rest of the estate should go to a nephew, previously passed over.

'The librarian had known the magnate, and had often been to his house: he had helped in cataloguing his collection. He saw that the witnesses were two old servants that had died soon after their master. The emotions are easy to understand: the librarian was proud of his library, a scholar, a lover of real English, and the father of a family; but he was also an honest man. He knew that the Donor had disliked the new Vice-Chancellor very much; also that the nephew was the Donor's next of kin, and poor.'

'Well, what did he do with the will?' said Jeremy.

'On second thoughts he thought it best to stuff it in the old oak chest?' said Lowdham.

'I don't know,' said Ramer. 'Of course it would have been easy and probably quite safe to suppress the will. But I found I had never finished the tale properly, though plenty of sequels could be invented. I found one or two ideas, not worked out, floating at the end. One was that the librarian went to the

Vice-Chancellor, who begged him to keep his discovery quiet; he gave way, and was later blackmailed by the Vice-Chancellor himself. But evidently that hadn't seemed satisfactory, or I'd lost interest in the whole thing beyond the recorded situation. I left a good many such yarns incomplete at that time.

'There's little merit in these stories, as you see. But they do illustrate one or two points about fragmentary memory, and about dream-storywriting. For it is not, of course, writing, but a sort of realized drama.'

'Elvish Drama,'[43] Jeremy interposed; 'there's something about it ...' But we had heard him on that topic before. 'Ramer has the floor!' we cried.

'Well anyway,' Ramer went on: 'the whole story as it is told becomes visible and audible, and the composer is inside it – though he can take his stand in some odd positions (often high up), unless he puts himself into the play, as he can at any moment. The scenes *look* real, but are feigned; and the composition is not complete like a "slice of life": it can be given in selected scenes, and compressed (like a drama). Also it can, when you're working over it again or merely re-inspecting it, be reviewed in any order and at varying speeds (like re-reading or reconsidering a book). I think that is one, though only one, of the reasons why the memory of such dreams, when any survives at all, is so often dissolving or jumbled. The dreamer is aware, of course, that he is author and producer, at any rate while he is at work asleep; but he can get far more absorbed by his work than a waking man is by any book or play that he is either writing or reading; and he can feel the emotions very strongly – excessively sometimes, because they are heightened by the excitement of combining authorship with an acting part; and in memory they may be exaggerated still more through getting dislocated, abstracted from the sounds and scenes that would explain them.

'The cases I've cited are without any symbolism. Just plain emotional situations. I can't say much about symbolic or mythical significances. Of course they exist. And really I can only put them back one stage. For the dreamer can work on myth, and on fairy-tale, quite as much as on novelette. I did. I do. And with a more complete text, so to speak, the excerpted scenes are often much easier to understand, and the functions of the symbols are plainer – but their final solution recedes.

'There are good dreams, apparently of the sort I mean, quoted in books. My own were not so good: the ones I used to

remember when awake, that is; they were only significant
fragments, more statically pictorial, seldom dramatic, and
usually without figures of humane shape.[44] Though I sometimes
retained the memory of significant words or sentences without
any scenery: such as *I am full of sovereign remedies*. That
seemed a wise and satisfactory utterance. I have never yet found
out why.

'Here are some of my fragments of this kind. There is the
empty throne on the top of a mountain. There is a Green Wave,
whitecrested, fluted and scallop-shaped but vast, towering
above green fields, often with a wood of trees, too; that has
constantly appeared.[45] I saw several times a scene in which a
wide plain lay before the feet of a steep ridge on which I stood;
the opposing sky was immense, rising as a vertical wall, not
bending to a vault, ablaze with stars strewn almost regularly
over all its expanse. That is an omen or presage of catastrophe.
A dark shape sometimes passes across the sky, only seen by
blotting out the stars as it goes. Then there is the tall, grey,
round tower on the sheer end of the land. The Sea cannot be
seen, for it is too far below, too immeasurably far; but it can be
smelt. And over and over again, in many stages of growth and
many different lights and shadows, three tall trees, slender, foot
to foot on a green mound, and crowned with an embracing halo
of blue and gold.'

'And what do you think they all mean?' asked Frankley.

'It took me quite a time, far too long, to explain the very
minor story of the librarian,' said Ramer. 'I could not embark
tonight on even one of the immense and ramified legends and
cosmogonies that these belong to.'

'Not even on the Green Wave?' said Lowdham;[46] but Ramer
did not answer him.

'Are the Blessed Trees religious symbolism?' asked Jeremy.

'No, not more than all things mythical are; not directly. But
one does sometimes see and use symbols directly religious, and
more than symbols. One can pray in dreams, or adore. I think I
do sometimes, but there is no memory of such states or acts, one
does not revisit such things. They're not really dreams. They're
a third thing. They belong somewhere else, to the other
anchorage, which is not to the Body, and differ from dreams
more than Dream from Waking.

'Dreaming is not Death. The mind is still, as I say, anchored
to the body. It is all the time inhabiting the body, so far as it is *in*

anywhere. And it is therefore in Time and Space: attending to them. It is meant to be so. But most of you will agree that there has probably been a change of plan; and it looks as if the cure is to give us a dose of something higher and more difficult. Mind you, I'm only talking of the seeing and learning side, not for instance of morality. But it would feel terribly *loose* without the anchor. Maybe with the support of the stronger and wiser it could be celestial; but without them it could be bitter, and lonely. A spiritual meteorite in the dark looking for a world to land on. I daresay many of us are in for some lonely Cold before we get back.

'But out of some place beyond the region of dreams, now and again there comes a blessedness, and it soaks through all the levels, and illumines all the scenes through which the mind passes out back into waking, and so it flows out into this life. There it lasts long, but not for ever in this world, and memory cannot reach its source. Often we ascribe it to the pictures seen on the margin radiant in its light, as we pass by and out. But a mountain far in the North caught in a slow sunset is not the Sun.

'But, as I said, it is largely a rest-time, Sleep. As often as not the mind is inactive, not making things up (for instance). It then just inspects what is presented to it, from various sources – with very varying degrees of interest, I may say. It's not really frightfully interested in the digestion and sex items sent in by the body.'

'What is *presented* to it, you say?' said Frankley. 'Do you mean that some of the presentments come from outside, are *shown* to it?'

'Yes. For instance: in a halting kind of way I had managed to get on to other vehicles; and in dream I did it better and more often. So other minds do that occasionally to me. Their resting on me need not be noticed, I think, or hardly at all; I mean, it need not affect me or interfere with me at all; but when they are doing so, and are in contact, then my mind can use *them*. The two minds don't tell stories to one another, even if they're aware of the contact. They just are in contact and can learn.*[47] After

* See the further discussion of this point on the following Night 62. N.G. [Only a fragment of that meeting is preserved, and the only part that could correspond to this note is as follows. ' "How can the dreamer distinguish them?" said Ramer. "Well, it seems to me that

all, a wandering mind (if it's at all like mine) will be much more interested in having a look at what the other knows than in trying to explain to the stranger the things that are familiar to itself.'

'Evidently if the Notion Club could all meet in sleep, they'ld find things pretty topsy-turvy,' said Lowdham.

'What kind of minds visit you?' asked Jeremy. 'Ghosts?'

'Well, yes of course, ghosts,' said Ramer. 'Not departed human spirits, though; not in my case, as far as I can tell. Beyond that what shall I say? Except that some of them seem to know about things a very long way indeed from here. It is not a common experience with me, at least my awareness of any contact is not.'

'Aren't some of the visitors malicious?' said Jeremy. 'Don't evil minds attack you ever in sleep?'

'I expect so,' said Ramer. 'They're always on the watch, asleep or awake. But they work more by deceit than attack. I don't think they are specially active in sleep. Less so, probably. I fancy they find it easier to get at us awake, distracted and not so aware. The body's a wonderful lever for an indirect influence on the mind, and deep dreams can be very remote from its disturbance. Anyway, I've very little experience of that kind – thank God! But there does come sometimes a frightening ... a sort of knocking at the door: it doesn't describe it, but that'll

the chief divisions are *Perceiving* (free dreams), *Composing and Working*, and *Reading*. Each has a distinctive quality, and confusion is not as a rule likely to occur, while it is going on; though the waking mind may make mistakes about disjointed memories. The divisions can be subdivided, of course. *Perceiving* can be, for instance, either inspections and visits to real scenes; or apparitions, in which one may be deliberately visited by another mind or spirit. *Reading* can be simply going over the records of any experiences, messing about in the mind's library; or it can be perceiving at second hand, using minds, inspecting *their* records. There's a danger there, of course. You might inspect a mind and think you were looking at a record (true in its own terms of things external to you both), when it was really the other mind's composition, *fiction*. There's *lying* in the universe, some very clever lying. I mean, some very potent fiction is specially composed to be inspected by others and to deceive, to pass as record; but it is made for the malefit of Men. If men already lean to lies, or have thrust aside the guardians, they may read some very maleficial stuff. It seems that they do." ']

have to do. I think that is one of the ways in which that horrible sense of *fear* arises: a fear that doesn't seem to reside in the remembered dream-situation at all, or wildly exceeds it.

'I'm not much better off than anyone else on this point, for when that fear comes, it usually produces a kind of dream-concussion, and a passage is erased round the true fear-point. But there are some dreams that can't be fully translated into sight and sound. I can only describe them as resembling such a situation as this: working alone, late at night, withdrawn wholly into yourself; a noise, or even a nothing sensible, startles you; you get prickles all over, become acutely self-conscious, uneasy, aware of isolation: how thin the walls are between you and the Night.

'That situation may have various explanations here. But out (or down) there sometimes the mind is suddenly aware that there *is* a Night outside, and enemies walk in it: one is trying to get in. But there are no walls,' said Ramer sombrely. 'The soul is dreadfully naked when it notices it, when that is pointed out to it by something alien. It has no armour on it, it has only its being. But there is a guardian.

'He seems to command precipitate retreat. You could, if you were a fool, disobey, I suppose. You could push him away. You could have got into a state in which you were attracted by the Fear. But I can't imagine it. I'd rather talk about something else.'

'Oh!' said Jeremy. 'Don't stop there! It's been mostly digressions since the meteorite. My fault largely. Won't you go on?'

'I should like to, if the Club can bear it. A little longer. I only meant: I'd rather get back to the visions and the journeys. Well, apart from such dangers – which I've not experienced often or thought much about – I think that what one calls "interests" are sometimes actually stimulated, or even implanted by contacts. As you might get a special interest in China, through being visited by a Chinaman, especially if you got to know him and something of his mind.'

'Have you gone to any Celestial China?' asked Frankley. 'Or anywhere more interesting than your invented tales: something more like Emberü?'

'I've never *gone* anywhere,' said Ramer, 'as I've tried to explain. But I suppose I could say that I've *been* in places, and I'm still busy trying to sort out my observations. If you mean places off the Earth, other heavenly bodies: yes, I've seen several besides Emberü, either through other minds, or by vehicles and records; possibly by using light.* Yes, I've been to several strange places.

'The one I told you about, Green Emberü,[48] where there was a kind of organic life, rich but wholesome and longeval: that was where I landed when I first fell wide asleep. It seems a long while ago now. It is still very vivid to me, or was until last week.' He sighed.

'I cannot remember the original again now, somehow; not when awake. I've an idea that writing these memories up, re-telling them in waking life and terms, blurs or erases them in waking memory; overlays them into palimpsests. One can't have it both ways. Either one must bear the pains of not communicating what one greatly desires to share, or one must remain content with the translation. I wrote that account for you, and all I'll have now is that, and stirrings and faint traces of what lies beneath: the vision of Emberü!

'It's the same with Ellor. Ellor!' he murmured. 'Ellor Eshúrizel! I drew it once in words as best I could, and now it *is* words. That immense plain with its silver floor all delicately patterned; the shapely cliffs and convoluted hills. The whole world was designed with such loveliness, not of one thought, but of many in harmony; though in all its shapes there was nowhere any to recall what we call organic life. There "inanimate nature" was orderly, symmetrical, unconfused, yet intricate, beyond my mind's unravelling, in its flowing modulations and recollections: a garden, a paradise of water, metal, stone, like the interwoven variations of vast natural orders of flowers. Eshúrizel! Blue, white, silver, grey, blushing to rich purples were its themes, in which a glint of red was like an apocalyptic vision of essential Redness, and a gleam of gold was like the glory of the Sun. And there was music, too. For there were many streams, water abundant – or some fairer counterpart, less wayward, more skilled in

---

* Jones says that Ramer explained: 'I think that as the *seeing* in free dream is not done with eyes, it is not subject to optical laws. But light can be used, like any other mode of being. The mind can, as it were, travel back up-stream, as it can go back into the historical record of other things. But it seems tiring: it requires a great energy and desire. One can't do it often; nor can one go to an indefinite distance of Time and Space.' N.G.

the enchantment of light and in the making of innumerable
sounds. There the great waterfall of Öshül-küllösh fell down its
three hundred steps in a sequence of notes and chords of which I
can only hear faint echoes now. I think the En-keladim dwell
there.'[49]

'The En-keladim?' asked Jeremy softly. 'Who are they?'

Ramer did not answer. He was staring at the fire. After a
pause he went on. 'And there was another world, further away,
that I came to later. I won't say very much. I hope to look on it
again, and longer: on Minal-zidar the golden, absolutely silent
and quiescent, a whole small world of one single perfect form,
complete, imperishable in Time, finished, at peace, a jewel, a
visible word, a realization in material form of contemplation
and adoration, made by what adoring mind I cannot tell.'

'Where is Minal-zidar?' asked Jeremy quietly.

Ramer looked up. 'I don't know where or when,' he
answered. 'The travelling mind does not seem very interested in
such points, or forgets to try and find out in the absorption of
beholding. So I have very little to go on. I did not look at the sky
of Minal-zidar. You know, if you were looking at the face of
somebody radiant with the contemplation of a great beauty or a
holiness, you'ld be held by the face for a very long time, even if
you were great enough (or presumptuous enough) to suppose
that you could see for yourself. Reflected beauty like reflected
light has a special loveliness of its own – or we shouldn't, I
suppose, have been created.

'But in Ellor there seemed to be lights in the sky, what we
should call stars, not suns or moons, and yet many were much
larger and brighter than any star is here. I am no astronomer, so
I don't know what that may imply. But I suppose it was
somewhere far away, beyond the Fields of Arbol.'[50]

'Fields of Arbol?' said Lowdham. 'I seem to have heard that
before. Where do you get these names from? Whose language
are they? Now that would really interest me, rather than
geometry and landscape. I should use *my* chances, if ever I got
into such a state, for language-history.'[51]

'Arbol is "Old Solar" for the Sun,' said Jeremy.[52] 'Do you
mean, Ramer, that you can get back to Old Solar, and that
Lewis* did not merely invent those words?'

* Referring to *Out of the Silent Planet* and *Perelandra*, which we
had all read some time ago, under pressure from Jeremy (while he was

'Old Solar?' said Ramer. 'Well, no. But of course I was quoting Lewis, in saying Fields of Arbol. As to the other names, that's another matter. They're as firmly associated with the places and visions in my mind as *bread* is with Bread in your minds, and mine. But I think they're *my* names in a sense in which *bread* is not.*

'I daresay it depends on personal tastes and talents, but although I'm a philologist, I think I should find it difficult to learn strange languages in a free dream or vision. You *can* learn in dreams, of course; but in the case of real visions of new things you don't talk, or don't need to: you get the meaning of minds (if you meet any) more directly. If I had a vision of some alien people, even if I heard them talking, their *sense* would drown or blur my reception of their *sounds*; and when I woke up, if I remembered what had been said, and tried to relate it, it would come out in English.'

'But that wouldn't apply to pure names, proper nouns, would it?' said Lowdham.

'Yes, it would,' said Ramer. 'The voice might say *Ellor*, but I should get a glimpse of the other mind's vision of the place. Even if a voice said *bread* or *water*, using "common nouns", I should be likely to get, as the core of a vague cloud (including tastes and smells), some particular glimpse of a shaped loaf, or a running spring, or a glass filled with transparent liquid.

'I daresay that you, Arry, are more phonetical, and more sound-sensitive than I am, but I think even you would find it difficult to keep your ear-memory of the alien words unblurred

---

writing his book on *Imaginary Lands*). See note to Night 60, p. 164. Jeremy was an admirer of the *Public-house School* (as he himself had dubbed them), and soon after he became a Lecturer he gave a series of lectures with that title. Old Professor Jonathan Gow had puffed and boggled at the title; and J. had offered to change it to *Lewis and Carolus, or the Oxford Looking-glass*, or *Jack and the Beanstalk*; which did not smooth matters. Outside the Club J. had not had much success in reviving interest in these people; though the little book of anonymous memoirs *In the Thirsty Forties, or the Inns and Outs of Oxford* attracted some notice when it came out in 1980.   N.G.

*Lowdham says that Ramer told him after the meeting that he thought *Minal-zidar* meant Poise in Heaven; but *Emberü* and *Ellor* were just names. *Eshúrizel* was a title, signifying in an untranslatable way some blend or scheme of colours; but *Öshül-küllösh* meant simply Falling Water.   N.G.

by the impact of the direct meaning in such dreams. If you did, then very likely it would be only the sounds and not the sense that you'ld remember.

'And yet ... especially far away outside this world of Speech, where no voices are heard, and other naming has not reached ... I seem to hear fragments of language and names that are not of this country.'

'Yes, yes,' said Lowdham. 'That's just what I want to hear about. What language is it? You say not Old Solar?'

'No,' said Ramer, 'because there isn't any such tongue. I'm sorry to disagree with your authorities, Jeremy; but that is my opinion. And by the way, speaking as a philologist, I should say that the treatment of language, intercommunication, in tales of travel through Space or Time is a worse blemish, as a rule, than the cheap vehicles that we were discussing last week. Very little thought or attention is ever given to it.[53] I think Arry will agree with me there.'

'I do,' said Lowdham, 'and that's why I'm still waiting to hear where and how you got your names.'

'Well, if you really want to know what these names are,' said Ramer, 'I think they're my *native* language.'

'But that is English, surely?' said Lowdham. 'Though you were born in Madagascar, or some strange place.'

'No, you ass! Magyarország, that is Hungary,' said Ramer. 'But anyway, English is *not* my native language. Nor yours either. We each have a native language of our own – at least potentially. In working-dreams people who have a bent that way may work on it, develop it. Some, many more than you'ld think, try to do the same in waking hours – with varying degrees of awareness. It may be no more than giving a personal twist to the shape of old words; it may be the invention of new words (on received models, as a rule); or it may come to the elaboration of beautiful languages of their own in private: in private only because other people are naturally not very interested.

'But the inherited, first-learned, language – what is usually mis-called "native" – bites in early and deep. It is hardly possible to escape from its influence. And later-learned languages also affect the natural style, colouring a man's linguistic taste; the earlier learned the more so. As Magyar does mine, strongly – but all the more strongly, I think, because it is in many ways closer to my own native predilections than English is. In language-invention, though you may seem to build only out of material taken from other acquired tongues, it is those elements most near to your native style that you select.

'In such rare dreams as I was thinking about, far away by oneself in voiceless countries, then your own native language bubbles up, and makes new names for strange new things.'

'Voiceless countries?' said Jeremy. 'You mean regions where there is nothing like our human language?'

'Yes,' said Ramer. 'Language properly so called, as we know it on Earth – token (perceived by sense) plus significance (for the mind) – that is peculiar to an embodied mind; an essential characteristic, the prime characteristic of the fusion of incarnation. Only *hnau*, to use Jeremy's Lewisian word again, would have language. The irrational couldn't, and the unembodied couldn't or wouldn't.'

'But spirits are often recorded as *speaking*,' said Frankley.

'I know,' Ramer answered. 'But I wonder if they really do, or if they make you hear them, just as they can also make you see them in some appropriate form, by producing a direct impression on the mind. The clothing of this naked impression in terms intelligible to your incarnate mind is, I imagine, often left to you, the receiver. Though no doubt they can cause you to hear words and to see shapes of their own choosing, if they will. But in any case the process would be the reverse of the normal in a way, outwards, a translation from meaning into symbol. The audible and visible results might be hardly distinguishable from the normal, even so, except for some inner emotion; though there is, in fact, sometimes a perceptible difference of sequence.'

'I don't know what spirits can do,' said Lowdham; 'but I don't see why they cannot make actual sounds (like the Eldil in *Perelandra*): cause the air to vibrate appropriately, if they wish. They seem able to affect "matter" directly.'

'I dare say they can,' said Ramer. 'But I doubt if they would wish to, for such a purpose. Communication with another mind is simpler otherwise. And the direct attack seems to me to account better for the feelings human beings often have on such occasions. There is often a shock, a sense of being touched in the quick. There is movement from within outwards, even if one feels that the cause is outside, something other, not you. It is quite different in quality from the reception of sound inwards, even though it may well happen that the thing communicated directly is not strange or alarming, while many things said in the ordinary incarnate fashion are tremendous.'

'You speak as if you *knew*,' said Jeremy. 'How do you know all this?'

'No, I don't claim to *know* anything about such things, and I'm not laying down the law. But I feel it. I *have* been visited, or spoken to,' Ramer said gravely. 'Then, I think, the meaning was direct, immediate, and the imperfect translation perceptibly later: but it was audible. In many accounts of other such events I seem to recognize experiences similar, even when far greater.'

'You make it all sound like hallucination,' said Frankley.

'But of course,' said Ramer. 'They work in a similar way. If you are thinking of diseased conditions, then you may believe that the cause is nothing external; and all the same something (even if it is only some department of the body) must be affecting the mind and making it translate outwards. If you believe in possession or the attack of evil spirits, then there is no difference in process, only the difference between malice and good-will, lying and truth. There is Disease and Lying in the world, and not only among men.'

There was a pause. 'We've got rather away from Old Solar, haven't we?' said Guildford at last.

'No, I think what has been said is very much to the point,' said Ramer. 'Anyway, if there is, or even was, any Old Solar, then either Lewis or I or both of us are wrong about it. For I don't get any such names as *Arbol* or *Perelandra* or *Glund*.[54] I get names much more consonant with the forms I devise, if I make up words or names for a story composed when awake.

'I think there might be an Old Human, or Primitive Adamic – certainly was one, though it's not so certain that all our languages derive from it in unbroken continuity; the only undoubted common inheritance is the aptitude for making words, the compelling need to make them. But the Old Human could not possibly be the same as the Prime Language of other differently constituted rational animals, such as Lewis's Hrossa.[55] Because those two embodiments, Men and Hrossa, are quite different, and the physical basis, which conditions the symbol-forms, would be *ab origine* different. The mind-body blends would have quite different expressive flavours. The expression might not take vocal, or even audible form at all. Without symbols you have no language; and language begins only with incarnation and not before it. But, of course, if you're going to confuse language with forms of *thought*, then you can perhaps talk about Old Solar. But why not Old Universal in that case?[56]

'However, I don't think the question of Old Solar arises. I don't think there are any other *hnau* but ourselves in the whole solar system.'

'How can you possibly know that?' asked Frankley.

'I think I know it by looking,' Ramer answered. 'I only once anywhere saw what I took to be traces of such creatures, but I'll tell you about that in a minute.

'I'll grant you that there is a chance of error. I have never been very interested in people. That's why when I first began to write, and tried to write about people (because that seemed to be the thing done, and the only thing that was much read), my efforts were so footling, as you see, even in dream. I'm now abnormally little interested in people in general, though I can be deeply interested in this or that unique individual; and the fewer I see the better I'm pleased. I haven't scoured the Fields of Arbol seeking for them! I suppose in dream I might have ignored or overlooked them. But I don't think it's at all likely. Because I like solitude in a forest and trees not manhandled, it does not follow that I shall overlook the evidence of men's work in a wood, or never notice any men I meet there. Much the reverse!

'It's true that I've not seen the solar planets often, nor explored them thoroughly: that's hardly necessary in most cases, if you're looking for any conceivable organic life resembling what we know. But what I *have* seen convinces me that the whole system, save Earth, is altogether barren (in our sense). Mars is a horrible network of deserts and chasms; Venus a boiling whirl of wind and steam above a storm-racked twilit core. But if you want to know what it looks and sounds like: a smoking black Sea, rising like Everest, raging in the dusk over dim drowned mountains, and sucking back with a roar of cataracts like the end of Atlantis – then go there! It is magnificent, but it isn't Peace. To me indeed very refreshing – though that's too small a word. I can't describe the invigoration, the acceleration of intellectual interest, in getting away from all this tangle of ant-hill history! I am *not* a misanthrope. To me it's a more inspiring and exacting, a much more responsible, perilous, lonely venture: that Men are in fact *alone* in EN.[57] In EN. For that is the name to me of this sunlit archipelago in the midst of the Great Seas.

'We can cast our own shadows out on to the other islands, if we like. It's a good and lawful form of invention; but an invention it is and proceeds out of Earth, the Talkative Planet. The only *hnau* ever to dwell in red *Gormok* or in cloud-bright *Zingil*[58] will be put there by us.'

'What reason have you for thinking that you've seen them at all, and not other places in remoter Space?' asked Frankley.[59]

'Well, I went to them in a more questioning mood,' said Ramer, 'and I looked for such signs as I could understand. They were planets. They went round the Sun, or a sun, in more or less the ways and times the books say, so far as I could observe. And the further heavens had much the same pattern, just the same to my little knowledge, as they have here. And old *Eneköl*, Saturn,[60] is unmistakable; though I suppose it is not quite impossible that he has his counterpart elsewhere.'

'Won't you describe what you saw there?' said Frankley. 'I once tried to describe a Saturnian landscape myself,*[61] and I should like to know if you support me.'

'I do, more or less,' said Ramer. 'I thought so at once when I landed there, and I wondered if you had been there too, or had heard some reliable news – though you may not remember it when awake. But it is getting late. I am tired, and I am sure you all are.'

'Well, something to wind up with!' Jeremy begged. 'You haven't really told us very much news yourself yet.'

'I'll try,' said Ramer. 'Give me another drink, and I'll do my best. As I haven't had time, when awake, either to name or to translate half of the shapes and sensations, it is impossible for me to do more than suggest the thing. But I'll try and tell you about one adventure among my deep dreams: or high ones, for this occurred on one of the longest journeys I have ever had the opportunity or the courage for. It illustrates several curious things about this sort of venture.

'Remember that dream-sequences dealing with astronomical exploration or space-travel are not very frequent in my collection. Nor in any one's, I should think. The chances of making such voyages are not frequent; and they're ... well, they take a bit of daring. I should guess that most people never get the chance and never dare. It is related in some way to *desire*, no

* In *The Cronic Star*. This appeared in his volume *Feet of Lead* (1980). One of the critics said that this title, taken with the author's name, said all that was necessary. N.G.

doubt; though which comes first, chance or wish, is hard to say – if there's any real question of priority in such matters. I mean: my ancient attraction to waking stories about space-travel, was it a sign that I was really already engaged on exploration, or a cause of it?

'In any case I have only made a few journeys, as far as I yet know; few, that is, compared with other activities. My mind "adream" is perhaps not daring enough to fit waking desire; or perhaps the interests I'm most conscious of awake are not really fundamentally so dominant. My mind actually seems fonder of mythical romances, its own and others'. I could tell you a great deal about Atlantis, for instance; though that is not its name to me.'

'What *is* its name?' asked Lowdham sharply, leaning forward with a curious eagerness; but Ramer did not answer the question.

'It's connected with that Fluted Wave,'[62] he said; 'and with another symbol: the Great Door, shaped like a Greek 𝝅 with sloping sides.[63] And I've seen the En-keladim, my En-keladim, playing one of their Keladian plays: the Drama of the Silver Tree:[64] sitting round in a circle and singing in that strange, long, long, but never-wearying, uncloying music, endlessly unfolding out of itself, while the song takes visible life among them. The Green Sea flowers in foam, and the Isle rises and opens like a rose in the midst of it. There the Tree opens the starred turf like a silver spear, and grows, and there is a New Light; and the leaves unfold and there is Full Light; and the leaves fall and there is a Rain of Light. Then the Door opens – but no! I have no words for that Fear.'

He stopped suddenly. 'That's the only thing I've ever seen,' he said, 'that I'm not sure whether it's invented or not.[65] I expect it's a composition – out of desire, fancy, waking experience, and "reading" (asleep and awake). But there is another ingredient. Somewhere, in some place or places, something like it really happens, and I have seen it, far off perhaps or faintly.

'My En-keladim I see in humane forms of surpassing and marvellously varied beauty. But I guess that their true types, if such there be, are invisible, unless they embody themselves by their own will, entering into their own works because of their love for them. That is, they are *elvish*. But very different from Men's garbled tales of them; for they are not lofty indeed, yet they are not fallen.'

'But wouldn't you reckon them as *hnau?*' asked Jeremy. 'Don't they have language?'

'Yes, I suppose so. Many tongues,' said Ramer. 'I had forgotten them. But they are not *hnau*; they are not bound to a given body, but make their own, or take their own, or walk silent and unclad without sense of nakedness. And their languages shift and change as light on the water or wind in the trees. But yes, perhaps *Ellor Eshúrizel* – its meaning I cannot seize, so swift and fleeting is it – perhaps that is an echo of their voices. Yes, I think Ellor is one of their worlds: where the governance, the making and ordering, is wholly in the charge of minds, relatively small, that are not embodied in it, but are devoted to what we call matter, and especially to its beauty. Even here on Earth they may have had, may have still, some habitation and some work to do.

'But I'm still wandering. I must go back to the adventure that I promised to tell. Among my few travel-sequences I recall one that seemed to be a long inspection (on several occasions) of a different solar system. So there does appear to be at least one other star with attendant planets.[66] I thought that as I wandered there I came to a little world, of our Earth's size more or less – though, as you'll see, size is very difficult to judge; and it was lit by a sun, rather larger than ours, but dimmed. The stars too were faint, but they seemed to be quite differently arranged; and there was a cloud or white whorl in the sky with small stars in its folds: a nebula perhaps, but much larger than the one we can see in Andromeda. Tekel-Mirim[67] it was, a land of crystals.

'Whether the crystals were really of such great size – the greatest were like the Egyptian pyramids – it is hard to say. Once away from Earth it is not easy to judge such things without at least your body to refer to. For there is no scale; and what you do, I suppose, is to focus your attention, up or down, according to what aspect you wish to note. And so it is with speed. Anyway, there on Tekel-Mirim it was the inanimate matter, as we should say, that was moving and growing: into countless crystalline formations. Whether what I took for the air of the planet was really air, or water, or some other liquid, I am not able to say; though perhaps the dimming of sun and stars suggests that it was not air. I may have been on the floor of a wide shallow sea, cool and still. And there I could observe what was going on: to me absorbingly interesting.

'Pyramids and polyhedrons of manifold forms and symmetries were growing like ... like geometric mushrooms, and growing from simplicity to complexity; from single beauty amalgamating into architectural harmonies of countless facets and reflected lights. And the speed of growth seemed very swift. On the summit of some tower of conjoined solids a great steeple, like a spike of greenish ice, would shoot out: it was not there and then it was there; and hardly was it set before it was encrusted with spikelets in bristling lines of many pale colours. In places forms were achieved like snowflakes under a microscope, but enormously larger: tall as trees some were. In other places there were forms severe, majestic, vast and simple.

'For a time I could not count I watched the "matter" on Tekel-Mirim working out its harmonies of inherent design with speed and precision, spreading, interlocking, towering, on facet and angle building frets and arabesques and frosted laces, jewels on which arrows of pale fire glanced and splintered. But there was a limit to growth, to building and annexation. Suddenly disintegration would set in – no, not that, but reversal: it was not ugly or regrettable. A whole epic of construction would recede, going back through shapeliness, by stages as beautiful as those through which it had grown, but wholly different, till it ceased. Indeed it was difficult to choose whether to fix one's attention on some marvellous evolution, or some graceful devolving into – nothing visible.

'Only part of the matter on Tekel-Mirim was doing these things (for "doing" seems our only word for it): the matter that was specially endowed; a scientist would say (I suppose) that was of a certain chemical nature and condition. There were floors, and walls, and mighty circles of smooth cliff, valleys and vast abysses, that did not change their shape nor move. Time stood still for them, and for the crystals waxed and waned.

'I don't know why I visited this strange scene, for awake I have never studied crystallography, not even though the vision of Tekel-Mirim has often suggested that I should. Whether things go in Tekel-Mirim exactly as they do here, I cannot say. All the same I wonder still what on earth or in the universe can be meant by saying, as was said a hundred years ago (by Huxley, I believe) that a crystal is a "symmetrical solid shape assumed spontaneously by lifeless matter".[68] The free will of the lifeless is a dark saying. But it may have some meaning: who can tell? For we have little understanding of either term. I leave it there. I merely record, or try to record, the events I saw, and they were too marvellous while I could see them in far Tekel-Mirim for speculation. I'm afraid I've given you no glimpse of them.

'It was on one occasion, returning – or should I say "back-dreaming"? – from Tekel-Mirim, that I had the adventure that I'll close with. Speed, as I said, like size is very difficult to judge with no measure but vague memories of earth-events far away. Maybe I had been speeding up, that is moving quickly down Time in Tekel-Mirim, so as to get as long a story or sequence as I could. In Tekel-Mirim I must have been not only far away in Space but in a time somewhat before my earth-time, or I should have overrun the point for my withdrawal. For I had to withdraw on that visit earlier than my body usually summons me. A determination of my own will, set before I went to sleep, had fixed a time of waking, for an appointment. And the hour was coming near.

'It is no good harking back, when you do not want to repeat but to see on; and so I withdrew, with my mind still so filled with the wonder of Tekel-Mirim that I could not even adream, and still less awake, recall the transitions or the modes of travelling, until my attention was loosened from my recollections and I found that I was looking at a twinkling sphere. I knew that I had seen it, or something like it, on one of my other journeys; and I was tempted to examine it again. But time was running on, and dimly, like a remote shred of a dream (to one awake) I was aware of my body beginning to stir unwillingly, feeling the returning will. So there and then I "harked back" suddenly with as great an effort as I could manage; and at the same time I closed in to look for a while at this strange ball.

'I found a horrible disorderly shifting scene: a shocking contrast to Tekel-Mirim, and after Emberü and Ellor intolerable. Dark and light flickered to and fro over it. Winds were whirling and eddying, and vapours were rising, gathering, flashing by and vanishing too quick for anything to be discerned but a general ragged swirl. The land, if that is what it was, was shifting too, like sands in a tide, crumbling and expanding, as the sea galloped in and out among the unsteady edges of the coast. There were wild growths, woods you could hardly say; trees springing up like mushrooms, and crashing and dying before you could determine their shapes. Everything was in an abominable flux.

'I came still closer. The effort to attend carefully seemed to steady things. The flicker of light and dark became much slower; and I saw something that was definitely a small river, though it waggled a little, and broadened and narrowed as I looked at it. The trees and woods in its valley held their shapes now for some time. Then "*Hnau* at last!" I said to myself; for in the vale, down by the river among the trees I saw shapes, unmistakable shapes of houses. At first I had thought that they were some kind of quick-growing fungus, until I looked more steadily. But now I saw that they were buildings, but still fungus-buildings, appearing and then falling to pieces; and yet their agglomeration was spreading.

'I was still rather high above it all, higher than a man in a very tall tower; but I could see that the place was crawling or rather boiling with *hnau* of some sort – if they were not very large ant-creatures, endowed with amazing speed: darting about, alone or in bunches, bewilderingly; always more and more of them. Often they went shooting in or out like bullets along the tracks that led to the horrible, crumbling, outgrowing sore of house-shapes.

' "This really is frightful!" I thought. "Is this a diseased world, or is it a planet really inhabited by may-fly men in a sort of tumultuous mess? What's come to the land? It's losing most of its hair, going bald, and the house-ringworm goes on spreading, and starting up in fresh patches. There's no design, or reason, or pattern in it." And yet, even as I said this, I began to see, as I looked still more carefully, that there were in fact some shapes that did suggest crude design, and a few now held together for quite a long while.

'Soon I noticed down by the river, near the heart of the agglomeration, where I had observed it beginning, several constructions that endured. Two or three had some real form, not without an echo of beauty even to one fresh from Tekel-Mirim. They continued standing, while the ringworm ate its way further and further around them.

' "I must have a really close look," I thought; "for if there are *hnau* here, it is important, however nasty they may be; and I must take some notes. Just a look, and then I must be off. Now, what is that thing like a great fluted mushroom with an odd top? It hasn't been here as long as some of the other larger things." With that I came right down.

'Of course, if one really concentrates on things – especially to observe their static forms, not their changes, as I'd been doing in

Tekel-Mirim – then they tend to halt, as it were. The speed is in you, when you're not tied to a time-clock of a body. So as I bent my attention, I lost all the acceleration that the excitement of Tekel-Mirim had induced. Things stood still for a moment, rock-hard.

'I was gazing at the Camera.[69] I was about thirty feet above the ground in Radcliffe Square. I suppose I had at first been seeing the Thames Valley, at a huge speed; and then, slower and slower, Oxford since I don't know when, since the beginning of the University probably.

'The clock on Saint Mary's struck 7 a.m. – and I woke up for my appointment. To go to Mass. It was the morning of the feast of Saint Peter and Saint Paul, June 29th 1986, by our reckoning. That's all for tonight! I must go to bed.'

'Well, I must be off too,' said Cameron. 'Thanks for a very enterrtaining evening!'

MGR. NG. PF. AAL. RD. WTJ. RS. JJ. JJR.

NOTES

1   The Great Storm of June 12th, 1987: my father's 'prevision' was only out by four months. The greatest storm in living memory struck southern England, causing vast damage, on October 16th, 1987. It is curious in the light of this to read Mr. Green's remarks (p. 158): 'it may well be that the predictions (notably of the Storm), though genuine and not coincidences, were unconscious: giving one more glimpse of the strange processes of so-called literary "invention", with which the Papers are largely concerned.'

2   *O.S.B.*: 'Order of Saint Benedict'.

3   For the title as typed in the final text D, but subsequently rejected, see p. 153 note 2.

4   In A and B the report of Night 54 is absent (cf. Mr. Green's Foreword, p. 156: 'Many Nights are represented only by a few lines, or by short entries, of which Nights 54 and 64 have been included as specimens').

5   I cannot explain *The Canticle of Artegall*. Irish *arteagal* = 'article'; and an isolated note of my father's reads: 'My/The Canticle of Night in Ale', 'Artegall', 'article Artegall'. But this does not help very much.

6   In B Night 60 is Night 251, without date (see p. 149).

7   I have mentioned (p. 150) a page that preceded text A and carries the identifications of members of the Notion Club with members of the Inklings. On this page are found two brief, abandoned

openings for *The Notion Club Papers*. In the first Ramer asks Latimer (predecessor of Guildford) for his opinion of his story. With ' "Yes, I suppose it'll do," I answered' this opening breaks off, and is followed by:

> When I had finished reading my story, we sat in silence for a while. 'Well?' I said. 'What do you think of it? Will it do?' Nobody answered, and I felt the air charged with disapproval, as it often is in our circle, though on this occasion the critical interruptions had been fewer than usual. 'Oh, come on. What have *you* got to say? I may as well get the worst over,' I urged turning to Latimer. He is not a flatterer.
>
> 'Oh yes, it'll do, I suppose so,' he answered reluctantly. 'But why pick on me? You know I hate criticizing offhand and still in the heat of listening – or the chill.'

Here this second opening was abandoned. It is presumably to be connected with the word 'Self' written under *Ramer* at the head of the page (p. 150).

8   David Lindsay, author of *A Voyage to Arcturus*, published in 1920, to which Guildford refers subsequently (see note 9).

9   Cf. my father's letter to Stanley Unwin of 4 March 1938, concerning *Out of the Silent Planet* (*Letters* no. 26):

> I read 'Voyage to Arcturus' with avidity – the most comparable work, though it is both more powerful and more mythical (and less rational, and also less of a story – no one could read it merely as a thriller and without interest in philosophy religion and morals).

10   *Cavorite* was the substance 'opaque to gravitation' devised by the scientist Cavor in H. G. Wells's *The First Men in the Moon* (1901).

11   For 'the Great Explosion' see Mr. Green's Foreword, p. 157, and p. 186.

12   *Ransom:* Dr. Elwin Ransom was the Cambridge philologist who in *Out of the Silent Planet* went under duress to Mars (Malacandra), and in *Perelandra* went to Venus by the mediation of the Oyarsa of Malacandra (see next note).

13   At the beginning of *Perelandra* the *Eldils* are described thus:

> For Ransom had met other things in Mars besides the Martians. He had met the creatures called *eldila*, and specially that great eldil who is the ruler of Mars or, in their speech, the *Oyarsa* of *Malacandra*. The eldila are very different from any planatary creatures. Their physical organism, if organism it can be called, is quite unlike either the human or the Martian. They do not eat, breed, breathe, or suffer natural death, and to that extent resemble thinking minerals more than they resemble anything we should recognise as an animal. Though they appear on planets and may even seem to our senses to be

sometimes resident in them, the precise spatial location of an eldil at any moment presents great problems. They themselves regard space (or 'Deep Heaven') as their true habitat, and the planets are to them not closed but merely moving points – perhaps even interruptions – in what we know as the Solar System and they as the Field of Arbol.

14 *Old Solar*: cf. *Perelandra* Chapter 2, in which Ransom speaks to Lewis before his journey to Venus begins:

'... I rather fancy I am being sent because those two blackguards who kidnapped me and took me to Malacandra, did something which they never intended: namely, gave a human being a chance to learn that language.'

'What language do you mean?'

'*Hressa-Hlab*, of course. The language I learned in Malacandra.'

'But surely you don't imagine they will speak the same language on Venus?'

'Didn't I tell you about that?' said Ransom ... 'I'm surprised I didn't, for I found out two or three months ago, and scientifically it is one of the most interesting things about the whole affair. It appears we were quite mistaken in thinking *Hressa-Hlab* the peculiar speech of Mars. It is really what may be called Old Solar, *Hlab-Eribol-ef-Cordi*.'

'What on earth do you mean?'

'I mean that there was originally a common speech for all rational creatures inhabiting the planets of our system: those that were ever inhabited, I mean – what the eldils call the Low Worlds. ... That original speech was lost on Thulcandra, our own world, when our whole tragedy took place. No human language now known in the world is descended from it.'

For Ramer's observations on this subject see p. 203 and note 55.

15 In the original text A (still followed in B) Dolbear, waking up, says with reference to these words of Guildford's ('Incarnation. By being born'): 'Then try reincarnation, or perhaps transcarnation without loss of memory. What do you say, Ramer?'

16 *Arry*, for *Arundel*, became the name by which Lowdham was known in text C; in the earliest lists of members of the Notion Club he was simply *Harry Loudham*. For the significance of this see pp. 233–4, 281–2.

17 *New Erewhon*: *Erewhon* (= 'Nowhere') is the title of a satire by Samuel Butler (1872). *News from Nowhere*: a fantasy of the future by William Morris (1890).

18 *Turl Street* or *the Turl* is a narrow street running between High Street and Broad Street in Oxford, onto which open the gates of Ramer's college Jesus, Guildford's college Lincoln, and Exeter College.

19   In B Night 61 is Night 252, without date (see p. 149).

20   B has *Harry Loudham*: see note 16.

21   In the 'Prose Edda' the Icelander Snorri Sturluson tells of
       Skidbladnir:
              'Skíðblaðnir is the best of ships and made with great skill ...
              Certain dwarves, the sons of Ívaldi, made Skíðblaðnir and gave
              the ship to Freyr; it is so large that all the Æsir [gods] can man
              it with their weapons and equipment of war, and it has a
              favourable wind so soon as the sail is set, wherever it is bound;
              but when it is not going to sea it is made of so many pieces and
              with such great cunning that it can be folded up like a napkin
              and kept in one's pouch' (*Snorra Edda, Gylfaginning* §42).

22   The Battle of Bosworth Field (1485), in which King Richard III
       was defeated and slain by Henry Tudor (Henry VII). A has here
       'at any period before the accession of Richard II' (1377). On
       Frankley's *horror borealis* see pp. 151–2, 159.

23   '*Yes, 1938,*' *said Cameron*: in A this observation is given to
       Loudham, and rather surprisingly Latimer's comment is much as
       Guildford's in the final text: 'whose memory is like that. I doubt
       if he ever read the book. Memoirs of the courts of minor 18th
       century monarchs are his natural browsing-ground.' Yet at this
       earliest stage Loudham's interest in Norse was perhaps already
       present, since it is he who makes the joke about Skidbladnir
       immediately before. As B was written the remark was still
       attributed to Loudham, and Guildford's comment remains the
       same as in A; later Loudham was changed to Franks (the earlier
       name of Frankley) and then to Cameron. See pp. 281–2.

24   *Last Men in London* by Olaf Stapledon (1932).

25   *hnau*: rational embodied beings.

26   I have added the footnote from the third manuscript C; it
       is not in the final typescript D, but was perhaps omitted in-
       advertently.

27   In A there is no reference to the Glacier or any mention of what
       the scene in the book was; but a later addition in the margin runs:
              and the chief difference (since both were now inner) is that
              the one is tinged with sadness for it is past, but the other,
              the Glacier, is not so tinged, has only its own proper flavour,
              because it is not past or present with reference to the world.

28   In A Dolbear does not speak at this point; Ramer says: 'And the
       will to remember can be strengthened; and the memory enlarged.
       (Dolbear helped me in that: I suppose that is what made him so
       suspicious.) Now here comes another thread.' Thus neither
       Emberü nor any other name appear here in A; in B the name is
       Gyönyörü, changed subsequently to *Emberü*.

29   Following this, the text of Ramer's remarks in A and B is different
       from that in the final form. I give the B version:

A living body can move in space, but not without an effort (as in a leap), or a vehicle. A mind can move more freely and very much quicker than a living body, but not without effort of its own kind, or without a vehicle. [*Added*: This is distinct from the instantaneous movement of thought to objects already in its grasp as memory.] And Space and Time do exist as conditions for it, especially while it is incarnate, and certainly if it is (largely for that reason) interested in them and studying them. How and how far in either dimension can it jump, without a vehicle? I asked myself. It probably cannot travel in empty Space, or eventless Time (which is the duration of empty Space): it would not be aware of it, if it did, anyway. How far can it jump over it? How can it jump at all?

The mind uses the memory of its body . . .

30   For the source of Lowdham's allusion to the Pig on the Ruined Pump see the Foreword.

31   The Banbury Road leads north out of the centre of Oxford. I do not think that there was any special reason for the choice of this particular late Victorian house (the reference to it only enters in C, where my father first wrote 'No. *x* Banbury Road', changing this subsequently to 'No. 100'). Mr. Green, the putative editor of the *Papers* refers in his Foreword (p. 157) to poltergeist activity at this house in the early years of the twenty-first century.

32   *Gunthorpe Park in Matfield*: so far as I can discover, the only Matfield in England is in Kent, but there is no Gunthorpe Park in its vicinity.

33   *Emberü*: A has here: 'Not if you mean for getting such news as I put into that tale you've heard', and no name appears; B has, as at the previous occurrence (note 28) *Gyönyörü > Emberü*.

34   My father once described to me his dream of 'pure Weight', but I do not remember when that was: probably before this time.

35   Of this experience also my father spoke to me, suggesting, as does Ramer here, that the significance did not lie in the remembered passage itself. See Ramer's subsequent remarks on this topic, pp. 189 ff.

36   See pp. 157, 167. A has here: 'pictures as unlike as seeing a small flower growing and a whole world shattered'; B places the great explosion 'in the sixties'.

37   The intervention of James Jones (see p. 159) first appears in C. In B Ramer's explanation of what he meant by *deep dreams* is given in a footnote by Guildford ('Ramer said later . . .').

38   In B Dolbear replies differently to Lowdham ('If I was to reveal some of the situations I've seen you in, Harry my lad'). His pregnant remarks 'You walk in disguises, even when awake. But they'll slip, my lad, one day. I shouldn't wonder if it was fairly soon' entered in the C text.

39 A continues from this point:

... on this sort of activity – the best bits and passages, especially, those that seem to come suddenly when you're in the heat of making. They sometimes fit with an odd perfection; and sometimes good in themselves don't really fit.

B has here:

... on this sort of activity. Those scenes that come up complete and fixed, that I spoke of before, for instance. I think that those really good passages that arise, as it were, suddenly when you're abstracted, in the heat of making, are often long-prepared impromptus.

40 *it's one I made up years ago:* i.e., made up in dream.

41 In A, and (at first) in B, Ramer interpreted the first of his 'fragments' far more elaborately, giving the entire plot of the story. This is, as Ramer admitted, 'not very interesting'; and as B was first written Loudham says (in answer to Ramer's 'Do you want another case?') 'Not particularly, unless it's better than the last, which I don't expect.'

42 Geoffrey of Monmouth (died in 1155), author of *The History of the Kings of Britain*, a chief contribution to the popularity, outside the Celtic lands, of King Arthur and 'the Matter of Britain'. Such a manuscript leaf as this in Ramer's dream-narrative would be of superlative importance in the study of the Arthurian legend.

43 *Elvish Drama.* In A it is Ramer himself who speaks of 'elf-drama' ('it is not writing but elf-drama'), and again in B, which has:

'... For it is not of course writing, but a sort of realized drama. The Elvish Drama that Lewis speaks of somewhere.'

'Not Lewis, said Jeremy. 'It comes in one of those essays of the circle, but it was by one of the minor members.'

The passage in question comes from the essay *On Fairy-Stories*, which my father had delivered at the University of St. Andrews in 1939, but which was not published until two years after the writing of *The Notion Club Papers*, in the memorial volume *Essays Presented to Charles Williams* (Oxford 1947). The passage is interesting in relation to Ramer's discourse and I cite a part of it:

Now 'Faërian Drama' – those plays which according to abundant records the elves have often presented to men – can produce Fantasy with a realism and immediacy beyond the compass of any human mechanism. As a result their usual effect (upon a man) is to go beyond Secondary Belief. If you are present at a Faërian drama you yourself are, or think that you are, bodily inside its Secondary World. The experience may be very similar to Dreaming and has (it would seem) sometimes (by men) been confounded with it. But in Faërian drama you are in a dream that some other mind is weaving, and the knowledge of that alarming fact may slip from your grasp. To experience *directly* a Secondary World: the potion is too strong, and you give to it Primary Belief, however marvellous the events. You are deluded – whether that is the intention of the elves (always or at any time) is another question. They at any rate are not themselves deluded. This is for them a form of Art, and distinct from Wizardry or Magic, properly so called. J. R. R. Tolkien, *The Monsters and the Critics and Other Essays*, 1983, p. 142; cf. also p. 116 in that edition of the essay ('In dreams strange powers of the mind may be unlocked . . .').

44   *of humane shape:* texts B, C, and D all have *humane*; cf. p. 206 ('humane forms') and note 55 below.

45   Cf. my father's letter to W. H. Auden of 7 June 1955 (*Letters* no. 163):

. . . the terrible recurrent dream (beginning with memory) of the Great Wave, towering up, and coming in ineluctably over the trees and green fields. (I bequeathed it to Faramir.) I don't think I have had it since I wrote the 'Downfall of Númenor' as the last of the legends of the First and Second Age.

By 'beginning with memory' I believe that my father meant that the recurrence of the dream went as far back in his life as his memory reached. – Faramir told Éowyn of his recurrent dream of the Great Wave coming upon Númenor as they stood on the walls of Minas Tirith when the Ring was destroyed ('The Steward and the King', in *The Return of the King*, p. 240).

46   This remark of Lowdham's is absent from B and first enters in C; cf. note 38.

47   In B the footnote at this point does not derive as in the final text largely from Mr. Green but entirely from Nicholas Guildford, citing Ramer: 'Later Ramer enlarged on this point, in the course of a discussion of the various kinds of "deep dreams", and how the dreamer could distinguish them. He divided them . . .' What follows is closely similar to the later version of the note, but it ends thus: ' "Made for the Malefit of Men," he said. "To judge by the ideas men propagate now, their curious unanimity, and obsession, I should say that a terrible lot of men have thrust aside the Guardians, and are reading very maleficial stuff." N.G.' There was thus at this stage no reference to 'Night 62' (see p. 222 and note 2).

The word *maleficial* is occasionally recorded, but *malefit*, occuring in both versions of this note, is a coinage echoing *benefit*, as if ultimately derived from Latin *malefactum* 'evil deed, injury'.

48   The world *Emberü* has not been named in A (see notes 28, 33), but at this point Ramer says in A: 'The one I told you about,

Menelkemen' (Quenya, 'Sky-earth'). In this original text the description of Menelkemen is (though briefer) that given in the final text of Ellor Eshúrizel, 'that immense plain with its floor of silver', ending with the account of the great waterfall, here called *Dalud dimran* (or perhaps *dimron*), with *Eshil dimzor* written above and *Eshil külü* (> *külö*) in the margin. There is no mention here of the *En-keladim*. At the end of the description of Menelkemen Jeremy asks 'Where is it, do you think?', which in the final text he asks after Ramer's description of the third world, Minal-zidar (p. 199).

In B (as originally written) Ramer says 'The one I told you about, Emberü the golden', and here the description of Emberü is that of Minal-zidar in the final version:

'. . . I wrote that account (not the frame) some time ago, and all I'll have now is that, and stirrings and faint traces of what lies beneath: the first vision of Emberü: golden, absolutely silent and quiescent, a whole small world of perfect form, imperishable in Time . . .'

This description of Emberü ends, as does that of Minal-zidar in the final text, with 'made by what adoring mind I cannot tell'; then follows: 'And there was Menel-kemen.'

At this point in B my father stopped, struck out what he had written about 'the first vision of Emberü', and wrote instead: 'the first vision of Emberü: that immense plain with its silver floor all delicately patterned . . .' – which in the final text is the description of Ellor Eshúrizel. Here the great waterfall is called *Öshül-külö*, and Ramer says: 'I think the Enkeladim dwell there.' My father then inserted in B, after 'the first vision of Emberü', the words ' "It is the same with Ellor. Ellor!" he murmured. "Ellor Eshúrizel! I drew it once in words as best I could, and now it *is* words. That immense plain with its silver floor . . .'; and (all these changes being made at the time of composition) introduced at the end of the description of Ellor the third world, 'Minal-zidar the golden'.

Thus the images were developed and separated into distinct 'world-entities' in rapid succession. In A *Menelkemen* is the only world that Ramer describes, the world of the story that he had read to the Notion Club, the inorganic, harmonious world of metal, stone, and water, with the great waterfall. In B the world that Ramer described in his story is *Emberü* (replacing *Gyönyörü* of the earlier parts of the manuscript), the silent 'golden' world; but this was changed immediately (reverting to A) to make Emberü 'that immense plain with its silver floor', and then changed again to make this description that of a second world, *Ellor Eshúrizel*, while the 'golden' world becomes a third scene, *Minal-zidar*. The final stage was to call the first world *Green*

Emberü, 'where there was a kind of organic life, rich but wholesome and longeval.'

49 On the *En-keladim* see p. 206 and notes 64, 65, and pp. 397, 400.

50 *the Fields of Arbol*: the Solar System in Lewis's novels (see note 13).

51 In A it is Dolbear, not Loudham, who asks: 'Where do you get all these names from? Who told you them? That [would] interest me more really than the geometry and landscape. I should, of course as you know, use my chance if I got into such a state for language-research.' In B this was still said by Dolbear, changed to Guildford and then to Loudham. See p. 151.

52 At this point both A and B continue with an account of Jeremy's attempt to arouse interest in the works of Lewis and Williams, which in the final text is put into a footnote of Guildford's here. I give the text of B, which follows that of A very closely but is clearer.

'*Arbol* is "Old Solar" for the Sun,' said Jeremy. 'Do you mean that you can get back to Old Solar, [*struck out:* or Old Universal,] and that Lewis was right?'

Jeremy was our Lewis-expert, and knew all his works, almost by heart. Many in Oxford will still remember how he had, a year or two before, given some remarkable lectures on Lewis and Williams. People had laughed at the title, because Lewis and all that circle had dropped badly out of fashion. Old Bell-Tinker, who was still Chairman of the English Board then, had boggled and puffed at it. 'If you must touch such a subject,' he snorted, 'call it Lewis and cut it Short.'

Jeremy had retorted by offering to change the title to 'Lewis and Carolus or the Oxford Looking-glass'. 'Or "Jack and the Beanstalk", if you like,' he added, but that was too recondite a joke for the English Board. I believe, before Jeremy spoke up, few even of the Twentieth Century experts could have named any work of Williams, except perhaps *The Octopus*. That was still occasionally played, because of the great revival of missionary interest after the Far-eastern martyrdoms in the sixties. *The Allegory of Love* was all of Lewis that the academicians ever mentioned (as a rule unread and slightingly). The other minor lights were only known by the few who read old C. R. Tolkien's little books of memoirs: *In the Roaring Forties*, and *The Inns and Outs of Oxford*. But Jeremy had made most of our club read some of those people (the Public-house School as it was called); though beside Jeremy only Ramer and Dolbear bothered with Tolkien père and all the elvish stuff.

'"Old Solar"?' said Ramer. 'Well, no. . . .

'Old Bell-Tinker' derives his name from a book of translations of

Anglo-Saxon literature by Bell and Tinker. His very bad joke 'call it Lewis and cut it Short' refers to the *Latin Dictionary* by Lewis and Short. The title of Jeremy's lectures, which aroused laughter, is omitted, but was presumably the same as in the final text, *The Public-house School* (because the Inklings met in pubs). 'Few bothered with Tolkien père and all the elvish stuff' was doubtless no more than a self-deprecating joke – but implies that the 'elvish stuff' had at least been published! (cf. p. 303 and note 14). *In the Roaring Forties* is a pun on the name of the regions of the southern oceans, between forty and fifty degrees south, where there are great winds.

53　Since Ramer's criticism of the standard of linguistic invention characteristic of tales of space-travel and time-travel follows immediately on his denial that there could be any such language as Old Solar, he appears to be including Lewis in his criticism. Some years before, however, in his letter to Stanley Unwin of 4 March 1938 (*Letters* no. 26), my father had said of *Out of the Silent Planet*:

> The author holds to items of linguistic invention that do not appeal to me . . .; but this is a matter of taste. After all your reader found my invented names, made with cherished care, eye-splitting. But the linguistic inventions and the philology on the whole are more than good enough. All the part about language and poetry – the glimpses of its Malacandrian nature and form – is very well done, and extremely interesting, far superior to what one usually gets from travellers in untravelled regions. The language difficulty is usually slid over or fudged. Here it not only has verisimilitude, but also underlying thought.

54　*Glund:* the name of Jupiter in Old Solar (also *Glundandra*).

55　*I think there might be an Old Human, or Primitive Adamic* . . .: A has here: 'But I think there might be, certainly was, an Old Humane or Adamic. But it could not possibly be the same as the Prime Language of Hrossa, *Hressa-hlab*.' This was retained in B (with Old Human for Old Humane: see note 44). The *Hrossa* were one of the three totally distinct kinds of *hnau* found on Malacandra; the language of the Hrossa was *Hressa-hlab*, which is 'Old Solar': see note 14.

56　*Old Universal:* see the beginning of the passage given in note 52.

57　*En:* this name appears already in A, with various predecessors, *An, Nor, El*, all struck out immediately.

58　*Gormok, Zingil:* in A Ramer's name for Mars is the Elvish word *Karan* ('red'); Venus was *Zingil* in A, though immediately replacing another name that cannot be read.

59　In A it is Jeremy who speaks at this point, asking: 'How do you know you've been there?' And Ramer replies: 'I don't: I have seen the places, not been there. My body's never travelled. I have seen the places either indirectly through other records, as you could say you'd seen Hongkong if you'd looked at many long accurate coloured films of it; or directly by using light. But how I know what the places are is another matter.'

60   Saturn is not mentioned in A. B has: 'And *Gyürüchill*, Saturn, is unmistakable'. *Gyürüchill* was changed to *Shomorú*, and then to old *Eneköl*.

61   *The Cronic Star* (in the footnote by Guildford at this point): Saturn (in astrology the leaden planet). *Cronic* is derived from *Kronos*, the Greek god (father of Zeus) identified by the Romans with Saturn; wholly distinct etymologically from *chronic*, derived from Greek *chronos* 'time'.

62   On the 'Fluted Wave' see p. 194.

63   In A Ramer says here: 'I could tell you about Atlantis (though that's not its name to me, nor Númenor): it is connected with that Fluted Wave. And the Door ᛏ [which is connected with the Meg(alithic) >] of the Megalithic is too.' In B he speaks as in the final text, but says again 'though that's not its name to me, nor Númenor' – the last two words being later strongly struck out, and Loudham's question (asked with 'a curious eagerness') 'What *is* its name?' inserted (when the peculiar association of Lowdham with Númenor had entered: see notes 38, 46). In the final text of the *Papers* the emergence of the name *Númenor* is postponed until Part Two (p. 231).

64   A has here: 'But I've seen my Mârim [*changed probably at once to* Albarim] playing one of their Albar-plays: the drama of the Silver Tree.' In A the name *En-keladim* has not occurred (see note 48). With 'the Drama of the Silver Tree' cf. the citation from *On Fairy-Stories* given in note 43.

65   In A Ramer says: 'I don't think that's invented: not by me anyway. It seems to take place on this earth in some time or mode or [?place].' In A he goes straight on from 'Atlantis' to his final story.

In B Ramer comments on the Drama of the Silver Tree as in the final text, as far as 'something like it really happens, and I have seen it, far off perhaps or faintly.' Then follows:

I guess that the true types of my Enkeladim are invisible, unless they turn their attention to you. That is, they are Eldilic in Lewis's terms, in some lesser rank [*added:* or perhaps like Tolkien's Unfallen Elves, only they were embodied].

All this was struck out, and replaced on a rider by the final text, as far as 'entering as it were into their own works because of their love for them.' Then follows: 'that is, that they are of a kind other than Lewis's Eldila (even of lesser rank); and yet not the same as Tolkien's Unfallen Elves, for those were embodied.'

The original B text continues with 'I think [Emberü >] Ellor is one of their worlds ...', as in the final form. Against *Ellor* is a footnote:

    Ramer said that it was queer how the syllable cropped up: first in Tolkien's Eldar, Eldalie, then in Lewis's Eldil, and then in his Ellor. He thought it *might* be an 'elvish' or Keladian word. The Enkeladim are language-makers. NG.

66   Here the fair copy manuscript C ends, and the typescript D from here on follows B (see p. 146).

67   In A the name was *Tekel-Ishtar*, becoming *Tekel-Mirim* before the manuscript was completed.

68   Thomas Huxley, *Physiography*, 1877, cited in the *Oxford English Dictionary*.

69   The Radcliffe Camera, a great circular domed building standing in Radcliffe Square, Oxford, on the south side of which stands St. Mary's church and on the north side the Bodleian Library. *Camera* is used in the Latin sense 'arched or vaulted roof or chamber' (Latin *camera* > French *chambre*, English *chamber*).

[PART TWO][1]

Night 62.[2]   Thursday, March 6th, 1987. [Of this meeting only half a torn sheet is preserved. The relevant part will be found in the note to Night 61, p. 195. There appears to have been further discussion of Ramer's views and adventures.]

Night 63.   Thursday, March 13th, 1987. [Only the last page of the record of this meeting is preserved. The discussion seems to have proceeded to legendary voyages of discovery in general. For the reference to the *imrám* see Night (69).][3]

[Good] night Frankley!'

    Lowdham seemed to feel a bit guilty about his ragging; and when the meeting finally broke up, he walked up the High with Ramer and myself. We turned into Radcliffe Square.[4]

    'Played the ass as usual, Ramer,' said Lowdham. 'Sorry! I felt all strung up: wanted a fight, or a carouse, or something. But really I was very interested, especially about the *imrám*.[5] Underneath we Nordics[6] have some feelings, as long as the Dago-fanciers will only be reasonably polite.' He hesitated. 'I've had some rather odd experiences – well, perhaps we'll talk about it some other time. It's late. But in the vac. perhaps?'

'I shall be going away,' said Ramer, a trifle coldly, 'till after Easter.'

'Oh well. But do come to the meetings next term! You must have lots more to tell us. I'll try and be good.'

It was a cool clear night after a windy day. It was starry in the west, but the moon was already climbing. At B.N.C.[7] gate Lowdham turned. The Camera looked vast and dark against the moonlit sky. Wisps of long white cloud were passing on an easterly breeze. For a moment one of them seemed to take the shape of a plume of smoke issuing from the lantern of the dome.

Lowdham looked up, and his face altered. His tall powerful figure appeared taller and broader as he stood there, gazing, with his dark brows drawn down. His face seemed pale and angry, and his eyes glittered.

'Curse him! May the Darkness take him!' he said bitterly. 'May the earth open ——' The cloud passed away. He drew his hand over his brow. 'I was going to say,' he said. 'Well, I don't remember. Something about the Camera, I think. Doesn't matter. Good night, chaps!' He knocked, and passed in through the door.

We turned up along the lane. 'Very odd!' I said. 'What a queer fellow he is sometimes! A strange mixture.'

'He is,' said Ramer. 'Most of what we see is a tortoise-shell: armourplate. He doesn't talk much about what he really cares for.'

'For some reason the last two or three meetings seem to have stirred him up, unsettled him,' I said. 'I can't think why.'

'I wonder,' said Ramer. 'Well, good night, Nick. I'll see you again next term. I hope to start attending regularly again.' We parted at the Turl end of the lane.

PF. RD. AAL. MGR. WTJ. JJR. NG.

Night 64. Thursday, March 27th, 1987.[8]

There was only one meeting in the vacation. Guildford's rooms. Neither Ramer nor Lowdham were present (it was a quiet evening). Guildford read a paper on Jutland in antiquity; but there was not much discussion. [No record of the paper is found in the minutes.]

PF. WTJ. JM. RS. JJ. RD. NG.

Night 65. Thursday, May 8th, 1987.[9]

This was the first meeting of Trinity term. We met in Frankley's rooms in Queen's. Jeremy and Guildford arrived first (in time); others arrived one by one at intervals (late). There was nothing definite on for the evening, though we had hoped for some more talk from Ramer; but he seemed disinclined to say anything further. Conversation hopped about during the first hour, but was not notable.

Lowdham was restless, and would not sit down; at intervals he burst into a song (with which he had, in fact, entered at about half past nine). It began:

> *I've got a very Briny Notion*
> *To drink myself to sleep.*

It seldom progressed further, and never got beyond:

> *Bring me my bowl, my magic potion!*
> *Tonight I'm diving deep.*
> *down! down! down!*
> *Down where the dream-fish go.*

It was not well received, least of all by Ramer. But Lowdham subsided eventually, into a moody silence – for a while.

About ten o'clock the talk turned to neologisms; and Lowdham re-entered in their defence, chiefly because Frankley was taking the other side. (No. Pure love of truth and justice. AAL)

Lowdham to Frankley: 'You say you object to *panting*, which all the younger people use now for *desire* or *wish*?'

'Yes, I do. And especially to *having a great pant for* anything; or worse *having great pants for* it.'

'Well, I don't think you've got any good grounds for your objection: nothing better than novelty or unfamiliarity. New words are always objected to, like new art.'

'Nonsense! Double nonsense, Arry!' said Ramer.[10] 'Frankley is complaining precisely because new words are *not* objected to. And anyway, I personally object to lots of old words, but I have to go on using 'em, because they're current, and people won't accept my substitutes. I dislike many products of old art. I like many new things but not all. There is such a thing as merit, without reference to age or to familiarity. I took to *doink* at once: a very good onomatopoeia for some purposes.'

'Yes, *doink* has come on a lot lately,' said Lowdham. 'But it's not brand-new, of course. I think it's first recorded, in the Third

Supplement to the N.E.D.,[11] in the fifties, in the form *dŏing*: seems to have started in the Air Force in the Six Years' War.'[12]

'And it's an onomatopoeia, mark you,' said Frankley. 'It's easy to appraise the merits of that kind of word, if you can call it a real word. Anyway, adopting that is not at all on all fours with misusing an established word, robbing Peter to relieve the poverty of Paul: lexicographical socialism, which would end by reducing the whole vocabulary to one flat drab Unmeaning, if there were no reactionaries.'

'And won't anybody give poor Peter his pants back?' Lowdham laughed. 'He's got some more pairs in the cupboard, you'll see. He'll just have to take to wearing modern *whaffing* and *whooshing*. And why not? Do you object to Language, root and branch, Pip? I'm surprised at you, and you a poet and all.'

'Of course I don't! But I object to ruining it.'

'But are you ruining it? Is it any worse off with *panting: whaffing* than with *longing:panting*? This is not only the way language is changed, it is how it was made. Essentially it consists in the contemplation of a relationship "sound : sense; symbol : meaning". It's not only when this is new (to you at any rate) that you can appraise it. At inspired moments you can catch it, get the thrill of it, in familiar words. I grant that an onomatopoeia is a relatively simple case: *whaff*. But "*to pant for* equals *to long for*" contains the same element: new phonetic form for a meaning. Only here a second thing comes in: the interest, pleasure, excitement, what you will, of the relation of old sense to new. Both are illumined, for a time, at any rate. Language could never have come into existence without the one process, and never have extended its grasp without the other. Both must go on! They will, too.'

'Well, I don't like this example of the activity,' said Frankley. 'And I detest it, when philologues talk about Language (with a capital L) with that peculiarly odious unction usually reserved for capitalized Life. That we are told "must go on" − if we complain of any debased manifestations, such as Arry in his cups. He talks about Language as if it was not only a Jungle but a Sacred Jungle, a beastly grove dedicated to Vita Fera,[13] in which nothing must be touched by impious hands. Cankers, fungi, parasites: let 'em alone!

'Languages are *not* jungles. They are gardens, in which sounds selected from the savage wilderness of Brute Noise are turned into words, grown, trained, and endued with the scents of significance. You talk as if I could not pull up a weed that stinks!'

'I do not!' said Lowdham. 'But, first of all, you have to remember that it's not *your* garden – if you must have this groggy allegory: it belongs to a lot of other people as well, and to them your stinking weed may be an object of delight. More important: your allegory is misapplied. What you are objecting to is not a weed, but the soil, and also any manifestations of growth and spread. All the other words in your refined garden have come into being (and got their scent) in the same way. You're like a man who is fond of flowers and fruit, but thinks loam is dirty, and dung disgusting; and the uprising and the withering just too, too sad. You want a sterilized garden of immortelles, no, paper-flowers. In fact, to leave allegory, you won't learn anything about the history of your own language, and hate to be reminded that it has one.'[14]

'Slay me with pontifical thunder-bolts!' cried Frankley. 'But I'll die saying *I don't like pants for longings.*'

'That's the stuff!' laughed Lowdham. 'And you're right of course, Pip. Both are right: the Thunder and the Rebel. For the One Speaker, all alone, is the final court of doom for words, to bless or to condemn. It's the agreement only of the separate judges that seems to make the laws. If your distaste is shared by an effective number of the others, then *pants* will prove – a weed, and be thrust in the oven.

'Though, of course, many people – more and more, I sometimes feel, as Time goes on and even language stales – do not judge any longer, they only echo. Their native language, as Ramer would call it, dies almost at their birth.

'It's not so with you, Philip my lad; you're ignorant, but you have a heart. I dare say *pants* just doesn't fit your native style. So it has always been with full men: they have had their hatreds among the words, and their loves.'

'You talk almost as if you'd seen or heard Language since its beginning, Arry,' said Ramer, looking at him with some surprise. It was a long time since Lowdham had let himself go at such length.

'No! Not since its beginning,' said Lowdham, while a strange expression came over his face. 'Only since – but ... Oh well!' He broke off and went to the window. It was dark but clear as glass in the sky, and there were many white stars.

The conversation drifted again. Starting from the beginnings of Language, we began to talk about legends of origins and cultural myths. Guildford and Markison began to have an argument about Corn-gods and the coming of divine kings or heroes over the sea, in spite of various frivolous interjections from Lowdham, who seemed curiously averse to the turn of the talk.

'The Sheaf personified,'* said Guild[ford. Here unfortunately one leaf is missing.] ......

[Jeremy] .... 'as you said. But I don't think one can be so sure. Sometimes I have a queer feeling that, if one could go back, one would find not myth dissolving into history, but rather the reverse: real history becoming more mythical – more shapely, simple, discernibly significant, even seen at close quarters. More poetical, and less prosaic, if you like.

'In any case, these ancient accounts, legends, myths, about the far Past, about the origins of kings, laws, and the fundamental crafts, are not all made of the same ingredients. They're not wholly inventions. And even what is invented is different from mere fiction; it has more roots.'

'Roots in what?' said Frankley.

'In Being, I think I should say,' Jeremy answered; 'and in human Being; and coming down the scale, in the springs of History and in the designs of Geography – I mean, well, in the pattern of our world as it uniquely is, and of the events in it as seen from a distance. A sort of parallel to the fact that from far away the Earth would be seen as a revolving sunlit globe; and that is a remote truth of enormous effect on us and all we do, though not immediately discernible on earth, where practical men are quite right in regarding the surface as flat and immovable for practical purposes.

'Of course, the pictures presented by the legends may be partly symbolical, they may be arranged in designs that compress, expand, foreshorten, combine, and are not at all realistic or photographic, yet they may tell you something true about the Past.

'And mind you, there are also real details, what are called facts, accidents of land-shape and sea-shape, of individual men and their actions, that are caught up: the grains on which the stories crystallize like snowflakes. There was a man called Arthur at the centre of the cycle.'

* [See Night 66, p. 236.]

'Perhaps!' said Frankley. 'But that doesn't make such things as the Arthurian romances real in the same way as true past events are real.'

'I didn't say *in the same way*,' said Jeremy. 'There are secondary planes or degrees.'

'And what do you know about "true past events", Philip?' asked Ramer. 'Have you ever seen one, when once it was past? They are all stories or tales now, aren't they, if you try to bring them back into the present? Even your idea of what you did yesterday – if you try to share it with anyone else? Unless, of course, you can go back, or at least see back.'

'Well, I think there's a difference between what really happened at our meetings and Nicholas's record,' said Frankley. 'I don't think his reports erase the true history, whether they're true in their fashion to the events or not. And didn't you claim to be able sometimes to re-view the past as a present thing? Could you go back into Guildford's minutes?'

'Hmm,' Ramer muttered, considering. 'Yes and no,' he said. 'Nicholas could, especially into the scenes that he's pictured or re-pictured fairly solidly and put some mental work into. We could, if we did the same. People of the future, if they only knew the records and studied them, and let their imagination work on them, till the Notion Club became a sort of secondary world set in the Past: they could.'

'Yes, Frankley,' said Jeremy, 'you've got to make a distinction between lies, or casual fiction, or the mere verbal trick of projecting sentences back by putting the verbs into the past tense, between all that and *construction*. Especially of the major kind that has acquired a secondary life of its own and passes from mind to mind.'

'Quite so!' said Ramer. 'I don't think you realize, I don't think any of us realize, the force, the daimonic force that the great myths and legends have. From the profundity of the emotions and perceptions that begot them, and from the multiplication of them in many minds – and each mind, mark you, an engine of obscured but unmeasured energy. They are like an explosive: it may slowly yield a steady warmth to living minds, but if suddenly detonated, it might go off with a crash: yes: might produce a disturbance in the real primary world.'

'What sort of thing are you thinking of?' said Dolbear, lifting his beard off his chest, and opening his eyes with a gleam of passing interest.

'I wasn't thinking of any particular legend,' said Ramer. 'But, well, for instance, think of the emotional force generated all down the west rim of Europe by the men that came at last to the end, and looked on the Shoreless Sea, unharvested, untraversed, unplumbed! And against that background what a prodigious stature other events would acquire! Say, the coming, apparently out of that Sea, riding a storm, [of] strange men of superior knowledge, steering yet unimagined ships. And if they bore tales of catastrophe far away: battles, burned cities, or the whelming of lands in some tumult of the earth – it shakes me to think of such things in such terms, even now.'

'Yes, I'm moved by that,' said Frankley. 'But it's large and vague. I'm still stuck a good deal nearer home, in Jeremy's casual reference to King Arthur. There you have a sort of legendary land, but it's quite unreal.'

'But you'll allow, won't you,' said Ramer, 'that the Britain of Arthur, as now imagined, even in a debased when-knights-were-bold sort of form, has some kind of force and life?'

'Some kind of literary attraction,' said Frankley. 'But could you go back to King Arthur's Camelot, even on your system? Of which, by the way, I'm not yet convinced: I mean, what you've told us seems to me very likely no more than an exceptionally elaborate, and exceptionally well-remembered form of what I call "dreaming" simply: picture-and-story-spinning while asleep.'

'And anyway: if legend (significant on its own plane) has gathered about history (with its own importance), which would you go back to? Which would you see, if you saw back?' asked Guildford.

'It depends on what you yourself are like, and on what you are looking for, I imagine,' Ramer answered. 'If you were seeking the story that has most power and significance for human minds, then probably that is the version that you'ld find.

'Anyway, I think you could – I think I could go back to Camelot, *if* the conditions of my mind and the chances of travel were favourable. The chances are not, as I told you, more than very slightly affected by waking desire. An adventure of that sort would *not* be the same thing as re-viewing what you'ld call Fifth-century Britain. Neither would it be like making a dream-drama of my own. It would be more like the first, but it would be more active. It would be much less free than the second. It would probably be more difficult than either. I fancy it might be the sort of thing best done by one or two people in concert.'

'I don't see how that would help,' said Frankley.

'Because different people have different views, or have indi-vidual contributions to make: is that what you mean?' asked Guildford. 'But that would be just as true of historical research or "backsight".'

'No, it wouldn't,' said Jeremy. 'You're mixing up history in the sense of a story made up out of the intelligible surviving evidence (which is not necessarily truer to the facts than legend) and "the true story", the real Past. If you really had a look back at the Past as it was, then everything would be there to see, if you had eyes for it, or time to observe it in. And the most difficult thing to see would be, as it always is "at present", the pattern, the significance, yes, the moral of it all, if you like. At least that would be the case, the nearer you come to our time. As I said before, I'm not so sure about that, as you pass backward to the beginnings. But in such a thing as a great story-cycle the situation would be different: much would be vividly real and at the same time ... er ... portentous; but there might be, would be, uncompleted passages, weak joints, gaps. You'd have to consolidate. You might need help.'

'You might indeed!' said Frankley. 'Riding down from Came-lot (when you had discovered just where that was) to most other places on the legendary map, you'd find the road pretty vague. Most of the time you'd be lost in a fog! And you'd meet some pretty sketchy characters about the court, too.'

'Of course! And so you would about the present court,' said Markison, 'or in any Oxford quadrangle. Why should that worry you? Sketchy characters are more true to life than fully studied ones. There are precious few people in real life that you know as well as a good writer knows his heroes and villains.'

'Riding down to Camelot. Riding out from Camelot,' mur-mured Lowdham. 'And there was a dark shadow over that too. I wonder, I wonder. But it is still only a tale to me. Not all legends are like that. No, unfortunately. Some seem to have come to life on their own, and they will not rest. I should hate to be cast back into some of those lands. It would be worse than the vision of poor Norman Keeps.'

'What on earth is he talking about now?' said Guildford.

'The cork's coming out pretty soon, I think,' grunted Dolbear without opening his eyes.

'Oh, Norman Keeps is our barber,'[15] said Frankley. 'At least that's what Arry and I call him: no idea what his real name is. Quite a nice and moderately intelligent little man: but to him everything beyond a certain vague distance back is a vast dark barren but utterly fixed and determined land and time called The Dark Ages. There are only four features in it: Norman Keeps (by which he means baronial castles, and possibly the house of any man markedly richer than himself); Them Jameses (meaning roughly I suppose the kings One and Two); The Squires (a curious kind of bogey-folk); and The People. Nothing ever happened in that land but Them Jameses shutting up The People in the Keeps (with the help of The Squires) and there torturing them and robbing them, though they don't appear ever to have possessed anything to be robbed of. Rather a gloomy legend. But it's a great deal more fixed in a lot more heads than is the Battle of Camlan!'[16]

'I know, I know,' said Lowdham loudly and angrily. 'It's a shame! Norman Keeps is a very decent chap, and would rather learn truth than lies. But Zigūr[17] pays special attention to the type. Curse him!'

Conversation stopped, and there was a silence. Ramer and Guildford exchanged glances. Dolbear opened his eyes quietly without moving his head.

'Zigūr?' said Jeremy, looking at Lowdham. 'Zigūr? Who is he?'

'No idea, no idea!' said Lowdham. 'Is this a new game, Jerry? Owlamoo,[18] who's he?' He strode to the window and flung it open.

The early summer night was still and glimmering, warmer than usual for the time of year. Lowdham leant out, and we turned and stared at his back. The large window looked west, and the two towers of All Souls' stuck up like dim horns against the stars.

Suddenly Lowdham spoke in a changed voice, clear and ominous, words in an unknown tongue; and then turning fiercely upon us he cried aloud:

Behold the Eagles of the Lords of the West! They are coming over Nūmenōr![19]

We were all startled. Several of us went to the window and stood behind Lowdham, looking out. A great cloud, coming up slowly out of the West, was eating up the stars. As it approached it opened two vast sable wings, spreading north and south.

Suddenly Lowdham pulled away, slammed the window down, and drew the curtains. He slumped into a chair and shut his eyes.

We returned to our seats and sat there uncomfortably for some time without a sound. At last Ramer spoke.

'*Nūmenōr? Nūmenōr?*' he said quietly. 'Where did you find that name, Arundel Lowdham?'

'Oh, I don't know,' Lowdham answered, opening his eyes, and looking round with a rather dazed expression. 'It comes to me, now and again. Just on the edge of things, you know. Eludes the grasp. Like coming round after gas. But it's been turning up more often than usual this spring. I'm sorry. Have I been behaving oddly or something, not quite my old quiet friendly self? Give me a drink!'

'I asked,' said Ramer, 'because *Nūmenōr* is my name for Atlantis.'[20]

'Now that *is* odd!' began Jeremy.

'Ah!' said Lowdham. 'I wondered if it might be. I asked you what your name was that night last term; but you didn't answer.'

'Well, here's a new development!' said Dolbear, who was now wide awake. 'If Arry Lowdham is going to dive where the dreams go and find the same fish as Ramer, we shall have to look into the pool.'

'We shall,' said Jeremy; 'for it's not only Ramer and Arry. I come into it too. I knew I had heard that name as soon as Arry said it.[21] But I can't for the life of me remember where or when at the moment. It'll bother me now, like a thorn in the foot, until I get it out.'

'Very queer,' said Dolbear.

'What do you propose to do?' said Ramer.

'Take your advice,' said Jeremy. 'Get your help, if you'll give it.'

'Go into memory-training on the Rufus-Ramer system and see what we can fish up,' said Lowdham. 'I feel as if something wants to get out, and I should be glad to get it out – or forget it.'

'I'm a bit lost in all this,' said Markison. 'I've missed something evidently. Philip has told me a bit about the Ramer revelations last term, but I'm still rather at sea. Couldn't you tell us something, Lowdham, to make things a little clearer?'

'No, really, I'm feeling frightfully tired,' said Lowdham. 'You had better read up the records, if Nick has written them out yet.[22] I expect he has. He's pretty regular, and pretty accurate, if a bit hard on me. And come along to the next meeting. And we'd better make that in a fortnight's time, I think. You can have my room, if you think you can all get in. We'll see what we have got by then. I've nothing much to tell yet.'

The conversation then dropped back uncertainly towards the normal, and nothing further occurred worth noting.

As we went out Lowdham said to Ramer: 'D'you think I could come round and talk to you, and to Rufus, some time soon?'

'Yes,' said Ramer. 'The sooner the better. You come too, Jeremy.'

MGR. PF. RD. JM. JJ. RS. AAL. WTJ. NG.

Night 66.   Thursday, May 22nd, 1987.

A crowded evening. Lowdham's rather small room was pretty packed. The idea of Arry 'seeing things' was sufficiently astonishing to attract every member who was in Oxford. (Also I am supposed to keep more bottles in my cupboard than some that I could name. AAL)

Lowdham seemed in a bright and rather noisy mood again; reluctant to do anything but sing. Eventually he was quietened and got into a chair.

'Well now,' said Markison, 'I've read the records. I can't say I've made my mind up about them yet; but I'm very interested to hear how you come into such business, Arry. It doesn't seem in your line.'

'Well, I'm a philologist,' said Lowdham, 'which means a misunderstood man. But where I come in is, I think, at the point you've mentioned: at *Arry*. The name Arry, which some of you are pleased to attach to me, is *not* just a tribute to my vulgar noisiness, as seems assumed by the more ignorant among you: it is short not for Henry or Harold, but for Arundel. In full *Alwin Arundel Lowdham* your humble jester, at your service.'

'Well, what has that got to do with it?' said several voices.

'I'm not quite sure yet,' said Lowdham. 'But my father's name was Edwin.'[23]

'Illuminating indeed!' said Frankley.

'Not very, I think,' said Lowdham. 'Not illuminating, but puzzling. My father was an odd sort of man, as far as I remember. Large, tall, powerful, dark. Don't stare at me! I'm a reduced copy. He was wealthy, and combined a passion for the sea with learning of a sort, linguistic and archaeological. He must have studied Anglo-Saxon and other North-western tongues; for I inherited his library and some of his tastes.

'We lived in Pembrokeshire, near Penian:[24] more or less, for we were away a large part of the year; and my father was always going off at a moment's notice: he spent a great deal of his time sailing about Norway, Scotland, Ireland, Iceland, and sometimes southward to the Azores and so on. I did not know him well, though I loved him as much as a small boy can, and used to dream of the time when I could go sailing with him. But he disappeared when I was only nine.'

'Disappeared?' said Frankley. 'I thought you told me once that he was lost at sea.'

'He disappeared,' said Lowdham. 'A strange story. No storm. His ship just vanished into the Atlantic. That was in 1947, just forty years ago next month. No signals (he wouldn't use wireless, anyway). No trace. No news. She was called *The Éarendel*.[25] An odd business.'

'The seas were still pretty dangerous at that time, weren't they?' said Stainer. 'Mines all over the place?'

'Not a spar at any rate was ever found,' said Lowdham. 'That was the end of *The Éarendel*: a queer name, and a queer end. But my father had some queer fancies about names. I am called Alwin Arundel, a mouthful enough, out of deference to prudence and my mother, I believe. The names he chose were Ælfwine Éarendel.

'One of the few conversations I remember having with him was just before he went off for the last time. I had begged to go with him, and he had said NO, of course. "When can I go?" I said.

'"Not yet, Ælfwine," he said. "Not yet. Some time, perhaps. Or you may have to follow me."

'It was then that it came out about my names. "I modernized 'em," he said, "to save trouble. But my ship bears the truer name. It does not look to Sussex,[26] but to shores a great deal further off. Very far away indeed now. A man has more freedom in naming his ship than his own son in these days. And it's few men that have either to name."

'He went off next day. He was mad to be at sea again, as he had been kept ashore all through the Six Years' War,[27] from the summer of 1939 onward, except I believe just at the Dunkirk time in 1940. Too old – he was fifty when the war broke out, and I was only a year; for he had married late – too old, and I fancy a good deal too free and unbiddable to get any particular job, and he had become fiercely restless. He only took three sailors with him,[28] I think, but of course I don't know how he found them, or how they ever managed to get off, in those days of tyranny. I fancy they just cleared out illegally, somehow. Whither, I wonder? I don't think they meant to return. Anyway I never saw him again.'

'I can't see the connexion of this thread at all yet,' said Guildford.

'Wait a bit!' said Ramer. 'There is a connexion, or we think so. We've discussed it. You'd better let Arundel have his say.'

'Well – as soon as he'd gone ... I was only nine at the time, as I said, and I had never bothered much about books, let alone languages, naturally at that age. I could read, of course, but I seldom did ... as soon as my father had gone, and we knew that it was for good, I began to take up with languages, especially making them up (as I thought). After a time I used to stray into his study, left for years it was, just as it had been when he was alive.

'There I learned a lot of odd things in a desultory way, and I came across some sort of a diary or notes in a queer script. I don't know what happened to it when my mother died. I only found one loose leaf of it among the papers that came to me. I've kept it for years, and often tried and failed to read it; but it is mislaid at present. I was about fourteen or fifteen when I got specially taken with Anglo-Saxon, for some reason. I liked its word-style, I think. It wasn't so much what was written in it as the flavour of the words that suited me. But I was first introduced to it by trying to find out more about the names. I didn't get much light on them.

'*Éadwine* friend of fortune? *Ælfwine* elf-friend? That at any rate is what their more or less literal translation comes to. Though, as most of you will know (except poor Philip), these two-part names are pretty conventional, and not too much can be built on their literal meaning.'

'But they must originally have been made to have a meaning,' said Ramer. 'The habit of joining, apparently at random, any two of a list of beginners and enders, giving you Spear-peace and Peace-wolf and that sort of thing, must have been a later development, a kind of dried-up verbal heraldry. *Ælfwine* any-

way is one of the old combinations. It occurs outside England,
doesn't it?'

'Yes,' said Lowdham. 'And so does *Éadwine*. But I could not
see that any of the many recorded Ælfwines were very suitable:
Ælfwine, grandson of King Alfred, for instance, who fell in the
great victory of 937; or Ælfwine who fell in the famous defeat
of Maldon, and many others; not even Ælfwine of Italy, that
is Albuin son of Auduin, the grim Langobard of the sixth
century.'[29]

'Don't forget the connexion of the Langobards with King
Sheaf,'[30] put in Markison, who was beginning to show signs of
interest.

'I don't,' said Lowdham. 'But I was talking of my earliest
investigations as a boy.'

'Nor the repetition of the sequence: Albuin son of Auduin;
Ælfwine son of Éadwine; Alwin son of Edwin,' said Ramer.[31]

'Probably deliberately imitated from the well-known story of
Rosamund,'[32] objected Philip Frankley. 'Arry's father must have
known it. And that's quite enough to explain Alwin and Ælfwine,
when you're dealing with a family of Nordic philologues.'

'Perhaps, O Horsefriend of Macedon!'[33] said Lowdham. 'But
it doesn't take in *Éarendel*. There's little to be found out about
that in Anglo-Saxon, though the name is there all right. Some
guess that it was really a star-name for Orion, or for Rigel.[34] A
ray, a brilliance, the light of dawn: so run the glosses.[35]

Éalá Éarendel engla beorhtost
ofer middangeard monnum sended!'

he chanted. ' "Hail Earendel, brightest of angels, above the
middle-earth sent unto men!" When I came across that citation
in the dictionary I felt a curious thrill, as if something had
stirred in me, half wakened from sleep. There was something
very remote and strange and beautiful behind those words, if I
could grasp it, far beyond ancient English.

'I know more now, of course. The quotation comes from the
Crist; though exactly what the author meant is not so certain.[36]
It is beautiful enough in its place. But I don't think it is any
irreverence to say that it may derive its curiously moving quality
from some older world.'

'Why *irreverent*?' said Markison. 'Even if the words do refer
to Christ, of course they are all derived from an older pre-
christian world, like all the rest of the language.'

'That's so,' said Lowdham; 'but *Éarendel* seems to me a

special word. It is not Anglo-Saxon;[37] or rather, it is not *only* Anglo-Saxon, but also something else much older.

'I think it is a remarkable case of linguistic coincidence, or congruence. Such things do occur, of course. I mean, in two different languages, quite unconnected, and where no borrowing from one to the other is possible, you will come across words very similar in both sound and meaning. They are usually dismissed as accidents; and I daresay some of the cases are not significant. But I fancy that they may sometimes be the result of a hidden symbol-making process working out to similar ends by different routes. Especially when the result is beautiful and the meaning poetical, as is the case with *Éarendel*.'

'If I follow all this,' said Markison, 'I suppose you are trying to say that you've discovered *Éarendel*, or something like it, in some other unconnected language, and are dismissing all the other forms of the name that are found in the older languages related to English. Though one of them, *Auriwandalo*, is actually recorded as a Langobardic name, I think. It's odd how the Langobards keep cropping up.'

'It is,' said Lowdham, 'but I am not interested in that at the moment. For I do mean that: I have often heard *éarendel*, or to be exact *éarendil*, *e-a-r-e-n-d-i-l*, in another language, where it actually means Great Mariner, or literally Friend of the Sea; though it also has, I think, some connexion with the stars.'

'What language is that?' said Markison, knitting his brows. 'Not one I've ever come across, I think.' (He has 'come across' or dabbled in about a hundred in his time.)

'No, I don't suppose you've ever met it,' said Lowdham. 'It's an unknown language. But I had better try and explain.

'From the time of my father's departure I began to have curious experiences, and I have gone on having them down the years, slowly increasing in clearness: visitations of linguistic ghosts, you might say. Yes, just that. I am not a *seer*. I have, of course, pictorial dreams like other folk, but only what Ramer would call marginal stuff, and few and fleeting at that: which at any rate means that if I see things I don't remember them. But ever since I was about ten I have had words, even occasional phrases, ringing in my ears; both in dream and waking abstraction. They come into my mind unbidden, or I wake to hear myself repeating them. Sometimes they seem to be quite isolated, just words or names. Sometimes something seems to "break my dream"[38] as my mother used to say: the names seem to be connected strangely with things seen in waking life, suddenly, in some fleeting posture or passing light which transports me to some quite different region of thought or imagination. Like the Camera that night in March, Ramer, if you remember it.

'Looking at a picture once of a cone-shaped mountain rising out of wooded uplands, I heard myself crying out: "Desolate is Minul-Tārik, the Pillar of Heaven is forsaken!" and I knew that it was a dreadful thing. But most ominous of all are the Eagles of the Lords of the West. They shake me badly when I see them. I could, I could – I feel I could tell some great tale of Nūmenor.

'But I'm getting on too fast. It was a long time before I began to piece the fragments together at all. Most of these "ghost-words" are, and always were, to all appearance casual, as casual as the words caught by the eye from a lexicon when you're looking for something else. They began to come through, as I said, when I was about ten; and almost at once I started to note them down. Clumsily, of course, at first. Even grown-up folk make a poor shot, as a rule, at spelling the simplest words that they've never seen, unless they have some sort of phonetic knowledge. But I've still got some of the grubby little note-books I used as a small boy. An unsystematic jumble, of course; for it was only now and again that I bothered about such things. But later on, when I was older and had a little more linguistic experience, I began to pay serious attention to my "ghosts", and saw that they were something quite different from the game of trying to make up private languages.

'As soon as I started looking out for them, so to speak, the ghosts began to come oftener and clearer; and when I had got a lot of them noted down, I saw that they were not all of one kind: they had different phonetic styles, styles as unlike as, well – Latin and Hebrew. I am sorry, if this seems a bit complicated. I can't help it: and if this stuff is worth your bothering about at all, we'd better get it right.

'Well, first of all I recognized that a lot of these ghosts were Anglo-Saxon, or related stuff. What was left I arranged in two lists, A and B, according to their style, with a third rag-bag list C for odd things that didn't seem to fit in anywhere. But it was language A that really attracted me; it just suited me. I still like it best.'

'In that case you ought to have got it pretty well worked out by now,' said Stainer. 'Haven't you got a *Grammar and Lexicon of Lowdham's Language A* that you could pass round? I wouldn't mind a look at it, if it isn't in some hideous phonetic script.'

Lowdham stared at him, but repressed the explosion that seemed imminent. 'Are you deliberately missing the point?' he said. 'I've been painfully trying to indicate that I do *not* believe that this stuff is "invented", not by me at any rate.

'Take the Anglo-Saxon first. It is the only known language that comes through at all in this way, and that in itself is odd. And it began to come through *before* I knew it. I recognized it as Anglo-Saxon only after I began to learn it from books, and then I had the curious experience of finding that I already knew a good many of the words. Why, there are a number of ghost-words noted in the very first of my childish note-books that are plainly a beginner's efforts at putting down spoken Old English words in modern letters. There's *wook, woak, woof* = crooked, for instance, that is evidently a first attempt at recording Anglo-Saxon *wōh*.

'And as for the other stuff: A, the language I like best, is the shortest list. How I wish I could get more of it! But it's *not* under my control, Stainer. It's not one of my invented lingoes. I have made up two or three, and they're as complete as they're ever likely to be; but that's quite a different matter. But evidently I'd better cut out the autobiography and jump down to the present.

'It's now clear to me that the two languages A and B have got nothing to do with any language I've ever heard, or come across in books in the ordinary way. Nothing. As far as it is possible for any language, built out of about two dozen sounds, as A is, to avoid occasional resemblances to other quite unrelated tongues: nothing. And they have nothing to do with my inventions either. Language B is quite unlike my own style. Language A is very agreeable to my taste (it may have helped to form it), but it is independent of me; I can't "work it out", as you put it.

'Any one who has ever spent (or wasted) any time on composing a language will understand me. Others perhaps won't. But in making up a language you are free: too free. It is difficult to fit meaning to any given sound-pattern, and even more difficult to fit a sound-pattern to any given meaning. I say *fit*. I don't mean that you can't assign forms or meanings arbitrarily, as you will. Say, you want a word for *sky*. Well, call it *jibberjabber*, or anything else that comes into your head without the exercise of any linguistic taste or art. But that's code-making, not language-building. It is quite another matter to find a relationship, sound plus sense, that satisfies, that is when made *durable*. When you're just inventing, the pleasure or fun is in the moment of invention; but as you are the master your whim is law, and you may want to have the fun all over again, fresh. You're liable to be for ever niggling, altering, refining, wavering, according to your linguistic mood and to your changes of taste.

'It is not in the least like that with my ghost-words. They came through made: sound and sense already conjoined. I can no more niggle with them than I can alter the sound or the sense of the word *polis* in Greek. Many of my ghost-words have been repeated, over and over again, down the years. Nothing changes but, occasionally, my spelling. They don't change. They endure, unaltered, unalterable by me. In other words they have the effect and taste of real languages. But one can have one's preferences among real languages, and as I say, I like A best.

'Both A and B I associate in some way with the name *Númenor*. The rag-bag list has got pretty long as the years have gone on, and I can now see that, among some unidentified stuff, it contains a lot of echoes of later forms of language derived from A and B. The Númenorean tongues are old, old, archaic; they taste of an Elder World to me. The other things are worn, altered, touched with the loss and bitterness of these shores of exile.' These last words he spoke in a strange tone, as if talking to himself. Then his voice trailed off into silence.

'I find this rather hard to follow, or to swallow,' said Stainer. 'Couldn't you give us something a bit clearer, something better to bite on than this algebra of A and B?'

Lowdham looked up again. 'Yes, I could,' he said. 'I won't bother you with the later echoes. I find them moving, somehow, and instructive technically: I am beginning to discern the laws or lines of their change as the world grew older; but that wouldn't be clear even to a philologist except in writing and with long parallel lists.

'But take the name *Númenóre* or *Númenor* (both occur) to start with. That belongs to Language A. It means Westernesse, and is composed of *núme* "west" and *nóre* "folk" or "country". But the B name is *Anadúnê*, and the people are called *Adúnāim*, from the B word *adún* "west". The same land, or so I think, has another name: in A *Andōre* and in B *Yōzāyan*,[39] and both mean "Land of Gift".

'There seems to be no connexion between the two languages there. But there are some words that are the same or very similar in both. The word for "sky" or "the heavens" is *menel* in Language A and *minil* in B: a form of it occurs in *Minul-tārik* "Pillar of Heaven" that I mentioned just now. And there seems to be some connexion between the A word *Valar*, which seems to mean something like "The Powers", we might say "gods" perhaps, and the B plural *Avalōim* and the place-name *Avallōni*. Although that is a B name, it is with it, oddly enough, that I associate Language A; so if you want to get rid of algebra, you can call A Avallonian, and B Adunaic. I do myself.

'The name *Ëarendil*, by the way, belongs to Avallonian, and contains *ëare* "the open sea" and the stem *ndil* "love, devotion": that may look a bit odd, but lots of the Avallonian stems begin with *nd*, *mb*, *ng*, which lose their *d*, *b*, or *g* when they stand alone. The corresponding Adunaic name, apparently meaning just the same, is *Azrubēl*. A large number of names seem to have double forms like this, almost as if one people spoke two languages. If that is so, I suppose the situation could be paralleled by the use of, say, Chinese in Japan, or indeed of Latin in Europe. As if a man could be called Godwin, and also Theophilus or Amadeus. But even so two different peoples must come into the story somewhere.

'Well there you are. I hope you are not all bored. I could give you long lists of other words. Words, words, mostly just that. For the most part significant nouns, like *Isil* and *Nīlū* for the Moon; fewer adjectives, still fewer verbs, and only occasional connected phrases. I love these languages, though they are only fragments out of some forgotten book. I find both curiously attractive, though Avallonian is nearest to my heart. Adunaic with its, well, faintly Semitic flavour belongs more nearly to our world, somehow. But Avallonian is to me beautiful, in its simple and euphonious style. And it seems to me more august, more ancient, and, well, sacred and liturgical. I used to call it the Elven-Latin. The echoes of it carry one far away. Very far away. Away from Middle-earth altogether, I expect.' He paused as if he was listening. 'But I could not explain just what I mean by that,' he ended.

There was a short silence, and then Markison spoke. 'Why did you call it Elven-Latin?'[40] he asked. 'Why Elven?'

'I don't quite know,' Lowdham answered. 'It seems the nearest English word for the purpose. But certainly I didn't mean *elf* in any debased post-Shakespearean sort of sense. Something far more potent and majestic. I am not quite clear what. In fact it's one of the things that I most want to discover. What is the real reference of the *ælf* in my name?

'You remember that I said Anglo-Saxon used to come through mixed up with this other queer stuff, as if it had some special connexion with it? Well, I got hold of Anglo-Saxon through the ordinary books later on: I began to learn it properly before I was fifteen, and that confused the issue. Yet it is an odd fact that, though I found most of these words already there, waiting for me, in the printed vocabularies and dictionaries, there were some – and they still come through now and again – that are not there at all. *Tíwas*,[41] for instance, apparently used as an equivalent of the Avallonian *Valar*; and *Nówendaland*[42] for *Númenóre*. And other compound names too, like *Fréafíras*,[43] *Regeneard*,[44] and *Midswípen*.[45] Some were in very archaic form: like *hebaensuil* "pillar of heaven", or *frumaeldi*; or very antique indeed like *Wihawinia*.'[46]

'This is dreadful,' sighed Frankley. 'Though I suppose I should be grateful at least that Valhalla and Valkyries have not made their appearance yet. But you'd better be careful, Arry! We're all friends here, and we won't give you away. But you will be getting into trouble, if you let your archaic cats out of your private bag among your quarrelsome philological rivals. Unless, of course, you back up their theories.'[47]

'You needn't worry,' said Lowdham. 'I've no intention of publishing the stuff. And I haven't come across anything very controversial anyway. After all Anglo-Saxon is pretty near home, in place and time, and it's been closely worked: there's not much margin for wide errors, not even in pronunciation. What I hear is more or less what the received doctrine would lead me to expect. Except in one point: it is so slow! Compared with us urban chirrupers the farmers and mariners of the past simply mouthed, savoured words like meat and wine and honey on their tongues. Especially when declaiming. They made a scrap of verse majestically sonorous: like thunder moving on a slow wind, or the tramp of mourners at the funeral of a king. We just gabble the stuff. But even that is no news to philologists, in theory; though the realization of it in sound is something mere theory hardly prepares you for. And, of course, the philologists would be very interested in my echoes of very archaic English, even early Germanic – if they could be got to believe that they were genuine.

'Here's a bit that might intrigue them. It's very primitive in form, though I use a less horrific notation than is usual. But you had better see this.' He brought out from his pocket several scraps of paper and passed them round;

> *westra lage wegas rehtas, wraikwas nu isti.*

'That came through years ago,[48] long before I could interpret it, and it has constantly been repeated in various forms:

> *westra lage wegas rehtas, wraikwas nu isti.*
> *westweg wæs rihtweg, wóh is núþa*

and so on and on and on, in many snatches and dream-echoes, down from what looks like very ancient Germanic to Old English.

> *a straight way lay westward, now it is bent.*

It seems the key to something, but I can't fit it yet. But it was while I was rummaging in an Onomasticon,[49] and poring over the list of Ælfwines, that I got, seemed to *hear* and *see*, the longest snatch that has ever come through in that way. Yes, I said I wasn't a *seer*; but Anglo-Saxon is sometimes an exception. I don't see pictures, but I see letters: some of the words and especially some of the scraps of verse seem to be present to the mind's eye as well as to the ear, as if sometime, somewhere, I had seen them written and could almost recall the page. If you turn over the slips I gave you, you'll see the thing written out. It came through when I was only sixteen, before I had read any of the old verse; but the lines stuck, and I put them down as well as I could. The archaic forms interest me now as a philologist, but that's how they came through, and how they stand in my note-book under the date October 1st 1954. A windy evening: I remember it howling round the house, and the distant sound of the sea.

> *Monath módaes lust mith meriflóda*
> *forth ti foeran thaet ic feorr hionan*
> *obaer gaarseggaes grimmae holmas*
> *aelbuuina eard uut gisoecae.*
> *Nis me ti hearpun hygi ni ti hringthegi*
> *ni ti wíbae wyn ni ti weoruldi hyct*
> *ni ymb oowict ellaes nebnae ymb ýtha giwalc.*

It sounds to me now almost like my own father speaking across grey seas of world and time:

> My soul's desire over the sea-torrents
> forth bids me fare, that I afar should seek
> over the ancient water's awful mountains
> Elf-friends' island in the Outer-world.
> For no harp have I heart, no hand for gold,
> in no wife delight, in the world no hope:
> one wish only, for the waves' tumult.

'I know now, of course, that these lines very closely resemble some of the verses in the middle of *The Seafarer*, as that strange old poem of longing is usually called. But they are not the same. In the text preserved in manuscript it runs *elþéodigra eard* 'the land of aliens', not *aelbuuina* or *ælfwina* (as it would have been spelt later) 'of the Ælfwines, the Elven-friends'. I think mine is probably the older and better text – it is in a much older form and spelling anyway – but I daresay I should get into trouble, as Pip suggests, if I put it into a "serious journal".[50]

'It was not until quite recently that I picked up echoes of some other lines that are not found at all among the preserved fragments of the oldest English verses.[51]

> *Þus cwæð Ælfwine Wídlást Éadwines sunu:*
> *Fela bið on Westwegum werum uncúðra,*
> *wundra and wihta, wlitescéne land,*
> *eardgeard ælfa and ésa bliss.*
> *Lýt ænig wát hwylc his langoð síe*
> *þám þe eftsíðes eldo getwæfeð.*

'Thus spake Ælfwine the Fartravelled son of Éadwine:

> There is many a thing in the west of the world unknown to men; marvels and strange beings, [a land lovely to look on,] the dwelling place of the Elves and the bliss of the Gods. Little doth any man know what longing is his whom old age cutteth off from return.

'I think my father went before Eld should cut him off. But what of Éadwine's son?

'Well, now I've had my say for the present. There may be more later. I am working at the stuff – as hard as time and my duties allow, and things may happen. Certainly I'll let you know, if they do. For now you have endured so much, I expect you will want some more news, if anything interesting turns up.

If it's any comfort to you, Philip, I think we shall get away from Anglo-Saxon sooner or later.'

'If it's any comfort to you, Arry,' said Frankley, 'for the first time in your long life as a preacher you've made me faintly interested in it.'

'Good Heavens!' said Lowdham. 'Then there must be something *very* queer going on! Lor bless me! Give me a drink and I will sing, as the minstrels used to say.

> *Fil me a cuppe of ful gode ale,*
> *for longe I have spelled tale!*
> *Nu wil I drinken or I ende*
> *that Frenche men to helle wende!'*[52]

The song was interrupted by Frankley. Eventually a semblance of peace was restored, only one chair being a casualty. Nothing toward or untoward occurred for the remainder of the evening.

AAL. MGR. WTJ. JM. RD. RS. PF. JJ. JJR. NG.

Night 67.   Thursday, June 12th, 1987.[53]

We met in Ramer's rooms in Jesus College. There were eight of us present, including Stainer and Cameron, and all the regulars except Lowdham. It was very hot and sultry, and we sat near the window looking into the inner quadrangle, talking of this and that, and listening for the noises of Lowdham's approach; but an hour passed and there was still no sign of him.

'Have you seen anything of Arry lately?' said Frankley to Jeremy. 'I haven't. I wonder if he's going to turn up at all tonight?'

'I couldn't say,' said Jeremy. 'Ramer and I saw a good deal of him in the first few days after our last meeting, but I haven't set eyes on him for some time now.'

'I wonder what he's up to? They say he cancelled his lectures last week. I hope he's not ill.'

'I don't think you need fret about your little Elf-friend,' said Dolbear. 'He's got a body and a constitution that would put a steamroller back a bit, if it bumped into him. And don't worry about his mind! He's getting something off it, and that will do him no harm, I think. At least whatever it does, it will do less harm than trying to cork it up any longer. But what on earth it all is – well, I'm still about as much at sea as old Edwin Lowdham himself.'

'Sunk, in fact,' said Stainer. 'I should say it was a bad attack of repressed linguistic invention, and that the sooner he brings out an Adunaic Grammar the better for all.'

'Perhaps,' said Ramer. 'But he may bring out a lot more besides. I wish he would come!'

At that moment there was the sound of loud footsteps, heavy and quick, on the wooden stairs below. There was a bang on the door, and in strode Lowdham.

'I've got something new!' he shouted. 'More than mere words. Verbs! Syntax at last!' He sat down and mopped his face.

'Verbs, syntax! Hooray!' mocked Frankley. 'Now isn't that thrilling!'

'Don't try and start a row, O Lover of Horses[54] and Horseplay!' said Lowdham. 'It's too hot. Listen!

'It's been very stuffy and thundery lately, and I haven't been able to sleep, a troublesome novelty for me; and I began to have a splitting headache. So I cleared off for a few days to the west coast, to Pembroke. But the Eagles came up out of the Atlantic, and I fled. I still couldn't sleep when I came back, and my headache got worse. And then last night I fell suddenly into a deep dark sleep – and I got this.' He waved a handful of papers at us. 'I didn't come round until nearly twelve this morning, and my head was ringing with words. They began to fade quickly as soon as I woke; but I jotted down at once all I could.

'I have been working on the stuff every minute since, and I've made six copies. For I think you'll find it well worth a glance; but you fellows would never follow it without something to look at. Here it is!'

He passed round several sheets of paper. On them were inscribed strange words in a big bold hand, done with one of the great thick-nibbed pens Lowdham is fond of. Under most of the words were glosses in red ink.[55]

I

(A) O   *sauron*   *túle*   *nukumna* ... *lantaner*   *turkildi*
     and   ?   came   humbled ...   fell   ?

nuhuinenna   ... *tar-kalion*   *ohtakáre*   *valannar* ...
under shadow ...   ?   war made   on Powers ...

númeheruvi   *arda*   *sakkante*   *leneme*   *ilúvatáren* ...
Lords-of-West   Earth   rent   with leave   of   ?   ...

ëari	*ullier*	*ikilyanna*	... *númenóre*	*ataltane*
seas	should flow	into chasm	... Numenor	fell down

* * *

(B)
Kadō	*zigūrun*	*zabathān*	*unakkha*	... *ēruhīnim*
and so	?	humbled	he-came	... ?

dubdam	*ugru-dalad*	... *ar-pharazōnun*	*azaggara*
fell	?shadow under ...	?	was warring

avalōiyada	... *bārim*	*an-adūn*	*yurahtam*	*dāira*
against Powers	... Lords	of-West	broke	Earth

sāibēth-mā	*ēruvō*	... *azrīya*	*du-phursā*	*akhāsada*
assent-with	?-from	... seas	so-as-to-gush	into chasm

... *anadūnē*	*zīrān*	*hikallaba*	... *bawība*	*dulgī*
... Numenor	beloved	she-fell down	... winds	black

... *balīk*	*hazad*	*an-nimruzīr*	*azūlada*
... ships	seven	of ?	eastward

II

(B)
Agannālō	*burōda*	*nēnud*	... *zāira*	*nēnud*
Death-shadow	heavy	on-us	... longing (is)	on-us

... *adūn*	*izindi*	*batān*	*tāidō*	*ayadda:*	*īdō*
... west	straight	road	once	went	now

kātha	*batīna*	*lōkhī*
all	roads	crooked

(A)
Vahaiya	*sín*	*Andóre*
far away	now (is)	Land of Gift

(B)
Ēphalak	*īdōn*	*Yōzāyan*
far away	now (is)	Land of Gift

(B)
Ēphal	*ēphalak*	*īdōn*	*hi-Akallabēth*
far	far away	now (is)	She-that-hath-fallen

(A)
Haiya	*vahaiya*	*sín*	*atalante.*[56]
far	far away	now (is)	the Downfallen.

'There are two languages here,' said Lowdham, 'Avallonian
and Adunaic: I have labelled them A and B. Of course, I have
put them down in a spelling of my own. Avallonian has a clear
simple phonetic structure and in my ear it rings like a bell, but I

seemed to feel as I wrote this stuff down that it was not really spelt like this. I have never had the same feeling before, but this morning I half glimpsed quite a different script, though I couldn't visualize it clearly. I fancy Adunaic used a very similar script too.

' "I believe these are passages out of some book," I said to myself. And then suddenly I remembered the curious script in my father's manuscript. But that can wait. I've brought the leaf along.

'These are only fragmentary sentences, of course, and not by any means all that I heard; but they are all that I could seize and get written down. Text I is bilingual, though they are not identical, and the B version is a little longer. That's only because I could remember a bit more of it. They correspond so closely because I heard the A version, a sentence at a time, with the B version immediately following: in the same voice, as if someone was reading out of an ancient book and translating it bit by bit for his audience. Then there came a long dark gap, or a picture of confusion and darkness in which the word-echoes were lost in a noise of winds and waves.

'And then I got a kind of lamentation or chant, of which I have put down all that I can now remember. You'll notice the order is altered at the end. There were two voices here, one singing A and the other singing B, and the chant always ended up as I have set it out: A B B A. The last word was always *Atalante*. I can give you no idea of how moving it was, horribly moving. I still feel the weight of a great loss myself, as if I shall never be really happy on these shores again.

'I don't think there are any really new words here. There are a lot of very interesting grammatical details; but I won't bother you with those, interesting as they are to me – and they seem to have touched off something in my memory too, so that I now know more than is actually contained in the fragments. You'll see a lot of query marks, but I think the context (and often the grammar) indicates that these are all names or titles.

'*Tar-kalion*, for instance: I think that is a king's name, for I've often come across the prefix *tar* in names of the great, and *ar* in the corresponding Adunaic name (on the system I told you about) is the stem of the word for "king". On the other hand *turkildi* and *ēruhīnim*, though evidently equivalent, don't mean the same thing. The one means, I think, 'lordly men', and the other is rather more startling, for it appears to be the name of

God the Omnipotent with a patronymic ending: in fact, unless I am quite wrong, "Children of God". Indeed, I need not have queried the words *ēruvō* and *ilúvatáren*: there can't really be any doubt that *ēruvō* is the sacred name *Ēru* with a suffixed element meaning "from", and that therefore *ilúvatáren* means the same thing.

'There is one point that may interest you, after what we were saying about linguistic coincidence. Well, it seems to me a fair guess that we are dealing with a record, or a legend, of an Atlantis catastrophe.'

'Why *or?*' said Jeremy. 'I mean, it might be a record *and* a legend. You never really tackled the question I propounded at our first meeting this term. If you went back would you find myth dissolving into history or history into myth? Somebody once said, I forget who, that the distinction between history and myth might be meaningless outside the Earth. I think it might at least get a great deal less sharp on the Earth, further back. Perhaps the Atlantis catastrophe was the dividing line?'

'We may be able to deal with your question a great deal better when we've got to the bottom of all this,' said Lowdham. 'In the meantime the point I was going to bring up is worth noting. I said "Atlantis" because Ramer told us that he associated the word Nūmenor with the Greek name. Well, look! here we learn that Nūmenor was destroyed; and we end with a lament: *far, far away, now is Atalante. Atalante* is plainly another name for Nūmenor-Atlantis. But only after its downfall. For in Avallo-nian *atalante* is a word formed normally from a common base *talat* "topple over, slip down": it occurs in Text I in an emphatic verbal form *ataltane* "slid down in ruin", to be precise. *Atalante* means "She that has fallen down". So the two names have approached one another, have reached a very similar shape by quite unconnected routes. At least, I suppose the routes are unconnected. I mean, whatever traditions may lie behind Plato's *Timaeus,*[57] the name that he uses, Atlantis, must be just the same old "daughter of Atlas" that was applied to Calypso. But even that connects the land with a mountain regarded as the pillar of heaven. Minul-Tārik, Minul-Tārik! Very interesting.'

He got up and stretched. 'At least I hope you all think so! But, good lord, how hot and stuffy it is getting! Not an evening for a lecture! But anyway, I can't make much more out of this with only words, and without more words. And I need some pictures.

'I wish I could *see* a little, as well as hear, like you, Ramer. Or like Jerry. He's had a few glimpses of strange things, while we worked together; but he can't hear. My words seem to waken his sight, but it's not at all clear yet. Ships with dark sails. Towers on sea-washed shores. Battles: swords that glint, but are silent. A great domed temple.[58] I wish I could see as much. But I've done what I can. *Sauron. Zigūrun, Zigūr.* I can't fathom those names. But the key is there, I think. *Zigūr.*'

'Zigūr!' said Jeremy in a strange voice.[59] We stared at him: he was sitting with his eyes closed, and he looked very pale; beads of sweat were on his face.

'I say, what's the matter, Jerry?' cried Frankley. 'Open the other window, Ramer, and let's have some more air! I think there's a storm brewing.'

'Zigūr!' cried Jeremy again, in a remote strained voice. 'You spoke of him yourself not long ago, cursing the name. Can you have forgotten him, Nimruzīr?'[60]

'I had forgotten,' Lowdham answered. 'But now I begin to remember!' He stood still and clenched his fists. His brow lowered, and his eyes glittered. There was a glimmer of lightning far away through the darkening window. Away in the west over the roofs the sky was going dead black. There came a distant rumour of thunder.

Jeremy groaned and laid his head back.

Frankley and Ramer went to him, and bent over him; but he did not seem to notice them. 'It's the thunder, perhaps,' said Frankley in a low voice. 'He seemed all right a few minutes ago; but he looks pretty ghastly now.'

'Leave him alone,' growled Dolbear. 'You'll do no good hovering over him.'

'Would you like to lie down on my bed?' said Ramer. 'Or shall I get the car out and run you home?'

'Are you feeling ill, old man?' said Frankley.

'Yes,' groaned Jeremy without moving. 'Deathly. But don't trouble me! Don't touch me! *Bā kitabdahē!*[61] Sit down. I shall speak in a moment.'

There was a silence that seemed long and heavy. It was then nearly ten o'clock, and the pale sky of summer twilight was pricked by a few faint stars; but the blackness crawled slowly onwards from the West. Great wings of shadow stretched out ominously over the town. The curtains stirred as with a presage of wind, and then hung still. There was a long mutter of thunder ending in a crack.

Lowdham was standing erect in the middle of the floor, looking out of the window with staring eyes. Suddenly:

'Narīka 'nBāri 'nAdūn yanākhim,'[62] he shouted, lifting up both his arms. 'The Eagles of the Lords of the West are at hand!'

Then all at once Jeremy began to speak. 'Now I see!' he said. 'I see it all. The ships have set sail at last. Woe to the time! Behold, the mountain smokes and the earth trembles!'

He paused, and we sat staring, oppressed as by the oncoming of doom. The voices of the storm drew nearer. Then Jeremy began again.

'Woe to this time and the fell counsels of Zigūr! The King hath set forth his might against the Lords of the West. The fleets of the Nūmenoreans are like a land of many islands; their masts are like the stems of a forest; their sails are golden and black. Night is coming. They have gone against Avallōni with naked swords. All the world waiteth. Why do the Lords of the West make no sign?'[63]

There was a dazzle of lightning and a deafening crash.

'Behold! Now the black wrath is come upon us out of the West. The Eagles of the Powers of the World have arisen in anger. The Lords have spoken to Ēru, and the fate of the World is changed!'[64]

'Do you not hear the wind coming and the roaring of the sea?' said Lowdham.

'Do you not see the wings of the Eagles, and their eyes like thunderbolts and their claws like forks of fire?' said Jeremy. 'See! The abyss openeth. The sea falls. The mountains lean over. Urīd yakalubim!' He got up unsteadily, and Lowdham took his hand, and drew him towards him, as if to protect him. Together they went to the window and stood there peering out, talking to one another in a strange tongue. Irresistibly I was reminded of two people hanging over the side of a ship. But suddenly with a cry they turned away, and knelt down covering their eyes.

'The glory hath fallen into the deep waters,' said Jeremy weeping.

'Still the eagles pursue us,' said Lowdham. 'The wind is like the end of the world, and the waves are like mountains moving. We go into darkness.'[65]

There was a roar of thunder and a blaze of lightning: flashes north, south, and west. Ramer's room flared into a blistering light and rocked back into darkness. The electric light had

failed. At a distance there was a murmur as of a great wind
coming.

'All hath passed away. The light hath gone out!' said Jeremy.

With a vast rush and slash rain came down suddenly like
waterfalls out of the sky, and a wind swept the city with wild
wings of fury; its shriek rose to a deafening tumult. Near at
hand I heard, or I thought I heard, a great weight like a tower
falling heavily, clattering to ruin. Before we could close the
windows with the strength of all hands present and heave the
shutters after them, the curtains were blown across the room
and the floor was flooded.

In the midst of all the confusion, while Ramer was trying to
find and light a candle, Lowdham went up to Jeremy, who was
cowering against the wall, and he took his hands.

'Come, Abrazān!'[66] he said. 'There is work to do. Let us look
to our folk and see to our courses, before it is too late!'

'It is too late, Nimruzīr,' said Jeremy. 'The Valar hate us.
Only darkness awaits us.'

'A little light may yet lie beyond it. Come!' said Lowdham,
and he drew Jeremy to his feet. In the light of the flickering
candle that Ramer now held in a shaking hand, we saw him
drag Jeremy to the door, and push him out of the room. We
heard their feet stumbling and clattering down the stairs.

'They'll be drowned!' said Frankley, taking a few steps, as if
to follow them. 'What on earth has come over them?'

'The fear of the Lords of the West,' said Ramer, and his voice
shook. 'It is no good trying to follow them. But I think it was
their part in this story to escape from the very edge of Doom.
Let them escape!'

And there this meeting would have ended, but for the fact
that the rest of us could not face the night and dared not go.

For three hours we sat huddled up in dim candle-light, while
the greatest storm in the memory of any living man roared over
us: the terrible storm of June 12th 1987,[67] that slew more men,
felled more trees, and cast down more towers, bridges and other
works of Man than a hundred years of wild weather.*

---

* The centre of its greatest fury seems to have been out in the
Atlantic, but its whole course and progress has been something of a
puzzle to meteorologists — as far as can be discovered from accounts it
seems to have proceeded more like blasts of an explosion, rushing
eastward and slowly diminishing in force as it went.   N.G.

When at last it had abated in the small hours, and through the rags of its wild retreat the sky was already growing pale again in the East, the company parted and crept away, tired and shaken, to wade the flooded streets and discover if their homes and colleges were still standing. Cameron made no remark. I am afraid he had not found the evening entertaining.

I was the last to go. As I stood by the door, I saw Ramer pick up a sheet of paper, closely covered with writing. He put it into a drawer.[68]

'Good night – or good morning!' I said. 'We should be thankful at any rate that we were not struck by lightning, or caught in the ruin of the college.'

'We should indeed!' said Ramer. 'I wonder.'

'What do you wonder?' I said.

'Well, I have an odd feeling, Nick, or suspicion, that we may all have been helping to stir something up. If not out of history, at any rate out of a very powerful world of imagination and memory. Jeremy would say "perhaps out of both". I wonder if we may not find ourselves in other and worse dangers.'

'I don't understand you,' I said. 'But at any rate, I suppose you mean that you wonder whether they ought to go on. Oughtn't we to stop them?'

'Stop Lowdham and Jeremy?' said Ramer. 'We can't do that now.'

MGR. RD. PF. RS. JM. NG.   Added later AAL. WTJ.

Night 68.   June 26th, 1987.

Frankley's rooms. A small attendance: Frankley, Dolbear, Stainer, Guildford.

There is not much to record. Most of the Club, present or absent, were in one way or another involved in examinations, and tired, and more bothered than is usual at this season.*

---

* The extraordinary system of holding the principal examinations of the year in the summer, which must have been responsible for an incalculable amount of misery, was still in force. During the period of 'reforms' in the forties there was talk of altering this arrangement, but it was never carried out, though it was one of the few thoroughly desirable minor reforms proposed at the time. It was the events of the summer of 1987 that finally brought things to a head, as most of the examinations had that year to be transferred to the winter, or held again after the autumn term.   N.G.

Things had been rather shaken up by the storm. It had come in the seventh week, right in the middle of the final examinations; and amongst a lot of other damage, the Examination Schools had been struck and the East School wrecked.

'What a time we've been having, ever since old Ramer started to attend again!' said Frankley. 'Notion Club! More like the Commotion Club! Is there any news of the Commoters?'

'D'you mean Lowdham and Jeremy?' said Stainer. 'Promoters, I should say! I've never seen anything better staged – and with Michael Ramer, as a kind of conniving chorus. It was wonderfully well done!'

'Wonderfully!' said Dolbear. 'I am lost in admiration. Think of their meteorological information! Superb! Foreseeing like that a storm not foretold, apparently, by any station in the world. And timing it so beautifully, too, to fit in neatly with their prepared parts. It makes you think, doesn't it? – as those say, who have never experienced the process. And Ramer says flatly that he was bowled over, altogether taken by surprise. Whatever you may think of his views, it would be very rash to assume that he was lying. He takes this affair rather seriously. "Those two are probably dangerous," he said to me; and he wasn't thinking merely of spoofing the Club, Stainer.'

'Hm. I spoke too hastily, evidently,' said Stainer, stroking his chin. 'Hm. But what then? If not arranged, it was a very remarkable coincidence.'

'Truly remarkable!' said Dolbear. 'But we'll leave that question open for a bit, I think; coincidence or connexion. They're both pretty difficult to accept; but they're the only choices. Pre-arrangement is impossible – or rather it's a damned sight more improbable, and even more alarming. What about these two fellows, though? Has anything been heard of them?'

'Yes,' said Guildford. 'They're alive, and neither drowned nor blasted. They've written me a joint letter to lay before the Club. This is what they say:

Dear Nick,
We hope every one is safe and sound. We are. We were cast up far away when the wind fell, but we're dry again at last; so now we're off, more or less in the words of the old song, 'on some jolly little jaunts to the happy, happy haunts where the beer flows wild and free'. In due course (if ever) we'll let our colleges have our addresses. A.A.L.

That is the end of Arry's great big fist. Jeremy adds:

> We are researching. More stuff may come through, I think.
> What about a vacation meeting? Just before the racket of
> term. What about Sept. 25th? You can have my rooms. Yrs.
> W.T.J.'

'What about the racket of the vacation!' said Frankley.
'They're damned lucky not to be in the schools[69] this year, or
they'ld have to come back, wherever the wind may have blown
them. Any idea where that was, Nick?'

'No,' said Guildford. 'The postmark is illegible,[70] and there's
no address inside. But what about the proposed meeting? I
suppose most of us will be about again by then.'

September 25th was agreed to. At that moment Michael
Ramer came in. 'We've heard from them!' Frankley cried.
'Nicholas has had a letter. They're all right, and they're off on a
holiday somewhere: no address.'

'Good!' said Ramer. 'Or I hope so. I hope they won't wreck
the British Isles before they've finished.'

'My dear Ramer!' Steiner protested. 'What do you mean?
What can you mean? Dolbear has been preaching the open
mind to my incredulity. He had better talk to you. The other
extreme is just as bad.'

'But I haven't any fixed opinions,' said Ramer. 'I was merely
expressing a doubt, or a wild guess. But actually I am not really
very much afraid of any more explosions now. I fancy that that
force has been spent, for the present, for a long time to come
perhaps.

'But I *am* a little anxious about Arry and Wilfrid themselves.
They may quite well get into some danger. Still we can only wait
and see. Even if we could find them we could do no more. You
can't stop a strong horse with the bit between its teeth. You
certainly could not rein Arry in now, and Wilfrid is evidently
nearly as deeply in it as Arry is.

'In the meantime I have got something to show you. Arry
dropped a leaf of paper in my room that night. I think it is the
leaf of his father's manuscript that he told us about. Well – I've
deciphered it.'

'Good work!' said Guildford. 'I didn't know you were a
cryptographer.'

'I'm not,' Ramer laughed, 'but I have my methods. No, no –
nothing dreamy this time. I just made a lucky shot and landed

on the mark. I don't know whether Arry had solved it himself before he dropped it, but I think not; for if he had, he would have included it in the stuff he showed us. It's quite plain what held him up: it was too easy. He was looking for something remote and difficult, while all the time the solution was right on his own doorstep. He thought it was Nūmenorean, I guess; but actually it is Old English, Anglo-Saxon, his own stuff!

'The script is, I suppose, Nūmenorean,[71] as Arry thought. But it has been applied by someone to ancient English. The proper names, when they're not Old English translations, are in the same script, but the letters are then quite differently used, and I shouldn't have been able to read them without the help of Arry's texts.

'I wonder who had the idea of writing Anglo-Saxon in this odd way? Old Edwin Lowdham seems at first a likely guess; but I'm not so sure. The thing is evidently made up of excerpts from a longish book or chronicle.'

'Well, come on!' cried Frankley. 'How you philologists do niggle! Let's see it, and tell us what it says!'

'Here it is!' said Ramer, taking three sheets out of his pocket and handing them to Frankley. 'Pass it round! I've got a copy. The original is only a small octavo page as you see, written on both sides in a large hand in this rather beautiful script.

'Now, I said to myself: "If this is in one of Arry's languages, I can't do anything with it; no one but he can solve it. But he failed, so probably it isn't. In that case, what language is it most likely to be, remembering what Arry told us? Anglo-Saxon. Well, that's not one of my languages, though I know the elements. So when I'd made a preliminary list of all the separate letters that I could distinguish, I trotted round to old Professor Rashbold at Pembroke,[72] though I didn't know him personally. A grumpy old bear Arry has always called him; but evidently Arry has never given him the right sort of buns.

'He liked mine. He didn't care tuppence about what the stuff said, but it amused him to try and solve the puzzle, especially when he heard that it had defeated Arry. "Oh! Young Lowd-ham!" he said. "A clever fellow under that pothouse manner. But too fly-away; always after some butterfly theory. Won't stick to his texts. Now if *I* had had him as my pupil, I should have put some stiffening into him." Well, starting out with my guess that the stuff might be Anglo-Saxon, old Rashbold didn't take long. I don't know his workings. All he said before I left was: "Never seen this script before; but I should say it was a consonantal alphabet, and all these diacritics are vowel-signs. I'll have a look at it." He sent it back to me this morning, with a long commentary on the forms and spellings, which I am not inflicting on you, except his concluding remarks.

'"To sum up: it is in Old English of a strongly Mercian (West-Midland) colour, ninth century I should say.[73] There are no new words, except possibly *to-sprengdon*. There are several words, probably names and not Old English, that I have not succeeded in getting out; but you will excuse me from spending more time on them. My time is not unlimited. Whoever made the thing knew Old English tolerably well, though the style has the air of a translation. If he wanted to forge a bit of Old English, why did not he choose an interesting subject?"

'Well, I solved the names, as I told you; and there you have the text as old Rashbold sent it back, with the names put in. Only as my typewriter has no funny letters I have used *th* for the old thorn-letter. The translation is Rashbold's too.[74]

Hi alle sǽ on weorulde oferliodon, sohton hi nyston hwet; ah ǽfre walde heara heorte westward .... forthon hit swé gefyrn arǽdde se Ælmihtiga thæt hi sceoldan steorfan 7 thás weoruld ofgeofan .... hi ongunnon murcnian .... hit gelomp seoththan thæt se fúla deofles thegn se the Ælfwina folc (Zigūr) nemneth wéox swíthe on middangearde 7 he geáscode Westwearena meht 7 wuldor .... walde héalecran stól habban thonne Earendeles eafera seolf ahte ...... Thá cwóm he, (Tarcalion) se cyning up on middangeardes óran 7 he sende sóna his érendwracan to (Zigūre): heht hine on ofste cuman to thes cyninges manrǽdenne to búganne. 7 he (Zigūr) lytigende ge-éadmedde hine thæt he cwóm, wes thæh inwitful under, fácnes hogde Westfearena théode ..... swé adwalde he fornéan alle tha (Numenor)iscan mid wundrum 7 mid tácnum .... 7 hi gewarhton micelne alh on middan (Arminalēth)[75] there cestre on thæm héan munte the ǽr unawídlod wes 7 wearth nu to hǽthenum herge, 7 hi thér onsegdon unase[c]gendlic lác on unhálgum weofode ... Swé cwóm déathscua on Westfearena land 7 Godes bearn under sceadu féollon .... Thes ofer feola géra hit gelomp thæt (Tarcalione) wearth ældo onsǽge, thý wearth he hréow on móde 7 thá walde he be (Zigūres) onbryrdingum (Avalloni) mid ferde gefaran. Weron Westfearena scipferde swéswe unarímedlic égland on there sǽ .... ah tha Westfrégan gebédon hi to thǽm Ælmihtigan 7 be his léafe tosprengdon hi tha eorthan thæt alle sǽ nither gutan on efgrynde, 7 alle tha sceopu forwurdan, forthon seo eorthe togán on middum gársecge .... swearte windas asteogon 7 Ælfwines seofon sceopu eastweard adrǽfdon.

Nu sitte we on elelonde 7 forsittath tha blisse 7 tha eadignesse the iú wes 7 nu sceal eft cuman nǽfre. Ús swíthe onsiteth déathscua. Ús swíthe longath ..... On ærran mélum west leg reht weg, nu earon alle weogas wó. Feor nu is léanes lond. Feor nu is Neowollond[76] thæt geneotherade. Feor nu is Dréames lond thæt gedrorene.

All the seas in the world they sailed, seeking they knew not what; but their hearts were ever westward .... because so had the Almighty ordained it of old that they should die and leave this world .... they began to murmur .... It afterwards came to pass that the foul servant of the devil, whom the people of the ?Ælfwines name (Zigūr), grew mightily in middle-earth, and he learned of the power and glory of the *Westware* (Dwellers in the West) .... desired a higher throne than even the descendant of Earendel possessed ...... Then he, King (Tarcalion) landed on the shores of middle-earth, and at once he sent his messengers to (Zigūr), commanding him to come in haste to do homage to the king; and he (Zigūr) dissembling humbled himself and came, but was filled with secret malice, purposing treachery against the people of the Westfarers ..... Thus he led astray wellnigh all the (Numenore)ans with signs and wonders .... and they built a great temple in the midst of the town (of Arminalēth) on the high hill which before was undefiled but now became a heathen fane, and they there sacrificed unspeakable offerings on an unholy altar ... Thus came death-shade into the land of the Westfarers and God's children fell under the shadow .... Many years later it came to pass that old age assailed (Tarcalion); wherefore he became gloomy in heart, and at the instigation of (Zigūr) he wished to conquer (Avallōni) with a host. The ship-hosts of the Westfarers were like countless islands in the sea .... But the West-lords prayed to the Almighty, and by his leave split asunder the earth so that all seas should pour down into an abyss and the ships should perish; for the earth gaped open in the midst of the ocean .... black winds arose and drove away Ælfwine's seven ships.

Now we sit in the land of exile, and dwell cut off from the bliss and the blessedness that once was and shall never come again. The death-shade lies heavy on us; longing is on us ..... In former days west lay a straight way, now are all ways crooked. Far now is the land of gift. Far now is the ?prostrate land that is cast down. Far now is the land of Mirth that is fallen.

'Well, old Rashbold may not have found that interesting. But it depends what you're looking for. You people at any rate will find it interesting, I think, after the events of that night. You will notice that the original text is written continuously in bold-stroke hand (I don't doubt that the actual penman was old Edwin), but there are dividing dots at intervals. What we have is really a series of fragmentary extracts, separated, I should guess, by very various intervals of omission, extremely like Arry's snatches of Avallonian and Adunaic. Indeed this stuff corresponds closely to his (which in itself is very interesting): it includes all that he gave us, but gives a good deal more, especially at the beginning. You notice that there is a long gap at the same point as the break between his Text I and II.

'Of course, when old Rashbold said "the style has the air of a translation", he simply meant that the fabricator had not been quite successful in making the stuff sound like natural Anglo-Saxon. I can't judge that. But I daresay he is right, though his implied explanation may be wrong. This probably *is* a translation out of some other language into Anglo-Saxon. But not, I think, by the man who penned the page. He was in a hurry, or like Arry trying to catch the evanescent, and if he had had any time for translation he would have done it into modern English. I can't see any point in the Anglo-Saxon unless what he "saw" was already in it.

'I say "saw". For this stuff looks to me like the work of a man copying out all he had time to see, or all he found still intact and legible in some book.'

'Or all he could get down of some strongly visualized dream,' said Dolbear. 'And even so, I should guess that the hand that penned this stuff was already familiar with the strange script. It's written freely and doesn't look at all like the work of a man trying to copy something quite unknown. On your theory, Ramer, he wouldn't have had time, anyway.'

'Yes, it's a pretty puzzle,' said Frankley. 'But I don't suppose we shall get much forrarder[77] without Arry's help. So we must wait in patience till September, and hope for a light beyond the sea of Scripts. I must go. The scripts that are waiting for me are much longer and hardly more legible.'

'And probably more puzzling,' said Stainer. 'Surely there's no great mystery here, in spite of Ramer's attempts to create one. Here we have a specimen of old Edwin Lowdham's queer hobby: the fabrication of mythical texts; and the direct source of all Arry's stuff. He seems to have taken after his father, in more senses than one; though he's probably more inventive linguistically.'

'Really you're unteachable, Stainer,' said Dolbear. 'Why do you always prefer a theory that cannot be true, unless somebody is lying?'

'Who am I accusing of lying?'

'Well, wait until September, and then say what you've just said slowly and carefully to Arry, and you'll soon discover,' said Dolbear. 'If you've forgotten everything he said, I haven't. Good night!'

RD. PF. RS. MGR. NG.

Night 69.   Thursday, 25 September, 1987.

There was a large meeting in Jeremy's rooms. Jeremy and Lowdham had reappeared in Oxford only the day before, looking as if they had spent all the vacation examining rather than holidaymaking. There were eight other people present, and Cameron came in late.

After the experiences of June 12th most of the Club felt a trifle apprehensive, and conversation began by being jocular, in consequence. But Lowdham took no part in the jesting; he was unusually quiet.

'Well, Jerry,' said Frankley at last, 'you're the host. Have you arranged any entertainment for us? If not, after so many weeks, I daresay several of us have got things in our pockets.'

'That means that you have at any rate,' said Jeremy. 'Let's have it! We want, or at least I want, some time to tell you about what we've been doing, but there's no hurry.'

'That depends on how long your account of yourselves is going to take,' said Stainer. 'Did you do anything except drink and dawdle about the countryside?'

'We did,' said Lowdham. 'But there's no special reason to suppose that you'ld be interested to hear about it, Stainer.'

'Well, I'm here, and that indicates at least a faint interest,' said Stainer.

'All right! But if the Club really wants to hear us, then it's in for one or two meetings in which we shall take up all the time. Pip will burst, I can see, if he has to wait so long. Let him let his steam off first. What's it about, Horsey?'

'It'll explain itself, if the Club really wants to hear it,' said Frankley.

'Go on! Let's have it!' we said.

Frankley took a piece of paper out of his pocket and began.[78]

The Death of St. Brendan	At last out of the deep seas he passed,

The Death
of St.
Brendan

At last out of the deep seas he passed,
   and mist rolled on the shore;
under clouded moon the waves were loud,
   as the laden ship him bore   4
to Ireland, back to wood and mire,
   to the tower tall and grey,
where the knell of Cluain-ferta's bell[79]
   tolled in green Galway.   8
Where Shannon down to Lough Derg ran
   under a rainclad sky
Saint Brendan came to his journey's end
   to await his hour to die.   12

'O! tell me, father, for I loved you well,
   if still you have words for me,
of things strange in the remembering
   in the long and lonely sea,   16
of islands by deep spells beguiled
   where dwell the Elven-kind:
in seven long years the road to Heaven
   or the Living Land did you find?'   20

'The things I have seen, the many things,
   have long now faded far;
only three come clear now back to me:
   a Cloud, a Tree, a Star.   24
We sailed for a year and a day and hailed
   no field nor coast of men;
no boat nor bird saw we ever afloat
   for forty days and ten.   28
We saw no sun at set or dawn,
   but a dun cloud lay ahead,

and a drumming there was like thunder coming
    and a gleam of fiery red.   32

Upreared from sea to cloud then sheer
    a shoreless mountain stood;
its sides were black from the sullen tide
    to the red lining of its hood.   36
No cloak of cloud, no lowering smoke,
    no looming storm of thunder
in the world of men saw I ever unfurled
    like the pall that we passed under.   40
We turned away, and we left astern
    the rumbling and the gloom;
then the smoking cloud asunder broke,
    and we saw that Tower of Doom: 44
on its ashen head was a crown of red,
    where fires flamed and fell.
Tall as a column in High Heaven's hall,
    its feet were deep as Hell;   48
grounded in chasms the waters drowned
    and buried long ago,
it stands, I ween, in forgotten lands
    where the kings of kings lie low.   52

We sailed then on, till the wind had failed,
    and we toiled then with the oar,
and hunger and thirst us sorely wrung,
    and we sang our psalms no more.   56
A land at last with a silver strand
    at the end of strength we found;
the waves were singing in pillared caves
    and pearls lay on the ground;   60
and steep the shores went upward leaping
    to slopes of green and gold,
and a stream out of the rich land teeming
    through a coomb of shadow rolled.   64

Through gates of stone we rowed in haste,
    and passed, and left the sea;
and silence like dew fell in that isle,
    and holy it seemed to be.   68

As a green cup, deep in a brim of green,
   that with wine the white sun fills
was the land we found, and we saw there stand
   on a laund between the hills   72
a tree more fair than ever I deemed
   might climb in Paradise:
its foot was like a great tower's root,
   it height beyond men's eyes;   76
so wide its branches, the least could hide
   in shade an acre long,
and they rose as steep as mountain-snows
   those boughs so broad and strong;   80
for white as a winter to my sight
   the leaves of that tree were,
they grew more close than swan-wing plumes,
   all long and soft and fair.   84

We deemed then, maybe, as in a dream,
   that time had passed away
and our journey ended; for no return
   we hoped, but there to stay.   88
In the silence of that hollow isle,
   in the stillness, then we sang –
softly us seemed, but the sound aloft
   like a pealing organ rang.   92
Then trembled the tree from crown to stem;
   from the limbs the leaves in air
as white birds fled in wheeling flight,
   and left the branches bare.   96
From the sky came dropping down on high
   a music not of bird,
not voice of man, nor angel's voice;
   but maybe there is a third   100
fair kindred in the world yet lingers
   beyond the foundered land.
Yet steep are the seas and the waters deep
   beyond the White-tree Strand.'   104

'O! stay now, father! There's more to say.
   But two things you have told:
The Tree, the Cloud; but you spoke of three.
   The Star in mind do you hold?'   108

'The Star? Yes, I saw it, high and far,
   at the parting of the ways,
a light on the edge of the Outer Night[80]
   like silver set ablaze,   112
where the round world plunges steeply down,
   but on the old road goes,
as an unseen bridge that on arches runs
   to coasts than no man knows.'   116

'But men say, father, that ere the end
   you went where none have been.
I would hear you tell me, father dear,
   of the last land you have seen.'   120

'In my mind the Star I still can find,
   and the parting of the seas,
and the breath as sweet and keen as death
   that was borne upon the breeze.   124
But where they bloom those flowers fair,
   in what air or land they grow,
what words beyond the world I heard,
   if you would seek to know,   128
in a boat then, brother, far afloat
   you must labour in the sea,
and find for yourself things out of mind:
   you will learn no more of me.'   132

In Ireland, over wood and mire,
   in the tower tall and grey,
the knell of Cluain-ferta's bell
   was tolling in green Galway.   136
Saint Brendan had come to his life's end
   under a rainclad sky,
and journeyed whence no ship returns,
   and his bones in Ireland lie.   140

When Frankley stopped there was a silence. If he had hoped
for critical comments, adverse or favourable, he got none.

'Very odd indeed! Very odd!' said Lowdham at last. 'Have
you been in touch with our minds on the Ramer-system, Philip?
Anyway, when did you write that, and why?'

'There have been many more minds than yours, Arundel,
working on this theme, as has been pointed out before,' said
Ramer. 'Tell us about it, Philip!'

'There's nothing much to tell,' said Frankley. 'I woke up
about four days ago with the thing largely fixed, and the name
Brendan running in my head. The first dozen lines were already
made (or were still remembered), and some of the rest was too.
The pictures were quite clear for a while. I read the *Navigatio
Sancti Brendani*, of course, once upon a time, years ago, as well
as that early Anglo-French thing, Benedeit's *Vita*. But I've not
looked at them again – though perhaps if I did, I might find
them less dull and disappointing than I remember them.'

'I don't think you would,' said Lowdham; 'they're rather
dismal. Whatever merits they may have, any glimmer of a
perception of what they are talking about is not one of them,
trundling the magnificent theme to market like bunches of
neatly cut and dried flowers. The Old French thing may be very
interesting linguistically, but you won't learn much about the
West from that.

'Still that seems to be where you got your Volcano and Tree
from. But you've given them a twist that's not in your source.
You've put them in a different order, I think, making the Tree
further west; and your Volcano is not a hell-smithy, but
apparently a last peak of some Atlantis.[81] And the Tree in St.
Brendan was covered with white birds that were fallen angels.
The one really interesting idea in the whole thing, I thought:
they were angels that lived in a kind of limbo, because they were
only lesser spirits that followed Satan only as their feudal
overlord, and had no real part, by will or design, in the Great
Rebellion. But you make them a third *fair* race.'

'And that bit about the "round world" and the "old road",'
said Jeremy, 'where did you get that from?'

'I don't know,' said Frankley. 'It came in the writing. I got a
fleeting picture, but it's faded now.'

'The Parting of the Ways!' muttered Lowdham. 'What do you
know of that?'

'Oh, nothing. But, well – well, but you cannot really find or
see Paradise by ship, you know.'[82]

'No,' said Lowdham. 'Not in the High Legends, not in those
that have power. No longer. And it was seldom permitted
anyway, even before.' He said no more, and we all sat still for a
while.

The silence was finally broken by Markison. 'Well,' he said, 'I
hope you're not going to take the line of St. Brendan to the

monk: "you will learn no more of me." Have you two nothing
more to say?'

'Yes indeed!' said Jeremy. 'But we've not been to Paradise.'

'Where have you been then?'

'We ended up at Porlock[83] on the 13th, that's last Saturday
week,' said Jeremy.

'Why Porlock? Not a very exciting place, is it?'

'Not now, maybe,' Lowdham answered. 'You'll see a sort of
reason for it, though. But if you mean: did we wittingly pick on
Porlock? the answer is no.'

'We started off down in Cornwall, Land's End,' said Jeremy.
'That was just before the end of June.'

'Started off?' said Guildford. 'I got your letter on June 25th,
but that still leaves a bit of a gap. We last saw you on the night
of June 12th: not a date we're likely to forget in a hurry. What
happened during the next ten days?'

'Was it as long as that?' said Lowdham blankly. 'I don't really
know. We landed in a cove. I seem to remember the boat
grinding on rocks and then being flung up on the shingles. We
were damned lucky. She was holed and sinking, and we ought
to have been drowned. Or did I dream it?' He knitted his brows.
'Bless me, if I'm sure. D'you remember, Trewyn?'[84]

'No,' said Jeremy, thinking. 'No, I don't. The first thing I can
remember is your saying: "We'd better let Nick have a line to
know that we haven't been drowned." Yes, yes of course: we'd
been caught at sea in a storm of wind and lightning, and as you
all knew we had gone sailing, we thought you might be
anxious.'

'Don't you remember the night up in my rooms, the night of
the great storm?' said Ramer.

'Yes, I remember bringing some texts round,' said Lowdham.
'And I remember the Eagles. But surely the storm came afterwards, after we had started on our research tour?'

'All right,' said Dolbear. 'Don't bother with all that now;
there will be plenty of time to talk about it later. Get on with
your own tale.'

'Well,' said Jeremy, 'we stuck to the west coasts as much as
we could, staying by the sea, and walking as near to it as
possible, when we did not go by boat. Arry is an able seaman,
and you can still get small sailing craft in the West, and
sometimes an old sailor to help who can still handle a boat

without petrol. But after our wreck we did not sail again till we got round to North Devon. We actually crossed by boat from Bideford to South Wales in July, and then we went on to Ireland, right up the west coast of it by stages.

'We took a look at Scotland, but no further north than Mull. There seemed nothing for us there, no feel in the air at all. So we went back to Hibernia.[85] The great storm had left more traces there than anywhere, and not only in visible damage. There was a good deal of that, but much less than you would expect, and it did not interest us so much as the effect on the people and the stories that we found going about. People in Galway – well, for the matter of that, from Brandon Hill to Slieve League[86] – seemed to have been pretty well shaken by it, and were still scared for weeks afterwards. If the wind got up at all, as of course it did from time to time, they huddled indoors; and some would begin to trek inland.

'We both heard many tales of the huge waves "high as hills" coming in on the Black Night. And curiously enough, many of the tale-tellers agreed that the greatest waves were like phantoms, or only half real: "like shadows of mountains of dark black wicked water". Some rolled far inland and yet did little damage before, well, disappearing, melting away. We were told of one that had rolled clean over the Aran Isles[87] and passed up Galway Bay, and so on like a cloud, drowning the land in a ghostly flood like rippling mist, almost as far as Clonfert.

'And we came across one old man, a queer old fellow whose English was hardly intelligible, on the road not far from Loughrea.[88] He was wild and ragged, but tall and rather impressive. He kept pointing westward, and saying, as far as we could gather: "It was out of the Sea they came, as they came in the days before the days". He said that he had seen a tall black ship high on the crest of the great wave, with its masts down and the rags of black and yellow sails flapping on the deck, and great tall men standing on the high poop and wailing, like the ghosts they were; and they were borne far inland, and came, well, not a soul knows where they came.

'We could get no more out of him, and he went on westward and vanished into the twilight, and who he was or where he was going we did not discover either. Apart from such tales and rumours we had no real adventures. The weather was not too bad generally, and we walked a lot, and slept pretty well. A good many dreams came, especially in Ireland, but they were very slippery; we couldn't catch them. Arry got whole lists of ghost-words, and I had some fleeting pictures, but they seldom fitted together. And then, when we thought our time was up, we came to Porlock.

'As we crossed over the Severn Sea[89] earlier in the summer, Arry had looked back, along the coast to the south, at the shores of Somerset, and he had said something that I couldn't catch. It was ancient English, I think, but he didn't know himself: it faded from him almost as soon as he had spoken. But I had a sudden feeling that there was something important waiting for us there, and I made up my mind to take him back that way before the end of our journey, if there was time. So I did.

'We arrived in a small boat at Porlock Weir on Saturday, September 13th. We put up at The Ship, up in Porlock itself; but we felt drawn back shorewards, and as soon as we had fixed our rooms we went out and turned westward, going up onto the cliffs and along as far as Culbone and beyond. We saw the sun set, dull, hazy, and rather grim, about half past six, and then we turned back for supper.

'The twilight deepened quickly, and I remember that it seemed suddenly to grow very chilly; a cold wind sprang up from the land and blew out westward towards the dying sun; the sea was leaden. We both felt tired and anxious, for no clear reason: we had been feeling rather cheery. It was then that Arry turned away from the sea and took my arm, and he said quite clearly, and I heard him and understood him: *Uton efstan nú, Tréowine! Me ofthyncth thisses windes. Mycel wén is Deniscra manna to niht.*[90] And that seemed to break my dreams. I began to remember, and piece together a whole lot of things as we walked back to the town; and that night I had a long series of dreams and remembered a good deal of them.'

'Yes,' said Lowdham, 'and something happened to me at that moment, too. I began to *see* as well as to hear. Tréowine, that is Wilfrid Trewyn Jeremy, and I seemed to have got into the same dream together, even before we were asleep. The faces in the hotel looked pale and thin, and the walls and furniture only half real: other things and faces were vaguely moving behind them all. We were approaching the climax of some change that had begun last May, when we started to research together.

'Anyway, we went to bed, and we both dreamed; and we woke up and immediately compared notes; and we slept again and woke and did the same. And so it went on for several days, until we were quite exhausted. So at last we decided to go home; we made up our minds to come back to Oxford the next day, Thursday. That night, Wednesday, September 17th, something happened: the dreams coalesced, took shape, and came into the open, as you might say. It seemed impossible to believe when it was over that years had not slipped by, and that it was still Thursday, September 18th, 1987, and we could actually return here as we had planned. I remember staring incredulously round the dining-room, that seemed to have grown strangely solid again, half wondering if it was not some new dream-trick. And we went into the post-office and a bank to make sure of the date! Then we crept back here secretly, a week ago, and stayed in retreat until yesterday, conferring and putting together all we had got before we came out of hiding. I think I'll leave Trewyn to do the telling. He's better at it than I am; and he saw more, after the earlier scenes.'

'No!' said Jeremy. 'Alwin had better begin. The earlier part is his, more than mine. He remembers more of what was said by me than I do myself. Go on now, Arry!'

'Well', said Lowdham, 'it seemed to me like this. I woke with a start.[91] Evidently I had been dozing on a bench near the fire. The voices seemed to pour over me like a stream. I felt that I had been dreaming, something very odd and vivid, but I could not catch it; and for a minute or two the familiar scene in the hall seemed strange, and the English speech about me sounded alien and remote, although the voices were for the most part using the soft speech of western Wessex that I knew so well. Here and there I caught the tones of the Marchers from up beyond Severn-mouth; and I heard a few speaking queerly, using uncouth words after the manner of those from the eastern shires.

'I looked down the hall, hoping to see my friend Tréowine Céolwulf's son. There was a great crowd in hall, for King Éadweard was there. The Danish ships were in the Severn Sea, and all the south shores were in arms. The heathen earls had been defeated away up in the west marches at Archenfield, but the pirates were still at large off the Welsh coast, trying to get food and supplies, and the Devenish men and Somersets[92] were on guard. There had been a bitter affray at Watchet a few nights before, but the Danish men had been driven off. Porlock's turn might come.

'I looked round at the faces of the men: some old and worn,

some still young and keen; but they seemed dim, almost dreamlike in the wavering torches. The candles on the high table were guttering. A wind was blowing outside the great wooden hall, surging round the house; the timbers creaked. I felt tired. Not only because Tréowine and I had had a long spell of coastguard duty, and had had little sleep since the raid on Watchet; but I was tired of this woeful and dishevelled world, slipping slowly back into decay, as it seemed to me, with its petty but cruel wars, and all the ruin of the good and fair things there had been in my grandsires' days. The hangings on the wall behind the dais were faded and worn, and on the table there were but few vessels or candlesticks of gold and silver smithcraft that had survived the pillage of the heathen.

'The sound of the wind disturbed me and brought back to me old longings that I thought I had buried. I found myself thinking of my father, old Éadwine Óswine's son,[93] and the strange tales he had told me when I was a small lad and he a grizzled seaman of more than fifty winters: tales of the west coasts, and far islands, and of the deep sea, and of a land there was far away, where there was peace and fruitfulness among a fair folk that did not wither.

'But Éadwine had taken his ship, Éarendel, out into the deep sea long ago, and he never returned. What haven received him no man under heaven could tell. That was in the black winter, when Alfred went into hiding[94] and so many men of Somerset fled over sea. My mother fled to her kindred among the West Welsh[95] for a while, and I had seen only nine winters in this world, for I was born just before the holy Éadmund was done to death by the heathen.[96] I learned the Welsh tongue and much craft upon the wild waters, before I came back in full manhood to Somerset and the service of the good king in his last wars.[97]

'I had been in Íraland more than once; and wherever I went I sought tales of the Great Sea and what lay out upon it, or beyond, if haply it had any further shore. Folk had not much to tell for certain; but there was talk of one Maelduin[98] who had sailed to new lands, and of the holy Brendan and others. And some there were who said that there had been a land of Men away west in long days of yore, but that it had been cast down and those that escaped had come to Ériu[99] (so they called Íraland) in their ships, and their descendants lived on there, and in other lands about the shores of Gársecg. But they dwindled and forgot, and nought now was left of them but a wild strain in

the blood of men of the West. "And you will know those that
have it by the sea-longing that is on them," they said; "and it is
many that it draws out west to their death or to come never
back among living men".

'And I thought that maybe the blood of such men ran in my
father's veins and my own, for our kin had long been settled at
Glastonbury, where there was rumour of strange comers out of
the sea in days of old. And the sound of the winds and seas on
the west beaches was ever a restless music to me, at once a pain
and a desire; and the pain was keener in Spring, and the desire
stronger in Autumn. And now it was Autumn, and the desire
was scarcely to be borne; for I was growing old. And the seas
were wide. So I mused, forgetting once again where I was, but
not sleeping.

'I heard the crash of waves on the black cliffs, and sea-birds
wailing; snow fell. Then the sea opened before me, pale and
boundless. And now the sun shone above me, and the land and
the sound of it and the smell of it fell far behind. Tréowine was
beside me, and we were alone, going west. And the sun came
down and sank towards the sea before us, and still we sailed
west, on towards the setting sun, and the longing in my heart
drew me on against my fear and land-bound will. And so I
passed into night in the midst of the deep waters, and I thought
that a sweet fragrance was borne on the air.

'And suddenly I was brought back to Porlock and the hall of
the king's thegn Odda. Men were calling out for a minstrel, and
a minstrel I was, when the mood was on me. The king himself,
stern Éadweard Alfred's son – tired before old age he looked –
sent to me, bidding me sing or speak. He was a stern man, as I
say, but like his father in having an ear, when he had the time,
for the sound of the old measures. I rose and walked to the steps
of the dais, and bowed.

'"*Westu hál, Ælfwine!*" said the king. "*Sing me nú hwæt-
wegu: sum eald léoth, gif thu wilt.*"

'"*Ic can lýt on léothcræft, hláford,*" I said; "*ac this geworht'ic
unfyrn thé to weorthmynde.*"

'And then I began, and let my voice roll out; but my mouth
did not speak the words that I had purposed: of all that I had so
carefully devised against the event, in the night watches or
pacing on the cold cliffs, not a stave came out.

    Hwæt! Éadweard cyning Ælfredes sunu
    beorna béaggifa on Brytenríce

æt Ircenfelda[100] *ealdorlangne tír*
geslóg æt sæcce sweorda ecgum *

and all the rest, of such sort as kings look for: not a word of it.
Instead I said this: [101]

Monath módes lust mid mereflóde
forth tó féran, thæt ic feor heonan
ofer gársecges grimme holmas
Ælfwina eard út geséce.
Nis me tó hearpan hyge ne tó hringthege,
ne tó wífe wynn, ne tó worulde hyht,
ne ymb ówiht elles, nefne ymb ýtha gewealc.

Then I stopped suddenly, and stood confused. There was some
laughter, from those not under the king's eye, and a few
mocking calls. There were many folk in hall who knew me well,
and they had long been pleased to make a jest of my talk of the
Great Sea; and it now pleased them to pretend that I had spoken
of *Ælfwines eard*, as if I had a realm of my own out westward.

' "If England is not good enough, let him go find a better
land!" they cried. "He need go no further than Íraland, if he
longs for elves and uncouth wights, God save him! Or he can go
with the heathen to the Land of Ice that they say they have
found."

' "If he has no mind to sing for the raising of our hearts, let us
find a *scop* who will."

' "We have had enough of the sea," shouted one of the
Marchers. "A spell of Dane-hunting round the rim of Wales
would cure him."

'But the king sat gravely and did not smile, and many besides
were silent. I could see in his eyes that the words had touched
him, though I doubt not, he had heard others like them often
before.

' "Peace!" said old Odda of Portloca, master of the hall.
"Ælfwine here has sailed more seas than you have heard of, and

---

* Lowdham provides the following translations 'for Philip's benefit'.
'Greetings, Ælfwine,' said the king. 'Recite me something, some old
poem if you like.' 'I have little skill in poetry, my lord,' I said, 'but I
composed this in your honour a little while ago.'
'Lo! Éadweard the king, Alfred's scion, brave men's patron, in
Britain's island at Archenfield undying fame in battle reaped him with
reddened blades.'
For the translation of the next verses see Night 66, p. 244. N.G.

the lands of the Welsh and Irish are not strange to him. With the king's leave let him say what his mood bids him. It is no harm to turn from these sorry shores for a while and speak of marvels and strange lands, as the old verse-makers often did. Will you not speak us something by the elder poets, Ælfwine?"

'"Not now, lord," I said; for I was abashed and weary, and I felt as a man in a dream who finds himself unclad in the market-place. "There are others in hall. Men of the Marches I hear by their speech; and they were used to boast of their songcraft, before the Danes came. With the king's leave I will sit."

'At that a man from among the Marchers leapt to his feet and got leave to speak; and lo! I saw it was my friend Tréowine. A small dark man he was, but he had a good voice, if a strange way with his words. His father Céolwulf, I had heard, claimed to come of the kin of the kings that sat at Tamworth[102] of old; but Tréowine had come south many years before. Ere I had found a seat, he had a foot on the step and had begun.

'His verse was in the old style, indeed it was the work of some old poet, maybe, though I had not heard it before, and many words were dark to us of later times; but he gave them out strong and true, now loud, now soft, as the theme asked, without help of harp. Thus he began, and soon all the hall was stone-still:

> Hwæt! wé on geárdagum of Gársecge
> fyrn gefrugnon of feorwegum
> to Longbeardna londgemǽrum
> tha hí ǽr héoldon, íglond micel
> on North-théodum, nacan bundenne
> scírtimbredne scríthan gangan ...

'But if it was dark to some of our younger men of Wessex, it will be as night to you, who have passed so much further down the streams of time, since the old poets sang in Angel of the grey North-seas; so I have cast it into the speech of your age. And I have done so, for by chance, or more than chance, this song had a part in what befell after, and its theme was knit up with my own thoughts, and it whetted my longing the more.

King Sheave[103]

In days of yore out of deep Ocean to the Longobards, in the land dwelling that of old they held in the isles of the North, a ship came sailing, shining-timbered, without oar or mast, eastward floating. The sun behind it sinking westward with flame kindled the fallow water. Wind was wakened. Over the world's margin clouds grey-helméd climbed slowly up, wings unfolding wide and looming, as mighty eagles moving onward to eastern Earth, omens bearing.

Men there marvelled, in the mist standing of the dark islands in the deeps of time: laughter they knew not, light nor wisdom; shadow was upon them, and sheer mountains stalked behind them, stern and lifeless, evil-haunted. The East was dark.

The ship came shining to the shore driven, and strode upon the strand, till its stern rested on sand and shingle. The sun went down. The clouds overcame the cold heavens. In fear and wonder to the fallow water sad-hearted men swiftly hastened, to the broken beaches, the boat seeking gleaming-timbered in the grey twilight. They looked within, and there laid sleeping a boy they saw breathing softly: his face was fair, his form lovely; his limbs were white, his locks raven golden-braided. Gilt and carven with wondrous work was the wood about him. In golden vessel gleaming water stood beside him; strung with silver a harp of gold beneath his hand rested; his sleeping head was softly pillowed on a sheaf of corn shimmering palely, as the fallow gold doth from far countries west of Angol. Wonder filled them.

The boat they hauled, and on the beach moored it high above the breakers, then with hands lifted from the bosom its burden. The boy slumbered. On his bed they bore him to their bleak dwellings, dark-walled and drear, in a dim region between waste and sea. There of wood builded high above the houses was a hall standing, forlorn and empty. Long had it stood so, no noise knowing, night nor morning, no light seeing. They laid him there, under lock left him lonely sleeping in the hollow darkness. They held the doors. Night wore away. New awakened, as ever on earth, early morning; day came dimly. Doors were opened. Men strode within, then amazed halted; fear and wonder filled the watchmen. The house was bare, hall deserted; no form found they on the floor lying, but by bed forsaken the bright vessel dry and empty in the dust standing. The guest was gone.

Grief o'ercame them. In sorrow they sought him, till the sun rising over the hills of heaven to the homes of men light came bearing. They looked upward, and high upon a hill hoar and treeless gold was glimmering. Their guest stood there with head uplifted, hair unbraided; harpstrings they heard in his hand ringing, at his feet they saw the fallow-golden corn-sheaf lying. Then clear his voice a song began, sweet, unearthly, words in music woven strangely in a tongue unknown. Trees stood silent, and men unmoving marvelling harkened.

Middle-earth had known for many ages neither song nor singer; no sight so fair had eyes of mortal, since the earth was young, seen when waking in that sad country long forsaken. No lord they had, no king, nor counsel, but the cold terror that dwelt in the desert, the dark shadow that haunted the hills and the hoar forest: Dread was their master. Dark and silent, long years forlorn lonely waited the hall of kings, house forsaken without fire or food.

Forth men hastened from their dim houses. Doors were opened, and gates unbarred. Gladness wakened. To the hill they thronged, and their heads lifting on their guest they gazed. Grey-bearded men bowed before him and blessed his coming their years to heal; youths and maidens, wives and children, welcome gave him. His song ended. Silent standing he looked upon them. Lord they called him; king they made him, crowned with golden wheaten garland: white his raiment, his harp his sceptre. In his house was fire, food and wisdom: there fear came not. To manhood he grew, might and glory.

Sheave they called him, whom the ship brought them, a name renowned in the North-countries ever since in song; but a secret hidden his true name was in tongue unknown of a far country, where the falling seas wash western shores, beyond the ways of men since the world worsened. The word is forgotten and the name perished.

Their need he healed, and laws renewed long forsaken. Words he taught them wise and lovely: their tongue ripened in the time of Sheave to song and music. Secrets he opened, runes revealing. Riches he gave them, reward of labour, wealth and comfort from the earth calling, acres ploughing, sowing in season seed of plenty, hoarding in garner golden harvest for the help of men. The hoar forest in his days drew back to the dark mountains; the shadow lifted, and shining corn, white ears of wheat, whispered in the breezes where waste had been. The woods blossomed.

Halls and houses hewn of timber, strong towers of stone steep and lofty, golden-gabled, in his guarded city they raised and roofed. In his royal dwelling of wood well-carven the walls were wrought; fair-hued figures filled with silver, gold, and scarlet, gleaming hung there, stories boding of strange countries, were one wise in wit the woven legends to thread with thought. At his throne men found counsel and comfort and care's healing, justice in judgement. Generous-handed his gifts he gave. Glory was uplifted. Far sprang his fame over fallow water; through Northern lands the renown echoed of the shining king, Sheave the mighty.

'When he ended there was loud applause – loudest from those who understood least, so that men should perceive how well they could thread the old songs; and they passed a horn to Tréowine's hand. But ere he drank, I rose up, and there where I stood I finished his song for him:

Seven sons he begat, sire[104] of princes, men great of mood, mighty-handed and high-hearted. From his house cometh the seed of kings, as songs tells us, fathers of the fathers, who before the change in the Elder Years the earth governed, Northern kingdoms named and founded, shields of their people: Sheave begat them: Sea-danes and Goths, Swedes and Northmen, Franks and Frisians, folk of the islands, Swordmen and Saxons, Swabians, Angles, and the Longobards, who long ago beyond Mircwudu a mighty realm and wealth won them in the Welsh countries, where Ælfwine, Éadwine's son in Italy was king. All that has passed!

'And with that, while men still stared – for there were many that knew my name and my father's – I beckoned to Tréowine, and we strode from the hall into the darkness and the wind.

'And there I think I must end for tonight,' said Lowdham, with a sudden change of tone and voice that startled us: we jumped like men waked suddenly from a dream. It seemed as if one man had vanished and another had sprung up in his place, so vividly had he presented Ælfwine to us as he spoke. Quite plainly I had seen him standing there, a man very like Arry but not the same – rather taller and less thick, and looking older and greyer, though by his account he was just Arry's age it seemed; I had seen the glittering of his eyes as he looked round and strode out. The hall and the faces I saw in a blur behind him, and Tréowine was only a dim shadow against the flicker of far candles as he spoke of King Sheave; but I heard the wind rushing above all the words.

'Next meeting Tréowine and I will go on again, if you want any more of this,' said Lowdham. 'Ælfwine's tale is nearly done; and after that we shall flit more quickly, for we shall pass further and further from what Stainer would call History – in which old Ælfwine really walked, at least for the most part, I guess.

'If you haven't got a horn, fill me a mug! For I have done both Ælfwine's part and Tréowine's, and it is thirsty work, a minstrel's.'

Markison handed him a pewter tankard full. '*Béo thu blíthe æt thisse béorthege!*'[105] he said, for ancient English is only one of the innumerable things he knows.

Lowdham drained the tankard at a draught. And so ended the sixty-ninth night of the Notion Club. It was agreed to meet again in only one week's time, on October 2nd, lest the onset of term should hinder the further tales of Ælfwine and Tréowine.

WTJ. AAL MGR. RD. PF. RS. JM. JJR. NG.

Night 70.   Thursday, 2 October, 1987.

Here the typescript text ends, not at the foot of a page; and here the manuscript ends also, without the date-heading for the next meeting. It is certain that my father wrote nothing further. There are, however, two brief texts, written very fast in pencil but fortunately just about legible, which give a glimpse of what he had in mind. Though both obviously belong to the same time, it is not clear which preceded the other; the one that I give first was written on the back of a draft for the passage in E beginning 'It was then that Arry turned away from the sea' (p. 268).

The Danes attack Porlock that night. They are driven off and take refuge by swimming out to the ships and so to 'Broad Relic'.[106] A small 'cnearr'[107] is captured.

It is not well guarded. Ælfwine tells Tréowine that he has stores laid up. They move the boat and stock it the following night and set sail West.

The wind is from the East, and they sail on and on, and come to no land; they are exhausted, and a dreamlike death seems to be coming over them. They smell [? the] fragrance. *Swéte is blóstma bræþ begeondan sǽ*[108] says Ælfwine, and struggles to rise. But the wind changes: great clouds come out of the West. 'Behold the Eagles of the Lords of the West coming over Númenor' said Ælfwine, and fell back as one dead.

Tréowine sees the round world [?curve] below, and straight ahead a shining land, before the wind seizes them and drives them away. In the gathering dark [*or* dusk] he sees a bright star, shining in a rent in the cloud in the West. *Éalá Éarendel engla beorhtast.* Then he remembers no more.

'Whether what follows is my direct dream,' said Jeremy, 'or the dreams of Tréowine and Ælfwine in the deeps of the sea I cannot say.'

I woke to find myself

Here this sketch tantalisingly breaks off. On the same page and fairly certainly written at the same time stands this note:

The theory is that the sight and memory goes on with *descendants* of Elendil and Voronwë (= Tréowine) but *not* re-incarnation; they are different people even if they still resemble one another in some ways even after a lapse of many generations.

The second sketch is at first fuller (and may for that reason be thought to have followed the other), but then passes into an outline of headings and brief statements.

Danes attack that night but are driven off. Ælfwine and Tréowine are among those who capture a small ship that had ventured close inshore and stuck. The rest escape to 'Broad Relic'.

It is grey dawn ere all is over. 'Going to rest?' said Tréowine to Ælfwine. 'Yes, I hope so,' said Ælfwine, 'but not in this land, Tréowine! I am going – to seek a land, whence King Sheaf came, maybe; or to find Death, if that be not the name for the same place.'

'What do you mean?'

'I am sailing,' said Ælfwine. 'The wind blows westward. And here's a ship that knows the sea. The king himself has given it to me. I have handled many such before. Will you come? Two could make shift to sail her.'

'We should need more; and what of water and victual?'

'I have all prepared,' said Ælfwine, 'for this venture has long been brewing in my mind, and now at last chance and desire are matched. There is provision down in my house by the weir, and we'll find a couple of lusty men of Somerset whom I know. They'll go as far as Ireland at the least, and then we'll see.'

'Yes, you'll find madmen enough there,' said Tréowine, 'but I'll go with you so far at the least.'

When it was dark on the following night Ælfwine brought along Ceola (of Somerset) and Geraint (of West Wales) and we stowed her, and thrust her off. The east wind freshened, and we set sail and drove out into the dark waters. There's no need to make long tale of it: we bent our course past the horns of Pembrokeshire and so out to sea. And then we had a change of weather, for a wild wind from the South-west drove us back and northward, and we hardly made haven upon a long firth in the South-west of Ireland. I'd never been there before, for I was younger than Ælfwine. We sat out the storm there, and got fresh supplies, and then Ælfwine spoke of his desire to Ceola and Geraint.

Tréowine sees the straight road and the world plunging down. Ælfwine's vessel seems to be taking the straight road and falls [sic] in a swoon of fear and exhaustion.

Ælfwine gets view of the Book of Stories; and writes down what he can remember.

Later fleeting visions.

Beleriand tale.

Sojourn in Númenor before and during the fall ends with *Elendil* and *Voronwë* fleeing on a hill of water into the dark with Eagles and lightning pursuing them. Elendil has a book which he has written.

His descendants get glimpses of it.

Ælfwine has one.

On the same slip of paper and written at the same time as this second text is a note saying that Edwin Lowdham's page 'should be in Anglo-Saxon *straight*, without some scraps of Númenórean', and that 'the Anglo-Saxon should *not* be written in Númenórean script'. Finally there stands this last note: 'At end Lowdham and Jeremy can revisualize some more fragments, but it is hardly needed, as Lowdham and Jeremy have a vivid dream of the Fall of Númenor.'

From the beginning of this history, the story of the Englishman Ælfwine, called also Eriol, who links by his strange voyage the vanished world of the Elves with the lives of later men, has constantly appeared. So in the last words of the *Quenta Noldorinwa* (IV.165) it is said:

To Men of the race of Eärendel have they [*the tales of the Quenta*] at times been told, and most to Eriol, who alone of the mortals of later days, and yet now long ago, sailed to the Lonely Isle, and came back to the land of Leithien [*Britain*] where he lived, and remembered things that he had heard in fair Cortirion, the city of the Elves in Tol Eressëa.

He is seen in Tavrobel of Tol Eressëa translating *The Annals of Valinor* and *The Annals of Beleriand* from the work of Pengolod the Wise of Gondolin, and parts of his Anglo-Saxon text are preserved (IV.263, 281 ff.); the *Ainulindalë* was spoken to him by Rúmil of Tûn (V.156); the *Lhammas* of Pengolod was seen by Ælfwine 'when he came into the West' (V.167). To the *Quenta Silmarillion* his note is appended (V.203): 'The work of Pengolod I learned much by heart, and turned into my tongue, some during my sojourn in the West, but most after my return to Britain'; after which follow the lines of Ælfwine Wídlást that Arundel Lowdham heard, as Alboin Errol had heard them: *Fela bið on Westwegum werum uncuðra, wundra ond wihta, wlitescyne lond* ...

Crossing this theme, and going back to one form of the old story *Ælfwine of England* (II.322 and note 42), was the story that Ælfwine never set foot on the Lonely Isle. So in my father's sketches for those further reaches of *The Lost Road* that he never wrote, Ælfwine on the one hand (V.78) awakes on the beach of the Lonely Isle 'to find the ship being drawn by people walking in the water', and there in Eressëa he 'is told the Lost Tales'; but in other notes of that time (V.80), after 'the vision of Eressëa', the 'west wind blows them back', and they come to shore in Ireland. In the note to the final version of the poem *The Song of Ælfwine* (a version which I suggested was 'probably from the years after *The Lord of the Rings*, though it might be associated with the *Notion Club Papers* of 1945', V.100) it is told (V.103):

Ælfwine (Elf-friend) was a seaman of England of old who, being driven out to sea from the coast of Erin, passed into the deep waters of the West, and according to legend by some strange chance or grace found the 'straight road' of the Elvenfolk and came at last to the Isle of Eressëa in Elvenhome. Or maybe, as some say, alone in the waters, hungry and athirst, he fell into a trance and was granted a vision of that isle as it once had been, ere a West-wind arose and drove him back to Middle-earth.

In the first of the sketches just given Ælfwine and Tréowine are in sight of the 'shining land' when the wind drives them away; but in the second my father once more sees Ælfwine in the Lonely Isle looking at 'the Book of Stories'. But the whole conception has now developed a disturbing complexity: the Downfall of Númenor, the Straight Road into the West, the ancient histories in unknown language and unknown script preserved in Eressëa, the mysterious voyage of Edwin Lowdham in his ship *The Éarendel* and the single preserved page of his book in Anglo-Saxon, the 're-emergence' in his son Arundel (Éarendel) and his friend Wilfrid Trewin Jeremy of 'the sight and memory' of their forebears in distant ages communicated in dreams, and the violent irruption of the Númenórean legend into the late twentieth century – all framed within an elaborate foreseeing of the future (not without comic and ironic elements).

There is a slip of paper on which my father sketched out very rapidly ideas for what would become 'Part Two' of The Notion Club Papers; this was undoubtedly written before he began the writing of the manuscript E, but it is most conveniently given here.

Do the Atlantis story and abandon Eriol-Saga, with Loudham, Jeremy, Guildford and Ramer taking part.

After night 62.[109] Loudham, walking home with Guildford and Ramer, apologizes for appearing to scoff. They halt in Radcliffe Square and Loudham looks up at the Camera. It is starry, but a black cloud is coming up out of the West [changed at once to (but) caught like smoke in the moon a wisp of cloud seemed to be issuing from the lantern of the dome]. Loudham halts and looks up, passing [his] hand over his forehead. 'I was going to say,' he says, 'that – I don't know. I wonder.' He hopped into college and said no more.

Night 65. Truncated. It begins after lacuna. Conversation had been about myths, but Loudham had been restless, walking about twisting his handkerchief and making some unsuccessful jests.

Suddenly he went to the window. It was a summer night and he looked out, then spoke in a loud solemn voice. 'Behold the Eagles of the Lords of the West coming over Númenor.' We were startled. Some of us went and looked out. A great cloud was eating up the stars, spreading two vast dark wings south and north.

Loudham drew away. They discuss Númenor? Loudham's ancestry?

The words with which this sketch begins, 'Do the Atlantis story and abandon Eriol-Saga ...', are remarkable. In the first place, they seem to support the analysis of the way in which The Notion Club Papers developed that I have suggested at various points, and which I will state here in a more coherent form.

'Part One' of the Papers (not at this time conceived to be so) had reached the stage of the completed manuscript B (see p. 147 and note 4), and at this stage Harry Loudham was not seen as contributing greatly to the discussions of the Notion Club: a maker of jokes and interjections. Above all, he had no especial interest in the question of Atlantis or in names from unknown worlds. Examples of this have been pointed out in the notes to Part One.[110]

Only when the manuscript B was completed (and the text of 'Part One' of the *Papers* very largely achieved) did the thought enter: 'Do the Atlantis story.' With Loudham's standing beneath the Radcliffe Camera and staring up at the sky the whole course of the *Papers* was changed. Adjustments and additions were subsequently made to 'Part One', hinting at his peculiar 'affinity' with the legend of the downfall of the island empire, and changing the nature of his interests: for whereas in B Guildford could say of him (p. 214 note 23): 'Memoirs of the courts of minor 18th century monarchs are his natural browsing-ground', in the list of members of the Club given on p. 151 (made when B had been completed)[111] he has 'special interests in Icelandic and Anglo-Saxon'. And as the writing of 'Part Two' in the manuscript E proceeded he ceased to be Harry and became Arry, for Arundel (Éarendel).

But when my father wrote 'Do the Atlantis story' he also said that the 'Eriol-Saga' should be abandoned, although there is no mention of any such matter in the text of 'Part One'. The only explanation that I can see is that the 'Eriol-Saga' had been, up to this time, what my father had in mind for the further course of the meetings of the Notion Club, but was now rejecting in favour of 'Atlantis'.

In the event he did not do so; he found himself drawn back into the ideas that he had sketched for *The Lost Road* (see V.77–8), but now in a conception so intricate that one need perhaps look no further for an answer to the question, why were *The Notion Club Papers* abandoned?

NOTES

1   Pencilled at the head of the first page of the sole manuscript ('E') of 'Part Two' is 'The Strange [Investigation >] Case of Arundel Loudham', and the same title together with the number '[Part] II' is found on a separate title-page that seems to belong with E (p. 153 note 2). The second text of this Part, the typescript 'F', while distinct from the typescript D of Part One and with a separate pagination, has no title or heading before 'Night 62'. — *Loudham* is spelt thus in E at first, but becomes *Lowdham* in the course of the writing of the manuscript (p. 153 note 4).

2   In E there is no Night 62: see p. 195 (Guildford's footnote) and note 47.

3   In E there is no head-note to Night 63 except the word 'defective', and thus no reference to 'the *imrám*'. In the final text, the typescript F, the number of the night to which the mention of the *imrám* is referred was left blank; I have added '69', since on that night Frankley read his poem on Saint Brendan (pp. 261 ff.). — The bracketed opening word 'Good', supposed to be absent in the original, was added by the editor.

4   *the High:* High Street; *Radcliffe Square,* see p. 222 note 69.

5   For 'especially about the *imrám*' E has 'especially about the Enkeladim', changed soon to 'the Imrám'. For references to the *Enkeladim (En-keladim)* in Part One see pp. 199, 206–7, 221 note 65; and for the *imrama* (tales of seavoyaging) see V.81–2.

6   *Nordics:* E has 'philologists' (but Ramer himself was a philologist).

7   *B.N.C.:* the common abbreviation of Brasenose College, whose gate is in Radcliffe Square. The 'lane' along which Ramer and Guildford walked after Lowdham had left them is Brasenose Lane, leading from Radcliffe Square to Turl Street (p. 213 note 18). — For *The Camera* in the following sentence see p. 222 note 69.

8   On the inclusion of Night 64 see the Editor's Foreword, p. 156.

9   In E as originally written the entire opening of Night 65 had been lost, and the text only takes up with '[Jeremy] ... "as you said. ..."' — which is where in F the text takes up again after the loss of a page in the middle of the record of the meeting (p. 227). Thus in E the conversation concerning neologisms was at first lacking; it was added in to the manuscript subsequently.

10   In E it was Dolbear, not Ramer, who objected thus to Lowdham's remark. *Arry* (for *Harry*) entered in the course of the writing of E; see p. 213 note 16.

11   *N.E.D.: A New English Dictionary,* the actual title of the *Oxford English Dictionary* or *O.E.D.*

12   The expression *the Six Years' War* is used in the Foreword and several times in the text. In E my father called it here *the Second German War.*

13   *Vita Fera:* literally 'savage life' (*ferus* 'wild, untamed, savage, fierce').

14   Cf. p. 174: Frankley, according to Guildford, 'regards knowledge of his own language at any period before the Battle of Bosworth as a misdemeanour'.

15   *Norman Keeps* was an historical person, who expounded to my father the view of English history here recounted by Philip Frankley while plying his trade at the barbering establishment of Weston and Cheal in the Turl Street.

16   *Battle of Camlan:* the battle in which King Arthur and his nephew Modred fell.

17 *Zigūr:* the Adunaic name of Sauron, which is the name that Lowdham uses in E here.

18 *Owlamoo:* This was in fact the name of a bogey conceived by my brother Michael (and of which my father made a picture, dated 1928, now in the Bodleian Library); but of course Lowdham intended no more than any old absurd name: in E he says 'Wallamaloo, who's he?'

19 *Nūmenōr:* so F at all occurrences here (the long mark over the *o* being added subsequently); E has *Númenor.*

20 *Nūmenōr is my name for Atlantis:* see p. 221 note 63.

21 *I knew I had heard that name as soon as Arry said it:* see pp. 306–7.

22 A footnote to the text in E at this point reads: 'The records were supposed to be written up and presented for correction at the end of each term. Before being passed they were initialled by all persons mentioned in them. N.G.' Cf. the Note to the list of members of the Notion Club in F, p. 160.

23 *My father's name was Edwin:* in initial drafting (and in E as first written) Lowdham's father was called *Oswin Ellendel* (a 'modernisation' of *Elendil*) and he himself was *Alboin Arundel* (cf. Oswin Errol father of Alboin in *The Lost Road,* V.36 ff.). Oswin Loudham was at first to be a sailor by profession, or else the somewhat absentee Professor of Anglo-Saxon at Cambridge ('I believe he did know some Anglo-Saxon' said his son).

24 I have not been able to discover a place named Penian in Pembrokeshire.

25 *The Éarendel:* in E the ship was named *Éarendel Star.*

26 *It does not look to Sussex:* Arundel in Sussex (explained as Old English *hārhūn-dell,* 'hoarhound valley', the name of a plant) has of course no connection whatsoever with *Éarendel,* merely a likeness of sound.

27 E has 'the War of 1939' (see note 12).

28 *three sailors:* E has only 'And he'd had great difficulty in collecting any sort of crew.' Cf. the three mariners who accompanied Eärendel and Elwing on the voyage to Valinor in the *Quenta Silmarillion* (V.324, 327).

29 With this passage cf. V.37–8 and my commentary V.53–5.

30 *the connexion of the Langobards with King Sheaf:* see p. 227, and V.92 ff.

31 In E Ramer says: 'Nor the repetition of the sequence: *Alboin* son of *Audoin* = *Alwin* son of *Edwin.*' The addition in F of *Ælfwine son of Éadwine* is curious, since no actual Ælfwine son of Éadwine has been mentioned (merely the Old English forms of *Alwin* and *Edwin*). Possibly it should be understood that Ramer in his discussion with Lowdham before the present meeting

(p. 235) had learnt of the verses ascribed to *Ælfwine Wídlást Éadwines sunu* (p. 244).

32   *Rosamund*: see V.54.

33   *O Horsefriend of Macedon!* A Lowdham joke on Frankley's first name (of which one is reminded immediately above), referring to King Philip of Macedon, father of Alexander the Great (Greek *phil-ippos* 'horse-loving').

34   *a star-name for Orion, or for Rigel*: see p. 301 and note 6.

35   *the glosses*: translations into Anglo-Saxon of individual words in Latin manuscripts. See my father's (draft) letter written in August 1967 to a correspondent known only as Mr. Rang (*Letters* no. 297), in which he gave a long account of the relation between Anglo-Saxon *Éarendel* and the *Eärendil* of his mythology. The relevant part of this letter is reprinted in II.266, but without the footnote to the words 'To my mind the Anglo-Saxon uses seem plainly to indicate that it was a star presaging the dawn (at any rate in English tradition)':

> Its earliest recorded A-S form is *earendil* (*oer-*), later *earendel*, *eorendel*. Mostly in glosses on *jubar* = *leoma*; also on *aurora*. But also in *Blickling Homilies* 163, *se níwa éorendel* applied to St John the Baptist; and most notably *Crist* 104, *éalá! éarendel engla beorhtast ofer middangeard monnum sended*. Often supposed to refer to Christ (or Mary), but comparison with Blickling Homilies suggests that it refers to the Baptist. The lines refer to a *herald*, and divine messenger, clearly not the *sóðfæsta sunnan léoma* = Christ.

The last words of this note refer to the following lines in the poem *Crist*:

> *Éalá Éarendel engla beorhtast*
> *ofer middangeard monnum sended,*
> *ond sóðfæsta sunnan léoma,*
> *torht ofer tunglas – þú tída gehwane.*
> *of sylfum þé symle inlíhtes.*

'. . . and true radiance of the sun, bright above the stars – thou of thy very self illuminest for ever every season.' — The Blickling Homilies are a collection of Old English sermons preserved in a manuscript at Blickling Hall in Norfolk.

36   *E has 'what Cynewulf meant'*. Of Cynewulf, author of the *Crist* and other poems, nothing is certainly known beyond his name, which he preserved by setting the runic letters composing it into short passages in the body of his poems, so that the actual names of the runes (as for example the W-rune was called *wynn* 'joy') have a meaning in the context.

37   From this point to the end of Night 66 there are not two but three texts to be considered (as already noted, p. 147), for this part of the typescript F was rejected and replaced by a new

version, while both typescript versions differ radically from E in respect of Lowdham's linguistic discoveries. The divergences have many notable features, and the superseded versions are given separately, pp. 299 ff.

38 'That breaks my dream' was an expression of my mother's, meaning that something in waking life had suddenly reminded her of a passage in a dream. In the original version of Night 66 (p. 303) Jeremy says 'That breaks *my* dream!' when Lowdham's words suddenly recall to his mind the place where, in his dream, he had found the reference to Númenor. — The *Oxford English Dictionary* does not give the expression, and the only place that I have found it is in the *English Dialect Dictionary*, ed. Joseph Wright, *Break* 27 (3), with a reference to West Yorkshire.

39 *Yōzāyan*: this Adunaic name occurs in *Aldarion and Erendis* (*Unfinished Tales* p. 184): 'Do you not love the Yôzâyan?'

40 The term *Elf-latin* (also *Elven-latin*) occurs frequently in *The Lost Road* and *The Lhammas*: see the Index to Vol.V. Alboin Errol called the first language ('*Eressëan*') that 'came through' to him *Elf-latin*, but it is not explained why he did so.

41 *Tíwas*: *Tíw* was the name in Old English of the Germanic god equated with Mars (whence *Tuesday*, based on Latin *dies Martis*; French *Mardi*), and known in Old Norse as *Týr*. The name is generally derived from an earlier **Tiwaz*, cognate with Latin *deus* (< **deiwos*), and so meaning originally 'god'; in Old Norse the plural *Tívar* 'gods' is found, of which *Tíwas* (= 'Valar') is the unrecorded Old English equivalent that 'came through' to Lowdham.

42 *Nówendaland*: derived from the recorded Old English word *nówend* 'shipmaster, mariner'. For another occurrence of *Nówendaland* see p. 317.

43 *Fréafíras*: this word is found elsewhere (see p. 317) as a translation of the word *turkildi* in Lowdham's Fragment I (p. 246), which he translated 'lordly men' (p. 248): Old English *fréa* 'lord', often found also as the first element of compounds, and *fíras* 'men', a word used in Old English poetry (cf. IV.206, 208, 211–12).

44 *Regeneard*: this was no doubt used in reference to Valinor. In Old English the element *regn-* occurs in compounds with an intensive force ('greatness, power'), and also in proper names (as *Regenweald*, revived as *Reginald*). In the ancient Norse poems *Regin*, plural, meant the gods, the rulers of the world, and occurs in *Ragna-rök* 'the doom of the gods' (mistakenly transformed into 'the twilight of the gods' by confusion with the word *rökr* 'twilight'). Old English *eard* 'land, country, dwelling, home'; thus *Regeneard* 'God-home', Valinor.

45 *Midswípen*: a word *midja-sweipains* is found in Gothic,

apparently meaning 'cataclysm, flood of the middle(-earth)', *midja* being a reduced form of *midjun-* as in Gothic *midjungards* (the inhabited world of men, 'Middle-earth'). This is clearly the basis of Lowdham's unrecorded Old English *Midswípen*.

46 *hebaensuil:* in later spelling *heofonsýl*; cf. the Old English text given on p. 314. *frumaeldi:* 'First Age'. I cannot certainly interpret *Wihawinia*.

47 In *The Lost Road* (V.43) Oswin Errol tells Alboin: 'But you'll get into trouble, if you let your cats out of the bag among the philologists – unless, of course, they back up the authorities.' Like Edwin Lowdham, Oswin Errol had studied Old English (V.44).

48 *westra lage wegas rehtas, wraikwas nu isti:* the line 'came through' also to Alboin Errol in *The Lost Road* (V.43), but ending *nu isti sa wraithas*; see p. 304.

49 *Onomasticon:* alphabetic list of proper names, especially of persons.

50 In *The Lost Road* Ælfwine chanted a form of these lines in the hall before King Edward the Elder (V.84), where they are not given in an archaic form but in the spelling of the manuscript of *The Seafarer* (see V.85):

> Monað modes lust mid mereflode
> forð to feran, þæt ic feor heonan
> ofer hean holmas, ofer hwæles eðel
> elþeodigra eard gesece.
> Nis me to hearpan hyge ne to hringþege
> ne to wife wyn ne to worulde hyht
> ne ymb owiht elles nefne ymb yða gewealc.

A prose translation is given (whereas Lowdham translates into alliterative verse): 'The desire of my spirit urges me to journey forth over the flowing sea, that far hence across the hills of water and the whale's country I may seek the land of strangers. No mind have I for harp, nor gift of ring, nor delight in women, nor joy in the world, nor concern with aught else save the rolling of the waves.'

In *The Seafarer* the text is somewhat different:

> monað modes lust mæla gehwylce
> ferð to feran, þæt ic feor heonan
> elþeodigra eard gesece

(which is then followed by five lines omitted in Ælfwine's version); *mæla gehwylce* 'on every occasion', *ferð (ferhð)* 'heart, spirit', i.e. literally 'the desire of my spirit urges my heart on every occasion to journey'. These alterations reappear in Lowdham's version here, and they depend, I imagine, on my father's judgement that the preserved text of *The Seafarer* is corrupt.

The third line in *The Lost Road* text, *ofer hean holmas, ofer hwæles eðel*, not found in *The Seafarer*, is replaced in Lowdham's version by the less banal *ofer gársecges grimme holmas* (writing it in later spelling), 'over the grim waves of Gársecg (the ocean)'; for *Gársecg* see the references given in V.82.

The fourth line of Lowdham's version differs, as he points out, from that in *The Seafarer* in the reading *aelbuuina eard* (= later *ælfwina eard*) 'land of the Elf-friends' for *elþeodigra eard* 'land of strangers, aliens'; the substitution of *ælfwina* for *elþeodigra* requires the presence of the word *uut (út)* for metrical reasons. The text of *The Lost Road* follows *The Seafarer*.

In *The Notion Club Papers* Ælfwine's chant before the king (p. 272) is exactly as Lowdham's version here, but given in later spelling; see also p. 304.

51 These lines Alboin Errol recited to his father in *The Lost Road* (V.44) in precisely the same form, except that Ælfwine is not there called *Éadwines sunu*. For other appearances of these lines see V.55. In the translation the words 'a land lovely to look on' (*wlitescéne land*) have been added from the first typescript (see note 37): they were inadvertently omitted in the second.

52 Lowdham concludes his lecture in the manner of the ending of a medieval minstrel's romance, and with a swipe at Frankley. *or I ende*: 'before I end.'

53 From Night 67 onwards there are again only the manuscript E and the typescript F, the latter being the continuation of the revised typescript (see p. 147 and note 37 above).

54 *O Lover of Horses*: see note 33.

55 Lowdham's 'fragments' are inserted into the typescript on separate sheets. They are in two forms: a typescript, printed here, and a manuscript of two pages, reproduced as frontispieces to this book, representing Lowdham's copies 'in a big bold hand, done with one of the great thick-nibbed pens Lowdham is fond of', with 'glosses in red ink': for unglossed words there are however (unlike what Lowdham said of his copies, p. 248) no query marks. In the typescript text of the fragments the Avallonian and Adunaic words are given all in capital letters, but I print them here in italic, capitalising according to the manuscript version.

56 Comparison of the typescript text of the fragments printed here with the manuscript version reproduced as frontispieces will show that the only differences in actual word-forms are manuscript *hikalba* 'she fell' in I (B), where the typescript has *hikallaba*; manuscript *katha* 'all' in II, where the typescript has *kātha*; and manuscript *īdō* 'now' at all three occurrences in II, but *īdōn* at the last two in the typescript, with the gloss 'now (is)'. There are many minor differences in Lowdham's glosses.

The typescript text of the fragments was no doubt made to accompany the final typescript F of the narrative, but it is not clear to me whether it preceded or followed the manuscript pages. Earlier forms of these pages are given on pp. 311–12. For the form of the fragments in E see p. 309.

57 Plato's dialogue *Timaeus* is the source (together with the long unfinished dialogue *Critias*) of the legend of Atlantis, the great island empire in the western ocean which, expanding aggressively against the peoples of the Mediterranean, was defeated by the Athenians, and was swallowed up 'in a single day and night' by the sea, leaving a vast shoal of mud that rendered the waters impassable in the region where Atlantis had been. According to Plato, the story was told (about the beginning of the sixth century B.C.) by an Egyptian priest to Solon the Athenian, and it came down thence by several intermediaries to Critias, a relative of Plato's, who tells the story in the two dialogues. In the *Critias* a long and extremely detailed account of Atlantis is given, of its great city, the temple of Poseidon with its colossal statue of the god, the wealth of the land in all resources of minerals, animals, timber, flowers and fruits, the horse-racing, the bull-sacrifice, the laws governing the realm. At the end of this account the narrator tells that the men of Atlantis fell away from the justice, wisdom and virtue of earlier generations, and that Zeus, perceiving their debasement and corruption, and wishing to punish them, called all the gods together and spoke to them; but at this point the *Critias* breaks off unfinished. The story of the war with the Greeks and the downfall of Atlantis is told, very briefly, in the other dialogue, the *Timaeus*.

The eldest child of Poseidon (tutelary god of Atlantis) by a mortal woman became the first king, and Poseidon named him Atlas, 'and after him the whole island and ocean were called Atlantis.'

Ultimately the name *Atlas* is that of the Titan who upheld the heavens on his head and his hands, according to Hesiod in the far western regions of the earth, near the dwelling of the Hesperides. He was the father of the Pleiades, and also, in Homer, of Calypso, on whose island Ogygia Odysseus was shipwrecked.

58 Cf. *The Lost Road*, where Audoin Errol, son of Alboin, speaks to himself of his dreams (V.52): 'Just pictures, but not a sound, not a word. Ships coming to land. Towers on the shore. Battles, with swords glinting but silent. And there is that ominous picture: the great temple on the mountain, smoking like a volcano.'

59 E has here: ' "... But I've done what I can. *Sauron* and *nahamna* remain to be solved." "Sauron!" said Jeremy in a strange voice.'

Lowdham refers only to unknown Quenya words because, as will be seen more fully later, in E there was no Adunaic element in the fragments he received. The word *nahamna* preceded *nukumna* 'humbled' of the later text of the Quenya fragment (p. 246), and was uninterpretable also by Alboin Errol in *The Lost Road* (V.47).

60 The name *Nimruzīr* appears in Fragment I (B), 'seven ships of Nimruzīr eastward'. In E Jeremy addresses Lowdham as *Ēarendil*, changed subsequently to *Elendil*.

61 The Adunaic words *Bā kitabdahē!* are absent in E (see note 59).

62 In E Lowdham cries out: '*Es sorni heruion an!* The Eagles of the Lords are at hand!' This was changed later to 'The Eagles of the Powers of the West are at hand! *Sorni Nūmevalion anner!*' In an earlier, rejected version of the passage Lowdham's words were: '*Soroni númeheruen ettuler!*'

63 In E Jeremy speaks of 'the fell counsels of Sauron', not 'of Zigūr'. He says that 'Tarkalion has set forth his might', where F has 'the King', and the sails of the Númenórean ships are 'scarlet and black' ('golden and black', F). He ends in E: 'The world waits in fear. The Númenóreans have encompassed Avallon as with a cloud. The Eldar mourn and are afraid. Why do the Lords of the West make no sign?'

64 For 'The Lords have spoken to Ēru, and the fate of the World is changed' E has 'The Lords have spoken to Ilúvatar [> the Maker], and the counsel of the Almighty is changed, and the fate of the world is overturned.'

65 For the passage in F beginning 'See! The abyss openeth ...' E (as first written: the wording was changed in detail subsequently) has:

> 'Ah! Look! There is a chasm in the midst of the Great Seas and the waters rush down into it in great confusion. The ships of the Númenóreans are drowned in the abyss. They are lost for ever. See now the eagles of the Lords overshadow Númenor. The mountain goes up to heaven in flame and vapour; the hills totter, slide, and crumble: the land founders. The glory has gone down into the deep waters. Dark ships, dark ships flying into darkness! The eagles pursue them. Wind drives them, waves like hills moving. All has passed away. Light has departed!'
> There was a roar of thunder and a blaze of lightning ...

Thus there is no mention in E of Lowdham and Jeremy moving to the window and 'talking to one another in a strange tongue.'

66 For *Abrazān* E has *Voronwë*, 'Steadfast', 'Faithful'; this was the name of the Elf who guided Tuor to Gondolin, *Unfinished Tales* pp. 30 ff. Cf. Jeremy's second name, Trewin (see note 84).

67 On 'the Great Storm' see p. 157 and note 1.

68 The statement that Ramer picked up a piece of paper covered with writing and put it in a drawer is present in E as written. See note 70.

69 *in the schools:* acting as examiners in the final examinations, held at the end of the summer term (cf. Guildford's footnote on p. 253).

70 In E the letter was postmarked in London. — As E was written, the record of the meeting of Night 68 ended immediately after Guildford had read the letter aloud, with the words: 'We agreed to Thursday 25th of September', and is followed by Night 69 on that date. Thus, although at the end of Night 67 Guildford's statement that he saw Ramer pick up the leaf of Edwin Lowdham's manuscript and put it in a drawer was present in E as originally written, on Night 68 Ramer does not appear and the paper is not mentioned (which is why the account of Night 68 begins with the words 'There is not much to record' – words that should have been removed). In E Night 69 (the last meeting recorded in *The Notion Club Papers*) proceeds essentially as in F (pp. 260–77). The matter of 'Edwin Lowdham's page' on Night 68 was inserted into E, but the structure of the manuscript and its pagination show clearly that this was not done until the text of Night 69 had been completed.

71 In E Ramer's remarks about 'Edwin Lowdham's page' and his discovery that the language was Old English are very much the same as in F, but he gives an opinion about the dialect and date: 'He thought it was Númenórean, I guess. But actually it is just Old English – latish West Saxon, I think, but I'm no expert. The script is, I think, plainly Númenórean . . .' See further notes 72 and 74.

72 *Rashbold* is a translation of *Tolkien*: see p. 151. Pembroke is the college to which the professorship of Anglo-Saxon is attached, its holder being *ex officio* a fellow of the college. — In E Professor Rashbold does not appear, and it is Ramer himself who deciphered, transcribed, and translated the page ('And here's the transcription, with such a translation as I could make').

73 Cf. the third Old English version of *The Annals of Valinor*, of which I noted (IV.290) that the language is that of ninth-century Mercia. There are several references in my father's letters to his particular liking for and sense of affinity with the West Midlands of England and its early language. In January 1945 he had said to me (*Letters* no. 95): 'For barring the Tolkien (which must long ago have become a pretty thin strand) you are a Mercian or Hwiccian (of Wychwood) on both sides.' In June 1955 he wrote to W. H. Auden (*Letters* no. 163): 'I am a West-midlander by blood (and took to early west-midland

Middle English as a known tongue as soon as I set eyes on it)';
and in another letter of this time (*Letters* no. 165): '... it is, I
believe, as much due to descent as to opportunity that Anglo-
Saxon and Western Middle English and alliterative verse have
been both a childhood attraction and my main professional
sphere.'

74   The Old English version (not in the Mercian dialect, see note 71)
written to accompany the manuscript E is given on pp. 313–14,
and the representation of the original form of it in Edwin
Lowdham's *tengwar* on pp. 319–20. Of the subsequent Old
English (Mercian) version, printed here from F, my father began
a text in *tengwar* but abandoned it after a single page; this is
reproduced on p. 321.

75   *Arminalēth*: Adunaic name of the City of the Númenóreans,
found also in *The Drowning of Anadûnê*. In *The Fall of
Númenor* (§2) it was named *Númenos* (V.25, and in this book
p. 333). On the site of the temple see p. 384.

76   *Neowollond*: in Professor Rashbold's translation (p. 259) this is
rendered 'the ? prostrate land'; in the earlier Old English version
accompanying E, which was translated by Michael Ramer (note
72), the name (in the form *Niwelland*) is rendered 'the Land that
is fallen low' (pp. 314–15). Old English *neowol* (*néol, niwol*)
'prostrate, prone; deep, profound'; cf. the early names for
Helm's Deep, *Neolnearu, Neolnerwet*, VIII.23 note 6.

77   *forrarder*: 'further forward'.

78   On the texts and titles of this poem see the note on pp. 295–6,
where also the published version is given.

79   *Cluain-ferta*: Clonfert, near the river Shannon above Lough
Derg. The monastery was founded by Saint Brendan Abbot of
Clonfert, called the Navigator, about the year 559.

80   *a light on the edge of the Outer Night*: cf. the *Quenta
Silmarillion* (V.327): 'But [the Valar] took Vingelot [the ship of
Eärendel], and they hallowed it, and they bore it away through
Valinor to the uttermost rim of the world, and there it passed
through the Door of Night and was lifted up even into the
oceans of heaven.' The following line in the present text, *like
silver set ablaze*, is replaced in the final form of the poem
(p. 298, line 104) by *beyond the Door of Days*.

81   The passage Lowdham refers to is lines 33–52, where when 'the
smoking cloud asunder broke' they 'saw that Tower of Doom':
in the earliest text of the poem the mariners 'looked upon
Mount Doom' (p. 295).

82   Cf. the outline for *The Lost Road* in V.80, where 'Ælfwine
objects that Paradise cannot be got to by ship – there are deeper
waters between us than Garsecg. *Roads are bent*: you come
back in the end. No escape by ship.'

83 *Porlock:* on the north coast of Somerset.

84 *Trewyn:* Jeremy's second name is spelt *Trewin* in the lists of
    members of the Notion Club. The Old English name is
    Tréowine (which Lowdham uses subsequently, p. 268), 'true
    friend'; cf. the Elvish name *Voronwë* 'Steadfast' by which
    Lowdham names him in the text E (note 66).

85 *Hibernia:* Ireland (see note 99).

86 *Slieve League* is a mountain on the coast of Donegal, *Brandon
    Hill* on the coast of Kerry; thus Lowdham means 'all down the
    west coast of Ireland'.

87 The *Aran Isles* lie across the entrance to Galway Bay.

88 *Loughrea:* a town and lake to the east of Galway.

89 *the Severn Sea:* the mouth of the Severn.

90 'Let us hasten now, Tréowine! I do not like this wind. There is a
    great likelihood of Danes tonight.'

91 The opening of Lowdham's story is closely based on the account
    in *The Lost Road* (V.83), although there Ælfwine's part is
    reported by the narrator, and it is his son Éadwine that he looks
    for in the hall, not his friend Tréowine. For a brief account of
    the historical setting in the years of King Edward the Elder (son
    of King Alfred), the defeat of the Danes at Archenfield in
    Herefordshire, and the raids on Watchet and Porlock, see
    V.80–1.

92 *Devenish men and Somersets: Devenish* is Old English *Defenisc*
    'of Devon'; *Defnas, Defenas* 'men of Devon' is the origin of
    the name *Devon. Somersets* is from Old English *Sumorsǣte*
    'men of Somerset' with the later plural ending added; as with
    Defnas > Devon, Sumorsǣte became the name of the region
    Somerset.

93 Edwin Lowdham's father has not been mentioned, but as is seen
    here he was Oswin Lowdham.

94 *Alfred went into hiding:* in the Isle of Athelney in Somerset, in
    878.

95 *the West Welsh:* the people of Cornwall (Old English *Corn-
    wealas* 'the Welsh in Cornwall' became the name of the region,
    Cornwall). On Ælfwine's mother, who came 'from the West',
    see II.313, V.85.

96 Saint Edmund, King of East Anglia, was defeated by the Danes
    in 869 and (according to the tenth century life of the king)
    murdered by them: he was tied to a tree and shot through with
    many arrows. The Danish raids in the region of the Severn took
    place in 914, and thus 'Ælfwine' was about 45 years old at this
    time (see V.80, 85), since he was born 'just before' the death of
    Saint Edmund. Arry Lowdham was born in 1938, and was now
    48 or 49. Subsequently Guildford says (p. 276) that in his vision
    of Ælfwine in the hall at Porlock he had looked older than

Lowdham, 'though by his account he was just of Arry's age it seemed'.

97   *the good king in his last wars:* King Alfred (died 899).

98   *Maelduin:* see V.81–2.

99   *Ériu:* the Old Celtic name **Iveriu* (whence Latin *Hibernia*) became Irish *Eriu* (accusative case *Eirinn*, Erin). From the same source is Old English *Íras*, *Íraland*.

100   *æt Ircenfelda:* Archenfield in Herefordshire; see V.80 (the Old English *Ircingafeld* given there is an earlier form).

101   *Monath módes lust . . .:* on these verses see note 50.

102   *Tamworth:* in Staffordshire: the chief residence of the Mercian kings.

103   *King Sheave:* for discussion of the legend of 'Sheaf' and notes on the text of the poem see V.91–6.

Among the manuscripts of *The Lost Road* material (see V.85 ff.) there are two texts of the poem, the one (which I will here call 'V') written out in verse lines, the other ('P') written as prose. In *The Lost Road* I printed V only, since the two versions differ only in a few minor details. In V there is a short narrative opening, in which it is told that Ælfwine chanted the poem; in P there is only a title, *King Sheave*.

In the manuscript E of *The Notion Club Papers* it is not Tréowine who recites the poem, as it is the typescript F:

At that one of the Marchers leaped to his feet and got leave to speak. Even before I had found a seat beside Tréowine, whom I espied far down the hall, the fellow had a foot on the step and had begun. He had a good voice, if a strange way with his words. Céolwulf, as I heard later, was his name, and he claimed to come of the blood of their kings that sat at Tamworth of old. His verse was in the old style . . .

This was changed in pencil to the later account. In E there is only a direction 'Here follows the Lay of King Sheave', which stands at the bottom of page 42 in the manuscript. The text continues on another page with 'When he ended there was loud applause . . . and they passed a horn of ale to Céolwulf's hand.' When I edited *The Lost Road* I did not observe that this page is numbered 46, while the manuscript P of *King Sheave* (in which the poem is written out as prose) is numbered 43 to 45. Thus the manuscripts V and P, which I took to be 'obviously closely contemporary' (V.87), were in fact separated by some eight years: a misjudgement based on the fact of the texts being placed together in my father's archive and their close similarity, although the evidence of the pagination is perfectly clear.

The manuscript P, then, was written in 1945 on the basis of the much earlier V, and was the text from which the typescript F given here was taken (with a few further changes); and all differences between the text given on pp. 273 ff. in this book and that on pp. 87 ff. in *The Lost Road* belong to 1945.

The last eight lines of the supplementary part of the poem (*The Lost Road* p. 91, lines 146–53, beginning 'Sea-danes and Goths ...'), which do not appear in the manuscript V, also belong apparently to the time of *The Notion Club Papers*.

104 The text P has *sires*, but both V and the typescript F of the *Papers* have *sire*.

105 *æt thisse béorthege:* Old English *béorðegu* 'beer-drinking'.

106 I cannot explain the reference of 'Broad Relic'.

107 *cnearr:* 'ship', a very rare Old English word probably taken from Norse, since it is only applied to vessels of the Vikings.

108 'Sweet is the breath of flowers beyond the sea.'

109 *After night 62:* this is the later Night 63.

110 See p. 214 note 23; p. 194 and note 46; p. 199 and note 51; p. 206 and note 63.

111 That this list, following the revised title-page given on p. 149, was made after the completion of manuscript B is seen from the name *Frankley* for earlier *Franks* (p. 150).

Note on 'The Death of Saint Brendan' with the text of the published form 'Imram'

A great deal of work went into this poem, with its elaborate versification: there are no less than fourteen closely-written pages of initial working, and there follow four finished manuscript texts preceding the typescript text printed on pp. 261–4. Much further work on it followed later. It is notable, however, that already in the earliest text the final form reached in *The Notion Club Papers* was very closely approached: there is in fact only one passage that shows a significant difference (and this was corrected already on the first manuscript to the later form). This concerns lines 43–53, where the earliest text reads:

> then the smoking cloud asunder broke
> and we looked upon Mount Doom:
> tall as a column in high Heaven's hall,
> than all mortal mountains higher,
> the tower-top of a foundered power,
> with crown of redgold fire.

> We sailed then on ...

The first text bears the title *The Ballad of St. Brendan's Death*. The second text, which as the pagination shows belongs with the manuscript E of *The Notion Club Papers*, is entitled *The Death of St. Brendan*. The third (with this title) and the fourth (without title) are finely written manuscripts, and the fifth (with the title *The Death of St.*

Brendan pencilled in as shown on p. 261) is part of the typescript F of *The Notion Club Papers*.

The poem, entitled *Imram* (Irish: 'sailing, voyaging') was once previously printed, in the issue of the periodical *Time and Tide* for 3 December 1955 (where it was illustrated by a woodcut of Saint Brendan and the great fishes by Robert Gibbings, originally made for Helen Waddell's book of translations *Beasts and Saints*, 1934). Three further typescripts, all with the title *Imram*, clearly belong to the later time. I print here in its entirety the text as it was published in *Time and Tide*, for that is now scarcely obtainable, and although the opening and concluding verses underwent very little alteration my father greatly changed most of the poem from its form in *The Notion Club Papers*.

IMRAM

At last out of the deep sea he passed,
    and mist rolled on the shore;
under clouded moon the waves were loud,
    as the laden ship him bore   4
to Ireland, back to wood and mire
    and the tower tall and grey,
where the knell of Clúain-ferta's bell
    tolled in green Galway.   8
Where Shannon down to Lough Derg ran
    under a rain-clad sky
Saint Brendan came to his journey's end
    to find the grace to die.   12

'O tell me, father, for I loved you well,
    if still you have words for me,
of things strange in the remembering
    in the long and lonely sea,   16
of islands by deep spells beguiled
    where dwell the Elvenkind:
in seven long years the road to Heaven
    or the Living Land did you find?'   20

'The things I have seen, the many things,
    have long now faded far;
only three come clear now back to me:
    a Cloud, a Tree, a Star.   24

'We sailed for a year and a day and hailed
    no field nor coast of men;
no boat nor bird saw we ever afloat
    for forty days and ten.   28

Then a drumming we heard as of thunder coming,
   and a Cloud above us spread;
we saw no sun at set or dawn,
   yet ever the west was red.   32

'Upreared from sea to cloud then sheer
   a shoreless mountain stood;
its sides were black from the sullen tide
   up to its smoking hood,   36
but its spire was lit with a living fire
   that ever rose and fell:
tall as a column in High Heaven's hall,
   its roots were deep as Hell;   40
grounded in chasms the waters drowned
   and swallowed long ago
it stands, I guess, on the foundered land
   where the kings of kings lie low.   44

'We sailed then on all till winds failed,
   and we toiled then with the oar;
we burned with thirst and in hunger yearned,
   and we sang our psalms no more.   48
At last beyond the Cloud we passed
   and came to a starlit strand;
the waves were sighing in pillared caves,
   grinding gems to sand.   52
And here they would grind our bones we feared
   until the end of time;
for steep those shores went upward leaping
   to cliffs no man could climb.   56
But round by west a firth we found
   that clove the mountain-wall;
there lay a water shadow-grey
   between the mountains tall.   60
Through gates of stone we rowed in haste,
   and passed, and left the sea;
and silence like dew fell in that isle,
   and holy it seemed to be.   64

'To a dale we came like a silver grail
   with carven hills for rim.
In that hidden land we saw there stand
   under a moonlight dim   68
a Tree more fair than ever I deemed
   in Paradise might grow:
its foot was like a great tower's root,
   its height no man could know;   72

and white as winter to my sight
   the leaves of that Tree were;
they grew more close than swan-wing plumes,
   long and soft and fair.   76

'It seemed to us then as in a dream
   that time had passed away,
and our journey ended; for no return
   we hoped, but there to stay.   80
In the silence of that hollow isle
   half sadly then we sang:
softly we thought, but the sound aloft
   like sudden trumpets rang.   84
The Tree then shook, and flying free
   from its limbs the leaves in air
as white birds rose in wheeling flight,
   and the lifting boughs were bare.   88
On high we heard in the starlit sky
   a song, but not of bird:
neither noise of man nor angel's voice,
   but maybe there is a third   92
fair kindred in the world yet lingers
   beyond the foundered land.
But steep are the seas and the waters deep
   beyond the White-tree Strand!'   96

'O stay now, father! There is more to say.
   But two things you have told:
the Tree, the Cloud; but you spoke of three.
   The Star in mind do you hold?'   100

'The Star? Why, I saw it high and far
   at the parting of the ways,
a light on the edge of the Outer Night
   beyond the Door of Days,   104
where the round world plunges steeply down,
   but on the old road goes,
as an unseen bridge that on arches runs
   to coasts that no man knows.'   108

'But men say, father, that ere the end
   you went where none have been.
I would hear you tell me, father dear,
   of the last land you have seen.'   112

'In my mind the Star I still can find,
   and the parting of the seas,

and the breath as sweet and keen as death
    that was borne upon the breeze.   116
But where they bloom, those flowers fair,
    in what air or land they grow,
what words beyond this world I heard,
    if you would seek to know,   120
in a boat then, brother, far afloat
    you must labour in the sea,
and find for yourself things out of mind:
    you will learn no more of me.'   124

In Ireland over wood and mire
    in the tower tall and grey
the knell of Clúain-ferta's bell
    was tolling in green Galway.   128
Saint Brendan had come to his life's end
    under a rain-clad sky,
journeying whence no ship returns;
    and his bones in Ireland lie.   132

MAJOR DIVERGENCES IN EARLIER VERSIONS OF THE NOTION CLUB PAPERS (PART TWO)

(i) The earlier versions of Night 66

I have mentioned previously that from Lowdham's words 'Éarendel seems to me a special word. It is not Anglo-Saxon' (see p. 237 and note 37) there is a third text to be considered: for the part of the typescript F that follows from this point and extends to the end of Night 66 (p. 245) was rejected and replaced by another version. I shall refer to the rejected portion as 'F 1', and its replacement as 'F 2'. That this rewriting was carried out while the typescript was being made is seen from the fact that at the end of the rewritten section it is F 2 that continues to the end of the *Papers*.

For some distance the original manuscript E was followed closely in F 1 and for this part it is only necessary to give the text of the latter.

'In any case,' said Lowdham, 'Éarendel is not Anglo-Saxon. Or rather, it is and it isn't. I think it is one of those curious cases of "linguistic coincidence" that have long puzzled me. I sometimes think that they are too easily dismissed as "mere accident". You know the sort of thing that you can find in any dictionary of a strange language, and which so excites the amateur philologists, itching to derive one tongue from another that they know better: a word that is nearly the same in form and meaning as the corresponding word in English, or Latin, or Hebrew, or what not. Like *mare* 'male' in the New Hebrides and Latin *maris, marem*.[1] Or the example that used to be given as a frightful warning in the old text-books: that *popol* means 'people' or 'popular assembly' in Tamil, but has no connexion whatever with *populus* and its derivatives, and is really derived, they say, from a Tamil word for a mat for the councillors to squat on.

'I dare say some of these things are mere chance, or at least not very significant. Yet I think it also happens that a word-form may be arrived at by different routes, in far separated times and places, and yet the result may be the product of a hidden symbol-making process working out to a similar end. Or in any case the "accident" may touch off, as it were, deeper or sleeping mind-echoes, so that the similar form thus acquires similar significance or emotional content. Every language has words in which its genius seems to come to flash-point, words whose form, though it remains within the general style, achieves a brilliance or a beauty of universal virtue.'

'If I follow all this, and I'm not at all sure that I do,' said Markison, 'I suppose you are trying to say that you've discovered *Éarendel* or something like it in some strange language. Is that so?'

'I think I come in for a moment here,' said Jeremy, who had been as restless as a bird on a twig ever since the word *Éarendel* had cropped up. 'We've been trying to strengthen our recollections under tuition; but I've not had much success yet. Still I have succeeded in connecting *Númenor* a little more clearly with a library,[2] with something I came across once when I was working on Ghost-stories. I can't get it more exact, or I couldn't. But a result of the effort to remember has been to drag up a good many vague dream-scenes of that rather troubled searching-for-something-missing variety: wandering about in libraries looking for a lost book, getting dusty and worried.

'Then two nights ago I got a dream of which I still remember one fairly clear passage. I took down a folder, or a cardboard case, from a high shelf, and in it I found a manuscript. It was in an ornamental and rather archaic hand, yet I seem to remember that I knew that it was not really old (by the paper, or the ink, or something), but belonged to this century. Here and there were passages in an unknown character.'

'I've found that missing leaf of my father's book,' interposed Lowdham.[3] 'I've shown it to Jeremy, and he's quite certain that the character is the same. Though we've not succeeded in deciphering it. It's not any alphabet known to the books.'

'And what is more peculiar', said Jeremy, 'there is nothing at all to connect my dream-vision or dream-manuscript with Edwin Lowdham: the style of the hands is wholly different, though the letter-forms are the same. Old Edwin's is a large, black, broad-stroke round hand; mine was more delicate and pointed.

'Well, unfortunately I don't recollect anything very clear or connected about the contents of my dream-manuscript – I call it that because I begin to wonder if this dream is really founded on any waking experience at all – but it contained, I think, some kind of legendary history,[4] full of strange names all seeming to belong to the same language. This much I do remember: the name *Nūmenor* or *Nūmenōre* was frequent; and so was the name *Ëarendil*. Very nearly the same, you see, but actually spelt: *ë-a-r-e-n-d-i-l*, *Ëarendil*.

'So I think Arry must be right. It is a case of linguistic coincidence or congruence, and the key is not to be found in Anglo-Saxon. We need not bother with the connexions of English *Ëarendel* in the other related languages, like the proper names *Ōrendel*, and *Aurvendill*, or Saxo's *Horwendillus*.'[5]

'But is not *Auriwandalo* actually recorded as a name in Langobardic?' said Markison, who has a finger in most pies of learning. 'Odd how the Langobards crop up.'

'It is,' said Lowdham.

'Hm, yes, and there is a connexion between these names and the stars,' said Jeremy. 'Didn't Thor throw Aurvendil's toe up into the sky, Arry?[6] And *Ëarendil* certainly had a connexion with a star in the strange tongue. Somehow I feel sure of that.'[7]

'Yes, that's so,' said Lowdham; 'but in the unknown language it was only a legendary connexion, not a linguistic one, I think. *Ëarendil* meant Sea-friend.[8] I am quite sure of that, because – well, perhaps I'd better go on where I left off.

'From the time of my father's departure . . .

The following passage in E / F 1 was retained in the revised type-script F 2 (p. 237–8) as far as 'some great tale of Nūmenor' almost without change, and there is no need to repeat it. The only difference between the texts is in the name of the 'cone-shaped mountain', and this is a difference very important in determining the relation of the texts of *The Drowning of Anadûne* to those of *The Notion Club Papers*. Where F 2 has 'Desolate is *Minul-Tārik*, the Pillar of Heaven is forsaken!' the name in E is *Menelminda*, changed in pencil to *Meneltyúla*, while in F 1 it is *Menel-tūbel*, changed to *Menel-tūbil*.

From 'some great tale of Nūmenor', however, all three texts diverge among themselves, and the major divergence is between the manuscript E and the first typescript F 1. I continue now therefore with the text of E (cf. pp. 238 ff.).

'But most of the word-recollections are, as it were, casual; as casual as the words caught by the eye from a lexicon when one is looking for something else. It was a long time before I began to note them down, and use them for the language I was amusing myself by "making up". They did not fit, or rather they took control and bent that language to their own style. In fact it became difficult to tell which were my invented words and which the ghost-words; indeed I've a notion that "invention" gradually played a smaller and smaller part. But there was always a large residue that would not work in.

'I soon found, as I got to know more, that some of the ingredients were Anglo-Saxon, and other things: which I'll mention in a minute. But when I weeded them out there was still a large amount of words left over, and in worrying over these I made a discovery. They belonged to another ghost-language, and to one that was related to the other. I could perceive a good many of the laws or rules of change: for the Nūmenórean style was in most points the older, more archaic, while the other had been altered (as if by contact with our western shores) to a style much more like that of the older north-western tongues.'

'I don't follow all this,' said Stainer. 'Nor do I,' said both Markison and Guildford. 'Give them some of the examples you gave me, Arry,' said Ramer.

'Well,' said Lowdham hesitating, 'if I can remember any of the examples where the relationship is clear to lay folk (it is often rather complex). Yes, *lōme* is 'night' (but *not* 'darkness') and *lōmelinde* is 'a nightingale': I feel sure of that. In the second language it is *dūmh*, later *dū*; and *duilin*. I refer them to a Primitive Western *dōmi, dōmilindē*. *Alda* means a 'tree' – it was one of the earliest certain words I got – and *orne* when smaller and more slender like a birch or rowan; in the second language I find *galað*, and *orn* (plural *yrn*): I refer them to *galadā*, and *ornē* (plural *ornei*). Sometimes the forms are more similar: the Sun and Moon, for instance, appear as *Anār, Isil* beside *Anaur* (later

Anor) and *Ithil*. I liked first the one language and then the other in different linguistic moods,[9] but the older seemed always the more august, somehow, the more, I don't know ... liturgical, monumental: I used to call it the Elven-latin; and the other seemed more resonant with the loss and regret of these shores of exile' – he paused – 'but I don't know why I say that.'

'But why *Elven*-latin?' asked Markison.

'I don't quite know,' said Lowdham. 'I certainly don't mean Elves in any of the more debased post-Shakespearean sort of ways. Actually the language is associated in my mind with the name *Eressë*: an island, I think. I often call it Eressëan.[10] But it is also associated with names like *Eldar, Eldalie* which seem to refer to, well, something like Ramer's *Enkeladim*.'[11]

'That breaks *my* dream!' cried Jeremy.[12] 'Of course! Now I know. It wasn't a library. It was a folder containing a manuscript, on a high shelf in Whitburn's second-hand room,[13] that funny dark place where all sorts of unsaleable things drift. No wonder my dreams were full of dust and anxiety! It must have been fifteen years ago since I found the thing there: *Quenta Eldalien, being the History of the Elves, by John Arthurson*[14] – in a manuscript much as I've described it. I took an eager but hasty glance. But I had no time to spare that day, and I could find no one in the shop to answer any enquiries, so I hurried off. I meant to come back, but I didn't, not for almost a fortnight. And – then the manuscript had vanished! They had no record of it, and neither old Whitburn nor anyone else there remembered ever seeing any such thing. I recall now what a catastrophe it seemed to me at the time; but I was very busy with other work, and soon forgot all about it.'

'It certainly looks as if more than one mind had been working back along similar lines,' said Ramer. 'Several minds indeed; for our expert is at fault for once. Lewis also mentions the name somewhere.'

'So he does!' cried Jeremy. 'In a preface, was it? But he was quoting from someone, I think, from a source that hasn't been traced. And he used the form *numinor*. All the other sources have *númenor*, or *númenórë* – that's so, isn't it, Arry?'[15]

'Yes,' said Lowdham. '*nūmē* is West, and *nōrě* is kindred, or land. The ancient English was *Westfolde*, Hesperia.[16] But you wanted to know why *Elven*. Well, I got that from another line, too. You remember I mentioned that Anglo-Saxon used to come through mixed up with this other queer stuff? Well, I got hold of Anglo-Saxon through the ordinary books, of course, fairly early, and that confused the issue; though some words and names came through to me that are not in the dictionaries ...'

From here to the end of Night 66 the version in the original manuscript E is very close to the final form (pp. 242–5), though some elements are lacking, notably Lowdham's description of the ancient slowness and sonorousness of diction (p. 242): following Frankley's 'Unless, of course, you back up their theories' Lowdham goes on: 'As a matter of fact, I think they do. At least, here is a bit that came through very early, long before I could interpret it; and it has been repeated over and over again in various forms:

> Westra lage wegas rehtas   wraithas nu isti ...'[17]

The Old English lines beginning *Monað módes lust* are in later spelling, but have the same form as that in F 2 (see pp. 243–4 and note 50, and p. 272). There is no reference in E to the date of the 'coming through' of these lines, nor to its being an evening of high wind.

The remarkable feature of this original version is of course that Lowdham's two 'ghost-languages' were Quenya and Sindarin (or rather, the language that would come to be called Sindarin). Lowdham's account in this version thus maintains the linguistic experience of Alboin Errol in *The Lost Road* (cf. note 9): '*Eressëan* as he called it as a boy ... was getting pretty complete. He had a lot of Beleriandic, too, and was beginning to understand it, and its relation to Eressëan' (V.45).

The first typescript version F 1 follows the manuscript E at the beginning of the section just given ('But most of these word-recollections ...', p. 302), in Lowdham's description of how the 'ghost-words' 'soon took control and bent my [invented] language to their own style'; but when he comes to tell that as he sifted the 'large residue [of words] that would not work in' he made a discovery, his discovery is totally different from that in the original text. This is where Adunaic first appeared. It may be that my father had been long cogitating this new language; but even if this is so, it would seem that it had not reached a form sufficiently developed to enter as Lowdham's 'second language' in manuscript E. In fact, I doubt that it is so. It seems to me to be overwhelmingly probable that Adunaic actually arose at this time (see further p. 147).

I give here the text of F 1 from this point (corresponding to the E text on p. 302 and the final text F 2 on p. 238).

'I found, when I got to know more, that some of the ingredients were Anglo-Saxon and other related things: I'll deal with that in a minute; it was not a large part. Working over the rest, collecting and sifting it, I made a discovery. I had got *two* ghost-languages: Númenorean A and B. Most of what I had got at an early period was B; later A became more frequent, but B remained the most common language, especially in anything like connected passages; A was chiefly limited to single words and names, though I think that a lot of it is incorporated in my invented language.

'As far as I could or can see, these languages are unrelated, though they have some words in common. But in addition to these tongues there remains a residue, and I now see that it consists of some echoes of other later tongues that are later than Númenorean A and B, but are derived from them or from their blending. I can discern some of the laws or lines of change that they show. For the Númenorean tongues, I feel, are archaic and of an elder world, but the others are altered and belong to Middle-earth.'

'I don't follow all this,' said Stainer. Most of us felt the same, and said so.

'Couldn't you give them some of the examples that you gave to me, Arry?' said Ramer. 'Some of the important names, and a word or two; it would be clearer with something definite to go on.'

Lowdham hesitated. 'I'll try,' he said. 'But I shan't be able to give many examples of the later changed forms; the relations would seldom be clear, even to philologists, without many instances side by side in writing.

'Well, take the name *Númenor* or *Númenóre*. That belongs to language A. It means Westernesse, and is composed of *núme* "west" and *nóre* "folk" or "country"; but the B name is *Anadûn*, and the people are called *Adûnái*. And the land had another name: in A *Andóre*, and in B *Athânâti*; and both mean "land of gift". There seems no connexion between the two languages here; but in both *menel* means "the heavens". It occurs in the B name *Menel-tûbil* that I mentioned just now. And there seems to be some connexion between the A word *Valar*, which appears to mean something like "gods", and the B plural *Avalói* and the place-name *Avallóni*.

'The name *Ëarendil*, by the way, belongs to language A, and contains *eäre* "the open sea" and the stem *ndil* "love, devotion". The corresponding B name is *Pharazîr*, made of *pharaz* and the stem *iri-* [*changed in ink on the typescript to*: *Azrubêl*, made of *azar* "sea" and the stem *bel-*]. A large number of the names seem to have double forms like this, almost as if one people spoke two languages. If that is so, I suppose the situation could be paralleled by the use of, say, Chinese in Japan, or indeed of Latin in Europe. As if a man could be called Godwin and also Theophilus or Amadeus. But even so, two different peoples must come into the story somewhere.

'I don't know if you want any more examples; but the words for the Sun and Moon in A are *Anar* and *Isil* (or in their oldest form *Anār* and *Ithīl*); and in B they are *Ūri* and *Nīlu*. These words survive in not much changed shapes in the later languages that I spoke of: *Anor (Anaur)* and *Ithil*, beside *Uir*, *Ȳr* and *Nil*, *Njūl*. Again the A and B forms seem unconnected; but there is a word that often occurs and is nearly the same in both: *lōme* in A, and *lōmi* in B. That means "night", but as it comes through to me I feel that it has no evil connotations; it is a word of peace and beauty and has none of the associations of fear or groping that, say, "dark" has for us. For the evil sense I do not know the A word. In B and its derivatives there are many words or stems, such as *dolgu*, *ugru*, *nūlu*.

'Well, there you are. I hope you are not all bored. I love these languages. I call them Avallonian and Adunaic.[18] I find first the one and then the other more attractive, in different linguistic moods; but A, the Avallonian, is the more beautiful, with the simpler and more euphonious phonetic style. And it seems to me the more august, somehow, the more ancient, and, well, sacred and liturgical. I used to call it the Elven-latin. But the Adunaic is more resonant with the loss and regret of Middle-earth, these shores of exile.' He paused, as if he heard echoes from a great distance. 'But I do not know why I say that,' he ended.

There was a short silence, and then Markison spoke. 'Why did you call it Elven-latin?' he asked. 'Why Elven?'

'It seemed to fit,' Lowdham answered. 'But certainly I didn't mean *elf* in any debased post-Shakespearean sort of sense. ...

The remainder of Night 66 is the same as in F 2 (pp. 242–5), except that, as in E, Lowdham's account of the ancient mode of utterance is absent.

It will be seen that in F 1, as in E, Wilfrid Jeremy interrupts to speak of his 'dream-manuscript' (p. 300), found in a library, in which occurred the names *Númenor* and *Ëarendil*: the unknown character of some passages in it was the same as that of the single leaf preserved from Edwin Lowdham's 'notes in a queer script' (p. 235), which Arundel Lowdham had now found again; but that this passage is entirely absent in F 2 (p. 237). Subsequently, in E, Jeremy returns to the subject ('That breaks *my* dream!', p. 303), remembering both that he found – in waking life, years before – the manuscript not in a library but in the second-hand room of a bookshop, and that the manuscript bore the title *Quenta Eldalien, being the History of the Elves, by John Arthurson*; and this leads to a mention of Lewis's use of the name *Numinor*. This second interruption of Jeremy's is *not* in F 1, which is on the face of it strange, since his first speech was surely intended to lead on to his second. A probable explanation of this is that my father decided to discard this element of Jeremy's manuscript (perhaps as complicating excessively the already complex conception) while he was making the typescript, and that this was one reason why he produced the revised version at this point. But Jeremy's remarks at the previous meeting (Night 65, p. 232: 'I come into it too. I knew I had heard that name as soon as Arry said it. But I can't for the life of me remember where or when at the moment. It'll bother me now, like a thorn in the foot, until I get it out') should have been removed.

NOTES

1   The genitive and accusative cases *maris, marem* are given because the nominative is *mas* ('male').

2   Jeremy is referring to the earlier passage (Night 65, p. 232) in which he claimed that he himself had heard the name *Númenor*, but could not remember when.

3   In the revised text F 2 there is no mention of the missing leaf having been found under Night 66 – naturally enough, since it was at this meeting that Lowdham referred to it as having been mislaid (p. 235). It was an odd oversight in E and F 1 that at the same meeting Lowdham both first mentions it and says that he cannot find it at the present time, and also declares that he has found it and discussed it with Jeremy. In F 2 he brings the leaf to the next meeting (p. 248).

4   E has here: '... the contents of the dream-manuscript – I call it that, because I doubt now whether this dream is really founded on any waking experience at all; though I don't somehow doubt that such a manuscript exists somewhere, probably in Oxford: it contains, I think, some kind of legendary history ...'

5   *Ōrendel* in German, *Aurvandill* in Norse, *Horwendillus* in Latinized form in the Danish History of Saxo Grammaticus (latter half of the twelfth century). The form in Norse is *Aurvandill*, but at the occurrences of the name both in E and F 1 my father spelt it *Aurvendill*. See note 6.

6   In the 'Prose Edda' of Snorri Sturluson a strange tale is told by the god Thor, how he 'carried Aurvandill in a basket on his back

from the North out of Jötunheim [land of giants]; and he added
for a token that one of his toes had stuck out of the basket and
become frozen; and so Thor broke it off and cast it into the sky,
and made a star of it, which is called *Aurvandilstá* [Aurvandil's
Toe]' (*Snorra Edda, Skáldskaparmál* §17). Association of Aurvandill with Orion is the basis of the suggestions mentioned by
Lowdham earlier (p. 236): 'Some guess that it [Éarendel] was
really a star-name for Orion, or for Rigel' – Rigel being the very
bright star in the left foot of Orion (as he is drawn in the old
figure).

7   E has: 'And *Éarendil* certainly had a connexion with a star in the
strange tongue: I seem to remember that: like the ship' – the last
words being changed from 'And the ship was *Éarendel's Star*'.
Earlier in E (p. 284 note 25) the ship was called *Éarendel Star*.

8   In E Lowdham translates *Éarendil* as 'Lover of the Great Seas'; in
the final text F 2 as 'Great Mariner, or literally Friend of the Sea'
(p. 237).

9   This passage is modelled on Alboin Errol's words to his father in
The Lost Road (V.41), using the same examples, with the same
distinction in respect of the word *lōme* ('night' but not 'darkness'), the same note that *alda* was one of the earliest words to
appear, and the same remark that (in Alboin's words) 'I like first
one, then the other, in different moods.'

10 *Eressëan* was Alboin Errol's name for his first language, 'Elf-
latin'; the second was *Beleriandic*.

11 Cf. p. 221 note 65: the passage cited there from the B manuscript
of Part One, in which 'Tolkien's Unfallen Elves' and 'Tolkien's
Eldar, Eldalie' are referred to, though not struck out on that
manuscript, must by now have been rejected; it is clear that
Lowdham means that *Eldar, Eldalie* had 'come through' to him,
and that he only knew them so. See further note 14.

12 See p. 286 note 38.

13 *Whitburn:* see p. 149 and note 7.

14 My father's father was Arthur Tolkien; he was referring of course
to his manuscript of *The Silmarillion*, which had never been
published but had washed up, forgotten and disregarded, in the
second-hand room of a bookshop. The author of *The Silmarillion*
is disguised by a pseudonym; for no reference can now be made
to the works of *Tolkien*, least of all as having been published and
known to members of the Notion Club (see the citation from
manuscript B of Part One, p. 220 note 52 at end). — In a rejected
form of this passage the title of the manuscript was not *Quenta
Eldalien* but *Quenta Eldaron*.

15 Ramer's remark 'Lewis also mentions the name somewhere' is at
first sight puzzling, since it was Lowdham's mention of *Eldar,
Eldalie* that brought back to Jeremy's mind the manuscript by

'John Arthurson' that he had once seen, and the name *Númenor* has not been mentioned for some time. But Ramer was following his own thought, that 'several minds' had been 'working back along similar lines' (and of course it was the name *Númenor* that had originally caught Jeremy's attention and finally led to his recollection of the manuscript). — Jeremy's words 'In a preface, was it?' presumably refer to Lewis's preface to *That Hideous Strength*: 'Those who would like to learn further about Numinor and the True West must (alas!) await the publication of much that still exists only in the MSS. of my friend, Professor J. R. R. Tolkien.' But then why does Jeremy say 'from a source that hasn't been traced', since the source, though unpublished, was stated by Lewis? Such an untiring researcher as Wilfrid Jeremy would have found out who J. R. R. Tolkien was, even if now forgotten!

By 'All the other sources' Jeremy presumably means his own recollection of the manuscript by 'John Arthurson' and the name that had 'come through' to Ramer (p. 232) and Lowdham.

There are a number of references to *Numinor* in *That Hideous Strength*, as: 'Merlin's art was the last survival of something older and different — something brought to Western Europe after the fall of Numinor' (Chapter 9, §v); again with reference to Merlin, 'something that takes us back to Numinor, to pre-glacial periods' (Ch.12, §vi); (Merlin) ' "Tell me, slave, what is Numinor?" "The True West," said Ransom' (Ch.13, §i); other references in Ch.13, §v.

16   *Westfolde* (*folde* 'earth, land, country') seems not to be recorded in Old English. This is the same as *Westfold* in *The Lord of the Rings*. — *Hesperia*: 'western land' (*hesperus* 'western', 'the evening star').

17   Above the *th* of *wraithas* is written *kw* (see p. 287 note 48).

18   In F 1 Lowdham's words about *Avallóni* in F 2 (p. 241) are absent ('Although that is a B name, it is with it, oddly enough, that I associate language A; so if you want to get rid of algebra, you can call A Avallonian, and B Adunaic'). Thus there is no explanation in F 1 why he calls the A language *Avallonian* despite the fact that *Avallóni* is a B name.

(ii) The original version of Lowdham's 'Fragments' (Night 67)

In the manuscript E Lowdham's fragments are, like Alboin Errol's in *The Lost Road* (V.47) in one language only, Quenya ('Eressëan'). Lowdham bursts in to Ramer's rooms and tells of his visit to Pembrokeshire just as he does in F (p. 246), but he does not bring copies of the text that has come to him – he asks Ramer for a large sheet of paper to pin up on a board. Then he says: 'Well, here it is! It's Númenórean or Eressëan, and I'll put the text that I can remember

down first large, and the English gloss (where I can give any) under-
neath. It's fragmentary, just a collection of incomplete sentences.'

The first of the two fragments reads thus, as E was originally written
(the change of *ilu* to *eru* was very probably made at the time of
writing: for *ilu* 'the World' see IV.241–5):

ar	*sauron*	*túle*	*nahamna* ...	*lantier*	*turkildi*
and	?	came	?	... they-fell	?

unuhuine	... *tarkalion*	*ohtakáre*	*valannar* ...
under-shadow ...	?	war-made	on-Powers ...

Herunúmen	[*ilu* >] *eru*	*terhante*	... *Ilúvatáren* ...
Lord-of-West	world	sunder-broke ...	of-God ...

ëari	*ullier*	*kilyanna* ...	*Númenóre*	*ataltane.*
seas	they-should-pour	in-Chasm ...	Numenor	down-fell.

It will be seen that the Elvish here, apart from the curious change
from *ilu* to *eru*, is identical in its forms with that of Alboin Errol's first
fragment; and the only differences in the glosses are 'of-God' for
Alboin's 'of-Ilúvatar', 'sunder-broke' for 'broke', and 'they-should-
pour' for 'poured'. A few changes were made subsequently: *lantier* >
lantaner, *eru* > *arda*, *terhante* > *askante*, and the addition of *leneme*
'by leave' – the changed forms being found in the final version (p. 246)
with the exception of *askante*, where the final version has *sakkante*
'rent'.

Then follows (where in *The Lost Road* it is said: 'Then there had
seemed to be a long gap'): 'After that there came a long dark gap
which slipped out of memory as soon as I woke to daylight. And then I
got this:'

Malle	*tēna*	*lende*	*númenna*	*ilya*	*sī*	*maller*
road	straight	went	westward	all	now	roads

raikar ...	*turkildi*	*rómenna* ...	*núruhuine*
bent ...	?	eastward ...	death-shadow

mēne	*lumna* ...	*vahāya*	*sīn*	*atalante.*
on-us	is-heavy ...	far-away	now	?

This is also very close to Alboin Errol's second passage. The word
tēna 'straight' was changed from *tēra* (as in *The Lost Road*), perhaps
in the act of writing; otherwise the only differences in the Quenya
words are *mēne lumna* for *mel-lumna* in *The Lost Road* (glossed
'us-is-heavy'), and *sīn* for *sin*, where Lowdham's gloss was changed
from 'now' (as in *The Lost Road*) to 'now-is'. This fragment appears
in Adunaic in the final version (Fragment II, p. 247), apart from the
words *vahaiya sín Andóre / atalante.*

In E Lowdham makes the same observations as in F (pp. 247–8) about

his glimpse of the script, with the thought that these were passages out
of a book; and he says likewise 'And then suddenly I remembered the
curious script in my father's manuscript – but that can wait', without
however adding, as he does in F, 'I've brought the leaf along', although
at the end of the meeting, after the storm, Ramer picks up the leaf
from the floor and puts it in a drawer (p. 291, notes 68 and 70).
Lowdham remarks that 'there are some new words here', and that 'all
except *nahamna* I at once guessed to be names'. He naturally has less
to say in E about the language of the fragments than he does in F,
noting only that he thought that *Tarkalion* was a king's name and that
Turkildi was 'the name of a people: "lordly men", I think', and
commenting on *Atalante* in very much the same words as in F,
translating it as ' "It (or She) that is downfallen", or more closely
"who has slipped down into an abyss" '.

(iii) The earlier versions of Lowdham's 'Fragments' in Adunaic (Night 67)

There are two manuscript pages of Lowdham's fragments in Quenya
and Adunaic preceding those reproduced as frontispieces. The first of
these pages, here called (1), has interlinear glosses in English in red
ink; the second, (2), has not. In the Quenya fragment I (A) the
development from the form found in E to the final form (pp. 246–7)
can be observed, but there are only a few points to mention. The word
nahamna, which neither Alboin Errol nor Lowdham could translate,
became in (1) *kamindon*, still untranslatable but with the gloss -*ly*
beneath, and in (2) *akamna*, changed to *nukumna*. The name *herunū-
men* survived in (1) and (2), but was changed in the latter to
Nūmekundo (*númeheruvi* in the final form).

The Adunaic fragments, I (B) and II (B), underwent a great deal of
change, and I give here the text in (1), showing the changes made
carefully to the text in ink, but ignoring scribbled pencilled emendations which are mostly very difficult to interpret.

| *Kadō* | *zigūrun* | *zabathān* | [*hunekkū* >] *unekkū* ... | *eruhīn* |
| and so | ? | humbled | he-came ... | ? |

| *udūbanim* | *dalad* | *ugrus* | ... *arpharazōn* |
| fell | under | horror? shadow? ... | ? |

| *azgaranādu* | *avalōi*-[*men* >] *si* ... | *bārun-adūnō* |
| was waging war? | Powers on ... | the Lord of West |

| *rakkhatū* | *kamāt* | *sōbēthumā* | *eruvō* ... | *azrē* |
| broke asunder | earth | assent-with | of God ... | seas |

| *nai* [*phurusam* >] *phurrusim* | *akhās-ada.* | *anadūni* | *akallabi.* |
| might-flow | Chasm-into | Westernesse | fell in ruin. |

Adūnāim			*azūlada*	...	*agannūlō*	*burudan*
The Adunai (Men of W.)			eastward	...	death-shade	heavy-is

nēnum	...	*adūn*	*batān*	*akhaini*	*ezendi*	*īdō*	*kathī*
on-us	...	West	road	lay	straight	lo! now	all

batānī	*rōkhī-nam*	...	[*vahaia sīn atalante*]	...	*ēphalek*
ways	bent-are	...			far away

īdōn		*akallabēth*	...	[*haia vahaia sīn atalante*] ...
lo! now is		She-that-is-fallen	...

ēphal	*ēphalek*	*īdōn*	*athanātē*
far	far away	is now	Athanātē (the Land of Gift)

In the rejected typescript F 1 of Night 66 appears *Athānāti* (p. 305), where F 2 has *Yōzāyan* (p. 241).

In text (2) the final text of the fragments was very largely reached, but still with a number of differences. I list here all of these, in the order of the occurrence of the words in the final text, giving the final form first:

unakkha: unakkha > yadda > unakkha
dubdam: dubbudam > dubdam
ar-pharazōnun: ar-pharazōn > ar-pharazōnun
azaggara: azagrāra, with *azaggara* as alternative
bārim: bārun
yurahtam: urahhata > urahta
hikallaba (typescript), *hikalba* (manuscript): *hikallaba > hikalba*
bawība dulgī: dulgu bawīb
an-nimruzīr: nimruzīr
At the beginning of II *Adūnāim azūlada* retained from (1), then struck out
burōda nēnud: buruda nēnu
adūn izindi batān tāidō ayadda: adūn batān ēluk izindi yadda
īdō (manuscript) at last two occurrences, *īdōn* (typescript):   *īdōn*
hi-Akallabēth: Akallabēth

Eru. The appearance of the name *Eru* in these texts is interesting: Lowdham says (pp. 248–9) that he thinks that *ēruhīnim* in I (B) must mean 'Children of God'; that *ēruvō* 'is the sacred name *Ēru* with a suffixed element meaning "from"'; and that 'therefore *iluvatáren* means the same thing.' In a list of 'Alterations in last revision [of The Silmarillion] 1951' my father included *Aman, Arda, Eä, Eru,* and other names (V.338). It seems very probable that the name *Eru* (*Ēru*) — and *Arda* also — first emerged at this time, as the Adunaic equivalent of *Ilúvatar* (for the etymology of *Ēru* in Adunaic see p. 432). The appearance of *eru* in the E text (p. 310), replacing *ilu* 'world' and in turn displaced by *arda*, could be explained as the first emergence of *eru*, as a Quenya word, and with a different meaning.

(iv) Earlier versions of Edwin Lowdham's Old English text

Two texts of a longer Old English version are extant, the second of these, followed here, being a revision of the first but closely similar to it and accompanied by a translation. This version belongs with the manuscript E: there are no Adunaic names, and a complete facsimile of Edwin Lowdham's text in Númenórean script (*tengwar*) bears a page reference to the manuscript. In those passages where this version and the later one (pp. 257–8) can be compared many differences in the forms of words will be seen, for this does not represent the old Mercian dialect (see p. 291 note 71).

I give the text here as my father wrote it in a rapidly pencilled manuscript. The two sides of Edwin Lowdham's page in *tengwar* are reproduced on pp. 319–20; the *tengwar* text was directly based on the Old English that now follows, and (in intention) scarcely deviates from it. There are a very few minor differences in spelling between the two, including the last word, the name *Niwelland*, which in the *tengwar* text is given as *Neowolland* (p. 292 note 76).

Ealle sǽ on worulde hí oferlidon, sohton hí nyston hwæt ac ǽfre wolde hyra heorte westweard, forðamðe hí ofhyngrede wurdon ðære undéadlican blisse ðære *Eldalie* 7 swa hyra wuldor wéox swa ǽfre hyra langung 7 hyra unstilnes wurdon ðe má ætiht .... þá forbudon ða *Eldan* him on *Eresse* úp to cumanne, forðam hí mennisce wæron 7 déadlice 7 þéahþe ða Wealdend him langes lífes úðon ne mihton hí alýsan hí of ðære woruldméðnesse ðe on ealle men ǽr ðam ende færeð 7 hí swulton efne hyra héacyningas, *Éarendles* yrfenuman, 7 hyra líffæc þúhte ðam *Eldum* scort. Forðon hit swá gefyrn aráedde se Ælmihtiga ðæt hí steorfan sceoldon 7 þás woruld ofgyfan .... ac hí ongunnon murcnian, sægdon ðæt þis forbod him unryht þúhte. Þonne on dígle asendon hí scéaweras on *Avallon* ða dyrnan láre ðara *Eldena* to asméaganne; ne fundon ðeah nawðer ne rúne ne rǽd ðe him to bóte wǽron .... Hit gelamp siþþan ðæt se fúla Déofles þegn ðe Ælfwina folc *Sauron* nemneð wéox swíðe on middangearde 7 hé geaxode Westwarena miht 7 wuldor 7 ðæt hí gyt holde wǽren Gode; ongunnon úpahæfenlice swaðeah ... Þá gehyrde Westwarena cyning æt his sǽlidum be *Saurone* ðæt he wolde cyning béon ofer eallum cyning-um 7 héalicran stól habban wolde ðonne *Éarendles* afera sylf ahte. Þonne sende hé *Tarcalion* se cyning bútan Wealdendra rǽde oþþe *Eldena* his ǽrendracan to *Saurone*, abéad him ðæt he on ofste on Westfoldan cwóme þǽr to ðæs cyninges manrǽdenne to búganne 7 hé *Sauron* lytigende geéadmédde hine ðæt he cwóm, wæs þeah inwitful under, fácnes hogode Westwarena þéode. Þá cwóm he úp æt sumum cyrre on *Rómelonde* ðære hýðe 7 sóna adwealde fornéan ealle ða *Númenóriscan* mid wundrum 7 mid tácnum; forðam he mihte mycel on gedwimerum 7 drýcræftum . . . . 7 hí geworhton mycelne ealh on ðam héan 'munte' ðe *Meneltyúla* – ðæt is to secganne Heofonsýl – hátte – se ðe ǽr wæs unawídlod; dydon ða hálignesse to hæðenum hearge 7 þær onsægdon unasecgendlíce lác on unhalgum wéofode . . . swa cwóm se déaþscúa on Westfarena land . . . .

Þæs ofer fela géara hit gelamp ðæt *Tarcalione* wearþ yldo onsǽge 7 þý wearð he hréow on móde 7 þa wolde he be *Saurones* onbryrdingum *Avallon* mid fyrde gefaran, forðamðe *Sauron* him sægde ðæt ða *Eldan* him on wóh éces lífes forwyrnden . . . . . wæron Westwarena scipfyrda swaswa unarímedlic ígland on ðære sæ 7 hyra mæstas gelíce fyrgenbéamum on beorghliðum, 7 hyra here-cumbol gelíce þunorwolcnum; wæron hyra segl blódréad 7 blacu . . . . . Nú sitte wé on elelande 7 forgytað ðære blisse ðe iú wæs 7 nú sceal eft cuman nǽfre. Ús swíðe onsitt Déaþscúa. Wóh biþ seo woruld. Feor nú is Niwelland ð.

I cannot explain the ð at the end of this text, which stands at the end of a line but not at the end of the page, and which must have a significance since the symbol for *th* concludes the version in *tengwar* (and concludes the page). The translation reads thus:

All the seas in the world they sailed, seeking they knew not what; but their hearts were turned ever westward, for they were become greatly desirous of the undying bliss of the Eldalie, and as their power and glory grew so was their longing and their unquiet ever the more increased . . . . Then the Eldar forbade them to land on Eresse, for they were of human kindred and mortal; and albeit the Powers had granted them long life, they could not release them from the weariness of the world that comes upon all men ere the end, and they died, even their high-kings, descendants of Éarendel; and their life-span seemed short to the Eldar. For thus had the Almighty ordained it, that they should die and leave this world . . . . But they began to murmur, saying that this prohibition seemed to them unjust. Then they sent out in secret spies to Avallon to explore the hidden knowledge of the Eldar; but they discovered neither lore nor counsel that was of any avail to them . . . .

It came to pass afterward that the foul servant of the Devil whom the people of the Ælfwinas call Sauron grew mightily in the Great Lands, and he learned of the power and glory of the Westware, and that they were still faithful to God, but were behaving arrogantly nonetheless . . . Then the King of the Westware heard news from his

mariners concerning Sauron, that he desired to be King over all Kings and to have a more exalted throne than even the heir of Earendel himself possessed. Then he, Tarkalion the King, without counsel either of the Powers or of the Eldar, sent his ambassadors to Sauron, commanding him to come with all speed to Westfolde, there to do homage to the King. And Sauron, dissembling, humbled himself and came, being filled with malice beneath, and designing wickedness against the people of the Westware. He landed then one day at the haven of Rómelonde, and straightway he deluded well nigh all the Númenóreans with signs and wonders; for he had great craft in phantoms and in wizardry ... and they builded a great temple on that high mountain that was called Meneltyúla (that is to say the Pillar of Heaven), which before was undefiled, and there they did sacrifice unspeakable offerings upon an unholy altar ... thus came the Deathshadow upon the land of the Westware
....

Many years afterward it came to pass that old age assailed Tarkalion, so that he became exceedingly sad in mind, and he determined then (being goaded by Sauron) to invade Avallon with an army; for Sauron said to him that the Eldar refused to him the gift of everlasting life, wrongfully ..... The fleets of the Númenóreans were as uncounted islands in the sea and their masts were like unto tall trees upon the mountain-sides, and their war-banners like to thunder-clouds, and their sails were bloodred and black ....

Now we dwell in the land of exile and forget the bliss that once was and now shall come again never. Heavy lies upon us the Deathshadow. Bent is the world. Far now is the Land that is fallen low.

At the end the following bracketed sentence was added subsequently: '[that is Atalante which was before called Andor and Vinyamar and Númenor.]'

A remarkable feature of this text is the ascription to the *Eldar* of a ban on Númenórean landing in Eressëa, and still more the statement that Sauron told Tarkalion that the *Eldar* 'refused to him the gift of everlasting life'; on this see pp. 355–6.

Of names in this text the following may be noted. There is an Old English form *Eldan* for 'Eldar', with genitive plural *Eldena*, dative plural *Eldum*. For *Meneltyúla* (in the first draft of this version *Menelmindo*) see p. 302, and for *Heofonsýl* p. 242 and note 46. The statement that Sauron landed 'at the haven of *Rómelonde*' (in the first draft *Rómelónan*) is interesting: with *Rómelonde* 'East-haven' cf. the great harbour of *Rómenna* 'Eastward' in the later form of the legend. Also notable is the name *Vinyamar* of Númenor in the addition at the end of the translation: with this cf. *Vinya* 'the Young', 'the New Land' in *The Fall of Númenor* (V.19, 25, and in this book p. 332) and in *The*

Lost Road (V.64). Later *Vinyamar* 'New Dwelling' became the name of the house of Turgon on the coast of Nevrast, before he removed to Gondolin (Index to *Unfinished Tales*).

With the sails of the Númenórean ships that were 'bloodred and black' cf. p. 290 note 63, where Jeremy sees them as 'scarlet and black' in E, but 'golden and black' in F.

There are several other Old English texts and scraps of texts extant. In one of these a much fuller account of the drowning of Númenor is given, to which I append a translation:

Ac þá þá Tarcaligeones foregengan dyrstlæhton þæt híe on þæt land astígen and híe þǽr dydon micel yfel ond atendon Túnan þa burg, þá hréowsode Ósfruma and he gebæd him to þam Ælmihtigan, and be þæs Scyppendes rǽde 7 léafe onhwierfed wearþ worulde gesceapu. Wearð Ósgeard from eorþan asundrod, 7 micel æfgrynde ætíewde on middum Gársecge, be éastan Ánetíge. 7 þa sǽ dufon niþer inn on þæt gin, ond mid þam bearhtme þara hréosendra wætera wearþ eall middangeard afylled; 7 þara wætergefealla se þrosm stanc up oþ heofon ofer þara écra munta héafdu.

Þǽr forwurdon eall Westfarena scipu, and adranc mid him eall þæt folc. Forwurdon éac Tarcaligeon se gyldena 7 seo beorhte Iligen his cwén, féollon bútú niþer swaswa steorran on þystro and gewiton seoþþan of eallra manna cýþþe. Micle flódas gelumpon on þam tíman and landa styrunga, and Westfolde þe ǽr Númenor hátte wearð aworpen on Gársecges bósm and hire wuldor gewát.

But when those who went before Tarcalion dared to go up into the land, and did there great evil and set fire to the city of Túna, then the Lord of the Gods grieved, and he prayed to the Almighty; and by the counsel and leave of the Creator the fashion of the world was changed. Ósgeard [Valinor] was sundered from the earth, and a great abyss appeared in the midst of Gársecg [the Ocean], to the east of Ánetíg [the Lonely Isle]. And the seas plunged down into the chasm, and all Middle-earth was filled with the noise of the falling waters; and the smoke of the cataracts rose up to heaven above the heads of the everlasting mountains.

There perished all the ships of the Westfarers, and all that people were drowned with them. There perished also Tarcalion the golden and bright Ilien his queen; they fell both like stars into the darkness and passed out of all men's knowledge. There were great floods in that time and tumults of the lands, and Westfolde, which before was named Númenor, was cast down into the bosom of Gársecg, and its glory perished.

Tol Eressëa, the Lonely Isle, is named *Ánetíg* in the Old English version of the earliest *Annals of Valinor* (IV.281, etc.). In that work Valinor was *Godéþel* changed to *Ésa-eard* (IV.283), *Ésa* being the genitive plural of *Ós* 'god', as here in *Ósgeard* (Valinor) and in *Ósfruma* 'Lord of the Gods' (Manwë). *Tarcaligeon, Iligen* are Old English spellings representing *Tarcalion, Ilien.*

Comparison of this text with *The Fall of Númenor* §§6–8 (pp. 336–7) will show a close relation between the two. I think it very probable that this text represents my father's original idea for the single preserved page of Edwin Lowdham's manuscript, before he decided that the page should consist, in Ramer's words (p. 259), of 'a series of fragmentary extracts, separated, I should guess, by very various intervals of omission'.

A portion of this text is also found written in *tengwar*, with an interlinear gloss in modern script. This, I think, was the first of the texts in *tengwar* (see the next section).

Other Old English names found in these papers are *Ealfæderburg* 'the mountain of Allfather (Ilúvatar)' as an alternative name for *Heofonsȳl* 'Pillar of Heaven'; *Héafíras* 'High Men', of the Númenóreans (cf. *Fréafíras* mentioned below); and *se Malsca*, of Sauron (cf. *Malscor*, a name of Morgoth found in a list of Old English equivalents of Elvish names associated with the *Quenta*, IV.209; an Old English noun *malscrung* 'bewitching, bewildering' is recorded).

Lastly may be mentioned a slip of paper giving the Quenya fragments in their original form (that is, in the form in which they are found in *The Lost Road* and preceding that in manuscript E, as is seen from *tēra* 'straight' for *tēna*, p. 310), with the usual English glosses and queries, but also with a translation into Old English (rapidly jotted down and hard to read):

7 Saweron cóm to hýþe. Gedruron Fréafíras under sceadu. Tarkalion wíg gebéad þam Héamægnum. Þa tocléaf Westfréa þas woruld be þæs Ælmihtigan léafe. 7 fléowon þa sǽ inn on þæt micle gin 7 wearþ Nówendaland ahwylfed.

Géo læg riht weg westanweard, nú sind alle wegas [?forcrymbed]. Fréafíras éastweard. Déaþscúa ús líþ hefig on. Nú swíþe feor is seo Niþerhrorene.

It is curious to see that *nahamna* (marked as usual with a query in the modern English gloss) was translated to *hýþe* 'to haven'. The Old English words *be ... léafe* 'with leave' correspond to dots in the Elvish text (the word *lenēme* being introduced here later in E, p. 310). *Fréafíras* and *Nówendaland* are mentioned by Lowdham (p. 242 and notes 42, 43) among names that have 'come through' to him which are not recorded in Old English. *Héamægnum: héah-mægen* 'great power'. *Westfréa* ('Lord of the West') was struck out and replaced by (apparently) *Regenríces Wealdend* ('Ruler of Valinor': cf. *Regeneard* p. 242 and note 44). No verb *(for)crymban* is recorded, but cf. Old English *crumb* 'crooked, bent', and *crymbing* 'curvature, bend'.

*(v) The page preserved from Edwin Lowdham's manuscript
written in Númenórean script*

My father's representations of this page are reproduced on pp. 319–21.
The first form, here called Text I, is written on both sides of a single
sheet as was Edwin Lowdham's, and represents the Old English text
given on pp. 313–14; as already explained, this was written to
accompany the account in the manuscript E. My father wrote it with
a dipping pen, and where the ink ran pale parts of many letters,
especially the fine strokes, are extremely faint in the original and
disappear entirely in reproduction. To remedy this I have worked over
a photocopy of the original and darkened the strokes to make them
visible; and I have added line-numbers in the margins to make my
commentary on the *tengwar* easier to follow.

Text **II** corresponds to the later Old English version in the typescript
F, but it covers only one side of a sheet and extends only to the words
swé adwalde he for(néan) (p. 257): at that point, as it appears, it was
abandoned. This may or may not relate to my father's note (p. 279):
'the Anglo-Saxon should *not* be written in Númenórean script'.

The reproductions of these pages are followed by commentaries on
the scripts, which differ in the two versions. These commentaries are
reproduced from my manuscript, since it would be very much more
difficult to print them.

Text I was written quickly and has a number of errors; Text II was
more carefully done. Some pages of notes accompany the original
texts, but these are very rough and difficult jottings and have not
proved of much help in deducing the structure. There can be no doubt
that these texts were to some degree experimental, especially in the use
of the diacritic marks and in the application of the script to Old
English.

In what I take to be the first of these *tengwar* texts (not reproduced),
corresponding to part of the Old English text given on p. 316, the
vowel-diacritics differ from the usage in Text I. Those used for o and y
in Text I are here used for u and o, while y is rendered by that for u
together with a single dot (= i), reflecting the historical origin of Old
English y in many instances from u followed by i in the next syllable.

The surviving page of Edwin Lowdham's manuscript
Text I, recto

The surviving page of Edwin Lowdham's manuscript
Text I, verso

The surviving page of Edwin Lowdham's manuscript
Text II

Text I

In the following analysis references to the text are by page and line-number, as '2 : 26' = line 26 of the verso page. The consonants are set out simply in alphabetical order, not according to phonetic function.

b ꝑ

c ꝗ ; ꞇ In Old English the letter c had 'front' and 'back' ('palatal' and 'velar') values, the front stop becoming [tš] as in *church* in later Old English. This distinction is represented here :

ꝗ for the back stop, as in ꝗ *ac* (1 : 2), ᚻᚳꝗ *folc* (1 : 20) ; ꞇ for the original front stop, as in ꞇᚱᛁ *cyrre* (2 : 6-7, where ꞇ is the last letter of line 6), ꝗᛁ *eces* (2 : 20). Thus the c in *undeadlican* (1 : 3) and in *deadlice* (1 : 7) is differently represented : ~ ꞇꝗᚱᛁ and ~ ꞇᛁꞇᛁ

d ꝺ For *ld* see *l*.

f ᛒ In Old English the letter f was used in medial positions between voiced sounds to represent the voiced spirant [v] ; thus ᛒ 'v' will be found in many words where the Old English text has f, as ꞇᛁᛒ *lifes* (1 : 8), ᛗᛁᛒᚾᛁ *næfre* (2 : 26).

g ꝙ, ꝺᛁ ; ᚳꝗ, ᚳᛁ In Old English the letter g (ᵹ) had not only front and back values but also stop and spirant. The back stop is represented here by ꝙ, as in ꝙᛁ *gode* (1 : 22) ; also in *ng*, where the nasal is indicated by a horizontal line above : ꞇꝙꝙ *langung* (1 : 4).

The back spirant has the vertical rising not descending, ꝺ, as in λꝺᛁ *hogode* (2 : 6), ᛗᛚꞇꝺ *unhalgum* (2 : 14).

The front stop is represented by ᚳᛁ. In late Old English this became [dž] as in *judge* ; this appears in the words *secganne* (2:11), *unasecgendlice* (2:13-14), where *cg* is a graph for *gg*, hence the mark of doubling placed below the sign : ᛒ *secganne*.

The front spirant, which in Modern English has become *y* initially or has combined to form diphthongs, has the vertical rising, *ccl*, as in *þegn* (1:19), ~ ~*gearde* (1:21), *igland* (2:22), *fyrgen* [cf. *Firien* in LR] (2:22), *segl* (2:24).

h λ; ꝺ   The breath [h], only found initially, is represented by λ. The voiceless back spirant [χ] is represented by ꝺ (cf. ꝺ under *g*), as in *þeah* (1:17), *ealh* (2:10), *woh* (2:20).

ht may be represented by a combinatory sign as in *þuhte* (1:11), or as in *mihton* (1:8), according to the front or back position of the spirant (cl, ꝺ); but the verticals may be written separately, as *ahte* (1:26).

l ᛏ; *ld* as in *wuldor* (1:4)

m m

n m

p p   (written þ in *upahæfenlice* 1:22)

r ᚾ

s ᛒ; at the end of words often written as a curl, as for example in *facnes* (2:5). As in the case of *f*, in Old English *s* was used in medial positions between voiced sounds to represent the voiced spirant [z]. The only example of [z] in the text is *alysan* (1:8), where it is written with the sign ᛤ.

sc (becoming in the course of Old English [ʃ] as in *ship*) is written with a combinatory sign as in *scort* ['short'] (1:11), *deapscua* (2:15).

t   þ   For *ht* see *h*.

th   ƀ; ð   In Old English, as with *f/v*, *s/z*, the voiceless spirant (as in Modern English *thin*) and the voiced (as in *other*) appear in different positions in words, but in this case there were two symbols, the barred *d* 'ð' and the Runic 'þ' ('*thorn*'). These were not used, however, to distinguish the sounds.

    The Old English text uses the signs indiscriminately, as is commonly the case in O.E. manuscripts; thus for example both *þeah* and *ðeah* occur. But it is curious that although the distinction between ƀ and ð was phonetic, between voiceless and voiced, no use is made of it: thus we find *ƀið* at 2:5 (where the text in modern script has *þeah*) but *ðið* at 1:17 (where it has *ðeah*).

v   ð   On the frequent occurrence of ð where the Old English word is spelt with an *f* see under *f*. The only other instance is *aƀođ* Avallon (2:18).

w   ȝ   In *ȝreow hreow* (2:17) the sign u 'u' is used (see under *Vowels*).

    hw is represented by ƕ as in *ƕæt hwæt* (1:1).

x   ƕ   as in *weox* weox (1:20).

z   ʒ   See under *s*.

Vowels

Vowels are normally expressed by diacritic signs (*tehtar*):

a	/	i	.
æ	∴	o	'
e	..	u	∩
		y	ς

These precede the consonant if placed *above* it and follow it if placed below, as in *ðære* ðære, *ende* ende. The diacritics of o and u are not used in the subscript position.

The diacritics are very frequently borne on 'carriers', the short carrier ı being used for short vowels and the long carrier ȷ for long vowels (as *bȷ sǽ*, 1:1).

The Old English diphthongs are not represented by simple signs or diacritics: thus *heorte* (1:2) The diphthong *ea* as representing [æɑ] is written with the diacritics of *æ* and *a*, as *westweard* (1:2); but *e+a* in *ᵹearde* (1:21).

The glide 'i, y' is ɑ in *Meneltyúla* (2:11), *iú* (2:26).

In certain positions (chiefly in prefixes and finally) *a* is written as a letter, ɑ, though not invariably: so *swa hyra* (1:4), *swa arædde* (1:12); also always ɑ in *Sauron*. Long *a* has both letter and diacritic in *má* (1:5) Similarly *u* may be written as a letter; so *nú* (2:26), *scúa* (2:27).

Other signs

Doubling is shown by two inclined strokes beneath the letter, or in the case of τ within it: as *Eresse* (1:6), *ealle* (1:1).

A horizontal line above the letter represents a nasal in such combinations as *nd, ng, mp*, as *ende* (1:9), *cyning* (1:23); in *nn* it therefore acts as a doubling sign, as *þonne* (1:15).

The Old English sign ꝥ *ond, and* 'and' is used (1:21 &c).

Errors

The text was written quickly, and there are a number of unquestionable errors, as for example: for *Éarendles* in 1:10, for *Eldum* in 1:11, 'Sauron' in 2:4, for *gefaran* in 2:19. In some cases apparent errors may reflect indecision or rejected forms, as ᵹ for r in *æfre* 1:4 (*næfre* 2:26), *unryht* 1:14, and *he* for *hi* twice in 1:1 and again in 1:2.

Text II

In this form of the script the values of the *tengwar* are the same, the differences from Text I lying chiefly in the use of the vowel diacritics.　In Text II the diacritics follow the consonants; and while *i, o, u, y* remain the same those representing *a, æ, e* are now:

a　∴

æ　..

e　╱

Thus *gefyrn* in Text I (1:12) is written [tengwar], but in Text II [tengwar] (line 2).

Further, the diacritics of *o* and *u* can be written subscript, as for example in [tengwar] *weorulde*, [tengwar] *ofer-liodon*, both in line 1.

As in Text I the Old English diphthong written *ea* but phonetically [æa] is represented by the diacritics of *æ* and *a*, thus [tengwar] *heara* in line 2; on the other hand, in [tengwar] *Westwearena* (lines 6–7) *ea* is represented by *e+a*.

In Text II long vowels can be shown by a subscript ɹ; this is evidently the tail of the long carrier ɹ. So [tengwar] *sæ* (line 1), [tengwar] *þás* (3), [tengwar] [tengwar] *wéox swíðe* (6).

A problem lies in the representation of names. Ramer says of the text that the proper names, when they are not Old English translations, are in the same script, 'but the letters are then quite differently used'.　In the Old English text in modern script these names are set within brackets. In Text II appear only *Zigūr* (*Zigūre*) and *Tarcalion*, which are placed between marks of citation and represented thus:

line 5　[tengwar]　*Zigūr*

line 10　[tengwar]　(*to*) *Zigūre*

line 11　[tengwar]　*Zigūr*

line 8　[tengwar]　*Tarcalion*

ᚻᚩ is here used with the value 'z'. (It is a feature of the script in Text II that ᚻ and ᚻᚩ (= 'th') are often but not always / with the vertical stroke extended downwards, to a greater or lesser degree : so �becþᚩᚱᚩ (*forðon*, line 2), ᚷᛒᚩᚱᚩ (*seoþþan*, line 4), þᚩᚩp (*þæt*, line 3), but ᛒᚳᛞᚱᚩ (*þegn*, line 5). In ᚻᚩ = 'z' the vertical is not extended downwards; but whether this distinction, not in any case very clearly marked, is significant I cannot say.)

The other consonants in *Zigūr*, and in *Tarcalion*, are not different from those used to represent the Old English; but the use of the diacritics is mysterious. In *Zigūr(e)* · = *i*, ⌐ = *u*, / = *e*, and a subscript ɟ = long vowel, as in the rest of the text; but in one case of *Zigūr* a single dot is placed under *r*, in the other not. In *Tarcalion* single dots are placed under *r* and *n*; ⊙̈ᵢ presumably represents *lio* (but with ·· = *i*), but there is no representation of the two occurrences of *a* in the name.

In this text there is only one clear error: this is the word ᛚᚷᛄ 'sté' in the last line of the page, for ᛚᚷᛄ *swé* ('so'), written as ᛚᚤᛄ in line 2.

PART THREE

THE DROWNING
OF ANADÛNÊ

With the Third Version of
THE FALL OF NÚMENOR

And Lowdham's Report on
THE ADUNAIC LANGUAGE

THE DROWNING OF ANADÛNÊ

(i) The third version of The Fall of Númenor

Before coming to *The Drowning of Anadûnê* it is necessary to turn
first to the original narrative of the legend of Númenor, which arose in
close association with *The Lost Road* (see V.9). This, *The Fall of
Númenor*, is extant (in addition to an initial sketch) in two versions,
given in V.13 ff., which I called FN I and FN II, the second being
closely similar to the first for the greater part of its length. Some
subsequent work was done on this text during the period of the
writing of *The Lord of the Rings*, including a rewriting of the passage
describing 'the World Made Round' and a development of the
concluding section concerning Beleriand and the Last Alliance (see
V.31 ff.); but since the name *Ondor* appears in the latter passage it
can be dated before February 1942, when *Ondor* became *Gondor*
(VII.423); at that time my father was working on Book III of *The Lord
of the Rings*.

Now there is a further text of *The Fall of Númenor* in fine
manuscript, which I referred to but did not print in Vol.V; I noted
there that 'this version, improved and altered in detail, shows however
very little further advance in narrative substance,' and concluded therefore that it belongs to the same period as the revisions just referred to,
i.e. to a relatively early stage in the writing of *The Lord of the Rings*.
Since *The Drowning of Anadûnê* shows such an extraordinary departure from *The Fall of Númenor* I give the third version of the latter
in full here, calling it 'FN III', to make comparison of the two works
easier. I have again introduced the paragraph numbers that I inserted
in the earlier versions; and various alterations that were made to FN III
subsequently are shown as such.

The Last Tales

1. The Fall of Númenor

§1   In the Great Battle, when Fionwë son of Manwë overthrew Morgoth, the three houses of the Men of Beleriand were
friends and allies of the Elves, and they wrought many deeds of
valour. But men of other kindreds turned to evil and fought for
Morgoth, and after the victory of the Lords of the West those
that were not destroyed fled back east into Middle-earth. There
many of their race wandered still in the unharvested lands, wild

and lawless, refusing the summons alike of Fionwë and of Morgoth to aid them in their war. And the evil men who had served Morgoth became their masters; and the creatures of Morgoth that escaped from the ruin of Thangorodrim came among them and cast over them a shadow of fear. For the gods [> Valar] forsook for a time the Men of Middle-earth who had refused their summons and had taken the friends of Morgoth to be their lords; and men were troubled by many evil things that Morgoth had devised in the days of his dominion: demons, and dragons and ill-shapen beasts, and the unclean orcs, that are mockeries of the creatures of Ilúvatar; and the lot of men was unhappy.

But Manwë put forth Morgoth, and shut him beyond the World in the Void that is without; and he cannot [> could not] return again into the World, present and visible, while the Lords are [> the Lords of the West were] enthroned. Yet his will remaineth, and guideth [> remained, and guided] his servants; and it moveth [> moved] them ever to seek the overthrow of the gods [> Valar] and the hurt of those that obey [> obeyed] them. When Morgoth was thrust forth, the gods [> Valar] held council. The Elves [> Eldar] were summoned to return into the West; and those that obeyed dwelt once more in Eressëa, the Lonely Isle; and that land was named anew Avallon: for it is hard by Valinor and within sight of the Blessed Realm. But to men of the three faithful houses rich reward was given. Fionwë son of Manwë came among them and taught them; and he gave them wisdom, and power, and life stronger than any others have of mortal race. [*Added:* and the span of their years, being unassailed by sickness, was thrice that of Men of Middle-earth, and to the descendants of Húrin the Steadfast even longer years were granted, / even to three hundreds [> as is later told].][1]

§2   A land was made for them to dwell in, neither part of Middle-earth, nor of Valinor; for it was sundered from either by a wide sea, yet it was nearer to Valinor. It was raised by Ossë out of the depths of the Great Water, and it was established by Aulë and enriched by Yavanna; and the Eldar brought thither flowers and fountains out of Avallon, and they wrought gardens there of great beauty, in which at times the children of the Gods [> Valar] would walk. That land the Valar called Andor, the Land of Gift; and by its own folk it was at first called Vinya, the Young; but in the days of its pride they named it Númenor, that is Westernesse, for it lay west of all lands inhabited by mortals;

yet it was far from the true West, for that is Valinor, the land
of the Gods. But the glory of Númenor was thrown down [>
overthrown] and its name perished; and after its ruin it was
named in the legends of those that fled from it Atalantë, the
Downfallen.

Of old the chief city and haven of that land was in the midst
of its western coasts, and it was called Undúnië [> Andúnië],²
because it faced the sunset. But the high place of the king was at
Númenos in the heart of the land, the tower and citadel that was
built by Elros son of Ëarendel [>Ëarendil], whom the gods and
elves and men chose to be the lord [> who (was) appointed to
be the first lord] of the Númenóreans. He was descended from
the line of both Hador and Bëor, fathers of Men, and in part
also from both the Eldar and the Valar, for Idril and Lúthien
were his foremothers. But Elros and all his folk were mortal;
for the Valar may not withdraw the gift of death, which cometh
to men from Ilúvatar. [*This passage, from 'He was descended
...', was struck out and replaced by the following rider:* 'Now
Elrond, and Elros his brother, were descended from the line of
both Hador and of Bëor, fathers of Men, and in part also both
from the Eldar and the Valar, for Idril and Lúthien daughter of
Melian were their foremothers. None others among Men of the
Elder Days had kinship with the Elves, and therefore they were
called Halfelven. The Valar indeed may not withdraw the gift of
death, which cometh to Men from Ilúvatar, but in the matter
of the Halfelven Ilúvatar gave them judgement. And this they
judged: choice should be given to the brethren. And Elrond
chose to remain with the Firstborn, and to him the life of the
Firstborn was given, and yet a grace was added, that choice was
never annulled, and while the world lasted he might return, if he
would, to mortal men, and die. But to Elros, who chose to be a
king of men, still a great span of years was granted, seven times
that of mortal men; and all his line, the kings and lords of the
royal house of Númenor, [*added:* being descended from Húrin,]
had long life even according to the span of the Númenóreans,
for some of the kings that sat at Númenos lived four hundred
years. But Elros lived five hundred years, and ruled the Númenóreans four hundred years and ten. Thus, though long in life
and assailed by no sickness, the men of Númenor were mortal
still.] Yet the speech of Númenor was the speech of the Eldar of
the Blessed Realm, and the Númenóreans conversed with the
Elves, and were permitted to look upon Valinor from afar; for

their ships went often to Avallon, and there their mariners were suffered to dwell for a while.

§3 In the wearing of time the people of Númenor grew great and glorious, in all things more like to the Firstborn than any other of the kindreds of Men; yet they were less fair and less wise than the Elves, though greater in stature. For the Númenóreans were exceedingly tall, taller than the tallest of the sons of men in Middle-earth. Above all arts they nourished ship-building and sea-craft, and became mariners whose like shall never be again, since the world has been diminished. They ranged from Eressëa in the West to the shores of Middle-earth, and came even into the inner seas; and they sailed about the North and the South and glimpsed from their high prows the Gates of Morning in the East. And they appeared among the wild men and filled them with wonder and dismay; for men in the shadows of the world deemed that they were gods or the sons of gods out of the West. Here and there the Númenóreans sowed good seed in the waste-lands, and they taught to the wild men such lore and wisdom as they could comprehend; but for the most part the men of Middle-earth feared them and fled; for they were under the sway of Sauron and the lies of Morgoth and they believed that the gods were terrible and cruel. Wherefore out of that far time are descended the echoes of legends both bright and dark; but the shadow lay heavy upon men, for the Númenóreans came only seldom among them and they tarried never long in any place. Upon all the waters of the world they sailed, seeking they knew not what, yet their hearts were set westward; and they began to hunger for the undying bliss of Valinor, and ever their desire and unquiet increased as their power and glory grew.

§4 The gods forbade them to sail beyond the Lonely Isle and would not permit them to land in Valinor; for the Númenóreans were mortal, and though the Lords of the West had rewarded them with long life, they could not take from them the weariness of the world that cometh at last, and they died, even their kings of the seed of Eärendel, and their span was brief in the eyes of the Elves. And they began to murmur against this decree, and a great discontent grew among them. Their masters of knowledge sought unceasingly for secrets that should prolong their lives; and they sent spies to seek hidden lore in Avallon; and the gods were angered.

§5 Now it came to pass [added: in the days of Tar-kalion,

and twelve kings had ruled that land before him,]³ that Sauron, servant of Morgoth, grew strong in Middle-earth; and he learned of the power and splendour of the Númenóreans, and of their allegiance to the gods; and he feared lest they should come and wrest from him the dominion of the East and rescue the men of Middle-earth from the Shadow. And the king from his mariners heard also rumour of Sauron, and it was reported that he would make himself a king, greater even than the king of Númenor. Wherefore, taking no counsel of the gods or of the Elves, Tar-kalion the king sent his messengers to Sauron and commanded him to come and do homage. And Sauron, being filled with malice and cunning, humbled himself and came; and he beguiled the Númenóreans with signs and wonders. Little by little Sauron turned their hearts towards Morgoth, his master; and he prophesied to them, and lied, saying that Morgoth would come again into the world. And Sauron spake to Tar-kalion, and to Tar-ilien his queen, and promised them life unending and the dominion of the earth, if they would turn unto Morgoth. And they believed him, and fell under the Shadow, and the greater part of their people followed them. And Tar-kalion raised a great temple to Morgoth upon the Mountain of Ilúvatar in the midst of the land; and Sauron dwelt there, and all Númenor was under his vigilance. [*This passage, from 'upon the Mountain of Ilúvatar ...', was struck out and replaced by the following:* in the midst of the city of Númenos,⁴ and its dome rose like a black hill glowering over the land; and smokes issued from it, for in that temple the Númenóreans made hideous sacrifice to Morgoth, beseeching the Lord of Darkness to deliver them from Death. But the hallowed place of Ilúvatar was upon the summit of the Mountain Menelmin, Pillar of Heaven, in the midst of the land, and thither men had been wont to climb to offer thanksgiving. There only in all Númenor Sauron dared never to set his foot, and he forbade [any] to go there under pain of death. Few dared to disobey him, even if they so wished, for Sauron had many eyes and all the ways of the land were under his vigilance. But some there were who remained faithful, and did not bow to him, and of these the chief were Elendil the fair, and his sons Anárion and Isildur, and they were of the royal blood of Ëarendel, though not of the line direct.]

§6 But in the passing of the years Tar-kalion felt the oncoming of old age, and he was troubled; but Sauron said that the bounty of Morgoth was withheld by the gods, and that to obtain plentitude of power and freedom from death the king must be master of the West. And the fear of death was heavy upon Tar-kalion. Therefore at his command the Númenóreans made a great armament; and their might and skill had grown exceedingly in those days, for they had in these matters the aid of Sauron. The fleets of the Númenóreans were like a land of many islands, and their masts were like a forest of mountain-trees, and their banners like the streamers of a thunderstorm, and their sails were scarlet and black. And they moved slowly into the West, for all the winds were stilled, and all the world was silent in the fear of that time. And they encompassed Avallon; and it is said that the Elves mourned and sickness came upon them, for the light of Valinor was cut off by the cloud of the Númenóreans. Then Tar-kalion assailed the shores of Valinor, and he cast forth bolts of thunder, and fire came upon Túna, and flame and smoke rose about Taniquetil.

§7   But the gods made no answer. Then the vanguard of the Númenóreans set foot upon the forbidden shores, and they encamped in might upon the borders of Valinor. But the heart of Manwë was sorrowful and dismayed, and he called upon Ilúvatar, and took power and counsel from the Maker; and the fate and fashion of the world was changed. The silence of the gods was broken and their power made manifest; and Valinor was sundered from the earth, and a rift appeared in the midst of the Great Sea, east of Avallon.

Into this chasm the Great Sea plunged, and the noise of the falling waters filled all the earth, and the smoke of the cataracts rose above the tops of the everlasting mountains. But all the ships of Númenor that were west of Avallon were drawn down into the abyss, and they were drowned; and Tar-kalion the golden and bright Ilien his queen fell like stars into the dark, and they perished out of all knowledge. But the mortal warriors that had set foot upon the Land of the Gods were buried under fallen hills; there it is said they lie imprisoned in the Caves of the Forgotten until the day of Doom and the Last Battle.

§8   Then Ilúvatar cast back the Great Seas west of Middle-earth and the Empty Lands east of it, and new lands and new seas were made; and the world was diminished, for Valinor and Eressëa were taken from it into the realm of hidden things. And thereafter, however a man might sail, he could never again reach the True West, but would come back weary at last to the place of his beginning; for all lands and seas were equally distant from the centre of the earth. There was flood and great confusion of waters in that time, and sea covered much that in the Elder Days had been dry, both in the West and East of Middle-earth.

§9   Númenor, being nigh to the east of the great rift, was utterly thrown down, and overwhelmed in the sea, and its glory perished, and only a remnant of all its people escaped the ruin of those days. Some by the command of Tar-kalion, and some of their own will (because they still revered the gods and would not go with war into the West) had remained behind when the fleets set sail, and they sat in their ships upon the east coast of the land, lest the issue of war should be evil. Therefore, being protected for a while by the wall of their land, they avoided the draught of the sea; and many fled into the East, and came at length to the shores of Middle-earth.

Small remnant of all the mighty people that had perished were those that came up out of the devouring sea upon the wings of the winds of wrath, and shorn were they of their pride and power of old. But to those that looked out from the seaward hills and beheld their coming, riding upon the storm out of the mist and the darkness and the rumour of water, their black sails against the falling sun, terrible and strong they seemed, and the fear of the tall kings came into lands far from the sea.

§10   For lords and kings of men the Númenóreans became, and nigh to the western shores of Middle-earth they established realms and strong places. Some few were indeed evil, being of those who had hearkened to Sauron and still did not forsake him in their hearts; but the most were those of good will who had revered the gods and remembered the wisdom of old. Yet all alike were filled with the desire of long life upon earth, and the thought of death was heavy upon them. Their fate had cast them east upon Middle-earth, but their hearts still were westward. And they built mightier houses for their dead than for their living, and endowed their buried kings with unavailing treasure; for their wise men hoped still to discover the secret of prolonging life, and maybe of recalling it. Yet it is said that the span of their lives, which had of old been thrice that of lesser men, dwindled slowly; and they achieved only the art of preserving incorrupt the dead flesh of men. Wherefore the kingdoms of the western world became a place of tombs and

were filled with ghosts. And in the fantasy of their hearts, amid
the confusion of legends concerning half-forgotten things that
once had been, they imagined in their thought a land of shades,
filled with the wraiths of the things that are upon the mortal
earth; and many deemed that this land was in the West and
ruled by the gods, and that in shadow the dead should come
there, bearing with them the shadows of their possessions, who
could in the body find the True West no more. Therefore in after
days many would bury their dead in ships, setting them forth in
pomp upon the sea by the west coasts of the ancient world.

§11   Now the blood of the Númenóreans remained most
among men of those western lands and shores; and the memory
of the primeval world abode most strongly there, where the old
paths to the West had aforetime set out from Middle-earth. For
the ancient line of the world remained in the mind of Ilúvatar,
and in the thought of the gods, and in the memory of the world,
as a shape and plan that has been changed and yet endureth.
And it has been likened to a plain of air, or to a straight vision
that bendeth not to the curving of the earth, or to a level bridge
that rises slowly above the heavy air. Of old many of the exiles
of Númenor could still see, some clearly and some more faintly,
the paths to the True West; and they believed that at times from
a high place they could descry the peaks of Taniquetil at the end
of the Straight Road, high above the world. Therefore they built
very high towers in those days, and their holy places were upon
the tops of mountains, for they would climb, if it might be,
above the mists of Middle-earth into the clearer air that doth
not veil the vision of things far off.

§12   But ever the number of those that had the ancient sight
dwindled, and those that had it not and could not conceive it in
their thought scorned the builders of towers, and trusted to
ships that sailed upon the water. But they came only to the lands
of the new world, and found them like to those of the old and
subject to death; and they reported that the world was round.
For upon the Straight Road only the gods could walk, and only
the ships of the Elves could journey; for being straight that road
passed through the air of breath and flight and rose above it,
and traversed Ilmen in which no mortal flesh can endure;
whereas the surface of the earth was bent, and bent were the
seas that lay upon it, and bent also were the heavy airs that were
above them. Yet it is said that even of those Númenóreans of
old who had the straight vision there were some who did not

comprehend this, and they were busy to contrive ships that should rise above the waters of the world and hold to the imagined seas. But they achieved only ships that would sail in the air of breath. And these ships, flying, came also to the lands of the new world, and to the East of the old world; and they reported that the world was round. Therefore many abandoned the gods and put them out of their legends. But men of Middle-earth looked up with fear and wonder seeing the Númenóreans that descended out of the sky; and they took these mariners of the air to be gods, and some of the Númenóreans were content that this should be so.

§13 Yet not all the hearts of the Númenóreans were crooked; and knowledge of the days before the Downfall and of the wisdom descended from the Elf-friends, their fathers, was long preserved among them. And the wisest among them taught that the fate of Men was not bounded by the round path, nor set for ever upon the straight. For the round has no end, but no escape; and the straight is true, but has an end within the world, and that is the fate of the Elves. But the fate of Men, they said, is neither round nor ended, and is not complete within the world.

But even the wisdom of the wise was filled with sorrow and regret; and they remembered bitterly how the ruin was brought about and the cutting off of Men from their portion of the Straight Path. Therefore they avoided the shadow of Morgoth according to their power, and Sauron they held in hatred. And they assailed his temples and their servants, and there were wars among the mighty of Middle-earth, of which only the echoes now remain.

The concluding section (§14) of the earlier versions of *The Fall of Númenor* concerning Beleriand (see p. 331) was omitted in FN III.

Accepting the conclusion (see p. 331) that the version just given, as it was originally written, comes from a much earlier stage in the writing of *The Lord of the Rings* than do *The Notion Club Papers*, it seems almost certain that the alterations and additions made to it belong to the period of the *Papers* and *The Drowning of Anadûnê*. The chief evidence for this[5] lies in the addition to §5 stating that Tar-kalion was the thirteenth king of Númenor, and in the correction in §5 of the description of the temple: it was not on the Mountain of Ilúvatar, but 'in the midst of the city of Númenos' (see notes 3 and 4).

The most remarkable, and indeed astonishing, feature of these later additions to FN III is the statement in §2 that while 'the life of the Firstborn' was given to Elrond in accordance with his choice, 'yet a grace was added, that choice was never annulled, and while the world lasted he might return, if he would, to mortal men, and die.' To my present knowledge no such thing is said elsewhere of the Choice of Elrond; and contrast Appendix A (I, i) to *The Lord of the Rings*: 'At the end of the First Age the Valar gave to the Half-elven *an irrevocable choice* to which kindred they would belong.' This passage in FN III concerning Elrond and Elros reappeared years later in the *Akallabêth*, but with this sentence removed (*The Silmarillion*, p. 261).

NOTES

1   On the threefold span of the Númenóreans see p. 378, §13. – *The descendants of Húrin the Steadfast*: presumably an inadvertence, for Huor, father of Tuor, father of Eärendil; but *Húrin* is repeated in the addition to §2. Cf. the note given in VII.6, 'Trotter is a man of Elrond's race descendant of Túrin', where *Túrin* is presumably a slip for *Tuor*.

2   *Undúnië*: *Andúnië* is the form in FN II, but on the amanuensis typescript made from FN II (V.31) the form was changed to *Undúnië*.

3   Tar-kalion became the fourteenth (not the thirteenth) king of Númenor by correction of the second text of *The Drowning of Anadûnê* (see p. 381, §20).

4   On uncertainty with regard to the site of the temple see p. 384, §32.

5   On the back of the slip carrying the long addition to §2 concerning Elrond and Elros are rough notes in which there is a reference to the Adunaic language; but these are not dateable.

(ii) *The original text of* The Drowning of Anadûnê

It will become very evident that *The Drowning of Anadûnê* was as closely associated with Part Two of *The Notion Club Papers* as was the original *Fall of Númenor* with *The Lost Road*. I shall give first the original draft, and postpone observations about it to the conclusion.

The draft is a typescript of extreme roughness, with a great many typing errors, and I have little doubt that my father, for some reason, and for the first time, composed a primary draft entirely *ab initio* on a typewriter, typing at speed. Certainly there is no trace among all this great collection of texts and notes of any still more 'primary' narrative (although there are preliminary sketches which are given later, pp. 397 ff.). I print it here essentially as it was typed, correcting the obvious errors and here and there inserting punctuation, but ignoring subsequent correction. Such correction is largely confined to the opening paragraphs, after which it ceases: it looks as if my father saw that it would be impossible to carry out a wholesale rewriting on a single-spaced typescript with narrow margins. In any case these corrections were taken up into the second text, which I also give in full. One name that was consistently changed, however, is *Balāi* > *Avalāi*, as far as §16, where *Avalāi* appears in the typescript as typed. I have extended the marks of length over vowels throughout the text: my father's typewriter having no such marks, he inserted them in pencil, and often omitted them.

The numbered paragraphs have of course no manuscript warrant: I have inserted them to make subsequent reference and comparison easier. This first text has in fact little division into paragraphs, and my divisions are made largely on the basis of the following version.

I shall refer to this text subsequently as 'DA I'. It had no title as typed, but *The Drowning of Númenor* was pencilled in afterwards.

§1   Before the coming of Men there were many Powers that governed Earth, and they were Eru-bēnī, servants of God, and in the earliest recorded tongue they were called Balāi. Some were lesser and some greater. The mightiest and the chieftain of them all was Mēlekō.

§2   But long ago, even in the making of Earth, he pondered evil; he became a rebel against Eru, desiring the whole world for his own and to have none above him. Therefore Manawē his brother endeavoured to rule the earth and the Powers according to the will of Eru; and Manawē dwelt in the West. But Mēlekō remained, dwelling in hiding in the North, and he worked evil, and he had the greater power, and the Great Lands were darkened.

§3   And at the appointed time Men were born into the world, and they came in a time of war; and they fell swiftly under the domination of Mēlekō. And he now came forth and appeared as a Great King and as a god, and his rule was evil, and his worship unclean; and Men were estranged from Eru and from the Balāi, his servants.

§4   But there were some of the fathers of Men who repented, seeing the evil of King Mēlekō, and their houses returned with sorrow to the allegiance of Eru, and they were befriended by the Balāi, and they were called the Eruhil, the children of God. And the Balāi and the Eruhil made war on Mēlekō, and for that time they destroyed his kingdom and threw down his black throne. But Mēlekō was not destroyed and he went again for a while in hiding, unseen by Men. But his evil was still ever at work, and cruel kings and evil temples arose ever in the world, and the most part of Mankind were their servants; and they made war on the Eruhil.

§5   And the Balāi in grief withdrew ever further west (or if they did not so they faded and became secret voices and shadows of the days of old); and the most part of the Eruhil followed them. Though it is said that some of these good men, simple folk, shepherds and the like, dwelt in the heart of the Great Lands.

§6   But all the nobler of the Eruhil and those closest in the friendship of the Balāi, who had helped most in the war on the Black Throne, wandered away until they came to the last shores of the Great Seas. There they halted and were filled with dread and longing; for the Balāi for the most part passed over the sea seeking the realm of Manawē. And there instructed by the Balāi men learned the craft of ship-building and of sailing in the wind; and they built many small ships. But they did not dare to essay the deep waters, and journeyed mostly up and down the coasts and among the nearer isles.

§7   And it was by their ships that they were saved. For evil men multiplied in those days and pursued the Eruhil with hatred; and evil men inspired by the evil spirit of Mēlekō grew cunning and cruel in the arts of war and the making of many weapons; and the Eruhil were hard to put to it to maintain any land in which to dwell.

§8   And in those dark days of fear and war there arose a man among the Eruhil and his name was Earendil the Sea-friend, for his daring upon the sea was great. And it came into his heart that he would build a ship greater than any that had yet been built, and that he would sail out into the deep water and come maybe to the land of Manawē and there get help for his kinsfolk. And he let build a great ship and he called it Wingalōtē,[1] the Foam-flower.

§9   And when it was all ready he said farewell to his sons and his wife and all his kin; for he was minded to sail alone. And he said: 'It is likely that you will see me never again, and if you do not, then continue your war, and endure until the end. But if I do not fail of my errand, then also you may not see me again, but a sign you will see, and then have hope.'

§10   But Earendel[2] passed over the Great Sea and came to the Blessed Realm and spoke to Manawē.

§11   [Rejected at once: And Manawē said that he had not now the power to war against Mēlekō, who moreover was the rightful governor of Earth, though his right might seem to have been destroyed by his rebellion; and that the governance of the earth was now in the hands of] And Manawē said that Eru had forbidden the Balāi to make war by force; and that the earth was now in the hands of Men, to make or to mar. But because of their repentance and their fidelity he would give, as was permitted to him, a land for the Eruhil to dwell in if they would. And that land was a mighty island in the midst of the sea. But Manawē would not permit Earendil to return again amongst Men, since he had set foot in the Blessed Realm, where as yet no Death had come. And he took the ship of Earendil and filled it with silver flame and raised it above the world to sail in the sky, a marvel to behold.

§12   And the Eruhil on the shores of the sea beheld the light of it; and they knew that it was the sign of Earendil. And hope and courage was born in their hearts; and they gathered their ships, small and great, and all their goods, and set sail upon the deep waters, following the star. And there was a great calm in those days and all the winds were stilled. And the Eruhil came to the land that had been set for them, and they found it fair and fruitful, and they were glad. And they called that land Andōrē,[3] the land of Gift, though afterward it was mostly named Nūmenōrē, Westernesse.

§13   But not so did the Eruhil escape the doom of death that had been pronounced upon all Mankind; and they were mortal still; though for their fidelity they were rewarded by a threefold span, and their years were long and blissful and untroubled with sickness, so long as they remained true. And the Nūmenōreans grew wise and fair and glorious, the mightiest of men that have been; but their number was not great, for their children were few.

§14   And they were under the tutelage of the Balāi, and they took the language of the Balāi and forsook their own; and they wrote many things of lore and beauty in that tongue in the high tide of their realm, of which but little is now remembered. And they became mighty in all crafts, so that if they had had the mind they might easily have surpassed the evil kings of Middle-earth in the making of weapons and of war; but they were as yet men of peace; and of all arts they were most eager in the craft of ship-building, and in voyaging was the chief feat and delight of their younger men.

§15   But the Balāi as yet forbade them to sail westward out of sight of the western shores of Nūmenōr; and the Nūmenōreans were as yet content, though they did not fully understand the purpose of this ban. But the purpose was that the Eruhil should not be tempted to come to the Blessed Realm and there learn discontent, becoming enamoured of the immortality of the Balāi, and the deathlessness of all things in their land.

§16   For as yet the Balāi were permitted by Eru to maintain upon earth upon some isle or shore of the western lands still untrodden (it is not known for certain where; for Eärendel alone of Men came ever thither and never again returned) an abiding place, an earthly paradise and a memorial of that which might have been, had not men turned to Mēlekō. And the Nūmenōreans named that land Avallondē the Haven of the Gods, for at times when all the air was clear and the sun was in the east they could descry, as them seemed, a city white-shining on a distant shore and great harbours and a tower; but only so when their own western haven, Andūniē of Nūmenōr, was low upon the skyline, and they dared not break the ban and sail further west. But to Nūmenōr the Avalāi came ever and anon, the children and the lesser ones of the Deathless Folk, some-times in oarless boats, sometimes as birds flying, sometimes in other fair shapes; and they loved the Nūmenōreans.

§17   And so it was that the voyages of the men of Western-esse in those days went east and not west from the darkness of the North to the heats of the South and beyond to the nether darkness. And the Eruhil came often to the shores of the Great Lands, and they took pity on the forsaken world of Middle-earth; and the young princes of the Nūmenōreans would come among the men of the Dark Ages, and they taught them language (for the native tongues of men of Middle-earth were yet rude and unshapen) and song, and many arts, such as they could compass, and they brought them corn and wine.

§18   And the men of Middle-earth were comforted, and in some places shook off somewhat the yoke of the offspring of Mēlekō; and they revered the memory of the Men out of the Sea and called them Gods, for in that time the Nūmenōreans did not settle or dwell in Middle-earth for long. For though their feet were set eastward their hearts were ever westward.

§19   Yet in the end all this bliss and betterment turned to evil again, and men fell, as it is said, a second time. For there arose a second manifestation of the power of darkness upon earth, and whether that was but a form of the Ancient or one of his old servants that waxed to new strength, is not known. And this evil thing was called by many names, but the Eruhil named him Sauron, and men of Middle-earth (when they dared to speak his name at all) named him mostly Zigūr the Great. And he made himself a great king in the midst of the earth, and was at first well-seeming and just and his rule was of benefit to all men in their needs of the body; for he made them rich, whoso would serve him. But those who would not were driven out into the waste places. Yet Zigūr desired, as Mēlekō before, to be both a king over all kings and as a god to men. And slowly his power moved north and south, and ever westward; and he heard of the coming of the Eruhil and he was wroth. And he plotted in his heart how he might destroy Nūmenōr.

§20   And news came also to Nūmenōr and to Tarkalion the king, Earendel's heir (for this title had all the kings of Nūmenōr, and they were indeed descended in unbroken line from Elros the son of Earendel), of Zigūr the Great, and how he purposed to become master of all Middle-earth and after of the whole world. And Tarkalion was angered, for the kings of Nūmenōr had grown very glorious and proud in that time.

§21   And in the meanwhile evil, of which once long ago their fathers had tasted, albeit they had after repented, awoke again in the hearts of the Eruhil; for the desire of everlasting life and the escape from death grew ever stronger upon them as their lot in the land of Nūmenōr grew more blissful. And they began to murmur in their hearts (and anon more openly) against the doom of men; and especially against that ban which forbade them to sail west or to visit the Blessed Realm.

§22   'For why should the Avalāi sit in peace unending there,' said they, 'while we must die and go we know not whither, leaving our own home; for the fault was not ours in the beginning; and is not the author of evil Mēlekō himself one of the Avalāi?'

§23   And the Avalāi knowing what was said, and seeing the cloud of evil grow, were grieved, and they came less often to Nūmenōr; and those that came spoke earnestly to the Eruhil; and tried to teach them of the fashion and fate of the world, saying that the world was round, and that if they sailed into the utmost West, yet would they but come back again to the East and so to the places of their setting out, and the world would seem to them but a prison.

§24   'And so it is to those of your strange race,' said the Avalāi. 'And Eru does not punish without benefit; nor are his mercies without sternness. For we (you say) are unpunished and dwell ever in bliss; and so it is that we do not die, but we cannot escape, and we are bound to this world, never again to leave it, till all is changed. And you (you murmur) are punished, and so it is that ye die, but ye escape and leave the world and are not bound thereto. Which therefore of us should envy the other?

§25 'Ye us maybe, for of you is required the greater trust, knowing not what lies before you in a little while. But whereas we know nothing of the mind of Eru in this (for he has not revealed anything of his purpose with you unto the Avalāi), we say to you that that trust, if you give it, will not be despised; and though it take many ages of Men, and is yet beyond the sight of the Avalāi, that Iluvatar the Father will not let those perish for ever who love him and who love the world that He has made.'

§26 But only a few of the Nūmenōreans harkened to this counsel. For it seemed hard to them, and they wished to escape from Death in their own day, and they became estranged from the Avalāi, and these came now no more to Nūmenōr save seldom and in secret, visiting those few of the faithful. Of whom the chief was one Amardil and his son Elendil (who was called also Earendil for his love of the sea, and for his father, though not of the elder line which sat upon the throne of Nūmenōr, was also of the blood of Earendil of old).

§27 But Tarkalion the king fell into evil mood, and the worship of Eru upon the high place the mountain of Meneltyūlā in the midst of the land was neglected in those days.

§28 But Tarkalion hearing of Sauron determined, without counsel of the Avalāi, to demand his allegiance and homage; for he thought that no king so mighty [could] ever arise as to vie with the lords of Nūmenōr; and he began in that time to smithy great hoard of weapons of war, and he let build great ships; and he sailed into the east and landed upon Middle-earth, and bade Sauron come and do homage to him. And Sauron came, for he saw not his time yet to work his will with Nūmenōr, and he was maybe not a little astonied at the majesty of the kings of men; and he was crafty. And he humbled himself and seemed in all things fair and wise.

§29 And it came into the heart of Tarkalion the King that for the better keeping of Sauron and his new promises of fealty he should be brought to Nūmenōr as his own hostage. And to this Sauron assented willingly, for it chimed with his own desire. And Sauron looking upon Nūmenōr in the days of its glory was indeed astonied; but his heart within was all the more filled with hatred.

§30 Such was his craft and cunning that ere long he became closest to the counsels of the King; and slowly a change came over the land, and the hearts of the Faithful, the Avaltiri, were darkened.

§31 For with subtle arguments Sauron gainsaid all that the Avalāi had taught. And he bade them think that the world was not a closed circle; and that therein there were many lands yet for their winning, wherein was wealth uncounted; and even yet, when they came to the end thereof, there was the Dark without, out of which came all things. 'And Dark is the Realm of the Lord of All, Mēlekō the Great, who made this world out of the primeval darkness. And only Darkness is truly holy,' said he.

§32 And Tarkalion the King turned to the worship of the Dark and of Mēlekō the Lord thereof. And the Meneltyūlā was deserted in those days and none might ascend it under pain of death, not even those of the faithful who yet kept Eru in their hearts. But Sauron let build on a hill in the midst of the city of the Nūmenōreans, Antirion the Golden, a great temple; and it was in the form of a circle at the ground, and its walls were fifty feet thick, and they rose five hundred feet, and they were crowned with a mighty dome, and it was wrought all of silver, but the silver was black. And this was the mightiest of the works of the Nūmenōreans, and the most evil, and men were afraid of its shadow. And from the topmost of the dome, where was an opening or great louver, there issued ever and anon smoke, and ever the more often as the evil of Sauron grew. For there men sacrificed to Mēlekō with spilling of blood and torment and great wickedness; and ofttimes it was those of the faithful that were chosen as victims. But never openly on the charge that they would not worship Mēlekō; rather was cause sought against them that they hated the King or falsely that they plotted against their kin and devised lies and poisons.

§33 And for all this Death did not depart from the land. Rather it came sooner and more often and in dreadful guise. For whereas aforetime men had grown slowly old, and laid them down as to sleep in the end when they were weary at last of this world, now madness and sickness assailed them, and yet they were afraid to die and go out into the dark, the realm of the lord

they had taken. And men made weapons in those days and slew
one another for little cause.

§34   Nonetheless it seemed that they prospered. For their
wealth increased mightily with the help of Sauron, and they built
ever greater ships. And they sailed to the Middle-earth to get
them new wealth; but they came no longer as the bringers of
gifts, but as men of war. And they hunted the men of Middle-
earth and enslaved them and took their goods; but they built
fortresses and great tombs upon the western shores in those
days. And men feared them, and the memory of the kindly kings
of the Elder Days faded in the world and was overlaid with
many a dread legend.

§35   Thus waxed Tarkalion the King to the mightiest tyrant
that had yet been seen in the world since the rule of Mēlekō;
and yet nonetheless he felt the shadow of death approach as his
days lengthened. And he was filled with anger and with fear.
And now came the hour that Sauron had planned. For he spoke
now to the King saying evil of Eru, that he was but a phantom, a
lie devised by the Avalāi to justify their own idleness and greed;
and that the Avalāi withheld the gift of everlasting life out of
avarice and fear lest the kings of men should wrest the rule
of the world and the Blessed Realm from them. 'And though
doubtless the gift of everlasting life is not for all, and only for
such as are worthy, being men of might and pride and great
lineage, still,' said Sauron, 'it is against all justice that this gift,
which is his least due, should be withheld from Tarkalion the
King, mightiest of the sons of Earth. To whom only Manawē
can compare, if even he.' And Tarkalion being besotted and also
under the shadow of Death, for his span was drawing to an end,
harkened to him, and devised war against the Avalāi. Long
was he in pondering this design, and it could not be hidden
from all.

§36   And in those days Amardil, who was of the royal house
as has been told, and faithful, and yet so noble and so well-
beloved of all save the most besotted of the people, that even in
the days of Sauron the King dared lay no hand on him as yet,
he learned of the secret counsels of the King, and his heart was
filled with sorrow and great dread. For he knew that Men could
not vanquish the Avalāi in war, and that great ruin must come
upon the world, if this war were not stayed. Therefore he called
his son Elendil Earendil and he said to him: 'Behold, the days
are dark and desperate; therefore I am minded to try that rede

which our forefather Eärendil took: to sail into the West (be there ban or no ban) and speak to the Avalâi, yea even to Manawê himself if may be, and beseech his aid ere all is lost.'

'Would you then bewray the King?' said Elendil.

'For that very thing do I purpose to go,' said Amardil.

'And what then, think you, is like to befall those of your house whom you leave behind, when your deed becometh known?'

§37   'It must not become known,' said Amardil. 'I will prepare it in secret and I will set sail at first into the East, whither many ships daily set out, and then round about. But you and your folk, I counsel that you should prepare yourself ships and put on board all such things as your heart cannot bear to part with, and lie ready. But you should hold your ships in the eastern havens; and give out among men that you purpose, maybe, when all is ready to follow me into the East. And I think not that your going will be letted; for the house of Amardil is no longer so dear to our kinsman on the throne of Eärendil that he will grieve over much if we seek to depart. But do not take many men with you, or he may become troubled because of the war that he now plots, for which he will need all the force that he hath. Do not take many, and only such as you may be sure that they are faithful. Even so open not your design to any.'

§38   'And what design is this that you make for me?'

'Until I return I cannot say. But to be sure it is like to be flight far from fair Andôrê that is now so defiled, and from our people; east or west the Avalâi alone shall say. But it is likely enough that you shall see me never again, and that I shall show you no sign such as Eärendil our sire showed of old. But hold you ever in readiness, for the end of the world that we have known is at hand.'

§39   And it is said that Amardil set sail at night and went east and then about, and he took three servants with him, dear to his heart, and never again were they heard of by word or sign in this world; nor is there any tale or guess of their fate. But this much may be seen, that men could not be a second time saved by any such embassy; and for the treason of Nûmenor there was no easy assoiling. But Elendil abode in the east of the land and held him secret and meddled not in the deeds of those days; and looked ever for the sign that came not. At whiles he would journey to the western shores of the land and gaze out at the sea, and sorrow and yearning was upon him, for he had loved his father – but further he was not suffered to go; for Tarkalion was now gathering his fleets in the havens of the west.

§40   Now aforetime in the isle of Nūmenōr the weather was ever fair, or leastways apt to the liking and needs of men, rain in due seasons and in measure, and sunshine, now warm now cooler, and winds from over the sea; and when the wind was in the west it seemed to many that it was filled with a fragrance, fleeting but sweet, heart-stirring, as of flowers that bloom for ever in undying meads and have no names on mortal shores. But now that too was changed. For the sky itself was darkened and there were storms of rain and hail in those days, and ever and anon the great ships of the Nūmenōreans would founder and return not to haven. And out of the West there would come at whiles a great cloud, shaped as it were an eagle with pinions spread to the North and to the South; and slowly it would creep up blotting out the sunset – for at that hour mostly was it seen; and then uttermost night would fall on Nūmenōr. And soon under the pinions of the eagles was lightning borne, and thunder rolled in the heaven, such a sound as men of that land had not before heard.

§41   Then men were afraid. 'Behold the Eagles of the Lords of the West coming over Nūmenōr!' they cried, and they fell upon their faces. And some would repent, but others hardened their hearts and shook their fists at heaven, and said: 'The Lords of the West have made the war. They strike the first blow, the next shall be ours.' And these words were spoken by the King and devised by Sauron.

§42   But the lightnings increased and slew men upon the hills and in the meads, and ever the darts of greatest fury smote at the dome of the Temple. But it stood firm.

§43   And now the fleets of the Nūmenōreans darkened the sea upon the west of the land, like an archipelago of mighty isles, and their masts were as forests, and their banners red as the dying sun in a great storm and as black as the night that cometh after. But the Eagles of the Lords of the West came up now out of the dayfall, in a long line one behind the other, as if in array of battle, and as they came their wings spread ever wider, until they embraced the heavens.

§44   But Tarkalion hardened his heart, and he went aboard his mighty ship Andalōkē and let spread his standard, and he gave the order for the raising of anchors.

§45   And so the fleet of the Nūmenōreans set forth into the teeth of the storm, and they rowed resolutely into the West; for they had many slaves. And when the storm had abated the sky cleared, and a wind came up out of the East (by the arts of Sauron, some have said), and there was a false peace over all the seas and land while the world waited what should betide. And the fleets of the Nūmenōreans sailed out of sight of Andūniē and broke the ban, and held on through three nights and days; and they passed out of the sight of all watchers.

§46   And none can tell the tale of their fate, for none ever returned. And whether they came ever in truth to that haven which of old men thought that they could descry; or whether they found it not or came to some other land and there assailed the Avalāi, who shall say, for none know. For the world was changed in that time, and the memory of all that went before is become dim and unsure.

§47   But those that are wisest in discernment aver that the fleets of the Nūmenōreans came indeed to Avallondē and encompassed it about, but that the Avalāi made no sign. But Manawē being grieved sought the counsel at the last of Eru, and the Avalāi laid down their governance of Earth. And Eru overthrew its shape, and a great chasm was opened in the sea between Nūmenōr and Avallondē and the seas poured in, and into that abyss fell all the fleets of the Nūmenōreans and were swallowed in oblivion. But Avallondē and Nūmenōrē that stood on either side of the great rent were also destroyed; and they foundered and are no more. And the Avalāi thereafter had no local habitation on earth, nor is there any place more where memory of an earth without evil is preserved; and the Avalāi dwell in secret or have faded to shadows, and their power is minished.

§48   But Nūmenōr went down into the sea, and all its children and fair maidens and its ladies, and even Tar-Ilien the Queen, and all its gardens and halls and towers and riches, its jewels and its webs and its things painted and carven, and its laughter and its mirth and its music and its wisdom and its speech, vanished for ever.

§49   Save only the very top of Meneltyūlā, for that was a holy place and never defiled, and that maybe is still above the waves, as a lonely isle somewhere in the great waters, if haply a mariner should come upon it. And many indeed after sought it, because it was said among the remnant of Nūmenōr that those with holy sight had been able from the top of Meneltyūlā to see the haven of Avallondē, which otherwise only those could see who sailed far westward. And the hearts of the Nūmenōreans even after their ruin were still set westward.

§50   And though they knew that Nūmenōr and Avallondē were no more they said: 'Avallondē is no more and Nūmenōr is not; yet they were, and not in this present darkness; yet they were, and therefore still are in true being and in the whole shape of the world.' And the Nūmenōreans held that men so blessed might look upon other times than those of their body's life, and they longed ever to escape from the darkness of exile and see in some fashion the light that was of old. 'But all the ways are now crooked,' they said, 'that once were straight.'

§51   And in this way it came to pass that any were spared from the downfall of Nūmenōrē; and maybe that was the answer to the errand of Amardil. For those that were spared were all of his house and kin. For Elendil had remained behind, refusing the King's summons when he set out to war, and he went aboard ship, and abode there riding out the storm in the shelter of the eastern shore. And being protected by the land from the great draught of the sea that drew all down into the abyss, he escaped from death in that time. And a mighty wind arose such as had not before been, and it came out of the West, and it blew the sea into great hills; and fleeing before it Elendil and his sons in seven ships were carried far away, borne up on the crests of great waves like mountains of Middle-earth, and they were cast at length up far inland in Middle-earth.

§52   But all the coasts and seaward lands of Middle-earth suffered great ruin and change in that time. For the earth was sorely shaken, and the seas climbed over the lands and shores foundered, and ancient isles were drowned and new were uplifted, and hills crumbled and rivers were turned to strange courses.

§53   And here ends the tale to speak of Elendil and his sons who after founded many kingdoms in Middle-earth, and though their lore and craft was but an echo of that which had been ere Sauron came to Nūmenōr, yet did it seem very great to the men of the wild.

§54   And it is said that Sauron himself was filled with terror at the fury of the wrath of the Avalāi and the doom of Eru, for it was greater far than any that he had looked for, hoping only for the death of the Nūmenōreans and the defeat of their proud king. But he himself sitting in his black seat in the midst of his temple laughed when he heard the trumpets of Tarkalion sound for battle; and he laughed yet again when he heard afar the noise of the thunder; and a third time even as he laughed at his own thought (thinking what he would do now in Middle-earth, being rid of the Eruhil for ever) he was caught in the midst of his mirth, and his temple and his seat fell into the abyss.

§55   [*Rejected at once*: It was long before he appeared in visible form upon the earth again] But Sauron was not of mortal flesh, and though he was robbed of that form in which he had wrought evil for so long, as Zigūr the great, yet ere long he devised another; and he came back unto Middle-earth and troubled the sons of Elendil and all men beside. But that cometh not into the tale of the Downfall of Nūmenōr, Atalante the downfallen, as the exiles ever after named her whom they had lost, the land of Gift in the midst of the Sea.

★

There are two definitive clues to the date of this text. One is that at the foot of one of its pages are typed the words 'Ramer discusses the feeling of lost significance' (see pp. 183, 189); and the other is that the name of the Pillar of Heaven in Númenor is *Meneltyūlā*, which appears as a pencilled correction of the original name *Menelminda* in the manuscript E of Part Two of *The Notion Club Papers* (p. 302), while the next text of the *Papers* (the typescript F 1) has *Menel-tūbel*, changed to *Menel-tūbil*. It is thus certain that this first draft of *The Drowning of Anadûnê* was written in the course of work on Part Two of *The Notion Club Papers*, and can indeed be placed, presumably, precisely between the manuscript E and the typescript F 1.

Comparison with the text of the third version of *The Fall of Númenor* (FN III) given on pp. 331 ff. will show that this is an entirely new work, an altogether richer conception, and with many remarkable differences. But comparison with the much later *Akallabêth* (in the published *Silmarillion*, pp. 259–82) will also show that it is the direct ancestor of that work, to a much greater extent than *The Fall of Númenor*, although that also was used in the *Akallabêth*.

One of the most extraordinary features of this text lies in the conception of the *Balāi*, whom I shall call rather the *Avalāi*, since this name superseded the other before the typing of DA I was completed. At the beginning (§1) this is a name, 'in the earliest recorded tongue', of the *Eru-bēnī*, 'servants of God', who 'governed Earth'; 'some were lesser and some greater', and 'the mightiest and the chieftain of them all was Mēlekō', brother of Manawē (see V.164, note 4). In §4 it is told that certain of the fathers of Men who repented, and who were named *Eruhil* 'Children of God', made war on Mēlekō in concert with the Avalāi and cast him down; but (§5) in grief at the evil works of Men the Avalāi withdrew ever westwards ('or if they did not so they faded and became secret voices and shadows of the days of old'), and the most part of the Eruhil followed them. And when they came to the shores of the Great Sea (§6) the Avalāi 'for the most part passed over the sea seeking the realm of Manawē', but the Eruhil of the western coasts were taught by the Avalāi the craft of ship-building.

After the coming of the Eruhil to Númenor 'they took the language of the Avalāi and forsook their own' (§14); and the Avalāi 'forbade them to sail westward out of sight of the western shores of Nūmenōr' (§15). The Avalāi dwelt somewhere in the West unknown to Men, who called that land *Avallondē*, translated 'the Haven of the Gods', for at times they could see a distant city far off in the West; and 'to Nūmenōr the Avalāi came ever and anon, the children and the lesser ones of the Deathless Folk, sometimes in oarless boats, sometimes as birds flying, sometimes in other fair shapes' (§16). Avalāi came to Númenor and attempted to persuade the Eruhil of the error of their thoughts (§§23–5); and when the fleets of Númenor came to Avallondē the Avalāi 'laid down their governance of Earth' (§47). At the Cataclysm Avallondē and Nūmenōrē were overwhelmed and swallowed up, 'and the Avalāi thereafter had no local habitation on earth ... and [they] dwell in secret or have faded to shadows, and their power is minished' (§47).

Who then are the Avalāi? Looking no further than the present text, the name must be said to represent the whole 'order' of deathless beings who, before the coming of Men, were empowered to govern the world within a great range or hierarchy of powers and purposes. Looking at it in relation to the earlier narrative, *The Fall of Númenor*, the distinction between 'Gods' and 'Elves' is here lost. In that work, after the Great Battle in which Morgoth was overthrown, 'the Elves were summoned to return into the West; and those that obeyed dwelt once more in Eressëa, the Lonely Isle; and that land was named anew Avallon: for it is hard by Valinor ...' (FN III §1, p. 332); and 'the speech of Númenor was the speech of the Eldar of the Blessed Realm, and the Númenóreans conversed with the Elves, and were permitted to look upon Valinor from afar; for their ships went often to Avallon, and there their mariners were suffered to dwell for a while' (FN III §2, p. 333). *The Fall of Númenor* was a vital and far-reaching extension of the legends embodied in the *Quenta Silmarillion*, but it was congruent with them. This earliest text of *The Drowning of Anadûnê*, in which the Elves are not distinctly represented, and Valinor and Eressëa are confused, is not.

Even more startling perhaps is the loss in this narrative of the

conception that the world was made round at the Downfall of
Númenor. Here, the Avalāi, coming to Númenor and attempting to
teach the Eruhil 'of the fashion and fate of the world', declared to
them 'that *the world was round*, and that if they sailed into the utmost
West, yet would they but come back again to the East and so to the
places of their setting out, and the world would seem to them but a
prison' (§23); but when Sauron came to Númenor he 'gainsaid all that
the Avalāi had taught. And he bade them think that *the world was not
a closed circle*' (§31). Most striking is a hastily pencilled passage
written alongside §§49–50, which was not taken up in the following
text: 'For they believed still *the lies of Sauron that the world was plain*
['flat'; see footnote to p. 392], until their fleets had encompassed all
the world seeking for Meneltyūlā, and they knew that it was round.
Then they said that the world was bent, and that the road to
Avallondē could not be found, for it led straight on.' No direction is
given for the insertion of this; but I think that it was intended to
replace the sentence at the end of §50: ' "But all the ways are
now crooked," they said, "that once were straight." '

In this connection the earlier version of the Old English text (the
single preserved leaf of Edwin Lowdham's book) that accompanied
the manuscript E of *The Notion Club Papers* (pp. 313–15) is interesting. In the Old English it was the *Eldar* who forbade the Númenóreans
to land on Eresse (whereas in *The Fall of Númenor* it was the Gods
who imposed the ban on sailing beyond Tol Eressëa, §4), because they
were mortal, although it was 'the Powers' (*Wealdend*) who had
granted them long life; and very remarkably Sauron declared to
Tarkalion that 'the *Eldar* refused to him the gift of everlasting life'.
The Númenóreans are here said to have 'sent out in secret spies to
Avallon to explore the hidden knowledge of the Eldar' (a reminiscence
of FN §4: 'they sent spies to seek hidden lore in Avallon'). The
reference of *Avallon* is not explained in the Old English text, but it is
surely the same as *Eresse* (in FN §1 Eressëa was renamed Avallon); yet
Tarkalion determined to invade Avallon, because Sauron said that the
Eldar had denied him everlasting life (whereas in FN §6 the fleets of
the Númenóreans, having 'encompassed Avallon', 'assailed the shores
of Valinor').

This Old English version came in point of composition between the
completion of manuscript E of the *Papers* and the writing of DA I.[4]
There is thus a development from a text in which both 'the Powers'
and 'the Eldar' appear, but in which the Eldar have powers far greater
and of a different order than could properly be ascribed to them, to a
text (DA I) in which 'the Powers' (Valar) and 'the Eldar' are confused
under the single term *Avalāi*; and in the Old English the name *Avallon*
seems to be used confusedly (in contrast to the earlier *Fall of
Númenor*), while in DA I *Avallondē* is a vague term, related to the
vagueness of the name *Avalāi*.

The further development and the significance of these extraordinary departures is discussed later: see pp. 391 ff. and 405 ff.

In this text DA I there are many other important developments in the legend of Númenor which were retained in the later story. The Ban now becomes more severe, for the Númenóreans are not permitted 'to sail westward out of sight of the western shores of Nūmenōr' (§15); the importance of the eastward voyages emerges, the coming of 'the Men out of the Sea' at first as teachers and enlighteners of the men of Middle-earth (§17), but afterwards as oppressors and enslavers (§34); and the 'Avalāi' are remembered as coming out of the West to Númenor, and attempting to avert the growing hostility to the Ban. The temple is now built, not on the Mountain sacred to Ilúvatar, but 'in the midst of the city of the Nūmenōreans, Antirion the Golden' (§32), and ascent of the Mountain is forbidden under pain of death. The 'Faithful' (named Avaltiri, §30) are referred to, and the story of Amardil (for later Amandil) and his son Elendil is told, with the statement that although Amardil was not of the elder line from which came the kings of Númenor, he also was descended from Eärendil (§§26, 36, 38). These are only the most striking new developments in the narrative, and moreover comparison with the Akallabêth will show that some of the prose itself remained unchanged into the final form.

It seems that in DA I Adunaic was at the point of emergence, with Eru-bēnī, Avalāi, and Zigūr (said to be the name of Sauron among the men of Middle-earth, §19).

NOTES

1   Wingalōtē: in the Quenta (Index to Vol.IV) the form was Wingelot > Vingelot, in the Quenta Silmarillion (Index to Vol.V) Vingelot. Wingalōtē was subsequently corrected to Vingalōtē on this type-script (see p. 377, §8).

2   The form Earendel occurs also in §§16, 20, but it was clearly no more than a casual reversion. Already in the manuscript E of Part Two of the Papers Wilfrid Jeremy notes that the name that he saw in his 'dream-manuscript' was Earendil, not Earendel.

3   Andōrē: Andor in The Fall of Númenor (§2) and The Lost Road (V.65).

4   The matter of 'Edwin Lowdham's page' was inserted into manuscript E of the Papers after the manuscript was completed so far as it went (see p. 291 note 70), and the name of the Pillar of Heaven in the accompanying Old English text was already Meneltyúla (p. 314; for earlier Menelminda in E), as in DA I, so that this name is not here indicative of relative date. On the other hand, in the Old English text Sauron built the great temple on the Meneltyúla itself,

not in the midst of the city, which is good evidence that it was the earlier composition. So also, the ban upon landing on Eressëa in the Old English text (p. 313) was clearly a development from the original story in *The Fall of Númenor* (§4), that the Númenóreans must not sail beyond Eressëa, towards that in DA I that they must not sail beyond sight of the western coasts of Númenor.

(iii) The second text of The Drowning of Anadûnê

This text, 'DA II', is a typescript typed with care and almost free of error. A paper folded round it, in my father's writing, bears my name and the words 'Fair copy   Anadūnē'. DA II represents so great an advance on and elaboration of DA I that (since it is almost free of alterations or hesitations during the original typing) it is hard to believe that no drafting intervened between the two, although there is no trace now of anything of the sort; but I do not think that I typed DA II (see p. 389, §28).

The title is *The Drowning of Anadûnê*. A fair number of alterations were pencilled on the typescript, and in addition several passages were rewritten or extended on typewritten slips attached to the body of the text. These are ignored in the text printed, but all changes of any substance are recorded in the commentary on DA II, pp. 376 ff.

I give the text in full, although this involves a certain amount of repetition especially in the latter part of the narrative, for the sake of clarity in the commentary and in making comparison with the *Akallabêth*. The paragraphs are numbered to provide convenient reference to DA I. In DA II both long marks and circumflex accents are used (inserted in pencil); the circumflex superseded the long mark, as is seen from the fact that it is found chiefly in corrected or added passages and on corrected names, and only here and there in the original text. The third text of *The Drowning of Anadûnê* uses the circumflex exclusively, and it is more convenient to do the same here.

THE DROWNING OF ANADÛNÊ

§1   Before the coming of Men there were many Powers that governed the Earth, and these were the Eru-bênî, servants of God. Many were their ranks and their offices; but some there were among them that were mighty lords, the Avalôi, whom Men remembered as gods, and at the beginning the greatest of these was the Lord Arûn.

§2   But it is said that long ago, even in the making of the Earth, the Lord Arûn turned to evil and became a rebel against Eru, desiring the whole world for his own and to have none above him. Therefore his brother Amân endeavoured to rule the Earth and the Powers according to the will of Eru; and Amân dwelt in the West.

But Arûn remained on Earth, dwelling in hiding in the North, and he worked evil, and he had the greater power. And the Earth was darkened in that time, so that to Arûn a new name was given, and he was called Mulkhêr, the Lord of Darkness; and there was war between Mulkhêr and the Avalôi.

§3   At the appointed hour Men were born into the world, and they were called the Eru-hîn, the children of God; but they came in a time of war and shadow, and they fell swiftly under the domination of Mulkhêr, and they served him. And he now came forth and appeared as a Great King and as a god; and his rule was evil, and his worship unclean, and Men were estranged from Eru and from his servants.

§4   But some there were of the fathers of Men who repented, seeing the evil of the Lord Mulkhêr and that his shadow grew ever longer on the Earth; and they and their sons returned with sorrow to the allegiance of Eru, and they were befriended by the Avalôi, and received again their ancient name, Eruhîn, children of God. And the Avalôi and the Eruhîn made war on the servants of Mulkhêr; and for that time they destroyed his kingdom and threw down his temples. But Mulkhêr fled and brooded in the darkness without, for him the Powers could not destroy. And the evil that he had begun still sprouted like a dark seed in Middle-earth, bearing bitter grain, which though it were ever reaped and burned, was never at an end. And still cruel kings and unholy temples arose in the world, and the most part of Mankind were their servants; for Men were corrupt and still hankered in their hearts for the Kingdom of Arûn, and they made war on the Eruhîn and pursued them with hatred, wheresoever they might dwell.

§5   Therefore the hearts of the Eruhîn were turned westward, where was the land of Amân, as they believed, and an abiding peace. And it is said that of old there was a fair folk dwelling yet in Middle-earth, and Men knew not whence they came. But some said that they were the children of the Avalôi and did not die, for their home was in the Blessed Realm far away, whither they still might go, and whence they came, working the will of Amân in all the lesser deeds and labours of the world. The Eledâi they were named in their own tongue of old, but by the Eruhîn they were called Nimrî, the Shining Ones, for they were exceeding fair to look upon, and fair were all the works of their tongues and hands. And the Nimrî became sorrowful in the darkness of the days and withdrew ever westward; and never again was grass so green, nor flower so fair, nor water so filled with light when they had gone. And the Eruhîn for the most part followed them, though some there were that remained in the Great Lands, free men, serving no evil lord; and they were shepherds and dwelt far from the towers and cities of the kings.

§6   But those of the Eruhîn who were mightiest and most fair, closest in friendship with the Nimrî, most beloved by the Servants of God, turned their faces to the light of the West; and these were the children of the fathers that had been most valiant in the war upon Mulkhêr. And at the end of journeys beyond memory they came at last to the shores of the Great Seas. There they halted and were filled with great dread, and with longing; for the Nimrî passed ever over the waters, seeking the land of Amân, and the Eruhîn could not follow them.

Then such of the Nimrî as remained in the west of the world took pity on the Eruhîn, and instructed them in many arts; and the Eruhîn became wiser in mind, more skilled in hand and tongue, and they made for themselves many things that had not before been seen. In this way the dwellers on the shore learned the craft of ship-building and of sailing in the wind; and they built many fair ships. But their vessels were small, and they did not dare to essay the deep waters; for though their desire was to the unseen shores, they had not as yet the heart for the wastes of the Sea, and they sailed only about the coasts and among the hither isles.

§7   Yet it was by their ships that they were saved and were not brought to nought. For evil men multiplied in those days, and pursued the Eruhîn with hatred; and the men of Middle-earth, being filled with the spirit of Mulkhêr, grew cunning and cruel in the arts of war and the making of many weapons, so that the Eruhîn were hard put to it to maintain any land in which to dwell, and their numbers were diminished.

§8   In those dark days of fear there arose a man, and his daring upon the Sea was greater than that of all other men; and the Nimrî gave him a name and called him Ëarendil, the Friend of the Sea, Azrabêl in the language of the Eruhîn. And it came into the heart of Azrabêl that he would build a ship, fairer and more swift than any that men had yet made; and that he would sail out over deep water and come, maybe, to the land of Amân, and there get help for his kinsfolk. And with the help of the

Nimrî he let build a ship, fair and valiant; white were its
timbers, and its sails were white, and its prow was carven in the
light of a silver bird; and at its launching he gave it a name and
called it Rôthinzil, Flower of the Foam, but the Nimrî blessed it
and named it also in their own tongue, Vingalôtë. This was the
first of all the ships of Men to bear a name.

§9   When at last his ship was ready, then Azrabêl said
farewell to his wife and to his sons and all his kin; for he was
minded to sail alone. And he said to them: 'It is likely that ye
will see me never again; and if ye do not, then harden your
hearts, and cease not from war, but endure until the end. But if I
do not fail of my errand, then also ye may not see me again; but
a sign you will see, and new hope shall be given to you.'

§10   And it was at the time of evening that Azrabêl set forth,
and he sailed into the setting sun and passed out of the sight of
men. But the winds bore him over the waves, and the Nimrî
guided him, and he went through the Seas of sunlight, and
through the Seas of shadow, and he came at last to the Blessed
Realm and the land of Amân and spoke unto the Avalôi.

§11   But Amân said that Eru had forbidden the Avalôi to
make war again by force upon the kingdoms of Mulkhêr; for
the Earth was now in the hands of Men, to make or to mar. Yet
it was permitted to him, because of their fidelity and the
repentance of their fathers, to give to the Eruhîn a land to dwell
in, if they would. And that land was a mighty island in the midst
of the sea, upon which no foot had yet been set. But Amân
would not permit Azrabêl to return again among Men, since he
had walked in the Blessed Realm where yet no death had come.
Therefore he took the ship Rôthinzil and filled it with a silver
flame, and raised it above the world to sail in the sky, a marvel
to behold.

§12   Then the Eruhîn upon the shores of the Sea beheld the
new light rising in the West as it were a mighty star, and they
knew that it was the sign of Azrabêl. And hope and courage
were kindled in their hearts; and they gathered all their ships,
great and small, and their wives and their children, and all the
wealth that they could bear away, and they set sail upon the
deep waters, following the star. And there was a great calm in
those days and all the winds were stilled. So bright was
Rôthinzil that even at morning men could see it glimmering in
the West; and in the cloudless night it shone alone, for no other
star might come beside it. And setting their course towards it the

Eruhîn came at last to the land that had been prepared for them, and they found it fair and fruitful, and they were glad. And they called that land Amatthânê the Land of Gift, and Anadûnê, which is Westernesse, Nûmenôrë in the Nimrian tongue.

§13   But not so did the Eruhîn escape the doom of death that had been pronounced upon all Mankind, and they were mortal still, although for their faithfulness they were rewarded by life of threefold span, and their years were full and glad and they knew no grief nor sickness, so long as they remained still true. Therefore the Adûnâi, the Men of Westernesse, grew wise and fair and glorious; but their numbers increased only slowly in the land, for though sons and daughters were born to them fairer than their fathers, and they loved their children dearly, yet their children were few.

§14   Thus the years passed, and the Adûnâi dwelt under the protection of the Avâlôi, and in the friendship of the Nimrî; and the kings and princes learned the Nimrian tongue, in which much lore and song was preserved from the beginning of the world. And they made letters and scrolls and books and wrote in them many things of wisdom and wonder in the high tide of their realm, of which all is now forgot. And they became mighty in all other crafts, so that if they had had the mind, they would easily have surpassed the evil kings of Middle-earth in the making of war and the forging of weapons; but they were become men of peace. In ship-building still was their chief delight, and this craft they followed more eagerly than all others; and voyaging upon the wide seas was the chief feat and adventure of their younger men.

§15   But the Avalôi forbade them to sail so far westward that the coasts of Anadûnê could no longer be seen; and the Adûnâi were as yet content, though they did not fully understand the purpose of this ban. But the purpose of Amân was that the Eruhîn should not be tempted to seek for the Blessed Realm, nor desire to overpass the limits set to their bliss, becoming enamoured of the immortality of the Avalôi and the land where all things endure.

§16   For as yet Eru permitted the Avalôi to maintain upon Earth, upon some isle or shore of the western lands (Men know not where), an abiding place, an earthly memorial of that which might have been, if Mulkhêr had not bent his ways nor Men followed him. And that land the Adûnâi named Avallôni, the Haven of the Gods; for at times when all the air was clear and the sun was in the east they could descry, as then seemed, a city white-shining on a distant shore, and great harbours, and a tower. But this only from the topmost peak of their island could the far-sighted see, or from some ship that lay at anchor off their western shores, as far as it was lawful for any mariner to go. For they did not dare to break the ban. And some held that it was a vision of the Blessed Realm that men saw, but others said that it was only a further isle where the Nimrî dwelt and the little ones that do not die; for mayhap the Avalôi had no visible dwelling upon Earth.

And certain it is that the Nimrî had some dwelling nigh unto Anadûnê, for thither they came ever and anon, the children of the Deathless Folk, sometimes in oarless boats, sometimes as birds flying, sometimes by paths that none could see; for they loved the Adûnâi.

§17   Thus it was that the voyages of the Adûnâi in those days went ever eastward and not west, from the darkness of the North to the heats of the South, and beyond the South to the Nether Darkness. And the Eruhîn came often to the shores of the Great Lands, and they took pity on the forsaken world of Middle-earth. And the princes of the Adûnâi set foot again upon the western shores in the Dark Years of Men, and none now dared withstand them; for most of the peoples of that age that sat under the shadow were now grown weak and fearful. And coming among them the sons of the Adûnâi taught them many things. Language they taught them, for the tongues of men on Middle-earth were fallen into brutishness, and they cried like harsh birds or snarled like the savage beasts. And corn and wine the Adûnâi brought, and they instructed men in the sowing of seed and the grinding of grain, in the shaping of wood and the hewing of stone, and in the ordering of life, such as it might be in the lands of little bliss.

§18   Then the men of Middle-earth were comforted, and here and there upon the western shores the houseless woods drew back, and men shook off the yoke of the offspring of Mulkhêr, and unlearned their terror of the dark. And they revered the memory of the tall Sea-kings, and when they had departed called them gods, hoping for their return; for at that time the Adûnâi dwelt never long in Middle-earth nor made any habitation of their own: eastward they must sail, but ever west their hearts returned.

§19   Thus came the lightening of the shadow upon the Earth and the beginning of betterment, of which the songs of men preserve still the distant memory like an echo of the Sea. And yet in the end new good turned again to evil, and Men fell, as it is said, a second time. For there arose a second manifestation of the power of darkness upon Earth: a new shape of the Ancient Shadow, it may be, or one of its servants that drew power from it and waxed strong and fell. And this evil thing was called by many names; but its own name that it took in the arising of its power was Zigûr, Zigûr the Great. And Zigûr made himself a mighty king in the midst of the Earth; and well-seeming he was at first, and just, and his rule was of benefit to all men in the needs of the body. For he made them rich, whoso would serve him; but those who would not he drove out into the waste places. Yet it was the purpose of Zigûr, as of Mulkhêr before him, to make himself a king over all kings, and to be the god of Men. And slowly his power moved north and south, and ever westward; and he heard of the coming of the Eruhîn, and he was wroth, and he plotted in his heart how he might destroy Anadûnê.

§20   And tidings of Zigûr came also to Anadûnê, to Ar-Pharazôn the king, heir of Azrabêl; for this title had all the kings of Amatthânê, being descended indeed in unbroken line from Indilzar son of Azrabêl, and seven kings had ruled the Adûnâi between Indilzar and Ar-Pharazôn, and slept now in their deep tombs under the mount of Menel-Tûbal, lying upon beds of gold. For high and glorious had grown the kings of Amatthânê; and great and proud was Ar-Pharazôn, sitting upon his carven throne in the city of Ar-Minalêth in the noontide of his realm. And to him came the masters of ships and men returning out of the East, and they spoke of Zigûr, how he named himself the Great, and purposed to become master of all Middle-earth, and indeed of the whole world, if that might be. Great was the anger of Ar-Pharazôn when he heard these things, and he sat long in thought, and his mood darkened.

§21   For it must be told that evil, of which once long ago their fathers had partaken, albeit they had after repented, was not banished wholly from the hearts of the Eruhîn, and now again was stirring. For the desire of everlasting life, to escape from death and the ending of delight, grew ever stronger upon them as their lot in the land of Amatthânê grew more full of bliss. And the Adûnâi began to murmur, at first in their hearts and anon in words, against the doom of Men; and most of all against that ban which forbade them to sail into the West or to seek for the land of Amân and the Blessed Realm.

§22   And they said among themselves: 'Why do the Avalôi sit in peace unending there, while we must die and go we know not whither, leaving our own home and all that we have made? For the fault was not ours in the beginning, seeing that Mulkhêr was stronger and wiser than our fathers; and was not he, even the Lord Arûn, author of this evil, one of the Avalôi?'

§23   And the Nimrî reported these words to the Avalôi, and the Avalôi were grieved, seeing the clouds gather on the noon-tide of Amatthânê. And they sent messengers to the Adûnâi, who spoke earnestly to the king and to all who would listen to them, teaching them concerning the fashion and fate of the world.

'The doom of the world,' they said, 'One alone can change, who made it. And were you so to voyage that, escaping all deceits and snares, you came indeed to the Blessed Realm, little good would it do to you. For it is not the land of Amân that maketh its people deathless, but the dwellers therein do hallow the land; and there you should rather wither the sooner, as moths in a flame too bright and hot.'

But Ar-Pharazôn said: 'And doth not Azrubêl [sic] my father live? Or is he not in the land of Amân?'

To which it was answered: 'Nay, he is not there; though maybe he liveth. But of such things we cannot speak unto you. And behold! the fashion of the Earth is such that a girdle may be set about it. Or as an apple it hangeth on the branches of Heaven, and it is round and fair, and the seas and lands are but the rind of the fruit, which shall abide upon the tree until the ripening that Eru hath appointed. And though you sought for ever, yet mayhap you would not find where Amân dwelleth, but journeying on beyond the towers of Nimroth would pass into the uttermost West. So would you but come at the last back to the places of your setting out: and then the whole world would seem shrunken, and you would deem that it was a prison.

§24   'And a prison, maybe, it hath indeed become to all those of your race, and you cannot rest anywhere content within. But the punishments of Eru are for healing, and his mercies may be stern. For the Avalôi, you say, are unpunished, and so it is that they do not die; but they cannot escape and are bound to this world, never again to leave it, till all is changed. And you, you say, are punished, and so it is that you die; but you escape, and leave the world, and are not bound thereto. Which of us therefore should envy the other?'

§25   And the Adûnâi answered: 'Why should we not envy the Avalôi, or even the least of the deathless? For of us is required the greater trust, knowing not what lieth before us in a little while. And yet we too love the world and would not lose it.'

And the messengers answered: 'Indeed the mind of Eru concerning you is not known to the Avalôi, and he hath not yet revealed it. But earnestly they bid you not to withhold again that trust to which you are commanded and your fathers returned in sorrow. Hope rather that in the end even the least of your desires shall have fruit. For the love of this Earth was set in your hearts by Eru, who made both it and you; and Eru doth not plant to no purpose. Yet many ages of men unborn may pass ere that purpose is made known.'

§26   But few only of the Adûnâi gave heed to this counsel. For it seemed hard to them and full of doubt, and they wished to escape from Death in their own day, not waiting upon hope; and they became estranged from the Avalôi, and would no longer receive their messengers. And these came now no more to Anadûnê, save seldom and in secret, visiting those few that remained faithful in heart.

Of these the chief was one Arbazân, and his son Nimruzân, great captains of ships; and they were of the line of Indilzar Azrabêlo, though not of the elder house, to whom belonged the crown and throne in the city of Arminalêth.

§27   But he Ar-Pharazôn the king fell into doubt, and in his day the offering of the first-fruits was neglected; and men went seldom to the hallow in the high place upon Mount Menel-Tûbal that was in the midst of the land; and they turned the more to works of handicraft, and to the gathering of wealth in their ships that sailed to Middle-earth, and they drank and they feasted and they clad themselves in silver and gold.

And on a time Ar-Pharazôn sat with his counsellors in his high house, and he debated the words of the messengers, saying that the shape of the Earth was such that a girdle might be set about it. 'For if we shall believe this,' he said, 'that one who goeth west shall return out of the East, then shall it not also be that one who goeth ever east shall come up at last behind the West, and yet break no ban?'

But Arbazân said: 'It may be so. Yet nought was said of how long the girdle might be. And mayhap, the width of the world is such that a man would wear the whole of his life, or ever he encompassed it. And I deem it for a truth that we have been set for our health and protection most westward of all mortal men, where the land of those that do not die lies upon the very edge of sight; so that he that would go round about from Anadûne must needs traverse well nigh the whole girdle of the Earth. And even so it may be that there is no road by sea.' And it has been said that at that time he guessed aright, and that ere the shape of things was changed, eastward of Anadûne the land stretched in truth from the North even into the uttermost South, where are ices impassable.

But the king said: 'Nonetheless we may give thought to this road, if it may be discovered.' And he pondered in his secret thought the building of ships of great draught and burden, and the setting up of outposts of his power upon far shores.

§28   Thus it was that his anger was the greater, when he heard those tidings of Zigûr the Mighty and of his enmity to the Adûnâi. And he determined, without counsel of the Avalôi or of any wisdom but his own, that he would demand the allegiance and homage of this lord: for in his pride he thought that no king could ever arise so mighty as to vie with the heir of Azrabêl. Therefore he began in that time to smithy great hoard of weapons of war, and he let build great ships and stored them with arms; and when all was ready he himself set sail into the East, and he landed upon Middle-earth; and he commanded Zigûr to come to him and to swear him fealty. And Zigûr came. For he saw not his time yet to work his will with Anadûne; and he was maybe for the time astounded by the power and majesty of the kings of men, which surpassed all rumour of them. And he was crafty, well skilled to gain what he would by subtlety when force might not avail. Therefore he humbled himself before Ar-Pharazôn, and smoothed his tongue, and seemed in all things fair and wise.

§29   And it came into the heart of Ar-Pharazôn the king that, for the better keeping of Zigûr and his oaths of fealty, he should be brought to Anadûne, and dwell there as a hostage for himself and all his servants. And to this Zigûr assented willingly, for it chimed with his desire. And Zigûr coming looked upon Anadûne and the city of Ar-Minalêth in the days of its glory, and he was indeed astounded; but his heart within was filled the more with envy and with hate.

§30   Yet such was his cunning that ere three years were past he had become closest to the secret counsels of the king; for flattery sweet as honey was ever on his tongue, and knowledge he had of many hidden things; and all the counsellors, save Arbazân alone, began to fawn upon him. Then slowly a change came over the land, and the hearts of the Faithful grew full of fear.

§31   For now, having the ear of men, Zigûr with many arguments gainsaid all that the Avalôi had taught. And he bade men think that the world was not a circle closed, but there lay many seas and lands for their winning, wherein was wealth uncounted. And still, should they at the last come to the end thereof, beyond all lay the Ancient Darkness. 'And that is the Realm of the Lord of All, Arûn the Greatest, who made this world out of the primeval Darkness; and other worlds he yet may make and give them in gift to those that serve him. And Darkness alone is truly holy,' he said and lied.

§32   Then Ar-Pharazôn the king turned back to the worship of the Dark, and of Arûn-Mulkhêr the Lord thereof; and the Menel-tûbal was utterly deserted in those days, and no man might ascend to the high place, not even those of the Faithful who kept Eru in their hearts. But Zigûr let build upon a hill in the midst of the city of the Eruhîn, Ar-Minalêth the Golden, a mighty temple; and it was in the form of a circle at the base, and there the walls were fifty feet in thickness, and the width of their base was five hundred feet across the centre, and they rose from the ground five hundred feet, and they were crowned with a mighty dome; and it was wrought all of silver, but the silver was turned black. And from the topmost of the dome, where was an opening or great louver, there issued smoke; and ever the more often as the evil power of Zigûr grew. For there men would sacrifice to Mulkhêr with spilling of blood and torment and great wickedness, that he should release them from Death. And ofttimes it was those of the Faithful that were chosen as victims; but never openly on the charge that they would not worship Mulkhêr, rather was cause sought against them that they hated the king and were his rebels, or that they plotted against their kin, devising lies and poisons. And these charges were for the most part false, save that wickedness breeds wickedness, and oppression brings forth murder.

§33   But for all this Death did not depart from the land.
Rather it came sooner and more often and in dreadful guise. For
whereas aforetime men had grown slowly old and laid them
down in the end to sleep, when they were weary at last of the
world, now madness and sickness assailed them; and yet they
were afraid to die and go out into the dark, the realm of the lord
that they had taken; and they cursed themselves in their agony.
And men took weapons in those days and slew one another for
little cause, for they were become quick to anger; and Zigûr, or
those whom he had bound unto himself, went about the land
setting man against man, so that the people murmured against
the king and the lords and any that had aught that they had not,
and the men of power took hard revenge.

§34   Nonetheless for long it seemed to the Adunâi that they
prospered, and if they were not increased in happiness yet they
grew more strong and their rich men ever richer. For with the
aid of Zigûr they multiplied their wealth and they devised many
engines, and they built ever greater ships. And they sailed with
power and armoury to Middle-earth, and they came no longer
as the bringers of gifts, but as men of war. And they hunted the
men of Middle-earth and took their goods and enslaved them,
and many they slew cruelly upon their altars. For they built
fortresses and temples and great tombs upon the western shores
in those days; and men feared them, and the memory of the
kindly kings of the Elder Days faded in the world and was
darkened by many a tale of dread.

§35   Thus Ar-Pharazôn the King of the land of the Star of
Azrabêl grew to the mightiest tyrant that had yet been seen in
the world since the reign of Mulkhêr, though in truth Zigûr
ruled all from behind the throne. And the years passed, and
lo! the king felt the shadow of Death approach as his days
lengthened; and he was filled with rage and fear. And now came
the hour that Zigûr had planned and long awaited. And Zigûr
spoke to the king, saying evil of Eru, that he was but a phantom,
a lie devised by the Avalôi to justify their own idleness and
greed.

'For the Avalôi,' said he, 'withhold the gift of everlasting life
out of avarice and fear, lest the kings of Men should wrest from
them the rule of the world and take for themselves the Blessed
Realm. And though, doubtless, the gift of everlasting life is not
for all, but only for such as are worthy, being men of might and
pride and great lineage, yet against all justice is it done, that this

gift, which is his least due, should be withheld from the King, Ar-Pharazôn, mightiest of the sons of Earth, to whom Amân alone can be compared, if even he.' And Ar-Pharazôn, being besotted, and walking under the shadow of Death, for his span was drawing to an end, harkened to Zigûr; and he began to ponder in his heart how he might make war upon the Avalôi. Long was he in preparing this design, and he spoke of it to few; yet it could not be hidden from all for ever.

§36 Now there dwelt still in the east of Anadûnê, nigh to the city of Ar-Minalêth, Arbazân, who was of the royal house, as has been told, and he was faithful; and yet so noble had he been and so mighty a captain of the sea that still he was honoured by all save the most besotted of the people, and though he had the hatred of Zigûr, neither king nor counsellor dared lay hand on him as yet. And Arbazân learned of the secret counsels of the king, and his heart was filled with grief and great dread; for he knew that Men could not vanquish the Avalôi in war, and that great ruin must come upon the world, if this war were not stayed. Therefore he called his son Nimruzân, and he said to him: 'Behold! the days are dark and desperate. Therefore I am minded to try that rede which our forefather Azrabêl took of old: to sail into the West (be there ban or no ban), and to speak to the Avalôi, yea, even to Amân himself, if may be, and beseech his aid ere all is lost.'

'Would you then bewray the King?' said Nimruzân.

'For that very thing do I purpose to go,' said Arbazân.

'And what then, think you, is like to befall those of your house whom you leave behind, when your deed becometh known?'

§37 'It must not become known,' said Arbazân. 'I will prepare my going in secret, and I will set sail into the East, whither daily many ships depart from our havens, and thereafter, as wind and chance may allow, I will go about through south or north back into the West, and seek what I may find.

'But you and your folk, my son, I counsel that you should prepare yourself other ships, and put aboard all such things as your hearts cannot bear to part with, and when the ships are ready you should take up your abode therein, keeping a sleepless watch. And you should lie in the eastern havens, and give out among men that you purpose, when you see your time, to set sail and follow me into the East. Arbazân is no longer so dear to our kinsman upon the throne that he will grieve over much, if we seek to depart for a season or for good. But let it not be seen that you intend to take many men, or he may become troubled because of the war that he now plots, for which he will need all the force that he may gather. Seek out rather the Faithful that are known to you, and let them lie ashore at call, if they are willing to go with you. But even to these men do not tell more of your design than is needful.'

§38   'And what shall that design be, that you make for me?' said Nimruzân.

'Until I return, I cannot say,' his father answered. 'But to be sure most like is it that you must fly from fair Amatthânê that is now defiled, and lose what you have loved, foretasting death in life, seeking a lesser land elsewhere. East or West, the Avalôi alone can say.

'And it may well prove that you shall see me never again, and that I shall show you no such sign as Azrabêl showed of old. But hold you ever in readiness, for the end of the world that we have known is now at hand.'

§39   And it is said that Arbazân set sail in a small ship at night, and steered first eastward and then went about and passed into the West. And he took three servants with him, dear to his heart, and never again were they heard of by word or sign in this world; nor is there any tale or guess of their fate. But this much may be seen that Men could not a second time be saved by any such embassy, and for the treason of Anadûnê there was no easy assoiling. But Nimruzân did all that his father had bidden, and his ships lay off the east coast of the land, and he held himself secret and did not meddle with the deeds of those days. At whiles he would journey to the western shores and gaze out upon the sea, for sorrow and yearning were upon him, for he had greatly loved his father; but nought could he descry but the fleets of Ar-Pharazôn gathering in the havens of the west.

§40   Now aforetime in the isle of Anadûnê the weather was ever apt to the liking and the needs of men: rain in due seasons and ever in measure, and sunshine, now warm now cooler, and winds from over the sea; and when the wind was in the West, it seemed to many that it was filled with a fragrance, fleeting but sweet, heart-stirring, as of flowers that bloom for ever in undying meads and have no names on mortal shores. But all this was now changed. For the sky itself was darkened, and there were storms of rain and hail in those days, and violent winds; and ever and anon a great ship of the Adûnâi would founder and return not to haven, though never had such a grief betid before since the rising of the Star. And out of the West there would come at whiles a great cloud, shaped as it were an eagle, with pinions spread to the North and to the South; and slowly it would loom up, blotting out the sunset (for at that hour mostly was it seen), and then uttermost night would fall on Anadûnê. And anon under the pinions of the eagles lightning was borne, and thunder rolled in heaven, such a sound as men of that land had not heard before.

§41   Then men grew afraid. 'Behold the Eagles of the Lords of the West!' they cried; 'the Eagles of Amân are over Anadûnê!' and they fell upon their faces. And some few would repent, but the others hardened their hearts and shook their fists at heaven, and said: 'The Lords of the West have desired this war. They strike first; the next blow shall be ours.' And these words the king himself spoke, but Zigûr devised them.

§42   Then the lightnings increased and slew men upon the hills, and in the fields, and in the streets of the city; and a fiery bolt smote the dome of the Temple and it was wreathed in flame. But the Temple was unshaken; for Zigûr himself stood upon the pinnacle and defied the lightnings; and in that hour men called him a god and did all that he would. When therefore the last portent came they heeded it little; for the land shook under them, and a groaning as of thunder underground was mingled with the roaring of the sea; and smoke appeared upon the top of Menil-Tûbal [sic]. But still Ar-Pharazôn pressed on with his designs.

§43   And now the fleets of the Adûnâi darkened the sea upon the west of the land, and they were like an archipelago of a thousand isles; their masts were as a forest upon the mountains, and their sails were like a brooding cloud; and their banners were black and golden like stars upon the fields of night. And all things now waited upon the word of Ar-Pharazôn; and Zigûr withdrew into the inmost circle of the Temple, and men brought him victims to be burned. Then the Eagles of the Lords of the West came up out of the dayfall, and they were arrayed as for battle, one after another in an endless line; and as they came their wings spread ever wider, grasping all the sky; but the West burned red behind them, and they glowed like living blood beneath, so that Anadûnê was illumined as with a dying fire, and men looked upon the faces of their fellows, and it seemed to them that they were filled with wrath.

§44   Then Ar-Pharazôn hardened his heart, and he went aboard his mighty ship, Aglarrâma, castle of the sea; many-oared it was and many-masted, golden and sable, and upon it the throne of Ar-Pharazôn was set. Then he put on his panoply and his crown, and let raise his standard, and he gave the signal for the weighing of the anchors; and in that hour the trumpets of Anadûnê outrang the thunder.

§45   And so the fleets of the Adûnâi moved against the menace of the West; and there was little wind, but they had many oars, and many strong slaves to row beneath the lash. The sun went down, and there came a silence; and over the land and all the seas a dark stillness fell, while the world waited for what should betide. Slowly the fleets passed out of the sight of the watchers in the havens, and their lights faded upon the sea, and night took them; and in the morning they were gone. For at middle night a wind arose in the East (by Zigûr's art, it is said), and it wafted them away; and they broke the ban of the Avalôi, and sailed into forbidden seas, going up with war against the Deathless Folk, to wrest from them life everlasting in the circle of the world.

§46   And who shall tell the tale of their fate? For neither ship nor man of all that host returned ever to the lands of living men. And whether they came in truth to that harbour which of old the Adûnâi could descry from Menel-Tûbal; or whether they found it not, or came to some other land and there assailed the Avalôi, it is not known. For the world was changed in that time, and the memory of all that went before is unsure and dim.

§47   Among the Nimrî only was word preserved of the things that were; of whom the wisest in lore of old have learned this tale. And they say that the fleets of the Adûnâi came indeed to Avallôni in the deeps of the sea, and they encompassed it about; and still all was silent, and doom hung upon a thread. For Ar-Pharazôn wavered at the end, and almost he turned back; but pride was his master, and at last he left his ship and strode upon the shore. Then Amân called upon Eru, and in that hour the Avalôi laid down the governance of the Earth. But Eru showed forth his power, and he changed the fashion of the world; and a great chasm opened in the sea between Anadûnê and the Deathless Land, and the waters flowed down into it, and the noise and the smoke of those cataracts went up to heaven, and the world was shaken. And into the abyss fell all the fleets of the Adûnâi and were swallowed in oblivion. But the land of Amân and the land of his gift, standing upon either side of the great chasm in the seas, were also destroyed; for their roots were loosened, and they fell and foundered, and they are no more. And the Avalôi thereafter had no habitation on Earth, nor is there any place more where a memory of a world without evil is preserved; and the Avalôi dwell in secret, or have become as shadows and their power has waned.

§48 In an hour unlooked-for this doom befell, on the seventh evening since the passing of the fleets. Then suddenly there was a mighty wind and a tumult of the Earth, and the sky reeled and the hills slid, and Anadûnê went down into the sea with all its children, and its wives, and its maidens, and its ladies proud; and all its gardens and its halls and its towers, its riches and its jewels and its webs and its things painted and carven, and its laughter and its mirth and its music and its wisdom, and its speech, they vanished for ever. And last of all the mounting wave, green and cold and plumed with foam, took to its bosom Ar-Zimrahil the Queen, fairer than silver or ivory or pearls; too late she strove to climb the steep ways of Menel-Tûbal to the holy place, for the waters overtook her, and her cry was lost in the roaring of the wind.

§49 But indeed the summit of the Mountain, the Pillar of Heaven, in the midst of the land was a hallowed place, nor had it ever been defiled. Therefore some have thought that it was not drowned for ever, but rose again above the waves, a lonely island lost in the great waters, if haply a mariner should come upon it. And many there were that after sought for it, because it was said among the remnant of the Adûnâi that the far-sighted men of old could see from Menel-Tûbal's top the glimmer of the Deathless Land. For even after their ruin the hearts of the Adûnâi were still set westward.

§50 And though they knew that the land of Amân and the isle of Anadûnê were no more, they said: 'Avallôni is vanished from the Earth, and the Land of Gift is taken away, and in the world of this present darkness they cannot be found; yet they were, and therefore they still are in true being and in the whole shape of the world.' And the Adûnâi held that men so blessed might look upon other times than those of the body's life; and they longed ever to escape from the shadows of their exile and to see in some fashion the light that was of old. Therefore some among them would still search the empty seas; 'but all the ways are crooked that once were straight,' they said.

§51   And in this way it came to pass that any were spared from the downfall of Anadûnê; and maybe this was the answer to the errand of Arbazân. For those that were spared were all of his house and kin, or faithful followers of his son. Now Nimruzân had remained behind, refusing the king's summons when he set out to war; and avoiding the soldiers of Zigûr that came to seize him and drag him to the fires of the Temple, he went aboard ship and stood out a little from the shore, waiting on the hour. There he was protected by the land from the great draught of the sea that drew all down into the abyss, and afterward from the first fury of the storm and the great wave that rolled outwards when the chasm was closed and the foundations of the sea were rocked.

But when the land of Anadûnê toppled to its fall, then at last he fled, rather for the saving of the lives of those that followed him than of his own; for he deemed that no death could be more bitter than the ruin of that day. But the wind out of the West blew still more wild than any wind that men had known; and it tore away sail and threw down mast and hunted the unhappy men like straws upon the water. And the sea rose into great hills; and Nimruzân, and his sons and people, fleeing before the black gale from twilight into night were borne up upon the crests of waves like mountains moving, and after many days they were cast away far inland upon Middle-earth.

§52   And all the coasts and seaward regions of the world suffered great ruin and change in that time; for the Earth was sorely shaken, and the seas climbed over the lands, and shores foundered, and ancient isles were drowned, and new isles were uplifted; and hills crumbled, and rivers were turned into strange courses.

§53   And here ends the tale to speak of Nimruzân and his sons who after founded many kingdoms in Middle-earth; and though their lore and craft was but an echo of that which had been ere Zigûr came to Anadûnê, yet did it seem very great to the wild men of the world.

§54   And it is said that Zigûr himself was filled with dread at the fury of the wrath of the Avalôi and the doom that Eru wrought; for it was greater far than aught that he had looked for, hoping only for the death of the Adûnâi and the defeat of their proud king. And Zigûr sitting in his black seat in the midst of his temple laughed when he heard the trumpets of Ar-Pharazôn sounding for battle; and again he laughed when he heard the thunder of the storm; and a third time, even as he laughed at his own thought (thinking what he would now do in the world, being rid of the Eruhîn for ever), he was taken in the midst of his mirth and his seat and his temple fell into the abyss.

§55 But Zigûr was not of mortal flesh, and though he was robbed of that shape in which he had wrought so great an evil, yet ere long he devised another; and he came back also to Middle-earth and troubled the sons of Nimruzân and all men beside. But that comes not into the tale of the Drowning of Anadûnê, of which all is now told. For the name of that land perished, and that which was aforetime the Land of Gift in the midst of the sea was lost, and the exiles on the shores of the world, if they turned to the West, spoke of Akallabê that was whelmed in the waves, the Downfallen, Atalantë in the Nimrian tongue.

★

I have shown (p. 353) that the original text of *The Drowning of Anadûne* (DA I) can be placed between the composition of the manuscript (E) of Part Two of *The Notion Club Papers* and the rejected section F 1 of the typescript, on the evidence of the name of the Pillar of Heaven: *Meneltyûlâ* in DA I (appearing as an emendation in E) but *Menel-tûbel* (>-*tûbil*) in F 1 (from here onwards, in comparative passages, I use the circumflex accent on all forms whatever the usage in the text cited). On the same basis the present text DA II belongs with F 1, since the Pillar of Heaven is here *Menel-Tûbal*, whereas the replacement section F 2 of the typescript of the *Papers* has *Minul-Târik*. Similarly DA II and F 1 agree in *Avalôi*, *Adûnâi* for F 2 *Avalôim*, *Adûnâim* (for the different forms of Adunaic names in F 1 and F 2 see pp. 240–1, 305).

On the other hand, DA II has *Anadûnê*, as does F 2, whereas F 1 has *Anadûn*; and F 1 had the Adunaic name of Eärendil as *Pharazîr*, changed on the typescript to *Azrubêl*, while DA II has *Azrabêl* from the first. In DA II appears the name *Amatthânê* of 'the Land of Gift', which supplanted the name in F 1, *Athânâti* (see p. 378, §12); F 2 has the final name, *Yôzâyan*.

From this comparison it is clear that the writing of DA II fell between the original and rewritten forms (F 1 and F 2) of Lowdham's account of Adunaic in Night 66 of *The Notion Club Papers*.

This greatly extended version of *The Drowning of Anadûnê* serves, looking further on, as an extraordinarily clear exemplification of my father's method of 'composition by expansion'. Separated by years and many further texts from the published *Akallabêth*, in DA II (most especially in the latter part of it) a very great deal of the actual wording of the *Akallabêth* was already present. The opening of DA II is totally distinct (for here the *Akallabêth* was expanded from *The Fall of Númenor*); but beginning with §12 (the sailing to Anadûnê following the Star) I calculate that no less than three-fifths of the precise wording of DA II was preserved in the *Akallabêth*. This is the more striking when one looks at it in reverse: for I find that, beginning at the same point in the *Akallabêth* (p. 260), only three-eighths of the latter (again, in precisely the same wording) are present in DA II. In other words, very much more than half of what my father wrote at this time was exactly retained in the *Akallabêth*; but very much less than half the *Akallabêth* was an exact retention from DA II.

A good deal of this expansion came about through the insertion (at different stages in the textual history) of phrases or brief passages into the body of the original text (and a small part of this belongs to the further textual history of *The Drowning of Anadûnê*). To a much greater extent the old narrative was transformed by the introduction of long sections of new writing. There were also significant alterations of structure.

There follows here a commentary, by paragraphs, on DA II, which includes all alterations of significance made to the text after it was typed, and also indications of the later expansions found in the *Akallabeth*.

Commentary on the second version

§1   In DA II the ambiguity of the term *Avalâi* in DA I is removed, and the *Avalôi* are 'mighty lords, whom Men remembered as gods', the Valar; while in §5 appear the *Nimrî* (Eldar). The phrase 'whom Men remembered as gods' was changed to 'who were before the world was made, and do not die'.

      This opening paragraph had been very roughtly rewritten on DA I nearly to its form in DA II, but for 'the Lord Arûn' the name was 'the Lord Kherū'.

§2   *his brother Amân* (DA I *Manawë*). In all the texts of *The Drowning of Anadûnê* Manwë is named *Amân*, and this is the sole reference of the name. *Aman* was one of the names that my father listed as 'Alterations in last revision [of *The Silmarillion*] in 1951' (see p. 312), and there seems good reason to suppose that *Amân* actually made its first appearance here, as the Adunaic name of Manwë.

§5   *some said that they were the children of the Avalôi and did not die.* In §16 the Nimrî are called, without any qualification of 'some said', 'the children of the Deathless Folk'. Cf. the opening of the *Quenta Silmarillion* (V.204, §2):

These spirits the Elves name the Valar, which is the Powers, and Men have often called them Gods. Many lesser spirits of their own kind they brought in their train, both great and small; and some of these Men have confused with the Elves, but wrongly, for they were made before the World, whereas Elves and Men awoke first in the World, after the coming of the Valar.

Though not mentioned in this passage, the conception of 'the Children of the Valar' is frequently encountered in the *Quenta Silmarillion*; and cf. especially *The Later Annals of Valinor* (V.110): 'With these great ones came many lesser spirits, beings of their own kind but of smaller might ... And with them also were later numbered their children ...' (see commentary on this, V.120–1).

Eledâi: this name is found elsewhere; see pp. 397 ff.

§7 *and were not brought to nought:* changed to 'and did not perish wholly from the Earth.'

§8 At the end of the opening sentence, '... than that of all other men', the following was added in:

for often he would launch his boat into the loud winds, or would sail alone far from the sight even of the mountains of his land, and return again hungry from the sea after many days.

Azrabêl: cf. the rejected section F 1 of the typescript of Part Two of the *Papers* (p. 305): '*Azrubêl*, made of *azar* "sea" and the stem *bel-*'. The form *Azrabêl* became *Azrubêl* in the course of typing the third text DA III; but there is a single occurrence of *Azrubêl*, as typed, in DA II (§23). On the significance of the two forms see p. 429.

Rôthinzil: this name is found in the *Akallabêth* (pp. 259–60).

Vingalótë: in DA I *Wingalôtê*; becoming *Wingalôtë* in DA III, and reverting to *Vingalôtë* in the final text DA IV.

§11 The concluding passage, beginning 'But Amân would not permit Azrabêl ...', was changed to read:

Azrubêl did not return to bear these tidings to his kindred, whether of his own will, for he could not endure to depart again living from the Blessed Realm where no death had come; or by the command of Amân, that report of it should not trouble the hearts of the Eruhîn, upon whom Eru himself had set the doom of death. But Amân took the ship Rôthinzil and filled it with a silver flame, and set therein mariners of the Nimîr, and raised it above the world to sail in the sky, a marvel to behold.

The form *Nimîr*, for *Nimrî*, appears in the third text DA III.

§12   The name *Amatthânê* ('the Land of Gift') was typed in subsequently over an erasure, but the erased form can be seen to have had eight letters, beginning with *A* and probably ending with *e*. In the text F 1 of Part II of the *Papers* the Land of Gift was *Athānāti* (p. 305), and *Athanātē* occurs in an earlier form of Lowdham's fragment II, p. 312; thus the erased name here was obviously *Athānāte*. Subsequently the name *Amatthânê* appears in DA III as typed.

To this paragraph a typewritten slip was attached, changing the passage following the words 'they set sail upon the deep waters, following the star':

And the Avalôi laid a peace on the sea for many days, and sent sunlight and a sailing wind, so that the waters glittered before the eyes of the Eruhîn like rippling glass, and the foam flew like shining snow before the stems of their ships. But so bright was Rôthinzil that even at morning men could see it glimmering in the West, and in the cloudless night it shone alone, for no other star might come beside it. And setting their course towards it, the Eruhîn came at last over leagues of sea and saw afar the land that was prepared for them, Zenn'abâr the Land of Gift, shimmering in a golden haze. Then they went up out of the sea and found a country fair and fruitful, and they were glad. And they called that land Gimlad, which is Starwards, and Anadûnê, which is Westernesse, Nûmenôrë in the Nimrian tongue.

This is virtually the text in the *Akallabêth* (pp. 260–1), apart of course from the names. *Zenn'abâr* was subsequently changed to *Zen'nabâr*, and then to *Abarzâyan* (which was the form in the third text DA III). The name *Amatthânê* was not lost, however: see p. 388, §23.

§13   The statement here and in DA I that the Eruhîn were rewarded by a life of threefold span goes back to a change made to FN II, §10 (V.28); cf. also Aragorn's words 'I have still twice the span of other men', p. 57, and the statement in Appendix A (I,i) to *The Lord of the Rings*: the Númenóreans were granted a span of life 'in the beginning thrice that of lesser Men'. For an account of my father's views on the longevity of the Númenóreans see *Unfinished Tales* pp. 224–5.

Between §13 and §14 there is a long passage in the *Akallabêth* in which Andúnië, the Meneltarma, Armenelos, and the tombs of the kings are referred to, and then the ancestry and choices of Elrond and Elros (this being closely derived from a long insertion to FN III §2: see pp. 333, 339–40).

§14 The opening sentence was changed to read:
Thus the years passed, and while Middle-earth went backward and light and wisdom failed there, the Adûnâi dwelt
under the protection of the Avalôi, and in the friendship of
the Nimrî, and increased in stature both of body and of mind.
With 'the kings and princes learned the Nimrian tongue, in
which much lore and song was preserved from the beginning of
the world' cf. FN III §2 (p. 333): 'the speech of Númenor was
the speech of the Eldar of the Blessed Realm'. In the *Akallabêth*
the linguistic conception is more complex (p. 262): the Númenóreans still used their own speech, but 'their kings and lords
knew and spoke also the Elven tongue [Sindarin], which they
had learned in the days of their alliance, and thus they held
converse still with the Eldar, whether of Eressëa or of the westlands of Middle-earth. And the loremasters among them learned
also the High Eldarin tongue of the Blessed Realm, in which
much story and song was preserved from the beginning of the
world ...' See note 19 to *Aldarion and Erendis* in *Unfinished
Tales*, p. 215.

§15 On the progressive restrictiveness of the Ban see p. 356 note 4.

§16 The vagueness of knowledge concerning the dwelling of the
Avalôi ('upon some isle or shore of the western lands (Men
know not where)') is retained from DA I, and the Adûnâi still
name it 'the Haven of the Gods', *Avallôni*, for *Avallondē* in DA
I. (In FN §1 the name *Avallon* was given to Tol Eressëa, 'for it is
hard by Valinor'. In both versions of Lowdham's exemplification of Númenórean names in *The Notion Club Papers*, pp.
241, 305, he refers to the place-name *Avallôni* without suggesting where or what it might be; and in the second version F 2 he
adds that although it is a name of his Language B, Adunaic, 'it is
with it, oddly enough, that I associate Language A', Quenya. In
both versions he calls Language A 'Avallonian'.) The Adûnâi
named the land of the Avalôi 'the Haven of the Gods', *Avallôni*,
'*for* at times ... they could descry ... a city white-shining on a
distant shore, and great harbours, and a tower.' But there now
enters in *The Drowning of Anadûnê* the idea of divergent
opinions concerning this vision of a land to the west: 'And some
held that it was a vision of the Blessed Realm that men saw, but
others said that it was only a further isle where the Nimrî dwelt
... for mayhap the Avalôi had no visible dwelling upon Earth.'
The latter opinion is supported by the author of *The Drowning
of Anadûnê*, since 'certain it is that the Nimrî had some dwelling
nigh unto Anadûnê, for thither they came ever and anon, the
children of the Deathless Folk ...'
This was retained through the two further texts of *The*

Drowning of Anadûnê without any significant change save the loss of the words 'the children of the Deathless Folk' (see the note on §5 above). In the *Akallabêth* the true nature of the distant city is asserted: 'But the wise among them knew that this distant land was not indeed the Blessed Realm of Valinor, but was Avallónë, the haven of the Eldar upon Eressëa, easternmost of the Undying Lands' (pp. 262–3). See further the commentary on §47 below.

Before 'the Blessed Realm' the name *Zen'namân* was pencilled on the typescript, and again in §23; in both cases this was struck through. See the commentary on §47.

The reference to 'their own western haven, Andūniē of Nūmenōr' in DA I is now lost. Andúnië had appeared in FN (§2, p. 333): 'Of old the chief city and haven of that land was in the midst of its western coasts, and it was called Andúnië, because it faced the sunset'; this reappears in the *Akallabêth*, p. 261.

§17 In *none now dared withstand them* 'now' was changed to 'yet'; this is the reading of the *Akallabêth*, p. 263.

The whole of §§17–18 was retained in the *Akallabêth*, with the exception of the reference to the brutish speech of the men of Middle-earth (repeated in the following texts of *The Drowning of Anadûnê*). In the *Akallabêth* there appears here a reference to the far eastern voyages of the Númenóreans: 'and they came even into the inner seas, and sailed about Middle-earth and glimpsed from their high prows the Gates of Morning in the East'; this was derived from FN §3 (p. 334; see V.20, commentary on §3). With this cf. the opinion expressed in §27, that there was no sea-passage into the East.

§19 *of which the songs of men preserve still the distant memory like an echo of the Sea*. The song of *King Sheave* is doubtless to be understood as such an echo.

In the *Akallabêth* the first mention of the emergence of Sauron is postponed to a much later point in the narrative, and it is not until §21 that the old version begins to be used again, with the murmurings of the Númenóreans against the Doom of Men and the ban on their westward sailing.

In DA I *Zigūr* is the name which the men of Middle-earth gave to Sauron; it is not said that it was the name that he took for himself.

§20 *Amatthânê:* at the first occurrence in this paragraph the name was left to stand, but at the second (and again in §21) it was changed to *Zen'nabâr* (see under §12 above).

Indilzar: Elros, first King of Númenor. The name was changed to *Gimilzôr* (and so appears in the subsequent texts).

In the later development of the Númenórean legend the name *(Ar-)Gimilzôr* is given to the twenty-third king (father of Tar-Palantir who repented of the ways of the kings and grandfather of Ar-Pharazôn; *Unfinished Tales* p. 223, *Akallabêth* p. 269).

seven kings: here Ar-Pharazôn becomes the ninth king, since it is expressly said that 'seven kings had ruled between Indilzar [Elros] and Ar-Pharazôn'. *Seven* was changed to *twelve*, and this remains into the final text of DA; he thus becomes the fourteenth king. In his long exposition of the 'cycles' of his legends to Milton Waldman in 1951 (*Letters* no. 131, p. 155) my father wrote of 'the thirteenth king of the line of Elros, Tar-Calion the Golden'. It may be that he was counting the kings 'of the line of Elros' and excluding Elros himself; but on the other hand, in an addition to FN III §5 (p. 335) it is said that 'twelve kings had ruled before him', which would make Ar-Pharazôn the thirteenth king including Elros. See further p. 433, Footnote 6.

Menel-Tubâl: see p. 375.

Ar-Minalêth replaces the name of the city in DA I (§32), *Antirion the Golden*; spelt *Arminalēth*, it occurs in the final form of the Old English text of 'Edwin Lowdham's page', pp. 257–8. *Arminalēth* remained into the earlier texts of the *Akallabêth*, with a footnote: 'This was its name in the Númenórean tongue; for by that name it was chiefly known. *Tar Kalimos* it was called in the Eldarin tongue.'

§23 The words 'the Avalôi were grieved' were changed to 'Amân was grieved'; so also the *Akallabêth* has 'Manwë' here (p. 264).

Amatthânê was not changed here (see under §20 above).

Azrubêl: see under §8 above.

In the *Akallabêth* the words of the 'messengers' of Manwë to the Númenóreans are still described as 'concerning the fate and fashion of the world', but the word *fashion* referred originally to their instruction as to its physical shape. In DA I the Avalāi said baldly 'that the world was round, and that if they sailed into the utmost West, yet would they but come back again to the East and so to the places of their setting out'; but now there enters (and this was retained in the following texts of DA) the conception of the Earth (which is 'such that a girdle may be set about it') as 'an apple [that] hangeth on the branches of Heaven', whose seas and lands are as 'the rind of the fruit, which shall abide upon the tree until the ripening that Eru hath appointed.' Nothing of this is left in the later work.

the towers of Nimroth: Nimroth was changed to *Nimrûn*, and so appears in the following texts; neither name is found elsewhere.

§24 The words 'till all is changed' were altered to 'for its life is theirs'.

§25 After 'For of us is required the greater trust' was added: 'and hope without assurance'; and 'he hath not yet revealed it' was changed to 'he hath not yet revealed all things that he hath in store'. Following this a further passage was added on a type-written slip:

But this we hold to be true that your home is not here, neither in the land of Amân, nor anywhere else within the girdle of the Earth; for the Doom of Men was not [*added:* at first] devised as a punishment. If pain it hath become unto you, as you say (though this we do not clearly understand), then is that not only because you must now depart at a time set and not of your own choosing? But this is the will of Eru, which may not be gainsaid; and the Avalôi do most earnestly bid you ...'

At the end of the words of the messengers was added: 'and to you it will be revealed and not to the Avalôim' (the plural ending -*m* in *Adûnâim*, *Avalôim* appears in the next text, DA III; see p. 375).

§26 From the refusal of all but a few of the Númenóreans to give heed to the counsel of the messengers the *Akallabêth* diverges altogether from *The Drowning of Anadûnê*, with the introduc-tion of a very long passage (pp. 265–270) in which the history of Númenor was vastly extended. Here it was also to the thirteenth king (but including Elros as the first: see *Unfinished Tales* pp. 218 ff., and under §20 above) that the messengers came, but he was Tar-Atanamir, and many kings would follow him before Ar-Pharazôn. There follows an account of the decadence of the Númenóreans in that age as their wealth and power increased, of their growing horror of death, and of their expansion into Middle-earth. The brief phrases of the opening of §27 are embedded in this. Then in the *Akallabêth* comes the arising of Sauron, told in entirely different terms from the story in the old version, with mention of Barad-dûr, of the One Ring, and of the Ringwraiths; and all the history of the division of the Númenóreans, the persecution of the Faithful under Ar-Gimilzôr and the banning of the Elvish tongue, and of the line of the Lords of Andúnië and the repentance of Tar-Palantir, the last king before Ar-Pharazôn.

Arbazân and his son *Nimruzân*: Amandil (in the *Akallabêth*) and Elendil. In DA I Elendil's father is *Amardil*; but the Elvish names do not appear again in *The Drowning of Anadûnê*.

Indilzar Azrabêlo was changed to *Indilzar Azrabêlôhin*, and then to *Gimilzôr* (see under §20 above).

§27 *Menel-Tûbal* was here changed to *Menil-Tûbal*, and subsequently.

Of the debate of Ar-Pharazôn with Arbazân on the possibility of sailing east and so coming upon the land of Amân from the west, retained in the following texts, there is no vestige in the *Akallabêth*. On Arbazân's surmise that there might be no eastern passage by sea see under §17 above. It is perhaps possible that an idea of the geographical conception here can be gained from the two maps accompanying the *Ambarkanta* in IV.249, 251: for in the first of these there is very emphatically no sea-passage, and in the North and South there are 'ices impassable', while in the second there are straits by which ships might come into the furthest East. But even if this were so it could of course have no more than a 'pictorial' relevance, for the second map exhibits the convulsions after the breaking of Utumno and the chaining of Melkor in the First Battle of the Gods (*Quenta Silmarillion* §21, V.213).

§28 The story of Ar-Pharazôn's expedition into Middle-earth and the submission of Sauron is much enlarged in the *Akallabêth*, but this enlargement entered already in the third text DA III (see p. 389, §28).

§31 For 'he bade men think that the world was not a circle closed, but there lay many seas and lands for their winning' (retained in the following texts) the *Akallabêth* (p. 271) has: 'he bade men think that in the world, in the east and even in the west, there lay yet many seas and many lands for their winning'.

The concluding passage of §31, 'And that is the Realm of the Lord of All . . .', was replaced by the following on a typewritten slip:

'And out of it the world was made; and the Lord thereof may yet make other worlds to be gifts to those who serve him, so that the increase of their power shall find no end.'

'And who is the lord of Darkness?' quoth Ar-Pharazôn.

And behind locked doors Zigûr spoke, and he lied, saying: 'It is he whose name is not now spoken, for the Avalôim have deceived you concerning him, putting forward the name of Eru, a phantom devised in the wickedness [> folly] of their hearts, seeking to chain Men in servitude to themselves. For they are the oracle of this Eru, which speaketh only what they will. But he that is their master and shall yet prevail will deliver you from this phantom; and his name is Arûn, Lord of All.'

Apart from names, this is almost the text of the *Akallabêth*.

§32 After the statement that Ar-Pharazôn 'turned back to the worship of the Dark' and that most of the people followed him, there enters in the *Akallabêth* (p. 272) the first mention of Amandil and Elendil, taking up the words of DA §26 and the opening sentences of §36 and greatly expanding them, with an account of the friendship of Ar-Pharazôn and Amandil in their youth, of Sauron's hatred of Amandil, and of his withdrawal to the haven of Rómenna.

The sentence 'and no man might ascend to the high place' was changed to 'for though not even Zigûr dared defile the high place, yet the king would let no man, upon pain of death, ascend to it'. The revised form appears in the *Akallabêth*, after which there is a long passage (pp. 272–3) concerning the White Tree of Númenor: of the king's reluctance to fell the Tree at Sauron's bidding, of Isildur's circumventing the guards about Nimloth and taking a fruit, narrowly escaping with many wounds, and of the king's then yielding to Sauron's demand. Then follows the description of the temple, not greatly changed from that in DA II, but with the addition that the first fire made on the altar was kindled with the wood of Nimloth. Of the White Tree of Númenor there is no mention in the texts of *The Drowning of Anadûnê*.

A puzzling reference to the site of the temple may be noticed here. This is in the final version of Edwin Lowdham's page in Old English, that appearing the typescript F 2 of Part Two of *The Notion Club Papers*. In the earlier Old English version (pp. 314–15) the temple was built 'on that high mountain that was called Meneltyúla (that is to say the Pillar of Heaven), which before was undefiled'. In the final version (pp. 257–8; certainly later than DA II, p. 375) it was built 'in the midst of the town of Arminalëth on the high hill which before was undefiled but now became a heathen fane'. Since the same words are used in both Old English texts the second version suggests a halfway stage, in which the temple was still built on the Pillar of Heaven (*on ðæm héan munte*), until now undefiled (*unawídlod*), but the Pillar of Heaven was in the midst of the city of Arminalëth. But this can scarcely be so, for already in DA I the story is present that the Meneltyúla was deserted, and that the temple was built on a hill in the midst of the city (Antirion).

In DA II both references to *Mulkhêr* were changed to *Arûn*, but *Arûn-Mulkhêr* was retained.

§35   For the passage following the words 'And Zigûr spoke to the king' the following (retained almost exactly in the *Akallabêth*) was substituted on a typewritten slip:

  saying that his might was now so great that he might think to have his will in all things and be subject to no command or ban. 'For behold! the Avalôim have possessed themselves of the land where there is no death; and they lie to you concerning it, hiding it as best they may, because of their avarice and their fear lest the kings of Men should wrest from them the Blessed Realm, and rule the world in their stead. And though, doubtless . . .

§38   *Amatthânê* was here changed to *Anadûnê* (see under §§20, 23 above).

§39   In the *Akallabêth* (p. 276) there enters at this point an account of the treasures that were put aboad the ships at Rómenna, with the Seven Stones ('the gift of the Eldar') and the scion of Nimloth the White Tree.

§43   *their banners were black and golden:* in DA I the banners were 'red as the dying sun in a great storm and as black as the night that cometh after.' So in the manuscript E of Part Two of the *Papers* the sails of the Númenórean ships were 'scarlet and black', but 'golden and black' in the typescript F (p. 290 note 63; 'scarlet and black' also in FN III §6, 'bloodred and black' in the earlier Old English text, pp. 314–15).

§44   *Aglarrâma, castle of the sea:* in the *Akallabêth* the name of the great ship of Ar-Pharazôn is *Alcarondas*, with the same meaning.

§47   The radically different conception of the Cataclysm (from both *The Fall of Númenor* and the *Akallabêth*), here derived from the Nimrî but in DA I attributed merely to 'the wisest in discernment', in which the Land of Amân itself foundered, remained in the following texts: 'the fleets of the Adûnâi came indeed to Avallôni in the deeps of the sea, and they encompassed it about', and 'a great chasm opened in the sea between Anadûnê and the Deathless Land . . . *But the land of Amân and the land of his gift,* standing upon either side of the great chasm [> rift] in the seas, *were also destroyed . . .*'

Against the name *Avallôni* is pencilled *Zen'namân*, and this name appears written beside 'the Blessed Realm' in §§16, 23, though there struck out. At the end of §47 is written, but struck out, *Zen'namân* and *Zen'nabâr*, i.e. 'Land of Amân' and 'Land of Gift' (for *Zen'nabâr* see under §12 above). The references to *Avallôni* seem to amount to this: the distant city glimpsed across the sea was named by the Adûnâi *Avallôni* 'Haven of the Gods' *(Avalôi)* because they thought that it was a vision of the Blessed Realm (§16). Some said that this was not so: it was only an isle on which the Nimrî dwelt that they could see. The question is not resolved; but the name *Avallôni* was nonetheless used in §47 to refer to the Land of Amân. The statement that *Avallôni* was 'encompassed' by the fleets of the Adûnâi is possibly to be associated with the words of §16, that the Avalôi dwelt 'upon *some isle* or shore of the western lands'.

Apart from the opinion held by some in Anadûnê that the land that they could see was an isle where the Nimrî dwelt, and the certainty that the Nimrî must have some dwelling near to Anadûnê, since they came there, Tol Eressëa is never referred to in *The Drowning of Anadûnê*.

The relation of the *Akallabêth* (pp. 278–9) to the earlier works in this passage is curious and characteristic. Just as in DA it is said that the fleets of Ar-Pharazôn 'came indeed to Avallôni ... and they encompassed it about', so in the *Akallabêth* they 'encompassed Avallónë'; but in the latter *Avallónë* is the eastern haven of Tol Eressëa, and the text continues: '*and all the isle of Eressëa*, and the Eldar mourned, for the light of the setting sun was cut off by the cloud of the Númenóreans.' My father was in fact turning back to *The Fall of Númenor* (§6, p. 336), which is almost the same here – but which has 'they encompassed Avallon', and lacks the words 'and all the isle of Eressëa': for in FN *Avallon* was the name of Eressëa itself.

The description of the 'changing of the fashion of the world' in the *Akallabêth* is almost exactly as in *The Drowning of Anadûnê*:

... and a great chasm opened in the sea between Númenor and the Deathless Lands, and the waters flowed down into it, and the noise and smoke of the cataracts went up to heaven, and the world was shaken. And all the fleets of the Númenóreans were drawn down into the abyss, and they were drowned and swallowed up for ever.

But whereas in *The Drowning of Anadûnê* this is followed by the statement that not only Anadûne but the Land of Amân also disappeared into the great rift, in the *Akallabêth* my father again turned to *The Fall of Númenor* (§§7–8), telling that the king and his warriors who had set foot in the Blessed Realm were 'buried under falling hills' and 'lie imprisoned in the Caves of the Forgotten, until the Last Battle and the Day of Doom'; and then, that 'Ilúvatar cast back the Great Seas west of Middle-earth ... and the world was diminished, *for Valinor and Eressëa were taken from it into the realm of hidden things.*' Thus the radical difference in the conception of the loss of the True West between *The Drowning of Anadûnê* and the *Akallabêth* was a *reversion* to that of *The Fall of Númenor*.

The passage 'Ilúvatar cast back the Great Seas ...' was a revision (see V.32) of the original form of *The Fall of Númenor* (V.16; the second text FN II is virtually the same), in which the World Made Round was more unequivocally expressed: the

Gods 'bent back the edges of the Middle-earth, and they made it into a globe ... Thus New Lands came into being beneath the Old World, and all were equally distant from the centre of the round earth ...'

This subject is further discussed on pp. 391 ff.

In the concluding sentence of §47 in DA II, 'and the Avalôi dwell in secret, or have become as shadows and their power has waned', my father was following DA I, where the name *Avalāi* is ambiguously used; in the next text DA III the sentence was changed (p. 391, §§46–7).

§48   *Ar-Zimrahil: Tar-Ilien* in DA I and in FN (§§5, 7); afterwards *Tar-Míriel*, whose Adunaic name was *Ar-Zimraphel* (*Unfinished Tales* p. 224, *Akallabêth* pp. 269–70).

§§49–50   This passage, despite many small changes in the expression, does not differ at all in its content from that in DA I, except for the addition at the end of §50 of 'Therefore some among them would still search the empty seas'. See further pp. 391 ff.

§51   After 'Nimruzân, and his sons and people' the words 'in their seven ships' were added – presumably they had been omitted unintentionally, since 'in seven ships' is present in DA I. In the *Akallabêth* there were nine ships, 'four for Elendil, and for Isildur three, and for Anárion two'. The sons of Elendil are not named, nor their number given, in *The Drowning of Anadûnê*.

(iv) The final form of The Drowning of Anadûnê

The extensive alterations to the text of DA II detailed in the preceding commentary were taken up into the third text, DA III, which was typed on the same machine and the same paper as DA II. More changes entered in DA III, and the completed typescript was then further altered. Finally another typescript, DA IV, was made, identical in appearance to the two preceding; in this the changes made to DA III were taken up, but the completed text was scarcely emended. With DA IV this phase in the development of the Númenórean legend comes to an end.

There follows here an account, paragraph by paragraph, of the alterations made between DA II, as emended, and the final form, excluding only very minor changes (such as 'appointed time' for 'appointed hour' in §3). In general I do not distinguish between those that entered in DA III and those that were made to it subsequently, appearing in DA IV as typed.

§1   *Avalôi* became *Avalôim* throughout; this is the form in the final text F 2 of Part Two of *The Notion Club Papers* (see p. 375).

Eru (*Eru-bênî, Eruhîn*) became *Êru* throughout. In the earlier form of Lowdham's fragments the name has a short vowel (p. 311), but in the final form a long (p. 247).

§5   The opening sentence was changed to read: 'And out of the sorrows of the world the hearts of the Êruhîn were turned westward, for there, as they believed, was the land of Amân and abiding peace.'
      Nimrî became *Nimîr* throughout.

§6   'filled with great dread, and with longing' > 'filled with longing'

§8   *Azrabêl* became *Azrubêl* throughout, at first by emendation of *Azrabêl* on DA III, and then as typed; see p. 377, §8.
      Vingalôtë > *Wingalôtë* > *Vingalôtë*, see p. 377, §8.

§12   The Adunaic name of 'the Land of Gift' in DA III was *Abarzâyan* (see p. 378, §12), changed to the final form *Yôzâyan*, which appears in DA IV and in the final text F 2 of *The Notion Club Papers* (pp. 241, 247). It is thus seen that DA III preceded F 2.

§13   'so long as they remained still true' was omitted.
      Adûnâi became *Adûnâim* throughout (cf. the note on *Avalôi*, *Avalôim*, §1 above).

§16   'to break the ban' > 'to break the ban of Amân'
      '(a vision of the Blessed Realm) that men saw' > 'that men saw by grace'
      'the children of the Deathless Folk' was omitted.

§19   'And yet in the end new good turned again to evil, and Men fell, as it is said, a second time' was omitted, the following sentence beginning 'But after an age there arose a second manifestation ...'
      '(he heard of the coming) of the Eruhîn' > 'of the Sea-kings out of the deeps'

§20   The name *Minul-Târik* of the Pillar of Heaven, replacing *Menel-Tûbal* (subsequently *Menil-Tûbal*) of DA II, first appears in DA III (see p. 375).

§21   'and now again was stirring' > 'and now the deep-planted seeds were stirring once again'

§23   For *Amatthânê* in DA II §§21, 23 (where it refers to 'the Land of Gift') the following texts have *Anadûnê*; but for *the Blessed Realm* in DA II §23 they have *Amatthâni, the Blessed Realm.* Thus *Amatthânê*, replaced in its application to Anadûnê in turn by *Zen'nabâr*, *Abarzâyan*, *Yôzâyan*, now reappears in the form *Amatthâni* as the name of Valinor; but *Avallôni* is retained in §§16, 47, 50. The etymology of *Amatthâni* is given in Lowdham's 'Report on Adunaic', p. 435.

§25 To the text of the typewritten rider attached to DA II and given
on p. 382 the following was added in DA III after the words 'nor
anywhere else within the girdle of the Earth': 'for it was not the
Avalôim that named you in the beginning Êruhîn, the children
of God.'
'who made both it and you' was omitted.

§26 *Arbazân* became *Aphanuzîr*, and *Nimruzân* became *Nimruzîr*,
in DA III. Jeremy calls Lowdham *Nimruzīr* in *The Notion Club
Papers*, pp. 250, 252, and the name appears in Lowdham's
fragment I (B), p. 247, 'seven ships of Nimruzīr eastward'.

§27 After the words of Aphanuzîr (Arbazân) 'It may be so' he
observes of the fraudulent argument of Ar-Pharazôn: 'Yet to go
behind a command is not to keep it'; and in the passage
following his speech the words 'where are ices impassable', first
changed to '. . . is ice . . .', were omitted.

§28 The story of the expedition of Ar-Pharazôn to Middle-earth was
much enlarged on a typewritten page inserted into DA III. The
new text is very close to that in the *Akallabêth* (p. 270), but
lacks the reference to the Havens of Umbar:
. . . and when all was ready he himself set sail into the East.
And men saw his sails coming up out of the sunset, dyed as
with scarlet and gleaming with red gold, and fear fell on them
and they fled far away. Empty and silent under the pale moon
was the land when the King of Anadûnê [> Yôzâyan] set foot
on the shore. For seven days he marched with banner and
trumpet, and he came to a hill, and he went up and set there
his pavilion and his throne; and he sat him down in the midst
of the land, and the tents of his host were laid all about him
like a field of proud flowers [> ranged all about him, blue,
golden, and white, as a field of tall flowers]. Then he sent
forth heralds and commanded Zigûr to come before him and
swear to him fealty.
A recollection of mine in connection with this passage is perhaps
worth mentioning. I remember my father, in his study in the
house in North Oxford, reading me *The Drowning of Anadûnê*
on a summer's evening: this was in 1946, for my parents left that
house in March 1947. Of this reading I recall with clarity that
the tents of Ar-Pharazôn were as a field of tall flowers of many
colours. Since the passage only entered with the text DA III, and
the naming of the colours of the flowers, 'blue, golden, and
white', was pencilled onto the typescript, appearing in the final
text DA IV as typed, my father was reading from DA III or DA
IV. I have the strong impression that the Adunaic names were
strange to me, and that my father read *The Drowning of*

Anadûnê as a new thing that he had written. This seems to support the suggestion I made earlier (p. 147) that the emergence of Adunaic and the evolution of a new form of the legend of the Downfall belong to the first half of 1946.

§30 This paragraph was rewritten to read:
> Yet such was the cunning of his mind, and the strength of his hidden will, that ere three years were passed he had become closest to the secret counsels of the King; for flattery sweet as honey was ever on his tongue, and knowledge he had of many things yet unrevealed to Men. And seeing the favour that he had of their lord, all the counsellors, save Aphanuzîr alone, began to fawn upon him. Then slowly a change came over the land, and the hearts of the Faithful were sorely troubled.

§31 At the end of the text on the replacement slip in DA II given on p. 383, §31, after 'his name is Arûn, Lord of All', was added: 'Giver of Freedom, and he shall make you stronger than they.'

§32 The description of the temple was changed on a retyped page of DA III by the alteration of the sentences following 'a mighty dome':
> And that dome was wrought all of silver and rose glittering in the sun, so that the light of it could be seen afar off; but soon the light was darkened and the silver became black. For in the topmost of the dome there was a wide opening or louver, and thence there issued a great smoke ...

To the second reference to Mulkhêr (> Arûn) in DA II was added 'Giver of Freedom' (cf. §31 above).

The final sentence of the paragraph became: 'These charges were for the most part false; yet those were bitter days, and wickedness begets wickedness.'

§36 The reply of Aphanuzîr (Arbazân) to Nimruzîr's question 'Would you then bewray the King?' was expanded to a form approaching that in the *Akallabêth* (p. 275):
> 'Yea, verily that I would,' said Aphanuzîr, 'if I thought that Amân needed such a messenger. For there is but one loyalty from which no man can be absolved in heart for any cause. And as for the ban, I will suffer in myself alone the penalty, lest all the Êruhîn become guilty.'

§38 'you must fly from fair Amatthânê that is now defiled, and lose what you have loved' > 'you must fly from the land of the Star with no other star to guide you; for that land is defiled. Then you shall lose what you have loved'

§39 'But this much can be seen that' was omitted.

§41   '(the Eagles of Amân) are over Anadûnê!' > 'overshadow Anadûnê!'

§43   'one after another in an endless line' > 'advancing in a line the end of which could not be seen'

§§46–7   This passage in DA II was closely preserved in the final form, including the reference to the fleets of the Adûnâim coming to 'Avallôni in the deeps of the sea', apart from an insertion and alteration following 'For Ar-Pharazôn wavered at the end and almost he turned back' in §47:

> His heart misgave him when he looked upon the soundless shores and saw the Mountain of Amân shining, whiter than snow, colder than Death, silent, alone, immutable, terrible as the shadow of the light of God. But pride was now his master, and at last he left his ship, and strode upon the shore, claiming that land for his own, if none should do battle for it.

This passage was retained in the *Akallabêth* (p. 278), with *Taniquetil* for *the Mountain of Amân* and *Ilúvatar* for *God*.

Following 'the land of Amân and the land of his gift' (near the end of §47) was added 'Amatthâni and Yôzâyan' (see under §23 above).

The final sentence of §47 was changed to read: 'And the Avalôim thereafter had no habitation on Earth, and they dwell invisible; nor is there any place more where a memory of a world without evil is preserved.' See p. 387 (§47, at end).

§§49–50

This crucial passage was at first retained in DA III in exactly the form that it had in DA II (pp. 373–4) with one difference (apart from *Minul-Târik* for *Menil-Tûbal*): the end of §50 was changed to read: 'Therefore some among them would still search the empty seas, *hoping to come upon the Lonely Isle. But they found it not*: "for all the ways are crooked that once were straight," they said.' Already in §49 as it appears in DA I the summit of the Pillar of Heaven is called '*a lonely isle* somewhere in the great waters', if it were to be found rising above the surface of the sea.

Since apart from the statements in §16 that the Nimîr must have dwelt near Anadûnê, and that some said that it was the island of the Nimîr that could be seen, Tol Eressëa is otherwise conspicuous by its absence from *The Drowning of Anadûnê*, and *Avallôni* is a name of the Blessed Realm, it is clear that my father used the name *Lonely Isle* of the summit of the Pillar of Heaven on Anadûnê with a deliberate intention of ambiguity.

Additional typewritten pages were substituted for the conclusion (§§49–55) of the narrative in DA III, and §50 was extended in a very remarkable way. The text was not further changed subsequently, and this is the final form of §§49–50 in *The Drowning of Anadûnê* (I give the passage in full for ease of comparison with the conclusion of the *Akallabêth* that follows):

Now the summit of Mount Minul-Târik, the Pillar of Heaven, in the midst of the land was a hallowed place, for there the Adûnâim had been wont to give thanks to Êru, and to adore him; and even in the days of Zigûr it had not been defiled. Therefore many men believed that it was not drowned for ever, but rose again above the waves, a lonely island lost in the great waters, if haply a mariner should come upon it. And many there were that after sought for it, because it was said among the remnant of the Adûnâim that the far-sighted men of old could see from the Minul-Târik the glimmer of the Deathless Land. For even after their ruin the hearts of the Adûnâim were still set westward; [§50] and though they knew that the world was changed, they said: 'Avallôni is vanished from the Earth, and the Land of Gift is taken away, and in the world of this present darkness they cannot be found; yet once they were, and therefore they still are in true being and in the whole shape of the world.' And the Adûnâim held that men so blessed might look upon other times than those of the body's life; and they longed ever to escape from the shadows of their exile and to see in some fashion the light that was of old. Therefore some among them would still search the empty seas, hoping to come upon the Lonely Isle, and there to see a vision of things that were.

But they found it not, and they said: 'All the ways are bent that once were straight.' For in the youth of the world it was a hard saying to men that the Earth was not plain* as it seemed to be, and few even of the Faithful of Anadûnê had believed in their hearts this teaching; and when in after days, what by star-craft, what by the voyages of ships that sought out all the ways and waters of the Earth, the Kings of Men knew that the world was indeed round, then the belief arose among them that it had so been made only in the time of the great Downfall, and was not thus before. Therefore they thought that, while the new world fell away, the old road and the path of the memory of the Earth went on towards heaven, as it were a mighty bridge invisible. And many were the rumours and tales among them concerning mariners and men forlorn upon the sea, who by some grace or fate had entered in upon

---

* *plain* is used in the lost sense 'flat'; but cf. the later spelling *plane* of the same word, and the noun *plain*.

the ancient way and seen the face of the world sink below them, and so had come to the Lonely Isle, or verily to the Land of Amân that was, and had looked upon the White Mountain, dreadful and beautiful, ere they died.

In the *Akallabêth* a good deal of this passage was retained, but given new bearings. I cite it here as it is printed in *The Silmarillion*, pp. 281–2 (some editorial alteration at the beginning and end does not affect the sense of the passage).

Among the Exiles many believed that the summit of the Meneltarma, the Pillar of Heaven, was not drowned for ever, but rose again above the waves, a lonely island lost in the great waters; for it had been a hallowed place, and even in the days of Sauron none had defiled it. And some there were of the seed of Eärendil that afterwards sought for it, because it was said among loremasters that the farsighted men of old could see from the Meneltarma a glimmer of the Deathless Land. For even after the ruin the hearts of the Dúnedain were still set westwards; and though they knew indeed that the world was changed, they said: 'Avallónë is vanished from the Earth and the Land of Aman is taken away, and in the world of this present darkness they cannot be found. Yet once they were, and therefore they still are, in true being and in the whole shape of the world as at first it was devised.'

For the Dúnedain held that even mortal Men, if so blessed, might look upon other times than those of their bodies' life; and they longed ever to escape from the shadows of their exile and to see in some fashion the light that dies not; for the sorrow of the thought of death had pursued them over the deeps of the sea. Thus it was that great mariners among them would still search the empty seas, hoping to come upon the Isle of Meneltarma, and there to see a vision of things that were. But they found it not. And those that sailed far came only to the new lands, and found them like to the old lands, and subject to death. And those that sailed furthest set but a girdle about the Earth and returned weary at last to the place of their beginning; and they said: 'All roads are now bent.'

Thus in after days, what by the voyages of ships, what by lore and star-craft, the kings of Men knew that the world was indeed made round, and yet the Eldar were permitted still to depart and to come to the Ancient West and to Avallónë, if they would. Therefore the loremasters of Men said that a Straight Road must still be, for those that were permitted to find it. And they taught that, while the new world fell away, the old road and the path of the memory of the West still went on, as it were a mighty bridge invisible that passed through the air of breath and of flight (which were bent now as the world was bent), and traversed Ilmen which flesh unaided cannot endure, until it came to Tol Eressëa, the Lonely Isle, and maybe even beyond, to Valinor, where the Valar still dwell and watch the unfolding of the story of the world. And tales and rumours arose along the shores of the sea concerning mariners and men forlorn upon the water who, by some fate or grace or favour of the Valar, had entered in upon the Straight Way and seen the face of the world sink below them, and so had come to the lamplit quays of Avallónë, or verily to the last beaches on the margin of Aman, and there had looked upon the White Mountain, dreadful and beautiful, before they died.

It will be seen that §49 and the first part of §50 (as far as 'But they found it not') in DA was largely retained in the *Akallabêth* (where however all this passage concerning the speculations of the Exiles was removed to the end of the work). But where DA has 'Avallôni is vanished from the Earth, and the Land of Gift is taken away' the *Akallabêth* has 'Avallónë is vanished from the Earth and the Land of Aman is taken away'. In DA Avallôni *is* the Land of Amân; in the *Akallabêth* it is the haven in Tol Eressëa (see p. 386). In DA those who searched the empty seas hoped to come upon 'the Lonely Isle', which is the summit of the Pillar of Heaven; in the *Akallabêth* they hoped to come upon 'the Isle of Meneltarma'.

In both versions the mariners who sailed west from Middle-earth seeking for the summit of Minul-Târik or Meneltarma discovered by their voyaging that the world was round; but in DA the words are 'that the world was indeed round', whereas in the *Akallabêth* they are 'that the world was indeed *made* round'.

In *The Fall of Númenor* it was explicit, the kernel of the legend of the Cataclysm, that the world was made round at the time of the Downfall (see pp. 386–7): this was the story, and within the story the rounding of the world at that time is a fact, unqualified. In *The Drowning of Anadûnê* the Nimîr (Eldar) had come to the Adûnâim and expressly taught that the world was *of its nature* round ('as an apple it hangeth on the branches of heaven', §23), but Zigûr coming had gainsaid it ('The world was not a circle closed', §31). In this work the author knows that the world is of its nature a globe; but very few of the Adûnâim had believed this teaching until the voyages of the survivors of the Downfall taught them that it was true (cf. the passage

written on the original text DA I, p. 355: 'For they believed still
the lies of Sauron that the world was plain, until their fleets had
encompassed all the world seeking for Meneltyūlā, and they
knew that it was round'). And so (as he recounts the tradition),
rather than accept the true nature of the Round World, 'the
belief arose among them that it had so been made only in the
time of the great Downfall, and was not thus before.' So it was
that the survivors of Anadûnê in the West of Middle-earth came
to the conception of the Straight Road: '*Therefore they thought
that, while the new world fell away, the old road and the path of
the memory of the Earth went on towards heaven, as it were a
mighty bridge invisible.*'

This is radically distinct from *The Fall of Númenor* (FN III
§11, p. 338): 'For the ancient line of the world remained in the
mind of Ilúvatar, and in the thought of the gods, and in the
memory of the world, as a shape and plan that has been changed
and yet endureth.' The author of *The Fall of Númenor* knows
that 'of old many of the exiles of Númenor could still see, some
clearly and some more faintly, the paths to the True West'; but
for the rationalising author (as he may seem to be) of *The
Drowning of Anadûnê* the Straight Road was a belief born of
desire and regret.

The author of the *Akallabêth* had both works before him, and
in this passage he made use of them both. I give again here the
concluding passage of the *Akallabêth* with the sources shown
(necessarily somewhat approximately): *The Drowning of Anadûnê* in italic, *The Fall of Númenor* (FN III §§8, 12) in roman
between asterisks, and passages not found in either source in
roman within brackets.

But they found it not. (And those that sailed far) *came only
to the new lands, and found them like to the old lands, and
subject to death.* (And those that sailed furthest set but a
girdle about the Earth and returned) *weary at last to the
place of their beginning;* *and they said: 'All roads are now
bent.'*

Thus in after days, what by the voyages of ships, what by
(lore and) *star-craft, the kings of Men knew that the world
was indeed* (made) *round,* (and yet the Eldar were permitted
still to depart and to come to the Ancient West and to
Avallónë, if they would.) *Therefore* (the loremasters of Men
said that a Straight Road must still be, for those that were
permitted to find it. And they taught) *that, while the new
world fell away, the old road and the path of the memory of
the* (West still) *went on, as it were a mighty bridge invisible*
(that) *passed through the air of breath and of flight* ((which

were bent now as the world was bent),) *and traversed Ilmen
which flesh unaided cannot endure,* (until it came to Tol
Eressëa, the Lonely Isle, and maybe even beyond, to Valinor,
where the Valar still dwell and watch the unfolding of the
story of the world.) *And tales and rumours* (arose along the
shores of the sea) *concerning mariners and men forlorn upon
the water who, by some fate or grace* (or favour of the Valar,)
had entered in upon the (Straight) *Way and seen the face of
the world sink below them, and so had come to* (the lamplit
quays of Avallónë, or verily to the last beaches on the margin
of) *Aman, and there had looked upon the White Mountain,
dreadful and beautiful, before they died.*

The intention that lay behind these aspects of *The Drowning of
Anadûnê* is discussed in the next section (v).

§51   The description of the gale that followed the Cataclysm was
rewritten in DA III to a form close to that in the *Akallabêth*
(p. 280), but still retaining the seven ships (see p. 387, §51):

But when the land of Anadûnê toppled to its fall, then he
[Nimruzîr] would have been drawn down and perished, and
deemed it the lesser grief, for no wrench of death could be
more bitter than the ruin of that day; but the wind took him,
for it blew still from the West more wild than any wind that
Men had known; and it tore away the sails, and snapped the
masts, and hunted the unhappy men like straws upon the
water; and the deeps rose up in towering anger.

Then the seven ships of Nimruzîr fled before the black gale
out of the twilight of doom into the darkness of the world;
and waves like moving mountains capped with snow bore
them up amid the clouds, and after many days cast them away
far inland upon Middle-earth.

On the text of DA IV *seven* was altered in a hastily scribbled
change to *twelve*.

§55   At first the conclusion in DA III retained the form in DA II, but
it was replaced by the following (with pencilled corrections as
shown, appearing in DA IV as typed):

And the name of that land has perished; for neither did men
speak of Gimlad, nor of Abarzâyan [> Yôzâyan] the Gift that
was taken away, nor of Anadûnê upon the confines of the
world; but the exiles on the shores of the Sea, if they turned
towards the West, spoke of Akallabê [> Akallabêth] that was
whelmed in the waves, the Downfallen, Atalantë in the
Nimrian tongue.

Akallabēth is the form in Lowdham's fragments (pp. 247, 312).

*

I have shown (p. 353) that the composition of the original draft DA I of *The Drowning of Anadûnê* fell between that of the sole manuscript E of Part Two of *The Notion Club Papers* and the first typescript F 1 of Night 66 in the *Papers*. The second text DA II fell between F 1 and the replacement F 2 (p. 375), as also did the third text DA III (p. 388, §12). The final text DA IV is the first in which the Adunaic name of 'the Land of Gift' is *Yôzâyan*, the form in F 2; it cannot be seen which of these two texts preceded the other, but this seems to be of slight importance. What is significant about these details, of course, is that they make it certain that the composition of *The Drowning of Anadûnê* was intertwined with and was completed within the same period as the further development of Part Two of *The Notion Club Papers*.

(v) The theory of the work

I turn now to the fundamental question, what is the significance of the extraordinary transformations of, and omissions from, the existing legends in the development of *The Drowning of Anadûnê*? I have headed this section *The theory of the work* because my father used the word in this connection, and because I believe and hope to show that there was a 'theory' behind it.

Before attempting to formulate an answer, there are three extremely curious texts to be considered. All three were written at great speed, dashed down in careless expression as words came to mind, and probably one after the other. Very obviously preceding the emergence of Adunaic, they are a series of sketches of the rapidly evolving conceptions that would underlie the new version of the Númenórean legend that my father was contemplating: the first of them is in fact headed *The theory of this version*.

This first essay, which I will call 'Sketch I', exceedingly rough and disjointed, led on to a second ('Sketch II') which followed I for some distance, enlarging and expanding it, but was then abandoned. It is convenient to give Sketch II first so far as it goes, and then the remainder of I.

Notes on this section will be found on pp. 410 ff.

Evil reincarnates itself from time to time – reiterating, as it were, the Fall.

There were 'Enkeladim' once on earth, but that was not their name in this world: it was *Eledāi* (in Númenórean *Eldar*).[1] After the First Fall they tried to befriend Men, and teach them to love the Earth and all things that grow in it. But evil also was ever at work. There were false Eldar: counterfeits and deceits made by evil, ghosts and goblins, but not always evil to look at. They terrified Men, or else deceived and betrayed them, and hence arose the fear of Men for all the spirits of the Earth.

Men 'awoke' first in the midst of the Great Middle Earth (Europe and Asia), and Asia was first thinly inhabited, before the Dark Ages of great cold. Even before that time Men had spread westward (and eastward) as far as the shores of the Sea. The [Enkeladim >] Eledāi withdrew into waste places or retreated westward.[2]

The Men who journeyed westward were in general those who remained in closest touch with the true Eledāi, and for the most part they were drawn west by the rumour of a land in or beyond the Western Sea which was beautiful, and was the home of the Eledāi where all things were fair and ordered to beauty. This was so for there was a great island in the Ocean where the Eledāi had first 'awakened' when the world was made: that is complete and ready for their operations.

Thus it is that the more beautiful legends (containing truths) arose, of oreads, dryads, and nymphs; and of the *Ljós-alfar*.[3]

At length Men reached the western shores of the Great Lands, and were halted on the shores of the Sea. The shock and awe and longing of that meeting has remained in their descendants ever since, and the Great Sea and the setting sun has been to them the most moving symbol of Death and of Hope for Escape.

In the margin of the text of this page, which ends at this point, my father wrote: 'The Almighty even after the Fall allowed an earthly paradise to be maintained for a while; but the Eledāi were bidden to withdraw thither as men spread – if they would remain as they had been: otherwise they would fade and diminish.'[4]

In times remote, when Men, though they had now wandered for many many lives upon the face of the Earth, were yet young and untutored (save such few kindreds as had become knit in friendship with the western Eledāi, and their language had become enriched, and they knew verse and song and other arts), evil once again took visible shape. A great tyrant arose, first as the war-lord of a tribe, but he grew slowly to a mighty king, magician, and finally a god. In the midst [*written above:* North?] of the Great Lands was the seat of this terrible dominion, and all about men became enslaved to him. In that time Darkness became terrible. The black power slowly extended westward; for Melekō[5] knew that there lingered the most powerful and beneficent of the Eledāi, and that their friendship with Men was the greatest obstacle to his complete dominion.

Those among Men of the West who were most filled with sea-hunger began to make boats, aided and inspired (as in much else) by the Eledāi, and they began to essay the waters, at first with fear, but with growing mastery of wind and tide, and of themselves. But now war broke out, for the forces of Melekō threatened the lands of the west marches of the sea. The Men of the West were strong, and free, and the Easterlings of Melekō were driven back again and again. But this was only a respite, for the Easterlings were innumerable, and the attack was ever renewed with greater force; and Melekō sent phantoms and demons and spirits of evil into the western lands, so that these also might become intolerable and a time of dread, when men cowered in their houses and looked no more on the stars.

The Eledāi had long disappeared. Some said they had died, or faded into nothing; some that they had never been, and were but the inventions of old-time tales; some few that they had passed over the Sea to their land in the West.

A mariner arose in that time who was called Earendel, and he was king of Men upon the west shore of the Great Sea in the North of the world. He reported that once taken by a great wind he had been borne far out of his course and had indeed seen many islands in the regions of the setting sun – and one most remote from which there came a scent as of gardens of fair flowers. And it came to pass that all the Men of the West who had not died or fallen or fled into waste places were now hemmed in a narrow land, a large island some say, and they were assailed by Melekō, but only because their land was an isle, divided by a narrow water from the Great Lands, were they able still to hold out. Then Earendel took his ship and said farewell to his people. For he said it was his purpose to sail into the West and find the Eledāi and ask for their help. 'But I shall not return,' he said. 'If I fail then the sea will have me, but if I succeed then a new star will arise in heaven.'

And what deeds Earendel did upon his last voyage is not known for certain, for he was not seen again among living Men. But after some years a new star did indeed arise in the West, and it was very bright; and then many men began to look for the return of the Eledāi to their aid; but they were hard pressed by evil.

Here Sketch II ends as a continuously written text, but my father added some scribbled and disjointed notes at the end, which include this passage:

Melekō was defeated with the aid of the Eledāi and of the Powers, but many Men had seceded to him. The Powers (under orders of Ilúvatar) withdrew the Eledāi to the Isle of Eresse, whose chief haven was westward, Avallon(de).[6] Those that remained in Middle-earth withered and faded. But faithful men of the Eruhildi (Turkildi) were also given an isle, between Eresse and Middle-earth.

Sketch I (written at extreme speed in soft pencil on small slips) was essentially the same as Sketch II, though much briefer, to the point where Earendel enters in the latter. In Sketch I, however, there was no reference to Earendel, and all that is told is that when there came a respite in the war with 'the tyrant' (who is not named in this text) 'and his Easterlings' the Men of the West set sail, having been instructed in the art of ship-building by 'the last lingering Enkeladim' and they landed 'on a large island in the midst of the Great Sea'. At the head of the page my father noted: 'The first to set sail was Earendel. He was never seen again.' Then follows (in very slightly edited form):

But there is another smaller isle out of sight to the West – and beyond that rumour of a Great Land [?uninhabited] in the West.

This island is called Westernesse Númenor, the other Eressëa.

The religion of the Númenóreans was simple. A belief in a Creator of All, Ilúvatar. But he is very remote. Still they offered bloodless sacrifice. His temple was the *Pillar of Heaven*, a high mountain in the centre of the island. They believed Ilúvatar to dwell outside the world altogether; but symbolized that by saying he dwelt in High Heaven.

[*Added:* But they believe he has under him Powers (Valar), some at his special command, some residing in the world for its immediate government. These though *good* and servants of God are inexorable, and . . . . hostile in a sense. They do not pray to them but they fear and obey them (if ever any contact occur). Some are Valandili (Lovers of the Powers).]

But they believe the world flat, and that 'the Lords of the West' (Gods) dwell beyond the great barrier of cloud hills – where there is no death and the Sun is renewed and passes under the world to rise again.

[*Struck out:* His servants for the governance of the world were Enkeladim and other greater spirits. *Added:* There were lesser beings – especially associated with living things and with making . . . – called Eldar.] These they asked for assistance in need. Some still sailed to Eressëa. [*In margin:* Elendili] But the most did not, and except among the wise the theory arose that the great spirits or Gods (*not* Ilúvatar) dwelt in the West in a Great Land beyond the sun. [*Bracketed:* The Enkeladim told them that the world was round, but that was a hard saying to them.] Some of their great mariners tried to find out.

They lived to a great age, 200 years or more, but all the more longed for longer life. They envied the Enkeladim. They grew mighty in ship-building, and began to adventure to sea. Some try to reach the West beyond Eressëa but fail to return.

The Pillar of Heaven in neglected by all but a few. The kings build great houses. The custom of sending their bodies adrift to sea in an east wind grows up. The east wind begins to symbolize Death.[7]

Some sail back to the Dark Lands. There they are greeted with awe, for they are very tall . . . . They teach true religion but are treated as gods.

Sauron comes into being.

He cannot prevail in arms against the Númenóreans who now have many fortresses in the West.

The text ends with a very rough sketch of the coming of Sauron and the Downfall. 'Sauron is brought to Númenor to do allegiance to Tarkalion'. He 'preaches a great sermon', teaching that Ilúvatar does not exist, but that the world is ruled by the Gods, who have shut themselves in the West, hating Men and denying them life. The one good God has been thrust out of the world into the Void; but he will return. In an added passage (but no doubt belonging to the time of the writing of the text) it is told, remarkably, that 'Sauron says *the world is round*. There is nothing outside but Night – and other worlds.'[8]

Sauron has 'a great domed temple' built on the Pillar of Heaven (see p. 384), and there human sacrifice takes place, the purpose of which is 'to add the lives of the slain to the chosen living'. The Faithful are persecuted, and chosen for the sacrifice; 'a few fly to Eressëa asking for help – but the Eressëans have departed or hidden themselves.' A vast fleet is prepared 'to assault Eressëa and go on to take the West Land from the Gods'; and the text ends with the bare statements that the fleet was sucked into the great chasm that opened, and that 'only those Númenóreans who had withdrawn east of the isle and refused to .... war were saved.' This is followed by a morass of names, including 'Elendil son of Valandil and his sons Árundil and Firiel', from which emerges 'Elendil and his sons Isildur and Anárion'. Finally there are some further notes: 'Sauron flees East also. The Pillar of Heaven is volcanic.[9] Sauron builds a great temple on a hill near where he had landed. The Pillar of Heaven also begins to smoke and he calls it a sign; and most believe him.'

The third text ('Sketch III') begins with a note on names: '*Ilūve Ilu:* Heaven, the universe, all that is (with and without the Earth); *menel:* the heavens, the firmament.'[10] Then follows:

In the beginning was *Eru* the One God (*Ilúvatar* the Allfather, *Sanavaldo* the Almighty). He appointed powers (*Valar*) to rule and order the Earth (*Arda*). One *Melekō*, the chief, became evil. There were also two kindreds of lesser beings, Elves : *Eldar* (**Eledāi*), and Men (*Hildi* = sons, or followers). The Eledāi came first, as soon as Arda became habitable by living things, to govern there, to perfect the *arts* of using and ordering the material of the Earth to perfection and beauty in detail, and to prepare the way for Men. Men (the Followers or Second Kindred) came second, but it is guessed that in the first design of God they were destined (after tutelage) to take on the governance of all the Earth, and ultimately to become Valar, to 'enrich Heaven', *Ilúve*. But Evil (incarnate in Melekō) seduced them, and they fell. They became immediately estranged from the Eldar and Valar. For Melekō represented their tutelage as usurpation by

Eldar and Valar of Men's rightful heritage. God forbade the Powers to interfere by violence or might. But they sent many messages to Men, and the Eldar constantly tried to befriend Men and to teach them. But the power of Melekō increased, and the Valar retreated to the isle of *Eresse* in the Great Seas far west of the Great Lands (*Kemen*) – where they had always had as it were a habitation and centre in their early strife with Melekō.[11]

Melekō now (because evil decreased him, or to further his designs, or both) took visible shape as a Tyrant King, and his seat was in the North. He made many counterfeits of the Eledāi who were evil (but did not always so appear), and who cozened and betrayed Men, and so increased their fear and suspicion of the true Eldar.

There was war between the Powers and Melekō (the second war: the first had been in the making of the world, before Elves and Men were). Though all Men had 'fallen', not all remained enslaved. Some repented, rebelled against Melekō, and made friends of the Eldar, and tried to be loyal to God. They had no worship but to offer firstfruits to Eru on high places. They were not wholly happy, as Eru seemed far off, and they dared not pray to him direct; and so they regarded the Valar as gods, and so were often corrupted and deceived by Melekō, taking him or his servants (or phantoms) for 'gods'. But in the war against the seats of Melekō in the North there were *three kindreds* of good men (sons of God, *Eruhildi*) who were wholly faithful and never sided with Melekō. Among these there was *Earendel*, and he was alone of Men partly of the kindred of the Eledāi, and he became the first of Men to sail upon the Sea. In the days of the Second War when Men and the remaining Eledāi were hard pressed he set sail West. He said: 'I shall not return. If I fail you will hear no more of me. If I do not fail a new star will arise in the West.' He came to Eresse and spoke the embassy of the Two Kindreds before the Chief of the Valar, and they were moved. But Earendel was not suffered to return among living men, and his vessel was set to rise in the sky as a sign that his message was accepted. And Elves and Men saw it, and believed help would come, and were enheartened. And the Powers came and aided Elves and Men to overthrow Melekō, and his bodily shape was destroyed, and his spirit banished.

But the Powers now withdrew the Eldar to Eresse (where they had themselves dwelled, but now they had no longer any local habitation on earth, and seldom took shape visible to Elves or Men). Those who lingered in Kemen were doomed to fade and wither. But in Eresse was long maintained an earthly paradise filled with all beauties of growth and art (without excesses), the dwelling of the Eldar, a memorial of what Earth 'might have been' but for Evil. But the Men (Eruhildi) of the Faithful Houses were allowed (if they would) to go and dwell in another isle (greater but less fair) between Eresse and Middle-earth. Elros son of Earendel was their first king, in the land of Andor also called Númenor: so that the kings of the Númenóreans were called 'Heirs of Earendel'. Earendel was not only partly of Elf-kin but he was an Elf-friend (*Elendil*), whence the Kings of Númenor were also called *Elendilli* (*Ælfwinas*). [*Marginal addition:* Elrond his other son elected to remain in Kemen and dwell with Men and the Elves that yet [?abode] in the West of Middle-earth.]

In that time the world was very forlorn and forsaken, for only fading Elves dwelt in the West of Middle-earth, and the best of Men (save others of the Eruhildi far away in the midst of Kemen) had gone westward. But even the Eruhildi of Númenor were mortal. For the Powers were not allowed to abrogate that decree of God after the fall (that Men should die and should leave the world not at their own will but by fate and unwilling); but they were permitted to grant the Númenóreans a threefold span (over 200 years).

And in Númenor the Eruhildi became wise and fair and glorious, the mightiest of Men, but not very numerous (for their children were not many). Under the tutelage of the Eressëans – whose language they adopted (though in course of time they altered it much) – they had song and poesy, music, and all crafts; but in no craft did they have such skill and delight as in ship-building, and they sailed on many seas. In those days they were permitted, or such of their kings and wise men who were favoured and called Elf-friends (*Elendilli*), to voyage to Eresse; but there they might come only to the haven of *Avallon(de)* on the east side of the isle and the city of [Túna >] Tirion on the hill behind, there to stay but a short while.[12] Though often the Elendilli craved to abide in Eresse this was not permitted to them by command of the Powers (received from God); for the Eruhildi remained mortal and doomed at the last to grow weary of the world and to die, even their high-kings the heirs of Earendel. And they were not suffered to sail beyond Eresse westward, where they heard rumour of a New Land, for the Powers were not willing that that land should as yet be occupied by Men. But the hearts of the Eruhildi felt pity for the forsaken world of Middle-earth, and often they sailed there, and wise men or princes of the Númenóreans would at times come among men in the Dark Ages and teach them language, and song, and arts, and bring to them corn and wine; and men of Middle-earth revered their memory as gods. And in one or two places nigh to the sea men of the western race made settlements and became kings and the fathers of kings. But at last all this bliss turned to evil, and men fell a second time.

For there arose a second manifestation of Evil upon Earth, whether the spirit of Melekō himself took new (though lesser) form, or whether it were one of Melekō's servants that had lurked in the dark and now received the [? counsel] of Melekō out of the Void and waxed great and wicked, tales differ. But this evil thing was called by many names, and the Eruhildi called him *Sauron*, and he sought to be both king over all kings, and to Men both king and god. His seat was southward and eastward in Kemen, and his power over Men (especially east and south) grew ever greater and moved westward, driving away the lingering Eledāi and subjugating more and more of the kindred of the Eruhildi who had not gone to Númenor. And Sauron learned of Númenor and its power and glory; and to Númenor in the days of Tarkalion the Golden (the [21st >] tenth in the line from Earendel)[13] news came of Sauron and his power, and that he purposed to take the dominion of all Kemen, and of all the Earth after.

But in the meanwhile evil had been at work [?already] in the hearts of the Númenóreans; for the desire of everlasting life and to escape death grew ever stronger upon them; and they murmured against the prohibition that excluded them from Eresse, and the Powers were displeased with them. And they forbade them now even to land upon the island. At this time of estrangement from Eledāi and Valāi Tarkalion hearing of Sauron determined without counsel of Eldar or Valar to demand the allegiance and homage of Sauron. ... [*sic*]

Númenor cast down.

Eresse and the Eledāi removed from the world save in memory and the world delivered to Men. Men of Númenórean blood could still see Eresse as a mirage [?on] a straight road leading thither.

The ancient Númenóreans knew (being taught by the Eledāi) that the Earth was round; but Sauron taught them that it was a disc and flat, and beyond was nothing, where his master ruled. But he said that beyond Eresse was a land in the [?utter] West where the Gods dwelt in bliss, and usurped the good things of the Earth.[14] And that it was his mission to bring Men to that promised land, and overthrow the greedy and idle Powers. And Tarkalion believed him, being hungry for life undying.

And the Númenóreans after the downfall still spoke of the Straight Road that ran on when the Earth was bent. But the good ones – those that fled from Númenor and took no part in the war on Eresse – used this only in symbol. For by 'that which is beyond Eresse' they meant the world of eternity and the spirit, in the region of Ilúvatar.[15]

Here this text ends, with lines drawn showing that it was completed. All the concluding passage (from 'The ancient Númenóreans knew ...'), concerning the shape of the world and the meaning of the Straight Road, was struck through, the only part of the text so treated.

It will be seen that in the latter part of Sketch III appear a number of phrases that survived into *The Drowning of Anadûnê* (such as 'men fell a second time', 'there arose a second manifestation (of Evil) upon Earth', 'this evil thing was called by many names').

It seems to me that there are broadly speaking two possible lines of explanation of my father's thinking at this time. On the one hand, many years had passed since the progressive development of 'The Silmarillion' had been disrupted, and during all that time the actual narrative manuscripts had lain untouched; but it cannot be thought that he had put it altogether out of mind, that it had not continued to evolve unseen. Above all, the relation between the self-contained mythology of 'The Silmarillion' and the story of *The Lord of the Rings* boded problems of a profound nature. This work had now been at a standstill for more than a year; but *The Notion Club Papers* was leading to the re-emergence of Númenor as an increasingly important element in the whole, even as the Númenórean kingdoms in Middle-earth had grown so greatly in significance in *The Lord of the Rings*.

It might seem at least arguable, therefore, that the departures from the 'received tradition' (not a line of which had been published, as must always be borne in mind) seen in my father's writing at this time represent the emergence of new ideas, even to the extent of an actual dismantling and transformation of certain deeply embedded concep-tions. Chief among these are the nature of the 'dwelling' of the Valar in Arda and the interrelated question of 'the shape of the world'; and the 'Fall of Men', seduced in their beginning by 'Mēlekō', but followed by the repentance of some and their rebellion against him.

On the other hand, it may be argued that these developments were inspired by a specific purpose in respect only of *The Drowning of Anadûnê*. Essentially this is the view that I myself take; but the other is not thereby excluded radically or at all points, for ideas that here first appear would have repercussions at a later time.

It will be seen that the 'sketches' just given are remarkably dissimilar in many points, although it is true that their haste and brevity, a certain vagueness of language, and my father's characteristic way of omitting some features and enlarging on others in successive 'outlines', make it often difficult to decide whether differences are more apparent than real. But I shall not in any case embark on any comparative analysis, for I think it will be agreed without further discussion that these 'sketches', taken with the opening texts of *The Drowning of Anadûnê*, give a strong impression of uncertainty on my father's part: they are like a kaleidoscopic succession of different patternings, as he sought for a comprehensive conception that would satisfy his aim.

But what was that aim? The key, I think, is to be found in the treatment of the Elves (*Enkeladim, Eledāi, Eldar, Nimrî* or *Nimîr*). For beyond a few very generalised ideas nothing is known of them: of their origin and history, of the Great March, of the rebellion of the Noldor, of their cities in Beleriand, of the long war against Morgoth. In the first text of *The Drowning of Anadûnê* this ignorance is extended beyond that of the 'sketches' to a total obscuration of the distinction between Valar and Eldar (see pp. 353–4), although in the second text the Eldar appear under the Adunaic name *Nimrî*. In the 'sketches' the isle of Eressëa (Eresse) appears, yet confusedly, for (in Sketch III) the Valar dwelt on Eresse, and it was to Eresse that Earendel came and spoke before 'the Chief of the Valar'; while in *The Drowning of Anadûnê* Tol Eressëa has virtually disappeared.

Where could such ignorance of the Elves be found but in the minds of Men of a later time? This, I believe, is what my father was concerned to portray: a tradition of Men, through long ages become dim and confused. At this time, perhaps, in the context of *The Notion Club Papers* and of the vast enlargement of his great story that was coming into being in *The Lord of the Rings*, he began to be concerned with questions of 'tradition' and the vagaries of tradition, the losses, confusions, simplifications and amplifications in the evolution of legend, as they might apply to his own – within the always enlarging compass of Middle-earth. This is speculation; it would have been helpful indeed if he had at this time left any record or note, however brief, of his reflections. But many years later he did write such a note, though brief indeed, on the envelope that contains the texts of *The Drowning of Anadûnê*:

> Contains very old version (in Adunaic) which is good – in so far as it is just as much different (in inclusion and omission and emphasis) as would be probable in the supposed case:
> (a) Mannish tradition
> (b) Elvish tradition
> (c) Mixed Dúnedanic tradition

The handwriting and the use of a ball-point pen suggest a relatively late date, and were there no other evidence I would guess it to be some time in the 1960s. But it is certain that what appears to have been the final phase of my father's work on Númenor (*A Description of Númenor, Aldarion and Erendis*) dates from the mid-1960s (*Unfinished Tales* pp. 7–8); and it may be that the *Akallabêth* derives from that period also.

At any rate, there is here unequivocal evidence of how, long afterwards, he perceived his intention in *The Drowning of Anadûnê*: it was, specifically, 'Mannish tradition'. It could well be that – while the 'sketches' preceded the emergence of Adunaic – the conception of such a work was an important factor in the appearance of the new language at this time.

It seems to me likely that by 'Elvish tradition' he meant *The Fall of Númenor*; and since 'Mixed Dúnedanic tradition' presumably means a mixture of Elvish and Númenórean tradition, he was in this surely referring to the *Akallabêth*, in which both *The Fall of Númenor* and *The Drowning of Anadûnê* were used (see pp. 376, 395–6).

I conclude therefore that the marked differences in the preliminary sketches reflect my father's shifting ideas of what the 'Mannish tradition' might be, and how to present it: he was sketching rapidly possible modes in which the memory, and the forgetfulness, of Men in Middle-earth, descendants of the Exiles of Númenor, might have transformed their early history.[16]

In *The Drowning of Anadûnê* the confusions and obscurities of the 'Mannish tradition' were in fact deepened, in relation to the preliminary sketches: in the submergence of the Elves under the general term *Avalāi* in DA I, and in the virtual disappearance of Tol Eressëa, with the name 'Lonely Isle' given to the summit of the Pillar of Heaven sought by seafarers after the Downfall. It is seen too in the treatment of 'Avallon(de)': for in the sketches (see note 12) this name appears already in the final application, the eastward haven in Tol Eressëa, while in DA I the reference of *Avallondē* is obscure, and in the subsequent texts *Avallôni* is used of the Blessed Realm (see pp. 379 §16, 385 §47). My father seems not to have finally resolved how to present the Blessed Realm in this tradition; or, more probably, he chose to leave it as a matter 'unsure and dim'. In Sketch III it is told that after the banishment of Melekō from the world the Powers 'had no longer any local habitation on earth', and the Land of the Gods in the far West seems to be presented as a lie of Sauron's (see note 14). In *The Drowning of Anadûnê* (§16) those in Anadûnê who argued that the distant city seen over the water was an isle where the Nimrî (Nimîr) dwelt held also that 'mayhap the Avalôi(m) had no visible dwelling upon Earth'; yet later it is recounted (§47, and still more explicitly in the revision made to this passage, p. 391) that Ar-Pharazôn set foot on the Land of Amân, and after the Land of Amân was swallowed in the abyss 'the Avalôi(m) thereafter had no habitation on Earth'.

The attempt to analyse and order these shifting and fugitive conceptions will perhaps yield in the end no more than an understanding of what the problems were that my father was revolving in his mind. But since there is no reason to think that he turned to the subject of Númenor again, after he had forced himself to return to the plight of Sam Gamgee at the subterranean door of the Tower of Kirith Ungol, until many years had passed, it is interesting to see what he wrote of it in his long letter to Milton Waldman in 1951 (*Letters* no. 131): and I reprint two extracts from that letter here.

Thus, as the Second Age draws on, we have a great Kingdom and evil theocracy (for Sauron is also the god of his slaves) growing up in

Middle-earth. In the West – actually the North-West is the only part clearly envisaged in these tales – lie the precarious refuges of the Elves, while Men in those parts remains more or less uncorrupted if ignorant. The better and nobler sort of Men are in fact the kin of those that had departed to Númenor, but remain in a simple 'Homeric' state of patriarchal and tribal life.

Meanwhile *Númenor* has grown in wealth, wisdom, and glory, under its line of great kings of long life, directly descended from Elros, Earendil's son, brother of Elrond. The *Downfall of Númenor*, the Second Fall of Man (or Man rehabilitated but still mortal), brings on the catastrophic end, not only of the Second Age, but of the Old World, the primeval world of legend (envisaged as flat and bounded). After which the Third Age began, a Twilight Age, a Medium Aevum, the first of the broken and changed world; the last of the lingering dominion of visible fully incarnate Elves, and the last also in which Evil assumes a single dominant incarnate shape.

The *Downfall* is partly the result of an inner weakness in Men – consequent, if you will, upon the first Fall (unrecorded in these tales), repented but not finally healed. Reward on earth is more dangerous for men than punishment! The Fall is achieved by the cunning of Sauron in exploiting this weakness. Its central theme is (inevitably, I think, in a story of Men) a Ban, or Prohibition.

The Númenóreans dwell within far sight of the easternmost 'immortal' land, Eressëa; and as the only men to speak an Elvish tongue (learned in the days of their Alliance) they are in constant communication with their ancient friends and allies, either in the bliss of Eressëa, or in the kingdom of Gilgalad on the shores of Middle-earth. They became thus in appearance, and even in powers of mind, hardly distinguishable from the Elves – but they remained mortal, even though rewarded by a triple, or more than a triple, span of years. Their reward is their undoing – or the means of their temptation. Their long life aids their achievements in art and wisdom, but breeds a possessive attitude to these things, and desire awakes for more *time* for their enjoyment. Foreseeing this in part, the gods laid a Ban on the Númenóreans from the beginning: they must never sail to Eressëa, nor westward out of sight of their own land. In all other directions they could go as they would. They must not set foot on 'immortal' lands, and so become enamoured of an immortality (within the world), which was against their law, the special doom or gift of Ilúvatar (God), and which their nature could not in fact endure.

. . .

But at last Sauron's plot comes to fulfilment. Tar-Calion feels old age and death approaching, and he listens to the last prompting of Sauron, and building the greatest of all armadas, he sets sail into the West, breaking the Ban, and going up with war to wrest from the gods 'everlasting life within the circles of the world'. Faced by this rebellion, of appalling folly and blasphemy, and also real peril (since the Númenóreans directed by Sauron could have wrought ruin in Valinor itself) the Valar lay down their delegated power and appeal to God, and receive the power and permission to deal with the situation; the old world is broken and changed. A chasm is opened in the sea and Tar-Calion and his armada is engulfed. Númenor itself on the edge of the rift topples and vanishes for ever with all its glory into the abyss. Thereafter there is no visible dwelling of the divine or immortal on earth. Valinor (or Paradise) and even Eressëa are removed, remaining only in the memory of the earth. Men may sail now West, if they will, as far as they may, and come no nearer to Valinor or the Blessed Realm, but return only into the east and so back again; for the world is round, and finite, and a circle inescapable – save by death. Only the 'immortals', the lingering Elves, may still if they will, wearying of the circle of the world, take ship and find the 'straight way', and come to the ancient or True West, and be at peace.

Three years later my father said in a letter to Hugh Brogan (18 September 1954, *Letters* no. 151):

Middle-earth is just archaic English for ἡ οἰκουμένη, the inhabited world of men. It lay then as it does. In fact just as it does, round and inescapable. That is partly the point. The new situation, established at the beginning of the Third Age, leads on eventually and inevitably to ordinary History, and we here see the process culminating. If you or I or any of the mortal men (or hobbits) of Frodo's day had set out over sea, west, we should, as now, eventually have come back (as now) to our starting point. Gone was the 'mythological' time when Valinor (or Valimar), the Land of the Valar (gods if you will) existed physically in the Uttermost West, or the Eldaic (Elvish) immortal Isle of Eressëa; or the Great Isle of Westernesse (Númenor-Atlantis). After the Downfall of Númenor, and its destruction, all this was removed from the 'physical' world, and not reachable by material means. Only the Eldar (or High-Elves) could still sail thither, forsaking time and mortality, but never returning.

A week later he wrote to Naomi Mitchison (25 September 1954, *Letters* no. 154):

Actually in the imagination of this story we are now living on a physically round Earth. But the whole 'legendarium' contains a transition from a flat world (or at least an οἰκουμένη with borders all about it) to a globe: an inevitable transition, I suppose, to a modern 'myth-maker' with a mind subjected to the same 'appearances' as ancient men, and partly fed on their myths, but taught that the

Earth was round from the earliest years. So deep was the impression made by 'astronomy' on me that I do not think I could deal with or imaginatively conceive a flat world, though a world of static Earth with a Sun going round it seems easier (to fancy if not to reason).

The particular 'myth' which lies behind this tale, and the mood both of Men and Elves at this time, is the Downfall of Númenor: a special variety of the Atlantis tradition. ...

I have written an account of the Downfall, which you might be interested to see. But the immediate point is that before the Downfall there lay beyond the sea and the west-shores of Middle-earth an *earthly* Elvish paradise Eressëa, and *Valinor* the land of the *Valar* (the Powers, the Lords of the West), places that could be reached physically by ordinary sailing-ships, though the Seas were perilous. But after the rebellion of the Númenóreans, the Kings of Men, who dwelt in a land most westerly of all mortal lands, and eventually in the height of their pride attempted to occupy Eressëa and Valinor by force, Númenor was destroyed, and Eressëa and Valinor removed from the physically attainable Earth: the way west was open, but led nowhere but back again – for mortals.

NOTES

1 The name *Eledāi* occurs in DA II (and subsequent texts) §5, as the name of the Nimrî (Nimîr) in their own language. On Michael Ramer's *Enkeladim* see pp. 199, 206 and note 65, 303.

2 Sketch I has here: 'The Great Central Land, Europe and Asia, was first inhabited. Men awoke in Mesopotamia. Their fates as they spread were very various. But the Enkeladim withdrew ever west.'

3 *Ljós-alfar:* Old Norse, 'Light-elves', mentioned in the 'Prose Edda' of Snorri Sturluson.

4 Cf. DA II (and subsequent texts) §16: 'For as yet Eru permitted the Avalôi to maintain upon Earth ... an abiding place' (DA I 'an abiding place, an earthly paradise').

In my father's exposition of his work to Milton Waldman in 1951 there is a passage of interest in relation to the opening of this sketch (*Letters* no. 131, pp. 147–8):

In the cosmogony there is a fall: a fall of Angels we should say. Though quite different in form, of course, to that of the Christian myth. These tales are 'new', they are not directly derived from other myths and legends, but they must inevitably contain a large measure of ancient wide-spread motives or elements. After all, I believe that legends and myths are largely made of 'truth', and indeed present aspects of it that can only be received in this mode; and long ago certain truths and modes of this kind were discovered and must always reappear.

There cannot be any 'story' without a fall – all stories are ultimately about the fall – at least not for human minds as we know them and have them.

So, proceeding, the Elves have a fall, before their 'history' can become storial. (The first fall of Man, for reasons explained, nowhere appears – Men do not come on the stage until all that is long past, and there is only a rumour that for a while they fell under the domination of the Enemy and that some repented.) The main body of the tale, the *Silmarillion* proper, is about the fall of the most gifted kindred of the Elves ...

Notable here is my father's reference to 'a rumour that for a while [Men] fell under the domination of the Enemy and that some repented', and see also the further citation from this letter on p. 408; with this cf. DA II (and subsequent texts) §§3–4:

At the appointed hour Men were born into the world, and they were called the Eru-hîn, the children of God; but they came in a time of war and shadow, and they fell swiftly under the domination of Mulkhêr, and they served him. ... But some there were of the fathers of Men who repented, seeing the evil of the Lord Mulkhêr and that his shadow grew ever longer on the Earth; and they and their sons returned with sorrow to the allegiance of Eru, and they were befriended by the Avalôi, and received again their ancient name, Eruhîn, children of God.

Of this there is no suggestion in the *Quenta Silmarillion* (V.274– 6); cf. however the suggestions in Chapter 17 of the published *Silmarillion* ('that a darkness lay upon the hearts of Men (as the shadow of the Kinslaying and the Doom of Mandos lay upon the Noldor) [the Eldar] perceived clearly even in the people of the Elf-friends whom they first knew').

At the head of the following page of the text is a very rough and disjointed note in which are named the *Eruhildi*, sons of God, descended from Shem or Japheth (sons of Noah).

5 *Melekō*: a footnote to the text states: 'He had many names in different tongues, but such was his name among the Númenóreans, which means Tyrant.' This is the form of the name in DA I, but with long first vowel: *Mēlekō*.

6 *Eresse* is the form in the earlier version of Edwin Lowdham's Old English text, pp. 313–14. – On the haven of *Avallon(de)* see note 12. In 'whose chief haven was westward' read 'eastward'.

7 In *The Fall of Númenor* (§10) ship-burial came to be practised by the Exiles on the western coasts of Middle-earth.

8 This (presumably) contradicts the earlier, bracketed, statement in this same text (p. 400): 'The Enkeladim told them that the world was round, but that was a hard saying to them.' The statement here is of course the opposite of the story in *The Drowning of*

Anadûnê (§§23, 31), where Sauron taught that the world was flat, contradicting the instruction of the messengers of the Avalôi(m). In Sketch III (p. 404) 'The ancient Númenóreans knew (being taught by the Eledāi) that the Earth was round; but Sauron taught them that it was a disc and flat, and beyond was nothing, where his master ruled.'

9   *The Pillar of Heaven is volcanic:* cf. Lowdham's comment on Frankley's poem (p. 265): 'Your Volcano is ... apparently a last peak of some Atlantis.'

10   On *Ilu, Ilúve*, see IV.241, V.47, 63, and the *Etymologies*, stem IL, V.361. The word *menel* first occurs here or in the manuscript E of Part Two of *The Notion Club Papers*, in the name *Menelminda* of the Pillar of Heaven (p. 302).

11   The first occurrence of the word *kemen* in the texts, but cf. the added entry stem KEM- in the *Etymologies*, V.363.

    where they had always had as it were a habitation and centre in their early strife with Melekō: the legend that the isle on which the Valar dwelt before Morgoth overthrew the Lamps was also that on which Ulmo ferried the Elves to Valinor, and which Ossë anchored to the sea-bottom far out in the ocean, so that it was named 'the Lonely Isle'. The original form of the story is found in *The Book of Lost Tales* ('The Coming of the Elves', I.118 ff.) and then in the successive versions of 'The Silmarillion': the 'Sketch of the Mythology' from the 1920s (IV.12, 14, 45), the *Quenta Noldorinwa* (IV.80, 86), and the *Quenta Silmarillion* (V.208, 221–2).

12   In the earlier version of the Old English text of the surviving page of Edwin Lowdham's manuscript (pp. 313–14) the Númenóreans were forbidden to land on Eresse. Here they may visit the isle, but only briefly, and only the haven of Avallon(de) and the city of [Túna >] Tirion 'on the hill behind'; subsequently the Powers, in their displeasure, transmuted this into a prohibition against landing on Eresse at all (p. 404). On the reference to 'the city of [Túna >] Tirion on the hill behind' see note 16.

    In notes added to Sketch II (p. 399), as well as in the present passage, 'Avallon(de)' appears as the name of the haven in Eresse, and this is where the final application of the name (later *Avallónë*) first appears (in FN III *Avallon* was still the name of the Lonely Isle, as it remained in the earlier Old English text referred to above).

13   *tenth in the line from Earendel:* this can be equated with the statement in DA II §20 (see the commentary, p. 381) if Earendel is himself numbered, as the first in the line though not the first king of Númenor.

14   This presumably implies that the idea of a land in the far West where the Gods dwelt was a lie of Sauron's. Earlier in the text

(p. 402) it has been told that the Gods had dwelt in Eresse, but after the final overthrow of Melekō 'they had no longer any local habitation on earth' (cf. also Sketch I, p. 400: 'except among the wise the theory arose that the great spirits or Gods ... dwelt in the West in a Great Land beyond the sun'). See further p. 407.

15 Cf. VIII.164 and note 37.

16 A curious case is presented by the statement in Sketch III, p. 403, that 'the city of [Túna >] Tirion' was 'on the hill behind the haven of Avallon(de)'; for Tún(a), Tirion was of course the city of the Elves in Valinor. One might suppose that Homer nodded here; but in the earliest draft of an Old English text for 'Edwin Lowdham's page' (p. 316), which closely followed *The Fall of Númenor* §6, it is told that the Númenóreans, landing in Valinor, set fire to the city of Túna. The statement in Sketch III is therefore more probably to be taken as intentional, an example of a famous name handed down in tradition but with its true application forgotten.

(vi) Lowdham's Report on the Adunaic Language

This is a typescript made by my father that ends at the bottom of its seventeenth page, at which point he abandoned it (there is no reason to suppose that further pages existed but were lost). That it belongs with the final texts DA III and DA IV of *The Drowning of Anadûnê* is readily seen from various names and name-forms, as *Nimīr, Azrubēl, Adūnāim, Minul-Tārik, Amatthāni* (see p. 388, §§5, 8, 13, 20, 23).

In printing 'Lowdham's Report' I have followed my father's text very closely indeed, retaining his use of capitals, italics, marks of length, etc. despite some apparent inconsistency, except where corrections are obvious and necessary. The only point in which I have altered his presentation is in the matter of the notes. These (as became his usual practice in essays of this sort) he simply interspersed in the body of the text as he composed it; but as some of them are very substantial I have thought it best to collect them together at the end. I have added no commentary of my own.

It may be noted that the 'we' of Lowdham's introduction refers to himself and Jeremy; cf. Footnotes 2 and 6 on pp. 432–3.

ADUNAIC

It is difficult, of course, to say anything about the pre-history of a language which, as far as my knowledge goes, has no close relations with any other tongue. The other contemporary language that came through together with Adunaic in my earlier 'hearings', and which I have called Avallonian, appears to be distinct and unrelated, at least not 'cognate'. But I guess that originally, or far back beyond these records, Avallonian and Adunaic were in some way related. It is in fact clear now that Avallonian is the Nimriyē or 'Nimrian tongue' referred to in the very early Exilic text that we have managed to get concerning the Downfall. In that case it must be the language of the Nimīr, or a western form of it, and so be the ultimate source of the languages of Men in the west of the Old World. Perhaps I should rather say that the glimpses of the 'Nimrian tongue' that we have received show us a language, itself doubtless much changed, that is *directly* descended from the primeval Nimrian. From that Nimrian in a later stage, but still older than the Avallonian, the ancestor of Adunaic was partly derived.

But Adunaic must then for a long time have developed quite independently. Also I think it came under some different influence. This influence I call Khazadian; because I have received a good many echoes of a curious tongue, also connected with what we should call the West of the Old World, that is associated with the name Khazad. Now this resembles Adunaic phonetically, and it seems also in some points of vocabulary and structure; but it is precisely at the points where Adunaic most differs from Avallonian that it approaches nearest to Khazadian.

However, Adunaic evidently again later came into close contact with Avallonian, so that there is, as it were, a new layer of later resemblances between the two tongues: Adunaic for instance somewhat softened its harder phonetic character; while it also shows a fairly large number of words that are the same as the Avallonian words, or very similar to them. Of course, it cannot always be determined in such cases whether we are dealing with a primitive community of vocabulary, or with a later borrowing of Avallonian terms. Thus I am inclined to think that the Adunaic Base MINIL 'heaven, sky' is a primitive word, cognate with the Nimrian Base MENEL and not borrowed from it at a later time; although certainly, if Menel had been so borrowed, it would probably have acquired the form Minil [*struck out:* and the actual Adunaic noun Minal could be explained as an alteration to fit Minil into the Adunaic declensional system]. On the other hand it seems plain that the Adunaic word lōmi 'night' is an Avallonian loan; both because of its sense (it appears to mean 'fair night, a night of stars', with no connotations of gloom or fear), but also because it is quite isolated in Adunaic. According to Adunaic structure, as I shall try to exhibit it, *lōmi* would require either a biconsonantal Base LUM, or more probably a triconsonantal Base LAW'M; but neither of these exist in our material, whereas in Avallonian *lóme* (stem *lómi-*) is a normal formation from an Avallonian biconsonantal Base LOM.

I will try now and sketch the structure and grammar of Adunaic, as far as the material that we have received allows this to be done. The language envisaged is the language about the period of the Downfall, that is more or less during the end of the reign of King Ar-Pharazōn. From that period most of the records come. There are only occasional glimpses of earlier stages, or of the later (Exilic) forms of the language among the descendants of the survivors. Some of our chief texts, notably *The Drowning*, are in point of time of composition Exilic: that is they must have been put together at some time later than the reign of Ar-Pharazōn; but they are in a language virtually identical with the 'classical' Adunaic. This is probably due to two causes: their drawing on older material; and the continued use of the older language for higher purposes. For the actual daily speeches of the Exiles seem in fact to have changed and diverged quickly on the western shores. Of these changed and divergent forms we have only a few echoes, but they sometimes help in elucidating the forms and history of the older tongue.

*

General Structure.

The majority of the word-bases of Adunaic were *triconsonantal*. This structure is somewhat reminiscent of Semitic; and in this point Adunaic shows affinity with Khazadian rather than with Nimrian. For though Nimrian has many triconsonantal stems (other than the products of normal suffixion), such as the stem MENEL cited above, these are rarer in Nimrian, and are mostly the stems of *nouns*.

The vocalic arrangements within the base, however, do not much resemble Semitic; neither does Adunaic show anything strictly comparable to the 'gradations' of languages familiar to us, such as the *e/o* variation in the Indo-European group. In an Adunaic Base there is a Characteristic Vowel (CV) which shares with the consonants in characterizing or identifying the Base. Thus KARAB and KIRIB are distinct Bases and may have wholly unrelated meanings. The CV may, however, be modified in certain recognized ways (described below under the Vowels) which can produce effects not unlike those of gradation.

In addition to the *triconsonantal* Bases, there existed also in Adunaic a large number of *biconsonantal* Bases. Many of these are clearly ancient, though some may have been borrowed from Avallonian, where the biconsonantal Base is normal. These ancient biconsonantal Bases are probably an indication that the longer forms are in fact historically a later development. A few of the commonest verbal notions are expressed by biconsonantal forms, though the verb form of Adunaic is usually triconsonantal: thus NAKH 'come, approach', BITH 'say', contrasted with SAPHAD 'understand', NIMIR 'shine', KALAB 'fall', etc. [*Footnote 1*]

A number of ancient elements also exist: affixes, pronominal and numeral stems, prepositional stems, and so on, that only show *one* consonant. When, however, a 'full word', a noun for instance, has a uniconsonantal form, it must usually be suspected that an older second consonant has disappeared. Thus *pâ* 'hand' is probably derived from a Base PA3.

Consonants.

The following is a table of the Consonants which Adunaic appears originally (or at an earlier stage) to have possessed: [*Footnote 2*]

	(a) p-series	(b) t-series	(c) c-series	(d) k-series
STOPS				
1. *Voiceless:*	P.	T.	C.	K.
2. *Voiced:*	B.	D.	J.	G.
3. *Voiceless aspirated:*	Ph.	Th.	Ch.	Kh.
CONTINUANTS				
4. *Voiceless:*	–	S.	2.	H.
5. *Voiced (weak):*	W.	L, R, Z.	Y.	3. ?.
6. *Voiced: Nasals:*	M.	N.	–	9.

[*Footnote 3*]

The sounds of the c-series: C, J, Ch, 2 were front or 'palatal' consonants originally; that is roughly consonants of the k-series made in the extreme forward or *y*-position, and they might be so represented, but the above notation has been adopted, because their later development was to simple consonants. The sign 2 represents a voiceless hissed Y, that is the German *ich*-laut, or a rather stronger form of the voiceless Y often heard initially in such an English word as *huge*.

It will be noted that the T-series is the most rich, and possessed *three* voiced continuants. The T-series is probably the most frequently employed in Base-formation; and is certainly the most used in pronominal and formative elements (especially those of uniconsonantal form). The P-series is the poorest and possesses no voiceless hiss; but it is very probable that one anciently existed, a voiceless w (as English *wh*), but became H prehistorically.

H represents the voiceless back hissing sound, the *ch* of Welsh, Gaelic, and German (as in *acht*). 3 is the corresponding voiced spirant, or 'open' G.

Adunaic employs affixion in word-formation, though more sparingly than Avallonian; and in contrast to Avallonian employs prefixion more frequently than suffixion: the latter is sparingly used in forming stems (where the two elements become merged), but is more frequent in inflexion (where the two elements usually remain distinct). The primitive Adunaic combinations of consonants, in consequence, are due mainly to the contact of the basic consonants, and are predominantly of the form 'Continuant + some other consonant', or *vice versa*. This is so, because the predominant (but not exclusive) form of the Adunaic Bases, when triconsonantal, is X + Continuant + X; or X + X + Continuant, where X = any consonant.

A much employed method of derivation, however, is the lengthening or 'doubling' of one of the basic consonants. The consonant doubled is usually either the medial or final consonant of the Base, though in certain formations the initial may be doubled (only *one* of the basic consonants is so treated in any one word).

Similar to this method, and so to some extent competing with it in functions, is the infixion of an homorganic nasal before the final, or less frequently the medial, basic consonant: thus B to MB; D to ND; G to NG. This method cannot, of course, be distinguished from doubling in the case of the Nasals. It is doubtful if it originally occurred before the other continuants: the apparent cases of NZ may be due to *NJ, which became NZ, or to the analogy of such cases. [*Footnote 4*]

Adunaic, like Avallonian, does not tolerate more than a single basic consonant initially in any word (note that Ph, Th, Kh, are simple consonants). Unlike Avallonian it tolerates a large number of combinations medially, and there consonants in contact are very sparingly assimilated. Finally, in the 'classical' period Adunaic did not possess consonant-combinations, since affixes always ended in a vowel or a single consonant; while basic stems were always arranged in the following forms: ATLA, TAL(A) in the case of biconsonantal bases; AK(A)LAB(A), (A)KALBA in the case of triconsonantals. But the omission of short final A (not I or U), both in speech and writing, was already usual before the end of the classical period, with the consequence that a large number of consonant combinations became final.

The following list will show the normal development of the more primitive consonants in later Adunaic. The consonants are here set out in the order of the former table, and not according to the phonetic classification.

	(a)	(b)	(c)	(d)
1.	P.	T.	S.	K.
2.	B.	D.	Z.	G.
3.	Ph.	Th.	S.	Kh.
4.	–	S.	S.	H.
5.	W.	L, R, Z.	Y.	– (G). –.
6.	M.	N.	–	(N) [*Footnote 5*]

It will be observed that the consonants have not suffered any very material change except in the case of the C-series, which has become dental (apart from Y, which remains unchanged). With the development of c, ch, 2 to s may be compared the development of Latin fronted c in part of the Romance area; and the development of Indo-European K to s in Slavonic. Similarly the development of J (fronted G) to z may be compared with the change of Indo-European fronted G and Gh to z in Iranian and Slavonic. The assumption of a primitive C-series is based partly on scraps of internal evidence (such as the presence of an infixion NZ, whereas infixion of Nasal does not occur before the genuine consonants); partly on early forms, especially some scraps of an early inscription, [*Footnote 6*] which shows two different s-letters and z-letters. The treatment of Avallonian loans is also significant; in early loans the Avallonian Ty and Hy (approximately equivalent to the English *t* in *tune* and *h* in *huge*) both become s in Adunaic: as for instance Adunaic *sulum* 'mast', *sūla* 'trump' from Nimrian *kyulumā*, *hyōlā*, Avallonian *tyulma*, *hyóla*.

In the earlier language Ph, Th, Kh had plainly been aspirated stops, as in ancient Greek. This is most clearly seen when these sounds came into contact with others (see below). But it appears from various signs in the spelling, from the later developments in Exilic, and from the actual pronunciations of words coming through in audible form, that before the Downfall these aspirates had become strong spirants: F (bilabial), Þ (as English voiceless *th*), and X (the *ach*-sound originally belonging to H, with which Kh now coalesced in cases where H had not gone on to the breath-H). At the same time the combinations PPh, TTh, KKh became the 'affricates' PF, TÞ, KX, and then the long or double spirants FF, ÞÞ, XX. PTh and KTh appear to have become FÞ, XÞ.

H was originally, as noted above, the voiceless back-spirant; but in the classical language it had usually become the breath H. So, always initially, and medially between vowels. It never, however, becomes silent in these positions. [*Footnote 7*] The spirantal sound of H was retained before S [*added*: and where long or doubled HH] (where it later therefore coalesced with Kh); and in some 'hearings' it seems to occur before T and Th, though usually before consonants it is heard as a breathless puff, having the timbre of the preceding vowel. On the development of H in other contacts, see below.

The original consonants w and y were weak (consonantal forms of the vowels U and I). Medially they disappeared prehistorically before the vowels U and I respectively. But initially they were strengthened, becoming more spirantal (though w remained bilabial); so that the initial combinations WU and YI remained. The same strengthening occurred between vowels (where w and y had not been lost). After consonants both w and y remained weaker, like English w and y. Before consonants and finally they were vocalized and usually combined with the preceding vowels to form diphthongs (see the *Vowels*). [*Footnote 8*]

The sound ʔ [see Footnote 1] had no sign in Adunaic script, except in the archaic inscription referred to above [page 418 and Footnote 6]. Presumably it disappeared very early. It cannot be determined whether it had ever been used medially as a base-forming consonant. Probably not.

3 became weakened, until in the classical period (parallel with the softening of the voiceless equivalent H to the breath-H) it merged with the adjacent vowels. This softening of the back spirants may be ascribed to Avallonian influence.

Initially 3 disappeared. Medially between vowels it disappeared also, and contractions often resulted (always in the case of like vowels, A3A to Ā); U3 + vowels became UW-, and I3 + vowel became IY-. Finally, or before a consonant, 3 became merged with the preceding vowel, which if short was consequently lengthened; as A3DA to ĀDA.

Assimilations in contact.

As noted above, these were only sparingly made, owing to the strong consciousness of the basic consonantal pattern in Adunaic. And even those assimilations most commonly made in actual speech are seldom represented in writing, except in the comparatively rare cases where the structure of the word was no longer recognized.

The nasals offer, however, a surprising exception to this conservative tendency, both in writing and speech. This is all the more remarkable, since the combinations MP, NT, NK seem not only easy to us, but are highly favoured in Avallonian. They were disliked in Adunaic, and tended to be changed even at the contact point of distinct words in composition: as *Amātthāni* from AMĀN + THĀNI 'the realm of Amān'.

The dental nasal N was in speech assimilated in position to following consonants of other series. It thus became M before P, Ph, B, and M; though notably NW remained unchanged (NW is a favoured combination in Avallonian); and 9 before K, Kh, G, H, 3. Where the nasal still remained a nasal, as in MB, NG, this change of position is often disregarded in writing.

After these changes in position the combinations of Nasal + Voiceless consonant all suffered change. In the combinations MP, MPh, NT, NTh, NK, NKh the nasal was first unvoiced, and then denasalized, the resulting combinations being PP, PPh, TT, TTh, KK, KKh. These changes were recognized as a rule in writing, though a diacritic was usually placed above the P, T, or K that resulted from a nasal; the evidence of the audible forms seems to show that this sign was etymological and grammatical, not phonetic. In old formations N + H became 9H and then HH (phonetically XX, long back voiceless spirant); but in contacts made after the weakening of H to breath-H, or remodelled after the event, NH remained and is heard as a voiceless NN with breath off-glide. NS became TS.

Since M did not become assimilated in position to following consonants there were the combinations MT, MTh, MK, MKh, MS, and MH. Parallel with the development described above these became PT, PTh, PK, PKh, PS, but no example of P-H for M-H is found. In the few cases of contact of M + H MH is written, and (as in the case of NH) a voiceless MM is heard.

Where the following consonant was voiced the changes are few (other than the changes in position described above). 3 after N or the infixed homorganic 9 does not disappear but becomes nasalized yielding 99, which became NG (phonetically 9G). NR, NL tended to become RR, LL, but usually with the retention of nasality (transferred to the preceding vowel), in speech; the change is not as a rule represented in writing, though such spellings as NRR, NLL are found. M3 became, in accordance with the general tendency of 3 to be assimilated to a preceding voiced sound, MM. MW became in speech MM (colloquially a preceding labial usually absorbs a following W), but this change is usually not shown in spelling.

Other assimilations are rarer and less remarkable. In speech there was a tendency for consonants in contact to be assimilated in the matter of voice; but this tendency is less strong than in, say, English, and is mostly disregarded in writing. Thus we usually find *Sapda* from Base SAPAD, and *Asdi* from Base ASAD, where *sabda* and *azda* may be spoken (though the z in such a form is only partly voiced and is not the same as the strongly buzzed sound of a basic z).

The aspirates Ph, Th, Kh have naturally a strong unvoicing tendency on the sounds that follow, and transfer their aspiration or audible breath off-glide to the end of the group. Thus Ph + D, or T, or Th became PTh (or strictly PhTh). Thus from Base SAPHAD is derived **saphdān* 'wise-man, wizard', becoming later *sapthān* (phonetically, as described above, *safpān*). But such combinations are not very common, and in perspicuous forms (such, for example, as arise in verbal or noun inflexion, or in casual composition) were liable to be remodelled, especially after the change of the aspirates to spirants; thus *usaphda* 'he understood' for *usaptha*.

The continuants W, Y; L, R, Z are pronounced voiceless after the aspirates, but otherwise suffer no change. They are also unvoiced after s and H. Before H and s the continuants L, R, Z were unvoiced, but w and y had already become vowels (u and I). M, N were unvoiced after the aspirates (while these remained as such), but not after other sounds; after the later developed spirants F, Þ, X the unvoicing of M, N was only partial.

After voiceless sounds 3 while it still remained an audible consonant became H. After voiced sounds it was assimilated to these, so that for instance B3, D3 became BB, DD. As noted above N3, 93, became 99 and then NG.

After voiced sounds H was not voiced but tended to unvoice the preceding consonant. Similarly where it preceded a voiced continuant (as in HR, HM, HZ, etc.); but before B, D, G it tended to become voiced, that is to become the same as 3, and so to disappear, being merged in the preceding vowel.

The Adunaic Vowels.

Adunaic originally possessed only the three primary vowels: A, I, U; and the two basic diphthongs AI, AU.

Each Base possessed *one* of these vowels: A, I, U as one of its essential components; this I call the CV (Characteristic Vowel).

The normal place of the CV was between the first and second basic consonant: thus NAK-, KUL'B.

The 2-consonant Bases could also add the CV at the end; and the 3-consonant Bases could add it before the last radical: NAKA, KULUB. These forms with two basic vowels may be called the Full forms of the Base.

Various other forms or modifications occurred.
(i) Prefixion of the CV: ANAK, UKULB, IGIML.
(ii) Suffixion of the CV in 3-consonant Bases: KULBU, GIMLI.
(iii) Suppression of the CV in its normal place, in which case it must be present in some other place: -NKA, -KLUB, -GMIL.

This 'suppression' of the normal CV can only occur in 2-consonant Bases where it is also suffixed. It also requires that the CV shall be prefixed: ANKA, UKLUB, IGMIL; or (more rarely) that some other formative prefix ending in a vowel shall be present: DA-NKA, DA-KLUB, DA-GMIL.

These modifications are seldom combined: that is, a basic form does not usually have the CV repeated more than twice (as UKULBU, KULUBU); though such a form as UKULB could not originally stand in Adunaic as a word, some other vowel than the CV was taken as the ending (as UKULBA).

One of the vowels of a basic stem must be either the CV or one of its normal modifications (described below); but the second vowel of the 'Full form' need not be the CV, but may be any one of the primary vowels (or their modification). Thus NAKA — NAKI, NAKU; KULUB — KULAB, KULIB. The prefixed vowel (as distinct from a separate formative prefix) must always be the CV; but the suffixed vowel may also vary: so KULBA, KULBI; GIMLA, GIMLU. [*Footnote 9*]

Every primary vowel A, I, U can show one of the following modifications:
(i)   Lengthening: Ā, Ī, Ū.
(ii) Fortification or A-infixion: Ā, AI, AU.
(iii) N-infixion: AN, IN, UN. [*Footnote 10*]

In the older language over-long vowels were recognized, and marked with a special sign, in my transcription represented by ^. These occurred: (i) as an actual basic modification: chiefly in 2-consonant Bases, and in any case only before the last basic consonant; (ii) as the product of the contraction of vowels, where one of the merged vowels was already long. Thus Base ZIR 'love, desire' produces both *zīr* and *zîr*; and also *zaira* and *zâir* 'yearning'.

Similar forms were sometimes produced by Bases with medial W, Y and lengthened CV: as Base DAWAR produces **dāw'r* and so *dâur* 'gloom'; *zāyan* 'land' produces plural **zāyīn* and so *zâin*.

Except in the oldest texts and 'heard' forms the diphthongs *ai, au* have become monophthongized to long (open) *ē* and *ō* respectively. The long diphthongs remained unchanged, and are usually heard, whatever their origin, as diphthongs with a long vowel as the first element, and a shorter one (always I or U) as the second element; though this second element is rather longer and clearer than in a normal diphthong: the intonation is 'rising-falling'.

The only source of *ē, ō* in Adunaic is the older diphthongs *ai, au*. The language consequently possesses no short *ĕ* or *ŏ*. Avallonian *ĕ* and *ŏ* are usually represented by *i* and *u*, respectively; though sometimes (especially in unstressed syllables before *r*, or where the Adunaic system favours it) both appear as *a*. In the earlier loans from Avallonian, presumably before the monophthongization of *ai, au*, Avallonian *ē* and *ō* appear as *ī* and *ū* respectively; but later they appear as *ē* and *ō*.

Contact of vowels.

This can be produced (i) by the loss of a medial consonant, especially 3; (ii) in suffixion, especially in the addition of the inflexional elements: *ĭ, ŭ, ă, āt, im*, etc.

If one or both of the components is long then the product is a long diphthong or an over-long vowel.

U contracts with U; I with I; and A with A.

After U a glide consonant w is developed (so *ŭ – ă, ŭ – ĭ* to *ŭwă, ŭwĭ*), as described above. Similarly after I a Y is developed (so *ĭ – ă, ĭ – ŭ* to *ĭyă, ĭyŭ*).

Earlier Adunaic also possessed the long diphthongs: ôi, ôu, and êi, êu. These were all contraction products, and êu was rare. In the classical period ôi (and êu) remained; but ôu became the over-long simple vowel ô, and similarly êi became ê.

These diphthongs were mainly found in inflexional syllables, where they appear to be produced by adding such inflexional elements as *-i, -u* direct to the uninflected form (come to be regarded as the stem) instead of to the etymological stem. Thus the plural of *manō* 'spirit', from **manaw-*, or **manau*, is *manôi*.

But similar forms can also be produced basically. Thus a Base KUY can produce by 'fortification' *kauy-* to *kōy, kôi*. A Base KIW can produce by 'fortification' *kaiw-* to *kēw, kêu*. It is possible that the inflexional forms are also, at least partly, of similar origin. If the plural inflexion was in fact originally YĪ not Ī (as it seems to be, because Y was lost before I medially) then the development would be so: *manaw, manau + yi* to *manōyi* to *manôi*; and similarly *izray, izrai + yī* to *izrēyī* to *izrêi* to *izrê*.

By the processes (i) of N-infixion, and consonant doubling; and (ii) of varying the position of the CV, and modifying it; and varying the vowels of the subordinate syllables, the Adunaic Bases, and especially those of 3-consonant form, were capable of an enormous number of derivative forms, without recourse to prefixion or suffixion. Naturally no single Base shows more than a few of the possible variations. In any case, any given derivative never shows two of the one *kind* of variation at the same time; for this purpose N-infixion and consonant doubling count as one kind of process; and Lengthening and A-fortification count as another. Alteration in the position of the CV, and variation of the subordinate vowels, can be combined with any other derivative process.

Even with these limitations such Bases as KULUB and GIMIL can for example develop the following variants (among other possible forms):

KULBU, -A, -I; KULAB, KULIB, KULUB; UKLUB — *Kulbō, -ā, -ē, -ū, -ī; kōlab, kōlib, kōlub, kulōb, kulēb, kulāb, kulūb, kulīb; uklōb, uklūb*

Kullub, -ib, -ab (with variants showing *-ūb, īb, āb, ēb, ōb*); *kulubba, kulubbi, kulabbu, kulabba, kulabbi, kulibbu, kulibbi, kulibba; kulumba* (also *kulimba, kulamba*, etc., though N-infixion is usually found with the CV preceding the nasal); *uklumba*; etc.

GIMLI, -A, -U; GIMAL, GIMIL, GIMUL; IGMIL with parallel variations, such as GĒMIL, GIMĒL, IGMĒL, GIMMIL, GIMILLA, etc.

The apparent gradations produced by these changes are:
Basic A: a —— ā —— â
Basic I: i —— ī —— î; ē —— âi
Basic U: u —— ū —— û; ō —— âu.

Declension of nouns.

Nouns can be divided into two main classes: *Strong* and *Weak. Strong* nouns form the Plural, and in some cases certain other forms, by modification of the last vowel of the Stem. *Weak* nouns add inflexions in all cases.

The stems of strong nouns were doubtless originally all Basic stems in one or other of the fuller forms: as NAKA, GIMIL, AZRA; but the strong type of inflexion had spread to most nouns whose stem ended in a short vowel followed by a single consonant. No nouns with a monosyllabic stem are strong.

The stems of Weak nouns were either monosyllabic, or they ended in a lengthened or strengthened syllable (such as *-ā, -ān, -ū, -ōn, -ūr*, etc.), or they were formed with a suffix or added element.

It is convenient also to divide nouns into Masculine, Feminine, Common, and Neuter nouns; though there is not strictly speaking any 'gender' in Adunaic (there is no m. f. or n. form of adjectives, for example). But the *subjective* case, as it may be called, differs in the four named varieties in the singular; and is formed differently in the plural neuter from the method employed in the m. f. and c. This arises because the subjective was originally made with pronominal affixes, and Adunaic distinguishes gender (or rather sex) in the pronouns of the third person.

All nouns are Neuter, except (i) Proper names of persons, and personifications; (ii) Nouns denoting male or female functions; and male or female animals, where these are specifically characterized: as 'master, mistress, smith, nurse, mother, son'; or 'stallion, bitch'.

Masculine or Feminine are the personifications of natural objects, especially lands and cities, which may have a neuter and a personalized form side by side. Often the 'personification' is simply the means of making a proper name from a common noun or adjective: thus *anadūni* 'western', *Anadūnē* f. 'Westernesse'. Abstractions may also be 'personified', and regarded as agents: so *Agān* m. 'Death', *agan* n. 'death'. In such cases, however, as *nīlō* n. 'moon', and *ūrē* n. 'sun', beside the personalized forms *Nīlū* m. and *Ūrī* f., we have not so much mere personification but the naming of real persons, or what the Adūnāim regarded as real persons: the guardian spirits of the Moon and the Sun, in fact 'The Man in the Moon' and 'The Lady of the Sun'.

Common are the noun *anā* 'homo, human being'; the names of all animals when not specially characterized; and the names of peoples (especially in the plural, as *Adūnāim*). [*Footnote 11*]

The stems of nouns can end in any single basic consonant, or in a vowel. It must be noted, however, that the original basic consonants w, y, ʒ have become vocalized finally, and that these final forms tend to become regarded as the actual stems. So *pā* 'hand' probably from **paʒa*, pl. *pâi*; *khâu* and *khō* 'crow' from **khāw* and **khăw*; pls. *khāwī(m)* and *khôi* (the latter should historically be *khăwī*).

Long consonants or combinations of consonants do not occur finally in classical Adunaic. [*Footnote 12*] The stems of nouns consequently can end only in one (or no) consonant. Suffixal elements usually end in a vowel, or in dental stops: *t*, *th*, *d*; or in continuants, especially *s*, *z*, *l*, *r*, the nasals *n* and *m*; less commonly in consonants of the other series such as *h*, *g*, *p*, *ph*, *b*, though *k* is not uncommon.

Where, however, a noun has a basic stem there is no limitation. Thus *pūh* 'breath'; *rūkh* 'shout'; *nīph* 'fool'; *urug* 'bear'; *pharaz* 'gold'. Such 'basic' forms are not very common, except as neuters; and they are very rare as feminines (since specifically feminine words are usually made with the suffixes -*ī*, -*ē* from the masculine or common stem). The only frequent f.

noun of this type is *nithil* 'girl'. The word *mūth* 'baby girl, maid-child' appears to be of this type, but is probably made with an affix *-th* (often met in feminines) from a base MIYI 'small'; cf. the m. form *mīk*, and the dual *miyāt* '(infant) twins'.

In compound nouns and names, however, a bare stem (often containing a lengthened or fortified vowel) is very frequent as a final element. In such formations, whatever the function of the stem used as a simplex, this final element very frequently has an agental force, and so requires the *objective* form in the preceding element (on the objective form see below). So *izindu-bēth* 'true-sayer, prophet'; *Azrubēl* p.n. 'Sea-lover'. Contrast the simplex *bēth* 'expression, saying, word'.

Masculine nouns usually have ō, ŭ, or ă in the final syllable. If they have affixed elements they end in -ō, or -ŭ; or in the favoured 'masculine' consonants *k, r, n, d* preceded by ō, ŭ, or ă.

Feminines usually have ē, ĭ, or ă in the final syllable; and if they have affixed elements (as is usual) they end in -ē or -ĭ; or in the favoured 'feminine' consonants *th, l, s, z* preceded by ē, ĭ, or ă.

Common nouns have 'neuter' stem forms, or favour the ending -ā or -ă in the final syllable.

Neuter nouns do not show ī, or ū, in the last syllable of their stems, nor do they employ suffixes that contain ū, ō, or ī, ē, as these are signs of the masculine and feminine respectively. [*Footnote 13*]

Nouns distinguish *three* numbers: *Singular*, *Plural*, and *Dual*. In most cases the Singular is the normal form, and the others are derived from it. There are, however, a good number of words with a more or less plural significance that are 'singular' (that is uninflected) in form, while the corresponding singulars are derived from them, or show a less simple form of the base. Thus *gimil* 'stars', beside the sg. *gimli* or *igmil* (the latter usually meaning a star-shaped figure, not a star in the sky). These plural-singulars are really collectives and usually refer to all the objects of their kind (either all there are in the world, or all there are in any specific place that is being thought or spoken of). Thus *gimil* means 'the stars of heaven, all the stars to be seen', as in such a sentence as 'I went out last night to look at the stars'; the plural of the singulars *gimli, igmil — gimlî, igmîl —* mean 'stars, several stars, some stars', and will in consequence be the only forms to be used with a specific numeral, as *gimlî hazid* 'seven stars'. Similarly in the title of the *Avalē* or 'goddess' *Avradī: Gimilnitīr* 'Star-kindler', the reference is to a myth, apparently, of her kindling all the stars of heaven; *gimlu-nitīr* would mean 'kindler of a (particular) star'.

The Duals are collectives or pairs, and mean 'both' or 'the two'. Hence they never require the article. They are made with a suffix *-at*. The Dual is only normally used of things that go in natural or customary pairs: as shoes, arms, eyes. For the expression of, say, two separate shoes not making a pair Adunaic would use the *singular* noun with the numeral 'two' *satta* following. But in the older language things only belonging together casually, where we should say 'the two', are sometimes put into the dual.

The chief use in classical Adunaic of the Dual was to make pair-nouns when (a) two objects are generally associated, as 'ears'; or sometimes (b) when they are generally contrasted or opposed, 'day and night'. The first case gives no difficulty: so *huzun* 'ear', *huznat* 'the two ears (of one person)'. In the second case, if the two objects are sufficiently different to have separate names, then either (a) the two stems can be compounded and the dual inflexion added at the end; or occasionally (b) one only of the stems is used, the other being understood, or added separately in the singular. Thus for 'sun and moon' are found *ūriyat, ūrinīl(uw)at*, and *ūriyat nīlō*.

Nouns distinguish *two* forms or 'cases' in each number: 1. *Normal* 2. *Subjective*. In addition in the singular only there is an *Objective* form.

The *Normal* (N) shows no inflexion for 'case'.

It is used in all places where *Subjective* (S) or *Objective* (O) are not obligatory. Thus: (i) as the object of a verb. It never immediately precedes a verb of which it is the object. (ii) Before another noun it is either (a) in apposition to it, or (b) in an adjectival or possessive genitive relation. The first noun is the one in the genitive in Adunaic (adjectives normally precede nouns). For that reason cardinal numerals, which are (except 'one') all nouns, follow their noun: *gimlī hazid* = 7 of stars. The two functions: apposition, and genitival adjective, were normally distinguished by stress and intonation. [*Footnote 14*] (iii) Predicatively: *Ar-Pharazōnun Bār 'nAnadūnē* 'King Pharazon is Lord of Anadune'. (iv) As subject when it immediately precedes a fully inflected verb. In that case the verb must contain the requisite pronominal prefixes. If the subjective is used the verb need not have any such prefixes. Thus *bār ukallaba* 'the lord fell', or *bārun (u)kallaba*; the latter is rather to be rendered 'it was the lord who fell', especially where both subjective and pronominal prefix are used. (v) As the base to which certain adverbial 'prepositional' affixes are added; such as *ō* 'from', *ad*, *ada* 'to, towards', *mā* 'with', *zē* 'at'.

The *Subjective* (S) is used as the subject of a verb. As shown above the subjective need not be used immediately before a verb with pronominal prefixes; an object noun is never placed in this position. The S. also represents the verb 'to be' as copula; cf. (iii) above. When two or more nouns in apposition are juxtaposed in Adunaic only the last of the series receives the subjective inflexion: thus *Ar-Pharazōn kathuphazgānun* = 'King Ar-Pharazon the Conqueror'. Contrast *Ar-Pharazōnun kathuphazgān* = 'King Ar-Pharazon is (was) a Conqueror'.

The *Objective* form (O) is only used in compound expressions, or actual compounds. Before a verb-noun, or verb-adjective (participle), or any words that can be held to have such a sense, it is then in an objective-genitive sense. Thus *Minul-Tārik* 'Pillar of Heaven', the name of a mountain. Here *minul* is the O. form of *minal* 'heaven', since *tārik* 'pillar' here means 'that which supports'. *minal-tārik* would mean 'heavenly pillar', sc. a pillar in the sky, or made of cloud. Contrast *Azru-bēl* (where *azru* shows the O. form of *azra* 'sea') 'Sea-lover', with *azra-zāin*.

Plural nouns are seldom (and Dual nouns never) placed in such a position. When a plural noun is so used it always stands in *object* and not adjectival or possessive relation to the noun that follows, so that the plural nouns need no special objective form. The genitive of a plural noun can only be expressed with the prefix *an-* described in the note above [see Footnote 14]; thus *Ārū'nAdūnāi* 'King of the Anadunians'.

Plurality is expressed in Adunaic either by *ī* as the last vowel of the stem before the final consonant (in strong nouns), or by the suffixion of the element *-ī*. It is suggested above that the suffix originally had the form *-yī* [see page 424].

Duality is expressed by the suffix *-at*. There are no 'strong' forms.

The *Subjective*: in Neuter nouns this is expressed by *a*-fortification of the last vowel of the stem, in the case of strong nouns: as *zadan* with the S. form *zadān*; in weak nouns the suffix *-a* is used. In Masculine nouns, strong or weak, the suffix *-un* is used; in Feminines the suffix *-in*; in Common nouns the suffix *-an*, or *-n*. In plurals it has the suffix *-a* in Neuters, and in all other nouns the suffix *-im*.

The *Objective* has either the vowel *u* in the last syllable of the stem, or else the suffix *-u*.

Examples of Declension

Nouns may be divided as noted above [see page 425] into Strong and Weak. In *Strong* nouns the cases and plural stems are formed partly by alterations of the last vowel of the stem (originally the variable vowel of the second syllable of basic stems), partly by suffixes; in the *Weak* nouns the inflexions are entirely suffixal.

The Strong nouns may again be divided into Strong I, and Strong II. In I the variable vowel occurs before the last consonant (Base form KULUB); in II the variable vowel is final (Base forms NAKA, KULBA).

Neuter Nouns

Strong I

Examples: *zadan*, house; *khibil*, spring; *huzun*, ear.

Singular	N.	zadan	khibil	huzun
	S.	zadān	khibēl	huzōn
	O.	zadun	khibul	huzun, huznu [*Footnote 15*]
Dual	N.	zadnat	khiblat	huznat
	S.	zadnāt	khiblāt	huznāt
Plural	N.	zadīn	khibīl	huzīn
	S.	zadīna	khibīla	huzīna

The Dual usually shows, as in the above examples, suppression of the final vowel before the suffix *-at*; but the final vowel of the N. form is often retained, especially where suppression would lead to the accumulation of more than two consonants, or where the preceding vowel is long: so usually *tārikat* 'two pillars'.

In all nouns the N. and S. of Duals was only distinguished in earlier texts. Before the Exilic periods the ending *-āt* was used for both N. and S. This doubtless was due to the coalescence of N. and S. in the very numerous class Strong II.

Strong II

Examples: *azra*, sea; *gimli*, star; *nīlu*, moon.

Singular	N.	azra	gimli	nīlu
	S.	azrā	gimlē	nīlō
	O.	azru	gimlu	nīlu
Dual	N.	azrāt, -at	gimlat, -iyat	nīlat, -uwat
	S.	azrāt	gimlāt, -iyāt	nīlāt, -uwāt
Plural	N.	azrī	gimlī	nīlī
	S.	azrīya	gimlīya	nīlīya

Beside the normal plural *gimli* there exists, as noted above [see page 427], also the plural with singular form *gimil* (declined like *khibil*, only with no plural or dual forms), in the sense 'the stars, all the stars' or 'stars' in general propositions. Other plurals of this type are not uncommon: such as *kulub* 'roots, edible vegetables that are roots not fruits', contrasted with *kulbī* 'roots' (a definite number of roots of plants).

The dual forms N. *azrat*; N. *gimlat*, S. *gimlāt*; N. *nīlat*, S. *nīlāt* are archaic, but in accordance with the basic system of Adunaic, and show a parallel suppression of the variable vowel to that seen in *zadnat*, etc. The later forms are due to the growth of the feeling that the final vowels of the N. forms *azra*, *gimli*, *nīlu* are suffixal and invariable, so that *-āt* was added to the N. form without suppression, producing *azrāt*, *gimilyat*, *nīluwat*. Later forms show *-āt* in both N. and S. owing to the predominance numerically of the nouns with final *-a*.

Weak

Here belong monosyllabic nouns; and disyllabic nouns with a long vowel or diphthong in the final syllable, such as *pūh*, breath; *abār*, strength, endurance, fidelity; *batān*, road, path.

Singular	N.	pūh	abār	batān
	S.	pūha	abāra	batāna
	O.	pūhu	abāru	batānu
Dual	N.	pūhat	abārat	batānat
	S.	pūhāt	abārāt	batānāt

Plural   N. pūhī   abārī   batānī [*Footnote 16*]
           S. pūhīya abārīya batānīya

Masculine, Feminine, and Common Nouns

M., F., and C. nouns only differ in the Singular Subjective, where the suffix -*n* is usually differentiated by the insertion of the sex or gender signs *u*, *i*, *a*. In later, but still pre-exilic, texts the Feminine Objective often takes the vowel *i* (so *nithli* for *nithlu*) owing to the association of the vowel *u* with the masculine. Feminine nouns are seldom of 'basic' form, that is few belong to Strong declension I*a*, since specifically feminine words are usually formed from the M[asculine]

Here Lowdham's 'Report' breaks off at the foot of a page (see p. 436). The 'footnotes' to the text now follow.

Footnote 1

In reckoning the number of consonants in a Base it must be observed that many bases originally began with weak consonants that later disappeared, notably the 'clear beginning' (or possibly the 'glottal stop') for which I have used the symbol ?. Thus Base ?IR 'one, alone', from which is derived a number of words (e.g. *Ēru* 'God'), is a biconsonantal base.

Footnote 2

In so far as this table differs from the list of the actual consonants of our records, it is arrived at by deduction from the observable changes occurring in word-formation, from variations in spelling in the written documents 'seen' by Jeremy, from the treatment of Avallonian loan-words, and from the alteration of the older forms that have been occasionally noted.

Footnote 3

Adunaic did not possess, as independent Base-forming elements, nasals of the C- or K-series. The latter (here symbolized by 9), the sound of *ng* in English *sing*, occurs, however, as the form taken (a) by an 'infixed' nasal before consonants of the K-series, and (b) by the dental nasal N (not M) when it comes in contact with a consonant of the K-series in the process of word-formation. On 'infixion' see below [see p. 417 and Footnote 4]. Doubtless Adunaic originally possessed similarly a nasal of the C-series, but as these all became dentals, except Y, if it occurred at all, it could only occur in NY. In this combination, however, the Adūnāim appear to have used the same sign as for dental N.

Footnote 4

Nasal-infixion is of considerable importance in Avallonian; but does not seem to occur at all in Khazadian; so that this element in Adunaic structure may be due to Avallonian influence in the prehistoric period.

Footnote 5

This sound only occurs in the combination NG, for which Adunaic employed a single letter.

Footnote 6

Jeremy could not see this very clearly; it was perhaps already very old and partly illegible at the period to which his 'sight' was directed. We believe it to have been on some monument marking the first landing of Gimilzōr, son of Azrubēl, on the east coast of Anadūnē. It cannot have been quite contemporary, since the texts seem to speak of the Adunaic script as being only invented after they had dwelt some little time in the island. It is likely, nonetheless, to date from a time at least 500 years, and quite possibly 1000 years, before the time of Ar-Pharazōn. This is borne out both by the letter-forms and by the archaism of the linguistic forms. The length of the period during which the Adūnāim dwelt in Anadūnē cannot of course be computed at all accurately from our scrappy material; but the texts seem to show that (a) Gimilzōr was young at the time of the landing; (b) Ar-Pharazōn was old at the time of the Downfall; (c) there were twelve kings in between: that is practically 14 reigns [see p. 381, §20]. But members of the royal house seem often to have lived to be close on 300; while kings seem normally to have been succeeded by the *grandsons* (their sons were as a rule as old as 200 or even 250 before the king 'fell asleep', and passed on the crown to their own sons, so that as long and unbroken a reign as possible might be maintained, and because they themselves had become engrossed in some branch of art or learning). This means that the realm of Anadūnē may have lasted well over 2000 years.

Footnote 7

Apparent cases, such as the variation between pronominal *u-* and *hu-*, are due to the existence of two stems, one beginning with a weak consonant (3 or ?), the other with the intensified н-form.

Footnote 8

In composition or inflexion a 'glide' w was developed between u and a following vowel (other than u), and this developed into a full consonant in Adunaic. Similarly a y was developed between ı and a following vowel (other than ı). The best representation of Adunaic w in English letters is probably *w*; but I have used *v* in the Anglicizing of Adunaic names.

Footnote 9

Note that these variations are only permitted where the CV is in normal position; such forms as AN'KU, UKLIB are not permitted.

Footnote 10

These modifications are not held to change the identity of the CV, so that they can occur together with vowel-variation in subordinate syllables: thus from Base GIM'L a form GAIMAL is possible.

N-infixion, though not strictly a vocalic change, is included here because it plays a similar part in grammar and derivation to Lengthening. It only occurs before a medial or final radical (never as in Avallonian before the initial), and there is limited to occurrence before the Stops and z (on which see above [p. 417]).

Footnote 11

Common nouns can be converted into M. or F. when required by appropriate modifications or affixes; or, naturally, separate words can be used. Thus *karab* 'horse', pl. *karīb*, beside *karbū* m. 'stallion', *karbī* 'mare'; *raba* 'dog', *rabō* m. and *rabē* f. 'bitch'. *anā* 'human being', *anū* 'a male, man', *anī* 'a female'; beside *naru* 'man', *kali* 'woman'. *nuphār* 'parent' (dual *nuphrāt* 'father and mother' as a pair), beside *ammī, ammē*, 'mother'; *attū, attō* 'father'.

Footnote 12

In most of our records from approximately the time of the Downfall final -*ă* was in fact often omitted in speech, not only before the vocalic beginning of another word, but also (especially) finally (i.e. at the end of a sentence or phrase) and in other cases; so that the spoken language could have various final consonant combinations.

Footnote 13

This use of ŭ and ĭ (and of ō from *au*, ē from *ai*) as m. and f. signs runs through all Adunaic grammar. *u* and *i* are the bases of pronominal stems for 'he' and 'she'. The use of the affixed elements -ū and -ī finally to mark gender (or sex): as in *karbū* 'stallion', or *urgī* 'female bear', is in fact probably a close parallel to such modern English formations as 'he-goat', 'she-bear'.

Footnote 14

In apposition each noun was separate and had an independent accent. In the genitive function the preceding or adjectival noun received a louder stress and higher tone, the second noun being subordinated. These combinations are virtual compounds. They are often in Adunaic script joined with a mark like a hyphen (–) or (=), or are actually compounded. Even when they are not conjoined the end of one noun is often assimilated to the following, as in *Amān-thāni* to *Amāt-thāni*, *Amatthāni* 'Land of Aman'. Adunaic has another way of expressing the genitive, where the nexus is not quite so close: by the adjectival prefix -*an*. Though this resembles the function of English 'of', it is not a preposition (Adunaic prepositions are in fact usually 'postpositions' following their noun); it is the equivalent of an inflexion or suffix. Thus *thāni anAmān*, usually *thāni 'nAmān* 'Land of Aman'. The same prefix occurs in *adūn* 'west, westward', *adūni* 'the West', *anadūni* 'western'. Other examples of the adjectival use are: *kadar-lāi* 'city folk', *azra-zāin* 'sea-lands, sc. maritime regions', *Ar-Pharazōn* 'King Pharazon'.

Footnote 15

The O. form *huznu*, borrowed from the nouns of Strong II and Weak, is frequently found in nouns whose final vowel is *u*. It occurs also in nouns with other final vowels (as *zadnu*), but less frequently.

Footnote 16

Dissyllabic nouns with a long final syllable (containing *a*) sometimes, especially in the older texts, make a strong plural by change of *a* to *i*, but not other strong forms: so *batīn*, *batīna* 'roads'.

*

Of further material on Adunaic in addition to 'Lowdham's Report' there is not a great deal, and what there is consists almost entirely of preliminary working, much of it very rough, for the text given above. From the point where it breaks off (at the beginning of the section on Masculine, Feminine, and Common Nouns, p. 432), however, drafting in manuscript is found for its continuation. The complexities of the passage of these nouns from 'strong' to 'weak' declension are rather obscurely arranged and presented, and there are illegibilities. I have been in two minds whether to print this draft; but on the whole it seems a pity to omit it. The form given here is somewhat edited, by removal of repetition, small clarifications of wording, omission of a few obscure notes, and the use of the macron throughout in place of the confusing mixture of macron and circumflex in the manuscript.

Masculine, Feminine, and Common nouns only differ in the Singular Subjective, where the suffix is M. *-un*, F. *-in*, C. *-(a)n*. Feminines also are very rarely 'basic', being nearly always formed with suffix from a masculine or common noun [see p. 426].

M. and F. nouns also have mainly become weak, since as a rule they show lengthening in the stem (final syllable) as a formative not an inflexional device.

Therefore corresponding to Neuter Strong I we have a small class I(a) as *tamar* 'smith', and a diminishing variety I(b) as *phazān* 'prince, king's son'. Corresponding to Neuter Strong II there is a small class II(a) of mainly common nouns as *raba* 'dog', and II(b) of nouns ending in *ū* (masc.), *ī* (fem.), *ā* (common); to which are joined nouns ending in *ō* (masc.) and *ē* (fem.) [on which see below]. These have usually become weak.

Strong I(a)

Examples: *tamar*, m. 'smith'; *nithil*, f. 'girl'; *nimir*, c. 'Elf'; *uruk*, c. 'goblin, orc.'

Singular					
	N.	tamar	nithil	nimir	uruk
	S.	tamrun	nithlin	nimran	urkan
	O.	tamur-	nithul-	nimur-	uruk-
		(tamru-)	(nithlu-)	(nimru-)	(urku-)
Dual		tamrăt	nithlăt	nimrăt	urkăt
Plural	N.	tamīr	nithīl	nimīr	urīk
	S.	tamrim	nithlim	nimrim	urkim

I(b)

Examples: *phazān* 'prince'; *banāth* 'wife'; *zigūr* 'wizard'.

Singular				
	N.	phazān	banāth	zigūr
	S.	phazānun	banāthin	zigūrun
	O.	(phazūn-)	(banūth-)	(zigūr-)
		phazānu-	banāthu-	zigūru
Dual		phazānăt	banāthăt	zigūrăt
Plural	N.	phazīn	banīth	zigīr
	S.	phazīnim	banīthim	zigīrim

Here belong only masculines with *ā*, *ū* in final syllables and feminines with *ā*. And these may all be declined weak: plural *phazānī, -īm, banāthī, zigūrī*, etc.

II(a)

There are very few M., F., C. nouns here since such have normally long final stems and have become weak. Here belong chiefly archaic *naru* 'male', *zini* 'female' (beside *narū, zinī*), and nouns denoting animals, as *raba* 'dog'.

Singular				
	N.	naru	zini	raba
	S.	narun	zinin	raban
	O.	naru-	zinu-	rabu-
Dual		narăt	zinăt	rabăt
Plural	N.	narī	zinī	rabī
	S.	narīm	zinīm	rabīm

Nouns corresponding to II(b) have all become weak except *anā* 'human being', which makes plural *anī* beside weak *anāi*.

Singular	N.	anā	Dual	anāt	Plural	N.	anī
	S.	anān				S.	anīm
	O.	anū-					

Weak (a)

Here belong nouns ending in a consonant. These are seldom 'basic' (except as described above in compounds).
Examples: *bār* 'lord'; *mīth* 'little girl'; *nūph* 'fool' [but *nīph* p. 426].

Singular	N.	bār	mīth	nūph
	S.	bārun	mīthin	nūphan (or m.f. *núphun, -in*)
	O.	bāru-	(mīthu-)	nūphu- (f. nūphi-)
			mīthi-	
Dual		bārăt	mīthăt	nūphăt
Plural	N.	bārī	mīthī	nūphī
	S.	bārīm	mīthīm	nūphīm

Weak (b)

Here belong (i) masculines and feminines ending in *ū* and *ī* and common nouns in *ā*. Also (ii) a new class, masculines in *ō*, feminines in *ē*. These are not quite clear in origin. They appear to derive (a) from basic stems in *aw, ay*; (b) from *-aw, -ay* used as m. f. suffixes as variants of *u, i*; (c) from common nouns in *a* + m. *u*, f. *i*, instead of varying vowel. So *raba > rabau > rabō*. These are specially used in f., since *rabī* would appear the same as the common plural.

Examples: *nardū* 'soldier'; *zōrī* 'nurse'; *mānō* 'spirit'; *izrē* 'sweetheart, beloved'; *anā* 'human'. To this class (especially in plural) belong many names of peoples as *Adūnāi*.

Singular	N.	nardū	zōrī	mānō	izrē
	S.	nardūn	zōrīn	mānōn	izrēn
	O.	nardū-	zōrī- (arch.	mānō-	izrē (izrāyu)
			zōrīyu)		
Dual		nardŭwăt	zōrĭyăt	mānōt	izrēt (izrayăt)
				(mānawăt)	
Plural	N.	nardŭwī	zōrī	mānōi	(izrē) izrēnī
	S.	nardŭwīm	zōrīm	mānōim	(izrēm) izrēnīm

Other rough pages are interesting as showing that a major change in my father's conception of the structure entered as the work progressed: for the Adunaic noun at first distinguished five cases, Normal, Subjective, Gentitive, Dative, and Instrumental. To give a single example, in masculine nouns the genitival inflexion was *ō* (plural *ōm*); the dative *-s, -se* (plural *-sim*); and the instrumental *-ma* (plural *-main*), this being in origin an agglutinated post-position meaning 'with', and expressing an instrumental or comitative relation. At this stage the masculine *bār* 'lord' showed the following inflexional system (if I interpret it correctly):

Singular	N.	bār	Dual	bārut	Plural	bāri
	S.	bārun		bārut		bārim

G.	bārō	bārōt	bāriyōm
D.	bārus	bārusit	bārisim
I.	bāruma	bārumat	bārumain

Of notes on other aspects of Adunaic grammar there is scarcely a trace: a few very rough jottings on the verb system are too illegible to make much of. It can be made out however that there were three classes of verbs: I Biconsonantal, as *kan* 'hold'; II Triconsonantal, as *kalab* 'fall down'; III Derivatives, as *azgarā-* 'wage war', *ugrudā-* 'overshadow'. There were four tenses: (1) aorist ('corresponding to English "present", but used more often than that as historic present or past in narrative'); (2) continuative (present); (3) continuative (past); (4) the past tense ('often used as pluperfect when aorist is used = past, or as future perfect when aorist = future'). The future, subjunctive, and optative were represented by auxiliaries; and the passive was rendered by the impersonal verb forms 'with subject in accusative'.

I have remarked before on the altogether unmanageable difficulty that much of my father's philological writing presents: I wrote in *The Lost Road and Other Writings* (V.342):

It will be seen then that the philological component in the evolution of Middle-earth can scarcely be analysed, and most certainly cannot be presented, as can the literary texts. In any case, my father was perhaps more interested in the processes of change than he was in displaying the structure and use of the languages at any given time – though this is no doubt due to some extent to his so often starting again at the beginning with the primordial sounds of the Quendian languages, embarking on a grand design that could not be sustained (it seems indeed that the very attempt to write a definitive account produced immediate dissatisfaction and the desire for new constructions: so the most beautiful manuscripts were soon treated with disdain).

'Lowdham's Report' is thus remarkable in that it was allowed to stand, with virtually no subsequent alteration; and the reason for this is that my father abandoned the further development of Adunaic and never returned to it. This is emphatically not to suggest, of course, that at the moment of its abandonment he had not projected – and probably quite fully projected – the structure of Adunaic grammar as a whole; only that (to the best of my knowledge) he wrote down no more of it. Why this should have been must remain unknown; but it may well be that his work was interrupted by the pressure of other concerns at the point where 'Lowdham's Report' ends, and that when he had leisure to return to it he forced himself to turn again to *The Lord of the Rings*.

In the years that followed he turned into different paths; but had he returned to the development of Adunaic, 'Lowdham's Report' as we have it would doubtless have been reduced to a wreck, as new conceptions caused shifts and upheavals in the structure. More than likely, he would have begun again, refining the historical phonology – and perhaps never yet reaching the Verb. For 'completion', the achievement of a fixed Grammar and Lexicon, was not, in my belief, the over-riding aim. Delight lay in the creation itself, the creation of new linguistic form evolving within the compass of an imagined time. 'Incompletion' and unceasing change, often frustrating to those who study these languages, was inherent in this art. But in the case of Adunaic, as things turned out, a stability was achieved, though incomplete: a substantial account of one of the great languages of Arda, thanks to the strange powers of Wilfrid Jeremy and Arundel Lowdham.

INDEX I

To Part One *The End of the Third Age*

This first index is made with the same degree of fulness as those to the previous volumes dealing with the history of the writing of *The Lord of the Rings*. As before, names are mostly given in a 'standard' form; and certain names are not indexed: those occurring in the titles of chapters etc.; those of the recipients of letters; and those appearing in the reproductions of manuscript pages. The word *passim* is again used to mean that in a long run of references there is a page here and there where the name does not occur.

Arnor   56, 128–9, 135. See *Aragorn*.
Arod   Horse of Rohan. 70, 72; Legolas's horse 120, 123. See *Hasufel*.
Arwen   59, 61, 66, 108, 110, 124–5; called *Undómiel* 59, 66, *Evenstar* 66–7; *the Queen* 66, 118, 127. The white jewel, her gift to Frodo, 67, 108–10; the choice of Arwen 66, 125. For earlier names of Elrond's daughter see *Finduilas* (1).

Bag End   3, 52, 79–80, 84–5, 88, 90–1, 93–4, 97–8, 100, 102–7, 112, 117, 121, 126, 132–3, 135.
Baggins   79, 108; *Bagginses* 111, 113
Baggins, Bilbo   47–8, 52–3, 64, 72, 74, 92, 109–14, 121–2, 132. His mailcoat, see *mithril*; his books of lore 64, 72, 111, and see *Red Book of Westmarch*.
Baggins (and *Bolger-Baggins*), *Bingo*   3, 37, 53
Baggins, Frodo   3–14, 18, 21–2, 24–5, 27, 29–53 *passim*, 56, 61–2, 64, 66, 70–114 *passim*, 121–3, 125, 129, 132, 135; *Frodo of the Nine Fingers* 44, 83, *Frodo of the Ring* 125; Old English *Fróda* 47. His character in the Scouring of the Shire 80, 93, 95, 103; his sicknesses after his return 108–10, 112; the Praise of Frodo and Sam at Kormallen 46–7, and at Edoras 62, 70–1
Bagshot Row   88, 108; called *Ruffians' End* 108
Bamfurlong   (1) Village in the Eastfarthing (replaced by Whitfurrows). 107. (2) Maggot's farm. 107
Bandobras Took   See under *Took*.
Barad-dûr   5–11, 24, 29, 38, 40, 43. See *Dark Tower, (The) Eye*.
Baranduin, Bridge of   117, 128; *(i) Varanduiniant* 129. See *Brandywine*.
Baravorn   Aragorn's translation of *Hamfast* (Gamgee). 121, 126, 129. (Replaced *Marthanc*.)
Barrow-downs   29, 77
Barrowfield   At Edoras. 68, 73; *Barrowfields* 62, 73
Battle of Unnumbered Tears   44
Battle Plain   7, 13
Beregond   Man of Minas Tirith. 59. See *Berithil*.
Beren   13, 45
Beril   Aragorn's translation of *Rose* (Gamgee). 117, 121. (Replaced by *Meril*.)
Berithil   Man of Minas Tirith. 52, 59. (Replaced by *Beregond*.)
Big Folk   Men (as seen by hobbits). 117, 126
Bilbo Baggins   See under *Baggins*.
Bill the Pony   (52), 78
Black Gate   45, 55. See *Morannon*.
Black Land   46. See *Mordor*.
Black Rider(s)   5–7
Bodleian Library   136

elanor Golden flower of Lórien. (114–15), 124, 132. For Sam's daughter *Elanor* see under *Gamgee*.

Elbereth Varda. 112

Eldamar Elvenhome, the region of Aman in which the Elves dwelt. 58

Elder Days 68

Elendil 56, 58–9; *the Horn of Elendil (Windbeam)* 4

Elessar (The) Elfstone, Aragorn. 52, 58, 117, 119, 128. See *Aragorn*.

Elf-friends 92; *Elf-maid* 134, *Elf-prince* 92

Elfhelm the Marshal Rider of Rohan. 59

Elfstone, (The) Aragorn. 64, 66–7, 117, 119, 128; the green stone 56; Sindarin *Edhelharn* 128–9. See *Elessar*.

Elladan Son of Elrond. 57, 66, 127

Ellonel Transient name preceding Arwen. 66. See *Finduilas* (1).

Elrohir Son of Elrond. 57, 66, 127

Elrond 25, 33, 52–3, 58–9, 63–4, 66–7, 69, 109, 111, 115, 119, 124–5, 132; *Council of Elrond* 71. *Sons of Elrond* 57, (63); see *Elladan, Elrohir*.

Elven- *Elven-cloak* 14, 29, 48, 50 (and see *Lórien*); *-grace* 122; *-light* 125; *-lord* 49; *-maid* 132

Elves 7, 9, 14, 26, 52–3, 58, 89, 109, 111, 115–16, 119, 123–5, 127, 132

Elvish (with reference to language) 58, 72, 117–18, 121, 126, 132; Elvish cited 30, 46–7, 51, 56–7, 62, 64, 68, 70, 72–3, 112, 128–9; (with other reference) 8, 26, 34, 69, 116, 125

Emmeril Original name of the wife of Denethor. 54. See *Finduilas* (2).

Emrahil Transient name preceding *Arwen*. 66. See *Finduilas* (1).

Emyn Muil 7

Encircling Mountains (about the plain of Gondolin) 44. See *Gochressiel, (Mountains of) Turgon*.

Ents 7, 9, 53, 63, 71, 116, 119, 123; *Entwives* 63, 116, 120, 123; *Entings* 71

Éomer, King Éomer 7, 48, 52, 54–5, 57, 61–3, 66–8, 73, 123

Eorl the Young 68, 72

Éowyn 52, 54–5, 57, 59, 62–3, 68, 123; *Lady of Rohan* 62

Ephel Dúath 22, 32, 35

Erebor The Lonely Mountain. 119

Erech, Stone of Erech 15–17; the *palantír* of Erech 15

Ered Lithui The Ash Mountains. 11, 32, 35; *the north(ern) range* 33, 39

Ered Nimrais 16. See *White Mountains*.

Eressëa See *Tol Eressëa*.

Erien Replaced, and replaced by, *Arien*. 120–1. See *Arien, Eirien*.

Ethir Anduin 15–16; *the Ethir* 15

Etymologies In Vol.V, *The Lost Road*. 73

Holdwine   Merry Brandybuck's name in Rohan. 68
Houses of Healing   54

Ildramir   Transient name replacing *Imrahil*. 66
Imlad Morghul   The vale of Morghul. 43
Imrahil   55, 66; and see *Dol Amroth, Ildramir*.
Ioreth   Woman of Gondor. 55; earlier spelling *Yoreth* 55
Iorhael   Aragorn's translation of *Frodo* (Gamgee). 126, 129; earlier
    spelling *Iorhail* 117, 135
Isengard   53, 63–4, 68, 71, 74, 82–3, 91, 95, 103, 106, 120, 123; *the
    Circle of Isengard* 136
Isenmouthe   33–6, 38, 41, 43. See *Carach Angren*.
Isen, River   64, 69, 76
Isildur   15; the standard of Isildur 15
Ithilien   7–8, 20, 49–50, 116; *Prince of Ithilien* (Faramir) 61, 70

Keleborn   See *Celeborn* (1) and (2).
Kheled-zâram   Mirrormere. 135
Kings' Norbury   76. See *Fornost Erain*.
King, The   See *Aragorn*.
Kirith Gorgor   The great pass into Mordor. 8, 11, 20, 34. [Kirith
    Gorgor originally not separated from Gorgor(oth): see 32–3.]
Kirith Ungol   The high pass or cleft above the Morgul Vale. 8–10,
    (14, 18), 20, 22, 25.
    The Tower of Kirith Ungol guarding the pass (including
    references to *the Tower* and to *Kirith Ungol* in this sense) 7–10,
    12–14, 18, 20–7, 29–30, 51 (some references are imprecise,
    whether to the pass or the fortress, 11, 25, 31, 35–6). *The turret*
    (or *horn-turret*) of the Tower (visible from the western side of the
    pass) 18, 20, 22, 24, 26–7; *the under-gate, brazen door, brazen
    gate* 18, 21–2, 24, 26, 28; the fortress described 18–20, 22, 26.
    Original sense, the main pass into Mordor, 28
Kormallen, Field of   45–6, 49–50, 55, 83, 92; *Cormallen* 105

Lagduf   Orc of the Tower of Kirith Ungol; earlier name *Lughorn*. 26
Lamedon   15–16
Lameduin, River   16–17; *Lamedui* 15–16; *Fords of Lameduin* 16;
    Mouths of Lamedui(n) 15–16
Landroval   See *Lhandroval*.
Lanhail   'Plain-wise', Aragorn's name for Samwise. 118. See
    Panthael.
Last Alliance, The   20
Laurelindórenan   The old Elvish name of Lórien used by Treebeard,
    earlier *Laurelindórinan*. 73
Lebennin   15–16
lebethron   Tree of Gondor. 55
Legolas   48–9, 57, 61, 63, 70–1, 116, 120, 123

INDEX II

To Part Two *The Notion Club Papers* and Part Three *The Drowning of Anadûnê*

In view of the great array of names occurring in these two parts of the book this second index is a little more restricted in scope than the first, especially in the reduction or omission of explanatory identification in many cases, and to some extent in the amount of cross-reference to related names. A number of names occurring in the Notes to Part Two that are casual and insignificant outside the immediate context have been omitted, but very few from the actual texts of the Papers. Inevitably the choice between omission and inclusion in such cases is rather arbitrary. In the case of names from the works of C. S. Lewis and from Michael Ramer's accounts of his experiences their provenance is indicated by '[Lewis]' and '[Ramer]', often without further explanation.

The exclusions mentioned in the note to Index I are made here also; and names are similarly given in 'standard' form, especially in the matter of accents and marks of length: thus the circumflex is generally used in Adunaic names.

Members of the Notion Club are included under the surname, and references include the initials of members and pages on which the person speaks but is not named. All names of streets, colleges and other buildings in Oxford are collected under the entry *Oxford*. O.E. = Old English.

Many names and groups of names have given exceptional difficulty in organisation and presentation, for there are here not only several languages, changing forms within the languages, rejections and replacements of names, but also shifting identities and intended uncertainty of reference.